The Power of Averborn

The Power of Averborn

Bounders, Book 3

Saoirse Temple

Published by Saoirse Temple, 2025

This is a work of fiction. Similarities to real people, places, or events are entirely coincidental.

THE POWER OF AVERBORN

First edition. September, 2025

Copyright ©2025 Saoirse Temple

ISBN: 978-1-0697505-7-0

Written by Saoirse Temple

Also by Saoirse Temple

Bounders Series

The Fire of Orhowyn (Book 1)

The Amber Chalice (Book 2)

Dear Diary Style Files

Dear Diary; Punctuation Can't Save the World (But It Did Save Grandma)

Dear Diary; I have 99 Problems and All of Them Are Numbers

Dear Diary; I Think the Alphabet is Gaslighting Me

Dear Diary; I've Committed a Capital Offence

Dear Diary; I Don't Think That Word Means What I Think It Means vi

For Kurt

Prologue

The teal dragon lifted its head. The effort was costly after many days without food or water. Still, through the brain-fog, it knew that something was… different. The men, with their lab coats and clipboards, were milling about as they normally did, huddled on the opposite side of the chamber. Even after all this time, they were afraid to get too close. The teal beast may not have its magic, it may be weak, but it still had teeth and claws. It could still cause harm.

It sniffed the air, hoping its olfactory senses could tell it what was happening. All it could smell was the sterile scent of the stone walls and the barely contained fear of the men. There were nine of them that day. Nine smug, frightened bastards cooking up another way to torture the dragon. *What will it be today?* It wondered. *Shock? Poisoned meat? Rip out a few more of my scales?*

Then it heard something strange. The clinking of metal. The rattling of chains.

My chains!

The teal dragon forced itself up onto its legs. Across the room, the men stopped talking. They turned to look at the dragon, curious at first, uncertain yet as to why it had risen.

The rattling morphed into a rumble that started out low, almost as if it came from far away. Beneath the dragon, the stone floor began to shake. Above its head the ceiling cracked, showering it with a curtain of dust.

The men just stood there, trying to stay upright, unsure what was happening. A few of them looked at the dragon, accusing it with their eyes. One of them tried to run to the door, but was pitched to the floor as the shaking grew more violent. No one attempted to help him, and before he could scramble back up to his feet, a large chunk of rock from the ceiling fell on him, crushing him as his companions looked on in horror.

The dragon instinctively pressed itself against the wall to which it had been chained for sixteen years. If the ceiling collapsed, this would not save it, but it might lessen the damage.

Dust and falling debris obscured the men from the dragon's vision, but a sudden wave of fresh air and the screams of the men told it that that side of the room no longer existed. Peering through the cloud, it saw slivers of blue sky and the

1

expanse of an ocean. The sight, the first glimpse of nature it had seen since it had been imprisoned in this fortress, brought tears to its one remaining eye.

Suddenly, it felt itself start to fall. For a brief second, it thought it was free and began to unfurl its wings—a skill it almost forgot it possessed. Then, just as suddenly, it stopped falling; the chain around its neck tightening as the floor dropped out from under it while the wall continuing to hold.

The dragon twisted around to face the wall. It scrambled to find purchase for its talons in the smooth stone. Flailing and screeching in desperation, it hung there, strangling at the end of the chain until it passed out. Finally, a last ferocious tremor shook the wall loose and the dragon tumbled 500 feet down into the cold ocean water.

A mile out, the passengers and crew of a passing ship witnessed the destruction of the fortress. While the captain shouted orders, the crew scrambled to turn the bow into the oncoming waves. They couldn't outrun them; this was their best chance of not being swamped and possibly capsized.

On board were a group of six very large men, passengers who were supposed to be delivered to the same fortress they had just watched fall into the drink. The leader, far from being upset about the turn of events, told the captain to take them to the site. This was met with vehement resistance, and settled with a bag of gold.

"We will recover dragon," the leader said.

This time, all it took to convince the captain was a slight tilt of the head and a single raised eyebrow. Accompanied by six hands on six sword hilts.

It took most of the rest of the day, but eventually the teal dragon's body was recovered and hoisted onto the deck of the ship. The six very large passengers worked into the night to revive the beast.

"You should have let me die," the teal dragon croaked when the passengers' ministrations were finally successful.

"Dying is not good," the leader said. "Living is good. You live now! Where we should take you?"

"Take me to the nearest Boundary to Thraeh," the dragon said. "Preferably one that goes to Epoh."

Chapter One

Princess Meg stood in front of her full-length mirror, admiring the dress she was wearing. The midnight-blue gown had belonged to her mother, Queen Alex. It was the same one Alex had worn the night Meg's father had been crowned King of Epoh, and tonight Meg was wearing it to the grand ball in celebration of her, and her twin brother Hart's, sixteenth birthday. The elegant gown, made of elven silk, hugged her diminutive figure like a second skin, only flaring slightly from the hips and falling to the floor in shimmering folds.

Like her mother's had been, Meg's hair was a mass of unruly, blond curls; a halo of gold around her cherubic face. She had pinned it back with sapphire-studded combs that matched the simple sapphire pendant she wore around her neck.

As she stared at her reflection, she wondered what her mother had been like. She'd heard the stories—all the stories—about King Arthur's cute hippie girl wife and how the two of them had come from another world called Earth to rule the people of Epoh. But the stories were just stories, second-hand memories of a woman Meg only barely remembered and suddenly dearly missed right then. A knock on the door tore Meg away from her thoughts and she turned to greet her visitor.

Meg's lady's maid, Renata, opened the door to let Prince Hart, Meg's younger twin brother, enter the room.

"Look at you!" Hart exclaimed. He wasn't used to seeing his sibling in a dress. "You are absolutely stunning, big sister!"

Meg smiled up at her tall and handsome brother. "You're looking pretty spiffy yourself, little brother," she said as she welcomed Hart's affectionate embrace. "Is it time?"

"Almost," Hart said. "Father asked if we could join him in his chambers before we head down to the great hall."

Meg sighed. "Seriously? He's going to make me climb two flights of stairs in these shoes?" She lifted the hem of her dress to reveal a pair of strappy heels that their Aunt Anayah had conjured up to match her dress.

"I could carry you," Hart offered, turning his back to her and squatting down.

And much to Renata's horror, Meg hiked her skirts up above her knees, jumped onto her brother's back and disappeared in a flurry of elven silk and gleeful teenage giggling.

"Harpur help us all!" Renata sighed as she watched Prince Hart piggy-back the future queen of Epoh down the hall toward the stairs. "I suppose I should just be happy that she agreed to put on a dress!"

"Who are you talking to?"

Renata turned to see Lady Anayah and Sir Davynn approaching from the other direction and was pleased to see them decked out in grand finery. Anayah wore an emerald-green sheath that clung to her curves and complimented her bright, auburn hair, which fell in cascading waves to her waist. She was the epitome of beauty and grace. Her handsome husband, Davynn Willhart, looked sophisticated in a charcoal-grey tuxedo-like suit with a cummerbund that matched Anayah's gown. Behind them, Alexa, nine, Brodie, seven, and young Caleb, just turned four, followed their parents. The children's excitement at being allowed to attend the celebration was palpable and Renata couldn't help but wonder at the wisdom of putting white shirts on the precocious little boys. Then again, Anayah was a witch. A snap of her fingers would take care of any stain her progeny was likely to decorate themselves with.

"It appears that all my years of service to the princess have left me vexed to the point of talking to myself now," Renata said with good humour. "That girl is a force to be reckoned with."

"What has she done now?" Anayah asked with equal good humour. Then with some concern, she asked, "She did put on the gown, didn't she?"

"Aye," Renata confirmed. "She did. And with almost no complaint, I might add. I was beginning to wonder if I was dressing a changeling of some sort. Then Prince Hart arrived to escort her to King Arthur's chambers and he carried her off on his back! Can you imagine?"

Anayah and Davynn both laughed. They could imagine. Being piggy-backed up the stairs was no surprise when it came to Meg. But Anayah would have to actually see the princess in a dress to believe it.

"We are on our way up there as well," Anayah said. "Would you mind watching these three for us for a while? We'll fetch them again when we come back down for the party."

"It would be my pleasure," Renata assured the witch and the knight. "Come, children! Let's wait for your parents in the library."

With the little ones looked after, Davynn offered his wife his arm. "Or," he said with a mischievous smile, "I could carry you up on my back."

4

Anayah rolled her eyes. "Not in this dress." She slipped her own arm through Davynn's and together they proceeded to the king's private chambers.

They had just reached the last flight of steps when a tall, silver-haired elf came bounding up behind them. He was dressed in leaf-green leggings and an elaborately embroidered, matching vest under a tailored, grey, knee-length coat. A pair of dark-grey leather boots enveloped his feet and calves. He slapped Davynn on the back as he leapt ahead of the knight and his pretty wife, and kept going without a word.

"Good to see you, Sok!" Davynn called up after the elf.

"Likewise!" Sok's voice drifted back down the stairwell.

The knight and the witch continued on their way with a shake of their heads. They found the door to King Arthur's private chambers open and, oddly, unguarded. Davynn, who was the captain of the guard, made a note to find out what happened to the sentries that were supposed to be keeping the king safe. Not that Arthur was in any imminent danger. The Kingdom of Epoh had not come under any real threat for centuries. But it was always better to be safe than sorry. Besides, the guards had come in handy once or twice when Arthur had found a spider in his rooms. He was a good king, but his bravery ended somewhat dramatically at eight-legged, creepy-crawly things. Davynn's question about the guards was answered when he entered the main room and found them drinking ale with the king on the sofas.

"What is this?" the knight demanded with a glower aimed directly at Arthur.

"Oh, relax, Davynn," Arthur said. "I invited them in."

Anayah placed a calming hand on her husband's arm. "Let's not get too caught up in protocol right now," she whispered.

Both of the guards drained their cups and returned to their posts outside Arthur's rooms. Davynn closed the door on them and turned to Arthur. "You really need to stop treating your guards like they are your friends." He felt another squeeze on his arm from Anayah, but ignored it.

"And you need to lighten up!" Arthur smiled at his friend and raised his own cup to his lips.

This time, Anayah's warning squeeze included fingernails. Davynn flinched, but acquiesced. Sort of. "We'll talk later."

"Personally, I have given up on trying to get Arthur to behave like a proper king," Sok said, pouring Davynn a cup of ale. "I think it has something to do with being from Earth that prevents him from understanding the importance of his role."

"I think it has something to do with being practical," Arthur replied. "Why do I need guards outside my door anyway?"

"Because I said so," Davynn answered.

Anayah rolled her eyes again and sighed. She snapped her fingers and conjured herself a cup of tea—even after all these years, there was never any tea available—as she turned to the young prince and princess standing next to the fire, seemingly in deep conversation. "Meg, you look wonderful!" Anayah announced as she approached. "And Hart, you are just too handsome!"

"Thank you, Aunt Anayah," Meg said. She smiled brightly, but Anayah saw something in her eyes that belied her outward glee.

"Thank you, Aunt Anayah," Hart said with a slight bow.

Anayah looked closely at the twins, but decided that now was not the time to probe into whatever was going on with them. "Tonight promises to be quite spectacular," she said with a winning smile of her own.

"Indeed," Hart agreed. "Meg and I are both excited to finally be coming of age."

Meg's face scrunched up in a grimace. Her hand strayed subconsciously to her hip, but the hilt of her sword was not there. Anayah watched the gesture with interest.

"Don't worry, big sister," Hart said to his diminutive sibling, "Elanfoil is safe in the armory."

Elanfoil was the name of the dwarven-forged sword that was gifted to Meg by the king of the dwarves to mark the auspicious occasion of her sixteenth birthday. King Röggenar was terribly fond of the twins and, in spite of Arthur's resistance to the gesture, had forged swords for both the prince and the princess. While Hart had hung his, a blade named Arggengrayl, above the hearth in his rooms, Meg had immediately commissioned an intricately tooled-leather scabbard from the elves and had worn it proudly ever since. At her father's request, albeit somewhat grudgingly, Meg had agreed not to wear it with her gown to the birthday celebration that night.

When she realized that Hart had noticed that she had reached for her sword, Meg's face flushed with embarrassment. "I know," she said, averting her gaze from her brother's amusement. "Just habit, that's all."

6

"Nothing is going to go wrong," Hart assured her.

"Are you expecting something to happen tonight?" Anayah couldn't help herself. She'd seen how serious the twins had seemed a moment before.

Meg appeared to consider how to answer. "No," she said at last, again affecting a cheerful smile. "I'm sure everything will be just grand."

Anayah smiled back and excused herself. She caught Davynn's eye and nodded her head toward the door. When her husband extricated himself from some debate between Sok and Arthur and joined her in the hallway, he was hoping for a display of affection. Instead, he was greeted with pursed lips and hooded eyelids—and not in a good way.

"What did I do?" he asked, assuming the consternation was directed at himself.

"You didn't do anything," Anayah said. "I need you to keep an eye on the twins tonight."

"Why?" Davynn asked, somewhat relieved that he wasn't the reason for his wife's displeasure.

"I'm not sure," Anayah said. "But something is bothering Meg and it seems to have happened since she and Hart arrived up here. Just keep an eye on them both and if you see or hear anything strange, let me know."

"Of course!" Davynn leaned in to kiss his wife and was rewarded with a quick peck on the lips. More may have been forthcoming, but right then two more arrivals showed up for the pre-party party.

Hiro, a Krist from the world of Mysturna, and Bon, an android from Earth's future, glided around the corner on Hiro's hover gilly, a telepathically controlled chariot of sorts, that he used to get around in. Standing only four feet tall, Hiro used the hover gilly to keep up with his much-longer-legged friends. Bon, one of those longer-legged friends, was a frequent passenger on the hover gilly. The two had grown to be nearly inseparable since coming to live in Epoh. Their bond was forged in Hiro's laboratory, where they worked on science projects, mostly involving the marriage of technology and magic. For the past sixteen years, they had been trying to invent a hover gilly for the Epohian guards. But they had yet to find a way to enable the non-magical human guards to effectively make use of an essentially magical vehicle.

To both Anayah and Davynn's surprise, the Krist and the android had foregone their usual grey robes in favour of something a little more daring. Hiro was dressed in purple and gold stripes. Bon was sporting a rather dashing tartan kilt and tam, complete with a leather sporran.

"Why are you wearing a skirt?" Davynn blurted when Bon stepped down from the hover gilly.

"It's not a skirt," Anayah explained. "It's a kilt."

"Looks like a skirt to me," Davynn said. "What's the difference?"

"Kilts are worn on Earth by…" Bon began, but was interrupted before he could fully educate the knight on traditional Scottish attire.

"It's an Earth thing," Anayah said to her confused husband. "I'll explain it all to you later. Bon, you look amazing! I've always thought kilts were rather sexy."

Bon, who normally resembled Obi-Wan Kenobi in his typical monotone grey robes tilted his head to one side. "I was not trying to be sexy."

Anayah laughed. "Still," she said, "if you weren't an android, I guarantee you'd have the ladies swooning."

"I'm not wearing a kilt!" Davynn asserted, sensing his wife's imagination was taking flight.

"We'll see!" Anayah said, patting her horrified husband on the cheek before sidling back into Arthur's private chambers.

"Perhaps these costumes were not the best idea," Bon said quietly to Hiro.

"Perhaps not," Hiro agreed with his signature giggle, looking down at his own brightly-coloured robes. "I can't believe she thought your kilt was sexier than this."

Davynn shook his head in disbelief and followed Anayah.

"Oh, good…" Arthur began when he saw the hover gilly glide through the door. Then he took in how Hiro and Bon were dressed. "Orhowyn's eyeballs! What are you two wearing?"

Everyone in the room stopped talking and turned to look at the Krist and the android. Meg had to clamp her hand over her mouth to keep from laughing. Hart's jaw dropped toward the floor. Sok's eyeballs nearly popped out of his head.

"Is that a kilt?" the elf asked as he approached Bon.

"It is," Bon confirmed. "How is it you know about kilts?"

8

"Harpur wore one once. I thought he had lost his mind, but when he explained what it was… Well, I thought it was pretty sexy."

"I don't know which is more disturbing," Arthur began, "Harpur wearing a kilt, or you thinking Harpur looked sexy in one."

Harpur Diggins was, at one time, the Dragon Lord of the Kingdom of Epoh. To all intents and purposes, he had died shortly after Meg and Hart were born, killed by a challenger who had subsequently abandoned the kingdom a few months later. While it was not common knowledge that dragons possessed complex magic, most of those gathered that day in Arthur's private chambers remembered their friend in both his dragon and human guises. Only Meg and Hart had no real recollection of the great purple dragon and all that he had sacrificed for Arthur; they only had the stories that Arthur, Sok, Anayah, Davynn, Hiro and Bon told them. But those stories had become like memories and neither of the twins could imagine the gruff and surly Harpur in anything resembling a skirt.

"I didn't say that I thought Harpur was sexy in a kilt. I said that I thought kilts were sexy," Sok said defensively.

Arthur turned to his senior advisor and best friend. "Your only experience with kilts was one wrapped around Harpur, right?"

"Right." Sok nodded.

"So, how did you make the mental leap from that image to the general conclusion that kilts are sexy?"

"Anayah!" Sok said, waving his hand to encompass all the males in the room.

Without hesitation, the witch snapped her fingers and everyone, save herself and Meg, were dressed in full Scottish regalia.

"Ak!" Davynn squealed as he leapt behind a chair to hide himself. "Anayah, get his off me!"

"Yep," Meg said with a droll lilt in her voice, "that's pretty sexy."

"I like it!" Sok said enthusiastically.

"Me too," Hart agreed. Then he slapped Meg's hand away from the hem of his kilt. "Stop that!"

"I just wanted to see what you are wearing under there," Meg said with a smirk.

"I have to admit, it's not half bad," Arthur chimed in. "But some shorts would be prudent, Anayah. If you don't mind."

Anayah shrugged and snapped her fingers. "Is that better?" she asked, receiving nods from everyone but Davynn.

"I'd prefer to have my pants back," the knight snapped.

"Oh, come on, Davynn," Arthur said, "be a sport. You have to admit that they are comfortable."

Davynn sighed. "Fine! But if anyone makes a crack about this at the ball…"

"Yeah, yeah," Anayah said dismissively. "Are we ready to go down to the hall?"

"Not yet," Arthur said. "We're still waiting for King Röggenar and Elder Dhonna to arrive. I invited them to come up for a toast before the festivities begin."

While they waited for the dwarf king and the elven guild master to arrive, Arthur, Sok and Hart compared notes on the virtues of kilt-wearing. Davynn, however, was trying to figure out how to sit in a skirt, something that was proving to be extremely awkward for the masculine knight. No matter how he arranged his legs, he felt either prissy or exposed. At last, he resolved not to sit down for the duration of the celebration. Hiro and Bon discussed making kilts their usual attire and Anayah and Meg watched it all in abject amusement.

At last, the door opened and a tall elf wearing a sparkling, gold kaftan between her shock of shortly-cropped, crimson hair and bare feet entered accompanied by a short, stalky, elaborately bearded dwarf wearing a leather jerkin emblazoned with jewels over leather pants tucked into leather boots. An enormous gold amulet hung from a thick, gold chain around his neck.

"No one told me we were cross-dressing for the occasion," King Röggenar said by way of a greeting.

"Ah, Röggenar! Welcome!" Arthur said. "What do you think of our fine new kilts?" The King of Epoh actually did a pirouette in front of the dwarf.

Davynn planted his face in his palm and swore under his breath.

"Harpur's heaving haunches!" Elder Dhonna exclaimed. "Have you all gone mad?"

"Not at all!" Arthur replied. "These were Bon's idea. On Earth kilts are often worn at special occasions."

"Well, I'm not wearing one," Röggenar announced with gruff finality.

"Your loss!" Arthur said. "Come, let me pour you some ale."

10

"If Röggenar doesn't have to wear one, I don't either," Davynn said, trying to sound as gruffly final as the dwarf had.

Anayah decided that she had pushed her husband as far as she dared. She snapped her fingers and returned Davynn's tuxedo.

"Thank you," the knight said, wondering how he was going to have to pay for not playing along. Then he sat down on the sofa feeling comfortable, but not altogether at ease.

Arthur poured King Röggenar a cup of ale and then made sure everyone else's cups were filled as well. Now that everyone was there, it was time for the toast he'd planned to commemorate his children's shared sixteenth birthday. He stepped to the hearth and beckoned Meg and Hart to join him. When the twins were positioned on either side of him, he raised his cup and cleared his throat.

"Sixteen years ago, these two wonderful young people came into our lives. Since then, they have brought endless joy to this old castle. It has been such a privilege watching them grow and learn and become the wonderful adults that stand before us now." Arthur turned to his daughter. "Meg, you are amazing. You're smart and funny and about the best damned archer the royal guard has ever known. Am I right, Davynn?"

Davynn nodded. "She split four arrows dead center yesterday!"

Meg bowed with a flourish of pride.

Arthur turned to Hart. "And you, my son, you are incredible! Every day, I see you making life better for all the people of Colwygshire and beyond. Your mother predicted you would become a scientist only hours after you were born. I only wish she could be here with us now. She would have been as proud of you both as I am.

"To Meg and Hart, the apples of my eye. I love you both so much!"

"To Meg and Hart," the others echoed before tipping their cups and drinking to the royal twins.

Sok stepped forward and bowed to the prince and princess. "Live long and prosper!"

While the others confirmed the elf's sentiment, Arthur's eyebrows shot up in surprise. "How very Vulcan of you, Sok. Where did you hear that term?"

"What do you mean? What is a Vulcan?" The elf sensed he had stumbled upon yet another *Earthism* from Arthur's past.

"It's not a bad thing," Arthur said. "Live long and prosper is a Vulcan blessing of sorts. I haven't heard it since before I came to Epoh. It just surprised me to hear you say it."

Sok wanted to move on; these kinds of things often led to confusion. But he couldn't help himself. "Vulcan is a country on Earth, right?"

"Not exactly," Arthur said. "It's a fictitious planet from the Star Trek series. But with your ears, you'd fit right in!"

"So, there are no real Vulcans?" Sok probed. He had a vague understanding of the thing Arthur called television, but it still baffled him that Arthur seemed to identify with the make-believe entities that were represented on it.

"No, there are no real Vulcans," Arthur confirmed. "Although, there is a town not far from where I come from…"

Sok held up his hand. "Stop. I don't want to know. I'm sorry I said anything."

Arthur laughed at his senior advisor. "Don't be, Sok. It was really very touching."

A knock at the door drew everyone's attention. Arthur excused himself to go and answer it. When he opened the door, one of the guards put an envelope in the king's hand.

"From Berryl, I believe, Sire," he said, peeking over Arthur's shoulder at the ale table.

"Thank you," Arthur said and closed the door again.

He looked at the wax seal on the back of the envelope and knew immediately that whoever sent the enclosed missive, it was definitely not Berryl, a member of the city council and former advisor to the Athur's predecessor, King Gnik. The wax was teal in colour, for one thing, and instead of a calligraphic B, the embossed image was a dragon. Arthur opened the envelope and removed the folded vellum containing a short note…

> *Dearest Arthur;*
>
> *Meet me in your chambers after the entertainment starts tonight. I have a plan to bring Harpur back to Epoh.*
>
> *Morgaine Fayle*

Arthur gasped.

"What is it, Father?" Hart asked, seeing the confusion on Arthur's face.

"Nothing," Arthur said. "It's nothing to be concerned about." He returned the note to the envelope and then tucked it into his sporran. "I think it is time we all headed down to the great hall. Finch will skin us alive if we let dinner get cold."

Not a single person in the room with Arthur believed that the note was nothing to be concerned about. But only Bon noticed the twins suddenly touch their foreheads as if they had felt something hot between their eyes. While the others, focused on Arthur as they were, began to file out of the room, the android moved closer to the twins.

"You feel it, too, don't you?" Meg whispered to her brother.

Hart forced his hand away from his face. "Let's just go down to the hall and enjoy the party. We'll figure this out later." He offered his sister his arm and escorted her into the hallway and down the stairs.

Chapter Two

The great hall was filled to capacity with people from all across the kingdom. Elves, dwarves and humans mingled throughout the vast space, sharing stories, renewing acquaintances, eagerly anticipating the arrival of the twins so that they might all acknowledge the coming-of-age of the prince and princess. The only race that was not represented at the celebration was the Fae; they preferred to keep to themselves. And the elves preferred it that way. The long-standing rivalry between the elves and the Fae remained at a precarious standoff. Where the elves considered the Fae to be unnatural abominations, the Fae simply resented the elves for thinking so. As far as Arthur was concerned, the Fae were strange and unpredictable beings, and it was better for everyone if they just stayed in their territory and didn't bother anyone.

There were, as far as anyone was aware, no dragons present either.

Had Harpur Diggins been alive, he, of course, would have been there to help usher Meg and Hart into adulthood. But he was long dead, killed by Karrys Evergreen shortly after the twins had been born. It had taken Arthur a long time to accept the demise of his friend, but now, with the words on the note he'd received burning in his brain, he had an inexplicable, nagging feeling that he should remember something more about Harpur's death.

As they entered the great hall, Arthur couldn't help but scan the crowd for the hulking form of Harpur Diggins in his human guise, a giant of a man standing well over six feet tall with skin the colour of poisonwood, violet eyes and a neatly trimmed beard as black as pitch. He was rarely seen without his top hat and ascot, perfectly knotted and pinned with a large amethyst brooch. For years he had carried an ornate walking stick, but that had been lost during a desperate fight to kill three wraiths that were terrorizing Colwygshire under the directions of the murderous Edlyngton Bloomregaard, who had killed King Gnik and attempted to usurp the crown. The precious cane had never been found and Harpur, for reasons unknown, had never replaced it.

Not seeing anyone that even remotely resembled Harpur Diggins, Arthur didn't know whether to feel disappointed or relieved. It had been sixteen years since Harpur had lost the challenge to Karrys and, if he had somehow survived, Arthur was uncertain that he would be able to forgive the dragon for abandoning the kingdom, which was now under the lordship of a bronze dragon named Glynnis Warwyrm.

For the most part, Glynnis Warwyrm left the peoples of Epoh alone. He had no interest in what the four races did as long as they also left him alone. After Karrys Evergreen had inexplicably left Epoh, the dragons had held a contest to appoint a new Dragon Lord to the kingdom and Glynnis had killed eight other dragons to win the title. It had been argued that Harpur's twin sons, Framanjesk and Phiercesten, should inherit Epoh and rule it jointly, but in the end, it was decided that Harpur would not have been pleased to see his sons given a kingdom to rule that they hadn't earned. Neither of them had put their names in to compete in the contest either, knowing that they would have to fight against each other at some point.

And so, Glynnis Warwyrm sent eight other magnificent dragons to their deaths for the privilege of ruling over Epoh and had accepted the terms set out by the Dragon Council to allow the four races that Harpur had welcomed into the kingdom to live there under his protection. He had rather hoped that the elves and the Fae would go to war and annihilate each other, taking the dwarves and humans with them. He could have used that as an excuse to exile them all, but, to his great chagrin, the races remained settled in mutually beneficial cooperation with one another, and he was left charged with their general protection. Every once in a while, however, he would grow bored and burn some crops or steal some livestock, but he always gave fair warning and never broke his vow to keep the people safe.

Still, it was always disconcerting when the great, bronze beast would assert his sovereignty and wreak havoc in the kingdom. There wasn't much the people could do about it, other than to get out of his way and hope that he didn't cross the line. Since his appointment as Dragon Lord, only three humans and one elf had been killed during his raids, and they had all been foolish enough to vainly try to stop him.

Arthur took his seat at the head table while the others all followed suit. Two chairs remained empty. One to Arthur's immediate right in honour of Queen Alex, and one to Meg's immediate left in honour of Harpur Diggins. This practice was Arthur's way of ensuring that his cute hippie girl wife and the Dragon Lord who had brought him to this world were never forgotten. While many had hoped that Arthur would take a new wife and Alex's seat would be filled, the two empty chairs had become an accepted, albeit heartbreaking, reminder of the love the King of Epoh held for these two special people. For Arthur, there could never be replacements for Queen Alex and Harpur Diggins and the chairs would stay empty as long as he wore the crown.

As the festivities progressed through a lavish dinner and the requisite speeches, Arthur continued to scan the crowd for the possible author of the note in his sporran. No one among those gathered in the great hall stood out in any significant way. He didn't know everyone there personally, however, and that did not help him in singling out a plausible suspect, until the entertainment started and a striking, raven-haired woman wearing an eye patch and dressed in teal leggings and a split-tail jacket caught his eye. The woman wore a top hat with a purple hat band and a cream-coloured ascot, pinned with a large amethyst brooch. She was sitting at the back of the room near the door and, at once, Arthur felt a sense of familiarity. When she stood and moved toward the exit, he followed her with his eyes. Before she left, she turned and smiled at Arthur, tipping her hat and nodding at him. Just like Harpur might have done.

Arthur's breath caught in his throat. He jumped from his chair and excused himself from the table, saying that he had to visit the loo. No one in the crowd noticed the king leaving, but the entire head table watched with suspicion as he ran out of the hall, not toward the water closet next to the kitchens, but toward the stairs that lead up to the south tower where his private chambers were located. There was no need for discussion, one-by-one they made their own excuses and followed Arthur's egress from the great hall.

When Arthur reached his private chambers, he finally understood the value of having guards at his door. "Do not, under any circumstances, allow anyone to enter my rooms," he ordered the two bored sentries. "Do you understand?"

"Yes, sire," the watchmen said in tandem. "Is there a problem, sire?"

The only problem Arthur could think of was keeping Anayah from zapping herself into his chambers once she and the others figured out that he hadn't gone to the loo. He would have to ward the room and hope it kept her out long enough for him to find out who this Morgaine Fayle was, and what she wanted.

"I just need some time to myself for a while," he answered. "It's been an emotional day."

The two guards exchanged sardonic looks. "Indeed, sire," said the guard on the left. "We won't let anyone in."

"What if it's Sok?" the other guard inquired.

"Especially if it's Sok!" Arthur ordered. Then seeing the look of dread at having to face Sok's anger at being denied entry, he added. "I will lock the door from the inside as well. Try to convince them that I didn't come up here."

With that, the King of Epoh entered his rooms and closed and locked the door, leaving the guards to wrestle with their orders. He was about to cast a warding spell to prevent anyone else from entering magically when he was startled by a voice behind him.

"I've already done that."

16

Arthur spun around to find the raven-haired woman from the great hall sitting in a wing chair next to the sofas. The same chair that Arthur usually sat in. The same chair that Harpur Diggins had always sat in when he was alive.

Arthur approached his guest, studying her closely. She was indeed a striking woman. Her complexion was pale in contrast to her ebony locks and her unpatched eye was a deep sapphire-blue, flecked with violet. Her elbows rested on the arms of the chair and he noticed that the fingernail on her left index finger was, unlike the others, marbled with a streak of black.

"I know you from somewhere," Arthur said, trying to remember where he'd seen this woman before.

The woman nodded, but said nothing else.

Arthur reached into his sporran and retrieved the note. "Morgaine Fayle, I presume?"

"For now, that will do," Morgaine said. "Sit down, Arthur."

Arthur frowned at the directive. He wanted to rebel, but something made him acquiesce. "Harpur is dead," he announced, deciding to cut to the chase. He tossed the note onto the low table between them.

"Not exactly," Morgaine said. "Tell me, Arthur, what do you remember about my... uh, Harpur's death?"

Arthur frowned at the bizarre correction. "Just that Harpur was weak from having lived in human form for so many years on Earth and that he was challenged by another dragon named Karrys Evergreen. He lost the challenge and was killed. Then, a few months later, she imprisoned two of my friends in her lair and then just disappeared from Epoh, never to be seen again."

"That's all you remember?" Morgaine probed.

"What more is there? It was awful. I don't like to talk about it." Arthur squirmed uncomfortably. He sensed that there was much more to the woman sitting across from him than met the eye. And, quite frankly, what met the eye was a lot.

"I appreciate that," Morgaine said with a rueful smile. "So, no one has ever offered an explanation for what happened to Karrys Evergreen?"

Arthur considered his answer carefully. "Well, Sok, my senior advisor, has always believed that Harpur wasn't actually killed in the challenge. He continually tries to convince us that Harpur somehow managed to take over Karrys' body and is alive and well, probably living on Whyte Avenue... That's a street in a city on

Earth where I came from originally. But that's just Sok being Sok. He's got quite an active imagination. Besides, if Harpur was still alive somehow, he would never have abandoned us like that."

Morgaine nodded. Her rueful smile faded at the accusation. "The elf is far more perceptive than is good for him sometimes," she said.

Again, Arthur frowned. "How do you know Sok? And what do you mean by *more perceptive?*"

"We'll get to that," Morgaine said. "And Bon has never said anything to you about… that time?"

The frown deepened. "How do you know Bon? And what would he have told me? He doesn't remember anything more than the rest of us do."

Morgaine stood up and went to the table next to the balcony doors. "Ale?" she offered. She didn't wait for Arthur to reply; she filled two cups and handed one to Arthur before walking over to the bookcase against the wall separating the sitting room from Arthur's bed chamber. She scanned the titles until her eyes settled on an unassuming book, which she pulled from the shelf. Sitting down again in the wing chair, she started to open the book. "Arthur, there's something I have to show you…"

Before she could continue, a cacophony of shouting broke out in the hallway outside Arthur's chamber door.

"Open this door immediately!" Sok's voice penetrated the thick oak portal as if it wasn't there.

"King Arthur is not here," one of the guards said in a quaking voice.

"He left orders not to let anyone in," the other guard said, sounding only slightly more assertive.

"I don't care!" Sok shouted. "Open this door!"

Morgaine's smile returned. "Some things never change, do they?"

It was obviously a rhetorical question, so Arthur didn't bother to reply.

"Let's go somewhere a little more private," Morgaine said, standing up and beckoning him to do the same.

Arthur stared at the mottled fingernail. *Where do I know her from?* he wondered. He stood up as well, assuming he was about to be zapped away from the castle and let Morgaine place her hand on his shoulder. Just as they disappeared in a plume of teal smoke, he heard Anayah's voice, "The room has been warded. I can't zap us in!"

A moment later, Arthur found himself standing in a small cave high on a mountain top overlooking Braydon Wood from the south. He moved to the entrance and looked out, but quickly stepped back. A shear drop invoked his vertigo and he pushed himself against the back wall, needing to feel its solidity. Several minutes passed before he could open his eyes again.

"Still afraid of heights?" Morgaine asked. "I should have warned you."

"Where are we?" Arthur croaked.

"We are in a cave above the Fae Lands," Morgaine said. "More importantly, we are where no one is likely to disturb us."

Arthur wished he'd brought his ale with him. "You were going to show me something…"

"I was," Morgaine confirmed. "But we might as well get comfortable. This might take some time."

Morgaine snapped her fingers and two purple velvet wing chairs appeared. She gestured, inviting Arthur to make himself comfortable, so he forced himself away from the cave wall and took a seat across from the mysterious woman who held the book she'd taken from his rooms out to him.

Arthur studied the cover. "The Gargoyles of Rednow," he read the title. "Did you bring me here to read a book?"

"Open it," Morgaine said.

Arthur frowned at the raven-haired woman. "You do realize that tonight is my children's birthday celebration. I'd rather not waste it reading about gargoyles. I think you should take me back to the castle now."

"Open it," Morgaine repeated. "I think you will find it most interesting."

Arthur's frown deepened, but he opened the book, hoping that whatever this nonsense was all about would be revealed quickly so he could return to Meg and Hart's birthday party. As he lifted the thick, leather-bound cover, a sheaf of folded papers slipped out from between the pages. A sudden jolt of familiarity shot through Arthur as he unfolded the papers. Recognizing his own hand writing, he looked up at Morgaine.

"What is this?" he asked.

"Read it," Morgaine said.

Trepidation seeped into Arthur's veins and sent a shiver down his back. He started to read the lengthy missive, a sense of awe and horror filling him as he took in a most fascinating tale of things that simply could not have happened. When at last he reached the end, he looked up, once again, at Morgaine.

"I don't understand." His voice was barely a whisper.

"Harpur knew his end was coming when he saw me in court one day," Morgaine began, filling the gaps in the dispatch Arthur had just read. "He left to go see Elder Dhonna, whom he had convinced to help him put an elaborate plan into action. He had hoped to keep his plan a secret—at least as long as possible—but his friends sensed that something was amiss and would not give up trying to help him. You, Arthur, had the foresight to record everything you knew and hide it in that book before Harpur erased your memory."

All at once, Arthur remembered everything. It had all begun with Morgaine Fayle appearing in court one day, and Harpur sneaking out as if to avoid her. The dragon-wizard's strange behaviour had puzzled Arthur and Sok at the time, but then Harpur Diggins often behaved oddly. They had been concerned, though not overly at first.

Later, Arthur had met with Morgaine Fayle, who told him that she was interested in acquiring property in Epoh. While he believed she wanted to buy land, she was, in fact, the dragon Karrys Evergreen, come to challenge Harpur for rulership over the kingdom. And Arthur had written it, and everything that transpired during the following weeks, down so that if Harpur did erase his memory, he would still know what had happened. The problem was that Arthur hid the pages in a book so unfathomably dull, he never found it again.

"So, you're…" Arthur couldn't bring himself to say it.

"I am," Morgaine said.

Arthur's mind was reeling from the revelation he'd just been privy to, emotions ricochetting off every corner of his mind. Relief. Excitement. Anger. Fear. Disbelief. They all vied for dominance over his psyche. The only one that couldn't quite make it into the mix was acceptance.

Morgaine watched Arthur carefully. Expecting another of his infamous meltdowns, she was prepared to knock him out if she had to. But Arthur was so overwhelmed with the knowledge that Harpur Diggins was actually still—sort of—alive, he skipped the meltdown altogether and sat in his chair in catatonic withdrawal. The dragon-wizardess was left not knowing what to do next, or how to get him out of it. She elected to let his dazed state run its course until, eventually, Arthur blinked and sat up straight.

"What are we going to do?" he asked.

"Are you okay?" Morgaine countered.

"I'm not sure," Arthur admitted. "Part of me wants to punch you in the face."

"I wouldn't recommend that," Morgaine said with a smile. "But perhaps I should be thankful to be trapped in a woman's body."

"Perhaps you should," Arthur said, though he was almost certain that even if Harpur Diggins was in his usual human guise, he would not be brave enough to punch the dragon-wizard in the face. "But you haven't answered my question."

Morgaine sighed. She stood up and walked to the back of the cave, stopping near the spot where Arthur had been pressed against the wall earlier. She waved her hand and an aperture open up in the rock. From it, Morgaine retrieved a golden chalice with a large amber stone embedded into its side. She handed it to Arthur.

"Harpur's holy heartbeat!" Arthur jumped out of his chair and held the Amber Chalice up to examine it. Then he turned, ashen-faced and hopeful, to Morgaine. "It really is you, isn't it?"

Morgaine nodded. Then she braced herself for Arthur's abrupt embrace.

"This is so weird!" Arthur sobbed as he held onto his long-lost friend. "You're a…"

"Yes, I think that's obvious," Morgaine said, extricating herself from Arthur's arms. "And weird is an understatement."

"Where have you been? Why did you leave us?" Arthur's excitement was palpable. But before Morgaine could respond, his demeanor shifted radically away from glee to anger. "Let me rephrase that! Where the hell have you been all this time? How could you just abandon us like that?"

Morgaine had been expecting this. Sooner or later, Arthur was going to lose it and she knew that this was likely just the beginning of a doozy of a meltdown! "Sit down, Arthur, and let me explain."

"Explain? Explain what? That you duped us all into helping you survive a challenge so you could take off and leave us for sixteen years. Sixteen years, Harpur! And not a single word in all that time. Did you ever even consider what that was like for us? Did you even think about how hard it was for us to lose you?"

"It was hard for me too, Arthur. Please sit down and let me…"

"Don't you dare tell me to sit down!" Arthur started backing away from Morgaine.

"Arthur, stop," Morgaine said, her eyes widening in alarm.

"You stop!" Arthur shouted. "How could you do this to us?" He backed farther away.

"Arthur, please stop…"

But it was too late. Arthur took another step backward and fell out of the cave. His terrified screams echoed off the mountainsides.

Morgaine had no choice but to follow the shrieking king. She leapt through the cave entrance and, as soon as she was clear of the small opening, transformed into the teal dragon, Karrys Evergreen, once again. She spotted Arthur, flailing and screeching, dangerously close to the steep cliff. Worse, though, he had let go of the chalice. She watched it bounce of the rockface, splitting into two pieces on impact.

"Orhowyn's balls!" Karrys groaned as she dove straight down after Arthur. "At least he had the good sense to wear shorts under his kilt."

She had to get beneath him and turn her belly to the mountain to catch him. She reached out with her left hind foot and caught Arthur as she pumped her wings to keep herself from smashing into the rocks and crushing him. With her right foot, she pushed off the cliff and spun her huge body around to gain altitude again. The moment Arthur felt her talons pluck him out of the air, he passed out and hung limply in her grasp.

Karrys' first priority was to get somewhere safe. In dragon form, Glynnis could very well sense her presence and come looking for her. The last thing she needed right then was a confrontation with the ruling dragon of Epoh. Had they been in the north, she would have crossed the mountains into the plains, but the mountains in the south bordered on two other kingdoms, both of which were also ruled by dragons who would not welcome Karrys either. If she was recognized, she'd have to explain her whereabouts over the past sixteen years, and that was not part of the plan. Not yet.

Her best bet was to find somewhere to land and transform, then zap them back to the cave. Karrys circled to her left and headed toward a plateau that was large

22

enough for her to land on. The moment she touched down, she transformed back into Morgaine and lifted Arthur, still unconscious, over her shoulder. With a snap of her fingers, she zapped them both to the safety of the small cave and laid the inert king down on the ground.

"You're still a bit of an idiot, aren't you?" she said aloud, though her words fell on unconsciously deaf ears. "You better hope that your new Dragon Lord didn't sense me here."

While she waited for Arthur to come around, she called the pieces of the Amber Chalice from where they had fallen at the bottom of the cliff. To her dismay, she discovered a crack in the amber stone that was embedded into the side of the cup. For centuries, it had contained the essence of a Fae girl who had been killed by elves. But now, that essence had been freed and the spirit of Willow, the Fae girl, was loose somewhere in Braydon Wood. All Harpur could do about that at the moment was hope that she remained in her ethereal form and did not take on a body of any kind. As for the Amber Chalice itself, it was now useless, a relic that could neither help nor harm. Karrys tossed the pieces to the ground and bent to revive Arthur from his stupor.

The king groaned and opened his eyes. "Am I dead?"

"No," Morgaine answered, "but you should be. Seriously, Arthur, you really do need to get your fits of pique under control."

Arthur sat up and rubbed the back of his neck. "In my defense, I have every right to be pissed off at you."

"Actually, you don't," Morgaine said. "And if you had just let me explain, you would have known that. Instead, you had to go off halfcocked and nearly get yourself killed. Not to mention the danger you put us both in by making me transform. If Glynnis sensed my presence here, he will come looking for me."

Morgaine moved to the entrance and scanned the sky for any sign of Glynnis Warwyrm. She was relieved to see none, but she still felt the urgent need to get out of Epoh as soon as possible.

"Well, are you going to explain where you've been and why you abandoned us, or not?" Arthur crawled farther away from the entrance and sat with his back to the cave wall. Having got his memories back, he needed to know what had kept Harpur from returning for so long, but he also needed to let the adrenaline rush pass.

"I was in prison," Morgaine said quietly. She moved away from the entrance of the cave and settled on the ground next to Arthur.

Arthur let that sink in for a moment. "Like dragon prison? The dragons found out what you did?"

"Yes," Morgaine said, "and no. I was imprisoned, but not here—on Thraeh."

"Where, then?"

"After I left Epoh, I went back to Earth. I needed time to figure out what to do. Long before Karrys challenged me, I had planned on using the Amber Chalice to transfer my soul into my challenger's body. I would continue to rule over Epoh and protect you and Alex… I'm sorry about Alex, Arthur. I know how much you loved her." Arthur didn't respond, so Morgaine continued. "It didn't occur to me that I would be challenged by a female. But once Karrys had made the challenge, I had no choice but to go through with the plan. So, I had you retrieve the Amber Chalice from the Fae, hoping to keep you busy and distracted long enough to get the challenge over with before you and the others figured it out and tried to interfere."

"But Sok and Anayah weren't so easy to fool, were they?" Arthur interjected.

"Alas, no." Morgaine sighed. "If it wasn't for Elder Dhonna, the whole thing would have fallen apart. How is my dear friend, by the way?"

"Elder Dhonna? She's still barefoot and crimson-haired. She misses you, though." Arthur paused. "We all do."

Morgaine sighed again. "Anyway, once the deed was done, things were not as simple as I had envisioned they would be. Bon knew everything and Karrys' magic did not work on him to wipe his memory. He agreed to be my prisoner for the duration of his stay in Epoh, but Anayah wouldn't accept that and I knew that my secret would not remain a secret for long with her determination to free the android from the evil new Dragon Lord. So, I fled. It was irresponsible of me, I know. I've been beating myself up about it for sixteen years, Arthur. You can't possibly make me feel worse than I already do."

Arthur didn't know how to respond to that. He reached over and picked up the pieces of the chalice that Morgaine had dropped and stared at them. "So, you went to Earth. Obviously, you didn't stay there. What happened?"

Morgaine sat down next to Arthur. "I couldn't stay on Earth, for obvious reasons. Eventually, even if I stayed in a remote place, I would have been spotted. Can you imagine what would happen if a dragon was found living on Earth?"

Arthur shrugged. "The government of whatever country you were found in would have covered it up."

Morgaine scowled at that. "Make me a resident of Area 51, I suppose?"

"Or someplace like that," Arthur agreed. "You can't get much more alien than a dragon."

"Well, I decided to go to another world where dragons are common. Unfortunately, dragons on that world are feared and hunted. They possess no magic, and Karrys' magic didn't work there either. I was set upon by a band of dragon slayers and was overwhelmed. They were going to kill me, but dragons of Karrys' colour were unheard of and so they put me in chains and took me to a facility to study me."

"Like Area 51…"

"It was more like a mad scientist's laboratory from some old B horror movie." Morgaine shifted to cover up the revulsion the memory invoked. "They kept me sedated so I couldn't use my fire. They pried scales off my body. They tried to feed me virgins!"

Arthur turned and stared at Morgaine in horror. "I'm so sorry, Harpur. I can't imagine how awful that must have been for you. How did you escape?"

Morgaine released a derisive snort. "I guess fate stepped in. The facility where I was being kept was built on a cliff overlooking an ocean. There was an earthquake. The walls crumbled. I was hurled from my cell into freezing water. I was weak and the sedative they gave me left me unable to do anything but sink into the depths. Part of me was relieved that it was over. I just wanted to let the ocean take me and be done with it all…"

Arthur remained quiet. He felt terrible for yelling at Harpur, but focusing on what Morgaine was saying helped keep his mind off the fall from the cave. He couldn't even look at the entrance.

"Do you remember Frode?" Morgaine asked.

"The Drengrokil? How could I forget him? He made you look tiny," Arthur said. "I mean he made Harpur look small."

"The Drengrokil have giant blood in their veins," Morgaine concurred, ignoring Arthur's confusion over talking to Harpur in Morgaine's body.

"What of him?"

"He rescued me."

Arthur's eyebrows shot upward. "Frode rescued you?"

"He and his men were on a ship off shore when the quake hit. They saw me hit the water and, in spite of the rough seas, sailed in to pull me out of the water. I don't remember all that happened, but several hours later I woke up on the deck of his ship, unchained and surrounded by very large men with very large swords. Once Frode explained that he had pulled me out of the water and meant no harm, I asked him to get me to a Boundary back to Thrach and he agreed to help me." Morgaine explained.

"Does he know who you really are?" Arthur asked.

Morgaine sighed. "No." She did not elaborate further.

"How long have you been here?"

"Long enough to come up with a plan to return Karrys' body to her," Morgaine said. "But you dropped the one thing that would have enabled me to do that." She took one of the pieces of the Amber Chalice from Arthur and frowned at the wreckage.

Arthur handed Morgaine the other half of the chalice and stood up, staying close to the back wall. "Well, I think we need to get that broken cup to Hiro and Bon at the castle and let them get to work on fixing it." He held out a hand to help Morgaine to her feet.

Morgaine stared, perplexed, at Arthur's outstretched hand. Finally, she got it. "Arthur, I know this is weird, but you really have to remember who it is you're actually talking to." Morgaine stood up, without Arthur's assistance.

The raven-haired beauty handed Arthur the cup and sighed while, inwardly, Harpur Diggins weighed his options. They did need to get out of the cave. And, if anyone could repair the chalice, it was Hiro and Bon. Then there was Willow's essence floating around in Braydon Wood, about to cause Orhowyn only knew what mayhem. But there wasn't much he could do about that just then. It would take forever to find her while in human form. And he couldn't exactly go flying around as a dragon in Karrys' body looking for the spirit of the Fae girl. Glynnis would definitely notice that.

Harpur's inner debate lasted all of ten seconds. "Might as well get this over with. I was going to ask you to keep it to yourself, but we both know that's not going to happen."

Arthur shook his head, not in disagreement, but in confirmation of his inability to keep such a big secret. There was no point in pretending. "There're going to be questions. Sok and Anayah, at the very least, would see right through any lie I attempted to tell them. I think you're right; you might as well get it over with."

26

Morgaine took Arthur by the arm and raised her hand to zap them back to the castle. "Wait," she said, releasing him again. "I think I better take this with us."

She moved over to the wall where the chalice had been and waved her hand. Another niche opened up and from it, she pulled a large, leather-bound book. "My life book."

"I was wondering what had happened to that," Arthur said. "It is still being written?"

Every dragon had a life book that magically recorded the details of their life. The last time Arthur had seen Harpur's life book, it had ended with his death in the meadow that spread out in front of the entrance to his lair. When Arthur had first come to Epoh, Harpur had given it to him to read, but the writing was all but illegible and he had never been able to decipher its contents. For a time, it had been kept in a vault in Arthur's bed chamber, but it had disappeared, along with Arthur's memories of the vault and all that had happened when Harpur had supposedly died.

Morgaine opened the book and flipped to the back pages. There was a sketch of Karrys Evergreen in chains, surrounded by the dragon slayers that had captured her. The next several pages chronicled her imprisonment and the experiments that had been performed on her. There was a picture of Frode standing next to her unconscious body on the deck of his ship after the earthquake. The last page showed Morgaine and Arthur standing in a cave, reading the book.

"I suspect that all this has been added since I returned. I doubt that any of it could have been written while I was not here on Thraeh." Morgaine closed the book and tucked it under her arm. "Shall we?"

Arthur took hold of Morgaine's arm this time, allowing her to snap her fingers and zap them to his private chambers back in the castle.

The rooms were blessedly unoccupied. A fire was burning low in the hearth and candles burned in wall sconces around the room. Arthur placed the broken chalice on the low table between the sofas and lowered himself onto one. Morgaine deposited the book next to the chalice and sat down in the wing chair that Harpur had always favoured.

"What now?" Arthur asked.

"I suppose it's too late for you to return to the party," Morgaine said.

"I suppose it is," Arthur agreed. "Meg and Hart are going to be so upset with me for ruining the celebration."

"Technically, I ruined the celebration," Morgaine said. "Feel free to blame me."

Arthur raised his eyebrows and looked over at Morgaine. "Living in a female's body has mellowed you."

Morgaine snorted. "Don't even go there."

Arthur chuckled. "It's good to have you back, my friend," he said.

"I need something to eat," Morgaine replied, ignoring the heart-felt sentiment.

"Me too! Let's say we send down to the kitchen for some leftovers from the supper."

"Or…" Morgaine waved her hand above the table and plates of roast pheasant, venison, steamed vegetables, bread, and cheese appeared.

Arthur nodded with approval. "Yep, I think *or* will work just fine.

The two of them dug in, sating their appetites in silence. When they were full, Arthur stepped out onto the balcony and looked out over the sleeping city below. His thoughts were still reeling with all that had happened and he needed time to process. Morgaine joined him and handed him a freshly filled cup of ale. They clinked glasses and leaned against the railing.

"You recovered quickly from your fall," Morgaine said after a few minutes had passed. "I'm impressed, Arthur."

Arthur grunted. "I just try not to think too much about it when things like that happen."

"Do you fall out of mountain caves often?" Morgaine asked.

"That was a first," Arthur said. "But my penchant for getting into messes hasn't changed much since the last time you saw me. Somehow, I always manage to survive."

"I better let you get some sleep," Morgaine drained her ale and retreated back inside.

"Where are you going to go?" Arthur asked, following her.

"The innkeeper at the Shire's Bend likes me," Morgaine said with a sigh. "I'll get a room there."

"You can't stay in human form, Morgaine."

"I know. But I can't be a dragon either, not here."

"How long have you been in human form?"

"Not long enough to do any damage," Morgaine assured the worried king. "A few days isn't going to make a difference."

"Why don't you stay here," Arthur offered. "I'll take the sofa; you can sleep in the bed."

Morgaine cocked her head to one side. "Chivalry still lives," she said with a smile.

Arthur blushed. "It is kind of hard to keep things in perspective here, Harpur. I mean I know it's you, but... Well...," He waved his hand to indicate Morgaine's shapely figure. "...it's just weird."

Morgaine laughed. "Like I said, weird is an understatement. I'll tell you what. You sleep on the sofa and I will shrink your bed to make room to transform for the night. There's plenty of room for Karrys in your bed chamber."

Arthur shrugged. "Sure. Just let me get my night shirt." He walked into his bed chamber to change. "I thought it was too dangerous for you to be in dragon form," he said as he reemerged.

"First a kilt, then a night shirt," Morgaine said under her breath. Then, smiling at the sleepy king she answered his question. "The rooms are still warded. Hopefully, that doesn't catch Glynnis' attention."

A few minutes later, Arthur returned carrying a pillow and a blanket, which he spread out over one of the sofas. "What?" he asked when he noticed Morgaine staring at him.

"Nothing. I'm just making sure that I remember this." Morgaine turned and left Arthur rolling his eyes.

Chapter Three

The next morning, Arthur was woken up by a knock on the door. More accurately, it was a pounding rather than a knock. Someone's angry fist was connecting repeatedly with the hard oak, accompanied by that same someone's angry voice demanding entry.

"Arthur! I know you're in there. Open this door right now!"

"Coming, Sok!" Arthur called out as he untangled himself from the blanket and stumbled to the door.

"What in Harpur's name happened last night? Why did you lock us out of your rooms? Did you sleep on your sofa?" Sok had been heading for the jamba jug, but had stopped next to the sofa when he noticed the pillow and blanket.

"Am I not allowed to sleep on my sofa?" Arthur asked, rubbing the sleep from his eyes.

"Don't deflect," Sok said, continuing on to the table where he frowned at an empty jug. "You're out of jamba."

Arthur snapped his fingers and the empty jug was replaced by a full one. He had mastered simple magical feats since learning that he was a descendant of an Epohian wizard and had inherited magic powers. But he remained far from adept at it and tended to leave it to those with more finesse than himself. Refilling the jamba jug, however, was something he could do well.

"I think I'd rather have ale," Sok said, holding the jug up.

"It's like not even dawn yet. Drink the jamba," Arthur proceeded to fold his blanket, all the while glancing at the door to his bed chamber.

Jamba was a sweet, warm wine that folks in Epoh drank instead of coffee. Sok shrugged and poured himself a cup full. In protest, though, he did not pour one for Arthur. He did notice Arthur's glances at the bed chamber door.

"Well?" Sok said as he sat down on the sofa that Arthur had just woken up on. "Who's in there?"

"In where?" Arthur asked, pretending not to know what the elf was talking about.

"I am," Morgaine said as she emerged from Arthur's bed chamber.

"Whoa, Arthur! There's a woman in your bedroom!" Sok said, nearly choking on his jamba.

30

"That's not a woman," Arthur said with a wry smile. He walked over and poured two cups of jamba for himself and Morgaine. "*That* is Harpur!"

Morgaine, dressed in black leggings under a fitted black blazer accepted the jamba from Arthur and sat down in the wing chair. A teal ascot was tucked into the blazer and a black top hat with a teal hat band sat atop her flowing black locks. Her eye patch matched her ascot. She sipped her beverage while Sok coughed and spat his jamba across the table. With a wave of her hand, Morgaine saved Harpur's life book and the broken chalice by sliding them to the opposite end of the table.

"You okay, buddy?" Arthur asked, patting the elf's back before sitting down across from Sok.

"What did you say?" Sok gasped. "And please go put some pants on." He placed what remained of his jamba on the table, convinced he was safer not drinking it.

Arthur crossed his legs. "It turns out that you were right all along. Your cockamamie theory that Harpur had somehow survived the challenge was not so cockamamie after all. He goes by Morgaine Fayle now, but this is indeed our long-lost Harpur Diggins."

Morgaine smiled at Sok.

"Prove it," Sok challenged.

Arthur looked at Morgaine and nodded toward Sok, but she just shook her head.

"What? What was that?" Sok demanded to know.

"Give him his memories back," Arthur pleaded.

"No," Morgaine said.

"Why?"

"Yeah, why?" Sok said. "What memories?"

"Harpur... Karrys... Morgaine wiped all our memories so we wouldn't remember that we helped Harpur take over Karrys' body so he could keep being the Dragon Lord of Epoh after he died." Arthur explained.

"Karrys? Karrys Evergreen? I'm so confused." Sok picked up his jamba cup again, looked into its depths and then put it back down.

"Come on, Morgaine," Arthur said, "if you give him back his memories, he'll stop asking questions and he'll be more cooperative."

"No," Morgaine repeated. "Get Bon. Bon remembers."

"Bon remembers what?" Sok's eyes darted back and forth between Morgaine and Arthur.

"Get Bon," Morgaine repeated. Then she leaned back and drank her jamba with her eyes closed.

"If I get Bon, will you tell me what is going on?" Sok asked.

"I already told you. Sort of. I suspect that Bon will just tell you the same thing. Probably in greater detail, but, yes, I think one of us needs to get Bon up here." Arthur sipped from his own cup. Then he remembered the pages that he'd hidden inside The Gargoyles of Rednow. "Damn! I left what I had written about it in the cave."

Morgaine expected Arthur to ask her to conjure them back for him, but Arthur surprised her by doing it himself.

"Here," he said to Sok. "This explains everything."

The elf took the pages from Arthur and looked at them dubiously. "What is this?" he asked.

"It's everything that really happened when Harpur was defeated by Karrys Evergreen." Arthur sipped his jamba. "I wrote it all down, expecting Harpur to wipe our memories."

"So, where has it been all this time?" Sok asked, remaining doubtful.

"On the shelf, hidden inside a book," Arthur said. He leaned back and took another drink.

"And you just happened to forget where you put it?" Sok made a face at his friend.

"Harpur wiped our memories," Arthur quipped. "Remember?"

Sok glowered at the king and unfolded the pages. "It's your handwriting," Sok acknowledged.

Morgaine was making a sour face of her own. Inside, however, Harpur Diggins was enjoying the convivial mockery between the elf and the man that he had missed so much. Though he would never openly admit it. He had a reputation to preserve.

"If you don't believe that, you can read it in Harpur's..." Arthur looked up at Morgain. "You made the book invisible?"

Morgaine ignored Arthur's query about Harpur's life book. "Wasn't someone going to summon Bon?"

Arthur stood up and dispatched one of the guards to get Bon.

"You might want to get dressed, as well," Morgaine suggested, eyes still closed.

Arthur was comfortable in his night shirt, but he recognized that Bon was not likely to show up alone. "You could have let Sok look at the book as further proof."

"I could have," Morgaine agreed.

"Yep! You're definitely Harpur!" The night-shirted king repaired to his bedroom to change.

While Arthur debated whether to wear the kilt again, or put on his usual clothes, namely pants with a tunic, his mind kept wandering back to Morgaine's account of her time in the facility where she was experimented on. Knowing that Harpur was not only trapped in another dragon's body, but also imprisoned and, basically, tortured, hurt Arthur deeply. Part of him was angry with Harpur for erasing their memories. A bigger part was happy to have the grumpy old dragon back among them. He knew that he would forgive Harpur for what he'd done and he regretted what had happened to the chalice. If he had been responsible for keeping Harpur from executing whatever plan he had to get out of Karrys' body he would never forgive himself, though. He could only hope that Harpur would.

By the time Arthur settled on a comfortable pair of grey trousers and a royal-blue shirt, Sok had finished reading his account of the events leading up to Harpur's faux death. He had folded the pages and placed them on the table. As bizarre as the diarized narrative was, it actually made sense to the elf. Everything that Arthur had written was, at the very least, plausible. And it meshed with the theory he'd harboured ever since Karrys Evergreen had disappeared from Epoh.

Arthur reentered the main room just as Anayah, Davynn, Bon and Hiro had arrived. All of them looked at Morgaine, curious about her presence; only Bon recognized her.

"Anayah, Davynn, Hiro and Bon, this is Harpur Diggins," Sok said. "Harpur Diggins, this is Anayah, Davynn, Hiro and Bon. But you already know that."

Arthur rolled his eyes. "Sok, don't be an ass! I'm sorry, Morgaine." He turned to face his friends. "Guys, this is Morgaine Fayle."

Morgaine templed her fingers and smiled at the assembled group. "Actually, Arthur and Sok are both right. I am Morgaine Fayle. And I'm Harpur Diggins."

Anayah leaned closer to her frowning husband and whispered, "Any clue as to what is going on here?"

Davynn shook his head. "Let's just sit down and see how this plays out."

The pretty witch and the handsome knight took seats on the sofa facing Morgaine so they could watch the events as they transpired. They noticed that Bon had retreated away from the others and was watching Morgaine intently.

Hiro dismounted from his hover gilly and offered to produce breakfast from his satchel. No one objected, so he began setting plates of pastries and cakes on the low table. One of the plates failed to connect with the table and the Krist realized that an invisible item was responsible for the anomaly.

"What's this?" Hiro asked.

Morgaine looked at Hiro. "Nothing you need be concerned about. The plate won't hurt it."

Yes, but will it hurt the plate? Hiro wondered. He covertly felt the invisible object and determined that it was a rather large book. Taking a fruit-filled pastry, he sauntered over to stand beside Bon whom, he suspected, knew exactly what the large book was.

It appeared that everyone had the same idea as Anayah and Davynn—to wait and see how things unfolded on their own. Plagued with questions, and knowing that if the woman sitting in the wing chair really was Harpur, most of those questions would not be answered, at least not directly. The prudent thing to do was wait and listen. But, as they all settled into their chosen positions, an odd silence filled the room instead, all eyes on Morgaine, whose own eyes were locked on the spot where the invisible chalice rested next to the invisible book on the table. Even Sok held his tongue, though his own gaze kept straying to the space Harpur's life book occupied under the plate of pastries.

Finally, just as the fidgeting in the room reached its crescendo, the book and the chalice materialized and six pairs of eyes shifted away from Morgaine to focus on the three new objects in their midst.

"Is that what I think it is?" Sok broke the silence. He reached over, moved the plate of pastries and hefted the heavy tome onto his lap. He flipped it open to the center, revealing a coloured drawing of Harpur Diggins. "It is," he whispered as he let his fingers wander over the pages. "Where did you get Harpur's life book?" he asked, not taking his eyes off the picture of his friend. As much as the elf had insisted that Harpur was still alive over the years, he'd never quite allowed himself to believe it was true.

Arthur reached over and lifted Sok's hand so he could turn the pages to the back of the book. Sok gasped when he saw the drawing of Karrys Evergreen in chains. He turned the pages back to the page depicting Harpur's death in the meadow outside his lair. Davynn, Anayah and Hiro all moved closer, crowding around to see what Sok was seeing. Morgaine and Arthur leaned back in their chairs and let the others absorb what the book disclosed. Bon remained where he was by the fireplace and observed the others as they discovered what he had known all along.

Thus, absolved of his promise to keep Harpur's secret, the android wondered why, after all this time, Harpur had decided to return. He knew that all would be revealed soon enough and patience was his best ally for the time being. So, he remained apart, watching, listening... Recording.

Morgaine joined the android. "Thank you for not telling anyone. May I ask why you are still here? You were supposed to return to your own time long ago."

"You're welcome. It wasn't always easy. Sok is tenacious, even for an elf!" Bon said, receiving a knowing smile from Morgaine. "I did return to my world at the appointed time, only to find that my technology was being made redundant and I was to be dismantled. I escaped and came back to Epoh rather than succumb to oblivion. When I got back, I removed the components that allowed me to time travel and have been here ever since. Now, what about you? Where have you been all these years?"

Morgaine took a deep breath. "Imprisoned on another world."

In four short words, she had managed to convey the depth of the distress talking about it would cost her. Bon simply nodded his acknowledgement of whatever she'd been through. There was no need to extract further information until she was ready. "I'm sorry," he said. "What will you do now?"

"The plan was to use the Amber Chalice to release myself from Karrys, but our good King Arthur dropped it and... Well, you can see its condition. I'm hoping that you and Hiro can fix it." She called the broken pieces to her and handed them to Bon.

"I'm not a wizard," Bon said, looking at the damaged cup and noting the crack in the amber stone.

"No, but with your knowledge and Hiro's magic, perhaps there is a chance?"

"We'll do our best," Bon vowed. "But what happens if we do manage to repair it and restore its magic? What happens to you when you are released from Karrys' body?"

Morgaine turned to stare out the window. "I'm not sure now," she said. "I was planning on killing Glynnis and taking over his body. Trying this again." She paused. "But now I'm wondering if maybe it's time to let go. Arachovor is waiting for me."

Arachovor was the place that dragons believed their spirits went when they died. And Harpur had lived a long, long life. Watching Arthur and the others and realizing that they had done just fine without him, his plan felt wrong to him. He had spent sixteen years in another dragon's body, hearing her thoughts, feeling her feelings. He regretted having stolen her life from her the way he had. *Could I do it to another dragon? Do I even deserve to keep living?*

"Not many would be sorry to see Glynnis removed from this world," Bon said. "He's not the honourable dragon that you are, Harpur."

"Many would say that what I've done is not honourable either," Morgaine said.

"You did what you did out of love for these people," Bon countered, noting the wince his words elicited from Morgaine. "What if we could restore your own body?"

Morgaine turned back from the window and looked skeptically at the android. "That's impossible. My body was burned to dust."

"I cannot guarantee anything, but I do believe that there is a way," the android said enigmatically. "Leave it with me for a while. I will keep you apprised of my progress."

Morgaine did not respond.

"One more thing," Bon continued. "Will Karrys betray you to the dragons once she is free of you?"

"No," Morgaine answered. "Karrys and I have come to an accord. She wants her body back, of course, and she has come to terms with my reasons for doing what I did. She will not betray me."

"Excellent," Bon said. "Then let me and Hiro get to work on the chalice. Perhaps, young Hart can be of assistance. He is a rather gifted scientist. I would wager that he will come up with some novel approaches to the problem."

As if on cue, the door opened and Princess Meg and Prince Hart entered.

"There you are!" Meg said, rushing to her father's side. "We were so worried about you last night. What happened?"

Arthur let his daughter fall into his embrace, relieved that she wasn't upset with him for ruining the celebration. "I'm okay," he said, then gently pushed her back so he could stand up. "There's someone special I would like the two of you to meet."

The King of Epoh took his daughter's hand and beckoned to Hart to follow them over to where Morgaine stood next to Bon.

"Meg, Hart, this is Harpur Diggins," Arthur said, presenting his perplexed children to the strange raven-haired woman. "But you can call him Morgaine for the time being."

Meg and Hart looked questioningly at each other. Morgaine Fayle did not resemble the description they had been given of Harpur Diggins in any way.

"I don't understand," Meg said.

Hart's eyes grew wide with realization. He turned to Arthur. "Sok was right? Harpur is in… her?"

"That's just weird," Meg said, scowling at the notion of the surly old dragon-wizard they'd heard stories about all their lives being alive in the voluptuous woman standing before them.

"Meg!" Hart admonished his sister. "Some respect, please."

Morgaine, in spite of herself, wiped a tear from her eye. Except for the glimpse of the twins across the great hall the night before, Harpur hadn't seen them since they were tiny babies. Seeing them standing there, all grown up, was more than even Harpur's gruff heart could withstand. Morgaine pulled the prince and princess into her arms and hugged them. "I'm so happy to see you both again. I'm so sorry about your mother. Alex was a very special woman."

Arthur's own eyes widened in shock at the spectacle of Morgaine displaying such affection for the twins. This was entirely unexpected, but he quickly composed himself and smiled at the reunion between his friend and his children. Then he noticed the pieces of the chalice in Bon's hands. Clearly, Harpur had already set things in motion with the android. And he hoped with all his heart that Bon and Hiro could repair the magical artifact. All he wanted was to have Harpur really and truly back with them all.

Behind them, Sok, Anayah, Davynn and Hiro were still engrossed in the contents of Harpur's life book. As for Arthur, the script was a challenge for him. The only person he knew who could read it was Elder Dhonna. He wondered where she had gone after he'd left the castle with Morgaine the night before.

He left Hart, Meg and Morgaine to get acquainted and walked back to the sofas. "Did Elder Dhonna go back to Braydon Wood last night?"

Sok didn't look up from the book. "I think so," he said. "Anayah, you were the last one to talk to her when we left the council chambers. Do you know where she went?"

Anayah looked up at Arthur. "She and King Röggenar left together. She invited him back to the elven city to spend the night with her."

"Spend the night with her?" Sok parroted, tearing his eyes from the book. "What does that mean?"

Sok tended to be overly protective of the guild master and the thought of Elder Dhonna having relations with a dwarf was beyond his comprehension.

"Not like that!" Anayah said. "She offered him a room in her tree house. She wanted to show him a dagger she has to see if he could clean it up and replace some of the missing jewels on the hilt. Get your mind out of the gutter, Sok."

"I don't know what that means either," Sok said, "but you should have been more clear."

"And you shouldn't make assumptions," Anayah replied, not wanting to let him have the last word. "Turn the page, I want to know what happened next."

Arthur left them to the book and went to the door where he asked the guards to send a message to Elder Dhonna in Braydon Wood. He could have asked Anayah to quickly zap over there and fetch the guild master, but he didn't want to disturb her from the history lesson.

When he turned back and took in the activity taking place in his chambers, he felt an overwhelming sense of satisfaction wash over him. Eight of the most important people in the world to him were there and his heart swelled with love for them all. While Elder Dhonna would soon join them, he couldn't help but notice the permanent absence of Alex. A lump formed in his throat and he suddenly felt the need to be alone.

"I'm just going out for a bit," he announced. But no one seemed to have heard him. So, he quietly exited his chambers and made his way down to the gardens at the front of the castle where a memorial to Alex stood next to a dragonfoil tree that had appeared the spring after she had died in childbirth eleven years earlier.

The dragonfoil tree, at that time of year, appeared to be little more than a sapling, but as the spring and summer progressed, it would grow to a height of nearly twenty feet. Already, Arthur could see tiny buds that would become thick, silver-purple foliage. Come autumn, the leaves would fall, much like any other deciduous tree's leaves. Then, when the last leaf was freed from its branch, the entire tree would burst into flames and collapse in a simmering pile of ash.

Dragonfoil trees grew throughout Epoh. They were the legacy to the land left behind by Orhowyn Bravvenshyn when Xzynthyrius Dreamfinder had beaten him in a challenge for rulership over the kingdom. Arthur had once walked into the flames of one of the dragonfoils to fulfil an elven prophecy that had been given to Sok at the Well of the Ancients when the young elf had come of age. Years later, Harpur had chanced upon Arthur performing magic on Earth and had tried to ask him about how he had come to possess such power. Arthur, thinking Harpur was deranged, had fled and been struck and killed by a car. Harpur had revived him with his own blood in hopes of solving the mystery of a human wizard on a world that was supposed to be devoid of magic. Necromancy was not a typical practice of dragons; the result of such an act was unpredictable, often causing the recipient of the blood to grow scales or sprout wings. In Arthur's case, he had become impervious to fire and Harpur convinced Arthur that he was the subject of the vague prophecy that stated that Sok would help guide a lost child of Epoh home to become king. Together, the dragon-wizard and the elf had determined that Arthur would have to convince the people of Epoh of his right to rule as the human king. Arthur had hoped to pull a sword out of a stone, or some other less terrifying feat than walking into the deadly flames of a dragonfoil tree, but Harpur had insisted. And he had survived, obviously, but he was determined never to repeat the experience.

Arthur sat on the cold ground and leaned against Alex's memorial, a simple standing stone with a simple plague commemorating her short reign as his queen and as the love of his life. "Harpur's back," he said in a quiet voice. "He looks a little different, but it's really him. He was in a prison on another world all this time. They did awful things to him, Alex. Awful things."

Arthur stopped talking and allowed all the emotions that had been welling up since the night before to pour out of him in a torrent of tears. When, at last, he could speak again, he told Alex everything. "I just hope that I didn't screw up

39

Harpur's only chance to release himself from Karrys' body. I can't believe that I dropped the chalice and broke it. I wish you were here, my love. I need you now," he finished. Then Arthur covered his face with his hands and let a fresh deluge of tears begin to flow.

Elder Dhonna and King Röggenar were sitting on the balcony of her treehouse sipping tea and sharing stories of their long-ago youths. Röggenar was an entertaining, albeit hyperbolic, story-teller, and Elder Dhonna was enjoying being social simply for the sake of being social. She knew she should be concerned about Arthur's odd behavior at the twins' birthday celebration, but she also knew that whatever was going on would filter its way through to her in its own time. For now, she was content to spend such a fine spring morning in the company of the amusing king of the dwarves.

She had given the dagger she wanted repaired to Röggenar when they had first arrived in Braydon Wood the night before and he had assured her that it would be returned looking like new. He had some particularly lovely rubies that he thought would make nice embellishments and Elder Dhonna was pleased by the prospect of having her favourite gemstones added to the hilt. When he had asked her where she'd gotten such a fine weapon, she was a little embarrassed to admit that she could not remember where it had come from. It had, in fact, come from Harpur's hoard, along with several other small treasures that her dear friend had given to her before he died. But Elder Dhonna had no recollection of it and it never occurred to her that it was even a remote possibility. Where it came from made little difference to her; she just assumed that she had found it somewhere, probably on one of her foraging expeditions looking for medicinal plants that grew wild in Braydon Wood.

They had planned on returning to the castle early to check on Arthur, but relaxing with a cup of tea had unraveled any sense of urgency over what the king was up to and time had slipped by largely unnoticed. It wasn't until a castle guard arrived with a message that they even realized just how much time had already passed.

Elder Dhonna descended from her treehouse gracefully and waited, barefoot as usual, while Röggenar scrambled down the rope ladder somewhat more awkwardly. The stalky dwarf was used to climbing solid rock, but the swinging motion of the ladder left him a little less certain of his footing. When he finally made it to the ground, he tugged on his sleeves and grunted that they should make haste and not dilly-dally any further. Elder Dhonna stifled a giggle and followed the proud king away from her treetop home.

The guard, on horseback, rode ahead, leaving the elf and the dwarf to walk to the city. Elder Dhonna had to try to match her long-legged gait to Röggenar's shorter steps. Still, the dwarf found himself nearly jogging to keep up with the guild master. By the time they reached the castle, Röggenar was slightly out of breath and was not looking forward to the climb up four flights of stairs to Arthur's private chambers, which is where the guard had said Arthur and the others would be waiting for them.

"What is wrong with the council chambers?" Röggenar groused as they passed the main-floor door and began their ascent up into the tower.

"Do you want me to fetch the others and have them meet us down here?" Elder Dhonna offered.

For a moment, Röggenar considered it. "Nah," he said, "I can make it."

They started up the stairs and it was all Elder Dhonna could do to climb slowly and keep pace with the dwarf as he huffed and puffed his way to the top. When, at last, they arrived at their destination, the guards at the door let them right in. Röggenar went straight to the table, expecting a refreshing jug of ale, and was as disappointed as Sok had been to find only jamba in the vessel.

Elder Dhonna, however, took an immediate inventory of the people who were already present and noted both Arthur's absence and Morgaine's unexpected presence. As she studied the one-eyed woman in the top hat, a peculiar sense of familiarity washed over her. She was sure she had never seen her before. Yet, something in Morgaine's demeanor seemed to tug at her memory in a most disturbing way. She approached Anayah, who was sitting on the sofa across from Sok and as she passed her fellow elf, she saw the book opened on his lap.

"Where did that come from?" she gasped.

Sok looked up. "Oh, hi, Elder Dhonna! You're not going to believe what has happened."

Elder Dhonna's eyes went straight to Morgaine, who turned and smiled at her. "Bella Dhonna, how lovely it is to see you again."

Hearing the term of endearment that only Harpur Diggins had ever called her, Elder Dhonna blanched as she realized who was actually speaking. She froze and stared at Morgaine, trying to make sense of what she was seeing and hearing.

Seeing the distress that Elder Dhonna had fallen under, Morgaine waved her hand and the elf's true memories of a time she had tried hard to forget flooded back. To everyone's shock and chagrin, Elder Dhonna fainted. It was only

Davynn's quick reflexes that prevented her from hitting the floor as he leapt up and caught her in his arms.

Anayah abandoned the sofa to make room for Davynn to lay the swooning elf down. The witch then began to administer healing energy by laying her hands on Elder Dhonna's cheeks and temples. "Get some water," Anayah ordered.

Sok closed the book and set it down beside him on the sofa. He jumped up and ran to the table where the jamba jug stood. "There's only jamba! What do I do?"

Hiro reached into his satchel and produced a cup of water. He stood next to Anayah, waiting for Elder Dhonna to come to again. "I got this, Sok," he said to the panicking elf.

Sok filled a cup with the sweet, warm wine and drank it as if he'd intended to all along.

Elder Dhonna recovered quickly. She sat up and took the cup of water from the Krist, sipping it slowly as she processed Harpur's strange reappearance in the human guise of Morgaine Fayle.

"Are you alright?" Anayah asked, sitting beside the guild master.

"I'm fine," Elder Dhonna said. "Thank you."

Everyone watched Elder Dhonna, not sure what else to do or say.

"May I have a moment alone with…?" Elder Dhonna began.

"Morgaine," Arthur offered, reentering his chambers and hearing the guild master's request. "Morgaine Fayle."

For several seconds, no one moved. Then everyone scrambled to leave the room.

"We'll be in the council chambers," Arthur said as he ushered the others out of his private chambers and down the hall.

Elder Dhonna said nothing; she continued to sip her water and stare at the wall. When everyone had left, she placed the cup on the table and picked up Harpur's life book. "I haven't seen this in a long time," she said quietly. "I assume it continues from where we left off?"

Morgaine returned to the wing chair and sat down. "Everything is in there," she said.

Elder Dhonna opened the book and began flipping slowly through the pages. She seemed to be in no hurry to get to the end and read what had happened to

Harpur over the past sixteen years. When she reached the center pages with the portrait of Harpur, she paused. Like Sok had done, she ran her fingers over the image. A single tear fell from her eye, landing on the bottom of the right-hand page. She wiped it away and continued to look at the great purple dragon.

"You could have warned me that you were about to restore my memories," Elder Dhonna said.

"In hindsight, that may have been the better course of action," Morgaine replied.

"Hmph!" Elder Dhonna snorted. It was as close to an apology as she was likely to get from Harpur. "You've restored all the others' memories?"

"Just Arthur's," Morgaine said.

"I think I would prefer to hear what happened to you after you left us from you rather than read it," Elder Dhonna said. She appeared calm, but under her stoic exterior, she was seething with an unfettered anger at her oldest and dearest friend. It was all she could do to give Harpur the benefit of the doubt and not rebuff him for his prolonged absence.

Morgaine smiled. She could sense Elder Dhonna's wrath. But the elf deserved a proper explanation and so she did as she was bid and told Elder Dhonna about what had happened after Karry Evergreen had left Epoh. When she was done, Elder Dhonna closed the book and stood up.

At first, Morgaine wasn't sure if Harpur had been forgiven or not. Then Elder Dhonna held out her arms, inviting Morgaine into them. "Welcome back, you old fool!"

The two women stood embracing each other for a long time until Morgaine pulled away. Keeping her hands on Elder Dhonna's upper arms, the dragon-wizardess leaned back a little and said with a tearful smile, "Thank you for not saying that this is weird."

Elder Dhonna shook her head and wiped away her own tears. "Weird is a bit of an understatement. Now, how are we going to get you back to your old self?"

Morgaine laughed. "I had a plan…"

"I'm sure you did," Elder Dhonna interrupted, "But we both know how well your plans tend to work out."

"Yes," Morgaine agreed. "Arthur has already tossed a spanner into the works by breaking the Amber Chalice. It was my only hope of releasing myself from Karrys' body."

"Good old Arthur!" Elder Dhonna said with a sigh. "What are the options?"

"Hiro and Bon have been tasked with trying to repair the chalice. Short of that..." Morgaine paused and shrugged, "...I'm at a loss."

"And if they do manage to fix it, what then? What happens to you?" Elder Dhonna was at as much of a loss as Morgaine and Harpur.

"The plan was to subdue Glynnis and transfer my... Harpur's spirit into his body. But without the chalice..." Morgaine's voice trailed off.

"Not much of a plan," Elder Dhonna said. "Look what happened last time you did that! And what if Glynnis couldn't be subdued?"

Morgaine shrugged again and shook her head. "That wasn't an option."

"Like I said, not much of a plan." Elder Dhonna sat back down on the sofa.

"It's worth the risk. Anything must be better than being stuck with me forever." Morgaine sat down again as well.

"If you're expecting me to disagree with that, you're going to be disappointed," Elder Dhonna said.

Morgaine laughed again. "I know you don't mean that, Bella Dhonna."

"Don't be so sure."

After hearing what had happened to Harpur, Elder Dhonna's anger had abated. She couldn't imagine how difficult it must have been for Harpur to live imprisoned as he was for so long. Not just in the facility where he was experimented on, but in Karrys' body as well. She had never thought that Harpur's original plan to live in another dragon's body was a good idea and she had only gone along with it because she couldn't imagine losing Harpur altogether. Before her memories had been wiped, she had believed that Harpur would find a way to come back to them. Now that she had her memories back, she couldn't fathom how they might achieve such an elusive goal.

Morgaine watched Elder Dhonna mulling all this over for a few minutes. "Bon thinks that he might have a solution," she said.

Elder Dhonna, looked up hopefully. "Such as?"

"He didn't give me any details," Morgaine said, "but knowing Bon, it will be... interesting."

Elder Dhonna frowned. She had come to admire the android over the years, but he tended to rely on technology, which was foreign and vexing to her. "What's he going to do, build an android body for you?"

That hadn't occurred to Harpur. "I sincerely hope not!"

Arthur, Sok, Davynn, Anayah, Bon, Hiro, Röggenar, Meg and Hart were all sitting at the round table in the council chambers when Elder Dhonna and Morgaine Fayle joined them a couple hours later. The elf and the dragon-wizardess had spent the time catching up on Elder Dhonna's life since she and Harpur had last seen one another. There had been more tears, more laughter and more hugs, though Harpur would not have appreciated the others knowing anything about that. They took their seats, filling the only two empty chairs and proceeded to fill the plates that Hiro handed them with food from the platters that littered the large, oak table.

The conversation seemed to be about the events of the previous evening, particularly what to do with all the gifts the twins had received for their birthdays. Though they had specified on the invitations that no gifts were required, two large tables had been heaped with packages that now had to be dealt with. Some members of the citizenry seemed to be expecting a public gift opening. But neither Meg nor Hart had much interest in indulging them.

"You will have to go through them," Anayah pointed out. "And send thank you cards to everyone."

"Ugh!" Meg groaned. "Do I have to?"

"Yes, you have to," Arthur said. "It's the polite thing to do."

"But, Father, did you see them all? It will take hours to open them." Meg was envisioning all the archery practice she would have to miss.

"Not to mention the time it will take to write out the thank you cards," Hart said, envisioning all the time in the laboratory he would have to give up.

"Ugh!" Meg reiterated.

"Maybe Anayah can help you," Sok suggested.

"Me?" Anayah exclaimed. "I have plans for this afternoon."

"Oh, please, Aunt Anayah?" Meg begged. "You could do it in no time with your magic."

"You have magic of your own," Anayah said. "You both could use the practice."

"Bah!" Hart said.

Morgaine leaned forward with interest. "You inherited magic from your father?"

"Apparently," Meg said, clearly as unimpressed by this as she was uninterested.

"Meg's not very good at it," Hart explained.

Morgaine's eyebrows arched upward as she looked at Arthur. "What about you? Has your magic improved any over the years?"

"You saw me fall out of that cave," Arthur said. "If my magic was anything to write home about, you wouldn't have had to save my sorry butt."

"Indeed," Morgaine said.

"How does one fall out of a cave?" Sok asked. "Let me guess. It was on the side of a mountain and Arthur was having a meltdown."

Morgaine nodded. "That pretty much sums it up."

"How have you lived so long?" Sok asked Arthur.

"Just lucky, I guess," Arthur said.

Meg looked horrified. "Did you even try to save yourself, Father?"

"I was falling off the side of a mountain," Arthur said. "Using magic was the last thing on my mind."

"Maybe we all should practice more," Hart said. He was as horrified as his sister was at the thought of their father plummeting off a mountain. As he spoke, he began to feel a tingling sensation between his eyebrows. He looked at his sister and noticed that her hand had strayed to her own brow. He caught her eye and shook his head.

Morgaine had noticed too. "Are you two alright?"

"We're fine," Meg said, glancing sideways at her brother. "I just have a bit of a headache."

"Do you want some healing?" Elder Dhonna offered.

"I'll be okay," Meg said quickly. "Thank you, though."

Morgaine made a mental note to keep an eye on the twins. Across the table, Anayah renewed her own mental note to keep an eye on them. After Arthur had left the celebration the night before, she'd all but forgotten their odd behaviour. Bon, too, had noticed Meg touch her forehead, but rather than be concerned about the twins, he turned his attention to Morgaine and made a mental note to talk to her about it. He was certain that Harpur had some idea of what was happening to the twins.

Meg stood up and pushed her chair in. "I'm going to the archery range. Have a nice day, everyone."

"You are going to deal with the gifts first," Arthur said to his daughter's retreating back.

Meg stopped and balled her fists. "I promise I'll do it later."

"Now, young lady," Arthur said.

"Argh!" Meg moaned as she turned around. "Then Hart has to come too."

Hart slumped and sighed. "Fine! Let's get it over with." He grabbed a large pastry from the tray in front of his chair and stood up to accompany his sister. "I'll get some paper and a pen from the lab and join you in a minute."

"No need," Anayah said, snapping her fingers.

A pen and a note pad appeared in Hart's free hand. "Thanks, Aunt Anayah," he said with something less than enthusiasm.

"Maybe we should practice our magic," Meg said under her breath as Hart caught up to her. "Then we can just zap out of rooms before anyone can say anything to us."

Hart stifled a laugh as he held the door open for the princess. "After you, big sister," he said, waving good bye to everyone with the note pad.

"So, Bon" Elder Dhonna said when the door closed on the twins again, "I understand you have a plan to help Harpur."

Morgaine looked at the elf. "Not now," she whispered, but Elder Dhonna shushed her.

"I have some thoughts on the matter," Bon affirmed. "First, I must do some research. I will apprise you of my findings when I am ready."

Arthur perked up. This was the first he'd heard of any kind of plan to help Harpur and he wanted a quick solution. "Can you share your ideas with us, Bon? Maybe we can help."

"I think I would prefer to keep it to myself for the time being," the android said. "There is no guarantee that I can make it work and so I do not wish to get your hopes up. The most immediate problem, however, is the Amber Chalice." He had given the pieces of the broken chalice to Hiro to stow in his satchel—it wasn't just good for producing food on demand—and now he motioned for the Krist to bring them out. "First we will attempt to find a way to repair this."

All eyes were on the pieces that Hiro was holding up.

"Oh, look," Anayah said, reaching across Davynn to take one of the pieces, "the amber stone is cracked. Didn't it hold the spirit of one of the Fae?"

Morgaine had hoped no one would notice. "It did." She saw no point in prevaricating.

"Her name was Willow, right?" Arthur asked, craning his neck to see the cracked stone.

"It was," Morgaine confirmed.

"Does this mean that Willow's spirit is now free?" Davynn asked

"It does," Morgaine said.

"Are you telling us that a Fae spirit is running loose in Braydon Wood?" Sok sounded alarmed.

Morgaine took a deep breath. "When the cup broke and the amber cracked, Willow's spirit most likely escaped. But we were in the mountains above the Fae Lands, so it is also likely that her spirit is there. She will seek out her own kind."

"Most likely?" Sok's alarm amped up several degrees. "How long was it trapped in that stone? Does it know that it must remain in the Fae Lands? What if it possesses a new body? What if it possesses a tree?!"

"Calm down, Sok," Morgaine said. "Willow was a gentle Fae and she chose to have her spirit encased in the amber. Once my own situation is dealt with, I will ensure that she is safe and causes no harm."

"And what if your situation isn't dealt with?" Sok was out of his chair. "What if, while we're trying to fix you, that abomination runs amok in Braydon Wood?"

"She won't run amok, Sok," Morgaine said firmly. "Now sit down and stop overreacting."

"Overreacting?" Sok stepped away from his chair. "It's bad enough that we have to live next to those..." The elf waved his hands spasmodically in the general direction of the Fae Lands. "...things! But to have the spirit of a murdered Fae just out there... What if it is plotting revenge against the elves?"

It was no secret that Sok was not a fan of the Fae. Elves considered the Fae to be unnatural and had no use for them, but Sok simply loathed them. Morgaine saw an elven version of an Arthurian meltdown coming on. "If you don't sit down and calm yourself right now, I will freeze you where you stand and leave you there until the dragonfoil leaves drop."

It may have been Morgaine's voice that Sok heard, but it was Harpur's character behind the words. Not for a second did the elf doubt that Morgaine would follow through. He sat back down and tried to quell his rapid breathing.

"Sok has a point," Davynn said. "We don't know anything about this Fae creature."

"I do," Morgaine said. "And I promise you that she will not be a problem." It wasn't the first time that Harpur had lied to his friends. The truth was that he did not know what Willow might do with her new-found freedom. She had been gentle and kind when she was alive, but she was still a Fae and after hundreds of years in the amber stone, who knew what she might be capable of? Morgaine had to keep them all focused on releasing Harpur. "I think we should focus on the problem at hand. Hiro? Bon? Do you think that you can repair the chalice?"

Hiro spoke first, "I need to know everything you know about it as it was. Where did it come from? How was it made? Who made it?" He stopped as if to think. "Why was Willow's spirit trapped in the amber stone?"

Morgaine stared at the Krist through narrowed eyes. "I will tell you what I know. But leave Willow out of it. She has nothing to do with what we need the chalice to do. The amber stone was a device of convenience, that's all."

"Okay!" Hiro said. "Shall we go to the laboratory, then?"

Morgaine followed Hiro and Bon out of the council chambers, saying to the others as they also stood to follow, "We'll let you know what we discover."

Arthur, Sok, Davynn, Anayah, Elder Dhonna and Röggenar all sat back down.

"Who does she think she is?" Sok spat.

49

"She doesn't think she's anybody," Arthur said. "He knows he's Harpur."

"This is too weird," Sok said. "I'm going to Braydon Wood for a while."

"I'm going to take the children to the market," Anayah announced. "Elder Dhonna, would you like to come with us?"

The guild master nodded. "Röggenar? Do you want to come to the market?"

The dwarf king shrugged. "Why not?"

"I'm going to the guard house to… check on things," Davynn said. He didn't want to think about how much Anayah and the children would spend at the market.

Arthur was left alone in the council chambers. He poured himself a cup of ale, reached for a pastry and put his feet up on the oak surface of the big, round table, intending to relish a few moments of peace. Two bites into his pastry, Sok burst back through the door.

"Arthur! It's Glynnis! He's summoning you!"

Arthur held his cup an inch away from his lips and glared over it at his excited senior advisor.

"Hurry!" Sok commanded.

Arthur took a long drink of ale and then set it and the pastry down on the table. "What does he want?"

"I don't know, but he's circling the city clockwise. That means he wants to talk to you." Sok held the door open for Arthur.

"I thought circling counter-clockwise means he wants to talk to me." Arthur said as he started down the steps toward the road leading to the main gates.

"No, clockwise means he wants to talk to you. Counter-clockwise means he wants to talk to you and it's urgent."

"Isn't it always urgent?"

"Sometimes he just wants to talk to you."

"So, there's nothing to be worried about and this is a social call?"

"How would I know?"

"You know the difference between a clockwise circle and a counter-clockwise circle."

"Someone has to," Sok said. *Harpur knows you don't pay attention to these things.*

Arthur felt a surge of trepidation as he looked up and saw the huge, bronze dragon begin his descent into the field outside the city walls. The sun glinted off the golden-hued scales, a point of pride for Glynnis, making the Dragon Lord look like a giant sparkler in the sky. Arthur adjusted his crown and picked up the pace. Whatever Glynnis wanted, Arthur wanted to get it over with as quickly as possible.

"Any ideas on what this is about?" Arthur asked as they passed through the city gate and turned south on the Colwygshire Road.

"Maybe he's just checking in," Sok said.

"Checking in? When was the last time Glynnis checked in?"

"Never," Sok replied.

"Then why would you say that?"

"It's all I could think of."

They reached the end of the city wall and veered left off the road into the wide field that surrounded Colwygshire. Glynnis touched down about a hundred yards away and watched them approach through the new spring grass. Arthur and Sok stopped thirty feet in front of the dragon and waited for the dragon to speak first. It wasn't out of respect or protocol; they just had nothing to say.

"I didn't ask for the elf," Glynnis growled.

"Nevertheless, the elf is here," Arthur said, trying to sound bored and brave at the same time. "What do you want?"

In spite of himself, Glynnis was impressed. He'd always thought of the king as weak and cowardly. "There's another dragon in my kingdom."

Arthur and Sok looked at each other.

"Did you know there was another dragon in the kingdom, Sok?" Arthur asked.

Arthur and Sok looked back at Glynnis.

"No, sire," Sok answered. "But if there is, I do hope it's not here to challenge our esteemed Dragon Lord."

51

"Thank you for letting us know," Arthur said. "If we see it, we'll contact you."

Arthur and Sok turned as if to leave.

"I'm not finished with you yet," Glynnis snarled.

Arthur and Sok turned back. Neither spoke, hoping that Glynnis was just being authoritative and wanted to formally dismiss them.

Glynnis stared hard at the human and the elf. "Why did you say that about a challenge?"

Arthur and Sok both gulped.

"We really don't know anything about another dragon being in the kingdom," Arthur said.

"I just can't imagine why else another dragon might come here," Sok said and received an elbow to the ribs from Arthur.

"Really, Glynnis, we have no knowledge of a challenge. Sok was just being... Sok." Arthur received an elbow from Sok in return.

"If I find out you are lying to me, I'll..."

"Yes, yes," Sok said with a dismissive wave of his hand, "you'll burn us alive. Glynnis, you're being paranoid." Sok stepped to the side to avoid another elbow. "But even if there was another dragon in Epoh, it's nothing to do with us."

"We will see," Glynnis growled. Then he launched into the air and flew away over Braydon Wood toward his lair.

"What were you thinking?" Arthur rounded on Sok.

The elf shrugged. "I was thinking that if he thought he might be challenged, he'd leave us alone."

"Or, he'll be doubly alert," Arthur said.

"I didn't think of that," Sok said.

Arthur rolled his eyes and stalked away. "We better go and warn Morgaine."

Arthur and Sok walked back to the castle in silence. Arthur's guilt over having fallen out of the cave and forcing Morgaine to transform weighed heavily on him. He didn't treasure having to tell her that Glynnis had definitely sensed her presence.

Sok, on the other hand, was wondering why Glynnis hadn't used the counter-clockwise signal of circling over the city. What could be more urgent to the Dragon Lord than the threat of another dragon being in his kingdom? He felt not a modicum of guilt over having suggested that Glynnis might be facing a challenge. As Dragon Lords went, Glynnis was not an especially good one, and fearing for his sovereignty might be good for him. He might step up his game and try harder to gain the respect of his subjects. *But if Harpur were to challenge him… Well, first we have to get Harpur properly back!*

They entered Hiro's laboratory to find the Krist, the android and the dragon-wizardess pacing back and forth, each in deep thought, their paths crisscrossing mindlessly. Arthur and Sok stood in the doorway, waiting for them to crash into each other. But their seemingly disparate strides were paradoxically in perfect sync. Arthur cleared his throat to announce his and Sok's arrival.

"Ah, Arthur, Sok!" Bon said, stopping his measured gait and turning to welcome them. "We may have found a way of healing the chalice. It will take some time, but we are almost certain that it can be done.

"That was quick," Sok said, stepping up to the work bench on which the broken chalice rested and reaching for one of the pieces. "What was the pacing all about then?

"Don't touch that!" Morgaine said. She reached over and pulled Sok's hand away before he could pick it up.

"Why?" Sok asked as he quickly retracted his arm and peered at the chalice as if it was poisonous.

"Because I said so," Morgaine snapped and received an eye roll for her efforts.

"It's not like I'm going to break it any more than it already is," Sok said defensively.

"Let's just leave the chalice alone," Morgaine replied in a softer tone. Then she turned to Arthur. "How would you like to accompany me to the Fae Lands?"

Arthur screwed his face into a complicated knot of dubiousness. "Yeah, I don't think that I would like that very much at all."

With his memories restored, he recalled his last foray into the Fae Lands when he and Davynn had gone there to retrieve the Amber Chalice for Harpur sixteen years earlier. He had been caught in a snare that had left him hanging by his ankles from a tree. A Fae creature had cut him down after Davynn had assured it that they meant no harm, but he had no desire to repeat any such mistreatment from the Fae again.

"Nevertheless," Morgaine said, "we are going to the Fae Lands."

"Sorry, my friend," Sok said to Arthur, relieved not to be invited. "I'll look after things here at the castle while you are gone."

"Why do I need to go with you?" Arthur moaned.

"Because I…"

"…said so," Arthur finished. "You know that isn't a good reason."

"It's the only reason you need," Morgaine said. "We'll leave in the morning."

Then Arthur remembered why he had come to the laboratory in the first place. "I don't think it's a good idea for you to be wandering about the kingdom."

"Oh?" Morgaine looked at Arthur with interest at being challenged.

"That's right," Sok chimed in. "We just met with Glynnis and he knows there is another dragon in Epoh."

Morgaine took a deep breath and exhaled forcefully. "Why didn't you start with that?"

"You were pacing and then you dropped the Fae Lands bomb on me," Arthur said. "We don't have to still go there, do we?"

"Someone has to!" Morgaine said. "We need something they have."

"What something?" Sok asked.

"That's none of your concern," Morgaine said to the elf.

"Okay," Sok said, raising his hands to stop Morgaine's resistance to his involvement, "we all know that it *is* my concern and that I'm not going to just stand by and do nothing while you try to keep whatever you have planned a secret from me. And, in the process of not standing by and doing nothing, I'll probably mess up said plan, causing more harm and making you need to improvise a solution that will very likely lead to more problems requiring more plans. Really, it would be easier on everyone if you just included me in the plan and let me help."

Morgaine grimaced. "Or we could just go back to my earlier idea of freezing you until the dragonfoil leaves fall."

Sok's mouth dropped open. "You don't mean that!"

Arthur stepped between the elf and the dragon-wizardess. "You know he's right, Morgaine. Give him a job and keep him happy."

Morgaine had to agree. "Well, I can't send you to the Fae Lands. You'll probably kill one of the Fae and start a civil war."

"I have no desire to go to the Fae Lands," Sok agreed. "But if you tell me what you are planning, I can help here in the castle."

"Very well," Morgaine said. "I'll think of something for you to do. In the meantime, if Glynnis is aware of my presence in Epoh, I will need to stay put and keep a low profile. Arthur, you and Davynn will have to go to the Fae Lands and look for Willow."

"Willow?" Arthur repeated. "The Fae spirit?"

"That is correct."

"How does one find a Fae spirit?" Arthur was doubtful of a good outcome.

"Chances are she'll find you," Morgaine said. "She's familiar with your energy and she will seek help from someone familiar."

Arthur frowned. "Didn't she die like a million years ago? How can she possibly be familiar with me?"

"When you used the chalice to transfer me into Karrys, Willow would have sensed you." Morgaine made it sound so normal.

"Okay," Arthur said, "but I still don't know how I'm supposed to get a ghost to follow me back to the castle. Or why I would want to!"

"It's more a matter of need than want," Morgaine said. "Willow can heal the chalice."

"You're not seriously thinking of bringing a Fae back to the castle?" Sok said. "No! That's not a thing that can happen."

Morgaine flipped her long, black hair over her shoulders. "It's what... six moon cycles before the dragonfoil leaves fall?"

Sok snapped his mouth shut and stared at the dragon-wizardess. Not knowing how much control Karrys had over Harpur, he reminded himself that it was actually Harpur who was speaking and there was a good chance that Harpur would try to find some way to keep Sok from interfering. "I will go to Braydon Wood if that thing comes here."

"Good," Morgaine said. "That works for me." She turned back to Arthur who was shaking his head at the elf. "At least you still have faith in me."

Sok had the good grace to look somewhat penitent. He folded his arms and glared at the Morgaine, but kept his mouth shut.

"I suppose I need to go and give Davynn the good news," Arthur said.

"What good news?" Davynn asked, walking into the laboratory and making Sok jump. He held an apple in his hand and was paring thin slices off it with his knife.

"We're going to the Fae Lands!" Arthur announced.

Davynn looked from one occupant of the room to the next, waiting for the expanded version of Arthur's declaration. When no one offered an immediate explanation, he sat down on a stool and continued to eat his apple. "Okay," he said with a shrug. "When do we leave?"

"You see, Sok?" Morgaine looked at the pouting elf. "This is how a good citizen of Epoh responds to his Dragon Lord."

Sok squinted back at Morgaine. "You are not my Dragon Lord."

"And I never will be if you continue to make things difficult." Morgaine motioned for Arthur and Davynn to follow her out of the laboratory.

Sok tried to remain still, but he couldn't help himself; he followed them out into the hall.

Morgaine said nothing about the elf's intrusion. She led them through the conservatory and outside past the kitchen gardens to a small clearing where a gazebo stood nestled among the trees. Arthur rarely came to this place. It had been a favourite spot of Alex's and they had spent many peaceful hours there together. He wanted to ask Morgaine if they could talk somewhere else, but when the others settled on the benches, he decided not to make things awkward for them. He leaned against one of the supports and resolved to keep his emotions in check.

No one spoke for a while. Morgaine seemed lost in thought, while Davynn finished eating his apple and Sok stared at a dragonfoil tree growing at the edge of the clearing. Arthur hoped someone would find a reason to keep him from having to go to the Fae Lands.

Finally, Morgaine snapped out of her reverie and cleared her throat. "I can't stay here," she announced.

Arthur frowned. "We kind of need you to be here if we are going to release Harpur," he said.

Sok also frowned. "You mean release Karrys.

"For the sake of my sanity," Arthur said, "I am addressing the person I see, not the person I know I'm speaking to."

"Well, for the sake of my sanity, I'm trying to keep reminding myself that the person I see is not the person I'm speaking to," Sok countered.

"It would help if there weren't three different identities to deal with," Davynn offered. "I mean Harpur was Harpur whether he was in dragon or in human form. It was much simpler."

"Most dragons who transform into other guises use different names," Morgaine said. "It's so the people they interact with while not in dragon form don't cotton on to the fact that dragons can transform at all. Regardless of what you see before you, I am Harpur. Now can we get back to the matter at hand?"

"So, we should call you Harpur?" Sok asked.

"No," Morgaine said. "You should call me Morgaine. Just don't forget that you are talking to me... uh, Harpur."

"Yeah, we really have to get this all sorted out soon," Sok said. "It's just too..."

"Don't say weird," Morgaine warned.

"Well, it is weird," Arthur said.

Morgaine closed her eyes, pinched the bridge of her nose and shook her head. "Can we just get on with it?"

"Why don't we call you Morpur? Or Hargaine?" Sok suggested. "You know, combine at least two of you into one."

Morgaine stood up. "I think I will just take my chances with Glynnis and figure this out myself."

She started to stalk away, but Arthur caught her by the arm as she went to step past him. "Wait." He looked the dragon-wizardess in the eye. "Sok is just being Sok. You can always freeze him until the dragonfoil leaves fall if he gets too annoying. But please don't leave us again."

Morgaine looked back at Arthur and saw something behind his grey eyes that dissolved her frustration with the elf. "You know I can't stay here. It's not safe for any of us."

Arthur nodded. "Then tell us what you need us to do and we'll do it."

"Hey!" Sok shouted as what Arthur had said sunk in.

"Shut up, Sok!"

Chapter Four

Anayah, Elder Dhonna and King Röggenar fetched the children from the library where their nanny, a pretty, young girl named Joy, was reading to them from their favourite book of fairy tales. The three young people were torn between accompanying their mother and Elder Dhonna to the market and hearing the end of the story Joy was telling them.

Little Caleb thought it might be a good idea if Joy came with them and read while they walked, but the nanny had other things to attend to and promised to finish the story at bedtime. Caleb, not a fan of bedtime, was certain that he was somehow being duped, but he couldn't quite figure out how. As compensation, the young boy smiled at Röggenar and took his hand. "I'll walk with you today," he announced and led the surprised dwarf out of the library. Anayah and Elder Dhonna traded amused looks and silently wished the dwarf much luck. Then, after reminding Alexa and Brodie to stay close, they, too, left the library and headed out to the market.

As usual, the market square was teeming with shoppers, eager to get the best deals from the vendors who, in turn, were just as enthusiastic about making the most profit. Friendly and passionate bartering was accompanied by the sound of buskers singing and bards regaling the crowd with stories of long-ago battles, no doubt with facts embroidered to mythical proportion. Caleb wanted to stop and listen to a bard that was introducing the tale of the elven prophecy that told of Arthur becoming king. Of course, the boy knew the story by heart, but he never got tired of hearing how Arthur had come from far away and walked into a dragonfoil fire to fulfil his destiny.

"Go ahead," Röggenar told Anaya and Elder Dhonna. "I'll stay with young master Caleb and we'll find you later."

Anayah recapped the rules of behaviour for Caleb, who mustered all his willpower so as not to roll his eyes at his mother. "I know, Mother," he said. "I'll be good." He squeezed Röggenar's hand a little harder to let the dwarf know that he believed that he meant it. Thus, with a nod from the dwarf, Anayah and Elder Dhonna left them to hear the latest version of a story they had actually lived not so long ago.

Röggenar and Caleb settled on a low bench to the right of the bard, the closest they could get to the poet so that Caleb wouldn't miss a word. Röggenar, however, was not as interested as his young charge. Instead of listening to the story, he trained his ears, and eyes, on the crowd that had gathered to be entertained. Though most people were paying quiet attention, a few were talking amongst themselves and bits and snippets of their conversation found their way to the dwarfs keen hearing. For the most part, their chatter was benign enough, but a deep, gravelly voice coming from across the crowd, caught his attention. As he looked for the source of the low, rumbling whisper, he felt the hairs on the back of his neck stand up.

Searching the crowd, Röggenar finally spotted a cloaked and hooded figure standing next to a weathered, old man. The old man was pointing toward the castle, saying something that the dwarf couldn't quite make out.

"Are you certain?" the cloaked figure asked. "You saw her go inside?" The old man nodded. "Thank you, my friend."

Röggenar watched the cloaked figure press a coin into the old man's hand, then melt back into the throng and disappear. If he wasn't mistaken, the cloaked figure was Glynnis in human form. Never, in the sixteen years that Glynnis had been Dragon Lord of Epoh, had anyone ever mentioned seeing him take human form, so he knew he could be wrong. But the impression was strong and the dwarf king trusted his instincts.

A short while later, Röggenar saw Glynnis circling above the city for the second time that day. The crowd noticed the dragon as well and it was enough to draw their attention away from the bard, who reluctantly stopped speaking. There seemed little point in telling a story that no one was listening to.

All around them, people stopped what they were doing and looked up. Soon, the market was abuzz with speculation as to the dragon's intention and the crowd began to disperse in a somewhat less than orderly fashion. Röggenar held onto Caleb's hand and cautioned the boy to remain seated. The last thing he needed was to lose Anayah's youngest son in the rush that was quickly escalating toward panic.

"What's going on?" Caleb asked. "Why did the bard stop telling the story?"

"The Dragon Lord is circling the city again," Röggenar explained. "These people are worried that he might be here to raze the city."

Caleb looked up and watched the circling dragon above. "He's just flying around," the boy observed, not sure why everyone was acting so silly. "Why would he want to hurt us?"

"He probably doesn't," Röggenar replied, "He's probably just looking for something. Let's just sit tight for a bit and when it's safe, we'll go find your mother and Elder Dhonna."

Caleb seemed to see the wisdom in that. He watched the people running to and fro as if they didn't know which way to go. "Someone ought to tell them that if he wants to talk to Uncle Arthur, he flies deosil over the city."

Röggenar smiled at the boy's use of such a word. Then again, his mother was a witch and he'd probably been well schooled in the use of magical terms. Still, the dwarf was impressed that the lad not only knew the magical word for clockwise, but knew the Dragon Lord's signal for Arthur. But Glynnis' reappearance wasn't something to be ignored. "Indeed," he said. Then Röggenar spotted the old man that the cloaked figure had been speaking to. "Stay right here," he said to Caleb. "I mean it, don't move. I will be right back."

Caleb let go of Röggenar's hand and scooched back on the bench a little further. He watched the dwarf make his way through the crowd to the old man, but within seconds the throng closed in between them and he lost sight of his temporary guardian. Quite certain that Röggenar would return soon, Caleb turned his attention back to the madness surrounding him. A woman, carrying a small child, ran past. As she dodged a man running toward her, the child dropped the toy she had been holding. Without thinking, Caleb hopped off the bench, picked up the toy and ran after the woman to return it.

Röggenar caught up to the old man and took him by the arm, not only to get his attention to talk to him, but to lead him out of the swarm of people to somewhere he would be less likely to get knocked down and trampled. When they reached the relative safety of a market stall, Röggenar first asked if the man was okay.

"Aye," the disoriented and breathless septuagenarian wheezed. "Thank ye."

"That man you were speaking to back there before Glynnis showed up," Röggenar began, "what did he say to you?"

"He asked if I'd seen a woman with raven hair, possibly wearing a top hat. I told him that I had seen just such a woman going into the castle a day or two ago. Not sure when exactly; my memory isn't what it used to be." The old man was blessedly forthright. "Why do you want to know?"

Röggenar ignored the question. "Do you know who the man in the cloak was?"

"Never seen him before."

Röggenar nodded and thanked the old man. "You've been quite helpful," he said. "I need to get back to the boy I'm looking after. Will you be okay here?"

"I think so," the old man said. "It appears that Glynnis is flying back to his lair." He pointed to the west.

The dwarf king turned and saw Glynnis gliding away over Braydon Wood. "I have to go. Stay here until the crowd thins out a bit more." And with that he left the old man and started to make his way back to the bench where he'd left Caleb.

When he arrived, Caleb was nowhere to be seen and a new fear clutched at Röggenar's heart. He yelled the boy's name as he looked around in a panic of his own, but no one answered. Caleb was not there and Röggenar had no idea what direction he might have gone.

The crowd was thinning out, and that gave him a better view of the market area. The boy could not have gone far—on his own, at least—but that was small comfort. It was no comfort at all when he spotted Anayah, Elder Dhonna and the other children walking toward him.

"Where's Caleb?" Anayah asked as she approached the terrified dwarf. She let go of Alexa's hand and grabbed Röggenar's arm. "Röggenar, where is Caleb?"

"I'm so sorry, Anayah. I only left him for a minute." Röggenar spun around again and called Caleb's name.

Anayah stared at the dwarf king. Part of her wanted to scream at him. Part of her wanted to turn him into a toad. Rather than do either, she turned to Elder Dhonna. "He lost my son!"

Elder Dhonna looked at the two panic-stricken people. "Why don't you just zap Caleb back here from wherever he is?"

Anayah's ashen face brightened slightly. "Of course," she said. "What was I thinking?"

Elder Dhonna held her tongue. Anayah was not easily rattled like this; chiding her would be of no use to anyone. Instead, she waved her hand as if to say get on with it then.

Anayah snapped her fingers and a puff of red smoke appeared between her and Röggenar. And there stood little Caleb, none the worse for wear. He was holding a sweet between his fingers and was just about to pop it into his mouth.

"Where did you get that?" Anayah asked, grasping her son's arm before he could eat the candy.

Caleb suddenly realized he was back where he'd started. "Oh, hello, Mother. Did you just zap me here?"

"I asked you a question, young man," Anayah said firmly.

Caleb looked at the sweet and then back at his mother. "A lady gave it to me. I saved her baby's toy and returned it to them. She was ever so grateful. Said the baby couldn't sleep without it. Then she gave me this."

Anayah took the candy from her son and tucked it into her pocket. "You are not supposed to take candy from people you don't know," she said.

"Oh," Caleb said, staring at the pocket, "right! I forgot. But, Mother, she was a very nice lady, I'm sure."

"Never mind that," Röggenar said. "Where did you go, lad? I told you to stay put."

"I told you," Caleb said, not understanding what the fuss was about, "the nice lady's baby dropped her toy and I picked it up and returned it to her."

Anayah knelt down beside her son. "Caleb, King Röggenar told you not to move. Why didn't you do as you were told?"

Caleb scowled at his mother. A baby had dropped her toy. Any good future knight would ensure that the wee girl got it back. It all made perfect sense to him. But, even at such a tender age, Caleb understood two things. First, adults were strange and had a penchant for being dramatic over nothing. Second, if he hung his head just so and looked kind of sad and kind of sorry, adults were likely to tousle his hair and admonish him mildly for his disobedience. "I'm sorry," he said, looking up through his lashes and sticking his bottom lip out just a little bit.

From behind him, Röggenar tousled Caleb's hair. "That was very noble of you, but next time you're told to stay where you are, stay where you are."

"Yes, sir," Caleb said. Then he looked at his mother, expecting her to pick up where Röggenar had left off.

Anayah, however, was just relieved that her boy was safe and, since the dwarf had essentially stolen her only line, she shrugged and stood up again. "I'll deal with you later," she said to Röggenar, who knew he would have to take his lumps at some point and hoped that his news about the cloaked figure would contribute to leniency.

"Well, what do you think that was all about?" Elder Dhonna asked.

"Glynnis was in the market just before he flew over the city," Röggenar said.

Anayah and Elder Dhonna both looked at him with expressions of doubt.

"What do you mean?" Anayah asked.

"I mean that he was here in human form asking about a woman with black hair wearing a top hat," Röggenar said.

Anayah and Elder Dhonna looked at each other with deeper expressions of doubt.

"How do you know it was Glynnis?" Elder Dhonna asked.

The dwarf looked thoughtful for a moment. "Timing, what he was inquiring about... my gut!"

"What did he look like?" Anayah wanted to know.

"He was quite tall and he was wearing a rather non-descript cloak, so I couldn't see his face. But I know it was him." Röggenar hitched up his breeches and gave them a definitive nod as if to dare them to challenge him on the matter.

There seemed no need for further discussion. "We had better warn Harpur," Anayah said, scooping Caleb into her arms to speed up their walk back to the castle.

"You mean Morgaine," Röggenar corrected her.

"I mean all of them!" Anayah said and started marching away.

Elder Dhonna took Brodie by the hand while Röggenar latched onto Alexa and the four of them followed the witch.

Hiro and Bon, alone at last in the laboratory had determined that the spirit of Willow of the Fae was the best chance of repairing the chalice. But unless or until she could be found, there was little they could do about it. Instead, Bon shared his plan for helping Harpur when and if the chalice got fixed. As he explained the process to Hiro, the Krist took notes and found himself quite in awe of the challenge that the android was presenting to him. Bon's proposal was intriguing to say the least, but without the technology, he could only conclude that they would need some very powerful magic to complete the procedure.

"I'm sure that between Anayah and Elder Dhonna, the two of them will have no problem creating a spell," Hiro said.

"I'd rather not bring anyone else into this," Bon disagreed.

"You sound like Harpur," Hiro said with a giggle. "Why bother trying to keep it a secret? You know the others are going to insinuate themselves into any plan we come up with."

If Bon had been capable of it, he might have sighed. "I suppose you are right, but let's try to figure this out ourselves first. If we do not come up with anything by the time Harpur and Arthur return with Willow's spirit, then we can reach out to Anayah and Elder Dhonna."

Hiro nodded, though he didn't completely agree. His own magic was limited to what he could pull out of his satchel. Food he could do. Small things like blankets or spy glasses were a snap. But what Bon was asking for was something quite different. Something beyond his skills and abilities. "Where do we start?"

Bon looked down at his friend. "Do you know where we can get about a dozen unfertilized dragon eggs?"

Sok chose that moment to walk into the laboratory. "That's impossible!" he stated emphatically. "What do you want with a dozen dragon eggs anyway?"

"I told you," Hiro said to Bon.

Bon looked at the Krist and then back at Sok. "They are for an experiment I wish to conduct."

Good one, Hiro thought to himself. Then he hopped up onto a stool to sit and watch how this would play out.

"You have far more important things to do than tinker with experiments," Sok said. "You need to focus on finding a way to release Harpur from Karrys' body." Bon remained silent and the elf looked around for something to eat. "I could use a sandwich."

Hiro hopped back down from his stool and retrieved his satchel. From it, he produced a thick roast beef sandwich and handed it to Sok, who seated himself on the stool and began to eat. Neither of his companions spoke as they watched the elf bite into the generous pile of juicy meat. As he chewed, they could practically see the wheels begin to turn in Sok's mind. He was about to take his second bite when the wheels stopped and he turned to stare at the android.

"You're joking, right?" Sok said from behind the sandwich that was poised a few inches in front of his mouth.

Bon had no idea what assumption the elf had made, but he decided to let Sok reveal his conclusions rather than jump to any of his own and risk revealing his plan before knowing exactly what Sok thought he was doing. He shook his head and said nothing.

"Well, you can put that idea right out of your head," Sok said, taking another bite. "Dragons aren't like chickens. They don't just lay eggs for the sake of laying eggs. Even if they did, getting one, let alone a dozen, to give up an egg would be exceedingly difficult. You'd have to steal them. And that, my friend, would not end well."

Bon, grateful for the information, looked at Hiro. "I suppose that we will need Anayah's expertise after all."

Hiro was flabbergasted. "Are you suggesting that we ask Anayah to conjure a dozen dragon eggs right out of their mothers' bodies?"

Bon nodded. "Yes."

Sok nearly choked on his sandwich. "That's insane!" he gasped.

"Perhaps," Bon said. "But I cannot think of another way to get twelve dragon eggs."

"Sok is right," Hiro said, pulling another roast beef sandwich out of his satchel and hopping onto another stool. "We can't ask Anayah to do that. I doubt that she would agree to it anyway."

Bon fully understood the ethical dilemma his plan imposed on all of them. Stealing dragon eggs was not only morally objectionable, it was dangerous. He would have to table that aspect of his plan for the time being; there was another issue that needed to be addressed. "We also need some of Harpur's DNA."

"What is DNA?" Sok asked.

Bon considered explaining deoxyribonucleic acid and its function to the elf, but decided that would be an exercise in futility. "I need some of Harpur's blood, or a piece of his flesh. A scale would work."

Sok and Hiro both frowned.

"You know that Harpur's body was burned to ash sixteen years ago," Hiro said. "Where would we get such a thing from after all this time?"

"There has to be something of him left somewhere," Bon said.

Sok took another bit of his sandwich and chewed thoughtfully. He couldn't begin to imagine why Bon needed Harpur's blood or flesh; it sounded ghoulish to him.

He swallowed his food and then realized that he could also use a drink. "Hiro, can you please get me some ale?"

Hiro sighed and hopped back down off his seat. He produced two cups of ale from his satchel and handed one to Sok.

"Thank you," Sok said, and took a long pull from his cup.

"Where are Arthur, Davynn and Morgaine?" Hiro asked. He had no ideas to contribute and he thought a change of subject might be a good diversion.

"Arthur and Davynn are preparing to leave for the Fae Lands." He shuddered at the thought. "And Morgaine is going to Andonsheer for a while. It seems that Glynnis has sensed another dragon's presence in the kingdom and so she is going to leave until we need her to come back."

"Ah!" Hiro nodded. "That seems wise."

"I wonder if we could use some of her blood?" Bon mused.

Sok, about to bite into his sandwich, paused and squinted at the android. "How would Karrys' blood help Harpur?"

"I'm not sure that it would," Bon replied. "I'm just trying to cover all the bases here. It wouldn't hurt to have some on hand. Just in case."

"Well, you better hurry," Sok said, "Harpur's planning on leaving as soon as possible."

"Indeed," Bon said. "I'll go and find her… uh, him… straight away."

Sok and Hiro watched the android stride out of the laboratory.

"More ale?" Hiro asked.

Sok, with his mouth full of roast beef sandwich, nodded as he pushed his cup closer to Hiro. With nothing else to do but enjoy their snack, the elf and Krist settled in to fill their bellies and wait for the next development.

By the time Anayah and her entourage returned to the castle and made their way to Hiro and Bon's laboratory, only Sok and Hiro, and a huge pile of pastries were present. Young Caleb spied the treats and wiggled out of his mother's arms. His intention, instantly clear to the pretty witch, was dashed when the plate vanished just as his little hand was about to wrap itself around a particularly large pastry.

"Hey!" Sok hollered. "Put those back!"

"I'll return them when we leave," Anayah said. "It's far too close to supper and I don't need any fuss from that one…" She pointed at Caleb, returning his four-year-old glare with a very adult and far more effective glare of her own. The little boy held her gaze for a count of ten, until his mother's eyes narrowed slightly and he was forced to concede. "Where's Harpur?" Anayah demanded.

"Getting ready to leave for Andonsheer," Sok said as he gave Caleb a commiserating shrug.

"Why is he going to Andonsheer?" Elder Donna asked. There was a tone of disappointment in her voice.

"Glynnis sensed the presence of a dragon and confronted me and Arthur about it," Sok said. "Harpur, Morgaine and Karrys thought it was best that they leave."

"Where is Bon?" King Röggenar asked.

"Gone to find them before they leave so he can get some of their blood," Sok explained.

"Are we referring to Harpur in the collective plural now?" Anayah asked, not sure if it simplified things or made it all even weirder.

Sok shrugged again. "I thought I would try it out."

"Mother, I need to use the water closet," Alexa said.

"Go ahead," Anayah said to her daughter, "but come right back here. Maybe Sok will take you three upstairs to Joy while Elder Dhonna and I go look for Harpur."

"I need something to drink," Brodie announced.

"You're fine," Anayah said, shaking her head at Hiro, who was already reaching for his satchel.

"No fair!" Caleb whined. "Alexa gets to do everything she wants to."

Anayah pursed her lips and redoubled *the look*, holding it until her youngest son lowered his eyes. "Sok, would you mind taking these two upstairs for me and fetching Alexa from the water closet on your way?"

"Sure," Sok agreed, then drained his cup. "Come on, boys, let's go find your sister." As he passed Anayah, he leaned toward her and whispered. "It was just a pastry."

Anayah transferred the look to the elf. "I'll remind you that I am their mother."

"How could anyone forget?" Sok picked Caleb up and tossed the squealing youngster over his shoulder.

Brodie, three years wiser than his sibling, kept his own mouth shut, and followed Sok out of the laboratory.

"Honestly! It's like having four children half the time," Anayah said to Elder Dhonna, who was stifling an amused smirk.

"Let's go and see what's going on with the others," Elder Dhonna said. "Are you coming with us Röggenar?

"Actually, I think I'll stay here with Hiro, if you don't mind," the dwarf king decided.

"As you wish," Elder Dhonna said. "We'll find you later."

Anayah turned to leave the laboratory.

"Um, Anayah," Hiro called out to the witch's retreating back.

"What is it, Hiro?" Anayah stopped and turned.

"The pastries?"

Anayah rolled her eyes and snapped her fingers. The pastries reappeared and the dwarf smiled as the Krist filled two cups with fresh ale.

While Arthur and Davynn were preparing for their journey to the Fey Lands, Morgaine returned to Arthur's private rooms to stow Harpur's life book in the vault in the bed chamber. Knowing that Arthur now remembered the vault didn't leave her with any solid relief. But she hoped that he would leave it alone. Maybe if Arthur wasn't made aware of its presence in the vault, he wouldn't think to meddle with it. For the time being, it was as secure as it could be.

Speaking of meddling, Morgaine still hadn't come up with an assignment for Sok. Keeping the elf busy and out of trouble, as Arthur had pointed out, was imperative. *But what could he do that would occupy him long enough for the rest of them to figure out a plan and execute it without Sok messing things up?*

Morgaine did not have time to worry about it, though worry was something of an understatement. She had to get out of Epoh at least until Glynnis felt less threatened by her presence in his kingdom. Even in human form, the acknowledged dragon lord might still sense her, now that he was aware of her being there in dragon form.

She sealed the vault and left Arthur's bed chamber, intent on saying a quick good bye to Arthur before zapping herself to Andonsheer. As she reached for the handle on the outer door of the king's private chambers, the handle turned and one of the guards posted outside opened the thick oak portal to allow Bon to enter. Morgaine stepped back to make way for the android.

"Were you looking for me?" she asked.

"I was!" Bon said, stepping inside and closing the door on the curious guards. Morgaine waited for Bon to secure their privacy. "I need some of your DNA. And, though I am not entirely sure it will be necessary, a bit of Karrys' blood might come in handy."

Morgaine stared at the android. "DNA?"

"Yes," Bon said, matter-of-factly. "Are you aware of anything biological that might have survived your demise?"

Morgaine frowned. Remembering how his magnificent body had been burned to ash made Harpur wince inside of her. "I can't think of..." Morgaine broke off, as Harpur remembered something else entirely. Then she slumped and shook her head. "No. I can't think of anything that would have survived after all this time."

Bon didn't believe the dragon-wizardess. "There is something, isn't there? Tell me."

"It's impossible," Morgaine said.

"What is impossible?" Bon insisted.

"Seriously, Bon, forget it." Morgaine stepped forward to reach for the door handle again, but Bon put a hand against the wood and held it closed.

"Tell me what it is."

Morgaine sighed. "When I was on Mysturna trying to save Arthur and Sok from the Entanglement, I was forced to give a scale to the Forest of Dheersha." She looked at the android and shook her head. "But there's no way that evil place is going to give it back, even if it still exists."

Bon tilted his head as if in deep thought. He was scanning his files for all the information he had on the Forest of Dheersha. When he was done, he

70

straightened his head and nodded at Morgaine. "I think that will do quite nicely," he announced.

"Are you insane?" Morgaine asked. "How would you get it back from them? The trees are not going to just hand it over."

"I never thought that they would," Bon said, arranging his lips into a smile. "We are going to steal it from them!"

With that, Bon opened the door and marched out into the hallway, leaving a nonplussed and unenthusiastic Morgaine standing open-mouthed behind him. She needed to get out of Epoh, but she couldn't leave without knowing what Bon was up to. The idea of any of them returning to Mysturna and facing that vicious and malevolent forest again sent shivers through her body. Harpur had not liked being there the first time; he certainly didn't treasure the idea going there again. It was too big of a risk. Too many things could go wrong.

"Are you okay, miss?"

One of the guards was speaking to Morgaine. She glared at the sentinel. "No, I'm not okay!" she bellowed. "Apparently, I'm going to Mysturna to steal a scale from a murderous forest!"

The guards watched the dragon-wizardess storm down the hallway after the android and disappear into the stairwell.

"Any idea who she is?" asked the other guard.

"No, but that view makes this post worth it," said the first guard, still leering in the direction of Morgaine's footsteps.

"Watch it, soldier!" Morgaine's voice drifted back up from the stairwell. "Or I'll cook you for my breakfast."

The guards snapped to attention on either side of the door and didn't move until the end of their shifts.

It took some time, but eventually, Bon had gathered everyone in the council chambers. Clockwise from the east side of the huge, round oak table, sat Arthur, Morgaine, Davynn, Anayah, Bon, Hiro (standing on his hover gilly, rather than sitting on a chair), Elder Dhonna, Röggenar, and Sok. Bon had just announced that a contingent comprised from those there gathered needed to go to Mysturna to steal the scale Harpur had given to the Forest of Dheersha. Five of those there

71

gathered, all of the male persuasion, held various pieces of food inches from their open mouths where their hands had frozen upon hearing the android's blunt proclamation. It was as if Bon had cast that freezing spell Morgaine had threatened to use to keep Sok in line. Two of those there gathered, both of the female persuasion, had turned what might best be described as lethal, and incredulous, glares upon the android. The other two, Bon and Morgaine, simply waited for the kerfuffle this news was about to evoke to erupt. The delay lasted exactly eleven seconds—according to Bon's internal, earth-based timing mechanism. The verbal melee that followed lasted eight full minutes.

While questions and excuses, not to mention a few accusations, flew around the table like hard-flung dodge balls in a school gymnasium, Morgaine desperately tried to figure out some other way of obtaining a sample of Harpur's DNA. She deeply regretted mentioning it to Bon, but the astute and observant android had seen her reaction when the memory had popped into her head. She knew that Arthur, Sok and Anayah, who had been there when Harpur had torn the scale from his chest, would not want to return any more than Harpur did. Hiro, a native of Mysturna, often returned to his home world, but had little affection for the violent trees that made up the Forest of Dheersha. Davynn, who disliked the idea of Bounding to another world, would not go willingly. Röggenar, a mountain-dwelling dwarf, was no more fond of the notion of Bounding than Davynn was. As for Elder Dhonna, putting Harpur's oldest and dearest friend in such a potentially dangerous situation was unthinkable. There had to be a better way. If she wasn't in such a dire need to get out of Epoh before Glynnis found her, Morgaine would argue vehemently against such an action. She didn't even know what Bon needed the DNA for. But time was of the essence, as they say, and so, Morgaine made a decision.

The moment the shouting began to subside, the dragon-wizardess stood up. "We're all going to Mysturna!"

Another few seconds of astonishment-driven silence followed Morgaine's assertion.

"I can't go back there," Anayah said. "You know I've been banished from Mysturna!"

"You can wear a disguise."

"I'm not Bounding anywhere!" Davynn said, pounding the table with his fist.

"You'll survive."

"Davynn and I have to go find Willow," Arthur pleaded, suddenly quite happy about a trip to the Fae Lands.

"Willow can wait."

"I really should get back to my mines," Röggenar said. "I've been away too long already."

Morgaine looked at the dwarf. If anyone could—or should—be excused, it was Röggenar. But Morgaine couldn't afford to give any leeway to anyone. "The mines will still be there when we return."

"Will going to Mysturna help you?" Elder Dhonna asked.

Morgaine looked at Bon to answer, hoping the android would give them some information.

"I believe that it will," the android said, remaining enigmatic about the purpose of the scale.

Sok, who had not contributed an excuse, had been listening to Morgaine closely and had heard the sadness in her voice. He recognized, for the first time, that the dragon-wizardess' words really were Harpur's and that Harpur was not taking any of this lightly. He knew the danger he was putting them all in; he also knew that if anyone could free him from Karrys' body and restore him to his former glory, it was this motley crew of those there gathered. His friends. His dear, dear friends. "I'm in," the elf said.

"Thank you, Sok," Morgaine said quietly and quite sincerely. Then she turned back to the others. "I'm going to zap myself to Andonsheer and will meet you by the Boundary at first light tomorrow. But maybe before I go Bon can enlighten us as to his plans for retrieving the scale so we can properly prepare."

Bon leaned forward to speak, but before he could, Anayah interrupted. "You're forgetting that the Boundary to Mysturna was destroyed when we killed Bloomregaard's wraiths."

"We'll use the Boundary south of Andon," Morgaine replied to the increasingly anxious witch.

"The desert will kill us before we can all get to it!" Arthur moaned.

Fearing another meltdown on the part of the King of Epoh, Morgaine laid a gentle hand on his shoulder. "I'm sure that Anayah can conjure up a shield to protect you all. And Hiro's hover gilly can bend time to get you through the desert faster."

73

"You've thought of everything, haven't you?" Anayah sneered.

"I sure hope so," Morgaine said. "But we all know how these things tend to go for us. If we stick together, though, we'll get through this. Bon, please tell us you have a plan to get the scale and get us all back here unscathed."

Once again, Bon leaned forward. He waited a moment to see if anyone else was going to disrupt the proceedings. When no one did, he smiled and said, "I most certainly do. We are going to steal the Sphere first!"

Meg and Hart were sick of opening presents. They were almost halfway through, though, and half of the gifts they had opened were, essentially, the same things.

Hats.

Baseball caps, to be precise.

One hundred and four baseball caps.

When they had opened the first gift containing a pair of hats with funny sayings embroidered on them, they were slightly bemused. Having never seen such a cap before, the novelty was kind of delightful. By the twelfth gift containing a pair of baseball caps, their bemusement had deepened and verged on outright perplexity. They assumed that the caps were a new style and that all the gift-givers wanted to be the first to introduce the royal twins to it. By the fifty-second gift, they were already tired of the peculiar fashion trend.

Meg looked at the remaining presents and determined that roughly half again were of the same size and shape as the opened ones with baseball caps. She sighed. "I think it's a fairly safe guess that there are a bunch more of these odd hats in there."

Hart was wearing a dark blue cap with a crown embroidered around the circumference as if it had been fitted over the actual hat. For some reason, he found the redundancy, as well as the inaccuracy, amusing. The young prince was not the first in line for the crown; his older—by several minutes—sister was, technically, the heir to the throne. But a hat on top of a hat? Well, that was just funny. Meg was not amused. It wasn't that she had her heart set on being the queen someday. She was offended that someone thought that Hart was heir by reason of his gender. The hat that had accompanied Hart's was also blue and had a tiara embroidered on it. A silly, girly tiara. She refused to put it on.

"Let's call it a day," Hart suggested.

"Father told us we had to do this," Meg said.

"Father tells us we have to do all sorts of things," Hart argued. "Since when do you do everything that he tells you to do?"

Hart had a point. Meg had to wonder what had just happened to her. She hadn't wanted to open all these presents in the first place. Now she was arguing against ditching her duty in favour of spending time at the archery range. This was new. And just a little bit frightening. She had a sudden urge to pierce effigies with arrows.

"What are we going to do with all these presents?" she asked, hoping her clever brother had a plan.

"Let's zap them to our rooms. We can finish them later," Hart said.

Meg looked at Hart as if he had two heads. "Yeah, right!" she scoffed. "Like either of us could manage zapping one present to the right location. There are dozens here."

"We can do it," Hart insisted. "I have a theory."

As if on cue, Meg's forehead started to tingle and itch painfully. Her hand flew to her brow. "What's your theory?"

"This is my theory," Hart said, pointing to his own forehead, which was also tingling. "Whatever is causing this, it's enhancing our magic."

Again, Meg grimaced at her sibling in disbelief. "Little brother, what does an itchy forehead have to do with magic?"

"I don't know yet," Hart said. "But last night right before Father left the party, I felt the sensation really strongly and so I started experimenting."

Meg's eyes widened. "That was you who made the juggler's balls explode?"

Hart smiled mischievously. "I was also responsible for Finch's tail."

Meg actually giggled. "That was amazing! Why didn't you say something sooner?"

"I'm still not sure the two are actually connected, but I've been doing little things whenever I feel the itch and it's worked every time."

The princess looked at the mountain of gifts. "Let's do it!"

"Okay," Hart said. "We'll zap everything to your room…"

"Oh, sure," Meg interjected. "So, if anyone finds out, I'll get all the blame."

"Fine," Hart said, rolling his eyes, "we'll zap them to my room."

"Personally, I'd like to zap all these stupid hats to the guard's latrine." Meg scowled at the crown cap on her brother's head. "Especially that one!"

Hart put his hand on his head as if to save his hat. "No way! I'm keeping this hat," he said defensively.

"Let's zap the open presents to my room and the unopened ones to yours," Meg suggested.

"So I have to open them by myself? I don't think so."

"While you're opening the presents, I can start writing the thank you notes for the ones we've already opened."

Hart considered this arrangement and smelled a rat. Meg knew he thought her handwriting was atrocious and if she offered to do it, he'd feel compelled to do it for her. But Hart knew Meg knew what he thought of her penmanship and he was well aware that she was just trying to get him to write all the thank you notes. "Sounds good to me," he said, and before it registered that her ruse had backfired, Hart zapped all the unopen presents to his room. "Go ahead. It's your turn."

"Jerk," Meg mumbled under her breath. Then she waved her hand and all the opened presents, including the crown hat Hart was wearing, along with the list of names of the gift-givers disappeared from the hall.

For a second or two, the twins stared at the empty tables that had held their birthday presents.

"We better go see if they got there safely," Hart said.

Meg nodded. It's wasn't improbable that some of the uglier hats had ended up in the guard's latrine.

Arthur squinted at the ceiling. So did Sok. They were remembering the Sphere, an enormous, solid black globe of great sacred importance to the peoples of Mysturna. Bon had lived inside the Sphere, acting as a caretaker of sorts, when he was assigned to that world to gather data on the various people and creatures that inhabited it. Anayah had sought sanctuary with him there after escaping from her grief-mad aunt and had holed up with the android until Hiro had been able to construct a teleportation device from Arthur's old cell phone from Earth. The thing was at least ten stories high—and across for that matter—and neither Arthur, nor Sok could fathom how they could possibly steal it.

Anayah, in spite of being banished from her home world, was horrified by the idea of stealing the Sphere. Having lived inside it for nearly a year and a half, she had a basic understanding of its inner workings, but the Sphere was a holy place, a place of worship. One just doesn't steal such a thing, and one definitely doesn't simply walk away with a ten-story marble.

Hiro commenced doing complex calculations in his head. He wasn't sure how stealing the Sphere was going to assist them in recovering Harpur's scale from the Forest of Dheersha, but the challenge of pilfering such a large and unwieldy thing was nothing short of exciting to the curious Krist.

Harpur, as Morgaine, being the only other person in the room to have seen the Sphere, also had doubts about Bon's plan. Not about absconding with a sacred object, he didn't care about that, but a hundred-foot ball of… whatever it was made of… wasn't going to slip into anyone's pocket. Unless, of course, it was magically altered to fit in a pocket.

"So, we're just going to shrink it and walk away with it?" Morgaine asked. Next to her, she heard Arthur emit an epiphanous "Ahhh…"

"Not at all," Bon said. "We're going to fly it away."

While Anayah, still shocked and appalled by Bon's suggestion, struggled with the ethics of stealing a sacred object, Arthur's, "Ahhh…," became a, "Huh?" and was echoed by Sok.

Morgaine stroked her chin in the same manner that Harpur used to tug on his beard. "The Sphere is an air ship?"

"More accurately," Bon began to explain, "the Sphere is a space ship."

"A space ship?" Morgaine parroted.

"Indeed!" Bon gushed. "It didn't originate on Mysturna. During my time as the caretaker of the Sphere, I discovered many interesting things about it. I was unable to determine which world it came from, but it most probably came from a distant part of the galaxy that Mysturna belongs to. Sadly, much of the recorded history of the Sphere was damaged—probably when it crashed on Mysturna— and its occupants either died or blended into the native population. The technology is pre-magical, but verges on the natural evolutionary transition to

77

magic that occurs on most worlds. I would hazard to say that the technology of the Sphere is at about the same level as that on Earth in my time."

Arthur considered the implications. "So, Earth in your time is about to leave technology behind and convert to magic?"

"Within the next one to two hundred years," Bon confirmed.

"Cool," Arthur said.

"Very," Bon said. "The signs are there."

"Like what?" Arthur asked, curious about the future of his own home world.

"The population is decreasing at a rapid rate…"

"What do you mean?" Arthur interjected.

"Well, typically when a world is about to transition from technology to true magic, the population decreases dramatically, and that's what is happening on Earth right now. Or at least it was when I was last there. Since I can no longer time travel, I cannot specifically or with any conviction say that it continues do so. But it was decreasing in conjunction with the, also typical, peak in technology. Based on the rate of the decline in population along with the fact that technology was plateauing, I can quite confidently estimate that Earth will become entirely magically driven within the next two hundred years."

"People are dying?" Arthur was shocked.

"People are always dying, Arthur…" Bon didn't understand Arthur's question.

"Wait," Morgaine interrupted. "Didn't you say that your technology was being made redundant in favour of new technology?"

"I did," Bon agreed.

"Then how can you say that technology was, or rather I suppose it would be more correct to say will plateau in your time?" Morgaine asked.

Bon considered the question. It was a very good question and he was as impressed as an android can be at the dragon-wizardess' astute observation. "Technology can only go so far," Bon explained. "At a certain point there just is not anywhere else for it to go, and the technology that replaced my technology was, or, as you say, will be, the beginning of the end for technological advancement on Earth." He looked at Arthur and noted the king's furrowed brow. "If it helps, Arthur, from your perspective in time, magic won't manifest on Earth for another six to seven hundred years."

"And yet, you've already experienced its imminent conception," Hiro said.

"I have," Bon agreed again, "and I suppose I will again when the time actually comes."

Arthur, still upset by the fact that a lot of people were, or would someday be, dying, felt his brain straining to keep up with the whole time-travel thing. "So, what does people dying have to do with magic?"

"It is not so much that people die off as much as it is that people do not reproduce as prolifically," Bon replied.

That seemed to make Arthur feel a little better and he nodded his head in acceptance.

"I think we've gotten a little off track, here," Anayah said. "We were talking about the Sphere being a spaceship."

"Right," Bon said. "We were indeed."

"So...?" Anayah prompted.

"The Sphere is a spaceship," Bon said. "We've already established that."

Anayah clenched her teeth and began to rise from her chair in frustration, a frustration that her loving husband picked up on immediately. Davynn placed a gentle hand on Anayah's shoulder. "I think what Anayah wants to know is how does this help you get the scale from the murderous forest?"

"Of course!" Bon exclaimed in his best impression of a real person. "We will fly it to the forest, hover above the trees, emit a frequency that will, essentially, render the forest... uh, ineffectual, enter its lair..."

"The forest has a lair?" Morgaine perked right up at the mention of a lair. Both Karrys and Harpur missed their lair.

"Yes, it does." Bon indulged Morgaine. "All of the things they have collected over the centuries is stored beneath the forest in what is best and rightly termed a lair." He smiled at the smile on the dragon-wizardess' face, before continuing the outline of his plan. "We will enter the lair, find the scale and take it. Then we will return the Sphere to its rightful place and come back to Thraeh to... uh, help Harpur."

"Um... How big is this lair?" Arthur asked.

Bon hesitated. "It is quite large."

"And the scale could be anywhere in this lair, right?" Anayah prompted.

"That's why we need you," Bon said. "You can conjure it from wherever it is."

"Uh-huh," Anayah said. "Have you considered how angry this is going to make the Forest of Dheersha?"

"I have," Bon said, "but without Harpur's DNA, we aren't going to be able to... uh, help him. I am hoping that by the time the forest recovers, we'll be long gone."

"Hoping?" Arthur yipped. "How angry is the forest going to be?"

"Very angry," Anayah said. "Very, very angry!"

Arthur opened his mouth to say something. Then quickly shut it again and slumped back in his chair, seemingly the epitome of despair.

"By the way," Morgaine said, "you're not just helping me... I mean Harpur... you're helping Karrys too."

"If we pull this off and get Harpur back, we're helping all of us," Sok said. "Where are the pastries? Why are the pastries always gone?"

Satisfied, albeit a little surprised and bewildered, that the gifts had all ended up where they had intended them to end up, the twins went their separate ways. Meg made her way to the archery range while Hart descended the stairs with the intention of going to the laboratory. He made a slight detour, though, and found his way to the back door of the council chambers, entering just in time to hear Sok say something about getting Harpur back. Instead of announcing himself, he slipped to the left of the door and hid behind a pillar to listen to the conversation. He'd been doing this since he was a small boy, sneaking into the council chambers unnoticed to eavesdrop on his father and the others, gaining, in the process, a lot of advantage when it came to understanding how the kingdom worked. Usually, the minutia of royal politics was just that, minute and uninteresting, but hearing that there was a plan to bring a dead dragon back to life was intriguing to say the least.

Harpur's reappearance in the guise of Morgaine Fayle was something that Hart was most curious about. He understood that Harpur's spirit had been transferred into Karrys Evergreen's body, but Harpur's body was long gone, burned to ash by Karrys after she bested him in the challenge for Epoh. That Sok believed there was some way to reverse that was a matter that Hart needed to know more about, and it was unlikely that the group seated at the round table would speak candidly in his presence. He now suspected that the urgency to get the birthday gifts opened and dealt with was nothing more than a ruse to get himself and Meg out of the way. So, Hart hunkered down on the floor with his back to the pillar and prepared to listen.

From the conversation that followed Sok's assertion that everyone would benefit from Harpur's return, Hart gleaned that there was a plan for the nine people then sitting at the round table to travel to Mysturna to retrieve a scale that Harpur had given to a forest. Of course, Hart knew this story well. He'd heard it many times. What he couldn't figure out was what they needed the scale for. *Are they planning to grow a new Harpur from this long-lost plate of dragon armor? Is that even possible? What kind of powerful magic does a feat like that require?* Hart's mind started to wander as he pondered these questions, and his focus drifted away from the activity on the other side of the pillar. Deep in thought, Hart failed to notice that the conversation going on around the round table had stopped. The sound of a single chair scraping across the floor failed to register. The sound of soft-booted footsteps approaching failed to penetrate his contemplative preoccupation.

"Care to join us?"

Hart's head whipped up and around to see Sok standing over him with hands on hips, a patently sardonic smile on his face.

"Wha…? How…" Hart stuttered as he clambered to his feet.

Sok sighed. "Oh, please! We could hear you breathing from across the room."

Hart's features raced through a dozen or so expressions, all highlighted in red, until he finally settled on realization. "So…?"

"Yes, Hart, we always know when you're back here," Sok said.

"Even Father?" Hart whispered.

"Well, that's highly doubtful," Sok admitted. "Arthur could miss a wasp on his nose if someone didn't point it out to him."

Hart frowned at the elf. "That's not nice!"

Sok shrugged. "Nevertheless, I've seen it happen." He turned away from the prince and walked back to the table.

Hart composed himself and took a tentative step out from behind the pillar. All eyes were on him.

"What were you doing back there?" Arthur asked as his son seated himself next to King Röggenar, who kindly passed a tray of pastries to the embarrassed young man.

Before Hart could answer, he felt the itchy tingle between his eyes and his hand reflexively went to his brow. He looked across the table and saw Morgaine staring intently at him. As quickly as his hand had shot upward, he lowered it and retrieved a pastry from the tray. His eyes strayed away from the dragon-wizardess and settled on Anayah to his right. She was also staring at him and when their eyes met, the witch raised her own brows questioningly. Hart shook his head and looked away again. This time, his gaze met Sok's.

"Are you alright?" the elf asked, cocking his own head in curiosity. The interest that Hart's gesture had raised in Morgaine and Anayah had not gone unnoticed.

"I'm fine," Hart said. Then he bit into the pastry, hoping to stave off any further questions.

His hopes were dashed when Morgaine stood up. "Where's your sister?"

"The archery range," Hart said around the mouthful of pastry.

"Let's go find her." Morgaine walked around the table toward the main doors and waited for Hart to join her.

"What's going on?" Arthur asked, clearly confused about just about everything that had happened in the last few minutes.

Anayah stood up as well. "I think I will join you."

Morgaine shot the witch an appraising look through narrowed eyes. The look she received in return told her that there was no point in arguing. "Hart, we're waiting," she said to the prince who had his own eyes trained on his father. Hoping, no doubt, for an intervention.

Hart understood that Morgaine knew something about the strange sensations he and Meg were experiencing. And he guessed that Anayah knew that Morgaine knew something about it and was coming along to find out what Morgaine knew. But he wasn't sure he wanted to know what Morgaine knew and Anayah wanted to know. All he did know was that he did not want to disrupt Meg when she was playing with her bow and arrows; the princess did not take kindly to having her practice time intruded upon. He was also relatively sure that whatever light Morgaine could shed on what was happening to him and his sister, it was likely going to be a life-changing illumination. Hart did not want his life to change.

When Arthur merely shrugged, Hart rolled his eyes and stood up. He grabbed another pastry off the tray and then followed Morgaine and Anayah out of the council chambers. They had almost reached the main doors of the castle when the council chambers' door flew open and Elder Dhonna came dashing across the foyer after them.

"A moment, Harpur... uh, Morgaine," the guild master said. Morgaine fell back as Hart and Anayah exited the castle and waited for the elf to say whatever she had to say. "What have you done to the twins?" Elder Dhonna whispered.

Harpur tried to think of a good answer for his oldest and dearest friend, but he settled on the best version of the truth that he could offer at the moment. "It appears more than I intended," Morgaine replied. "If I'm right, Hart and Meg are about to... Well, let's just go find out if I'm right first."

"Harpur Diggins," Elder Dhonna hissed, "if any harm comes to those children..."

"I know," Morgaine said, "you'll never forgive me." The dragon-wizardess sighed on Harpur's behalf. "Harm is a highly subjective thing, Bella Dhonna. Some people might think that what I suspect is about to happen is a good thing."

Elder Dhonna blanched. She couldn't imagine what Morgaine meant, but she knew that if Harpur had had a hand in it, the intention and the actual outcome were probably two very different things. There was no time for speculation. The elf followed Morgaine out of the castle, joining Hart and Anayah on the steps. Whatever was about to transpire, Elder Dhonna felt a measure of trepidation as they made their way, first to the barracks where the guards were housed, and then through them to the training grounds where the guards were busy taking turns beating each other senseless with practice swords, staffs and other implements of destruction. Keeping well out of the way of the swinging and thrusting of said implements of destruction, Morgaine lead them past the grunting and groaning that accompanied the better-aimed blows and through a gate to the archery range where they found Meg nocking an arrow in a bow that was designed for a much larger person than the diminutive princess. Behind her, several of the larger persons that the bow was appropriately suited to stood watching, and waiting, to see how Meg was going to do with it.

Meg's own bow lay on a table along with three daggers, an ornate axe, a pile of coins and a bejeweled silver arm band. Hart gasped when he realized what was happening. Meg was betting her bow on the outcome of the shot she was about to take. He was about to step forward to stop his sister from almost certainly losing her pride and joy, but Morgaine placed a staying hand on his arm and shook her head.

Meg raised the big bow and drew back the string, bringing her curled first and middle fingers to the corner of her mouth. An interminable minute passed. Everyone could see the strain the princess' arms were under as she concentrated on controlling the enormous weapon. Her arms trembled and a bead of sweat trickled down from her temple. But she held her stance. The onlookers started exchanging puzzled looks among themselves. What was she waiting for?

Meg's eyes were inexplicably closed as she stood there quaking under the effort to keep the bow steady. The experienced archers that stood behind her could see that her aim was off; the arrow might hit the target, but it would never even come close to the bullseye, which is where it had to land in order for Meg to keep her own bow.

Without warning, Meg finally stopped shaking. She shifted her aim and loosed the arrow. No one moved. No one breathed. It was as if time slowed down while they all watched the projectile clear the bow and arc toward the target. The shaft seemed to flex and bend as it took flight. Then the fletching began to do its job, causing the arrow to spin and the missile to stabilize. Meg didn't open her eyes until she heard the tell-tale thud of the arrowhead piercing the target. Then she turned slowly and smiled as if the bullseye shot she'd just made was something she did on a regular basis, which it was. Just not with a bow that was as tall as she was.

Meg's smile was met by admiration, albeit admiration thickly frosted with grudge. This only served to broaden the princess' smile as she handed the large bow back to its large owner and retrieved her own from the table. She left the rest of the pot where it was and, spotting her brother and the others standing next to the gate, wandered over to find out why they were there.

"Impressive," Morgaine said as Meg drew close.

"Thank you," Meg said. "They didn't believe that I could do it with that bow."

And they were right, Morgaine thought to herself. "Is there somewhere we could go to talk?"

Meg's eyes slid sideways toward Hart, whose own eyes conveyed abject ignorance of what Morgaine might want to talk about. To drive the message home, he shrugged.

"We can go to Uncle Davynn's office," Meg suggested.

Morgaine raised her eyebrows at this, but chose to nod in acquiescence and gestured for Meg to lead the way. The dragon-wizardess couldn't imagine Davynn leaving his office open for the guards to come and go as they pleased, but maybe Meg had some special dispensation. Being the heir to the throne and all.

The five of them made their way back through the training grounds, past more grunting and groaning, through the barracks and into a small room that contained three dust-laden chairs haphazardly scattered about the space. And nothing else.

"This is Davynn's office?" Morgaine asked in wonder.

"He doesn't spend much time in here," Meg said.

"Clearly," Elder Dhonna said.

No one bothered with the chairs.

Meg and Hart each chose a spot to lean against the wall while Morgaine made her way to the small window opposite the door, which she seemed to be inspecting with some concern. Anayah and Elder Dhonna remained near the door with their arms folded, lips pursed and toes tapping in impatient, not to mention trepidatious, anticipation of whatever Morgaine had gathered them there to announce. Neither of them was expecting anything good.

"Well?" Anayah finally broke the silence.

"Well, indeed," Morgaine said, turning around to face the others. She then turned her attention to the twins. "Tell me what has been happening with your…" She pointed to her own forehead.

Meg and Hart exchanged looks that included a nearly imperceptible head shake from Meg. Hart, in turn, scrunched up his face as if to say, "She already knows," which was followed by an expression pleading for forgiveness for what he was about to do. Meg rolled her eyes.

"A few days ago, Meg and I started feeling this weird sensation between our eyes, a kind of tingling, itch. Sometimes it burns a little." He stopped. He shrugged. He averted his gaze. He hoped that Morgaine would see it as nothing to be concerned about and dismiss it.

Morgaine studied the twins for a few beats. "And?"

"And nothing." Hart shrugged again. "It's nothing."

"Meg's little trick with the long bow out there suggests otherwise," Morgaine said.

85

Meg's head snapped up and she stared at the dragon-wizardess. "What do you mean?" The innocence she intended was lost on all three of the women before her, dripping with over-kill as it was.

Morgaine began pacing back and forth between Hart and Meg, and Anayah and Elder Dhonna.

"So, nothing... physical has... changed?" Morgaine asked.

"Physical?" Anayah jumped on the adjective and put it in a choke hold.

Morgaine stopped pacing. She looked at Anayah with the same pleading for forgiveness expression that Hart had so recently leveled at Meg. "It won't be so bad," she said.

"What won't be so bad?" Meg, Hart, Anayah and Elder Dhonna asked in unison as they closed in on the dragon-wizardess—also in unison.

"Calm down," Morgaine said. "Let me start at the beginning."

But she didn't start. She enfolded herself in a protective ward and took some time to gather her thoughts.

"We're waiting," Anayah said through gritted teeth.

"Be quiet!" Morgaine barked. She, or rather Harpur, who was actually speaking through Morgaine's body, was addressing the voice in her head. But the others could not know that the real Morgaine Fayle was attempting to assert herself into the mix.

"Excuse me?" Anayah retorted in shocked offence.

Morgaine's head followed her eyes ceiling-ward. "Not you," she said to Anayah. "Karrys is pestering me to... colour the truth, so to speak."

The others had to remind themselves that there were two separate beings ensconced within the raven-haired woman that stood before them.

"Go on," Elder Dhonna said encouragingly. "What truth are you talking about?"

Morgaine decided to focus on the elf as she spoke. Harpur's oldest and dearest friend would be the one to understand what Harpur had intended and would, she was sure, be the voice of reason once the truth came out. But the protective ward she had surrounded herself with would deflect any initial, angry blows the guild master might reactively try to land on her person.

Though she had planned on starting at the beginning, Morgaine's mouth leapt directly to the end. "I believe that the twins are turning into dragons."

Chapter Five

Arthur sat at the round oak table with his hands clasped in front of himself. He nodded his head a couple of times. "Cool," he said calmly.

Not a single person sitting at the table with him believed for a second that Arthur thought the news he'd just received was, in any possible way, cool. And none of them took his outwardly tranquil response at face value. They all new that it was only a matter of seconds before the serenity shattered like fine crystal at an opera convention and they all waited for the forthcoming meltdown to ensue before engaging in further conversation. They didn't have to wait long.

Arthur slammed his fist onto the table top and stood up. Sok was already poised to pull Arthur's chair away, thus, freeing the king to retreat to the back of the council chambers and commence blithering incoherently for the next several minutes, thus, also freeing the others in the council chamber to discuss the situation coherently. In the end, everyone would come to terms with it all; Arthur just had to take a more scenic route to acceptance than his companions.

While the King of Epoh ranted and paced and gesticulated on the other side of the council chambers, the prince and princess did their best to keep their excitement in check. They were, understandably, feeling somewhat anxious. At the same time, unlike their father, they did think that the idea of becoming dragons was cool. What they lacked, besides age and experience, was information. Hart was concerned about how painful the transformation might be and he wondered if he would still be able to take on human form and continue to conduct science experiments. Meg was worried about the permanence of it. She thought it would be awesome to fly and breathe fire, but she wasn't too keen on having to give up archery and sword fighting. From the conversation going on around them, no one knew exactly how, or when, it would happen, only that Morgaine believed that the tingling itch the twins were experiencing was the initial symptom of a greater consequence to a decision that Harpur had made when the twins were tiny babies.

Before Harpur had left Colwygshire to return to his lair and face Karrys Evergreen in her challenge for the kingdom, he had visited the infant twins and placed a protective sigil on their foreheads, drawn in his own blood. He had intended the sigil to keep the twins safe from all manner of peril as they grew up. At the time, he had no way of knowing whether his plan to have Arthur magically transfer his spirit into Karrys' body would work. He had been relatively certain that he would not prevail over the younger, fitter dragon, and he had accepted his imminent demise at her hand, but whether his plan succeeded or not, he knew he would not be part of the twins' lives. The problem, Harpur now realized, was that his own magic back then had been terribly unreliable, and though he believed that the sigil would cause no harm, he hadn't taken into consideration that his blood could have undesirable side effects on the human babies.

It was well known that dragon blood could bring the dead back to life. Arthur was, after all, an excellent example of this. He had died in a car accident on Earth shortly after meeting Harpur for the first time and Harpur had resurrected him, knowing full well that in doing so, Arthur could experience some rather uncomfortable consequences. Such as growing scales, or sprouting wings, or possibly even breathing fire. In Arthur's case, the eventual corollary was that he became impervious to fire. All things considered, this was not that bad. However, since being resurrected, Harpur's blood flowed through Arthur's veins and, through genetic inheritance, it also flowed through the twins' veins. When Harpur introduced more of his blood into the twins' bodies via the sigil, a whole different, complex and ultimately problematic repercussion may have been created. Hart and Meg were about to grow scales, sprout wings and breathe fire. Imperviousness to fire was also a given, along with horns, tails and talons.

"Think of it like this," Morgaine said, hoping to belay the reasonable fear that permeated the room, "Meg and Hart will be humans with the ability to transform into dragons. In their dragon forms, they will have all the power and magic of dragons, but they will still be people. Most of the time."

"She could have led with that," Meg said to Hart.

This bit of information served to reduce the anxiety and increase the cool factor immeasurably for both of the twins.

"This could be fun," Hart admitted.

"But...?" Elder Dhonna prodded, effectively throwing cold water on the twins' relief.

"Until they get it under control, the transformations could be spontaneous and erratic. Partial transformations. Full transformations. Very possibly at the worst times..." Morgaine began.

"Like in the great hall during supper?" Hart asked.

"Or during combat practice?" Meg asked.

"Or in the laboratory when I'm working?" Hart asked.

"Or while I'm riding my horse?" Meg asked.

"Or when I'm having a bath?" Hart asked.

89

"All or any of the above," Morgaine confirmed.

As if on cue, Arthur's meltdown stopped melting down and the king suddenly rejoined the others at the table. "We are leaving for Mysturna immediately," Arthur announced. "All of us, Meg and Hart included. We will get Harpur's scale from the Forest of Dheersha and then return here so that Bon can get to work on…" He paused, giving the android an opportunity to expound on his plan for the scale. When no expounding ensued, Arthur continued, "… whatever it is that Bon is going to do with the scale. While Bon does his thing, Morgaine can help teach Meg and Hart how to be dragons. But not in Epoh. They will have to go somewhere safe where Glynnis can't sense them. I'm guessing that if one dragon in Epoh is upsetting to him, three will make him completely crazy. And I'm not going to stand by and let that worm harm my children.

"Sok, go and tell Berryl that he's in charge while we're gone. The rest of us will remain here until you get back. Then we'll immediately zap ourselves to Andon and get to the Boundary to Mysturna from there. Anayah, I assume you have some way of keeping us from frying in the desert before we get through the Boundary. I also trust that you will be able to conjure an effective disguise for our time on your home world. Davynn, don't even think about wiggling your way out of this. We need you. Elder Dhonna, Röggenar, I apologize for keeping you from your gardens and mines, but we need you too. As for the rest of you, thank you for your help.

"We shall henceforth be known as *the Fellowship of the Scale*! Now let's go get that scale and bring our beloved Harpur back!"

If he had been expecting a cheer, Arthur was disappointed. He didn't get booed either, so that was a plus. But still, he felt a little annoyed that his rousing speech and clever, motivational team name garnered nothing but sardonic and mordant (on the part of Davynn) stares in return.

"You heard the man," Morgaine said, standing up, "it's time to get this quest on the road."

"That's the spirit," Arthur said, smiling at the dragon-wizardess. "Thank you, Harpur… uh, Morgaine." Under his breath, he added, "I'll never get used to this."

Sok also rose from his chair. "I'll be right back," he said, as he started to walk toward the door. "I hope Berryl is close by. I wouldn't want to miss another journey to the Forest of Dheersha."

Getting eleven people out of Epoh and to Andon was not the smooth and covert operation that Morgaine would have preferred. First, Berryl proved harder to find than he should have been. He should have been hovering somewhere near the council chambers in case Sok needed him for some task. As a previous member of the King's Council, Berryl had a good measure of status, but since the King's Council had petered out in the years following Arthur's coronation, Berryl's life had become something less definable. His official position was Assistant to the Senior Advisor, a job that paid reasonably well, but amounted to hanging around outside the council chambers waiting for the Senior Advisor to require assistance. Which was relatively rare, but often consisted of unsavory tasks that Sok found unworthy of his own time and skill to accomplish.

Occasionally, however, Berryl was called upon to keep an eye on things at the castle in Arthur and Sok's absence, a duty that the rotund and unspectacular man relished with all the enthusiasm of a shark for free chum. Though he was forbidden to wear Arthur's crown when he was called upon to keep an eye on things for the king, he was permitted to wear a badge with a crown on it, indicating to all that he was the emissary of the king. He kept said badge in a pocket close to his heart and actually practiced pulling it out and pinning it in place so he was always ready when Sok sought him out for just such an assignment.

Berryl had made a habit of hanging around in the foyer of the castle, talking to guards and servants and visitors. He was the self-appointed concierge, giving directions and answering questions. He also picked up a good deal of information that he would otherwise not be privy to—Sok told him next to nothing about the day-to-day goings-on. But servants and guards, both of which were much more often in the presence of Arthur and Sok than Berryl was, were excellent sources of morsels and tidbits of intriguing intelligence. Assuming that Berryl was being kept informed anyway, they had no qualms about discussing what they had overheard in the council chambers, the hallways and even, upon occasion, the private chambers of the king, his children, and his advisors. Over the years, Berryl had gotten quite good at acting like he knew what they were talking about.

On that particular day, a maid had told him about the hats the twins had received as birthday gifts. She'd seen them in Meg's room when she went in to lay out Meg's dress for supper. Not that Meg would wear it, of course, but it was part of her job description. And there was always hope. She would not have bothered had she known the princess would not be attending supper in the great hall that night, but that would not happen until Davynn happened to remember to apprise Finch, the head cook, probably only minutes before supper was served.

Berryl was curious, and since there wasn't a lot happening in the foyer, he had made his way up to the princess' rooms and entered, telling the guards that he had been asked to ensure that Meg had enough bath salts in stock. The guards thought this was an odd thing for the Assistant to the Senior Advisor to be put in charge of, but who were they to question a superior? They granted Berryl access and resumed their positions on either side of the door.

A few minutes later, Sok arrived in the corridor and was about to ask the guards if they had seen Berryl when Berryl himself emerged from the princess' room. Upon seeing Sok, he tucked something inside his coat and clamped his left arm tightly to his side.

"What are you doing in there?" Sok asked.

"Nothing!" Berryl blurted.

"What did you put in your coat?" Sok asked, not believing Berryl at all.

"Nothing," Berryl said with less blurt and more indecision. He was too busy averting his eyes to put any emphasis on his denial.

Sok held out a hand and Berryl clutched his coat closed, pressing his arm as hard as he could into his side. "Give it to me."

The guards, though sympathetic toward the Assistant to the Senior Advisor, had no intention of invoking Sok's wrath. They stepped menacingly next to Berryl and the guard on his left nudged his arm, loosening its grip on whatever he had stashed under his coat. Before Berryl could adjust his hold on the item he so desperately wanted to keep Sok from finding, the guard lifted the back of his coat and reached under to snatch the hat away. He held it up for Sok to see and promptly joined the elf in making a what-the-hell-is that-? face.

"What in Orhowyn's name is that?" It was Sok's turn to blurt.

Sok took the hat from the guard and studied it curiously.

"It's a hat, sir," Berryl finally answered.

"A hat?" Sok looked questioningly from one guard to the other and received shrugs from both of them.

"I believe so, sir," Berryl said.

"And you took it from Meg's room?"

Berryl lowered his gaze again, but his mind was suddenly less concerned with being caught stealing from the princess and much more fascinated by the fact that Sok had invoked Orhowyn's name instead of Harpur's. Since Harpur's death, no one in Epoh had used Orhowyn's name when swearing an oath. Something was going on and Berryl just had to get through this hiccup in his attempt to pilfer the hat so he could investigate further.

"I didn't steal it, if that's what you were insinuating," Berryl said defensively. "I was sent to fetch it."

"By who?" Sok asked.

"But you said you were sent to make sure Princess Meg had enough bath salts!" the guard on Berryl's right accused.

"I said no such thing!" Berryl's defensive tone ratcheted up a notch. "Clearly you misunderstood me."

Sok handed the baseball cap back to the guard and instructed him to return it to Meg's room. "You," he added, pointing at Berryl, "will come with me."

The elf marched away without looking back. He knew that Berryl would comply.

"Where are we going, sir?" Berryl panted as he caught up to Sok.

"To your room," Sok said.

Berryl gasped. "But... But why, sir? My room is all the way over on the other side of the castle. And it's rather untidy at the moment. Perhaps you'd prefer to go to the council chambers?"

"I'd prefer if you'd be quiet," Sok growled. Then he quickened his gait, forcing his assistant to jog to keep up. It was rather effective at keeping Berryl from talking at all.

By the time they reached Berryl's quarters, the Assistant to the Senior Advisor was sweating profusely. His face was beet red and his breath was distressingly laboured.

"Open it," Sok said, pointing to the door.

Berryl had no choice. He pulled a key from his pocket and attempted to insert it into the lock with a shaky hand. Impatient, Sok grabbed the key and opened the door himself. When he pushed it open, it was his turn to gasp. The small space was littered with shoulder-deep piles of books and vases and candle sticks and knick-knacks and... Well, the list went on. And on. And on.

Sok entered the room agog at the cache of obviously stolen items. There were socks and figurines, shoes and paintings, doilies and bottles, perfume atomizers and hair clips. The elf could not believe what he was seeing. Yet he was not entirely surprised. He had long suspected that Berryl was stealing things. He just had no clue that his assistant's problem was this bad.

Sok exited the room and closed the door. He reinserted the key into the lock and turned it until he heard it click securely into place. Then the put the key into his pocket.

"Excuse me, sir," Berryl said, pointing at Sok's pocket, "but I'll be needing the key to my room."

Sok draped an avuncular arm around Berryl's shoulder and began leading his confused assistant away from his room. "Oh, I don't think you'll be needing the key. Not for a while, at least."

"I don't understand, sir," Berryl squeaked. He actually understood completely.

"Don't you, Berryl?" Sok asked. "Do I really have to spell it out for you?"

"No, sir," Berryl said, "I suppose not."

"Here's what's going to happen," Sok continued. "I'm going to hand you over to the guards who are going to lock you up until I get back."

"Back from where, sir?"

"That's not important. What is important is that I now have a big problem and very little time to solve it."

"I might be able to help you, sir." Berryl sounded hopeful.

"That's okay, Berryl. But thank you for offering. What I'd really like you to do is to spend the next few days in your cell thinking about what you have done. Can you do that for me?"

"Of course, sir," Berryl agreed. "But, sir, if I may?"

"Go ahead."

"If you're going away, who will look after things at the castle?"

"That, my friend, is no longer your concern." They had reached the end of the corridor. Three guards, heading to the mess hall came around the corner and stopped in front of Sok and Berry. "Ah! What excellent timing, gentlemen. Will you please escort my ex-assistant to the cells in the guard tower at the north gate and make him comfortable in one of them?"

"What'd he do?" one of the guards asked.

"Let's just say that I want Berryl here kept safe for a few days," Sok said.

"We were just going for lunch, sir," another guard said.

"I suspected as much." Sok removed his arm from around Berryl's shoulders and reached into a pocket. He retrieved three gold coins and handed them to the lunch-bound guards. "Skull's Keep is just around the corner from the guard tower. Why don't you all have lunch there. On me."

"We'd be happy to escort Sir Berryl to the cells, sir. Thank you, sir." The guard pocketed the coins and took Berryl by the arm.

Sok watched them retreat with their prisoner back in the direction they had come. "Oh, and make sure to tell Jack y Lebard to bring meals to the prisoner while he's there."

"You can count on us," the third guard called back.

I'm sure I can, Sok thought. He waited until they were out of sight and then followed in the same direction to make his way back to the council chambers. Berryl's kleptomania was an interesting development. Sok had been suspicious of Berryl for some time, but he had no idea the scope of the man's larcenous tendencies was as vast as the evidence indicated. There were hundreds and hundreds of stolen objects in Berryl's room, strewn about in a chaotic jumble without any care or concern. It was as if, once they had been acquired, they had lost all their value.

As Sok made his way back across the castle, he reflected on how this sort of thing did not happen in the elven community. Elves simply did not steal. There wasn't even a standard punishment set out for thievery and he wondered what the council would do if it ever faced with such a charge against one of its people.

Sok brushed Berryl and his burglary aside and turned his thoughts to appointing someone to look after things while *The Fellowship of the Scale*—Sok shook his head at Arthur's nonsensical whimsy—was on Mysturna trying not to get eaten by a forest. He considered using it as an excuse for himself to stay behind, but that seemed cowardly. He could suggest that Davynn stay behind and give the good knight a way out of having to Bound, a prospect that had the poor man shaking in his boots. Not that Sok considered Davynn's fear of Bounding cowardly; Bounding was a dangerous activity not to be taken lightly at all. Being human,

Davynn was more susceptible to the capricious nature of Boundaries and Sok could not bear the idea of seeing his friend get chewed up and spit out by an anomalous, albeit convenient, portal to another world. Thus, Sok decided, the mission could go forward without Sir Davynn Willhart.

And thus it was that the second delay in leaving for Mysturna occurred.

When Sok returned to the council chambers, the others were milling about in an aura of impatience. They expected Berryl to accompany Sok, and when the elf arrived sans temporary head of state, they, of course, had questions.

The first question came from Arthur. "Where is Berryl?"

"He's indisposed for the interim," Sok replied. "I'm afraid that he will be unable to fulfil his duty as Acting King while we're away."

"Acting King?" Arthur sputtered. "He's not the king, acting or otherwise. He's just…"

"Yes, yes," Sok said, cutting Arthur off, "I know. But this time we'll have to appoint someone else to act in your stead."

"He doesn't act in my stead!" Arthur argued. "He acts in your stead."

Morgaine closed her eyes and pinched the bridge of her nose.

"But if I were unable to act in your stead, him acting in my stead would, in actuality be him acting in your stead. Instead, I think Davynn should act in both our steads." Sok turned to the knight and winked.

Davynn, while rather pleased by Sok's solution, immediately began wrestling with his conscience. Like Sok, he did not want to appear to be a coward. Also, like Sok, and perhaps even more so, he did not relish the idea of being chewed up and spit out by an anomalous portal to another world. Even if that other world was his beloved wife's home world. "Is there no one else who could watch over things while we're gone?" the knight heard himself asking. It felt like the right thing to do and it was a good compromise between begging to stay and demonstrating his loyalty and courage.

"You want to break up the Fellowship before we even get started?" Arthur was appalled.

Morgaine un-pinched the bridge of her nose and opened her eyes. "I'm reasonably sure that the Fellowship of the Scale has as much chance of succeeding without Davynn as with him," she said to the disappointed king. Then turning to Davynn, she said, "You're in charge. We'll be back as soon as we can."

The dragon-wizardess gestured for everyone to gather around to prepare to zap to Andon.

"Wait!" Röggenar said. "I really don't see how I can be of any use to this... fellowship thing either. I don't even know what a fellowship is, come to think of it. I think I should get back to my mines and..."

"When it comes right down to it," Elder Dhonna said, "Morgaine and Bon are the only ones who really need to go at all. What's the point in so many of us going? We'll only draw more attention. And, if I'm not mistaken, this mission requires stealth."

Morgaine inhaled and exhaled forcefully. They were right; there was no need for eleven of them to go and steal back the scale. She and Bon could handle it quite well, probably better, certainly more efficiently and with much less chance of something going wrong, on their own. At first, she had insisted because Harpur wanted them all together. Now, Harpur needed not only to retrieve the scale, but to keep the twins safe. She couldn't leave them behind and she couldn't take them without Arthur, who, oddly, seemed rather more enthusiastic about going to Mysturna than was characteristic. Anayah and Hiro knew the lay of the land, though so did Bon. She needed Bon to fly the Sphere. But Anayah was not welcome on her home world and her presence constituted an unnecessary risk— for all of them, but especially for the witch. How many guides were strictly necessary anyway? The urgency to get out of Epoh forced Morgaine to make a decision.

"Arthur, Bon, Hiro, Hart, Meg and myself will go to Mysturna. Sok, you're more than welcome to join us if you wish." Morgaine waited for any opposition to her declaration.

"I'm still in," Sok said, moving to the side of the room where the diminished Fellowship were gathering.

Anayah squeezed her husband's hand and smiled up at him. "I'm going too," she announced.

Davynn closed his eyes and shook his head. But he didn't argue. He knew how important getting Harpur back was to his wife and he understood that she would keep herself as safe as possible. Still, it hurt that she would choose to go and leave him safely behind.

Anayah stood on her toes and kissed her husband's cheek. "I'll come back, I promise," she whispered. "I'll feel better if you're here with the children. I love you."

Davynn nodded. "I love you too." He wanted desperately to say he would go with her, but, instead, he would beat himself up for not being able to overcome his fear of Bounding for the rest of his life.

Elder Dhonna and Röggenar remained steadfast in their resolve to absolve themselves of participating in what they both considered a fool's errand. Both of them believed that they could, and would, be of more use in Epoh. They had already planned on doing everything they could to help Harpur; they just couldn't fathom what use Harpur's scale would be in the process of getting him back. All they could do was hope that the Fellowship came back in one piece. Or eight pieces, as it were, while they researched the deepest secrets of their peoples to figure out how to reverse Harpur's current condition.

It wasn't that they disliked Morgaine, or even her true persona as Karrys Evergreen, the dragon. It was more that they liked Harpur better. And while they both harboured some animosity toward Harpur's choices and the consequent outcomes of those choices, they also felt that their world would be better with Harpur fully and physically in it.

Finally, Morgaine believed, they were ready to go. She signaled to her fellow Fellowship members to join hands and then nodded at Anayah to zap them all to Andon so they could get on with their quest. A bright plume of red smoke enveloped the huddled eight and before anyone could find another excuse to delay the procedure, they vanished from the council chambers.

The three guards that Sok had ordered to take Berryl to the cells at the north gate completed their task after a long trek through the winding roads of Colwygshire from the castle to the gate, during which Berryl pleaded his innocence incessantly and attempted to bribe them with promises of promotions that he had no authority to sanction. He had even tried to pull rank on Sok, but that just made the guards laugh. Sure, Berryl held the title of Sir, but that was mere honorific; the man had never been knighted. And Sok could make their lives quite miserable should his orders be thwarted. Whatever Berryl had done to earn a stay in the cells, it was not their problem. Besides, they had a free lunch waiting for them at Skull's Keep.

Skull's Keep was a public house of great renown in the city. It was once the entrance to a labyrinth of catacombs that led out under the city walls, making Colwygshire vulnerable to attack should an enemy decide to infiltrate through the dark and winding tunnels that also served as a charnel house, housing the bones of thousands of long-dead citizens. While attack from an enemy was highly unlikely in Epoh, some fearful and paranoid king had deemed the catacombs a weak spot in the city's defenses and had ordered the tunnels sealed. An enterprising man remodeled the entrance, creating a pub and opening it for business a few centuries before our intrepid guards entered that day for their free lunch. Currently, it was owned and operated by a handsome, middle-aged man named Jack y Lebard, who had recently taken it over and, somehow, managed to make it even better than it had been before. The food was excellent. The ale was excellent. The service was also excellent. Not that the food, the ale and the service hadn't been good before Jack took over; Jack just seemed to bring an unnamable element to the establishment that raised the spirits of any and all who entered.

The publican was a slightly stocky man of average height who wore his auburn hair cropped short. His ginger beard was streaked with white and crow's feet radiated out from his twinkling blue-green eyes. He was always quick with a smile and had a knack for making people feel welcome and comfortable. Jack y Lebard was as kind and as generous a man as anyone could hope for. Everybody loved and admired him. At the same time, he ran Skull's Keep in a manner that made it clear he would brook no guff from its patrons. Respect was his due, and no one dared cross the line with Jack lest they find themselves smartly, and permanently, ejected through the door and into the street, propelled there by one of Jack's boots to their bottoms.

The three guards arrived to find a single empty table at the back of Skull's Keep, which they claimed and made themselves comfortable at. While they waited for a serving girl to take their orders, they each extracted a silver coin from their pockets and placed them in the niche in the wall above their table. When Skull's Keep had first been renovated, these niches were adorned with skulls from the catacombs. It was tradition to place a coin or two next to the skulls to honour the long-dead occupant of the niche. The money was, in turn, used to feed those who found themselves in need.

Within minutes, Jack himself approached the table and welcomed the guards to the inn. "What can I get for you gentlemen?" he asked with his deep and soothing voice.

Speaking for the three of them, one of the guards replied, "Venison stew and ale all around."

Jack looked at the two silent guards and took their nods as approval. "Clay bowls or trenchers?"

"Trenchers," the three guards said in unison.

"Excellent choice," Jack said. "I'll have Helena bring you your meals right away."

Helena was a strawberry-blonde with a pretty smile and a buxom figure. A young widow with two children, Helena longed to be free of her position as a server at Skull's Keep, but after losing her husband, she had no immediate plans to become a wife again. She loved her children; she just couldn't imagine having more and the correlation between being married and having babies was not lost on her. So, she served food and ale to all manner of men with whom she flirted just enough to ensure her tip jar was always full, but not enough to encourage greater expectations. The tips accumulated in a locked box under her bed in hopes of someday being enough to purchase a small house for herself and her daughters. In the meantime, Jack provided a safe home, a decent wage and a strong tolerance for her mischievous children.

When she delivered the stew and ale to the guards, Helena overheard them talking about Berryl's incarceration in the north gate cells.

"Do you think he really did whatever Sok claims he did?" one of the guards asked.

"Sok wouldn't have put him in the cells if he wasn't sure," another one replied.

"But what was he going on about just before we locked him up?" the third one asked.

"Something about Harpur Diggins might not be dead," the first guard said. "Utter nonsense."

"Here you go," Helena interrupted as she sidled up to the table. "Venison stew and ale all around." She began placing the trenchers and mugs in front of their respective consumers. The guards all leaned back to give Helena room to serve them. But they didn't lean too far back. Helena's cleavage was as appetizing as the aromatic stew. "Anything else for you boys?"

From a nearby table, the guards heard Jack clear his throat and they turned their full attention to their lunch. One of them mumbled a contrite thank you and declined any further service.

"Enjoy your lunch," Helena said with a smile. Then she turned toward Jack and nodded her head toward the kitchen.

Unsure what she wanted to see him about, Jack cast a warning glare at the guards before following her.

"What did they say to you?" Jack asked when he joined Helena in the kitchen. He tried to keep the protective-employer out of his tone, and failed miserably.

100

Helena shook her head at the publican. "Those guards are a good eight or ten years younger than me, so stop thinking what you're thinking."

"What guards?" a voice said from behind a stack of crates containing potatoes. It was Emmaline, chief cook at Skull's Keep. She poked her head out so she could see past the crates.

"Never you mind, girl," Jack admonished the spinster cook. "Get back to whatever you were doing over there."

Emmaline scrunched up her cherubic face in disgust. She was an amazing cook, but she missed out on all the fun stuff.

"One of them said something about Harpur Diggins still being alive," Helena told Jack.

"I don't believe it!" Jack didn't disbelieve the bar wench. He did disbelieve that what she heard was true.

"Well, neither do I," Helena said, "but what would make him say such a thing?"

"Why don't you go and flirt with them and see if you can get more information?" Emmaline came out from behind the stack of crates carrying a large pot of water, which Jack promptly took from her. She pointed to the fire place and he hung the pot over the flaming grate.

"I don't flirt!" Helena snapped at the Rubenesque cook.

"Right!" Emmaline snorted. "And I don't make the best venison stew in Epoh."

Emmaline did, in fact, make the best venison stew in Epoh.

"There will be no flirting," Jack said. "I'll go and talk to them."

"And say what?" Helena asked. "'I hear that Harpur Diggins may still be alive. What's up with that?'"

Jack scowled at his flippant daughter. "I'll be discreet."

The two women watched Jack exit the kitchen. Then they both shrugged and went back to their respective jobs.

Jack stopped at the bar to pull a pint of ale for himself and made his way to the back of the pub where the three guards were well into their stew. "May I join you?" He asked. He didn't wait for an answer and sat down in the only empty chair at the table.

The three guards exchanged bewildered looks. It was considered an honour to have Jack join you at your table, but none of the guards could imagine why the publican would choose to honour them.

"How's the stew?" Jack asked. The three guards, all with full mouths, nodded their approval of the delicious repast. Jack took a sip of his ale. "Anything exciting happening today?" he asked.

One of the guards swallowed his food and shook his head. "Nothing much. Sir Berryl is in jail."

"The assistant to the elf?" Jack asked, feigning surprise.

"The very same," another of the guards answered. "Sok had us lock him up just before we came here."

"What did he do?" Jack asked casually and took another sip.

"Sok didn't give us any details," the third guard said, "just said to lock him up and keep him safe."

"And Sir Berryl didn't say anything?" Jack prompted.

"Oh, he said a lot!" the first guard said. "Wouldn't shut up as a matter of fact."

"Oh?" Jack said. Another sip of ale disappeared from his cup.

"Annoying little fellow," the third guard said. "Kept trying to convince us that he was innocent. Of what, he didn't share. Even tried to get us to let him go in exchange for promotions."

All three guards laughed.

"Even if he could promote us," the second guard said, "there's no way I'd ever cross Sok."

"Me either," said the third guard.

"No way," said the first guard.

"That skinny elf?" Jack mocked. "He doesn't seem like he'd be much of a threat."

"Ha!" barked the second guard. "Sok is a force to be reckoned with, he is! I'd stay on his good side if I were you."

"Hmm…" Jack took another sip of ale. "I never would have guessed." This wasn't strictly true. Jack was well aware of Sok's status and power. Some said that he was more the king than the king was. "So, you've no idea why Sok had Sir Berryl locked up?"

"Probably because he's going mad," the third guard said.

"Going mad?" Jack's interest was truly piqued.

The first guard snickered. "He claimed that Harpur Diggins might still be alive."

Jack nodded. "That is mad. What makes him think that?"

All three guards shrugged.

"We didn't stick around to find out," said the second guard. "And we were tired of listening to him."

"By the way," the third guard said, "Sok told us to ask you to make sure that Berryl was well fed while he is locked up."

"Indeed!" Jack said. "I'll be sure to do that." He drained his cup and stood up. There was no need to continue grazing in a field when he could get the grass delivered. "Enjoy your meals, gentlemen. And it's on the house today."

The guards all looked up at the publican in surprise and thanked him for his generosity. Delighted by the fact that they had each gained a gold coin on Sok, they dug back into their trenchers and finished their lunches feeling pretty darn good about this turn of events.

Jack was not a particularly nosy person. For the most part, he kept to himself and didn't meddle in the affairs of others. But he was a clever man, and the recent appearances of Glynnis was a dot that he was sure connected directly to Sir Berryl's claim that Harpur Diggins could be alive. In all the time he had lived in Colwygshire, he had seen Glynnis but a handful of times, and while nothing of any consequence had come of those rare occurrences, for this one to be so closely followed by such a bizarre assertion from someone who, technically, should be in the know about such things, had to be more than just coincidence. Jack needed to know more. So, he had Emmaline prepare a couple of sandwiches and set off to the north gate to do as Sok had asked: make sure that Berryl was properly fed.

Andon was a small village that rested on the northern-most border of the Sands of Sancheera. The Sands of Sancheera was a vast desert and the hottest place on Thraeh. Its only living occupants were dragons, who loved the heat and found the desert a pleasing place to be. Its only drawback for the great beasts was that it contained no prey. If they wanted to eat, they had to find greener pastures, so to speak. It did, however, contain the Boundary that the Fellowship of the Scale required to get them to Mysturna.

When Arthur, Sok, Morgaine, Anayah, Hiro, Bon, Hart and Meg materialized near Andon's only well, a few of the locals stopped what they were doing—which was not a lot—took note of their arrival, and then continued doing not a lot. The reason they were not doing much was because it was midday, the hottest part of the day. Being located, as it was, on the edge of a desert, Andon was always hot, except at night, when the conditions that held the temperature at searing dropped it to something more akin to chilly.

Arthur immediately began to sweat. "Where is the Boundary again?" he asked.

Morgaine pointed south. "Out there."

Arthur squinted against the sun, but all he saw was the biggest heat mirage he'd ever seen. "Right," he said. "How far out there?"

"Far enough," Sok said, recalling the last time he had come through the Boundary in question. He and Harpur and Hiro had come through it once from Mysturna. It hadn't been a pleasant experience.

"Don't worry, Arthur," Morgaine said. "I know where it is and I will zap us to within Bounding distance. As soon as we land, Anayah and I will envelope each of you in a cooling ward that should last until we are all able to Bound through."

"Should last?" Arthur asked.

"You'll be fine. Hiro will Bound first since he's familiar with the land on the other side. Then you and Sok will go. You will land near a waterfall spilling into a deep creek. As soon as you're through, get into the water," Morgaine instructed.

"Why?" Arthur was growing suspicious.

"Trust me," Morgaine said.

"I think that Hart and Meg should go after Hiro," Arthur said, protective of his offspring.

"Meg and Hart will Bound with me after the rest of you are through," Morgaine said.

Arthur frowned. "I don't think so," he protested. "I don't want my kids in this heat any longer than necessary. Even with a cooling ward."

"Arthur," Morgaine began with strained patience, "Hart and Meg have never Bounded before. They will Bound with me so I can deal with anything that might come up during their jump."

"Like what?" Arthur was horrified. He already knew what a Bound gone bad could do to a person, but he asked before realizing he didn't want to hear it repeated out loud.

Morgaine's patience strained a little tighter. "Arthur, I promise you I will get them through safely. Now let's get going."

"Promise-schmomise!" Arthur cried. "They are my children!"

Anayah, anticipating another Arthurian meltdown, tapped Arthur on the shoulder. Instantly, he calmed down. "Meg and Hart are much better suited to the heat than the rest of us. They will be fine with Morgaine. Let's please just get going."

"Did you just magic-tranquilize me?" Arthur stared at the witch.

Anayah rolled her eyes. "Morgaine, I think we're ready." She stepped away from Arthur and warded herself within an icy-cold shield.

Morgaine wanted to make sure Arthur knew what he had to do once they reached the Boundary, but magic tranquilizers notwithstanding, she wanted to get Arthur and the others through it as quickly as possible. Her biggest concern lay with Meg and Hart. So far, they hadn't exhibited any signs of an impending transformation, but a shock could trigger one. Before she zapped them all to the Boundary, she checked on the twins. Finding them calm, even eager for their first Bound to another world, she snapped her fingers and in a teal puff of smoke the good people of Andon were left to continue doing not much without them.

The moment that they landed, Anayah felt her ward giving way to the heat. She quickly reinforced it and then spun even icier wards around Arthur, Sok, Hiro and Bon. As she and Morgaine had hoped, Arthur didn't notice that she had not warded the dragon-wizardess or the twins, who both seemed cool as cucumbers in the oppressive heat.

Though the sudden chill took Hiro's breath away, he managed to keep his senses and surged into the Boundary on his hover gilly.

Sok felt the cold wrap around himself and almost immediately begin to warm up. He looked at Arthur, who appeared to be swooning, and grabbed the king by the arm all but dragging him through the Boundary.

Bon seemed to be unaffected by either the heat or the cold and as soon as Sok and Arthur had disappeared, he took Anayah by the hand and, together, they leapt through.

Meg and Hart, having watched how the others had done it, stepped up to the Boundary, preparing to jump too, but Morgaine held them back.

"How are you feeling?" Morgaine asked the twins.

"Fine," said Hart.

"It's not that hot here," Meg said.

"Are you nervous?" Morgaine asked.

The twins shook their heads.

"Do you feel the tingling right now?"

Again, the twins shook their heads.

"We should go," Hart said. "I don't want Father to worry about us."

"Right," Morgaine said. "I want you both to put your arms around me. When I say, 'Get ready,' I want you both to hold your breath. When I say, 'Go,' we're going to jump into the center of the Boundary together. Got it?"

The twins nodded.

Morgaine held out her arms and when the twins had wrapped their own arms around her back, she led them up to the Boundary. "Get ready!" Morgaine heard Meg and Hart fill their lungs. "Go!"

The three of them jumped into the shimmering void of the Boundary.

Both Hart and Meg felt like their bodies had turned to rubber. But almost as soon as the sensation registered, they were through the Boundary and falling rather farther than they had expected. What they had expected was to land on solid ground. Instead, they fell into the deep creek Morgaine had instructed Arthur to get into as soon as he had passed through the Boundary.

A moment later they all surfaced and swam to the rocky creek bank.

"That was awesome!" Hart shouted as he pulled himself out of the water.

"Are we really on Mysturna now?" Meg asked in wonder.

Arthur was sitting on a rock and held his hand out to help Meg out of the creek. "You could have warned us," he snarled at Morgaine.

The dragon-wizardess smiled at Arthur. "I wasn't sure which side we'd come out on," she said by way of apology.

"What took you so long?" Sok asked. "Arthur was about to have another fit."

"I was not!" Arthur objected. "I was just wondering why they didn't jump right away."

No one bothered to argue.

Morgaine inspected the Fellowship members. Of the eight of them, Hiro was the only one who wasn't dripping wet from plunging into the creek. His hover gilly had kept him high and dry, as it were. Finding everyone whole, hale and hearty, if a little damp, Morgaine moved to an open area a short distance away from the group.

"Where are you going?" Arthur asked.

"I'm going to transform into my dragon form," Morgaine announced. "Meg and Hart can fly with me. The rest of you will fit in the hover gilly."

Meg actually clapped her hands in excitement. "Ooh! I've never flown with a dragon before. What do I do?"

"Don't look down," Arthur advised.

"I don't suppose you could dry my boots, Anayah?" Sok asked. "They're my favourite ones and I don't want them ruined."

"Just the boots?" Anayah asked.

"Well, if you don't mind, it is a bit chilly…" Sok gestured to include the rest of himself.

Anayah obliged. "Anyone else?"

All the other creek-soaked members of the Fellowship indicated that being dry would be more comfortable and, in a blink, they all found themselves no longer sopping wet.

A short distance away, Morgaine transformed into Karrys Evergreen, her true, magnificent, teal dragon form. She stretched her wings and let loose a short burst of flame from her enormous maw. Having been confined to human size and shape for several days, it felt good to be a dragon again. She—and Harpur—looked forward to the flight to the Sphere.

Meg and Hart both stared in awe at Karrys. It's not like they hadn't seen a dragon before, but they had never seen a transformation.

"Is that going to happen to us?" Meg mused.

"I sure hope so!" Hart said. Then he took his sister's hand and led her to where Karrys stood waiting for them.

While the others climbed aboard Hiro's hover gilly, Karrys told the twins to climb into her front feet. She then wrapped her long talons around them, holding them snuggly in place. "Hiro, lead the way!" Karrys called out as she launched into the sky and circled around to follow the crowded, flying chariot.

"I can't watch," Arthur said, turning away from the sight of his children dangling underneath a dragon. He leaned closer to Sok. "Tell her to be careful with them."

"First of all," Sok said, "keep in mind that Harpur is really in control over there. Meg and Hart couldn't be in better hands."

Arthur considered this and decided that it did give him some comfort. "And second?" he prompted the elf, assuming that if there was a first of all, there must also be a second of all.

"Second of all," Sok said with a smirk, "stop being such a nincompoop!"

A number of swift and complicated expressions passed over Arthur's face. "Where did you get that word from?" he spat out when he could finally speak.

"I probably picked it up from you," Sok said.

"Do you even know what it means?" Arthur tried to remember the last time he'd called anyone a nincompoop. It wasn't a regular part of his lexicon.

"Not really," Sok admitted. "But it sounds like it fits the situation."

"And what situation are you referring to, exactly?"

"Your nincompoopiness, of course," Sok said as if it should be obvious.

"That's not even a word!" Arthur ridiculed his friend.

"Well, it should be," Sok countered, "'cause you're dripping in it."

Arthur's face froze in a look that, if it had a name, might aptly be called *Huh?*

"Sok's right," Anayah, who knew what nincompoop meant, interjected.

"He is?" Arthur said.

"I am?" Sok said. He wasn't used to having Anayah back him up.

"You are being a bit of a fool," the witch confirmed.

"How so?" Arthur challenged while Sok relished his vindicated assumption.

"Meg and Hart are adults now," Anayah said. "It's time you started treating them as such."

Arthur frowned. "Just because the age of majority is set at sixteen, doesn't mean that kids magically become adults at that moment in their lives."

"And they never will if you don't stop treating them like they are six," Anayah argued.

Arthur made another face. This one might be called *I Don't Do That!* "I don't treat them like they are six," he said. "Twelve or fourteen, maybe, but not six."

"Just the other day you asked Hart if he had washed behind his ears." Sok was sure that was how a human parent would treat a six-year-old.

"I asked him if he had gotten all the green slime he'd splashed all over himself out of his hair!" Arthur couldn't believe he was having this conversation.

"Which is behind his ears!" Sok insisted.

Arthur put his hands up in surrender. "Fine! I'll start treating them more like adults." He paused for a moment. "But I'm still going to worry about them!"

As it happened, it was late summer in the region they found themselves in on Mysturna. And, to Karrys' relief, it was also dusk. She and Harpur had been concerned about flying around in a world that did not have dragons during the day time, but luck, it seemed, was on their side. As the two suns set behind them, though, Karrys wondered how well Hiro would be able to navigate in the dark. She also grew concerned about her companions growing tired and needing to sleep as the night wore on. Meg and Hart could, of course, sleep where they were, but the others would not be able to rest in the standing-only-room hover gilly, especially with its open back, out of which a slumbering body could easily fall. The luck that Karrys had been so grateful for was quickly waning.

Thankfully, her passengers were behaving themselves. Unlike Sok had been when flying with Harpur, Meg and Hart enjoyed the flight without having to constantly wiggle and squirm about in her grasp. She kept her grip snug, but not unduly tight, and took their relative stillness as a sign that they were comfortable and secure. Truth be told, Karrys was glad that Harpur's spirit was in control and had experience with ferrying passengers at high altitudes through the night sky. Soon enough, she relaxed and left the twins to do the same.

Karrys needn't have worried about anyone needing to fall asleep. It had been early afternoon when they left Epoh, so even though it was evening on Mysturna, no one was particularly tired. They were, nonetheless, hungry and it wasn't long before Sok and Arthur began pointing out the lack of inflight food.

"When are we going to stop for a snack?" Arthur inquired.

Karrys picked this up with her keen hearing and swiveled her head toward the hover gilly, which was on her left about twenty yards from her wingtip.

"I could go for a hamburger," Sok said.

"You just finished lunch," Anayah said.

"That was a while ago," Sok replied. "And here it has to be supper time already. It's getting dark."

Meg and Hart couldn't hear this exchange over the wind rushing past their ears. They were close enough to hear each other if they shouted, but the conversation happening in the hover gilly was lost on them.

"Hiro, Bon?" Karrys called out. "Is there somewhere nearby that we could set down and feed the gluttons?

Hiro giggled, as he so often did. There was little in life that didn't amuse the Krist. "We'll be at the hills south of the Forest of Dheersha in a very short time."

"Really?" Arthur was impressed. He'd expected to be trekking about Mysturna for days.

"Yes," Bon replied. "The southern edge of the forest is not that far from where we are."

"Are we talking minutes or hours?" Arthur asked.

"Somewhere in between," Bon said. "In Earth time, I'd say forty-five minutes. Give or take."

"But we need to get to the Sphere," Anayah said, somewhat nervously. The Forest of Dheersha, though vast, was not that far from Danaleedh, the city where Anayah was from and of which her estranged Aunt Analeetah was Doyenne.

110

"We'll veer south from the hills," Hiro said.

"Why not veer south now and go straight to the Sphere?" Anayah's alarm was palpable.

"We could," Bon offered, "but we'd have to pass over the Windy Mountains. The hover gilly wouldn't withstand the gusts."

Anayah should have known this. "But we'll stay well away from Danaleedh?"

"We will stay well away from Danaleedh," Bon assured her.

They flew on, and if anyone, other than Bon, had had the ability to measure time in minutes, they would have been impressed with the android's estimated time of arrival at the hills Hiro was taking them to. Precisely forty-four minutes and fifty-one seconds had passed from the time Bon had mentioned the duration of the flight they were on.

It was fully dark by the time they reached the hills. Both Bon and Karrys, the ones with the best night vision, were scanning for an appropriate place to land. Almost simultaneously, they identified a bare field that would have been perfect for their purposes. The only problem was that it seemed to already be occupied. A campfire blazed in the center of what appeared to be a semi-circle of red and yellow striped tents. About a half-dozen extremely large men could be seen milling about around the fire.

"Go around them to the north," Karrys instructed Hiro. "Maybe they won't notice us."

"We're quite close to the forest," Hiro shouted back, knowing that Karrys' hearing would have no difficulty picking up his words.

"Besides, if I'm not mistaken, they are friends," Bon added.

By then, all of the others had seen the fire. But they couldn't make out the details that Bon and Karrys could see.

"Friends?" Karrys asked. "What friends could we possibly have on Mysturna?"

"Frode!" Bon announced.

"Frode?"

"Frode?"

"Frode?"

"Frode of Ordyr, leader of the Drengrokil clan? He's here?" This last overstated and eight-times-magnified repetition of his companion Fellow-shippers' mixture of surprise, delight and mild chagrin at learning that the demi-giant Drengrokil leader might be a mere fifty yards below them, was issued from the mouth of the only elf among them. All eyes in the hover gilly and one more belonging to Karrys Evergreen focused on Sok. "What? I was just clarifying that we're all talking about the same Frode."

"How many Frodes do you know?" Arthur asked.

Sok shrugged. "It's been a long time since we've seen him. I don't know how many Frodes the rest of you have met in the meantime."

"Exactly none," Arthur said.

"What should we do?" Hiro called over to Karrys.

"Well, they've spotted us now. We might as well go and see what brings a witch hunter to Mysturna." Karrys banked to her right and circled upward, giving Hiro time and space to land the hover gilly.

Arthur and Sok looked over the side of the hover gilly and watched as Frode— for it was indeed Frode on the ground—and his men all drew their swords and stood in a line, ready to meet whatever threat was descending upon them.

"That's not very friendly. He must not recognize us," Sok said. Then he leaned dangerously over the side of the hover gilly and started shouting, "Hey, Frode! It's us, Sok and Arthur and Anayah and Bon and Hiro. Don't mind the dragon. She's harmless."

Frode understood Sok's words, but it took a few beats before he accepted them as truth. Until he saw Sok leap over the side of the hover gilly and run, unabashedly, toward him, he kept his sword raised. As the elf drew closer and Frode could finally see him clearly in the fire light, he finally lowered his weapon.

"Is my good friend, Sok!" he said in some surprise to see the elf.

"I already told you it was me," Sok said, coming to a halt in front of the mountainous Drengrokil warrior. Without warning, Frode threw his arms around Sok and scooped him up into a bone-crushing bear hug. "Oof!" Sok grunted as his breath was squeezed out of his lungs in a sudden gush.

"Is good to see you!" Frode said. "What brings elf to world of witches?"

Around him, Frode's men all lowered their own weapons and retreated back to the fire.

"We're on a quest to save Harpur Diggins," Sok said, gasping for breath and checking for broken ribs.

Frode looked down at Sok, puzzled. "Harpur Diggins is dead, no?"

"Well, yes," Sok said. "And no."

Frode's eyebrows furrowed, then bounced back up toward his hairline. "Ah! He is ghost!"

"Not exactly," Sok said, suddenly unsure if he should have said anything at all about Harpur. "Why would you think he's a ghost?"

"You said he's dead and he isn't dead. That means ghost, no?"

Arthur and Anayah joined them, followed by Hiro and Bon on the hover Gilly.

"What's this about ghosts?" Anayah asked.

"Ah," Frode said, sweeping Anayah up in a somewhat gentler hug than he'd dispensed on Sok. "Is pretty witch come to improve Drengrokils' view."

"Down boy," Anayah said, extricating herself from the big man's arms.

Frode repeated his bear hug routine for Arthur, but chose to only shake hands with Bon and Hiro. He was still slightly weirded out by Bon's androidism and he actually feared damaging the Krist.

"Come," Frode said, sweeping his hand toward the fire, "fire is warm and ale is cold. Men will prepare food for guests."

The Drengrokil had already set up stumps for the newcomers to the camp, and they made themselves comfortable while they waited for Morgaine and the twins to join them. Never having seen Karrys in her human form, Frode jumped up when the dragon-wizardess entered the light of the fire. He approached her slowly, examining her from head to toe and then bringing his gaze to settle on the black patch covering her left eye.

"Karrys Evergreen, no?"

"Hello, my friend," Morgaine said. "But in my human form, I'm known as Morgaine Fayle."

Frode bowed his head. Then snapped it back up in alarm as his own memories of his time in Epoh came back to him. Suddenly, Sok's words made sense. "So, plan was good! Plan worked! Why not tell Frode when we were together after rescue?"

113

Morgaine smiled at the giant man. "It was supposed to be a secret, Frode. I'm sorry."

"Do I speak to Karrys or…"

"Technically, you are speaking to Harpur. You always were. But it's simpler to call me Morgaine in this form and Karrys when I'm in dragon form."

Frode nodded and ran his hand through his thick, black hair. "Is very weird. But Frode will do his best." He then turned his attention to the twins, who were both staring up at him in awe. "And who are these young people?"

"Frode, I would like you to meet Princess Meg and Prince Hart. They are Arthur's children." Morgaine introduced the twins.

Frode turned to look at Arthur, impressed. He gave the king a thumb's up sign. "Welcome to Drengrokil's humble camp, your majesties. We are honoured by your presence."

Arthur leaned over to whisper in Sok's ear, "He never said he was honoured to be in my presence."

"Do you blame him?" Sok jibed.

"Why do you always do that?" Arthur asked, hurt.

"You make it so easy," Sok said, accepting a mug of ale from one of Frode's men. "Thank you."

"It's a good thing I like you." Arthur took a mug from the same man. "Thank you."

"Come! Sit!" Frode said to Morgaine and the twins. "Wolf, more ale for our new friends here."

"Uh…" Arthur began as he stood up to protest, "the twins will just have water."

Sok elbowed the doting and over-protective father in the ribs. "You're being a nincompoop again," he whispered.

"Fine," Arthur whispered back. "Never mind. They're adults. It's up to them," he said to the Drengrokil named Wolf.

Meg and Hart exchanged shocked looks.

"Who are you?" Hart asked his father as he and Meg seated themselves across the fire from Arthur.

"And what did you do with our real dad?" Meg added.

"Ha-ha!" Arthur mocked. "Drink your ale." He leaned close to Sok again. "If they get drunk…"

"Nincompoop." Sok sing-songed.

"Stop it already!"

Anayah tried to stifle her laugh, but Hiro giggled relentlessly.

"What means nincompoop?" Frode asked, unsure what was happening.

To Arthur's relief, Anayah shushed Sok and told Frode that it was a joke between the king and the elf and that she would explain later.

The evening reunion lasted far longer than Morgaine would have liked. She had hoped to get at least a little closer to the Sphere before they settled down to sleep. But what lay ahead was uncertain at best and crazy-stupid dangerous at worst. Since she expected the worst, she decided she might as well let the Fellowship enjoy this respite from the stress that waited for them.

The twins seemed a bit overwhelmed, but in a happy, joyful way. They showed no signs of transforming, though Morgaine continued to constantly monitor their demeanors.

To Arthur's further relief, both Hart and Meg imbibed only enough ale to get slightly tipsy. He, too, kept a more subtle eye on them, and he did have to bite his tongue once or twice, but he was determined to show Sok that he was not as big a nincompoop as the elf believed.

Since Sok had already let a good part of the cat out of the bag, the Fellowship, as a whole, filled in the gaps for the Drengrokil.

"Is good plan," Frode said. "Maybe Drengrokil come back to Epoh with you and see how things turn out."

"You're always welcome," Arthur said. "But what are you doing here on Mysturna anyway?"

Frode stroked his beard and thought about what to tell the Fellowship. "We have reason to believe that evil witch is… What is expression? …wreaking havoc? Yes?" He paused when Anayah sucked in her breath.

All eyes turned to the witch. Then all eyes turned back to the Drengrokil leader.

Morgaine took the reins of this potential crisis. "Do you know the name of this evil witch?"

"Analeetah," Frode said.

Anayah exhaled. "What do you indent to do to her?"

"Kill her," Frode said.

Anayah paled. "You can't!" Her voice was barely a whisper.

"Ladies in forest say we can," Frode replied. "Why does pretty witch want Drengrokil to spare evil witch?"

"What ladies in what forest?" Morgaine asked.

"Is there problem?" Frode asked in return, picking up on the tension.

Morgaine, much like the rest of the Fellowship of the Scale, was at a loss as to how to respond. There was, indeed, a problem. Anayah!

Morgaine caught Bon's eye and nodded toward Anayah. She needed someone to be ready in case Anayah reacted badly. The android moved to Anayah's side and, as he did, Sok stood up to reposition himself on her other side. Neither of them knew what they would do to stop Anayah if she did make an unfortunate decision; they were both powerless against her magic, but at least they might be able to distract her.

"Frode," Morgaine began, "can you tell us exactly how you came to be here and who asked you to kill Analeetah?"

"The ladies in the forest," Frode said, somewhat nonplussed. He pointed with his thumb toward the Forest of Dheersha. "I already said this."

"There are ladies living in the forest?" Morgaine probed.

"Many!" Frode said. "They live in fear of the evil Analeetah and want Drengrokil to kill her."

Morgaine looked at Bon and Hiro, who was also hovering close to Anayah. "I thought the forest wouldn't allow anyone to live in it."

Bon cocked his head to one side as he internally scanned his files for information. "There is no precedence for it in known history," the android said. "However, if the forest were to agree to it, there is no reason why people could not live within its boundaries."

116

"That makes no sense," Anayah said. "The forest has never allowed anyone to live there. It may grant passage through it, but always at a cost."

Morgaine studied the witch. Anayah seemed to have composed herself, but it would not do to let their guard down.

"All Drengrokil know is ladies in forest summoned us and said Analeetah is evil witch," Frode explained. "Asked us to kill her."

"How many ladies live in the forest?" Anayah asked. She was beginning to suspect that these ladies were not just any ladies.

"Twenty," Frode said, stroking his lush beard in thought. "Maybe more, maybe less."

That wasn't the number Anayah expected. "Only twenty?"

"Drengrokil only talked to one," Frode said. "But others were there. Twenty is only guess."

"Who did you talk to?" Anayah asked. "Where did you meet her?"

"Lady's name is Benebell," Frode answered. "We meet in forest. In Benebell's house."

Morgaine watched Anayah closely. Aware that the native Mysturnian would know better than she what questions to ask, the dragon-wizardess contented herself with listening. Maybe something would be revealed that would allow them to get the scale back without having to steal the Sphere. With a bit of luck, they might even find a way to get what they came for and get back to Epoh that night. But she still needed to be prepared in case Anayah did something rash.

Unfortunately, Frode could not tell them how or why the ladies came to live in the Forest of Dheersha. For all he knew, they had always lived there and there was nothing strange about it. He and his men had been summoned by the ladies and asked to get rid of the evil witch, Analeetah, who had gone mad with grief some years ago and was systematically destroying others of her kind. They had arrived on Mysturna earlier that same day and had walked into the forest where they met with an old, white-haired woman named Benebell who promised to pay them in gold when the deed was done.

"She say forest is too dangerous for Drengrokil to stay in," Frode said, wrapping up. And his men all laughed, "but we humour Benebell. She is nice lady. And this is good place for camp, no?"

"You were wise to humour her," Arthur said, shuddering at the memory of his last visit to the vile place.

Again, the Drengrokil warriors all laughed.

"He's right," Morgaine said. "You wouldn't have lasted very long in there."

The fearless men remained skeptical, but they stopped laughing.

Morgaine was about to ask Anayah if she had any idea who these ladies might be when something caught her eye and she turned to the twins.

Then she gasped.

All eyes in the camp turned in the direction of Morgaine's gaze. A collective gasp followed her example. Glowing purple-red sigils had appeared on Hart and Meg's foreheads. The sigils pulsed with menace and the twins appeared to both be in a trance.

Instantly, the Drengrokil all stood and drew their swords.

"Tell your men to stand down," Morgaine said to Frode, keeping her eyes on the twins.

The Drengrokil leader tore his gaze away from the twins and looked at Morgaine. "Tell children to stop…" he began, but didn't know precisely what was happening to Meg and Hart. Instinct told him that whatever it was, it wasn't good.

"Get everyone out of the camp," she ordered. Then she, too, stood up and approached the twins.

No one else moved.

Sok was the first to realize what was going on. "Orhowyn's silvery scales!" the elf shouted. "Run!" Sok grabbed Arthur by the arm and hauled the king to his feet. "That way," he said as he pushed Arthur forward in the direction of the trees beyond the tents.

Bon picked up Anayah and jumped onto the hover gilly, which Hiro directed to follow Sok and Arthur. Frode, still uncertain of the nature of the threat, watched the retreat in progress. For a moment, he considered having his men attack the twins. Then he turned back to see what Morgaine was going to do. His eyes widened and he started backing away from the fire, shouting something in the Drengrokil language to his men.

Morgaine approached the twins, both of whom were now engulfed in purple flames. Their eyes were closed and they wore serene expressions on their faces. Morgaine took this as a good sign; the transformation was happening slowly, but Hart and Meg did not seem to be in any pain. She wondered what had triggered their first transformation into dragons and if she could get them away from the fire and the tents before it went any further. This was new to Morgaine—and Harpur!

Shapeshifting was a tricky business at the best of times. It took practice, and changing from tiny humans into thirty-or-so-foot, winged beasts for the first time was not likely to be a smooth or graceful process. Morgaine considered zapping them away, but zapping them in their current state was out of the question. She had no idea what effect it might have on the transformation. All she could do, at that point, was get out of the way and hope for the best.

She turned around and started running toward the mesmerized Frode, who had stopped just outside the ring of stumps that they had been sitting on. "Sorry about your camp," she apologized in advance of what she anticipated as she nudged him further away from the fire. When he reluctantly started to follow her to safety, she added, "You can't kill Analeetah."

Frode may only have known Harpur Diggins by reputation, technically. But that reputation was more than enough to give him pause. "Drengrokil will wait. For now."

Chapter Six

Jack y Lebard entered the gate house at the north gate about ten steps behind Davynn, who was in the process of discovering that Berryl was therein incarcerated. Davynn, upon entering with the intention of checking in with the guards, stopped short when he saw Berryl sulking on the cot in his cell. His first thought was that he was going to have to have words with Sok. His second thought was that he'd have to be very careful about what he said. At least until he figured out what was going on.

He heard the door open and close behind him and turned to see Jack enter with a cloth covered tray, presumably for the prisoner. Jack hid his disappointment at seeing Davynn and smiled at the knight.

"Good afternoon, Sir Davynn," Jack said. "Where would you like me to put this?"

"Jack." Davynn acknowledged the publican. "The guards will take it." He motioned for Jack to hand over the tray.

One of the two guards on duty in the gate house took the tray and lifted the cloth cover to inspect the contents. It was, as it appeared, two sandwiches and a slice of pie, a new type of fruit-filled, plate-sized pastry that Emmiline had become quite famous for. This one was filled with apples. Davynn's stomach rumbled when the aroma of sweet, warm apples reached his nose. He made a mental note to stop over at Skull's Keep before he returned to the castle that day.

The guard thanked Jack and went to deliver the repast to Berryl, who was still sulking behind the cell bars.

Davynn busied himself with some papers on the guards' desk, looking for any clue as to why Berryl was being incarcerated at the north gate. Finding none, he motioned for the guards to come closer and asked them what reason Sok had supplied for the current state of Berryl's affairs. He was careful to couch the query in a way that did not reveal his own ignorance.

"We didn't speak to Sok, sir," the first guard said. "Sir Berryl was delivered here by three other guards who said that we were to keep him safe until Sok returned."

Davynn nodded sagely. "Did you log the incident?"

"Not yet, sir," the second guard said.

"Well, don't bother," Davynn instructed. "I will take care of that myself. Do you know where the guards that brought Berryl in are now?"

The two guards exchanged doubtful looks. Not logging a prisoner was strictly against protocol. An errant guard could end up being logged in himself for failing to follow procedure. They were both feeling lucky that they hadn't been chastised by Davynn for not having logged Berryl in yet. But neither of them knew the whereabouts of the guards who had brought Berryl to the north gate.

"I might be able to help you with that," Jack interrupted. He had been feigning interest in two ancient and faded wanted posters on the wall next to the door.

"Go on," Davynn said, wondering why Jack was still there.

"They took lunch over at Skull's Keep. They may still be there." Jack smiled as if he was glad to be of service.

"Thank you," Davynn said, extricating himself from behind the desk and walking over to the door. On his way past, he placed a hand on Jack's shoulder, indicating that it was time for the publican to return to his own establishment. Though disappointed that he hadn't gleaned even a bit more information, Jack wisely allowed himself to be ushered out of the guard house.

"I'll return for the tray later," Jack called back over his shoulder as he and Davynn exited through the door.

The guards watched them leave and then looked over at Berryl, who was munching morosely on his meal.

"Why *are* you here?" the first guard asked the prisoner.

Berryl looked up and shrugged. "A simple misunderstanding," was all he said.

One minute Meg was sitting on a stump drinking ale with the Fellowship and the Drengrokil. The next minute—or so it seemed to her, though in reality it was several—she was looking down at the campfire from above it and she thought that she might be floating in the air for some unknown and unfathomable reason. Turning her head to see if Hart was up there with her, she suddenly realized that she was not floating at all. She looked down at her body and gasped rather similarly to the way Morgaine had just a short time earlier. Only Meg's gasp was followed by a jet of purple-black flame, which only caused the princess to gasp again, and this led the first of the six tents in the camp to ignite.

Meg tried to back away from the burning tent, only to discover that she had no control over her body. Something on her lower back was preventing her from moving and when she tried to look over her shoulder to see what it was, she learned that her neck was rather longer and much more bendy than it should be. Her head swung around and connected with something that felt like a large tree trunk. The impact caused her to cry out, sending another jet of purple-black flame to flare from her mouth, which set the second tent on fire.

She pulled away from the tree trunk and found herself looking, not at a tree, but into the violet eyes of a dragon. Still unsure why her visual perspective was so incongruously higher than it should be, she attempted to back away again, and was reminded of the obstacle protruding from her lower back. She stumbled and fell and when her arm failed to reach out to break her fall, she felt something strange on her upper back begin to flap and flail. As she tumbled to the ground, she became aware that the dragon she had just come eye-to-eye with was also stumbling and flailing and generally behaving in a decidedly un-dragon-like manner.

Next to Meg, Hart was experiencing an anomalous inability to control his own body. Instead of falling down, though, the flapping things on his shoulder blades began to lift him off the ground, and it occurred to him that he had suddenly gained the ability to fly. For a moment, just before the panic set in, he wanted to test this newly acquired faculty. Then he realized that he had no idea how to land again and the flapping converted to thrashing, which led to crashing back to earth, and he promptly decided that it was in his best interest to remain absolutely still.

Meg, in a heap next to Hart, had come to the same conclusion. She stared at the dragon beside her and tried to calm herself so she could figure out what was happening to her. *Where is Hart?* she wondered, worried that the dragon might have trampled her beloved brother.

And then it hit her. She was a dragon.

And that meant that the dragon lying beside her must be Hart.

A wave of relief washed over the dragon-princess. It was quickly followed by another wave of panic.

I'm a dragon!

She took a moment to compose herself, then raised her head and tentatively looked around. All the tents were now on fire. Hart had landed on the camp fire, sending sparks in all directions. Between Meg's unfortunate aim and Hart's bulk, the canvas pavilions hadn't stood a chance. They were well and thoroughly engulfed in flames, along with all of the Drengrokil's personal possessions.

Oddly, Meg registered only a flicker of remorse for the warriors' loss. She was too enthralled by the quality of the flames to be concerned about a few material possessions. At first glance, the fire looked like any other fire; it was yellow and orange and danced merrily as it consumed its fuel. But the closer Meg looked, the stranger the flames seemed. They had substance and physicality that she had never noticed before. She thought that if she reached out and touched it, the flame would feel solid in her hand.

Speaking of hands… Meg tore her attention away from the burning tents and focused on her body. In human form, the princess stood five feet, two inches tall and weighed a mere one hundred twenty pounds, most of which was toned muscle. Now, however, she weighed several tons and measured nearly thirty feet from the tip of her nose to the tip of her tail. Small perhaps, for a dragon, but when one has spent one's entire life as a diminutive human, manipulating that much mass was a skill that she would need time to master.

Meg looked down at Hart, lying nearby. He wasn't moving, but she could see he was breathing. She wanted to say something to him, call out to him for some reassurance that he was okay, but the idea of opening her mouth caused her to hesitate. The last two times she had done that, she had set Frode's men's homes on fire. She didn't think that her dragon fire would harm Hart, but she still couldn't bring herself to risk doing him any harm. She wished that Morgaine had better prepared her for this. Then again, neither Morgaine, nor Harpur, really knew much about *this*, either. On the surface, it may seem like the difference between being dragons that could transform into humans and humans who could transform into dragons was moot, but it was normal for dragons to change into other creatures, whereas humans tended to remain human all of the time.

Then another thought occurred to Meg. *If I can become a dragon, I can become myself again.*

Not knowing exactly how the process worked, Meg tried imagining herself as herself. Nothing happened. She remained a very large and very unwieldy dragon. She tried again. Again, nothing happened. She needed help.

It finally occurred to Meg that no one was around. It made sense, of course, that the Fellowship and the Drengrokil had fled from the burning tents, but surely they wouldn't have abandoned her and Hart all together. They had to be close by. She looked around, amazed at how clear her vision was, and finally spotted Morgaine standing next to the remains of one of the tents. When she made eye-contact with the dragon-wizardess, she nodded her head to indicate that she was okay and that she would not do anything to cause further harm.

"Can you stand up?" Morgaine asked.

Meg decided that, even though the idea of forcing her bulk into an upright position was slightly terrifying, she couldn't just lay around in a heap on the ground forever. She rolled to her right, closer to Hart, who was also beginning to stir, and maneuvered her arms—*or are they legs?* Meg wondered—beneath her for leverage.

"Mind your wings!" Morgaine called.

Wings? Oh, right! Those floppy things on my back.

Meg concentrated on the floppy things on her back and eventually managed to tuck them in closer to her body.

"And your tail!"

I have a tail? Harpur's ashes! I have a tail!

Meg soon discovered that, while her tail was something of an obstacle in backing up, it was also a great counter-weight and by keeping it low, she could lift her upper body with something not unlike ease. Once she was finally up and balanced on her powerful back legs, she couldn't repress a sense of accomplishment and pride.

She wasn't quite ready to give the awesomeness of the situation its entire due, but she was definitely beginning to see the potential in being an enormous dragon. A dragon version of a smile tugged at her mouth.

She watched Hart struggle to his own feet, and the urge to hug him compelled her to take a step toward him to close the gap. But they soon discovered that hugging was not a natural form of affection for dragons and settled on an awkward hand clasp—one they managed to accomplish without gouging each other's palms.

Without thinking, Hart opened his mouth to speak to his sister, but instead of words, a stream of purple-black flame shot out of his huge maw. Meg drew back to avoid the heated vapor and felt the impulse to laugh take over. Fearing that she, too, would belch fire instead of a joyful, if slightly hysterical, guffaw, she clamped her own mouth shut. But in doing so, the pressure of the dragon fire built up in her chest and she was forced to release it, which only created a greater need to laugh hysterically. For the next while, purple-black dragon flame crisscrossed the clearing as the two fledgling dragons came to terms with their new paradigm.

All Morgaine could do was stay out of the way and wait it all out. The Fellowship and the Drengrokil had crept out of the trees they had been sheltering in and they all stood behind her, gaping at the scene before them. Everything the Drengrokil had possessed had been reduced to ashes. And, while this was of minor concern to Frode and his mountainous men, it was Meg and Hart that held everyone's attention.

The two dragons were magnificent. Their scales were metallic black with opalescent flashes of violet and silver. Black dragons were extremely rare, but looking through Morgaine's eye, Harpur was seeing something he'd never seen before. In his long life, never had there been one black dragon with such colouring, let alone two, and though it stood to reason, Meg and Hart being twins after all, he couldn't help but feel a measure of pride. He had, to all intents and purposes, created them when he put the sigils on their foreheads with his blood.

At the time, he had intended only to protect the tiny infants that they were. Knowing that he was likely going to Arachovor, the afterlife for dragons of honour, he had wanted to ensure that the twins would be safe and guarded. It never occurred to him that such a profound side effect would befall the prince and princess. Even if he had, he could never have imagined such a stunning result. If Morgaine had had control over her eye, she would have rolled it at Harpur's shameless display of unbridled hubris. Though, even she had to admit that she was impressed. If Harpur felt any chagrin, it was due to the undignified, and decidedly un-dragon-like, behavior Meg and Hart were exhibiting as they tried to gain control over themselves. He understood it; he just didn't like having to witness it.

Arthur was the last of the Fellowship to emerge from the trees. He elbowed his way past the Drengrokil and placed himself between Sok and Morgaine. "Are they my kids?" he asked in fascinated horror.

"I believe so," Sok said, not taking his eyes off the thrashing, flashing beasts that had been two teenagers a short while earlier.

Arthur promptly fainted.

All eyes briefly flicked to the fallen king.

"Leave him?" Sok asked of Morgaine.

"Leave him," Morgaine said.

No one argued. They were all thinking that an unconscious Arthur was better than a ranting Arthur. He'd come around on his own in due time.

Eventually, Meg and Hart began to settle. They appeared to have gained better control over their limbs and wings and tails, and their hysteria had subsided to a giddy thrill. They managed to turn themselves to face their audience, grinning with nervous pride.

Morgaine stepped forward and ordered them not to speak. Then she directed them to move farther away from the ruined camp to a more open area where she could help them learn to talk without setting anyone on fire.

The twins followed the dragon-wizardess. Neither of them had seemed to notice that their father had been rendered temporarily cataleptic, and, for that, Morgaine was quite thankful. While she tutored the twins on the basics of dragonhood—how to speak without burning everything around them to the ground and, eventually, how to transform back to their natural states as humans—the others stepped over Arthur's prone figure and began the process of cleaning up what remained of the Drengrokil camp.

Davynn and Jack entered Skull's Keep together after a short walk from the north gate during which the knight had questioned the publican on what he knew about Berryl's recent incarceration. Jack denied any knowledge of the circumstances surrounding Berryl's current fate, which was essentially true. And he didn't offer any information regarding the strange rumor of Harpur Diggins' possibly being un-deceased. It seemed prudent to the barkeep to keep that tidbit to himself. He did, however, point out the three guards that had brought Berryl to the north gate on Sok's instructions, who were, as he and Davynn arrived, about to vacate the premises. Davynn thanked Jack and made his way toward the guards.

"Sit," Davynn ordered the guards, who immediately sensed that something was amiss. It wasn't like Davynn made a habit of socializing with lowly sentries such as themselves.

"We are supposed to go back on duty, sir," the first guard said.

"Sit," Davynn repeated as he, himself, took a seat. The guards sat. "Now tell me exactly what instructions Sok gave to you when he had you bring Berryl to the north gate."

The guards exchanged looks. They couldn't see how they could have done anything wrong, but being interrogated by Davynn over an order from Sok was unusual enough to give them pause. Did Davynn somehow know they had kept the coins that Sok had given them to pay for their lunches? Even that seemed beneath the scrutiny of the captain of the guards.

"We were just following orders, sir," the second guard said.

Davynn's brow corrugated at the prevarication. He mulled over the option of investigating the guards' need to deflect, but decided to focus on what he originally came to find out, which was why Sok had Berryl locked up in a cell. "That's not what I asked."

"Technically, sir," said the third guard, "you didn't actually ask us anything."

Davynn suppressed the urge to jump all over the insubordination inherent in the guard's statement. "Fair enough," he said through gritted teeth. "Let me rephrase. What did Sok say to you when he ordered you to bring Berryl to the north gate?" *Why is this so difficult?* he wondered.

More uncertain looks were traded among the guards.

"He just told us to take Berryl to the north gate and to keep him safe until he returned," said the first guard. "May I ask where Sok has gone?"

"You may not," Davynn said. "What else did he say?"

"Just to have Jack bring the prisoner his meals," the second guard said.

"That's it?" Davynn prodded.

All three guards nodded.

"You're sure?" Davynn tried digging a little deeper, but the guards' shaking heads indicated that he wasn't going to get much more from them. He could, of course, ask Berryl—and he would—but he would have liked to have at least some inkling of what was going on before he did that. It struck him that Berryl might have protested Sok's decision to the guards on the way to the north gate. "Did Berryl say anything to you while you were escorting him?"

The guards' reactions were entirely unexpected. They averted their eyes and lowered their heads. They all mumbled various versions of the conversation between themselves and Berryl, none of which made any real sense, but were clearly not related in any way to the truth. Davynn sighed. "What did Berryl say to you?"

Finally, Davynn's glare got the better of the third guard. "He didn't tell us why he was being locked up, sir. But he did say something about Harpur Diggins not being dead."

Davynn tried to filter through this unanticipated revelation. *How does Berryl know?* There was no way that Sok would volunteer that information to Berryl. It was time to go and have a proper talk with the Assistant to the Senior Advisor. "Thank you, gentlemen," Davynn said, standing up and pushing his chair under the table. "Do not breathe a word of what Berryl said to you to anyone. You can have the afternoon off."

The guards were too shocked to thank their superior, but they had the good grace to wait until Davynn had left the pub before they whooped in celebratory relief.

Davynn was already back at the north gate before he remembered that he hadn't ordered a piece of pie while he was at Skull's Keep. He chastised himself inwardly and entered feeling a little grouchier than he intended to convey to the two guards within. "Wait outside," he barked. "I need to talk to Sir Berryl privately."

The guards quickly left the guard house and closed the door behind themselves without question. They weren't thrilled to have to stand outside, but Davynn's tone told them that there would be no use in complaining. At least not aloud and in his presence.

Davynn pulled a chair up to the cell in which Berryl sat despondently staring at the floor. As he sat down, he noticed that the pie Jack had brought was still uneaten. "You going to finish that?" Davynn asked.

"Help yourself," Berryl said with a sigh.

Davynn reached through the bars and retrieved the pastry. "Thanks," he said, forking a large bite into his mouth. He chewed and swallowed before continuing. "Sok's pretty upset with you." It wasn't, strictly speaking a lie; Sok would have had to be quite upset to lock anyone up.

"It was a misunderstanding," Berryl said, looking at Davynn with a protruding lip under baleful eyes.

Davynn took another bite of pie and dismissed the attempt to gain his sympathies. "How so? Sok seemed pretty clear to me."

"What did he tell you?" Berryl asked.

Damn, Davynn thought, not expecting to have the tables turned on him like that. "I'm here to hear your side of the story," Davynn parried, with a small measure of pride. "Walk me through what happened." He hid his smile by eating another forkful of pie.

Berryl considered his options. He was almost positive that Davynn didn't know what happened, but he couldn't be entirely certain that Sok hadn't told the knight anything. He settled on telling a partial truth. "I found something in Princess Meg's room and I wanted to find out what it was."

"What did you find?"

"A hat."

"I thought you said you wanted to find out what it was. Now you say it's a hat. I'm confused." Davynn paused his pie-eating while he waited for an answer.

"What I meant was that I wanted to find out what kind of hat it was. I've never seen one like it."

"Okay." Davynn shoved the pie into his mouth to buy time to compose his next question. "So, what were you doing in Meg's room in the first place? Sok didn't seem to know."

"I just popped in to check on things," Berryl said, but his eyes slid to the left and downward.

Liar! Davynn thought. "Do you often pop into the princess' room to check on things?"

"Well, no," Berryl said. "I happened to be passing by and I thought I heard a strange noise coming from inside. I thought the princess might be in trouble."

"Really? That's what you're going with?" Davynn had never taken Berryl for a particularly brave man. It was far more likely that, in such a situation, Sok's assistant would have ordered the guards to investigate.

Berryl took in a deep breath and blew it out forcefully. Even he wouldn't have bought that one if he'd been Davynn. "Very well," the Assistant said, "a maid told me that the princess had received some odd hats as birthday gifts. I was curious and I went in to see for myself." He left it at that, hoping Davynn wouldn't press for more information.

Davynn pressed for more information. "Go on."

"They were singularly odd hats! I think I must have forgotten to put one back when I left and... Well, Sok just happened to come by as I was leaving and seemed to think that I had stolen it and... Well, I didn't mean to steal it. It was just a really, really strange accessory!"

It made no sense that Sok would lock Berryl up for accidentally taking a hat. There had to be more to it than that. *And how odd can a hat be?* he wondered. He would have to go and check these hats out for himself. In the meantime, he decided to change tactics and delve into how—and how much--Berryl knew about Harpur. For this, he chose a more direct approach.

129

"So, I ran into the guards that brought you here and they told me you were saying something about Harpur Diggins being alive. What is that all about?"

Berryl was taken aback by this sudden change of subject. His eyes widened and his mouth dropped open. He regretted having said anything to the guards about it. "I... I'm sure it was just a slip of the tongue," he stammered.

"Who's tongue?" Davynn demanded.

"Why Sok's, of course."

"Sok told you that Harpur was alive?" Davynn couldn't begin to hide his disbelief.

"So, it's true?" Berryl leaned toward the bars that separated him from the knight, curiosity taking over his whole being.

"I didn't say that!" Davynn snapped. "Tell me what Sok said that made you think that Harpur is alive."

"To be accurate, I don't think that Harpur Diggins is alive. I merely suspect that he is alive."

Again, Davynn had to wonder why getting to the point had to be so painful. He slowly placed the plate that had held the pie on the floor and leaned forward as Berryl had done a few moments before. Only Davynn's lean was somewhat more menacing than Berryl's had been, and it caused Sok's assistant to draw away, in spite of the bars that separated him from the knight. "And to what do you attribute your suspicions?"

"It was something Sok said," Berryl said.

Davynn actually growled.

"He invoked Orhowyn by name! That's all it was. I'm sure it was just a slip of the tongue," he repeated.

Davynn had to admit that he would have been suspicious too. Sok was extremely diligent about using Harpur's name when swearing an oath. But at least the elf hadn't let the dragon out of the bag, so to speak, and all that was left for the knight to do was to put the fear of Harpur into the assistant to quell any further mention of his unfounded, albeit justified, suspicions.

"Have you mentioned this to anyone other than the guards that brought you here?" Davynn demanded.

"Who would I tell?" Berryl squeaked. "I'm locked up in a cell!"

Good point, Davynn conceded internally. "I will not have you spreading rumors. Do you understand me?"

Berryl nodded. "It was just a slip of the tongue. Nothing more, I'm sure. I won't speak of it again."

Davynn held Berryl in his glare for a moment. When the assistant finally lowered his own gaze, Davynn took his leave. He had to figure out what all this hat business was about.

Meanwhile, back on Mysturna, Arthur was just coming to.

He sat up slowly and looked around. In the moonlight, he could see the Drengrokil admiring six new tents that Anayah had conjured for them. Instead of red and yellow stripes, though, the new tents were solid green in colour. Frode seemed especially excited about this, though Arthur could not understand his elation. They were just tents.

"Is fantastic!" the huge Drengrokil leader gushed. "Will blend in to countryside better than old tents."

"You're welcome," Anayah said, sidestepping another rib-crushing hug from Frode.

Arthur hauled himself up off the ground and joined Sok, who was assisting Bon in laying a new fire for the camp. "I can't believe you just left me passed out like that. I could have been hurt."

"Are you hurt?" Sok asked, giving his king a quick once over to check for obvious injuries.

"Well, no, but…"

"Didn't think so," Sok interrupted. "Now that you're awake, I think Wolf could use some help with the stumps he's cutting." The elf pointed toward the trees next to the tents.

Arthur scowled at Sok's insensitivity. "Where are my children?"

"Good of you to think of them," Sok said sarcastically. "Meg and Hart are with Morgaine, learning how to be dragons. I'm sure they'll be back soon."

Arthur's face reddened with shame. Deep down, he understood why they had left him to recover on his own. "I'll go see if Wolf needs any help."

Sok nodded his head. "Good idea."

As Arthur made his way through the darkness in the direction Wolf was supposed to be, he passed by Frode and Anayah.

"You're awake!" Anayah said, stopping Arthur to pick a leaf out of his hair and brush some dirt off his shirt.

"Yeah," Arthur said. "Are Meg and Hart okay?"

"I'm sure they're fine," Anayah answered. "Are you okay?"

"Pride's a little bruised, but otherwise I'm good."

Anayah suppressed a smile. "I'm sure that seeing the twins in dragon form was a bit of shock for you. It was a bit of a shock for all of us."

"Thank you, Anayah," Arthur said. Then he continued on to find Wolf.

"King is sad?" Frode asked Anayah as he watched Arthur shuffle away.

"King is human," Anayah replied in a rather passable Drengrokil accent, which made Frode laugh.

"For witch, you are good person," Frode said.

"Just don't forget that I *am* a witch," Anayah said with a smile.

"Just don't forget I am witch hunter," Frode said with a wink.

For two beings that were natural enemies, the camaraderie between Anayah and Frode was a welcome alliance to the members of the Fellowship. No one from Epoh had any doubt, though, that the alliance was a tenuous one. The Drengrokil were witch hunters and it would take little provocation for Frode to change his mind about the pretty witch. Neither did they doubt that Anayah could hold her own if he did. Still, it was amazing how a crisis could draw people together and make them set their differences aside, though Sok, Hiro and Bon all considered that the witch and the Drengrokil may have adopted some form of the keep-your-enemies-close philosophy. As long as the camp got repaired and the mission could move forward, no one was going to interfere. But they would keep a close eye on the situation.

Arthur spotted Wolf, who was shouldering two large stumps intended for seating in the camp. The ease with which he hefted the thick sections of tree trunk, caused the recently comatose king to rethink his potential contribution to the task. Perhaps he could be of more help elsewhere. Besides, it appeared that Wolf had things well in hand. He decided to go and look for Morgaine and the twins instead and slipped into the darkness away from the camp. Both Bon and Sok noticed the clandestine detour away from duty.

"Do you want to follow him," Bon began, "or should I?"

"I'll go," Sok said with a sigh. "You finish up here and then see if Hiro can wrangle up something yummy from his satchel. I have a feeling we're all going to need some nourishment."

The android nodded and returned to tenting logs over a bed of kindling. It seemed that Anayah and Frode were almost done with the tents and basic necessities that had been lost in the fire. The Drengrokil warriors were busy doing Drengrokil warrior things. Hiro was already laying out food in his hover gilly. With any luck, Morgaine had the twins under control. And Arthur, albeit unbeknownst to himself, was under the safe watch of Sok. Bon's only real concern at the moment was whether or not the spontaneous blasts of dragon flame from the twins had drawn any local attention. He lit the fire and then moved away from its brightness to scan the trees around the camp with his night vision capabilities for any sign of unwanted and unwelcome visitors that might be lurking. And his efforts were almost instantly rewarded.

In the bushes, to Arthur's right as he made his way from the camp, was a figure that drew back as the king drew closer. Not an immediate threat, Bon surmised, but a potential one. *Benebell, perhaps?* Bon hypothesized. He moved over to where Anayah and Frode were still talking about improvements to the Drengrokil supplies and positioned himself where he could see the figure in the bushes.

"Do not react," he said to Frode and Anayah, both of whom remained sensibly still. "Someone is lurking in the bushes just south of the camp. Would Benebell be wanting to speak with you?"

Frode's hand moved to the hilt of his sword. "Where?" he whispered. The mountainous man displayed remarkable restraint, though Anayah sensed a distinct change in his demeanor.

"You're not going to harm her," Anayah hissed. "She's the one who invited you here."

Frode's eyes slid from the android to the witch. "Why does she lurk in bushes then?" he asked.

Bon witnessing the comradeship between the witch and the Drengrokil leader slip toward tension, decided to apprise Frode of the situation from Anayah's point of view. "Three things are possible," he began. "The first is that Benebell has come to talk to you and is uncertain about our presence in the camp. The second the person in the bushes is some other local who just happened to stumble upon us. The third is that Analeetah is the one lurking in the bushes."

Frode considered the android's words. "Frode is not expecting Benebell. Must be someone else."

"That is the most reasonable deduction," Bon replied. "I only know that there is a figure lurking in the bushes. I suggest, however, that, for Anayah's sake, you do not act rashly."

Again, Frode took a moment to deliberate. "Where is figure now?"

Bon turned his back to the figure in the bushes and gestured broadly toward the tents as he spoke. "She is in the bushes about..." He paused to do some calculations. "...fifty paces south of the camp on the right."

"Good idea," Frode said loudly, picking up on the android's ruse to appear as if he wasn't aware of the figure's presence. Then he walked over to Wolf and relayed Bon's intelligence to his second in command.

"I guess it's too late for my disguise," Anayah said as Hiro joined her and Bon.

"What has happened?" the Krist asked.

"Bon spotted someone lurking in the bushes just south of the camp," Anayah said. "Frode and his men are going to check it out. Where are Sok and Arthur?"

"Arthur headed off, presumably to look for Morgaine and the twins," Bon said. "Sok went after him."

"I'm going to zap myself over there and see how they are doing," Anayah said. She raised her hand to snap her fingers, but Bon took her by the wrist and shook his head.

"Do it from inside one of the tents," he instructed. "Whoever is out there, she might not know who you are and there is no advantage in giving away the fact that you are a witch."

"Right," Anayah said, feeling a little foolish. She walked to the nearest tent and ducked inside.

"Well," Hiro began with a sigh as he looked at all the food on the floor of his hover gilly, "I suppose I should put all that away again for the time being."

"No need," Bon said. "I am sure that someone will want to eat."

The capture of the figure in the bushes by the Drengrokil was over in seconds. Frode and his men worked together as if they were a single entity. Not a word was spoken between them, yet they surrounded and subdued the figure with incredible efficiency. For men of such imposing stature, their speed registered as a blur to Bon's ocular receptors. Hiro saw nothing at all until the figure was led into the camp and deposited on one of the stumps a few feet away from the hover gilly, which still contained the midnight feast he had prepared. Being the only members of the Fellowship in the camp to witness the apprehension, both were amazed, if a little irked, by the lack of details the efficacy of the Drengrokil's labours allowed.

The woman Frode and his men had captured was not Benebell. Nor was she Analeetah. She entered the camp, flanked by two of Frode's men, who made her look tiny, almost fairy-like. Her long, straight hair was tinted pink and floated around her pixie face and slender shoulders as if she was under water. She wore a plain, blue tunic over black leggings and her feet were ensconced in low-heeled, ankle boots. On her left wrist was a silver cuff adorned with symbols, presumably of the protection variety.

Bon studied her closely as she approached. She didn't seem overly afraid of the Drengrokil, but she projected an overt curiosity about the android and the Krist being among them. It seemed to Bon that she knew who he and Hiro were; her surprise was at finding them in the camp.

"What are you two doing here?" she asked as if her own presence was as normal as Ostremu stew.

"I might ask you the same thing," Bon replied. "Am I correct in assuming that you are one of the ladies who lives in the Forest of Dheersha?"

Hiro retrieved a cup of ale from the back of the hover gilly and stepped forward to hand it to the captive. "You are Alissah, are you not?"

Frode, taking this early exchange in with great interest, motioned for his men to relax their vigilant guard over the diminutive woman. Hiro's recognition of her warranted granting her the benefit of the doubt. For the moment.

"You know lady from bushes?" he asked the Krist.

"We have met," Hiro said. "Alissah is from Danaleedh."

"So, she is witch?" Frode asked, wondering if his decision to give her the benefit of the doubt had been somewhat premature.

"Of course, I am a witch!" Allisah said. "What did you think I was?" She then turned to Hiro. "I *was* from Danaleedh. Now, I live in the Forest of Dheersha with the others who have survived Analeetah's insanity."

Bon looked at Frode and noted that the Drengrokil leader seemed a little confused. Fearing that Frode might be feeling some measure of betrayal at discovering that the ladies of the forest were witches and was considering acting on it, the android figured that the faster any confusion was cleared up, the safer the comely young witch would be.

"How is it that you are able to live in the forest?" Bon asked.

Realizing too late that she had said more than she was supposed to by admitting she was a witch, Allisah tried to take a step back farther away from the imposing Drengrokil leader who was frowning down at her, but was blocked by the equally imposing figures of the two Drengrokil standing directly behind her. She had forgotten about her escorts into the camp. Reflexively, she raised her hand to zap herself back to the forest, but was quickly reminded that her magic no longer worked. Analeetah had seen to that.

Frode reacted to her gesture with a nod to the two warriors blocking Allisah's escape. In seconds, they had seized her, bound and gagged her and had deposited her on one of the stumps meant as seating.

"I'm sure that is not necessary," Bon said to Frode. "Please untie her."

"She is witch," Frode said as if that was reason enough to tie someone up.

"Not all witches are evil," Bon reasoned. "You don't tie Anayah up."

"Pretty witch is different," Frode replied with a lift of his chin. "She is friend. This witch is lying to Drengrokil."

Allisah's eyes widened above her gag and she shook her head in fearful protest.

"What did she lie about?" Hiro asked. "I know Allisah. Not well, mind you, but she hasn't said anything false."

"Benebell say that ladies in forest are not witches," Frode said.

"So, Benebell lied to you," Bon corrected his large friend.

"And by association, this witch lied too." Frode scowled down at the quaking figure on the stump. "Frode does not like liars."

Anayah chose to return to the camp at just that moment. Upon seeing Allisah bound like a turkey and sitting on the stump, she ran to the helpless young witch and began yanking on the ropes in an effort to free her. When the ropes did not budge, Anayah spun around to face Frode.

"Untie her!" she demanded, her eyes flashing dangerously, and fearlessly, at the Drengrokil leader.

Frode took a step back. Not in fear; he was making space to draw his sword if he needed to.

"Oh, stop that!" Anayah hissed. "I'm not afraid of you. Now, untie this girl. She is no threat to you."

Frode's eyebrows levitated a good two inches. "She is witch!" he said.

"So am I," Anayah replied.

Bon stepped forward and placed a hand on Anayah's arm. "Apparently, your friend here lives in the Forest of Dheersha."

"So what?" Anayah snapped. "According to Frode here, so does Benebell. What's the problem?"

"The problem is that Benebell told Frode that she and the others that are living in the forest are not witches, and now Frode is feeling… shall we say uncertain about the situation with Analeetah."

Anayah took a moment to process Bon's words. If Frode thought that he was being betrayed in any way, who knew what he would do? She had to sort this out. Without anyone getting hurt.

"Frode," she began, hoping to charm him into cooperating, "I would like to talk to Allisah alone. I think she would explain things to me if she wasn't so terrified…"

A series of grunts came from behind the gag as Allisah attempted to protest, but Anayah turned and gave her a warning glare to keep quiet.

When she was satisfied that Allisah got the message, Anayah turned back to Frode to complete her thought. "If she wasn't so terrified that you will kill her. I

137

promise that I will keep her here in the camp and I will tell you everything once I know what's really going on."

Frode squinted suspiciously at Anayah. "Witches do not hire witch hunters to kill other witches," he said. He wasn't willing to let his captive go, just because another witch—pretty as she might be—asked him to.

"I realize that isn't something that happens very often," Anayah replied. "But there are extenuating circumstances here. If you will allow me to have a private conversation with Allisah, I'm sure we can clear everything up for you. Please?"

Frode was admittedly torn. He liked Anayah, and he wanted to trust her. But she was a witch and he was a witch hunter. If he let her take his prisoner off somewhere alone, he couldn't be sure that Anayah wouldn't let her go. And then he wouldn't like her so much.

"No private talk," he said. "I go with you."

Anayah tried to think of a way to convince him that Allisah would only open up if she and Anayah were alone. But before she could form a convincing rationale, Bon stepped in.

"I will go as well," he said.

"Me, too," Hiro added.

And Anayah threw her hands up in the air. "We might as well all stay here, then. At least remove her gag so we can talk to her."

Frode nodded at his one of the men guarding Alissah. He complied with his leader's silent directive.

"What's going on?"

All eyes shifted to the south, the direction from which the rest of the Fellowship of the Scale was approaching. To both Bon and Hiro's relief, the twins were back to their normal, teenager size and shape. Arthur looked a little pale, though, and he seemed to be relying on Sok to keep him upright as he stumbled into the camp and collapsed onto the nearest stump. Morgaine just looked annoyed.

The speaker was Sok. In spite of having to support Arthur, he was the first to see Allisah all wrapped up in ropes, sitting on a stump and looking decidedly as annoyed as Morgaine. He deposited Arthur next to Allisah and motioned to Hiro to bring some ale for the king. Happy to comply, Hiro delivered a mug to Arthur, and, anticipating Sok's next question, handed the elf one as well.

As the rest of the group settled around the campfire, Anayah took Morgaine aside to discuss the situation with Allisah. Explaining Frode's reluctance to untie the young witch, and why, Anayah was relieved when Morgaine assured her that this new development would be taken care of.

To wit, Morgaine marched over to Frode and glared up at the half-giant with strained patience. "I don't really care about your little bargain with the ladies, or whatever they are, in the forest. We are here for one reason and one reason only; to steal the Sphere and use it to get my... uh, Harpur's scale back from the forest. You sort out your dilemma however you wish, but we are going to head south at dawn, get the Sphere, and then come back here and blast the damned forest with a disrupter ray to dampen its power while we break into its lair and find my... uh, Harpur's scale. If you are still here, I cannot be responsible for any effect on you or your men the Sphere has. Got it?"

Frode crossed his arms and adjusted his stance. He replied to the dragon-wizardess with an amused grunt.

Anayah, however was incensed. "Are you insane?

"You can't steal the Sphere," Allisah said, cutting Anayah off.

"Why not?" Bon asked.

"Because Analeetah blew it up," she said. "It's in a million pieces scattered all over the plain."

That silenced the whole camp.

For about fifteen seconds.

Then the shouting began.

The only ones not participating in the fracas were Arthur, Meg and Hart. And Frode's men. But that was because they were on alert and ready to draw their swords if need be.

Arthur was still reeling from having witnessed the twins transform from large, black dragons back to human beings. The reality of their condition was taking root, though, at the present moment, it was hovering somewhere between denial and anger. He'd seen it, but he couldn't quite believe it. And he was pissed off that Harpur had caused it to happen. There was a good deal of processing yet to be done.

As for the twins, they were wishing they were anywhere but where they were. They, too, were struggling with the reality of what had just happened to them. If they knew how to get back to the Boundary, they would have abandoned the Fellowship of the Scale and returned to Epoh where things were normal. It still hadn't entirely sunk in that, technically, they were no longer welcome in Epoh. As dragons, they would be encroaching on Glyniss' territory, and he had every right to banish them. Or worse. There was much to be learned.

The shouting finally ran its course and the shouters stood around seething silently. Except for Allisah who was still tied up and sitting on a stump. Weary of the nonsense, she leaned a little to her left and nudged Arthur with her shoulder.

"I don't suppose you could untie me, could you?"

Arthur looked at the bound witch and shook his head. "My children are dragons," he said.

Allisah blinked. "That's nice." She smiled sweetly so he wouldn't see that she thought he was quite bonkers.

"It really isn't," Arthur replied.

Sok noticed this brief exchange and tapped Bon on the shoulder. "So, Arthur's a wreck, Frode is being a jerk, and the Sphere is no longer an option. Tell me you have a plan."

"The sensible thing to do would be to interview Allisah and gather some intel," the android said.

"Intel?"

"Intelligence."

"I think that dragon has flown," Sok said. He approached Morgaine. "Tell me *you* have a plan."

"I plan on knocking that big oaf's head off," Morgaine said.

Sok rolled his eyes. "I was talking about the Sphere."

"Ask Bon," Morgaine said, "It was his idea to steal it."

"Anayah," Sok called out as he turned his back on the dragon-wizardess. "A word?"

Anayah looked at the elf. She couldn't decide if she was annoyed with him or not. She had been focused on Frode and Morgaine and didn't pay any attention to Sok's contribution to the arguments that were flying around the campfire. "What is it?" she huffed.

140

"What are we going to do about the Sphere?"

"Ask Bon! It was his plan!" The witch turned away and sat down beside Allisah. "I'll find a way to get you out of here," she promised the other witch. "But first tell me what you know about all this."

Allisah looked up at Frode for a moment. "He needs to hear this too."

Anayah wasn't happy, but she nodded her consent and waited for Frode to pull up a stump and get comfortable.

"What do you want to know?" Allisah asked.

Frode opened his mouth to say something, but Anayah held up her hand. "Tell us how you came to live in the forest and why Benebell hired the big guy here to kill Analeetah."

Allisah took a deep breath. Well, at least as deep as she could in the tight restraints that encircled her body from the shoulders down. "After you and Bon escaped, Analeetah went completely crazy. She was going to Bound to wherever you went to find you and kill you, but no one else in Danaleedh would go with her. So, she destroyed the Sphere."

Hearing the beginning of Allisah's tale, the others started to gather around. Soon, with cups in hand and snacks aplenty, the Drengrokil and the Fellowship of the Scale were all giving the young witch their rapt attention.

At first, the citizens of Danaleedh resisted Analeetah's obsession with getting revenge on Anayah, believing she would work through her grief and come to a place of acceptance, if not forgiveness. But as time went by, it became increasingly clear that if the Doyenne of Danaleedh could not direct her anger at its intended target, she would take her wrath out on the witches in the city. Fearful for their lives, many of the witches that had lived in Danaleedh left in search of safer havens. A few who stayed attempted to subdue Analeetah, but she had somehow become far too powerful and all who openly opposed her perished, usually gruesomely. Benebell finally led the last few witches out of Danaleedh and into the forest where they had been living in safety for the past ten years, give or take.

"But how did you get the forest to let you live there?" Anayah asked, fighting tears of anger and sorrow.

Allisah seemed to be having an internal debate about how to answer. The Forest of Dheersha had, for centuries, been considered a sentient lifeform. A brutal and unforgiving sentient lifeform, but a lifeform nonetheless. But this wasn't true. The Forest of Dheersha was enchanted.

"Our cuffs allow us to pass freely through the forest," Allisah said at last, hoping not to have to admit to knowing all that she knew.

"Where did you get the cuffs?" Bon asked. "Surely, the forest did not give them to you."

"Benebell gave them to us," she answered.

"Where did Benebell get them?" Anayah pressed.

Alissah sighed. She'd been out of the forest too long. If she didn't get back soon, her cuff would stop working and she would be exposed to Analeetah's sensory magic. "Benebell made them," she said. "She controls the Forest of Dheersha. But I'm not supposed to know that!"

Anayah gasped. "That can't be true."

"The forest has been enchanted for centuries," Alissah explained. "When the witch holding the magic that controls the forest dies, the enchantment is passed on to another witch to keep the forest under control."

"Magic doesn't work that way," Anayah said as if she was talking to a toddler. "When a witch dies, so does her magic. It can't be passed on."

Bon, who had been listening intently, spoke up. "Theoretically, I believe it is possible." He paused to scan his files. "It seems to me that it would be something akin to extracting a soul. It makes total sense to me that the soul of a witch is the seat of her magic. Take the soul, take the magic."

Anayah was horrified. "How do you know this?" she asked Alissah.

"I overheard Benebell asking another of our kind if she would assume the magic when Benebell dies."

"And who is this other witch?" Anayah asked. "What did she say?"

"I don't know which witch she was," Alissah admitted. "I was gathering mushrooms in the forest when I happened to hear the two of them talking. I hid behind a bush, but I couldn't see them. I'm not supposed to know. And I'm not supposed to be away from the forest for this long. If we leave the forest the magic in our cuffs starts to wear off. I don't know how much magic is left in mine, or if it will work to let me go back."

"Why on Mysturna would Benebell give you a cuff that fails like that?" Anayah was even more horrified.

"We do have to leave sometimes." Alissah answered. "But if we were to get caught by Analeetah, she could take the cuff and use it to get into the forest. The magic fades so that she can't do that."

"And what happens to a witch who gets caught?" Sok asked.

Alissah merely shrugged. "There's more," she whispered after a moment or two had passed.

"What is it?" Bon asked.

"Benebell is old. She isn't going to live much longer. If she doesn't find someone to assume the enchantment before she dies, the forest will revert back to its natural state." She didn't need to add that Analeetah would then be able to get to the witches who had taken sanctuary there.

"That's why she hired Frode, isn't it?" Sok exclaimed. "If she can't pass on the enchantment, your protection will be gone. But if Frode kills Analeetah, then it won't matter if the forest is enchanted or not."

Alissah nodded. "I guess. I just know that I don't want to be out of the forest if my cuff fails."

Anayah jumped up and stood in front of Frode. "Untie her. Please!"

Frode was still analyzing what he'd just heard. He couldn't help being suspicious of witches and he was trying to find the flaw in Alissah's story.

"Frode!" Morgaine snapped. "Now!"

The big man rose from his stump. "I will free witch," he said, feeling the eyes of the Epohians burrowing into him. "But if she is lying…"

Chapter Seven

The Colwygshire market was still bustling as Davynn passed through on his way back to the castle. Vendors and customers bargained to make the best deals. Buskers and bards entertained the crowds. Children begged their parents for treats. Parents tried to keep their children in sight. Old men sat on benches, gossiping while they waited for their wives to finish shopping. Old women multi-tasked, shopping and gossiping at the same time. As Davynn scanned the throng, he was pleased to see that all was well in the city, though he couldn't help shooting a nervous glance skyward looking for any sign of Glynnis' return.

But the knight had other things on his mind. Like what was so interesting about the hats that Meg and Hart had received, and why Sok had really locked Berryl away in a cell. He didn't, for a second, believe that Berryl had accidentally taken the hat from Meg's room. Instinctively, he assumed that the hat had somehow led Sok to something else, something worth imprisonment, and the elf had taken steps to end it. It was no stretch to add that Sok wanted to be there when Berryl was held accountable for whatever he had done. He wished there was some way to reach the elf. Since that was impossible, he'd just have to do a little digging for himself. Hopefully, he could figure this out and deal with Berryl quickly. There was no telling how long the Fellowship would be away.

He entered the castle through the main doors and started to cross the wide foyer to go up the stairs to Meg's room. The scene of the crime, he decided, was the best place to start to unravel the mystery. He had just reached the bottom of the staircase when he heard a voice call out from the council chambers. The voice made him wince.

"There you are! I've been looking for the skinny elf or the king to settle the supper menu, but you'll do. Save me climbing all the way up to the king's chambers just to find out if he wants chicken or fish. An old woman shouldn't have to go to all that trouble. These knees have seen better days, I dare say. And where is everyone anyway? Haven't seen one of them all afternoon."

Davynn pasted a smile onto his face and turned around to greet Finch, the head housekeeper. He'd forgotten to tell her that the king would not be in the great hall for supper that night. "Ah, Finch. You're looking lovely as usual today."

Finch planted her pudgy fists on her plump hips and scowled at Davynn. "Nonsense! Flattery will get you nowhere, young man. I'm a lady and you'd do well to remember that."

Davynn clamped his mouth shut to stifle his amusement. "My apologies, lady…"

"Don't lady me! Now where is King Arthur? I need to speak to him."

Davynn wanted to tell her to make up her mind, but thought better of it. "I meant to tell you that the king is away for a while. I'm not sure when he'll be returning, but I'm sure he would be more than okay with whatever you decide is best for supper."

"The king expects to be consulted, he does! What if I decide to serve fish and he wants chicken?"

"He's not here, so serve whatever you want. It won't matter."

"Of course it matters! Oh, never mind. I'll just wait for the king and talk to him when he gets back from wherever he's galivanted off to this time." She turned on her heels and started marching back to the kitchens. "Couldn't be bothered to let me know that he's not going to be here for supper, could he? Ruddy disrespectful if you ask me! Like I have time to fuss at the last minute. He'll just have to make do with fish. And if he has a problem with that, he'll just have to suffer…"

Davynn waited until Finch's words transferred from his earshot to the kitchen staffs', then ascended the stairs leading to the princess' rooms. When he arrived at his destination, he nodded at the guards, one of which quickly opened the door to let his captain inside. Upon entry, the knight was astounded at the pile of gifts in the corner of the room. Most of which, as it turned out, were weird hats with brims on one side and adjustable straps at the back of what appeared to be an oversized skull cap. He might not have guessed that they were hats at all if not for the incident with Berryl. Frankly, he couldn't blame Sok's assistant if he had actually stolen one; they were rather fascinating, albeit peculiar, things. Checking first to ensure that the door was closed, he picked up a brown leather one and put it on his head. He crossed the room to Meg's full-length mirror to see how it looked and was surprised by the effect. He thought it made him look rather dashing and he wondered if Hart might be willing to part with one or two. There did seem to be more hats than the prince and princess would ever need.

The hats gave him no clue as to why Sok had arrested Berryl, though. Other than their strangeness, they were just hats and he doubted that the twins would even have missed the one that Berryl had taken. It occurred to Davynn that Sok might have been jealous that Berryl had discovered them before he had. Then he pushed the thought aside; not even Sok would be that petty. *Would he?*

Davynn reluctantly returned the hat to the pile and left Meg's rooms, ordering the guards not to let anyone other than himself and Meg inside. "That includes maids," Davynn said before walking toward the stairs. He was just about to begin his descent when a new thought popped into his head. He stopped and turned back to the guards. "Would either of you happen to know where Sok and Berryl went after they left Meg's rooms?"

"I believe that I heard Sok say they were going to Sir Berryl's room, sir," the guard that had opened the door said.

"Thank you," Davynn said. "I don't suppose you know where Berryl's room is?"

Both guards shook their heads. "Sorry, sir, we don't know where it is," said the other guard.

"The housekeeper, Finch, would know, sir," the first guard offered.

Davynn forced a smile. "Thank you, again. I'll check with her." He waited until he had gone down a few steps before he winced once again. *Great! Twice in one day!*

He entered the kitchen hoping that Finch was busy elsewhere and someone else could help him. Luck was not on his side and his hopes were dashed when the stout castle icon met him at the door, covered in flour, her grey bun doing its best to escape the pins that held it atop her head. "Shoo! Out with ye! I'll not be having the supper preparations held up while the cooks make snacks for the king."

"I'm not here for food, Finch," Davynn said with strained patience.

"What are you here for then?" The housekeeper blinked at the knight in confusion.

"I need the key to Berryl's room. I was told that you might have it. And that you could tell me which room he occupies." He threw in the bit about the key since he'd just thought of it.

"Whatever do you need the key to Berryl's room for?" Finch continued to blink, but now her blinks held an aura of suspicion.

"That is none of your concern." Davynn decided it was time to pull rank. "Do you have it?"

"Of course, I have it!" Finch turned and marched to the opposite side of the kitchen and opened a cabinet on the wall. She took a moment to locate the required key and removed it from the hook on which it lived. She returned to Davynn, who, in spite of his projection of authority, remained close to the door. "I'll be wanting this back as soon as you're done with it. And don't think that I won't remember who I loaned it to."

Davynn took the key and smiled at the housekeeper. "Thank you, Finch," he said. "Now which room does it open?"

"Berryl's, of course! What room do you think it opens?" She threw her hands up in the air, releasing a blizzard of flour from the folds of her apron. Shaking her head, she turned her back on the knight and proceeded to bark orders at the cooks.

Shaking his own head, Davynn started to follow her to get the information he needed. A gentle hand on his arm stopped him. He looked down to see a pretty kitchen maid smiling up at him. "Take the corridor to the guard's mess hall. Berryl's room is the second last door on the left before you reach the hall."

"Thank you," Davynn said and quickly took his leave.

A few minutes later, Davynn slipped the key into the lock on the second to last door on the left in the corridor leading to the guard's mess hall. Berryl had lived in the castle for many years and Davynn would have thought he'd have better accommodations than a windowless room in an area that was primarily reserved for storage. Surely, even Berryl deserved better living quarters than this. The knight made a mental note, as he opened the door, to see what he could do about the situation once all this kerfuffle was resolved. Then he stepped inside and promptly figuratively crumpled up that mental note and threw it away. He couldn't believe what he was looking at.

Except for a small cot in one corner and a narrow wardrobe beside the bed, the room was devoid of furniture. The rest of the space was filled with piles of trinkets that more than one maid had lost her job over, having been accused of stealing them. There was jewelry and clothing and...

Davynn stopped and stared at the base of one of the piles. "Harpur's horns, my boots!" he said as he scooped up the purloined footwear.

Then he started looking more closely at the mounds. The closer he looked, the more he found that he recognized. A silver picture frame that had once held a sketch of Queen Alex. A candle stick that had sat on a table in the foyer. A vase that had held flowers at Arthur and Alex's wedding. There was more, but the thing that made Davynn's blood boil was a rag doll that had been made by a little girl named Lissa for Princess Meg when the twins were born. It had gone missing shortly after Queen Alex had died; the princess had cried for days. Arthur had a search party of guards comb the castle from top to bottom looking for it. He had even hired an artist to draw the doll and had reward posters put up throughout the city, hoping to have it returned to his inconsolable daughter. Clearly, Berryl had intervened in the search and prevented his own quarters from being examined.

Davynn had to leave. He locked the door behind him and went straight back to the north gate with his boots under one arm and the rag doll in his other hand.

When he burst into the guard house, Jack y Lebard was handing a tray of food containing a piece of pie for Berryl to one of the guards. The publican barely managed to edge around the desk to get out of Davynn's way as he stormed up to the cell where Berryl sat waiting patiently to be fed. The guard, sensing Davynn's displeasure, bade Jack to put the tray down and then quickly escorted him along with the second guard on duty out of the guard house. Jack, also sensing Davynn's displeasure, reluctantly allowed himself to be guided outside. He tried to look back in to see what was happening, but the second guard firmly closed the door and, thanking Jack for the snack, told him to move along. The barkeep didn't even get the chance to ask what the guards thought Davynn might be upset about. He returned to Skull's Keep, none the wiser, but all the more curious.

"Care to explain this?" Davynn snapped at Berryl through the bars. He held up the boots and the doll for the prisoner to see.

Berryl gasped. "I… I… don't know anything about those things." He backed as far away from the bars as he could, but appeared to be examining the items in Davynn's hands. "Isn't that Princess Meg's doll? Oh, she'll be so happy that you finally found it."

"And do you care to guess where I found it?" Davynn growled.

"Why, I can't begin to imagine," Berryl said, poorly feigning innocence.

Davynn glared at Sok's soon-to-be ex-assistant. "You live in the castle, don't you, Berryl?"

"I do." Berryl nodded.

"Where in the castle? Exactly!"

"Well… I mean… I mostly stay near the kitchens…"

"Where is your room, Berryl? Don't even think about lying to me." Davynn took a menacing step closer to the bars.

Berryl, unable to retreat any further into his cell, collapsed onto the cot and hung his head in abject shame. "I'm so sorry," he moaned.

"That is an understatement!" Davynn bellowed. Then taking a deep breath to calm himself, he continued through clenched teeth, "All I want to know is why?"

"I don't know why," Berryl cried. "I just can't help myself."

Davynn stared at the pathetic man on the cot. He believed Berryl. He just didn't know what to do about it. On the way to the north gate, he had been planning on having the guards transfer Berryl to the dungeons, so great was his wrath. But seeing the thief in such remorseful misery, Davynn couldn't bring himself to give the order. Instead, he left the guard house, taking the pie from the tray on his way out.

"Anything we need to be aware of?" one of the guards asked as his captain stomped away.

"Just keep him locked up until Sok returns and decides what to do with him," Davynn snarled.

"Should we get Jack to bring another piece of pie?" the other guard called.

Davynn stopped and turned back to the guards. "No! Regular meals only. And keep Jack away from the prisoner. Berryl is to have no communication with anyone except myself and Sok."

"Yes, sir," the guards said together in total bewilderment as Davynn disappeared around the corner.

"Was that a doll Sir Davynn was carrying?" one guard asked the other, opening the door for his duty partner.

"I think so," said the other guard. "And a pair of boots."

They entered the guard house to find Berryl on his cot, sobbing.

"Let's get our report done," the first guard suggested.

"Good idea," said the other guard.

Rarely, in the history of guard duty at the north gate had two guards been more eager to fill out a report.

Frode drew his sword and pointed it at Alissah. Out of the corner of his eye, he could see Anayah and Morgaine tensing, ready to strike if he so much as nicked Alissah with it. But he wasn't concerned. If they did react badly, his men would have them subdued before either of them could release any harmful magic. At least they would have Anayah under control; he wasn't quite as certain how they would fare with the dragon-wizardess and he had to remind himself that, as sultry and seductive as she appeared, Harpur Diggins was lurking behind those sapphire eyes.

With the flat of the blade, Frode lifted Alissah's chin, forcing her to look up at him. He had no intention of harming the young witch—yet—but he wanted everyone in the camp to know who he was. He was a witch hunter, and a damned good one. And he didn't appreciate being trifled with, especially by witches who lied to him.

Shifting his gaze to the left, he saw Morgaine daring him to hurt the girl. Harpur was getting anxious and it would take little provocation for him to release his current frustration at having his plans foiled yet again. On his right, Anayah, was more concerned about Alissah. Her focus was wavering between her fellow witch and Frode's hand, clenching the hilt of the enormous sword. Had he been prone to fear, he would have been more afraid of Anayah. She, he could tell, would try to kill him outright, whereas Morgaine would try to restrain him first and only resort to lethal measures if it became necessary. It was an interesting development and Frode tucked his intuited impressions away for future reference.

With a twist of his wrist, Frode drew the tip of the sword downward, slicing cleanly through the magical cords that bound the witch. The ropes crackled and sparked as they fell away to lay sizzling on the ground next to the stump. Allisah released the breath she had been holding, but her eyes remained on the tip of the sword that hovered just below her heart.

"Go back to forest now," Frode said. "Tell Benebell Frode wishes to talk to her."

He held the sword steady for a few beats before slowly withdrawing and sheathing it.

"Oh, cut the dramatics!" Morgaine said as Alissah stood and sidled closer to Anayah. "Now that's all cleared up, how are we going to get the scale, Bon?" She turned to the android.

"I think I might be able to get it," Anayah said. She had her arm wrapped protectively around Alissah's shoulders.

Frode motioned for his men to gather by the tents for some sort of Drengrokil confab. Not a single member of the Fellowship of the Scale had any doubt that the subject of the briefing involved Benebell and the witches in the forest. Morgaine, in particular, wanted to tune into that conversation, but alas, it was being conducted in the half-giants' native language, so she was forced to turn her attention to Anayah's proposed solution to their immediate problem, vis, retrieving the scale. And getting off Mysturna.

"What are you thinking, Anayah?" Morgaine asked.

"I'll go with Allisah back to the forest and ask Benebell to give it to me."

Simple. Clean. Efficient. Morgaine nodded her approval.

"You can't just walk into the forest," Arthur said.

Damned forest! Morgaine wracked her brain to find a way to get back to simple, clean and efficient.

"I think I can," Anayah said. She released Alissah and lifted the younger witch's hand to show everyone the cuff. "Correct me if I'm wrong, Alissah, but this protects based on contact, right?"

"I think so," Alisah said, "but it's made for me. I don't think its powers extend to anyone else."

"I think they do," Anayah said. "I think that as long as I'm touching you, the cuff will protect me too."

"Even if it does," Alissah said, "its powers are weakening. I'm not even sure if it will protect *me* anymore."

"There's only one way to find out," Anayah said. Still holding Alissah's arm, she snapped her fingers and the two of them vanished in a billowing plume of red smoke.

From next to the tents, Frode started to laugh. "Drengrokil know witches can't be trusted. Maybe now rest of you know it too."

"Oh, shut up, Frode," Morgaine snapped as she twisted to face him. "Anayah knows what she'd doing." *I hope.*

"We will see," Frode said, sitting down on a stump.

Anayah zapped herself and Alissah to the edge of the Forest of Dheersha a few hundred yards west of the Drengrokil camp. They landed a short way from the first of the multi-coloured trees at the border of the Forest. Anayah stood still because she needed to steel her courage to enter the Forest. Alissah stood still because she had serious doubts about her cuff's ability to grant them passage.

"Maybe I should go first to make sure the cuff is still working," Alissah said, holding up her cuff.

"I don't think so," Anayah said. She didn't want to voice her fear that Alissah would abandon her out loud. "We'll go in together."

"It's your funeral," Alissah said and took a step toward the trees.

"Wait," Anayah said. "Is there a way to tell if the cuff's magic is gone?"

Alissah shrugged. "Benebell said that the cuffs will glow an amber-yellow just before the magic dies. She never did say how much time we had."

There was no time to wrestle with logic. The only thing to do was to walk into the forest and see what happened. Anayah took Alissah by the hand and started walking toward the trees. As they reached the edge of the forest, the trees directly in front of them shifted to block their way. Anayah pulled her foot back just before it was crushed between the trunks.

Alissah squealed. "We have to get back to the camp!"

Anayah wasn't ready to give up that quickly. "Is there a way you can call someone from the forest to help us?"

The words had barely left her mouth when a large, grey bird took flight from a nearby bush just outside the border of the forest. This time Alissah groaned.

"It's just a bird," Anayah said.

"Please take us back to the camp," Alissah begged. "We aren't safe here. That bird is one of Analeetah's familiars. It's on its way to report us to her."

The witches of Danaleedh did not, as a rule, keep familiars. The fact that Analeetah had more than one spoke to the level of madness she had succumbed to.

"How many familiars does she have?" Anayah asked.

"Too many," Alissah said. "They are all over the place!"

"How did you get to the Drengrokil camp without them seeing you, then?"

"When the cuff's magic is working properly, they can't see us."

Anayah looked in the direction the bird had flown—a direct path to Danaleedh. They had some time, but not much. "Why did you go to the camp anyway?"

"I was out looking for moon flowers and I saw some strange purple lights flashing just above the trees," Alissah explained. "I went to see what they were."

"What if Analeetah had been causing them as a trap to lure one of you out of the forest so she could take your cuff?" Anayah was annoyed at the naivety Alissah had displayed.

"She couldn't see me either," Alissah churlishly retorted. "And I hadn't planned on being away this long. Can we go back to the camp now? We are safer with the giants than we are out here where Analeetah can easily pick us off."

Anayah agreed. But she still thought that they might be able to find a way to get into the forest before the bird delivered the news of their whereabouts to her once-beloved aunt. Then it occurred to her that Alissah could have easily zapped herself back to the camp if she was that worried about being caught. *Why hadn't she?*

"Why don't you just zap us into the forest?" Anayah asked.

"I would have if I could have as soon as your friend back there untied me," Alissah confessed. "But Analeetah saw to it that my magic won't work."

Anayah was horrified. "She extracted your magic?"

"No, she did the same thing to me that she did to you when she made you a prisoner at Wildwood. If she had extracted my magic, I wouldn't be standing here in full view of Analeetah's minions waiting for her to come and finish the deed. Can we please go back to the camp now?"

Anayah didn't have time to analyze all of this. She could see Alissah was growing anxious. But she had to wonder, then, why her own magic was working again. Analeetah had suppressed it after Anabettah had died, but it wasn't until after she had escaped to Epoh that it had returned. There was also the possibility that Alissah was, indeed, lying, and was actually on Analeetah's side. Even if that proved to be true, they were safer surrounded by seasoned witch hunters. She was just about to zap them back to the Drengrokil camp when a hand clamped around her mouth and she was dragged into the forest. Next to her, Alissah was being hauled into the trees as well.

Her first instinct was to zap herself away, but almost as fast as the hand had covered her mouth, two others had restrained her arms. In spite of her violent struggling, Anayah found herself being forced to the ground on her stomach, her hands held tightly together at the small of her back. The hand was gone from her mouth, but she had been magically gagged and was unable to scream, or protest verbally in any way.

She turned her head to see that Alissah had been let go and was standing a few feet away beside two other people. Whoever was holding her down, she couldn't see, but whoever it was, was strong and unrelenting. She decided to stop struggling, not because she was tired, but because she realized that her cooperation would probably be the fastest route to a more comfortable position. Anayah laid still, working to get her breathing under control and straining to hear… Anything.

Orhowyn's wicked wings! They've blocked my hearing!

Her strategy to stay still paid off. The grip on her hands loosened, though not enough for her to wiggle free. She forced herself to relax. She closed her eyes and thought about Davynn and the children. In a while, she started to drift off. How long she slept, she did not know. A gentle hand, shaking her shoulder, woke her and a soft voice asked if she was okay. When she opened her eyes, Anayah found herself in a cozy cottage, in a cozier bed, but the gentle hand and the soft voice must have been figments of her imagination.

Sunlight, muted by the thick foliage of the trees that surrounded the cottage, filtered through a small window across from the bed. It was morning.

Anayah sat up and pushed the covers aside so she could put her feet on the floor. To her surprise and dismay, she realized that someone had put her in a simple night gown. She looked around the small room for her clothes, but they were not there. No matter, she was a witch after all; she could just snap her fingers and change into something… less dreary.

Lifting her hand to snap her fingers, she noticed something else. Around her wrist was a cuff identical to the one that Alissah had been wearing. She took that as a good sign; whoever had brought her here was protecting her. She snapped her fingers.

The simple night gown was still there. *Not again!*

Anayah sighed and walked to the door. She needed to find Benebell and get the scale. And get her magic back. The door opened easily, but when she went to step through, a gentle warding prevented her from exiting the cottage. She sighed again.

"Hello!" she called through the warded doorway. "Anybody out there? Alissah?"

She could see other cottages, about a dozen or so filling a clearing in the forest. They were all simple structures with thatched roofs and brightly painted doors. She looked up and assessed the thatching above her, wondering if the warding encompassed the whole cottage, or if only the door and the one small window were protected. It was worth a look.

She closed the door and retrieved a chair from the small table in the centre of the room. Placing it next to a narrow shelf opposite the door, she stepped up onto it and then climbed onto the top of the shelf. Where the roof met the top of the cottage wall, Anayah was able to reach the thatching. She pushed her hand through the straw and was delighted to find that the roof was not warded. All she had to do was find a way to separate the bundles that were woven together with twine and tied to beams evenly spaced three feet apart. Thin cross-ties ran from the edge of the roof to the peak to support the thatching. There was just enough room between them for Anayah to squeeze through. She tried tugging on the twine to loosen it, but it didn't budge. She needed a knife, but a quick survey of the cottage did not offer one up.

There was no way of knowing how long it would be before someone came along, or if they would be friend or foe when they did. But someone would come, and Anayah had to have the upper hand. Without her magic, though, that was going to be tricky. Her only option was to pull the thatching out—a few stalks at a time.

By the time the hole was big enough for Anayah to climb through, the morning had all but passed. She was sweating from the heat of the suns beating down on her through the hole. The sooner she got out, the sooner she could start finding her way back to the camp. She had begun to worry about whether or not there was even a camp to go back to. She pushed her arms up between the beams, gripped the top of the wall and hoisted herself upward until she could spread her elbows, giving herself better leverage. Once her upper body was through, she managed to get one knee onto the wall and pull her other leg up behind her. It was only about a six-foot drop to the ground. She lowered her legs, followed by her upper body, then let go of the wall and let gravity do its thing.

The camp was on the south side of the forest, so all she had to do was follow the suns. Trusting that the cuff would protect her, she dashed toward the trees. Just as they had done when she tried to enter the forest the night before, the trees shifted to block her path. She stepped to her left to go around them, but the trees were faster and shifted again, this time moving forward to push her back as well.

Anayah stared at the cuff as if willing it to work and let her pass.

"It's been modified," a voice behind her said.

Anayah spun around to face a witch she once knew well.

"Lyrica?" Anayah was relieved. She and Lyrica had been good friends when she lived in Danaleedh. "I'm so glad to see you."

"I wish I could say the same," Lyrica said. "What are you doing here, Anayah?"

Anayah hesitated. Her brief sense of relief was vaporized by Lyrica's icy stare. "Didn't Alissah tell you?"

"She did. But I want to hear it from you."

Anayah studied her old friend. Once a cheerful soul with a ready smile, Lyrica now looked worn out and tired. Deep lines creased her brow and dark smudges of purple underscored her sunken eyes. She was thinner than Anayah remembered. It was as if the forest that sustained here was also depleting her. Anayah took a tentative step closer, hoping for a welcome embrace. Lyrica crossed her arms, making Anayah stop and maintain some distance.

"I'm here to speak to Benebell," Anayah said, deciding that playing it nice was not going to get her very far.

Lyrica glanced up at the hole in the roof of the cottage, then raised a quizzical eyebrow at Anayah. "I asked you what you were doing here."

"And I told you," Anayah said, crossing her own arms and pursing her lips to convey her impatience.

"Do you really think that you could waltz back here as if nothing had happened? As if we would have forgotten that you are the cause of all our trouble and sorrow?"

Anayah weighed her options. She could deny culpability and feign ignorance, or she could take her lumps and try to make amends. *If Lyrica is this pissed off at me, how does Benebell feel?* She was trapped in the Forest of Dheersha with an unknown number of excommunicated witches, who were just as trapped as she was, more or less. She decided to buy some time. "Is Alissah okay?"

For a fleeting moment, Lyrica was thrown off by Anayah's deflection, but she quickly composed herself. "What do you care?"

Anayah was about to say that she cared very much. She hadn't returned to Mysturna to cause any further harm and she certainly had never intended for things to get this bad for her sisters from Danaleedh. But before she could think of an appropriate reply, they were joined by two other witches. Alissah, supporting a stooped and hobbling Benebell, came around the corner of the cottage and stopped a few feet behind Lyrica.

Anayah gasped at the sight of the older witch. Benebell's bent frame was frail. Like Lyrica, she appeared to be wasting away. Her hair, once lush and long, had thinned; all that remained were straggly wisps of dull grey tufts through which her pink scalp showed. Her face was deeply lined, her nose a sharp hook above pale lips. Her rheumy eyes were rimmed with red. She could barely hold onto the tree-branch cane she needed to walk with. As much as Anayah wanted to run to Benebell and hug her, she didn't think that Lyrica would let her pass.

"Anayah, dear? Is that really you?" Benebell asked.

Anayah looked at Lyrica, silently asking for permission to approach. A few tense moments passed before the angry witch stepped aside and gestured for Anayah to come forward.

"Yes, it's me," Anayah said, kneeling down before Benebell. "I'm so happy to see you. How are you, Benebell?"

"Old. Dying," Benebell said with a dismissive shrug of her shoulders. "Alissah tells us that you are here to get a scale from the forest's hoard."

Anayah looked up at Alissah and saw the fear in her eyes. What she was afraid of was anyone's guess, but Anayah would have put money on having Anayah reveal what she knew about the true nature of the forest. She would have to tread carefully; she had no intention of throwing Alissah under the cart wheels.

"That is true," Anayah said. "Can you help me?"

"That depends," Benebell said. "What do you need it for?"

Truth be told, Anayah had no idea. Whatever Bon had up his sleeve, she hadn't been made privy to it. She had to improvise. "I need it to make a very powerful medicine for a friend of mine. It could save his life."

"And you can't procure a dragon scale in this other world of yours? I was given to believe that dragons are abundant there." Benebell was no fool.

"They are," Anayah said, "but dragons don't give their scales to anyone. When I remembered that… that there was one here, I came to see if I could bargain with the forest for it."

"So, you'll help someone on another world, but you won't lift a finger to set right all the damage you've done on this one." Lyrica sneered.

157

"Hush, now!" Benebell snapped. She teetered on her brittle legs and Alissah quickly wrapped an arm around her waist to keep her from falling.

Lyrica also ran to the aged witch's side. "You should be laying down. Let me help you back to your cottage."

But Benebell waved her off. "I will decide when I need to lay down. Stop your fussing, girl."

Still on her knees, Anayah wanted to move things along, but she didn't want to push Benebell too hard. "Why don't you conjure a chair for her?" she suggested.

"Why don't you?" Lyrica shot back, with a knowing smirk.

Benebell twisted her cane and a chair appeared. With Alissah's help she lowered herself onto it and let out a sigh. "I see you have discovered that your magic doesn't work in the forest," she said to Anayah.

"I thought it was the cuff that was suppressing my magic." She held up her arm to show the others the cuff on her arm. She also noticed that Benebell was the only one among them who was not wearing one.

"Lyrica, take Alissah and go help the others prepare lunch. I want to speak to Anayah alone. Come fetch me when it is ready." Benebell shooed the two away and waited for them to comply, which they reluctantly did.

Anayah watched them walk away, and when they were well out of earshot, she turned back to Benebell. "I am so sorry about all that has happened here…"

"I don't want your apologies, Anayah." Benebell cut her off. "I have a proposition for you."

"What's that?" Anayah asked tentatively… hopefully.

"I will get the scale from the forest's hoard for you." She paused, peering at Anayah, who could barely contain her joy at hearing this. "But you will come back here and govern the forest and keep the last remaining witches of Danaleedh safe from Analeetah."

"Benebell, I can't," Anayah said. "I have a husband in Epoh. I have three children. I can't abandon them."

Too late, Anayah realized her mistake. She should have asked Benebell what she meant by govern the forest.

Benebell snickered. "So, Alissah is aware of the enchantment. I thought so."

"I don't understand," Anayah said, not bothering to deny that she knew Benebell had enchanted the forest. Or that she had learned it from Alissah. "Why did you do it?"

"I didn't," Benebell said. "I merely maintain the enchantment."

"But how?"

"I will tell you…" Benebell coughed, "…as soon as you agree to my terms."

Anayah scrambled to find a way out of this mess. If she agreed, she would lose Davynn and the children. If she refused… Well, she could very well find herself stuck there anyway, as a prisoner. The only counter offer she could think of was almost unthinkable.

"What if I… deal with Analeetah for you?"

Again, Benebell snickered. "Analeetah is beyond *dealing with*, as you so diplomatically put it. She is too strong and too mad to kill. Do you think that no one has tried?"

Anayah slumped, dropping her head in despair. "Let me try. I have friends that will help."

"You mean that repulsive giant and his band of barbarians?"

"You hired them!" Anayah exclaimed.

Benebell waved her boney hand, brushing off her own stupidity. "I was desperate."

"Frode knows what he is doing." At least Anayah hoped he did.

"Be that as it may," Benebell conceded, "I doubt that the Drengrokil are any match for what Analeetah has become. Now, do you want the scale or not?"

"If I find a way to deal with Analeetah, can I go back to my husband and children?"

Benebell thought for so long, Anayah began to wonder if she had fallen asleep. But eventually, the old witch answered, "If you kill Analeetah, you can do whatever you wish."

Anayah blew out the breath she'd been holding and swallowed the growing lump in her throat. "I have to get the scale back to my friends," she said.

"Lyrica will accompany you," Benebell decreed. "But before nightfall tonight, you will assume governance over the forest."

That didn't leave Anayah much time. A hasty plan had formed while they were talking. She wasn't sure she could pull it off, but she had to try.

Benebell summoned the scale from the hidden hoard and handed it to Anayah. "Betray me, Anayah, and you will never see your husband and children again."

Swallowing another lump of fear, Anayah took the scale. "Thank you, Benebell." There was no need to say anything else.

Morgaine took the scale and eyed the indignant looking witch who had appeared with Anayah. "What happened to Alissah?"

"Alissah stayed in the forest to care for Benebell," Anayah explained in the vaguest of terms. "This is Lyrica. Lyrica, these are my friends."

"Pleased to meet you," Sok said from his stump, which only garnered a sneer from the new comer.

Frode stepped forward, hand on sword hilt. "Something is wrong," he said.

Lyrica all but hissed at the Drengrokil leader. "I'll say," she said, implying that Frode was the problem.

Anayah quickly repositioned herself between the two. "Frode, please don't make things worse than they are."

The big man looked down at the pretty witch. "What has pretty witch done?"

Morgaine was wondering the same thing. She sensed that the scale had cost Anayah dearly and Lyrica's presence was assurance that Anayah would pay. In full. But sensing that Anayah wouldn't—or couldn't—explain what had happened in the forest, the dragon-wizard decided that evasive action was required. While Lyrica's eyes were daring Frode to try something, Morgaine did do something. She froze Lyrica where she stood.

"Whoa!" Sok yelped upon seeing the ice-encrusted witch teetering precariously next to him. He handed Arthur his plate and stood up to examine the effect. And avoid having Lyrica fall on top of him. "We should probably move her away from the fire," he suggested, knocking on Lyrica's head to test the thickness of the ice.

Frode nodded at his men and two of them came over, picked up the witch and moved her farther away from the flames.

"Was that necessary?" Anayah asked with no conviction behind her annoyance.

"I don't know," Morgaine replied. "Was it?"

"Is good trick," Frode said. "Drengrokil must learn how freezing people works."

Next to him, Wolf was examining his sword as if trying to figure out how to make it shoot freezing water instead of bright red and scorching bolts of lightning.

Morgaine ignored the large men's fascination with her magical prowess. "Well, Anayah? Wanna tell us what's going on?"

"Mm... Not particularly," Anayah replied. "Is she dead?"

"Not particularly," Morgaine answered. "But she can't stay like that for too long."

Anayah looked over at where the Drengrokil had laid Lyrica down on the ground. "How long does she have?"

"How long does she need?" Morgaine countered.

"Until nightfall?"

Morgaine took a moment to consider the intensity of the magic. "I can make it work,"

Arthur elbowed Sok in the arm. "Do you have any idea what they are talking about?"

"I can't be certain, but if I had to guess, Anayah promised the witches in the forest that she would kill Analeetah in exchange for the scale. She has until sundown to do the deed or..." Sok didn't know what could possibly follow the 'or.'

"Wouldn't they have kept the scale until after Anayah killed Analeetah?" Arthur pointed out the hole in Sok's theory.

"That would make sense," Sok agreed, "but they are witches, and in my experience, witches don't always make sense."

Arthur nodded, then ate the last bite of his pancakes.

"I have to do this by myself," Anayah was saying to Morgaine and Frode. "I'd really appreciate it if you just took these guys back to Epoh. I'll follow you as soon as I can."

161

Morgaine had no intention of leaving without Anayah, but she couldn't agree to Anayah's terms too easily. "You know I can't do that."

"I know," Anayah said with a sigh of resignation. "But I'd appreciate it if you'd at least pretend to humour me."

Morgaine smiled. "As you wish. Consider yourself humoured."

"If I'm not back by the time the first sun sets completely…"

Morgaine didn't get the chance to answer; Anayah disappeared in a plume of red smoke. She turned instead to Frode. "I believe that your services are no longer required, big guy."

"You're not helping pretty witch?" Frode asked.

"I'm thinking about it," Morgaine replied. "I suspect, however, that we'd only make a bigger mess of things if we did."

Frode huffed. "Drengrokil were looking forward to killing witch." He sounded disappointed.

"I'm sure you will find another witch to kill, Frode," Morgaine said as she patted him on the arm.

On Frode's orders, his men broke down the camp. Arthur and Sok watched in fascination while the Drengrokil's camp dissolved into neat bundles on their backs.

"Where will you go?' Bon asked when they were done.

"There is witch infestation on Portac Six," Frode said. "We will go there." The men all moved to form a circle around Frode as he took a small device from his pocket, flipped it open, and spoke into it, "Mission aborted. Six to beam aboard."

"Prepare to transport," a voice coming from the device said, and a few seconds later, the Drengrokil vanished from Mysturna in six misty-blue rays of light.

Chapter Eight

Anayah reappeared in a copse of trees just outside the walls of Danaleedh. She had to assume that Analeetah was aware of her return to Mysturna; the bird she and Alissah had seen fly toward the city would have reported her presence near the forest. She regretted not warning Morgaine about the winged familiars, but it was too late for that. Hopefully, the dragon wizardess had decided to take the others back to Epoh and make sure they were safe. It wasn't likely. Knowing Harpur, he was devising a plan to cover all the bases as the self-appointed protector of them all. The sooner she dealt with Analeetah, the less time Harpur had to interfere.

Speaking of plans… Anayah didn't have one. She had no idea where Analeetah even was, or if she was alone in the city. While it was clear that most of the other witches had abandoned the mad witch, it was possible that a few had remained, either as loyal subjects or because they were too terrified to flee. Then there was the matter of the familiars. How many, and what form they took, were a mystery to her. What she needed was a way to gather intel. And that seemed like an impossible undertaking. She was left with two choices: march through the gates, call Analeetah out, and hope for the best; or become invisible, try to sneak in, and hope for the best. Neither prospect sounded appealing.

"Well, you can't just stand here all day and hope that Analeetah drops dead of boredom!"

Anayah squealed and spun around to see who was talking. "Mezzi? What are you doing out here?" Anayah was filled with both relief and trepidation.

The head-size, spider-like koobar lowered herself on a thin line of web to be eye-level with Anayah. "I could ask you the same thing," she said, "but I already know why you're here. You can't beat her, Anayah."

"I have to try."

"She knows you're here," Mezzi said. "The moment you step through the gates, she will kill you."

"There has to be a way," Anayah said. "I have to try."

"Go back to Epoh, Anayah. Forget about this place." Mezzi started to climb back up into the trees.

"I can't."

Mezzi lowered herself back down. "What have you done now?"

Anayah grimaced, half in shame, half in annoyance. She held up her arm to show the koobar the cuff around her wrist.

Mezzi gasped. "You didn't?"

"I didn't have a choice," Anayah snapped, this time entirely in annoyance. "If I ever want to see my husband and children again, I have to stop Analeetah."

"You're as mad as she is! What were you thinking?" Mezzi exclaimed.

"You must know something that will help me," Anayah begged.

"Do you know how many witches have tried to stop her? How many have died?" Mezzi was incredulous. "The only way anyone can stop Analeetah is to get to the magic she has stolen from other witches and release it. And no one can get to it. She has it warded and guarded day and night."

"Guarded by who?"

"Puremen warriors," Mezzi said.

It was Anayah's turn to be mystified. "That can't be true!"

Since the war between them and the witches several centuries earlier, the Puremen served no one. They had fought hard for their freedom, and, though the witches and the Puremen now lived peacefully with each other, servitude to any witch was considered a crime.

"When all this started, some of the Puremen agreed to help the witches of Danaleedh to overthrow Analeetah and contain her magically. As she grew stronger, some of the Puremen abandoned the cause, while others continued to fight. When it became clear that the witches intended to kill Analeetah, Kel Wyndrummer led a few men to parlay with Analeetah, to try to reason with her. They didn't return…" Mezzi left the implications hang in the air between them

"Kel is serving Analeetah?" Anayah felt faint.

Kel Wyndrummer had been a good friend to Anayah. He brought exotic spices and fabrics from all over Mysturna to Danaleedh, not to trade, but as gifts to the witches who he admired. At one time, he and Analeetah had been lovers, but Analeetah ultimately chose to come to Danaleedh to study magic and live as a witch. They had remained close, choosing to love each other differently, rather than let themselves become bitter and resentful. Anayah could not believe, though, that he would forsake his loyalty to his people to serve the grief-maddened Doyenne of Danaleedh.

"I don't think it was by choice," Mezzi said, again relying on inuendo to convey her message.

"What will his people do to him if he is ever freed?"

"It's hard to say," Mezzi answered. "They may take the fact that he was enchanted into account. But the Puremen are extreme in their convictions and are likely to decide that he asked for it by attempting to bargain with Analeetah. I don't like to even think about it, but he will be punished regardless of the circumstances. How, I can't say, but I suspect that Kel would rather die than have to face his people again after this."

Anayah felt sick. She looked up at the sky as if searching for the answer in the clouds. Half hoping to see Harpur flying overhead in Karrys' body, looking for her so he could share some Fae-brained plan he'd come up with, she let the desperation she was feeling wash over her. She thought about zapping herself back to the camp to see if Morgaine and the others were still there, but quickly dismissed the idea. She'd been rash in making the bargain with Benebell. To humble herself in front of her friends now was out of the question.

"Where does Analeetah keep the magic she stole?"

"You can't go in there, Anayah," Mezzi said. "She's waiting for you. She won't be merciful with you."

"Where is it?" Anayah demanded again.

Mezzi sighed. "She keeps it in a vault in your old room."

The koobar scuttled up the line of web and disappeared into the trees, leaving Anayah to wrestle with her conscience.

Sok laid on his back in the grass staring up at the sky. He was lost in his thoughts, which mostly involved trying to come up with a way to convince Morgaine that they should all go to Danaleedh and help Anayah. Even Arthur felt that it was wrong to let her face Analeetah alone. But Morgaine would not be moved and had made it quite clear that anyone who tried to leave would end up on the ground next to, and in the same condition as, Lyrica, who, oddly, was not melting in the growing warmth of the two suns.

After Anayah had left and the Drengrokil had—much to Arthur's amazement and delight—been *beamed up*, The Fellowship of the Scale had fallen into a loud and lengthy argument about what they should do. Morgaine wanted Hiro, Bon and Arthur to return to Epoh while she, Sok, Meg and Hart stayed to wait for Anayah. Arthur refused to leave his children on Mysturna. Sok pointed out that depending on Arthur's ability to get himself, the Krist and the android safely through the Sands of Sancheera was just begging for trouble, which gained him a dirty look from Arthur, but also helped to steel the king's resolve not to be separated from the twins. Bon and Hiro offered to take Arthur to Hiro's lair where they could also attempt to make some headway with the scale in preparation for Bon's plan. At this point, Arthur grew angry and demanded to know why everyone wanted to get rid of him. No one denied that they were trying to get rid of him, but neither did they confirm it.

Meg and Hart reminded everyone that they couldn't go back to Epoh in case Glynnis sensed they were dragons. They actually believed that this would help their father accept that they should stay, but it only served as the catalyst to another one of Arthur's famous meltdowns.

With Arthur out of the argument, Morgaine felt like she had a better chance of controlling the situation, and suggested, strongly, that Meg and Hart go off and practice transforming, becoming invisible and raising their fire. But she warned them not to even think about trying to fly, which elicited groans of protest from the prince and princess. Sok, however, took this as a sign that Harpur was formulating a plan, so he removed himself from the debate and sat down on a stump to wait for Morgaine to let something slip. If she thought that she was winning, she might acquiesce to a request, should the opportunity to make one arise. Bon and Hiro came to the same conclusion and began insisting that they should stay as well. They didn't say it out loud, but the hover gilly could come in handy. The argument ended with Morgaine capitulating as she turned her gaze meaningfully toward the frozen Lyrica. No one, save Arthur, who was still ranting on the other side of the fire pit, missed her point.

Arthur's mental breakdown ended, as it often did, with an elevated sense of clarity and decisiveness. "Here's what we're going to do," he said, raising a pointed finger and turning to face the group. "Hiro, Bon, Sok and I will take the hover gilly closer to the city and hide somewhere close to the gates. Morgaine, Meg and Hart are going to transform into dragons, become invisible, fly over Danaleedh and set Wildwood on fire. We'll smoke Analeetah out and then we'll all swoop in and capture her."

Sok, Bon and Hiro couldn't count the number of problems with that proposal, but Morgaine was grudgingly impressed. She had, indeed, been formulating a plan. And, except for the swooping and capturing parts, setting Wildwood on fire to smoke Analeetah out was part of it.

They watched Arthur march confidently over to the hover gilly and climb on board as if he expected them to follow along without question. Then they watched his confidence shatter when he turned around and saw them all just standing there staring blankly back at him.

"Aw, come on, guys," he said. "This will work."

From his reclined position in the grass, Sok opened his mouth to begin perforating Arthur's scheme with a few barbed comments, but Morgaine hushed him with a stern look and approached the hover gilly. She boarded the vehicle and wrapped her arm around Arthur's shoulders. "Arthur, I'm so glad that you are on board with this. Really, I am! But before we can do any swooping or capturing, let alone burn down a palace, don't you think we should try to find Anayah and make sure she doesn't get caught in the crossfire, so to speak?"

Arthur's face reddened. "To be fair," he said in his own defense, "we've started bigger things with fewer specifics before."

Morgaine couldn't think of a single instance where any plan they had all been involved in wasn't detailed to death, but she decided not to point that out, lest another argument ensue. "Well, this plan needs a few more specifics. You're sure you're alright with Meg and Hart flying over the city?"

"Is there a better alternative?"

"Probably not," Morgaine said. "But I will do everything in my power to keep them safe."

Arthur looked around and realized that Meg and Hart were not in the camp. "Where are they? You didn't send them into the city alone, did you?"

"They are about two feet behind Sok at the moment," Morgaine whispered into Arthur's ear.

Arthur looked over at the elf and watched a blade of grass detach itself from its roots and start tickling Sok's nose. Sok, however, was prepared. He had heard the footsteps in the grass as Meg and Hart had invisibly tried to sneak up on him. He had lowered his eyelids so they appeared to be closed and waited. When the grass touched his nose, he reached up to where he estimated the hand holding the grass was and clamped his hand around a slender arm. Thankful that it was Meg and not her larger, stronger brother, he pulled her arm toward himself while simultaneously wrapping his right leg around her waist and flipping her onto her back. With an agile twist, Sok straddled the startled princess and pinned her to the ground beneath him.

Meg yelped. Unable to hold the spell that kept her invisible, she reappeared and lay panting under Sok's deceptively strong grip. "How did you know?" she gasped.

"Just because you can't be seen, it doesn't mean that you can't be heard," Sok replied. He stood up and extended a hand to help Meg get back to her feet.

Arthur looked at Morgaine. "How did you know they were there?"

"I could see the grass being flattened as they walked through it," she said.

Hart, too, had become visible again. "Sorry, big sister. I guess we didn't think that through well enough."

"You see, Arthur?" Morgaine said. "Specifics are important." She jumped off the hover gilly and motioned for everyone to gather around.

Anayah came to the sensible conclusion that she couldn't simply walk through the gates into Danaleedh, invisible or otherwise, and expect to come out again alive. Neither could she stay standing in this copse all day. But if Analeetah knew she was there, what was *she* waiting for? Why didn't she come out and confront Anayah? She finally decided to swallow her pride and zap herself back to the camp and ask Morgaine to help her, but a rustle in the bushes made her turn around to see who was there.

"Kel!" Anayah looked at the Pureman with a mixture of dread and hope.

"You shouldn't have come here, Anayah," Kel said. A touch of sorrow tinged his tone, but his face remained impassive.

Like Lyrica, the once handsome man looked drawn and weary. The swarthy skin had faded. The sparkle in his eyes was gone. His dull black hair lay unbraided across his shoulders. A thick, jagged scar ran from his collar bone down his left arm, ending just above his elbow. But the wound that shocked Anayah was the shame that festered in Kel's heart.

"Kel, I'm so sorry."

Anayah stepped toward her old friend to embrace him, but Kel backed away from her, making room in the small clearing for two other Puremen to come in and take her by the arms. She tried to zap herself out of their grip, but the Puremen were fast and seized her hands, nearly crushing her fingers together so she could not snap her fingers. She yelled in pain as they dragged her out of the trees and toward the city gate.

Kel walked a few steps ahead of Anayah and her captors, ignoring her pleas to be let go. In desperation, she tried to appeal to him as the friend she once knew, but Kel refused to be swayed by nostalgia. Unable to wipe away her tears, Anayah stumbled just before they reached the gates. It was enough to make the Pureman on her right to let go of her hand. Anayah didn't hesitate; she snapped her fingers and left her abductors holding nothing but bright red smoke.

Davynn woke from a dead sleep, drenched in sweat, a feeling of dread consumed him. He flipped the covers back and went into the children's room to check on them. Caleb was curled up on his side with his thumb in his mouth. Brodie was clutching his wooden sword, and Alexa was snoring softly on the other side of the room. All three were safe and sound. He pulled the door closed again and wandered through the suite, listening for strange sounds, looking for any sign of an intruder. Finding nothing amiss, the knight put his trepidation down to a forgotten bad dream and returned to his bedroom.

Through the window, the first rays of the sun were doing their best to push the night aside. As much as he wanted to crawl back into bed, the emptiness on Anayah's side rendered that idea decidedly unappealing. He decided he might as well get dressed and order the children's breakfast. They would be stirring soon and Joy would be along before the sun rose above the mountains. He'd have everything ready for them.

On his way to the kitchens, he had to pass Meg's room. The guards posted outside her door nodded at their captain and wished him a good day. Davynn could see that they were tired after having stood sentry all night, a mindless task that served no real purpose. It had always been Sok who insisted that guards be posted outside the royal family's rooms, but, in reality, they could all be replaced with simple keys. These men deserved something better. Then again, what could they do? It wasn't like the royal guards were even necessary in the peaceful Kingdom of Epoh where there was next to no crime, and the threat of an invasion was practically mythical. Even during all the years that Harpur had been gone, Epoh had remained undisturbed by any external menace. For the first time since joining the royal guards, Davynn wondered if he hadn't been wasting his life.

169

Then he remembered Berryl and the many pilfered items he had stowed away over what must have been years. Initially, Davynn had been incensed by Berryl's thievery, but it occurred to him as he descended the stairs that this was not the act of a man driven by malicious intent. Berryl was a troubled soul, crying out through his compulsion to steal for... *What, exactly?* What had happened to him to make him turn to petty larceny? What hole in Berryl's life was he trying to fill by pocketing trinkets and hiding them in his room? Davynn decided that the first order of business that day—after breakfast with his children—would be to go and talk to Berryl and try to get to the bottom of his compulsion.

The knight entered the kitchens and looked around for Finch. She was standing by the ovens, supervising the extraction of a dozen loaves of bread by two kitchen maids with her back to the door. Technically, Davynn was supposed to give his breakfast order directly to the feisty housekeeper, but he wasn't up to listening to her complaints and protests over a request for eggs and bacon for himself and the children. How Anayah managed to get through these daily transactions with Finch without turning the woman into a rat or a bug was beyond Davynn's comprehension. It never occurred to him that his lovely wife had deftly circumvented Finch's grudging compliance by simply conjuring their breakfasts instead.

Davynn caught the eye of a scullery maid and beckoned her over. "Please have five plates of eggs and bacon, two mugs of jamba and three cups of juice sent up to my rooms."

"Has Mistress Anayah returned, then?" the maid asked.

"No, she hasn't," Davynn confirmed with a slight edge of sadness. "The children's nanny will be joining us for breakfast again."

The maid smiled. "I see," she said, giving Davynn the impression that she was seeing far more than there was to see.

"Until my wife returns, Joy is in charge of the children from dawn until dusk. If I hear any rumors suggesting anything else, I will be back here to deal with you. Now, get our meals together and have them delivered to my rooms immediately."

He didn't wait for a response; Finch was on the move and he barely made it out of the kitchens before she rounded on the suspicious-minded scullery maid, demanding to know why she was lurking at the doorway.

After breakfast, which was inexplicably—and much to the knight's chagrin—delivered by Finch herself, Davynn kissed Alexa, Brodie and Caleb good bye and headed out of the castle to go and have a chat with Berryl. By the time he reached the market square, vendors and customers had already gathered to sell and buy their goods for the day. He joined a cue at the pastry stall with the intention of purchasing three fruit-filled delicacies. When he was second in line, he felt a tap on his shoulder.

"There's fresh pies coming out of the oven any time now at Skull's Keep."

Davynn turned to see Jack y Lebard smiling at him, hand extended in friendship. "Jack," Davynn said, taking the publican's hand. "What can I do for you?"

"Nothing at all," Jack replied. "I just saw you here and thought I would let you know that fresh pies are ready at the pub."

Davynn fought to keep the skepticism off his face. Outside of Skull's Keep, he and Jack had never exchanged a word. He couldn't help but wonder what the man really wanted. While he searched for a reply, a distinct, and slightly impatient, ahem sounded behind him. It was Davynn's turn and the vendor wanted him to either purchase something or move along so the next person in line could.

Davynn apologized and asked for three pastries. Then he turned to Jack. "I'll stick with these for now, but I'll stop by Skull's Keep later for a slice of that pie."

Thinking that would satisfy both the vendor and Jack, Davynn paid for his order and was surprised to see that Jack had not moved on.

"If you're heading over to the north gate," Jack said, "I'll walk with you."

Davynn couldn't think of a good reason not to walk with the pub owner, so he thanked the pastry vendor and fell in step beside Jack. "That's quite the cart you got there," he said, referring to the tri-level wagon loaded with flour, eggs, casks of milk and a variety of fruit and vegetables that Jack was pulling behind himself.

"You like that, hey?" Jack said with pride. "I made it myself. Rolls right into the kitchen and doubles as a shelf, so there's no need to unload when I get back from the market."

"Clever," Davynn agreed. "I dare say Finch would love something like that in the castle kitchens."

"Well, send someone around if you like. I can have one made up in a day to two," Jack offered.

"I will discuss it with Sok," Davynn said. "He'll have to approve the purchase."

"Fair enough." Jack adjusted his grip on the wagon handle to move it over behind him as they entered a narrow roadway off the market square. "If you like, I can deliver a slice or two of pie to poor old Berryl. He seems a little down in that cell you got him locked up in."

Davynn now understood Jack's burst of friendliness. "That won't be necessary. Berryl isn't going to be there much longer."

"Oh? Letting him go, are you?"

"It's a definite possibility," Davynn admitted.

"Does his being incarcerated have anything to do with the rumor that Harpur Diggins is still alive?"

Davynn stopped walking, but with the weight of the wagon behind him, Jack was forced to take a few more steps before he could bring the heavy load to a full stop. When he did, he turned to see Davynn standing with his arms folded, a look of annoyance on his face.

"Forgive me," Jack said. "I didn't mean to pry."

"The thing is, Jack, I think you did mean to pry," Davynn said calmly. "Now it's my turn to pry. Where did you hear that rumor?"

"A couple of guards came in the day Berryl got locked up," Jack confessed. "They mentioned it in passing."

"I see," Davynn said. "And have you mentioned it in passing to anyone else?"

"I have not," Jack declared.

"Good! Keep it that way. I don't need such a ridiculous rumor spreading and causing a panic in the city."

The knight started walking again, hoping that he had quelled the publican's curiosity. Behind him, Jack tugged on the wagon to get it moving again, but didn't bother to try to catch up to the knight. He realized that he had overstepped and had no desire to push his luck. But he was now almost positive that there was something to the rumor. Subconsciously, he looked skyward. There was no purple dragon flying around to confirm his suspicion.

When Davynn reached the north gate and entered the guard house, Berryl was still asleep on his cot, and the two guards on duty were attempting to kill a fly that was buzzing about the room. Six silver coins lay on the desk, telling the knight that a wager was on to see which guard could kill it first. The guards snapped to attention, and the fly deftly escaped through the open door.

"Sorry to spoil your fun, boys," Davynn said. "I need a few minutes alone with the prisoner."

The guards shuffled past Davynn and, scooping up their coins on their way by, exited the guard house nearly as quickly as the fly had.

Alone with the snoring Berryl, Davynn pulled a chair up to the bars and sat down. He shouted at the prisoner with no effect. A sword was laying on a desk just out of reach of the cell. He retrieved it and used it to bang on the bars. Berryl sat up, blinking the sleep out of his eyes and stared at his visitor, who was holding out a fresh pastry for him. Taking it, Berryl asked the knight what he was there for.

"It seems to me," Davynn began, "that your little thieving habit wasn't really about stealing at all."

"It wasn't?" Berryl took a bite of the pastry.

"If it was, you wouldn't have kept all the things you stole; you would have sold them. Am I right?"

Berryl chewed thoughtfully on his pastry while he tried to decide if Davynn was setting a trap of some kind. "They weren't mine to sell," he said finally.

"They weren't yours to hide in your rooms either," Davynn pointed out, "but that's not the point."

"It's not?" Berryl took another bite. He was shrewd enough to know that he needed to stay engaged and not give away anything more than he had to.

"Here's what I think happened." Davynn took a bite of his own pastry and watched Berryl closely while he chewed and swallowed. He saw hope, but no sign of guile. "I think that after Arthur became king and your position on the council was phased out, you felt... abandoned? Displaced? Without purpose?"

That was exactly how Berryl had felt. He'd been an advisor to King Gnik for a long time, then suddenly he was reduced to standing outside the council chambers waiting for an elf—of all people—to send him on some demeaning errand. The first thing he had stolen was a pen that belonged to Sok. He wanted to get back at the elf for replacing him. And it felt... not good exactly, but satisfying somehow.

"I did," Berryl agreed. "I felt all of those things."

"Why didn't you say anything?" Davynn asked.

"What was I going to say?" Berryl replied. "Sok wouldn't have listened. He was too busy lording his station over everyone to notice me."

"He made you his assistant."

Berryl scoffed. "Assistant! He made me his servant."

"I don't believe that was his intention, Berryl," Davynn said, "but I can understand how you saw it that way. Why didn't you come to me or to Arthur?"

"You all went along with it. I thought you were like the elf."

That stung a bit. Learning that Berryl had thought so lowly of him all these years did not make the knight feel very good about himself. "I cannot speak for the others, but I am truly sorry, Berryl. I am ashamed of myself for not seeing how things had affected you. I should have been more aware."

Still waiting for the knight to spring a trap, Berryl nodded. "Does this mean I'm free to go?"

"Not exactly," Davynn said, standing up and returning the chair to its place behind the desk. "What you did was still wrong, and you are going to have to make amends."

Berryl braced himself. "Make amends? How?"

"I'm going to assign a couple of guards to watch over you while you sort through all the things you stole and return them to their owners."

Berryl's heart sank. "All of it?"

"All of it," Davynn said. "And I am going to talk to Sok and Arthur when they get back and see if we can find a better position for you.

Berry leapt to his feet. "You're going to put me back on the council?"

Davynn rubbed his chin. "No. I have something else in mind for you."

Berryl's heart sank again. "Please don't make me work in the kitchens! I won't survive under Finch's supervision!"

Davynn had to laugh. "I wouldn't sentence anyone to that fate!"

"What is it, then?"

"I can't tell you just yet. I have to talk to Sok and Arthur first. But as soon as I get all the particulars worked out, I will tell you. You have enough to worry about with returning the things you stole for now."

Berryl sat back down on the cot. "Thank you, Sir Davynn," he said. But he wasn't sure what he was thanking the knight for.

Chapter Nine

Anayah, in her haste to escape from the Puremen, had done something that very few witches ever manage to do. And never want to. With only a split second to react when the Pureman released her hand, she decided to zap herself to freedom. But she failed to direct her magic to a specific location.

There is always a risk when wielding magic, and things do occasionally go wrong. For an experienced and competent witch like Anayah, mistakes—like the one in the great hall where she dumped wine on Davynn's lap so long ago—rarely resulted in the catastrophic outcome of this particular endeavor. Instead of focusing on where she wanted to go, Anayah inadvertently split the magic between two locations. And, in the process, split herself between the both of them. Half of her landed in the camp; the other half of her ended up in her old room in Wildwood.

The half of Anayah that landed in the camp appeared as a ghostly apparition and was initially noticed by Bon, who, upon seeing her, immediately scanned his databanks for any possible explanation. In seconds, he concluded that one of two things had happened. The first, and most desirable reason for Anayah's spectral form, was that she was projecting an image of herself, similar to a hologram, in order to deliver a message to the group. But, to the best of his knowledge, witches did not possess the ability to accomplish such a feat. The other cause, the one Bon knew was most likely, was that she had committed a grave and irreversible mistake, which, in fact she had.

The look of terror on her face confirmed the android's worst fears. It was now only a matter of time before Anayah's lifeforce would dissolve as her molecular structure continued to break down. From the data Bon had stored, it was possible that she could still communicate, but her magic was useless. All he could do was attempt to get as much information from her as possible before she faded out of existence.

"Bon, where are you going?" Morgaine said as the android extracted himself from the group and walked to where Anayah was standing. "You need to pay attention."

"I believe that this is more important," Bon replied without stopping.

They had been fleshing out Arthur's vague plan, attempting to fill in the details in such a way as to convince themselves that they could safely rescue Anayah and support her efforts to eliminate Analeetah. So far, the plan had remained as vague as it had been when Arthur had so boldly first proposed it. The only course of action any of them could agree on was to have Morgaine, Meg and Hart transform into dragons, fly into Danaleedh, set fire to Wildwood, and hope for the best. Hiro had just suggested that he try to contact Mezzi who might know where Anayah was, and they were chewing on that morsel of belated brilliance, when Bon saw the witch's form appear and had walked away.

Sok was next to see Anayah standing a short distance away from where they were huddled in discussion next to the fire pit. He rose from the stump he's been sitting on and looked in horror at her.

"No," he whispered. "It's not possible."

"What's not possible?" Arthur asked, standing up as well. Then he, too, saw the witch—or what was left of her—though it didn't quite register that she was not entirely herself. "Oh, hey, Anayah. You're back!"

Sok ran toward Anayah and arrived by her side a few steps in front of Bon. He reached out a hand to touch her, but the android grabbed his wrist and pulled him back.

"Do not touch her!" Bon snapped.

As the others gathered closer to see what was going on, Morgaine pushed herself to the front of the group. Inside the raven-haired dragon-wizardess, Harpur Diggins felt like he was being crushed. Helplessness consumed him and he couldn't contain the grief of knowing Anayah only had a half a day at best before she was dead. Morgaine backed away from Anayah, tearing her own gaze away from the witch's pleading eyes. She turned and ran until she was far enough away to transform. Then she launched into the air and flew toward Danaleedh.

Bon immediately took charge. "Arthur, use your magic and put a protective shield around Anayah. Make sure it goes beneath the ground and encapsulates her completely. Meg, Hart, move away from here and transform. Go after Harpur and do whatever you can to help him."

Meg and Hart started running farther into the open area south of the camp. They had no idea what was going on, but they understood that something bad had happened to Anayah and that Harpur couldn't be left to his own devices. They couldn't imagine how they were going to stop him from doing something crazy, but they understood that they stood a better chance than anyone else.

Arthur watched his children run through the grass, transform into magnificent black dragons and launch themselves skyward. He cursed himself for including them in the plan to save Anayah, but he still didn't comprehend what was going on.

"Now, Arthur," Bon said.

"Why does she have to be shielded?"

"Just do it, Arthur," Sok said, wiping tears from his cheeks with the palm of his hand.

Confused and not at all as confident he could do it, Arthur closed his eyes and envisioned a glass capsule descending around Anayah. When it reached the ground, he saw it penetrate the grass and dirt, and enclose itself about two feet beneath her. He opened his eyes. Anayah had placed one hand on the inside of the glass; Sok had placed his own hand over hers.

"Can she hear us?" Bon asked.

Arthur looked at the android. "I don't know! You didn't specify that she needed to be able to hear you. What is going on?"

"I can hear you," Anayah said. She continued to look at Sok.

Bon placed himself next to Sok. "Tell us what happened, Anayah."

"Kel Wyndrummer and at least two other Puremen are serving Analeetah. I believe she enchanted them to make them her slaves." Anayah, overwrought with emotion, faltered, and needed a precious moment to compose herself. "They caught me just outside of the city gates. I tried to get away, but…"

Anayah didn't need to say it. She couldn't say it.

"Do you know where Analeetah is?" Bon asked.

"I think she is in Wildwood."

"Where is the rest of you?"

"In my old room in the palace."

Bon turned and walked to the hover gilly. "Arthur, come with me. Hiro, take us to the city."

"Wait!" Anayah called out. "You can't go there. It's too dangerous. Analeetah is keeping stolen magic in a vault in my room."

Bon retraced his steps. "Alissah was right? Analeetah can extract magic from other witches?"

Anayah nodded. "According to Mezzi, she stores it for when she needs it."

"And what would happen if the magic was released?"

"I'm not sure," Anayah said, "but I think it would turn on Analeetah if it wasn't controlled. That's what I was planning on doing."

The words surprised even Anayah. She had been so unsure of what she should do, but now this was the only thing that made sense. The magic would probably have retained at least some of the consciousnesses of the witches it was stolen from. Surely, they would want to avenge themselves and their sisters.

"Thank you, Anayah." Bon returned to the hover gilly. "Hurry, Hiro! We must warn Harpur."

"Maybe I should stay here," Arthur said before Hiro could position himself at the front of the hover gilly. "Sok might need me."

"We need you more," Bon said. There was no time for sentiment, and, like it or not, Arthur's magic was the only weapon the android had against the mad Doyenne of Danaleedh. He reached down and pulled Arthur into the hover gilly by the upper arm. The moment Arthur's feet touched the floor of the vehicle, Hiro launched it forward at time-bending speed.

Sok and Anayah watched their friends disappear over the trees. When their eyes met again, they both smiled, trying to be strong for each other.

"Make sure Davynn understands that this was my fault," the witch said. "Don't let him blame Harpur."

"I'll be blaming Harpur for the both of us," Sok assured her.

After leaving the north gate guard house, Davynn made his way to the training grounds to update the duty roster to include round-the-clock supervision over Berryl. While he briefed the chosen guards on what the assignment entailed, he began to second-guess himself. Not having Arthur or Sok to bounce his plan off of, he decided to take a ride to Braydon Wood and talk it over with Elder Dhonna.

He arrived at Elder Dhonna's tree house to find that she was not there. Assuming she would be at the Guild House, he tethered his horse to a tree and made his way there on foot. At the gate to the guild house gardens, as was customary, Davynn stopped and waited to be acknowledged before entering. A young elf tending to some early spring planting, hailed the knight from the patch of earth he was working and bade him enter the yard.

"Is Elder Dhonna about?" Davynn asked as he surveyed the freshly turned dirt surrounding the elf's bare feet.

"I haven't seen her yet today," the elf replied. "She may be in her tree house still."

"I was just there," Davynn said. "She was not."

"She does like to go foraging early in the day," the elf said. "Perhaps she's out in the forest somewhere."

"Hmm…" Davynn said, looking toward the forest trees beyond the city and scratching his beard. "Any idea where she might have gone?"

"It's hard to say," replied the elf. "She could be anywhere."

"Elder Dhonna doesn't let someone know where she's going when she leaves the city?" Davynn asked hopefully.

The young elf laughed. "We all wish she would," he said, "but our beloved guild master is not one to report her comings and goings to us."

Figures, Davynn thought to himself. "Well, thank you anyway. I'll wander around a bit and see if I can find someone who's seen her."

"Is it important?" the young elf asked as Davynn turned to walk away.

"Not really," Davynn said. "I was just hoping to chat with her a bit." He continued to and through the gate.

"Oh, wait!" the young elf called. "I do recall her saying something about a stray Fae spirit that needed to be rounded up."

Davynn stopped and turned back to the elf. "A what?"

The elf seemed to be trying to remember exactly what he'd overheard. "Elder Dhonna and that dwarf king… What's his name?"

"Röggenar," Davynn supplied.

"Yes, Röggenar, that's the one. He's been staying with Elder Dhonna and I heard them talking about going to the Fae Lands to look for a Fae spirit that escaped from… a chalice?"

Davynn took a moment to digest this information. He couldn't imagine Elder Dhonna going willingly to the Fae Lands. For any reason! While the guild master was not as overt about her disdain for the Fae as Sok was, she was definitely not the sort to go galivanting about looking for trouble with them. He reentered the yard and approached the young elf again.

"Tell me everything you heard," he ordered.

"Well, it wasn't much," the elf replied, wondering if he had inadvertently stepped into something he shouldn't have. "Elder Dhonna and King Röggenar were in the guild house last night and Elder Dhonna said something about a willow being loose in the Fae Lands. That didn't make much sense to me, but she was clearly upset about it. Then King Röggenar suggested that they go and round the Fae spirit up. At first, Elder Dhonna refused. I mean what elf would go to the Fae Lands? But the dwarf said that if Harpur was able to do it himself, he would and that as Harpur's friend, she should help him out. That didn't make any sense either. Harpur Diggins is dead. Everyone knows that! I didn't stick around to hear what else they said. I don't think Elder Dhonna would be too happy with me if she knew I was listening in on her private conversations."

A growing knot of anxiety swelled up in Davynn's chest as the elf spoke, but he managed to keep his expression neutral. "You're right, that doesn't make much sense. I'm sure it was nothing."

"If you say so," the elf said. "But I better get back to the gardening here. Elder Dhonna was adamant that this patch be planted right away."

"Right," Davynn said. "Looks like you have your work cut out for you." He thanked the young elf and turned to leave again. "By the way," he said, pausing at the gate, "you might want to keep this to yourself."

"What do I say if anyone else comes looking for Elder Dhonna? Folks are going to notice that she's not here."

"Tell them that she's gone foraging and leave it at that." He turned away a third time.

"Sir Davynn?" the elf called after him.

"Yes?"

"What do you think Elder Dhonna meant by a willow being loose in the Fae Lands?"

"You got me," Davynn lied. "When Elder Dhonna gets back, you can ask her."

"No way!" the elf said. "Then she'd know I was listening."

Davynn smiled. "I guess you'll never know then."

The knight hurried back to his horse. He didn't treasure a trip to the Fae Lands any more than any elf living in Braydon Wood, but if that's where Elder Dhonna and Röggenar went, he couldn't very well not go and look for them. *What in the world would possess those two to make them go look for Willow?* He wondered. *Harpur will have a fit if I don't go and sort this out.*

Davynn rode out of the elven city and back to the castle, his horse maintaining a fast canter beneath him. His biggest problem now was to decide what route to take to the Fae Lands. Since Karrys had moved the Fae to the farthest south-west corner of Epoh, there was no easy or direct route to get there. He could take the Colwygshire Road south and then turn east and follow the mountains, or he could angle through Braydon Wood. The first way was longer, as the dragon flies, but would be faster, he reasoned, since he would be on an open road for the first leg of the journey. Traversing the forest would mean zig-zagging through the trees, fording creeks, and climbing hills. While the elves had many trails through the woods, none of them led straight to the Fae Lands. He decided to take the Colwygshire Road.

But first he would need to gather some supplies and let the children know he would be away, possibly for a few days. He would also have to leave someone else in charge of things until he or Arthur, or Sok, or someone with some sort of authority returned to keep the order. Eowyn Hunter was his first, and only, choice. The young man had once harboured a fear-driven hatred for the Fae nearly as strong as the elves'. He had been but a boy at the time, but time had molded him into as fine a guard as Davynn had ever seen. Some greater responsibility would do the lad good.

"Wouldn't you rather I accompany you, sir?" Eowyn asked after Davynn had explained where he was going and, to a reasonable degree, why.

"You can't be in two places at the same time, Eowyn," Davynn said. "I need you here more than I need you out there. I'll be fine on my own."

"Very well, sir," Eowyn said. "I will not let you down, sir."

Davynn smiled at the younger man. "See that you don't." Then he mounted his horse and rode out of Colwygshire hoping that when he got back his wife and friends would be waiting safely for him to return.

The teal dragon reached Danaleedh in no time. As she banked to her right to start circling the city, she noticed Mag and Hart flying fast in her direction. Whether they were on their way to help—or to hinder—Karrys didn't know. Not that it mattered; she intended to incinerate Wildwood and destroy Analeetah once for all. Not even a witch as powerful as Analeetah was supposed to be could withstand dragon fire.

Looking down on the city, Harpur took in the desolation and decay that Analeetah's madness had instigated through Karrys Evergreen's eyes. Roofs sagged, walls had crumbled, and the streets were riddled with weeds and potholes. Gardens, neglected and overgrown, were filled with dead plants choked out by weeds. Outside the main entrance to the once glorious palace, three bodies lay bent and broken on the street.

Karrys, who had been blessedly quiet since the return to Epoh, felt Harpur's anger and remorse.

Karrys: This isn't your fault.

Harpur: I beg to differ.

Karrys: Is there no chance of saving Anayah?

Harpur: She will be dead by nightfall.

Karrys: They why are you doing this? You've got your scale. Let's leave this world; this is their problem now.

Harpur didn't answer. There was no real need for these telepathic conversations; Karrys could read his thoughts without engaging. But sometimes, like now, an exchange of dialogue separated the two minds that occupied this single body and both Harpur and Karrys felt oddly less isolated.

Karrys, having noticed Meg and Hart's approach, pushed Harpur to listen to reason.

Karrys: I think you should wait for the twins. They might have learned something from Anayah that could help us.

Harpur: What could they have learned in the short time since we left the camp?

Karrys: If I knew, I wouldn't be telling you to wait for them.

Internally, Harpur grunted. He had to concede that Karrys might have a point; the Puremen lying dead in front of Wildwood were an interesting and disturbing development. He changed direction to go and meet Meg and Hart. When he reached the city wall, he veered left and called for them to follow him. They landed on a low hill a few miles south of the city.

"Why aren't you invisible?" Karrys demanded.

"Why aren't you invisible?" Meg retorted.

"I want that witch to see her killer," Karrys snarled.

Hart debated telling Harpur that Analeetah would be seeing Karrys, not him, but he decided to keep this to himself. Instead, he passed on what Anayah had told them back at the camp.

Karrys swung her huge head back in the direction of Danaleedh. "The rest of Anayah is in Wildwood?"

"In her room to be precise," Meg added.

"If Analeetah hasn't discovered her there yet," Hart said.

Karrys looked back at the twins. From what they had told her, Harpur deduced that Kel Wyndrummer was among the three dead Puremen. Analeetah must have killed them for letting Anayah escape. It spoke to the depth of her madness and Harpur was glad that Anayah would probably never know what had happened to her friend. He and Karrys were the only ones who knew that Kel had paid the ultimate price for Anayah, and they intended to keep it that way. All they had to do was figure a way to get to the vault and release the magic inside it. There was nothing anyone could for the part of Anayah that was inside the palace.

"Where are those three going?" Meg suddenly asked.

Karrys and Hart turned around, just in time to see the hover gilly whipping toward the city with Hiro, Bon and Arthur on board. Karrys launched into the air to go and try to intercept them, leaving Meg and Hart without instructions. By the time they settled on following, Karrys was on her way back to them. The hover gilly came floating behind not long after, and they were all soon reunited on the side of the hill.

"We have to go and get Anayah out of Wildwood," Arthur was saying as Hiro drew the chariot to a stop next to Karrys.

"We are going to try," Bon said. "She will have to be encapsulated the same way you did for the Anayah at the camp. Then we can attempt to move her."

"So, what are we waiting for?" Arthur demanded.

"For you to be quiet," Karrys said.

184

Bon had filled Arthur in on Anayah's condition on the way from the camp. Rather than send the king into hysterics, it seemed to have steeled his resolve to rescue their friend. He simply could not accept that Anayah was beyond saving. In his heart, he was ready to do whatever needed to be done to fix this. He clamped his mouth shut and waited to be told what to do.

"Arthur, are you familiar with the layout of Wildwood?" Bon asked.

Arthur looked at Karrys as if asking for permission to speak. The dragon rolled her eyes. "Not really," he admitted. "It's been a long time since I was there and I wasn't there long enough to learn my way around."

"That is a problem," Bon said.

Karry shifted on her feet. What she had to say was not going to be easy for anyone to hear. "Your desire to help Anayah is noble, Bon. I need you—all of you—to understand that there is nothing that can be done for her. I am outraged by what has happened, and not a little remorseful about my part in it.

"When I left the camp, I was going to fly to Wildwood and burn it. I gave no thought to the consequences, and if Meg and Hart hadn't followed to apprise me of the situation, I would have done just that. It probably would have been a more merciful end for Anayah, but I am grateful that I will not have her death on my conscience."

"You didn't cause this," Arthur said after a moment of reflection. "Edlyngton Bloomregaard is responsible."

"Thank you, Arthur," Karrys said. "Be that as it may, I played a part in it. As did Anayah and Anabettah. None of us could have known how Analeetah would react. But that does not negate the choices any of us made, or our reactions in turn. I want nothing more right now than to kill Analeetah and end this. But I'm not going to do that."

"What are you going to do?" Meg asked. She could feel the dragon fire rising in her chest.

"I'm going home," Karrys said quietly.

The teal dragon braced for the onslaught, but no one spoke. They were all lost in their own thoughts, reliving or recalling the stories of a time long ago when Harpur saved Epoh from an evil despot and his enslaved wraiths. He was doing his job as Dragon Lord of the kingdom, nothing more. Anabettah's death, and Analeetah's reaction to it, were not his fault. Yet he carried the weight of it, and now it seemed that he would carry the weight of Anayah's death as well.

"She came here to help you," Meg said. "You can't just walk away from this without at least trying to help her."

"She cannot be helped!" Karrys roared. "She chose to come here. She made whatever bargain she made with Benebell. She chose to confront Analeetah. I will not put any of you in further danger to avenge the consequences of her choices."

A thick plume of purple-black smoke rose from Meg's snout as she backed farther down the hill. "Then I'll take care of it myself."

Arthur followed her. "Don't be ridiculous, Meg! You can't face Analeetah alone."

Meg stopped and looked at her horrified father. "You're right," she said. "I'm going to need your help."

She reached out with a front leg and wrapped her hand around Arthur, then launched a bit awkwardly into the air and turned back toward the city.

Not surprised, but deeply dismayed by Meg's impulsive behaviour, Hart followed his sister.

"I should have expected that," Karrys said to Bon and Hiro as she watched them fly away.

"Yes," Hiro said. "You really should have."

Chapter Ten

Davynn made his way south down the Colwygshire Road and wondered what was waiting for him in the Fae Lands. Alternating between a gentle canter and walking, he chose not to push his horse too hard. He camped the first night near the Fae Waters, the river that cut through Epoh from the mountains to the west and ended at the Crysteel Sea in the east.

The second night he made camp at the base of the mountains where the Colwygshire Road ended after leaving his horse stabled in a small village east of the road. He would have preferred to have kept his horse with him, but the Fae had an aversion to the beasts and he did not wish to risk the animal's safety once he reached the Fae Lands. He continued on foot at first light, following a trail westward into the lands that the Fae had occupied for centuries until Karrys Evergreen had banished them to the far south-western corner of the of the kingdom. The realization that it had actually been Harpur who had relocated the Fae suddenly struck the knight and, like harsh realities often do, left him feeling a little numb around the edges.

He had always assumed that an incident with the Fae that had nearly culminated in a war between them and the elves had been the catalyst for Karrys' decision to contain the Fae far from the elves, the humans and the dwarves in order to keep the peace. Now, though, he had to wonder if Harpur had some other reason for sending the Fae so far away. What that reason might be was anybody's guess. Davynn, as much as he liked and admired Harpur Diggins, had never been able to fathom the dragon's thought processes.

Slowly, he made his way through the forest, keeping to the base of the mountains as much as possible. There were few paths to follow. Where the elves were much in favour of cultivating the forest to incorporate clear trails, the Fae tended to travel among the trees in a more willy-nilly fashion, taking different routes to their destinations each time. Still, signs of the Fae remained in the old Fae Lands. Twice he came upon gathering places, where the Fae Queen hosted celebrations and fêtes to commemorate a seemingly endless list of events. The phases of the moon were a big deal for the Fae, for example, and every version of the moon's presentation was reason for a ritual, followed by a party. They celebrated the equinoxes and solstices as well. But something as simple as finding a shiny object was more than sufficient reason for a gathering and general revelry to break out.

The farther he went, the more he wished he hadn't come. Anayah and the others might already be back and here he was, wandering through Braydon Wood, looking for an elf and a dwarf who had no business interfering with the Fae. If he hadn't come, though, and Harpur returned to find that he had left Elder

Dhonna and Röggenar to their own devices, he would never hear the end of it. By the same token, Harpur might have preferred that he had stayed in Colwygshire and informed him right away. Truth be told, waiting a day or two more for Anayah, Sok and Morgaine to return and letting them deal with the situation might have been the far more efficient way to go. But duty compelled him to do what he could in the situation.

There were only a few ways this trek through the woods could go. He could find Elder Dhonna and Röggenar and convince them to go back to Colwygshire. He could find them and not convince them to abandon their quest, and end up wrangling a stray Fae spirit. He could go on to discover Elder Dhonna and Röggenar had already accomplished their mission and were safely back where they belonged. Or the Fae had found them. And there was no telling what the Fae might do to them. Davyn had never coveted magical ability for himself. But this was one of those times where it would have come in handy. All he could do was go on and hope for the best.

Sok could not bring himself to remove his hand from the glass surrounding Anayah. He didn't care what the others were up to. All he could think about was what was happening to her. Even in the short time since Morgaine, Meg, Hart, Arthur, Bon and Hiro had left the camp, Anayah had faded alarmingly. As the molecules that once held her body together fell apart, an ash-like substance drifted downward, pooling on the grass at her feet. He noticed that the cuff Benebell had put on Anayah's wrist had not been affected in the split when she had zapped herself to two places at the same time. He looked for her wedding ring, but the gold band was not on her finger. He wanted to ask her why it was missing when the cuff was still there, but he couldn't bring himself to remind her of Davynn and the children.

"Thank you for staying with me," Anayah said, breaking the silence at last.

"Someone had to," Sok replied.

"I'm glad it was you."

"What were you thinking?"

"Clearly, I wasn't," Anayah said through a rueful smile. "It's okay if you're angry with me. I'm a little angry with myself."

Sok closed his eyes to hide his feelings. He was angry. But he couldn't quite decide what he was angry about. "Who's going to keep me in line now?" he asked.

"Silkhar Ornathan Kluupentarajhar, you don't need anyone to keep you in line! In line is the last place you need to be kept!"

He opened his eyes again and looked at Anayah. "You remembered my name."

"I asked Elder Dhonna once what your name means. She told me that Silkar means joyful or playful and Ornathan means a gift from beyond. She didn't know what Kluupentarajhar means. She said it was a Fae name."

Sok couldn't help himself. He laughed. "It is, and it isn't," he said. "The Fae have no language of their own. They speak the common language, but they draw on the languages from where their magic originates for their names. Kluupentarajhar is an ancient elven name. Presumably, the Fae took it from the magic of an elf."

"That doesn't make sense," Anayah said. "Elven magic is limited to healing and plant magic... Oh!"

"Oh, indeed," Sok said. "It is believed that the Fae were created by a wizard who deliberately infused elven magic into plants, rocks, dirt. Eventually, other magic was used."

Anayah frowned. "I don't understand why you hate the Fae, then. If they were created from elves..."

Sok grimaced. "To be fair, I suppose, I don't hate the Fae. It's not their fault that they exist. I hate what they are. I hate that elves were used... Probably killed... to make them."

Anayah grew thoughtful. "Do you think that Analeetah extracted the magic from the witches the same way?"

Sok shrugged. "Possibly."

They fell silent. The suns climbed higher and then began their descent through the afternoon sky. As Anayah's molecular structure fell apart and fluttered to the ground, a weariness began to consume her. It would not be long before she would be unable to speak.

"You didn't tell me what Kluupentarajhar means," she whispered.

Sok smiled at the fading witch. "It means chaser of dreams."

Anayah nodded. "Sok?"

189

"Yes, Anayah?"

"Please don't be angry with Harpur."

"Who should I be angry with?"

"Me."

"I'm a little angry with you too," the elf said.

"Good bye, Sok," Anayah whispered. "Tell Davynn and the children that I love them."

"Good bye, Anayah."

"Meg!" Arthur yelled. "Put me down this instant!"

Dragon flight was never on the top of Arthur's list of favourite activities. He had, at one time, grown accustomed to flying with Harpur, but it had been many years ago. And Harpur was an experienced dragon, not the fledgling who had her claws clamped around his body that Meg was. Her grip was too loose, forcing Arthur to wrap his arms around one digit and hold on for dear life while his legs dangled sloppily through her barely-clenched fist. The higher they climbed, the more terrified Arthur became. He squeezed his eyes shut and held on as tightly as he could.

"Meg! I'm warning you! Put me down!"

"I can't do that, Father," Meg said. "I need you to help me rescue Anayah."

At this point, Arthur had accepted that Anayah was beyond saving. He was too busy worrying about his own wellbeing to put much effort into a rescue that would only, in the end, be an exercise in futility.

"Meg, please! For the love of Orhowyn stop this. You're going to get us both killed!"

Meg ignored her frightened father and continued toward the city. She was determined to prove the adults wrong about... Well, everything. The fact that she had no clue about the layout of the city, or even where Wildwood was seemed, to her, to be minor details. Arthur had been there; he could navigate for her. And perhaps he would. If his eyelids weren't all but welded shut.

"We're almost at the city," Meg called out. "Where is Wildwood?"

"How the hell should I know?" Arthur yelled back.

This was the first inkling that Meg's haphazard plan might not work. She had intended to land on the roof of Wildwood, transform and have Arthur zap them both inside. Once inside, Arthur would take them to Anayah and encapsulate her as he had back at the camp while she watched for any sign of Analeetah. As soon as Anayah was safely ensconced in the glass capsule, Arthur would zap them both back onto the roof and Meg would fly them all back to the hill, where, Karrys, Hart, Hiro and Bon would be patiently waiting for their triumphant return. Simple!

"What do you mean you don't know where Wildwood is? I thought you'd been here before."

"Yeah, like a million years ago!" Arthur shouted. He knew the palace was in the centre of the city, but he wasn't about to tell his dragon-daughter that. "Meg, I think I'm going to be sick."

"I think I see it! Is it a big building that looks like a giant elf house?"

"Yes," Arthur groaned. "Meg, you have to turn around and take us back to Morgaine and the others."

Arthur felt the sudden shift in speed as Meg prepared to land. He peeked with one eye and saw the dilapidated roof of Wildwood rushing up toward him.

"Meg, no! It's not going to hold you!"

And Arthur was right. The dry and withered branches of the trees that had grown to form the roof of the palace crumbled under the weight of the dragon. In a cacophony of splintering wood and snapping branches, Meg and Arthur tumbled down through the roof and crashed into the floor below it. For a second, it seemed that the floor would hold them, but it, too, gave way to Meg's bulk and they started to fall again.

Unprepared for what was happening, Meg started thrashing out with her front legs, trying to grab onto anything that might stop her from falling. In the process, she let go of Arthur, who managed to roll away from her enormous body before the next floor gave out and she continued to fall. Clinging to the stub of a broken branch, he watched in horror as Meg disappeared through the gaping hole in the floor only a few feet away from where he was hanging by his hands. Meg screamed in pain as the splintered ends of the tree limbs tore through her wings. When, at last, she hit the ground, she passed out and lay still.

Forgetting his fear of heights, Arthur swung his feet toward a landing from which hung the remnants of a staircase. Hoping it would hold long enough for him to reach his daughter, he scrambled down the dangling steps through a cloud of dust kicked up by Meg's downward plummet.

"Please don't be dead. Please don't be dead," he muttered repeatedly, punctuating it every few feet with, "You are in so much trouble!"

He reached the ground just as two large, black dragon hands ripped through the front wall of the palace followed by Hart's large head. He took in the scene and quickly assessed what remained of the structure. There was no way he would be able to enter in his dragon form without bringing the rest of Wildwood down on top of Meg and his father. He transformed and rushed to Meg's side.

Arthur threw his bruised and aching arms around his son. "Help her," he sobbed.

A moment later, Morgaine, Hiro and Bon arrived together on the hover gilly. Like Hart, they had seen Meg's fateful attempt to land on the roof of Wildwood and had rushed to the palace. Seeing Meg lying there so still sent the dragon-wizardess into a rage.

"Foolish child!" Morgaine yelled. And everyone knew she was speaking for Harpur.

"Is she dead?" Hiro whispered to Bon.

"No," Bon answered. He could see Meg's sides lift and fall with her shallow breath. "But she is."

Everyone looked to where the android was pointing. Two feet, clad in bright-red satin slippers protruded from beneath Meg's haunches.

"Is that...?" Arthur asked.

"Ding, dong, the witch is dead." Morgaine stepped over Meg's tail to get closer. She lightly kicked one of the feet to confirm her declaration.

Analeetah had been waiting in the foyer of the palace for Anayah to show up. She had sensed Anayah's magic when her split half had first arrived, but as soon as Anayah had materialized, her magic had dissolved and Analeetah assumed that Anayah had immediately zapped herself away again. *Probably too afraid to face me just yet.*

When Meg's disastrous landing attempt failed and Wildwood had started to disintegrate beneath her, Analeetah started to go up the stairs to investigate. Had she stayed where she was, she might have survived, but, too late, she found herself directly under the falling dragon and had no time to react before she was crushed to death by several tons of that same falling dragon.

"Isn't anyone going to help Meg?" Arthur asked, not caring about Analeetah's fate.

Morgaine made her way to Meg's head and crouched beside it, placing a gentle hand on her jaw. "There isn't much we can do until she comes to. With a bit of luck, she'll be able to transform and we can carry her out of here."

Morgaine stood up and examined Meg's wings. The shredded membranes would heal, but it would be a while before the princess flew again.

Bon recorded everything and saved the data. Then he turned to Hiro. "Do you know where Anayah's room is?"

"Third floor, north wing," the Krist replied.

"Do you think we can make it there with the hover gilly?"

Hiro looked up through the hole to where the third floor should have been. "We can try."

Bon informed the others, who were not inclined to leave Meg, that he and Hiro were going to see if they could find Anayah. No one objected, so the android and the Krist floated upward to the third story and began their search for Anayah's room.

They found it after winding through, over and around broken walls and scattered debris. Bureaus and tables and beds and clothing littered the rooms and hallways, pathetic reminders of the charm and grandeur Wildwood once possessed.

In the middle of the room stood a large, stone cube that had been riven into two pieces by some unidentified force. Bon examined the jagged edges of the crack and found ash-like particles adhering to the rough surface. More of the substance was dispersed across the top of the cube. Bon could see shards of broken glass glistening on the bottom of the hollow vault. On the floor, next to it, lay a simple gold ring. Bon picked it up and tucked it into a pocket in his robe.

"Anayah's not here," Hiro observed.

"I am afraid this is all that is left of her," Bon said, indicating the particles of ash.

Hiro hung his head and wept. "We didn't get to say good bye."

Bon gave the Krist a few moments with his grief. When Hiro was able to compose himself, the android asked if he could produce a vessel and a whisk broom from his satchel. Hiro complied without comment, and Bon used the broom to carefully sweep the ash into the urn. "We will take this back to Davynn," Bon announced. "He will want to have something to bury."

Hiro nodded solemnly and stowed the vessel in his satchel along with the whisk broom while Bon boarded the hover gilly for their return to the main floor. They were about to depart when Bon asked Hiro to stop.

"What is it?" Hiro asked. "Is something wrong?"

Bon went back to the vault and reached inside to retrieve a piece of broken glass. "If I am not mistaken, these held the magic Analeetah extracted from the witches." Hiro waited for the android to explain his concern. "The magic has escaped."

Still not certain what Bon was getting at, Hiro asked, "What of it?"

"The most likely conclusion is that there are now Fae living on Mysturna. Or there soon will be."

"I better find Mezzi and inform her," Hiro said. He had been wondering why the koobar hadn't greeted them when they arrived, and now he was more than a little concerned.

Bon reboarded the hover gilly and they made their way back to the foyer.

Meg was just beginning to stir when the hover gilly came to a stop next to her body. She groaned and lifted her head. Her pupils were dilated and her eyes rolled in their sockets as she tried to focus.

Morgaine and Hart were kneeling next to Meg's head, soothing her with hushing sounds and stroking her long neck. Arthur was standing a short distance away with one hand clamped over his mouth, caught in a father's worst nightmare.

"How is she?" Hiro asked.

Arthur could only shake his head.

"She's coming around," Morgaine said over her shoulder. "Her wounds are bad, but she's young and strong. As long as she can transform so we can get her out of here, we'll be able to fix her up."

Arthur swallowed the lump in his throat. He wanted to believe Morgaine, but Meg didn't look easily fixable. Her wings were in tatters and purple-red blood was splattered all over her body. Now, he really did feel like he was going to be sick.

"Arthur, come wait outside," Bon said, placing a hand on the king's shoulder and gently guiding him to the ruined entrance. "Morgaine will let us know when she's able to be moved."

Arthur allowed himself to led out of the palace. He recognized Kel among the three dead Puremen laying on the street and had to turn away. He didn't know what was worse, being inside and seeing Meg in such distress, or having to look at Anayah's dead friend.

Bon spotted a bench about twenty feet to the left of the entrance and guided Arthur to it. A thick, but withered bush conveniently blocked their view of the bodies and they settled themselves down to wait.

Hiro produced a flask of brandy from his satchel and handed it to Arthur. "I'm going to look for Mezzi."

Arthur watched the Krist float away on the hover gilly and sipped the strong liquor. "If she survives, I'm going to kill her," he said.

"Meg has always been impulsive," Bon said. "Her heart was in the right place, I believe."

"That's not the point!" Arthur said. "She nearly got herself killed today."

"Hold onto the nearly part," Bon advised. "Are you badly hurt?"

Arthur felt like he'd been run over by truck, but he was relatively sure nothing was broken. "I'll be okay. Thank you, Bon."

The brandy seemed to be helping stave off the worst of the shock, so Bon remained a quiet presence, watching closely, but not intruding on Arthur's thoughts. There was a small contusion on Arthur's forehead that was cause for concern, but his pupils were not excessively dilated for the light they were in. There was also a tear in his pants that revealed a deep scratch, but that was superficial and would heal on its own. He would watch for any signs of concussion and deal with it if he had to.

Hiro returned looking worried a short time later. "I can't find Mezzi anywhere," he said. "She isn't answering the scrying mirror and I'm afraid she might have been hurt when…" He didn't have to complete his thought; Bon and Arthur both knew what he was talking about.

Arthur had no affinity for the koobar. He found her giant spider-like body repulsive and her ability to talk creepy. But he knew how much she meant to Hiro. "I'm sure she's fine," he said. "She probably just scuttled off somewhere to hide."

"I hope so," Hiro said, but there wasn't much hope in his voice.

It was then that Arthur remembered Bon and Hiro had gone to look for Anayah. "Did you find Anayah's room?" he asked.

"We did," Bon said. "We were too late."

"Do you think the rest of her is still in the capsule?"

"I do not know," Bon admitted. "I hoped it might slow the process down, but I cannot say if it had that effect."

Arthur nodded. "What's taking so long in there?" He looked toward the entrance to Wildwood.

"Would you like me to go and check on their progress?" Hiro offered.

Arthur wasn't sure. If it was good news, then, yes, he wanted to know. If it was bad news, he wasn't ready for it. "Maybe we should give them a bit more time."

"I can get you something to eat, if you like," Hiro suggested.

Arthur shook his head. He was hungry. But having something to eat felt inappropriate in the circumstances. "Maybe some more brandy?"

Hiro took the empty flask and traded it for a full one.

Arthur unscrewed the cap and took a long drink just as Morgaine emerged from the palace.

"Hiro?" she called. "Can you bring the hover gilly inside, please?"

Arthur stood up. He swayed a little, but he assured Bon that it was just the brandy and he handed the flask back to Hiro. "Better put this away," he said.

"And you better sit back down," Hiro said as he floated toward Morgaine.

"How is she?" Arthur asked.

"She's fine," Morgaine said. "A little stiff and sore, but she'll pull through."

Arthur let out a sigh of relief and started to follow the hover gilly.

Hart met them at the entrance, holding Meg's small, human form in his arms. She was awake, but groggy, and when her eyes met Arthur's, they were instantly flooded with tears and shame. He wanted to hug her and scold her, but both those options would have to wait. He stood aside as Hart laid his sister down on the floor of the hover gilly, then he climbed in and sat next to her. Hart joined him on Meg's other side, and Bon took a position at the rear of the chariot.

"We are heading back to the camp to get Sok," Morgaine announced. "Then we really are going home."

Sok was lying in the grass next to the glass capsule when Morgaine, Arthur, Bon, Hiro, Meg and Hart finally returned to the camp. He was looking up at the sky, his hands folded behind his head, his legs bent with an ankle resting on the opposite knee. His eyes were red-rimmed from crying, but the tears had dried up, leaving streaks across his cheeks.

"Where is she?' Arthur asked when he saw that the capsule was empty.

"Gone," Sok said.

Morgaine approached and looked down at the elf. "I'm sorry, Sok."

"You should be."

Morgaine closed her eyes and clenched her teeth against the wave of grief that threatened to crack her composure. Harpur had lost two friends that day. He hoped that in time, he would be able to win one of them back.

"We are going back to Epoh," she said.

Sok uncrossed his ankle and sat up. Arthur took his hand and pulled him to his feet. He walked over to the hover gilly and saw Meg laying on the floor. "Is *he* responsible for this?" He motioned with his thumb toward Morgaine.

"Harpur is not responsible for this," Bon replied. "Meg acted of her own accord."

Sok snorted and climbed on board.

"Should we do something with this?" Arthur asked, referring to the capsule.

Bon approached with the urn he'd put Anayah's ash residue in at Wildwood. "If you will remove the capsule, I will collect the remains."

Arthur obliged and bent down to hold the vessel while Bon scooped the ash into it. "Sok is pretty upset," he said.

"I am sure he will come around in time. He is grieving and he needs someone to blame," Bon replied. He picked up the cuff that Benebell had put on Anayah's wrist and tossed it aside.

"When we get back to Colwygshire, I'll suggest Sok spend a few days in Braydon Wood," Arthur said as if he was expecting approval.

"A few days in Braydon Wood will probably do Sok good," Bon said, "but Morgaine cannot stay in Epoh. Glynnis won't stand for it."

Arthur had forgotten about Glynnis. Now he was also reminded that the twins couldn't stay in the kingdom either. *One thing at a time*, he told himself internally.

"What are we going to do about Lyrica?" Bon asked of Morgaine. "We can't just leave her here like this."

Morgaine looked at the frozen witch. She walked over and knelt down beside Lyrica. With a wave of her hand, Morgaine removed just enough of the ice to expose the witch so she could talk, but her hands remained restrained.

"We are leaving now," Morgaine said. "Analeetah is dead. So, Anayah's obligation to Benebell is over."

Lyrica strained against her icy bonds. "Let me go! I want to talk to Anayah!"

"That's not possible," Morgaine said. "I've made it so the ice will melt quickly after we are gone. You will be able to return to the forest, or go back to Danaleedh and try to repair it. We won't be bothering you again."

She stood and motioned for everyone to prepare to leave. Hart transformed into his dragon form and waited for the others to board the hover gilly so Hiro could guide them back to the Boundary.

Once Morgaine had transformed, Hart turned to her and asked, "Why didn't you tell Lyrica that Anayah is dead?"

"They don't deserve to grieve for her."

Chapter Eleven

It was a somber and cheerless arrival at the castle in Colwygshire for the Fellowship of the Scale. Morgaine's plan was to find Davynn and deliver the news about his wife to him privately. She had managed to bring them all through the Boundary and out of the Sands of Sancheera without incident and then back to the castle where she left them in Arthur's chambers. They needed time to process their grief and she was not, at the moment, welcome to stay and process hers with them. With a nod to Bon, whose neutrality gave her some comfort, she left through the oak door and descended the stairs to the council chamber, hoping to find the knight there. Before she left, however, she entered Arthur's bed chamber and placed the vessel containing Anayah's ashes in the secret vault where Harpur's life book and the broken chalice were stored. Bon had suggested waiting to give it to Davynn and Morgaine had agreed, but not until after he had heard the news.

The dark and empty council chamber felt cold and as unwelcoming as Arthur's rooms in the tower above. Harpur wondered if he would ever feel comfortable in this place again. But time was of the essence and Morgaine needed to find Davynn and then get out of Epoh before Glynnis sensed her presence again. Had she known in advance that the knight was not in the city and was wandering about the Fae Lands looking for Elder Dhonna and Röggenar, who were, in turn, looking for the stray Fae spirit of Willow, she might have avoided running into the dragon lord.

Glynnis, in his paranoid suspicion, was standing outside the council chambers in his human form, waiting for someone with even a modicum of intelligence to appear and tell him where the king and his cronies were and why Arthur had not complied to his latest summons. He was tall, cloaked and hooded, but his eyes and skin glistened with a bronze sheen. He also smelled like a dragon. Morgaine, unable to contain her surprise, stopped short. She considered backing back into the council chambers and zapping herself out of there, but it was too late. She also smelled like a dragon, and Glynnis recognized the scent. He turned and grinned, revealing bone-white and wickedly sharp teeth.

"Well, well, well," he hissed. "What do we have here?"

"I have no time for you right now, Glynnis." Morgaine took the assertive highroad. "I've got things I need to do." She started forward again, intent on passing the dragon lord and leaving the castle.

"Oh, I agree," Glynnis said. "And the first thing you need to do is explain to me who you are and why you are in my kingdom."

Morgaine stopped and turned back to face Glynnis. She studied his leathery face and decided he wasn't very good at assuming human form. Then again, vain creature that he was, he may have chosen to keep some of his dragon qualities on purpose. She decided on the truth. Or a version of it that suited her. "I am known as Morgaine Fayle in this form, but my name is Karrys Evergreen. I was once the sovereign ruler of Epoh, before they turned it over to you in my absence." This seemed to give Glynnis pause. He stared at Morgaine in utter disbelief and Morgaine used his uncertainty to her advantage. "You need not worry about me trying to take back rulership of your kingdom. I am here only to find and contain a wild Fae spirit that has escaped confinement and is loose in the Fae Lands. Once I have safely got her back under control, I will leave Epoh. You have nothing to fear from me."

"I don't believe you," Glynnis said. "Karrys Evergreen is dead. And there are no loose spirits in the Fae Lands. I would know."

"Come with me then," Morgaine said with a flip of her long, black hair. "I'll show you."

Glynnis watched Morgaine walk toward the castle doors. He was stunned by her audacity, and more than a little impressed. He'd heard about Karrys Evergreen and her aggressive ways. He followed, expecting to find her waiting at the top of the steps, but Morgaine was already melting into the crowds in the streets, heading toward the north gate.

When he caught up to her, Glynnis fell into step on her left. "That was rude."

"I'll be polite later. Right now, I have to find the captain of the guard and deliver some news to him."

"I thought you were going to prove to me that you are Karrys Evergreen and that there is a loose Fae spirit running amok in my kingdom."

"All in good time," Morgaine said, shouldering her way through a group of people blocking the way.

Not being as adept at maneuvering in human form as Morgaine was, Glynnis found himself trapped in the throng and being pushed sideways while the dragon-wizardess continued merrily on her way. Rather than cause an unwanted scene, Glynnis zapped himself out of his predicament and once again fell in step next to Morgaine. "You did that on purpose," he accused.

"It takes practice," Morgaine said with a wry smile. "I don't recommend you get too used to it."

"I don't intend to. Where are we going?"

Morgaine was finding Glynnis' civility amusing. If she wasn't in such a hurry to find Davynn, she might have actually enjoyed this encounter. "We are going to the north gate. I am hoping to find the captain there."

"He's not there," Glynnis said.

"Oh? How do you know that? Have you eaten him?"

Glynnis laughed. "I'm not all that fond of human flesh," Glynnis said. "They taste like chicken." Morgaine shot a sideways glance of disapproval at him. "I overheard a young guard a day or two ago telling another guard that the captain... Sir Davynn, I believe he is called... has gone in search of friends in the Fae Lands."

Morgaine stopped dead in her tracks. "What friends?"

"Oh, that I don't know. All I heard was that the captain had journeyed to the Fae Lands in search of an elf and a dwarf. Why they are there, I can't tell you."

Morgaine narrowed her eyes. "You aren't lying to me, are you?"

"Why would I do that?" Glynnis said. "You're being truthful with me. Are you not?"

Morgaine couldn't bring herself to trust Glynnis. "You don't mind if I get that confirmed, do you?"

"Go ahead," Glynnis said. "Waste more of your time."

Morgaine huffed, then spun on her heels and continued marching toward the north gate.

They walked for a while, not talking, both thinking about what the other might really be up to. Glynnis was certain that Morgaine was more than she appeared to be; Morgaine was wondering why Glynnis was being so obliging. Neither of them thought that any good was going to come out of it.

"Tell me, Morgaine," Glynnis said as they passed Skull's Keep, "how did this Fae spirit come to be loose in my kingdom?"

Jack y Lebard was sitting on a chair in front of the pub, dozing in the late afternoon warmth. With Berryl having been released, his curiosity about the whole affair had gone unsatisfied, but he knew that the news would spread eventually. Colwygshire was not so big that the crimes of a nobleman like Berryl would pass without notice. But when Glynnis' words penetrated his half-slumber as the two dragons in disguise passed by, he was instantly awake and intrigued.

Generally speaking, Jack knew little about the Fae and the implications of a Fae spirit being loose in the kingdom was lost on him. But the cloaked man who had asked the question and the sultry woman he asked the question of were odd enough on their own and it was easy to deduce that they were not among the regular citizenry. That they were discussing an issue with the Fae just added to the mystery and Jack couldn't help but stretch the kinks from snoozing on the chair and follow them to see if he could learn more.

When he realized that they were going to the north gate guardhouse, he had to wonder if they were somehow involved in whatever was going on with Berryl. He chided himself for not having some pie or something with him to use as excuse to enter the guardhouse, but he needn't have concerned himself. The strange man and woman were only inside for a minute. He didn't even have time to come up with a plan before they reemerged and walked quickly out through the north gate. As they rounded the wall and disappeared from sight, Jack heard the man say to the woman, "I told you your captain had gone to the Fae Lands."

Jack wanted to follow them to see if he could learn anything more, but common sense told him that these two were not folks to be trifled with. Besides, the supper hours were going to start soon at Skull's Keep and he needed to get back to work. "Berryl has been let go," Jack muttered to himself as he made his way back to the pub, "and Sir Davynn has gone to the Fae Lands. What on Thraeh is going on?"

He couldn't make the connection because there was no connection to be made, of course. But Jack felt that the coincidence was too great for the two events not to be related in some way. And the cloaked man and the raven-haired woman were just gravy on the meat of titillating conspiracy theories.

Had he followed Morgaine and Glynnis, he would have seen them walk to the middle of the grassy verge between the city and Braydon Wood and vanish. But he would not have heard their conversation.

"So you did," Morgaine said in reply to Glynnis' I-told-you-so remark. "May I have permission to fly as a dragon in your kingdom?"

"Not visibly," Glynnis said.

"Of course not!" Morgaine rolled her eyes at him.

"Just don't forget that I can sense you now better than ever. Don't do anything stupid."

Morgaine, rather than dignify that with a reply, became invisible and transformed into her dragon guise. She launched herself into the air and flew over Braydon Wood toward the Fae Lands. Glynnis followed suit, happy to shed his human form. Once they were well away from Colwygshire, he became visible again. He saw no reason for such stealth in his own kingdom and had only been invisible to prevent the people below from connecting him to his human form. He still felt the need to keep his magic a secret, though that myth had long since been dispelled by Harpur Diggins—at least in Epoh.

Karrys, too, was happy to fly as a dragon again. She was spending far too much time as a human and she knew the horrific toll it would take if she kept it up for long. She took advantage of the hours-long flight to the Fae Lands by swooping and circling and doing barrel rolls, relishing the sense of freedom being in the air invoked.

As they drew close to the border of the Fae Lands, Karrys spied a group of deer in a clearing and she realized how hungry she was. "Do you mind?" she asked Glynnis, who had also spotted the easy prey.

"Go ahead," he said. "I could use a snack myself."

Minutes later, the dragons had two screaming deer in their talons and were flying off to a nearby cliff to land and devour them. With their bellies full, Karrys and Glynnis moved to the edge of the cliff to survey the home of the Fae from their vantage point high above. It didn't take long for them to spot what they were looking for. To the west, near a swamp, Elder Dhonna and Röggenar were surrounded by a group of Faefolk. Directly below them Davynn was moving through the forest more or less toward the swamp. He was flanked by several Fae, but either he was unaware of them, or they were taking him to where the elf and the dwarf were being held.

"You go and help Davynn," Karrys said. "I'll go and save Elder Dhonna and Röggenar."

"Are you giving me orders in my own kingdom?" Glynnis asked.

"I'm merely making a suggestion." Karrys said. "How would you prefer to handle the situation?"

"I will go and free the elf and the dwarf," Glynnis said for no other reason than to be contrary. "You deal with the knight."

Karrys, still invisible, was glad that Glynnis couldn't see her sly smile. Had she suggested that she help Davynn, Glynnis would have insisted on the opposite. Her ruse had worked beautifully, and now she was free to speak with Davynn alone. At the same time, she was worried about what he might do to Elder Dhonna and Röggenar. "They were just here to help," she said. "Please don't punish them for coming into the Fae Lands."

"You're talking about the elf and the dwarf, I assume." Glynnis said. "I care not for the affairs of the lesser races and what goes on between them. Unless they break the peace, I have no issue with them moving about as they wish. I will caution the Fae and see the elf and the dwarf safely out of the Fae Lands. But what of this Fae spirit you said you were so concerned about? I still do not sense the thing."

Neither could Karrys. And that was worrisome. "She may have already taken on a body," Karry said.

"How long has this Willow been loose here?" Glynnis was beginning to feel suspicious again.

"The better question," Karrys began, "is: How long was she contained?"

Glynnis waited quietly for Karrys to continue while he kept an eye on the Fae surrounding Elder Dhonna and Röggenar. He could see that they were taunting the elf and the dwarf. It was only a matter of time before they went too far.

Karrys finally decided on the truth once again. Her only problem was how to tell it and not have Glynnis figure out that Harpur Diggins was the one really speaking to him. There was no good reason that Karrys Evergreen should know Willow's history. Hoping that something would come to her, Karrys told the story of the war between the elves and the Fae and how Willow had been found by Harpur Diggins outside his lair, fatally wounded by the elves. To end her suffering, she had begged Harpur to allow her spirit to be absorbed into a large amber stone that was embedded into the side of an old iron chalice. Harpur had done what she asked, then had hidden the chalice in the Fae Lands, hoping one day to free Willow if ever her desire for revenge subsided. To Harpur's knowledge, it had not.

"If Willow has taken on a new body and still seeks revenge on the elves..."

"She might try to rally the Fae to her cause." Glynnis finished for her. He was not happy to learn about this. "How is it you know about all of this?"

Karrys felt a measure of panic rise inside her. Glynnis might be something of a bully, but he wasn't stupid. "I... I..." Karrys was about to admit that Harpur's soul shared her body with her own when a thought occurred to her. "I have read Harpur's life book." It wasn't a lie.

Glynnis wasn't expecting that. "I see," he said. "I'm not going to ask how you happened to come across Harpur Diggins' life book. I suspect you have a story ready for that too. But do tell me how it is that you knew Willow had escaped the chalice."

Karrys just had to roll with modified versions of the truth and hope that Glynnis didn't think too deeply about it all. At least not until she was well away from Epoh and beyond his reach. She didn't want to answer any unasked questions, though—and there were a few that she was sure were on the horizon—so an outright lie had to make its appearance. "I dreamt it," she blurted out in desperation.

Glynnis raised his head and looked at the seemingly empty space next to him. "I would like to see you now."

"What if the Fae or the others notice me?" Karrys stalled.

"They are clearly focused on their own problems," Glynnis said. "I have granted you more leeway than you probably deserve, Karrys Evergreen. Face me like the fierce and ruthless dragon you are rumored to be."

This stirred enough animosity in Karrys and Harpur to enable Karrys to affect a stern and stoic expression. She became visible and looked Glynnis directly in the eye. Something in her eyes struck a measure of fear in him and he stepped away from her.

"I don't believe you dreamt that Willow had escaped, but I will leave that alone for now. I have two more questions for you before we rescue the knight, the elf and the dwarf."

"Ask what you will," Karry said.

"Where have you been these past years? Why did you abandon Epoh?"

Again, a mostly truthful answer seemed the best course of to follow. "I did not intend on abandoning Epoh. I was bored and went off to explore another world where I was imprisoned and experimented on. I was finally able to escape and I returned to Thraeh. I didn't know what to expect, so I have not yet revealed myself to our kind. What else do you want to know?"

Glynnis decided this was plausible enough. "Are you here to challenge me for the kingdom?"

Karrys laughed with relief at that. "I am not," she said sincerely.

"Very well," Glynnis said. "I think it is time to go down there and sort this mess out."

Karrys agreed. She needed to get away from Glynnis before things got out of control. "I will send Davynn on his way. Then I will seek out Willow and find a way to keep her from doing anything rash."

"I suggest you kill her," Glynnis said.

"If it comes to it, I will do what I must," Karrys assured the dragon lord.

"Then I want you out of my kingdom." Glynnis punctuated this statement with a coppery plume of smoke from his nostrils.

"I will leave as soon as I possibly can," Karrys said.

She didn't wait for Glynnis to say anything else. She launched herself off the cliff and circled down to land in a clearing that was directly in Davynn's path.

The knight was moving cautiously through the trees. The deeper he went into the Fae Lands, the more Faefolk gathered to follow him. Strangely, none of them attempted to challenge his progress, but Davynn interpreted this to mean that the Fae had already encountered Elder Dhonna and Röggenar and were watching him, herding him if truth be told, to wherever the elf and the dwarf were located. In a way, this made Davynn's job easier. The Fae Lands were not particularly vast, but they were vast enough. It could take days to find anyone in the thick woods. If the Fae were indeed covertly guiding Davynn, so be it. He would cross his bridges as he reached them.

Just before he arrived in the clearing, Davynn sensed the Fae that had been flanking him retreat and fade back into the depths of the forest. He paused to listen, but he heard nothing at first. He was just about to move forward again when the canopy above him was disturbed by a sudden gust of wind. He looked up to see Karrys Evergreen swooping down to land in the clearing. Relieved to see her and excited for news of how things had gone on Mysturna, he ran forward and stopped again at the edge of the clearing to wait until the enormous dragon had landed.

"Morgaine!" Davynn called as he entered the clearing. "I'm so glad to see you! When did you get back? Is Anayah with you?"

Karrys winced inwardly as she transformed into Morgaine and chose not to correct Davynn's mistake in calling her by the wrong name when she first landed. She understood the confusion her friends were experiencing under the circumstances. Instead, she smiled at Davynn and reached out to shake his hand. "I'm glad I found you. Davynn, we need to talk."

Instantly, the knight's good cheer turned to dread. "What happened? Is Anayah alright?"

Morgaine led Davynn to a fallen log and bade him to sit. She recounted the events on Mysturna as gently as she could, leaving nothing out. When she was done, she braced herself for his reaction, expecting an even greater anger and hatred than Sok had displayed. It didn't come. Davynn lowered his head and covered his eyes with his hand. He sat like that for what felt like ages to the anxious dragon-wizardess, whose grief was no less than his. Suddenly, Davynn did something that surprised and touched Morgaine deeply; he took her by the hand and thanked her. Unsure how to respond, Morgaine simply squeezed Davynn's hand and held it until he was ready to speak again.

"I always knew that one day she would go back there and try to fix things," he said at last. "She talked about Analeetah a lot and she blamed herself for what became of her beloved aunt. She often told me that she had to find a way to help her, to set things right again. Not long ago, she was talking about it again and she said the strangest thing. I'd forgotten about it, but now I wonder if she knew she was going to go back and that she wasn't coming home."

"What did she say?" Morgaine prompted.

"She said that she was sad that she wouldn't see Alexa and the boys grow up. I asked her what she was talking about, but she told me it was nothing and not to worry." Davynn wiped his eyes and looked at Morgaine. "I should have worried."

"I don't think there was anything you could have done," Morgaine said. "Anayah was about as stubborn as…"

"As Harpur?" Davynn suggested.

That made Morgaine smile. "I was going to say Sok, but you're probably right."

"How is Sok?"

Morgaine was unprepared for Davynn's compassion. "He hates me… I mean Harpur. I think they all do right now."

"That will pass," Davynn said, after he sorted out who he was actually talking to. Then fell silent for a while. "I came out here to find Elder Dhonna and Röggenar. It seems they have taken it upon themselves to find and capture Willow's spirit."

"I'm aware," Morgaine said. "Glynnis is saving them from the Fae as we speak. I can't sense Willow anywhere near here, though. I fear she may have taken a new body and is on her way to exact revenge on the elves."

"Can you handle it?" Davynn said. "I'm not in the mood for Fae hunting at the moment." Then he realized what Morgaine had said. "What do you mean Glynnis is saving them from the Fae?"

"Not to worry. Glynnis knows I am here. I have his permission to get you back to Colwygshire and to find Willow before she causes a war with the elves. But as soon as I do get her back under control, I must leave Epoh." Morgaine stood up and walked to the center of the clearing. "Would you like to fly back to the castle?"

"Not particularly," Davynn admitted. Hiro's hover gilly was one thing, but being clutched in a dragon's talon hundreds of feet above the ground was on par with Bounding. "Can you zap me back? I would like to see my children. We're going to need each other."

Morgaine took a moment to study the knight. She could see the grief in his eyes. His sorrow and pain were almost unbearable to witness. "I loved her too, you know? And I will miss her for the rest of my life."

"Thank you, Harpur," Davynn said through quivering lips. "I know you did. Anayah knew it too, even if she didn't always show it."

"Are you ready, then?" Morgaine asked, wanting to end this before she, too, broke down and cried.

"No," Davynn replied. "Honestly, there's a part of me that would rather not face Alexa, Brodie and Caleb. I'm not entirely sure I am brave enough to do that."

"You are," Morgaine said. "I know you are."

Davynn swallowed and nodded at the dragon-wizardess. "Will I see you again?"

"I'm not very welcome at the castle right now," Morgaine said.

"What about the scale? Will Bon and Hiro still try to use it to help you?"

"Bon will, I'm sure," Morgaine answered. "I can't say what Hiro will do. I am hopeful that his curiosity will get the better of him and he'll do it for the sake of learning, if not for me."

"Hiro's a good… Krist," Davynn said, suddenly realizing that Harpur being stuck in Morgaine's body was not, strictly speaking, the weirdest thing in his world.

"Go home to your children, Davynn. I left Anayah's ashes in the vault in Arthur's rooms. I thought you may want to have them. I will check in with Bon after I find Willow. Please let him know privately that I still want him to help if he can."

"I will. Good-bye, Harpur."

"Good-bye, Davynn. I'm so sorry."

Morgaine did not give Davynn time to say any more. She raised her hands and zapped him back to the castle to face the scariest thing the brave knight would ever have to deal with. Then she let the tears flow.

Bon stood by the fireplace in Arthur's chambers and took in the scene. Morose was the word he settled on to describe it. Arthur was seated on one of the sofas with his arm around Meg's shoulders. The princess' healing powers were working on everything but her grief. Hart sat facing them on the other sofa, head back, eyes closed. Hiro stood by the balcony doors, hands clasped behind his back. And Sok sat on the big wing chair propping his chin up with one hand while the fingers of his other hand drummed a rhythmic tattoo on the fabric of the chair's arm. He knew that Harpur was not entirely to blame, but his anger toward the dragon would not abate. Grief was not, as he had witnessed many times, conducive to common sense and reasoning. He would just have to feel the feelings and wait for the pain and anger to transmute into something better.

Bon approached Hiro and stood next to him. "May I have the scale?" he asked softly so the others could not hear him.

Hiro looked up at the android with a blank expression as if he hadn't understood the question. A few seconds passed as the Krist's mind switched gears. "Yes, of course," Hiro said. "Shall we go to the laboratory?"

Bon made his way over to the door and opened it to allow Hiro to float through on his little chariot. Two guards, posted outside as always, jumped to their feet in surprise. They hadn't realized that Arthur and the others had returned. Thankful that it was Bon and Hiro exiting the chambers and not Davynn, they stepped aside and stood at attention as if the android might not have noticed them slacking off.

"Where are you two going?" Sok asked before Bon could close the door.

"To the laboratory," Bon answered truthfully. Then he did close the door so as not to invite further inquiry.

"Do you think they are going to work on the scale?" Hart asked.

Sok looked at the young prince. This hadn't occurred to him. He stood up and started toward the door. "If they are, I'm going to put a stop to it!"

"Let them do what they need to do," Arthur said.

"What?" Sok stopped and glared at Arthur. "You want them to help Harpur after all he's done?"

"The faster they figure out how to free Harpur from Karrys, the faster we get him out of Epoh." Arthur felt Meg stir and lifted his arm so she could sit up.

"You don't mean that!" Meg said to her father. "You don't really want to get rid of Harpur, do you?"

"I think it would be best if he wasn't around," Arthur said. "We don't need him."

"I agree!" Sok said. "But I'm not inclined to help them either."

"So don't!" Arthur said. "Just please don't interfere. When Morgaine gets back, I'm going to tell her that she can't stay in the castle."

"Father, we have to help Harpur," Meg said. "We've all played a part is what's happened." She hung her head, ashamed of what she had done in Danaleedh. Not even the fact that her blunder had ended Analeetah's reign of terror over the witches would ever console her.

"At least you tried to do something!" Sok shouted. "We all know that there are no absolutes in magic, but Harpur didn't even try to help Anayah!"

Hart stood up and faced the angry elf. "You're right, Uncle Sok, there are no absolutes in magic. But in this case, there was nothing Harpur could have done. And you know as well as anyone that that is true."

Sok shook with the unabashed anger he now felt toward the young prince. It galled him to be corrected by the youth, especially because he knew that Hart was right. But he wasn't ready to forgive Harpur. He tried to stare Hart down, but Hart wouldn't budge. "I'm going to my rooms," Sok finally said, lowering his eyes and walking out.

Hart felt awful. "I'm sorry," he said to Sok's retreating back. But what he was actually sorry about was much bigger than those three short syllables could possibly contain.

Arthur stood up too. He dabbed at his tear-stained shirt where Meg's head had been resting. "We're all sorry, son," he said. "And I suppose we'll all be sorrier before this is over." He embraced Hart, holding his son tightly as much for his own comfort as for Hart's.

"I miss her," Meg said from the sofa.

Arthur released Hart and turned to Meg. "Why don't you two go and get cleaned up. A hot bath and some clean clothes will do us all some good. I'll have supper brought up here tonight. I don't think I could sit in the great hall and see Anayah's empty chair."

The twins nodded. Then, arm in arm, they left Arthur alone.

The one thing that Arthur disliked about his chambers was that the bathroom was on one side of the sitting room and the bedroom was on the other side. He considered this design flaw a huge bane to his existence. Even after all the years he had spent in the suite, he never failed to forget something in the bedroom that he needed in the bathroom, or, conversely, something in the bathroom that he needed in the bedroom. The item he most often forgot was a towel. For some reason, the towels were stored in a small, free-standing wardrobe in his bedroom and though he had intended to have it moved into the bathroom, where its presence made the most sense, he had never gotten around to it, and so it was that he stepped out of the huge bathtub and had nothing to hand with which to dry himself. Sometimes a robe was conveniently hung on a peg next to the door. But this was not one of those times.

With a sigh, he opened the door and, muttering to himself, began the nude and dripping thirty-pace walk to his bedroom. He'd taken only a few steps when Davynn appeared at the end of the sofa closest to him. This wasn't the first time that one of his friends had zapped into his chambers at just such an inopportune moment. Before Harpur had died, his sudden appearance had been almost a regular occurrence. Anayah, too, had materialized after a bath a few times. But this was Davynn's first experience with the disorganized ablutions of his king.

"Ahk!" Davynn croaked.

"Ahk!" Arthur bleated.

Arthur covered himself as best he could and sprinted the rest of the way to his bedroom. He grabbed a towel and dried the worst of the wetness off himself. Snatching a robe from the floor, he put it on and tied it tightly while he glared at the towel cabinet.

"Davynn?" he called from his room.

"Yes, Arthur?" Davynn called back, but did not come closer to the door.

"I need your help."

A few beats of silence ensued. "With what?"

"Just get in here."

Davynn poked his head around the corner and peeked into the room. Relieved to find Arthur in a relatively decent state, he entered. "What?"

"Help me move this cabinet into the bathroom," Arthur said as he positioned himself on one side and prepare to start pushing it toward the door. It didn't move.

"Those things weigh a ton," Davynn said. "We have one just like it in our room. Anayah's been nagging me to move it for…"

At the mention of Anayah's name, Arthur was jolted back to reality. He came out from beside the wardrobe and saw the fresh pain in Davynn's red-rimmed eyes. "I'm so sorry, Davynn. I wasn't thinking."

Davynn had to look away. "It's okay," he said softly.

Arthur led the knight out of his bed chamber to the sofas in the sitting room. Davynn sat heavily down while Arthur poured them both a cup of ale. Davynn took his, but did not drink.

"You spoke to Morgaine?"

"I did." Davynn stared at the floor.

"She wouldn't be stopped," Arthur said, and instantly regretted it.

"I know," Davynn said, choking back a sob. "I don't know how I'm going to live without her, Arthur. How did you get through it when Alex died?"

"I don't know if you ever get through it," Arthur said. "There are still times when I wake up and don't quite understand why she's not there. Then I lose her all over again."

Davynn nodded. "I haven't told the children yet."

Arthur remembered having to tell Meg and Hart that their mother was dead. It had been gut-wrenching. "Would you like me to be with you when you do?"

"Thank you," Davynn said, "but I think I have to do this alone."

Arhtur took a sip of his ale. "I'm here for you, Davynn. Anything you need or want, just ask."

"I want my wife back!" Davynn shouted. Then he wiped his eyes with the heel of his hand and looked up at his friend. "I'm sorry."

"Don't be," Arthur said. "You have every right to be angry. If Harpur had only…"

"Don't, Arthur. Please don't do that. It wasn't Harpur's fault."

"She might not be dead if it wasn't for what Harpur put into motion with Bloomregaard," Arthur said. A wave of angry blame washed over him again.

"I really want to blame someone too," Davynn said, "but Harpur doesn't deserve all of it. I bear as much blame as anyone. I could have gone with you, but I was too afraid to Bound." He stopped speaking as the realization that Meg and Hart were able to transform into dragons hit him. "Harpur's teeth and tail, Arthur! How are you coping with Meg and Hart becoming dragons?"

"Another thing we have to thank Harpur for!" Arthur spat. "You'd think that after living for as long as he has, he'd have figured out not to meddle with stuff like that. But no! The great Harpur Diggins had to go and turn my kids into flying, fire-breathing lizards." Davynn's eyes widened at the vehemence in Arthur's voice. "What happens when they get married and have kids of their own? Are my grandchildren going to be born with wings and tails? What's going to happen if Glynnis finds out? Are they even going to be able to stay in Epoh? Or will he banish them from the kingdom? I can't wait for Bon to do whatever it is he's going to do with Harpur's scale so that we can be done with him for good. I'm damned sure Glynnis isn't going to let Harpur hang around."

Davynn hadn't thought of that. He had assumed that Harpur would somehow become the dragon lord of Epoh again and they would all live happily ever after, so to speak. Clearly, that was no longer an option. At least not for all of them. Not now.

Overwhelmed and frightened for what the future might hold, Davynn placed his ale on the table and stood up. He needed to see his children. "I'm so sorry about the twins, Arthur. I'm sure they will be okay, though. They are smart and they are good people." He had to take a deep breath before he could go on. "Morgaine put Anayah's ashes in your vault. Is it okay to leave them there until I make arrangements for her funeral?"

Like Morgaine had been in the Fae Lands, Arthur was amazed by Davynn's composure and compassion. "Of course," he said. "Just let me know when you want them."

After Davynn left, Arthur got properly dressed and then sent one of the guards down to ask that supper for himself and the twins be brought up to his rooms. He also requested a maintenance man.

"A maintenance man, sire?" the first guard asked.

"You know, whoever does maintenance around the castle. Send him up."

The first guard looked at the second guard questioningly. The second guard shook his head and shrugged his shoulders.

"Is there someone in the castle who does repairs and that sort of thing?" Arthur asked.

"I'm sure there is, sire," the first guard said.

"Don't you know who that is?" Arthur asked.

"It's your castle, sire, don't you know?" the second guard volleyed back.

Arthur rolled his eyes. "Never mind. I'll get Sok to look into it."

"Very well, sire."

"As you wish, sire."

Arthur closed the door.

Sok did not, as he had claimed, go to his rooms. He had intended to, but as he reached the third floor where his rooms were located, he remembered Berryl and decided to go and make sure the scoundrel was still behind bars. On the way, he stopped at Skull's Keep and though it was quite busy already, Jack stopped what he was doing the instant he saw the elf enter to serve Sok personally.

"Just one of your pies and two ales," Sok said to the publican before Jack had a chance to greet him properly.

"Two ales?" Jack parroted. "Are you expecting someone to join you?"

"I'll be taking them with me," Sok said.

Jack frowned at this. "And where would you be taking them?" To which Sok responded with a look that all but withered Jacks resolve. "It's just that we are not in the habit of letting our dishes wander about with our customers."

"I'll bring them back," Sok snapped.

Jack took note of the strain in Sok's expression. "Of course! I meant no offence. But you do look a little… tired. Wouldn't you rather sit in here and relax while you eat your pie and drink your ale? There's a nice table in the back corner where you won't be disturbed."

Sok felt bad. Jack had no way of knowing what had happened and the elf knew it was unfair to take his frustration out on the publican like that. Jack was doing his job. "I apologize, Jack," Sok said as kindly as his grim spirits would allow. "It's been a dreadful week and I am a bit over tired. I am taking the pie and ale to the north gate, and I promise I will return your dishes when I'm done."

The north gate? Jack was certain that the food and drink were meant for Berryl. "If you're taking this to Berryl, I must tell you that, on Sir Davynn's orders, the prisoner has been released."

"What do you mean he's been released?" Sok was stunned.

"I saw two guards escorting Berryl toward the castle," Jack said. "I've been told I no longer need to bring his meals to the north gate."

"I'm going to kill Davynn!" Sok said. "I explicitly said that Berryl was to be kept in the cell until I got back."

"Well, now you'll have to wait until Sir Davynn gets back."

"What do you mean?" Sok asked.

"Rumor has it that Sir Davynn has gone to the Fae Lands." Jack placed the cups on a tray.

"Why on Thraeh would Davynn go there?" Sok was truly baffled.

"That I cannot tell you for sure, but I heard he went there to help some friends. Not sure what friends a knight like Sir Davynn would have in the Fae Lands, but the really strange thing is that not long ago I overheard a black-haired woman and a tall cloaked man say that they were going to the Fae Lands to do the same thing." Jack placed an apple pie and two forks on the tray with the ale.

"I see," Sok said, recalling Morgaine's tale about Willow's spirit getting loose when Arthur broke the Amber Chalice. "That's very interesting. I don't suppose you know who the black-haired woman and the tall cloaked man are?" He reached over and picked up one of the cups and tipped it to his lips.

Jack smiled. If he could keep Sok talking, he might learn some facts. He might even bring the conversation back around to Berryl and settle that mystery once and for all. "I've seen the woman once or twice, but the man is a stranger to me."

"Can you describe him?" Sok perched on a bar stool and took another drink.

"He was quite tall. Thin. He wore his cloak with the hood up, so I didn't get a good look at his face, but his hands were an odd colour, sort of a bronze colour." Jack watched as the wheels turned in Sok's head.

It couldn't possibly be! Sok thought as he made a mental leap he never imagined ever he'd have to make. *Glynnis? In human form? Wait until Arthur hears this!* "Bronze, you say? Must be visiting from some other kingdom."

"That crossed my mind too," Jack said. "Seems rather odd that three different people suddenly need to travel to the Fae Lands, though. I'll bet Berryl knows what's going on." He threw that in to test the water.

"What makes you say that?" Sok asked, curious as to what the publican was thinking.

"Well, it makes sense, doesn't it? First, Berryl gets himself locked up in the north gate cells. Then Davynn goes to the Fae Lands, I assume to investigate whatever Berryl is charged with. Then these other two show up and they go to the Fae Lands. Berryl is Davynn's friend. I'm not sure how the black-haired woman and the tall man fit in, but I suspect that they are in cahoots with Berryl. They both seemed a little shady to me." Jack watched Sok closely as he spoke, looking for confirmation of his theory, but the elf's expression remained neutral, if still a bit strained.

"Anything is possible," Sok said, then emptied his cup.

"Another?" Jack offered.

"I'll just drink this one," Sok said, taking the second cup of ale from the tray.

"What I can't figure out," Jack continued, "is what it all has to do with Harpur Diggins still being alive…"

Sok spat the mouthful of ale he's just drawn from his cup in a wide spray across the bar. "What did you say?" he coughed.

Jack, having managed to avoid being showered with ale, reached for a cloth and started mopping up Sok's mess. "I overheard a few guards talking about it the day Berryl was taken to the north gate." He saw anger paint itself across the elf's

216

face. "I'm sure they were mistaken! Probably it was the ravings of some drunk they picked up earlier, or something."

Sok didn't bother to respond. He wiped the ale off his chin with his hand and then stormed toward the door. He was about to exit when he stopped, turned back to the bar, grabbed the pie off the tray and then stormed all the way out.

"Don't forget to bring the pan back!" Jack called after Sok as he scratched his head in bewilderment.

"Did Sok just steal a pie?" Helena asked, returning to the bar with an armful of empty dishes. All she saw was the senior advisor to the king running out with a whole pie in his hands.

"Don't let me forget to put it on the castle account," Jack said, not dispelling the accusation.

Publican and bar maid both stood staring at the door until another customer got their attention by asking for his bill. Then it was back to business for Jack. He'd find out sooner or later what was really going on.

Glynnis had arrived at the swamp just as poor Röggenar was about to be dunked head-first into the middle of the stagnant water. The dwarf was hanging by his feet from a rope attached to a tree branch that grew out from the edge of the murky pool. How the Fae had managed to get the rotund little man out there was beyond the Dragon Lord's ability to fathom, but there he was, cursing the Fae in his native Dwarven, most likely so as not to offend the lady elf who was doing much the same thing in the ancient Elven tongue.

Some of the Fae scattered back into the forest upon Glynnis' arrival, but most stayed to see what the dragon wanted. A visit from Glynnis was rare and usually resulted in some reward for some deed the dragon lord requested of them. It didn't occur to them that he might be displeased with the capture and subsequent torment of unwelcome interlopers in their land. While elves were not forbidden to venture into the Fae Lands, they did so at their own peril. As far as the Fae were concerned, when an elf crossed the border, it was an act of aggression, if not war.

Glynnis folded his wings close to his body and stared down at the scene. He scanned the elemental creatures, until he found the one he was looking for, a squat and twisted being with goat-like eyes of yellow-green. Its body was formed from a charred log and its face was a salad of oak and holly leaves. Altogether a hideous example of the Faefolk, and the one that Glynnis assumed had orchestrated Röggenar's current dilemma. For effect, the bronze dragon blew a plume of smoke in the creature's direction and then turned his head to look at the dwarf. Elder Dhonna and Röggenar stopped swearing and wondered how much more trouble they were in.

"New tree ornament?" Glynnis hissed at the Fae.

"We are perfectly within our rights," the Fae creature responded. "They are trespassing in Fae territory."

"So they are," Glynnis said.

He swung his massive head toward Röggenar, opening his jaws as he drew near. The Faefolk all started whooping and dancing about in delight. They had never seen a dwarf being eaten by a dragon before—none of them had even seen a dwarf before—and were looking forward to an even more gruesome end to the intruder than they had planned.

As Glynnis' lethal mouth seemed about to clamp shut around the struggling dwarf, Elder Dhonna shook off her captors and picked up a hand-sized stone from the ground. She hurled it at Glynnis, shouting, "Don't you dare!"

The stone bounced harmlessly off the scales on Glynnis' neck and fell with a plop into the swamp. Glynnis paused and looked back at the elf, from whom the Fae were all backing away. He cocked his head and, instead of roasting her on the spot, chuckled derisively. "Ouch." Then he opened his mouth again and snapped the rope just above Röggenar's feet. As he set the terrified dwarf down on the ground next to Elder Dhonna, the Fae all groaned in abject disappointment.

Elder Dhonna stooped to untie Röggenar as quickly as she could, all the while avoiding Glynnis' eyes. She helped the dwarf to his feet and the two stood holding on to each other, not sure if they should be afraid or relieved.

"I suggest that the two of you make haste back to your own territories. And you can thank Morgaine Fayle next time you see her for your safe passage out of the Fae Lands. Don't let me catch either of you back here again, though. Next time I won't stop the Fae from having their fun with you." For added emphasis, Glynnis engulfed them in a thick, bronze puff of smoke.

While Röggenar was quite ready to comply, Elder Dhonna felt compelled to justify her actions. "We only came here to…"

"I know why you came here," Glynnis said, cutting the elf off. "The matter, which you should have reported to me, is being dealt with. Now, go."

They didn't hesitate this time. Elder Dhonna and Röggenar scurried away from the swamp, heading in a generally north-east direction.

"I told you this was a bad idea," Elder Dhonna chided her friend.

"Yes, you did," Röggenar said. "And now I know why. I've had my fill of Fae forever."

"But why did Glynnis let us go?" Elder Dhonna wondered aloud. "And how does he know about Willow?"

"He did say we had Morgaine to thank for his mercy," Röggenar said. "She must have told him."

"That would never happen!" Elder Dhonna said. "Morgaine would not allow her presence in Epoh to be known to Glynnis. He'd kill her!"

"I wouldn't have thought so either," the dwarf replied, "but what else could he have meant?"

Elder Dhonna had no answer to that. They walked on as quicky as Röggenar's short legs would allow. Had they been traveling in a slightly more easterly direction, they might have met Morgaine and Davynn in the clearing. As it was, they had missed the knight and the dragon-wizardess, passing several hundred yards to the north.

As soon as the elf and the dwarf were safely on their way and out of earshot, Glynnis turned back to the Fae creature, who was fuming mad, but containing it rather admirably. "Sorry to ruin your sport," Glynnis said. "Now, tell me, has anything else unexpected happened in your lands recently?"

The angry Fae creature glared at the dragon for a few beats, wondering how much it should say. Then the dragon fire glowing in Glynnis' chest made up its mind for it. "A Fae spirit appeared not long ago. It took on a body from a willow sapling that grew on the riverbank. We tried to warn it not to do that, but it only spoke the old tongue and did not understand us any better than we understood it. It seemed agitated and confused. The last time we saw it, it was moving toward elven territory." The creature pointed with its viny hands in roughly the same direction that Elder Dhonna and Röggenar had gone.

"Why didn't you stop it?" Glynnis asked, staring in the direction the Fae creature had indicated.

"None of our affair," the Fae said. "If it wants to stir up trouble with the elves, it can do it on its own."

Glynnis shot a parting plume of smoke at the elemental and launched into the sky. The Fae watched in disappointment as their dragon lord flew away. The one with the charred log for a body decided that surviving an encounter with Glynnis such as this was reason for celebration and announced that they should all prepare for a gathering later that night. Somewhat appeased, the others all started cheering and dispersed into the forest to do just that.

Glynnis spotted Morgaine and Davynn in the clearing, but waited until she had zapped Davynn back to the castle. "Tears?" Glynnis sneered as he set down and folded his wings. He wanted to say something about Morgaine using her magic in front of a human, but decided that she must have also wiped his memory and let it go. She had disrupted his kingdom enough, and he didn't need to let himself think that the lesser races were aware of dragons' true magical abilities.

"Are Elder Dhonna and Röggenar okay?" Morgaine said, wiping the offensive emanations from her cheeks.

"They are on their way back to where they belong," Glynnis said. "As is your stray Fae spirit. Though it's not a spirit any longer."

Morgaine took a deep breath and sighed heavily. "She has taken a body?"

"A willow sapling, if the Fae are to be believed," Glynnis confirmed. "It speaks only the old tongue, by the way. The Fae couldn't understand it, nor could it understand them. It cannot be allowed to take its revenge on the elves."

"I will take care of her," Morgaine said sadly.

"See that you do," Glynnis said. "I have given you all the latitude that I intend to give you. Find it, kill it and then leave my kingdom. Quickly."

Morgaine nodded, but said nothing. She waited for Glynnis to fly away again before she transformed into her dragon form and become invisible. She was not looking forward to what she had to do.

Sok burst into Arthur's chambers just as Arthur and the twins were about to sit down to dinner. Only three plates had been delivered, but that didn't stop Sok from pulling up a chair and helping himself to the food on the others' plates. His excitement was palpable and contributed to their forgiveness for his intrusion on their family repast. The pie didn't hurt either.

"Well?" Arthur finally said. "Are you going to tell us what's got you so riled up? Or are you going to make us guess?"

"You wouldn't be able to guess in a thousand turns of the sun," Sok said. Then he popped a piece of buttered bread into his mouth, thus stalling any further elucidation. Arthur and the twins continued to eat while they waited for him to explain. Finally, the elf swallowed the bread and opened his mouth to speak. Then he shut it again and jumped up to pour himself a cup of ale.

Meg shrugged. She didn't have much of an appetite, so she pushed her food around her plate with her fork and tried not to think about Anayah. Sok took this as a sign that grazing from her plate was probably his best bet, so he relieved her of her fork and stabbed a piece of meat with it. "You don't want this, do you?" Sok asked, holding the laden fork a few inches from his mouth.

"Take it," Meg said. She pushed her plate over to Sok and watched him add a chunk of carrot to the meat before shoveling it all into his mouth.

Arthur frowned at the elf. "I could have sent down for another plate," he said.

"No need," Sok replied. "This is enough for me."

Arthur's mouth dropped open. He was about to chastise Sok for his insolence, but Meg put a hand on her father's arm and said, "It's okay. I'm not that hungry."

Arthur sighed. "So, what wouldn't we guess in a thousand turns of the sun?"

"Guess where Davynn is," Sok said, sopping some gravy up with a piece of bread.

"I thought we wouldn't be able to guess," Hart said.

"It's something else you wouldn't be able to guess," Sok said. "I'm working up to that."

"Davynn is in his rooms telling his children that their mother is dead," Arthur said.

"No, he's not," Sok countered in a know-it-all sing-song voice.

"Yes, he is," Arthur insisted. "He left here a short while ago to do just that."

Sok raised a questioning eyebrow. "Are you sure?"

"Yes, I am sure," Arthur said.

Sok wondered if his intel was flawed. He chewed on his bread while he considered everything he'd learned from Jack at Skull's Keep. "I suppose it's possible," he finally conceded. "Guess where he was then."

"He was in the Fae Lands, looking for Elder Dhonna and Röggenar, who were there looking for Willow, hoping to trap her for Harpur," Arthur said. "Morgaine is there now dealing with it. She zapped Davynn back here a while ago." He took a good deal of pleasure in watching Sok's news bubble burst.

"Hmm… I should have thought of that," Sok said. "But there's more!"

"Do tell," Meg said, not really interested, but wanting to hurry Sok along.

"It seems that Glynnis has been snooping around Colwygshire in his human form." Sok shoved a forkful of meat into his mouth and grinned at the surprised looks on his dinner companions' faces.

"Glynnis?" Arthur repeated, as he so often did. "Here? In human form?"

"That's right!" Sok said. "And he and Morgaine went to the Fae Lands together."

"Davynn didn't say anything about Glynnis being there," Arthur said. He didn't believe Sok's story.

"That's impossible!" Hart said. "If Glynnis knew that Morgaine was here, he'd hardly go flying around the kingdom with her."

"He'd probably fry her on the spot," Meg added, her interest beginning to pique.

"Dragons can't burn other dragons," Hart corrected his sister. "They are impervious to each other's fire, just like they're impervious to… regular fire."

"You know what I mean," Meg said, not wanting to admit she was wrong.

Arthur's mind fast-forwarded. "If Glynnis knows Morgaine is here, he knows that Karrys is here. And if he knows Karrys is here, he has information that he could use against her. We have to warn her!" Arthur stood up, panic written all over his face.

"If Glynnis knows, and they went to the Fae Lands together, then Morgaine knows he knows, ergo Karrys knows," Sok said. "What do we need to warn her about?"

"Ergo?" Arthur stared at the elf.

"It means therefore," Sok said as if addressing a child.

"I know what it means," Arthur said. "What about Harpur?"

222

"Karrys, Morgaine, Harpur," Sok said, drawing a circle in the air with his finger, "all the same. Whatever one knows, they all know."

Arthur sat down again. "Okay. Let me get this straight. Elder Dhonna and Röggenar went to the Fae Lands to look for Willow. Davynn went after them. Morgaine and Glynnis went after the three of them. Morgaine sent Davynn back here." He held up a finger for each fact he recited. "Then what? Where are Elder Dhonna and Röggenar now? And how do you know that Glynnis was in the city in human form?"

"I don't know where Elder Dhonna and Röggenar are," Sok admitted. "As for Glynnis being in the city, Jack told me."

"Jack from Skull's Keep?" Hart asked.

"The very same" Sok said.

"How does Jack know it was Glynnis? No one's ever seen Glynnis in human form." Arthur was confused.

"He doesn't," Sok said. "I figured it out." He recounted what Jack had told him in the pub. "It makes sense."

"It really doesn't," Meg said. "I'm going to bed. I have a headache."

"Are you okay?" Arthur asked, concerned for his daughter.

"She just said she has a headache," Sok said, scowling at Arthur. Then he turned to Meg. "I can heal you if you like."

Meg was grateful for the offer. Her own healing powers were working wonders, but a little extra elf healing couldn't hurt. She left the table to go and sit on a sofa so she could be comfortable while Sok applied his ministrations. He had often used his healing powers to ease the many cuts and bruises she got while training and it always made her feel light and cheerful all over. She could use some lightness and cheer just then. Leaning back and closing her eyes, Meg waited for the soothing elven energy to relieve the pain in her brow.

Arthur took the opportunity to cut into the pie Sok had brought with him. "Is this one of Emmaline's?" he asked.

"Yes," Sok said, looking over his shoulder. "And just so you know, it will very likely appear as a charge on the castle account."

"I thought we agreed there would be no castle account at Skull's Keep," Arthur said, more because he felt he should than because he actually disapproved. Sok often abused the account, but... Well, there was pie on the table!

"You agreed," Sok said. "I just told you what you wanted to hear."

Hart shook his head and smiled. He held out his plate so Arthur could serve him a piece of pie. "I think Sok should wear the crown."

"Sok should not wear the crown," Sok said. "It's much easier to rule the kingdom when no one knows you're ruling it. That way, if you mess up, everyone blames the guy with the crown on his head."

Arthur rolled his eyes, but inwardly he had to admit that Sok was not all that far off the mark. "You were about to tell us how you figured out that Glynnis was here."

Before Sok could amaze them all with his brilliant powers of deduction, Davynn entered the room. His eyes and nose were red from crying. He stood just inside the door and sniffled. "I can't do this," he said hoarsely.

Arthur abandoned his pie and went to comfort the grieving knight. He did not offer platitudes; the knight didn't need them. "Come and sit. I'll get you some ale."

Davynn sat on the sofa across from Meg and watched the glowing blue energy from Sok's hands surround the princess' head. A fresh wave of tears flowed down his cheeks. "Anayah used to do that for me."

Meg opened her eyes, awash with guilt for being cared for while Davynn suffered so. "I'm okay now," she said, though she really wasn't. "Uncle Sok, maybe you can help Uncle Davynn."

Sok removed his hands and went to tend to the knight. But Davynn waved him away. He couldn't bear to receive healing just then. He did take the cup of ale from Arthur and he downed it all in three large gulps. Then he held the empty cup out for Arthur to refill.

It's going to be rough night, Arthur thought as he refilled the cup. He wished he had some of Hiro's sleeping draught to put in it. Knocking Davynn out seemed much more preferable to having to babysit him through a night of drunken anguish.

Anticipating what lay ahead for their king, Sok, Meg and Hart all made excuses to leave. Arthur kissed his daughter on the cheek and gave his son a hug. He wished them good night and sent them on their way. But he grabbed Sok by the arm as he headed for the door. "Oh, no! You're staying right here, my friend."

Sok sighed in resignation. At least there was pie!

Chapter Twelve

Killing the Fae was no easy task. Their bodies could be destroyed readily enough; that was not the issue. The Fae only took bodies so that they could experience the physical realm. They liked to dance and sing and feel the world in which they lived, but they understood, unlike most sentient beings, that the bodies they occupied were just shells designed for that purpose and nothing more. They didn't care much about how they looked, only how their bodies functioned. Unfortunately, the consciousness that the magic their essence was comprised of was limited. Magic was meant to be wielded by a greater consciousness and when it went astray, as it sometimes did, it sought to find a means by which it could experience itself, so to speak. Thus, Fae magic tended to be undisciplined. If there was anything to be thankful for, it was the fact that the Fae did not wield their magic indiscriminately, for every time they did, their essence was diminished. If they used too much of it, they died out, as did their magic. It was not a renewable resource as it was in a witch or a wizard. Perhaps this was because the stray magic was often the result of a spell gone wrong, misaimed or, possibly loosed through illness.

The Fae was a cunning race, but it was also quite a gullible one, collectively. Their love of gold was often their undoing. They liked to collect it because it made their magic stronger, otherwise they did not have any practical use for it. It did not serve as currency, and they did not craft it in any way. They just liked to have it around to touch and look at and feel the power it raised within them. It was the one thing that they took care of, possibly because it was not that easy to come by. It's not like the Fae were of a mind to mine it and gold was not the kind of thing that was found just lying around in a forest.

When Willow was injured by the elves centuries before, she did not use her magic to heal herself. Her wounds would have used up all of her essence and she would have died anyway. Instead, she suffered the pain of the arrows that pierced her wonderful body and waited for Harpur to find her. She told Harpur about the attack on the Fae by the elves, then, to end her suffering, Harpur drew her magical essence into the Amber Chalice. She was unable to resist the pull of the iron in the cup and went willingly to her prison. One of the gentlest Faefolk Harpur had ever known, Willow's pain and suffering at the hands of the elves nearly put an end to the elves being allowed to stay in Epoh. But once he had found and killed the elves who were responsible for Willow's destruction, he imposed strict rules and permitted the elves to stay and continue to tend to Braydon Wood.

Karrys had no trouble tracking Willow through Braydon Wood once she knew what she was looking for. The Fae's fear and confusion was like a beacon leading the dragon straight to her. After Willow had left the Fae Lands, she made the natural mistake of avoiding the elves' pathways and trails. Instinctively, she perceived them as dangerous, though they would have led her right to the elves. When she was forced to cross an obvious trail, she climbed the trees and moved through the canopy rather than risk exposing herself should anyone be traveling along them.

At first, Karrys planned to try to talk to Willow to explain that centuries had passed and that the warring between her race and the elves had ended. Harpur remembered the old language and communication would not have been a problem. He regretted not having freed her sooner, but he could never bring himself to return her to a world in which her gentle nature would not have been appreciated. So, he had kept her like a prize possession hidden beneath a standing stone that marked the border to the Fae Lands. Karrys and Harpur both knew that Glynnis was expecting them to end her once and for all.

Harpur: If we save her, Glynnis doesn't need to know. He just wants Willow removed from Epoh.

Karrys: What is your fascination with this Fae child?"

Harpur: She is unlike any other Fae creature. Willow is possessed of a magic that is different from the others. She was kind.

Karrys: Yet she is trying to exact revenge upon the elves.

Harpur: We aren't certain that is her intention. But she has been trapped in the Amber chalice for a long time. That must have taken a toll.

Karrys: Then why did you keep her imprisoned for so long?

Harpur: I thought I was protecting her.

Karrys (with disgust): So, what do you intend to do with her?

Harpur: We are going to burn her new body until it is almost destroyed. Then we will trap her essence again.

Karrys: The amber stone is cracked. What are you going to trap her in?

Harpur: I have something else in mind…

Karrys: You can't be serious?"

Karrys rarely attempted to exert control over her body, but she did so now.

Harpur: Relax! We're not going to take anything from the hoard.

He couldn't bring himself to think of the treasures in Glynnis' lair as belonging to Glynnis.

Karrys settled down a little.

Karrys: I don't like this.

Harpur: You don't like anything I do. There is a crystal orb in a small chest buried above the lair. We're going to use that.

Karrys: What if Glynnis knows it's there?

Harpur: That's unlikely.

Karrys: Harpur, don't do this. It's not worth the trouble it could cause. Let's just borrow some gold from the castle treasury and lure Willow to use her magic up with it.

Harpur: No! If we can save her, we will. Once Bon and Hiro have separated us, I will take Willow somewhere safe and make sure she is looked after.

Karrys: Well, we better hurry. Willow is about to meet her first elf.

Below, Karrys could see that Willow perched in a tree above a wide trail through Braydon Wood. Approaching from the west was an elf with scarlet hair and a dwarf.

A hand-drawn schematic covered the table in the center of Hiro's laboratory. The precise lines and measurements diagramed a highly technical machine design that neither Bon, nor Hiro, knew for sure would work once it was built. Bon had been working on it relentlessly for hours, drawing from the vast stores of data in his memory banks, and improvising here and there to compensate for the lack of material available in Epoh. Though complicated, Bon was relatively sure—about 92.6 percent—that he could build it. Whether it would produce the results he needed was yet to be discovered.

He called the machine, simply, and for the benefit of the Krist, a processor. It seemed the most apt and descriptive term for the machine's use, which was to extract the DNA Bon required to clone Harpur from the scale they had retrieved from Mysturna, which was a process. When finished, the processor would resemble a box nine inches square with a single button above a tiny drawer into which Bon would place a small sample cut from Harpur's scale. The actual process would take several hours to complete and, if it worked, would provide enough DNA for Bon to make a half dozen or so new Harpurs. The problem was procuring dragon eggs from which to grow the new Harpurs. Bon had thought to entice Anayah into conjuring them for him, but that was no longer an option. First, he would have to build and test the processor. With a bit of luck, a dozen dragon eggs would appear magically in the laboratory and he wouldn't have to concern himself with that bit.

He needed to talk to Morgaine.

But Morgaine was not available to talk to. Where she had gone and what she was doing was a mystery to the android for the moment, so he discussed the materials list for the processor with Hiro instead.

The Krist perused the list that Bon had handed to him and announced that all but two of the items were right there in the laboratory. He would have to search for the other two, but he thought that the elves might have them, or at least know where they might be found. However, it was getting late and a foray to Braydon Wood would have to wait until the morning.

With that settled, Bon and Hiro combed through the chaotically organized room for the parts and pieces they had on hand and deposited them on the table. Bon decided that he would start with what they had and work through the night. Hiro left him to it, saying that he wished to check in with Arthur and the others to see how they were doing.

"Send for me if you need me," Hiro said as he climbed aboard his hover gilly and drifted toward the door. "I'll be back as soon as I can."

Bon could not think of any reason he would need the Krist for the manufacture of the processor, but one never knew in this world. Still, it was far more likely that the Krist would have need of Bon's assistance. "Try not to need to send for me," Bon said.

Hiro giggled as he floated out into the hallway, leaving Bon to do his thing. He arrived a short time later at Arthur's chamber door and waited for the guards to open it for him. He entered to find Davynn, well into his cups, babbling about how Anayah's death was all his fault and he didn't think he would be able to go on without her. Sok and Arthur were arguing quietly in the corner next to the fireplace.

"A little bump on the head won't hurt him," Sok said. "Much."

"You're not going to bash Davynn in the head with a poker!" Arthur said.

A bit of grappling for sole possession of the fireplace poker ensued. Sok, the stronger of the two, won.

"I'm not going to bash him," Sok said, hefting the poker to test its weight and balance. "I'll only hit him hard enough to knock him out. He'll be fine."

"Ah, Hiro! I'm so glad to see you!" Arthur peeled when he saw the Krist floating toward him. "Tell this nitwit that he can't knock Davynn out with the poker."

Hiro shifted the hover gilly to block Sok from getting closer to Davynn. "Sok," Hiro said as he rifled through his satchel, "you cannot knock Davynn out with a poker." He held up a small brown bottle. "But you can knock him out with this."

"It's kind of small," Sok said. "I think the poker will have more impact."

Arthur rolled his eyes. "I think Hiro means the stuff inside the bottle."

"That's exactly what I mean." Hiro alighted from the hover gilly and handed the bottle to Arthur. "Just a few drops," he said. "Put that thing down, you fool! You're going to hurt someone." This was directed at Sok, who was still convinced that a clout on the head was the better way to go.

"Fool?" Sok was hurt. Then he turned to Arthur. "Nitwit? Where do you come up with these words?"

"How long have I known you?" Arthur asked the elf as he roofied Davynn's ale with the sleeping draught.

"A long time."

"And I've never called you a nitwit before?"

"Not that I recall."

"Huh! I'd have thought I'd used it a lot." He wrapped Davynn's hand around the doctored cup of ale. "Drink up, buddy, it's nighty-night time."

Davynn stared at the cup through bleary eyes, then took a long pull. "I think I'm gonna be sick," he slurred.

"Quick! Hiro, we need a bowl!" Arthur jumped away from the drunken knight in case Hiro wasn't fast enough.

But the little Krist was already on it. Hiro reached into his satchel and pulled out a large, metal bowl, which he passed to Arthur. Arthur had just enough time to switch the cup for the bowl in Davynn's hands before the knight vomited up a sea of consumed ale.

Arthur's face scrunched in disgust as wave after wave of bile-infused ale splashed into the bowl. When the puking finally stopped, Davynn looked up at him for a few seconds, then his head flopped back and he was blessedly unconscious. Arthur dove forward to stop the bowl from sliding off the knight's lap and somehow managed to move it safely to the low table between the sofas.

"Well, that was gross!" Arthur said. Then, not thinking, he lifted the cup in his hand to his lips and drank it.

"No!" Sok shouted, but it was too late. Arthur wobbled and then fell to the floor; he was snoring before he got there.

"I suppose I should put him to bed," Sok said. It was a rhetorical statement. "Nah. They'll both be fine." He started toward the door.

Hiro looked from Davynn to Arthur, then, with a shrug and a giggle, he followed Sok out.

Meg and Hart entered Meg's room after they left their father's chambers and were instantly reminded of the task they had abandoned before going to Mysturna. The hats, and a few other gifts, were still piled up where Meg had left them, except for two. Meg did not remember leaving one next to her mirror or one on her bed. She wasn't too worried about it, assuming that the maid had been in and had moved them.

Hart picked a hat out of the pile and placed it on his head. "What do you think is behind these hats?"

Meg looked at him. "I suspect that someone made one and they just caught on."

Hart took the hat off again and frowned at it. "But I've never seen anybody wearing one. Have you?"

Meg shook her head. "No, I haven't. But I think we have more important things to worry about than a bunch of goofy hats."

Hart tossed the hat back onto the pile and nodded. "I'm going to miss Aunt Anayah. I can't imagine how Davynn and the little ones must be feeling right now."

Meg flopped down on her bed. She picked up the hat and fiddled with it. "I will miss her too. But that's not what I was talking about."

Hart looked at his sister. "There's something else?"

Meg cocked her head to one side. "Yeah, little brother, there is something else. There's the matter of us being dragons."

Hart smiled proudly. "That's so cool."

"How cool do you think it will be when Glynnis finds out?" She smiled sardonically back at the puzzlement that replaced the proud smile on Hart's face.

"I didn't think of that," he said. "That would not be good, would it?"

"That would not be good," Meg confirmed with a slow shake of her head.

"What do you think we should do?" Hart sat down beside his sister.

"Well," Meg said with a sigh, "I think we need to talk to Morgaine. There's so much we don't know about being dragons yet. Plus, she might be able to protect us."

"If she's even still in Epoh, she probably won't ever come back here after the way Sok and Father reacted," Hart pointed out.

"Harpur has to come back so Bon can free him." Meg sounded more hopeful than she felt. "How do you suppose Bon is going to do that?"

Hart put his arm around Meg's shoulder and pulled her close. He kissed her hair. "Let's sleep on it, big sister. We'll figure this out tomorrow."

Meg yawned and tossed the hat onto the pile. "Good idea."

Hart left Meg's room and wandered down the hallway toward his own chambers. Grief had left him exhausted. All he could think about was climbing into his own bed and closing his eyes. A good night's sleep, he hoped, would clear his mind and make room for solutions to evolve. Meg's observations of the potential pitfalls of being dragons had certainly put a damper on things. And now, with Anayah gone and the castle divided, so to speak, the future had begun to take on a bleak outlook.

As the approached the door to his room, one of the guards turned the knob and pushed it open for him. He nodded his thanks and was just about to walk in when he caught a movement out of the corner of his eye. Someone was walking down the hall toward Davynn and Anayah's rooms, which were located around the corner. For a second, he thought it was Anayah, but he shook that notion off, attributing it to being over-tired. Neither of the guards seemed to have noticed and Hart didn't see any point in alerting them; the guards at Davynn's door would handle it. He bid the guards good night and retired to his bed.

Elder Dhonna and Röggenar had been walking along the path through Braydon Wood, on their way back to the elven city north of Colwygshire. The sun was setting and they decided to camp in a clearing near a creek that Elder Dhonna sometimes visited. They had lost their packs to the Fae and, with no provisions, had to improvise. Röggenar wasn't concerned about the chilly spring night; he still had his warm coat and boots. Elder Dhonna, though, was barefoot, as usual, and wearing a thin, mud-stained kaftan. The temperature was already dropping. For the elf, it would be an uncomfortable night.

Röggenar offered her his coat, but Elder Dhonna declined. "I'll be fine. Once we reach the clearing, I will start a fire. That will be enough."

As they walked on, Röggenar's stomach began to growl. It was too early in the season for berries and, without weapons, they had no way to hunt for food. Elder Dhonna scanned the ground around certain trees, looking for fallen nuts that might have survived the winter, but the forest animals had beaten her to them. There weren't many other options. They could chew on Faeroot, a type of thistle, which, if they could gather enough of the young plants, would sustain them through the night. It didn't sound terribly appealing to the dwarf, but Röggenar decided to be a good sport and helped Elder Dhonna pick a few of the plants whenever they spotted them growing next to the trail.

They were almost to the tree where Willow was hiding in wait for them, when an unexpected gust of wind rustled the treetops and they heard a startled shout from above.

"What in Harpur's name was that?" Elder Dhonna asked looking skyward.

Both dwarves and elves have fairly good night vision, but all they could make out against the dark sky was a willow branch seeming to float away.

"That was odd," Röggenar said, scratching his head.

"It was indeed," Elder Dhonna said. "Willows don't grow in this part of the forest. I wonder who shouted."

Röggenar called out, but his call went unanswered. "Maybe it was a bird of some kind," he suggested. He looked back up at the sky, but could no longer see the willow branch that had flown out of the trees.

Elder Dhonna was doubtful. She had never heard a bird call like that before. But she supposed it was possible that a wounded bird or animal could have made the noise. That was not a comforting thought. She didn't treasure meeting an injured creature without having her medicines with her to treat it. She would, of course, administer her healing magic if the animal would let her. Depending on what it was, and how bad its injuries were, getting close enough to help it at all could prove difficult. But there was no injured animal near them that night.

The shout they heard had come from Willow as she was snatched out of the tree by an invisible Karrys Evergreen, and the gust of wind they felt was from Karrys' wings as she closed in on her quarry. Elder Dhonna and Röggenar had no way of knowing this. Neither of them expected Karrys to have free rein to fly about the kingdom and they certainly didn't expect to find any Fae skulking about in the trees waiting to pounce on them from above. They continued walking on high alert, chewing on the Faeroot leaves and wishing for something tastier, if not more substantial. Nothing else odd happened by the time they reached the clearing and they relaxed their vigilance. Elder Dhonna built a fire, Röggenar insisted she take his coat, and they settled in for the remainder of the night.

"What do you think is going to happen to Willow when she's found?" Röggenar asked.

"What I'd like to know is how Glynnis found out about it," Elder Dhonna said.

"It had to have been Morgaine who told him," Röggenar insisted. "Why else would Glynnis have told us we have her to thank?"

"That makes no sense, though," the elf said. "Harpur would not be that reckless."

"Maybe we'll find out when we get back to the castle," Röggenar posited.

"I wish I had my satchel," Elder Dhonna said. "I could have zapped us back there with the dragonfoil ash."

As it was, it would take them another two days to walk back to Colwygshire. With a bit of luck, they would meet some other elves working in the forest who could give them some food.

"I wish I'd never convinced you to go," Röggenar said. "I'm sorry."

Elder Dhonna patted the dwarf on the shoulder. "It's alright. This isn't the stupidest thing I've tried to do for Harpur." She paused. "It's like he's never been gone."

They slept fitfully and woke blanketed by mist in the chilly dawn.

"Stop squirming!" Karrys said to the bundle of willow sticks and twigs that she held in her talons.

Willow did not comply and Karrys was forced to tighten her grip on the frightened Fae child. Before she had been injured and her essence entrapped in the amber stone by Harpur, Willow had been quite beautiful. She had fashioned a body out of fallen willow branches, weaving them together so perfectly that she appeared almost human. Her eyes sparkled green and her smile lit up the forest. Harpur believed that the magic of her essence had come from a human child. How it had ended up in Epoh, he never knew; there were few humans with magic anywhere on all of Thraeh. Unlike most Fae, Willow was kind and caring. She possessed compassion and Harpur had thought that, one day, Willow would become queen of the Fae.

He had kept her in the Amber Chalice for far too long, though. Whenever he had thought to free her and return her to the Fae Lands, something stopped him. Fear for her safety? A selfish desire to keep something precious hidden from the world? Perhaps. But no matter what it was, it was too late now. Willow was of a different age; she would struggle to adapt and to adjust. And Harpur couldn't bring himself to leave her with the Fae that lived in Braydon Wood now. Neither could he destroy her completely.

Karrys flew north-west, passing by Glynnis' lair high up on a mountain side. The cave was dark and devoid of its owner, leaving Karrys to wonder where the dragon lord might be. She couldn't sense him nearby and that bothered her. But it was his kingdom—for the time being—and he had every right to be out and about in it. His absence did give Karrys the opportunity she needed to retrieve the chest with the crystal she intended to trap Willow in from its hiding spot above Glynnis' lair. She zapped it out of the mountain into her hand and flew on toward the mountains bordering the neighbouring kingdom of Rednow. There, upon a ledge enshrouded by clouds, Karrys landed to do the deed she had to do.

Still holding a terrified Willow in her talons, Karrys opened the chest and drew out the crystal orb. She held it, so tiny in her huge dragon hand, and gazed into its depths. Minutes passed while Harpur, inside her, wrestled with his conscience. Then she felt Willow begin to use her magic to try to escape. If the Fae child used too much of it, she would die. Harpur couldn't let that happen. Not yet. He owed Willow a chance to live the life the elves had taken from her so long ago.

"I'm so sorry, little one," Karrys said aloud, in the old tongue. "It's not yet your time to live, or to die. I will make this right for you though. I will find a way to free you again. I promise."

The words were Harpur's, but they touched something in Karrys in a foreign and uncomfortable way. She should have been used to Harpur's compassion by now, but he never seemed to cease surprising her with it. She surrendered to his will and crushed Willow's body beyond repair, forcing her magic to abandon it. As soon as the magic was free, Karrys burned the remains to ashes, leaving nothing organic for it to claim as a new body. Not a leaf or a twig, not a single blade of grass was to be found on the ledge. Willow's essence, sensing the great forest far below, flew toward the cliff edge in a desperate attempt to reach the safety of the trees. But Karrys had warded the area, preventing her from getting away.

Without a body, the magic could not wield itself. It could only seek a new body. Willow's magic flew at the magical barrier that stood between it and the forest where it could easily re-incorporate. Had there been any loose rocks or even dried mud, the magic could have animated itself within that material, but here was nothing but the flat surface of the ledge and the sheer side of the mountain. The only thing Willow's magic could absorb itself into was the crystal orb, which Karrys had placed on the ground. It took some time; Willow was not as willing this time to be entrapped as she had been the first time, but eventually, the magic went to the crystal orb and dissolved into its center.

Karrys watched all of this with appalled attention. Dragons did not care this much for other dragons, let alone other races and beings. Part of her wished she could expel Harpur's spirit from her body and be done with him forever. Still, she tenderly lifted the crystal orb and held it gently in her hand. Where it had been flawlessly clear moments before, it now glowed with swirling strands of orange and purple and green mist. She placed it in the chest and zapped it back to the hideaway above Glynnis' lair.

For a while, she remained on the ledge. Harpur and Karrys, joined as one as they had been for sixteen years, reflected on the time they had shared. Each of them was so often amazed at how differently they perceived their mutual experiences. Karrys' indifference to Willow's fate, for instance, only deepened Harpur's sadness. Yet she was moved by how difficult it was for Harpur to do what he did. Where Karrys wouldn't have given a second thought to the Fae child, Harpur was filled with regret for not having served her better, now and in the past. Harpur saw Willow as a failure on his part to protect the citizens of Epoh when he had been their dragon lord. It was a job he had taken very seriously, even though he occasionally had to choose a path that kept him from his duties.

There was a time, not so long ago, when the peoples of Epoh had deferred to their dragon lord out of sheer fear. They assumed that they governed the kingdom and saw the resident dragon as something to be tolerated. When Harpur had gone to Earth to watch over Arthur, he had pretended to bargain with

Edlyngton Bloomregaard, then the Senior Bounding Guard in charge of monitoring and enforcing the laws of Bounding between Epoh and Earth. At the time, he thought he was empowering the people under his protection. He believed that by giving them opportunities to fend for themselves, they would grow and better themselves. For the most part, this was true. The fly in the ointment was Bloomregaard himself. He had used Harpur's absence to stage a coup that was designed to make him king. It had failed, of course, Harpur had seen to that. It had cost the dragon dearly, though. Eight years on Earth living in human form while he watched over Arthur had weakened him, and while luring three wraiths—Bloomregaard's pets—to their deaths inside a Boundary, he had been severely injured and unable to heal properly. Anayah's friend, Anabettah, had died trying to help him and Anayah's aunt, Analeetah, had been driven mad by the loss. Anayah had been imprisoned without her magic for a time, then spent many months trapped inside the Sphere, waiting to be rescued. Now she was dead too. Because of Harpur.

Harpur: I've made so many mistakes. Too many have paid too dearly for my hubris.

Karrys: And many more have thrived because of it. Not even a great dragon like Xzynthyrius Dreamfinder can get it right all the time.

Harpur chuckled ruefully. The reminder of his real name surprised and disturbed him. He had given it up after being injured in a challenge fight for Epoh by a strong, but inexperienced young dragon. A kind healer, named Harpur Diggins, had helped him regain his strength when his own healing abilities were unable to work fast enough. After the healer had died some years later, Xzynthyrius Dreamfinder had changed his name to honour the man who had saved him.

Karrys: There is great power in the names we choose. You are the colour of amethyst. Xzynthyr is the old name of that stone. It represents wisdom and peace, which have always been your guiding principles. And how many dreams have you helped others find? Perhaps it is time for you to take back your true power.

Harpur: Are you saying that Harpur Diggins diminished my power?

Harpur: I'm saying that Harpur Diggins changed it.

Harpur: Your sister, Karryl, was very dear to me.

Harpur: Karryl means challenger.

Again, Harpur chuckled.

Harpur: She was challenging. I think that's what drew me to her.

Karrys: She chose her own fate, Xzynthyrius. When she chose to challenge Khol for rulership over Rednow, she did it not just to be close to you; she did it because that was her nature.

Harpur cringed at the implication in Karrys' statement.

Harpur: I'm sorry I did this to you. I should have accepted my fate and died when you challenged me.

Karrys: Yes, you should have. But here we are.

Harpur: Well, let's go and see if Bon can help us both change our fates.

Harpur launched Karrys' body into the air and flew towards Colwygshire.

Karrys: I thought you told Glynnis that we would leave Epoh once the Fae girl was dealt with.

Harpur: I did. And we will. But first we must see if there is any hope for your freedom from me.

Karrys: And where will we go?

Harpur: We will hide among our kind in the Sands of Sancheera.

The next few days at the castle were filled with the busyness of finding ways to carry on living in the grip of grief. Anayah's death had created a new dynamic requiring an adjustment that Arthur and his friends were struggling to make. Oddly, it was Arthur they all turned to for guidance and he quickly realized that they saw him as an expert in dealing with such a profound loss. He had somehow managed to survive the death of his beloved wife, Alex; surely, he could guide them all through this. He wore the mantle as stoically as he could, saving his own sadness for those rare times, usually late at night alone in his chambers, when he didn't feel like he had to be strong for the others.

Like Earth, the world of Thraeh has the unfortunate habit of continuing to spin even when it seems like it should stop completely. But life goes on, and so did Arthur, Sok, Davynn, Hiro, Bon, Meg and Hart, albeit with heavy hearts and, in Davynn's case, a hurting head.

The knight, unaware of Arthur's inadvertent encounter with the sleeping draught, stumbled into the council chambers the morning after he'd drunk himself into oblivion and slumped into a chair across from Sok at the round table. He unconsciously chose a different chair from the one he usually sat in next to Anayah and the others all shifted uncomfortably in their own at the unexpected variation in the routine. They all wondered if they also shouldn't have sat in different chairs. But no one commented, and no one had the nerve to get up and move, though they all inwardly pondered the merits of forming a new order the next time they all gathered.

Missing from the ranks, of course, was Morgaine. It occurred to Arthur that she played a part in everything that had happened. He had finally gotten past blaming Harpur for Anayah's death, but he couldn't help but be annoyed by the fact that she was not present to help deal with the fallout. He sipped his jamba thoughtfully, not sure where to begin. It was clear that they all needed to talk about it; but he had no desire to stir up the high-running emotions that were silently ricocheting all around the room.

Bon ended Arthur's dilemma by announcing the obvious. "Morgaine will not be joining us today," he said as all eyes turned toward him. "She has gone to the Sands of Sancheera to await the results of my efforts to free Harpur's spirit from her body. At the request of Glynnis…"

"Did you say Glynnis?" Sok interjected.

"I did," Bon said, then continued while the elf stared at him. "At the request of Glynnis, Morgaine… or, more accurately, Karrys… found and contained the spirit of the Fae child Willow, that had been freed when Arthur dropped the Amber Chalice from a cave overlooking the Fae Lands. She then left Epoh, also at the request of Glynnis, to seek refuge in the desert until such time as I can perfect a method of cloning Harpur's body."

"You're going to clone Harpur?" Arthur asked.

"I am going to try," Bon amended.

"So, I was right that Glynnis knew Morgaine was here!" Sok exclaimed, once again rather proud of his deduction. "And he let her go?"

Bon looked at Sok. "That is correct. And, yes, he did."

"Why?" Sok was baffled. Happy to be right, but baffled by it also.

"Morgaine did not elucidate on the matter," Bon said. "She only told me what I am telling you. Glynnis dispatched her to take care of Willow. After that was done, he expected her to leave Epoh."

"What is this world coming to?" Sok said philosophically.

Arthur stared at his senior advisor. "Did you get that from me?"

Sok appeared to be combing through his memory. "Probably."

"May I continue?" Bon asked patiently.

"There's more?" Sok replied.

"Stop interrupting." Arthur admonished the elf. "Go ahead, Bon."

Sok sat back in his chair and nibbled on a piece of bacon.

"I need twelve dragon eggs." Bon waited for the others to digest this.

No one could even begin to fathom how to procure dragon eggs. No one but Arthur understood what Bon needed them for.

"You're planning on cloning a dozen Harpurs? I would think that one is enough." Arthur said.

"What does cloning mean?" Hart asked, seconds before Sok could.

"It's a process of creating an exact replica of a living being," Arthur said.

Meg shot forward in her chair. "Harpur's tail and top hat! Am I going to start laying eggs?"

"What?" Arthur shouted. "No!" Then he turned to Sok. "Is she?"

"How would I know?" Sok said. "I'm still stuck on replicating someone. That's not even possible."

"I assure you that it is," Bon said. Then he turned to the horrified princess. "Morgaine asked me to tell you that there is a book in the archives you and your brother need to read. It is called *Becoming a Dragon* and it will tell you everything you need to know about your dragon existences."

"Cool," Hart said. "I'll get it later."

"I have to read a book?" Meg scowled.

"I'll read it and give you the rundown," Hart patted his sister on the arm. He knew better than to expect Meg to study dragonhood, even if it would make her life easier.

"Good," Meg said. "I'll wait for your report."

"Can we get back to the matter at hand?" Arthur said. When the others finally settled down, he turned again to Bon. "Do you really need twelve?"

"It would be ideal. My calculations tell me that with twelve eggs, we have a seventy-three percent chance of getting one viable embryo."

"I see." Arthur stroked his chin. "Anyone want to take on getting twelve dragon eggs for Bon?" There were no takers. "Very well, we'll table that for now. Sok why aren't you taking notes?"

"I didn't know this was a formal meeting," the elf said. "I thought we were having breakfast."

"Well, it is. So, start writing." Arthur reached for a biscuit and cut it in half. He then piled scrambled eggs, bacon and cheese on it and put it back together. As he was about to take his first bite, he noticed everyone looking at him. "Egg McMuffin," he said, then pushed the tasty breakfast sandwich into his mouth, and wondered why he hadn't thought of recreating one of his favourite treats from his life on Earth sooner.

"I think," Hiro said with a giggle as he patted his stomach, "that we need to get caught up on what happened before we concern ourselves too much with what lies ahead."

An audible groan came from Davynn's side of the table.

Arthur sent a sympathetic glance toward the knight. "We'll all understand if you don't want to hear this, Davynn."

The knight lifted his head and winced. "I'm okay," he said.

No, you're not, Arthur thought. "Okay, then. Let's go around the table and fill each other in on what we know. I'll start. I was abducted by my daughter and dropped through a roof."

Davynn looked confused. "You were dropped through a roof?"

"Long story," Arthur said. "Sok, why don't you go next."

"Am I writing all this down too?" the elf said sarcastically.

"If you want to," Arthur said.

Sok rolled his eyes. He told his version of what happened after Anayah had zapped herself out of the Drengrokil camp, and then half back to the camp. "I stayed with Anayah while the others... didn't."

Davynn kept his eyes down. He swallowed. "I still can't believe she made a mistake like that."

241

Sok and Arthur exchanged looks, sharing their despair over their friend's stoic courage.

"Thank you, Sok," Arthur said. "Hart? Do you want to go next?"

"I thought we were going around..." A swift thump on his arm stopped him from finishing the sentence. If they had gone around the table, Davynn would have been next and Hart would have been last. Meg's sharp, physical reminder brough him up to speed. "Of course." He had little to add to Sok and Arthur's accounts other than find Meg on the ground floor of Wildwood and thinking his sister was dead too.

Meg, feeling foolish, added that she had killed Analeetah.

Bon was invited to go next. His contribution was to inform the group that the magic Analeetah had extracted from the witches had escaped and it was possible that it would form Fae.

"There were no Fae there before?" Arthur asked.

"According to Morgaine—and by Morgaine, I mean Harpur—no."

"How would Harpur know if there were Fae on Mysturna or not?" Sok asked.

"On Earth, the Fae are just myths," Arthur said.

"What happens to stray magic on Earth, then? Sok asked.

"There is no magic on Earth." Arthur reminded the elf.

"You were on Earth and you had magic. Sort of." Sok liked to poke fun at Arthur's lack of prowess when it came to wielding his powers.

"I was the only one," Arthur said.

"That we know of," Sok added.

"Regardless," Arthur snapped, "there are no Fae on Earth." He turned back to Bon. "Is that a problem?"

"If it is, it is not our problem," Bon said matter-of-factly. "Morgaine and I also discussed that. Since we no longer have any ties to Mysturna, we need not concern ourselves with the effect the Fae will have on that world."

"Excuse me," Hiro piped up, "but Mysturna is still my home. I still have ties to it."

"I apologize," Bon said to the Krist. "I assumed that you would not be returning."

"I would like to have the option," Hiro said. "I do intend to find out what happened to Mezzi."

"I think we can table the Fae on Mysturna issue for now as well," Arthur said. "And I think that concludes our business here..."

"Not quite," Davynn interrupted. "I haven't given my report."

Arthur looked at the knight. "I'm sorry, Davynn. Did something happen here while we were gone?"

Davynn looked at Sok. "Do you recall Sok telling us that Berryl would not be available to look after things at the castle while you were all away?"

"Vaguely," Arthur said.

"I was saving that for court," Sok said.

"For court?" Arthur parroted. "What is going on?"

"It seems that our esteemed Assistant to the Senior Advisor is a petty thief," Davynn said. "What Sok failed to tell us was that before you all left, he had Berryl imprisoned in the cells at the north gate for stealing."

"Sok?" Arthur said, turning to the elf.

"I caught him stealing from Meg's room," Sok explained as if it was no big deal. "So, I had him taken to the north gate to await trial. Which reminds me... Why did you let him go?"

"Berryl tried to steal something from my room?" Meg felt slightly violated.

"Some strange hat he found," Sok said. "I put it back. Then I went to Berryl's room and... Since you seem to have solved the case, Davynn, why don't you tell them what Berryl did."

"After I found Berryl had been locked up, I did some investigating. It appears that our Assistant to the Senior Advisor has been pilfering things from around the castle for quite some time. His room is filled with stuff he's taken. I found my missing boots. I also found Meg's rag doll," Davynn explained.

"You found my rag doll?" Meg squealed "Where is it?"

"It's safe in my rooms. I'll get it back to you as soon as I can."

"Thank you, Uncle Davynn," the princess said with deep sincerity.

"Technically, I found it first," Sok said. "I mean I discovered Berryl's crime."

"Thank you, Uncle Sok," Meg said with a roll of her eyes.

"I can't believe this," Arthur said. "Our Berryl, a thief? What else did he take?"

"It would be easier to show you," Davynn said.

The impromptu debriefing was adjourned by consensus. Everyone, except Meg and Hart, were curious to see what Davynn was talking about. Sok, was well aware, having seen Berryl's room already, but he tagged along, curious to see Arthur's reaction. Meg made for the archery range, eager to get in some practice, while Hart went to the archives to look for the book that Morgaine had recommended.

As Davynn led Arthur, Sok, Hiro and Bon to Berryl's room, Arthur's mind was on the hat that Berryl was accused of stealing.

"You said Berryl stole a hat?" He addressed the question to Sok.

"Yeah. At least I think it was a hat. I don't know what else it could be."

"What did it look like?"

"Like a bowl, with a strap on one side and a wide brim on the other side."

"Meg's room is full of them. Birthday gifts I assume," Davynn added. His head was finally beginning to clear, though a dull, throbbing ache still remained behind his eyes.

"Full of them?" Arthur was confused. "I only ordered two. One for Meg and one for Hart."

Everyone stopped walking.

"You know about the hats?" Davynn asked.

"They are called baseball caps," Arthur said. "I had two custom-made for the twins. Meg's says 'Daddy's Little Princess', and Hart's says 'That's what I do; I conduct experiments and I know things'."

"Apparently, half of Colwygshire also had custom... what did you call them?" Davynn asked.

"Baseball caps," Arthur said. "What do you mean half of Colwygshire had them made. I swore Rupert to secrecy!"

Rupert was Arthur's under-utilized valet who looked a lot like Ichabod Crane. His chief duty was, seemingly, to have clothing commissioned for Arthur that Arthur wouldn't be caught dead in and then keep them for himself. Arthur preferred to put on his own clothes and brush his own hair. Thus, poor, flamboyant Rupert had very little to do. Every now and then Sok would encourage Arthur to let Rupert do his proper job—it would have saved the castle a great deal of money—but Arthur would not give in. "It's creepy," he'd say. And Sok would sigh and let it go, thankful at least that they no longer had to have similar discussions about Arthur wearing his crown. That bone of contention between king and senior advisor had been long-since put to rest.

"You swore Rupert to secrecy? It's like you don't know him at all!" Sok continued walking.

They finally rounded the corner into the hallway where Berryl's room was. Two guards were standing in the hallway in front of an open door. "Where are we?" Arthur asked. "I don't think I've ever been down here before."

"Why would you?" Sok said. "This is only where all the castle stores are kept."

"Don't you keep track of all that stuff?"

"Yes, Arthur, I do." Sok came to a halt next to the door to Berryl's room.

"Well, then, there's no need for me to come down here, is there?" Arthur said.

Davynn asked the guards to step aside and let Arthur in.

"Crikey!" Arthur blurted out when he saw the piles of pilfered goods.

"Crikey?" Sok repeated. "You've been here for almost twenty years. Are you ever going to run out of weird Earth things to say?"

"Admit it, Sok, you liked that one. You're going to use it," Arthur said as he turned around in awe, trying to take it all in.

Sok held out his hand and rotated his wrist. "Eh. It's okay."

Arthur entered the room and tried to estimate the number of things Berryl had stolen. There were hundreds, if not thousands of things in piles, some of which reached the ceiling. Berryl poked his head out from behind one of the piles.

"Your majesty," he squeaked, "I wasn't expecting you."

Arthur picked up a scarf from one of the piles. Then he spotted a candle stick and picked it up. A jeweled hair comb caught his eye and he dropped the items in his hand and climbed over a pile at the end of the bed to get to it. It had

245

belonged to Queen Alex and she had been quite distraught when it had gone missing. "No doubt," he said. "Why did you do this?"

Davynn spoke up to explain. "He was displaced when you became king and made Sok your senior advisor. He felt abandoned, unvalued. This…" Davyn gestured at the piles of stolen items. "…was a cry for help; a way to be in control of his life."

Behind him, Sok scoffed. "That's ridiculous!"

Arthur understood that kleptomania was a mental illness. Like gambling, it was an addiction that, with proper therapy, could be controlled. He wasn't aware of any licensed therapists in Epoh, though, so getting Berryl the help he required was not possible.

"Actually, it isn't," Arthur said, earning a deep frown from the elf. "This sort of thing happens on Earth a lot." He turned back to Davynn. "How have you decided to handle this?"

"Berryl will be under guard day and night until he has returned everything here to its rightful owner."

"I'm making amends," Berryl said sheepishly from the other side of the pile he was working on.

This garnered another look of disbelief from Sok. "What's to stop him from just stealing more stuff after he's given all this stuff back?"

"Well, that is a discussion I think the three of us need to have in private," Davynn said.

Arthur tucked the hair comb into his pocket. "Shall we return to the council chambers?"

Leaving Berryl to his amends-making, they retraced their steps and took seats at the round table. This time Arthur, Sok, Bon and Hiro chose to sit in places other than they were accustomed to.

"In some kingdoms," Sok said, thinking that they were going to discuss a proper punishment for Berryl, "they cut thieves' hands off."

"We are not cutting Berryl's hands off, Sok," Arthur said. "The man is ill. He needs help, not to be made helpless."

Sok shrugged.

Arthur looked at Bon. "In Earth's future, how do they deal with something like this?""

"Mental health issues have been destigmatized on Earth. Everyone has access to free mental health care. This sort of thing is rare, as it is here. I would suggest that you find some way to restore Berryl's sense of purpose. As Davynn explained, the man was displaced when the court was restructured under your rule. It seems only right that you do what you are able to assist him." Bon ignored the scowl Sok was directing at him.

For the first time since he'd come to Epoh, Arthur realized how true this was. People gambled, but they didn't lose their shirts over it. People drank alcohol, but chronic alcoholism didn't plague society. There were no town drunks clogging up the jails. In fact, the jails were empty more than they were occupied; crime, in general, was relatively rare. When people had issues with each other, they worked it out. If they couldn't work it out, they brought the matter to court and accepted Arthur's decision. Places, like Skull's Keep, had a system that ensured that anyone falling on hard times didn't go hungry. Everyone was expected to contribute *and* to make their own way in life; it wasn't a socialist society. Yet socialism thrived beneath the guise of the monarchy. People were conditioned to help each other out when and how they could. Occasionally, fights broke out, but there were no gangs vying for control over territories. Success was generally measured against one's self, and not against one's neighbour. Women didn't fear walking around the city at night—or any time. There were no slums in Colwygshire. The affluent and the less fortunate lived side-by-side.

"Any thoughts on how to we can make that happen?" Arthur said after a while.

Davynn cleared his throat. "I propose that we make him a citizen advocate."

"A what?" Sok asked.

"Explain," Arthur prompted the knight.

"A citizen advocate," Davynn repeated. He hadn't worked out all the details, but he forged ahead with his idea. "Let Berryl sort through the petitions and deal with them on his own. Let him interview the complainants and negotiate a settlement. If they cannot come to an agreement with Berryl, then they can bring their petition to court for you to decide on."

"That's brilliant!" Arthur exclaimed. He looked at Sok. "Why didn't you think of this?""

"Why didn't you?" Sok shot back. "You're the one that hates holding court. Personally, I think it's a daffy idea."

"Daffy?" Arthur repeated. "I really do have to start watching what I say."

"It's not... daffy," Davynn tried out the word and decided that *it* was daffy, "at all. Berry will have had to face everyone he's wronged and they will get their property back. By the time he has gone through all that stuff, he's never going to want to steal again."

"You don't actually think this will work?" Sok was incredulous.

"I think it is most definitely worth a try," Bon interjected. "Locking him up, or cutting off his hands is not going to address the problem. Some responsibility might help him overcome his compulsion to steal."

"But shouldn't we make an example of him?" Sok persisted.

"To whom?" Arthur said. "We just established that this isn't a common problem in Epoh. Who would benefit from making an example of Berryl?"

"He should at least get a day in the stocks," Sok said under his breath.

Arthur leaned back in his chair and considered this latest turn of event.

"How did this happen?" He mused.

"Berryl picked things up and put them..." Sok began.

"No, I mean how did Epoh become so... utopian?" Arthur said.

"You-what-ian?" Sok asked.

"Ideal, well adjusted, peaceful, supportive," Arthur explained.

"Harpur insisted on it," Davynn said. "I think."

"It's not like there have never been times of trouble or conflict in Epoh," Sok added. "Harpur simply didn't stand for it."

"Huh!" Arthur said. "It's' hard to believe it could be that simple."

"Are we all in agreement, then?" Davynn asked.

Everyone looked at Sok. "When this fails, don't say I didn't warn you," he said.

"Great!" Arthur said cheerfully. "You can draft the job description for the position of Citizen Advocate."

248

"I get to choose what he can and cannot do?" Sok saw a silver lining in this assignment.

"You get to write out a draft of what his duties should be," Arthur said, clasping his hands on the table. "Then the rest of us will look it over and we'll all decide what the position will be."

Sok grimaced, but he didn't protest.

I have to go and check in on the children," Davynn said, relatively happy that was settled. "I told them I would have lunch with them."

Arthur ordered lunch for himself and asked for it to be delivered to his chambers. He arrived at his door to find it open and the guards missing. He poked his head inside and looked around. "Hello?" he called. No one answered. He stepped inside and called out again. Again, he received no answer. A quick check into the bath and bed chambers revealed no intruders, so he closed the door and poured himself a cup of jamba, Epoh's answer to coffee. Then he sat down in the big wing chair closest to the fireplace to wait for his food to be delivered. He had just gotten settled with his feet on the low table between the sofas, when a kerfuffle erupted outside his door. He listened for a moment, trying to identify the cause, so he could decide if it was something he needed to get up for.

Suddenly, the door opened and the guards that should have been guarding his chambers when he arrived burst in with their swords drawn and grim looks on their faces that fell somewhere on the spectrum between suspicion and terror. Arthur looked at the guards and then at their swords. "Is something wrong?" he asked.

"Sire," the first guard said in a voice that was at least one full octave above normal. "You shouldn't be here."

"Where should I be?" Arthur asked, thinking that perhaps he'd forgotten an important appointment of some kind.

"Anywhere but here, sire," the second guard said with a voice appropriately pitched to support a distinct lack of confidence.

"And why is that?" Arthur asked, more interested in than concerned by the palpable discomfort the guards were displaying.

"We saw a…" the first guard began, but was stopped by an elbow to his chest administered by the second guard.

"There was an intruder, sire," the second guard said.

Arthur's eyes shifted to take in the room. "And where is this intruder now?"

"We're not sure, sire," the first guard said.

"We lost it," the second guard said and received a reciprocal elbow to his own chest.

"It?" Arthur asked, beginning to wonder if he should be more concerned.

"Her," the first guard corrected. "We lost her."

"Probably just a maid," Arthur said rationally and, he hoped, dismissively.

"It wasn't no maid as we ever saw in the castle," the second guard said.

Arthur frowned. "Well, there's no one here now. Get back to your post and close the door on your way out." He leaned back in his chair and sipped his jamba.

"Sire, we really must insist that you vacate your chambers until such time as the… uh, intruder can be apprehended," the first guard said.

Arthur took a deep breath and blew it out through his lips. "I appreciate your concern for my safety, I really do, but there is no one here but us and I would like to enjoy some peace and quiet for a while. Now return to your posts and stop bothering me!"

The guards looked at each other. Disobeying an order from the king was a court martial offence, but they didn't want to leave Arthur alone in his chambers either.

"Sire, if I may…?" the second guard began.

"No!" Arthur snapped. "You may not!" The guards stood where they were for a moment, unsure of what they should do. "Get out!" Arthur yelled, turning in his chair to glare at them.

"Yes, sire," they said, bowing and backing out of the room.

Alone with his thoughts, Arthur drank his jamba and let his mind drift. He thought about Anayah and how her death was going to impact life at the castle. He thought about Harpur and whether or not Bon would be able to free him from Karrys' body. He thought about Davynn and the children. He thought about Alex. And he thought about something he hadn't thought about in a very long time. From the moment they had Bounded to Mysturna, he'd had a sense that something was missing. Try as he might, he couldn't put his finger on what it was. Then it struck him. In his past adventures, when things had gotten tough, his guardians had appeared. They hadn't been all that useful and the guidance they dispensed was more baffling than clarifying, but they had been there all the same.

They had first appeared as Ralph and Holly, an amorous couple dressed in fig leaves and little else. They had been more of an embarrassment than anything, constantly pawing at each other—or worse! The next time they showed up, they called themselves Jack and Diane and were dressed like pirates. While they had been a little less embarrassing, they were no more helpful. Except for the warning they had given him just before they disappeared.

"Your efforts will succeed," Diane said.

"But you will not know it," Jack finished.

He wasn't sure at the time if his guardians were warning him that Harpur was going to wipe his memory, but he'd had enough experience with that tactic not to let any doubt prevent him from doing the only thing he could think of to thwart that possibility. He had zapped himself back to this very room and spent hours recording the events that had led up to the day Karrys had killed Harpur in the meadow outside of his lair.

Those pages were still lying on the table and he picked them up. "All this time," Arthur whispered as he thumbed through them, "it was right here. It was all right here."

Obviously, Arthur's counter measure against having his memory wiped hadn't worked. But he had to give himself a pat on the back for the ingenious effort.

Laughing to himself, he took the pages to the vault in his bedroom and tucked them next to Harpur's life book.

"Next time I'll use a book someone is actually likely to read!"

Chapter Thirteen

Lunch with Alexa, Brodie and Caleb was not the messy, noisy affair that it usually was. The children picked away at their meals, uninterested in eating, as they tried to make peace with knowing they would never see their mother again. Every now and then, they would look at Davynn as if willing him to fix this. He couldn't wait to finish his stew and get back to work so he wouldn't have to face their disillusionment. Even Joy seemed to be silently begging him to bring Anayah back.

He had thought that keeping busy and being distracted, would get him through this. His plan was to bury his grief in his job and hope that the pain would pass. But when he went to leave, Caleb burst into tears again.

The little boy threw his arms around his father's legs and yelled, "You can't go, Father! If you go, you won't come back."

Davynn covered his eyes with his hand and squeezed them to stop his own tears from escaping. At the table, Alexa and Brodie were staring wide-eyed at their father, and Joy was pressing the corner of her apron to her own eyes.

How am I going to do this?

In that instant, the knight made a decision. He gently pulled Caleb's arms free and lifted the child up.

"I need you to be brave for just a little while," he said softly. "Can you do that?"

Caleb nodded. "I'll try."

"That's good, Caleb. I know you can do it." Davynn held his son, still sobbing, against his chest. "I have to go and talk to Uncle Arthur and Eowyn. I promise I won't be long."

"You'll come back?"

"Of course, I'll come back. And I won't take very long either."

"Okay." Caleb sniffled.

Davynn put Caleb down and told him to go and finish his lunch.

"We'll be fine," Joy assured him as he quickly left.

He made his way through the castle, taking a shortcut past the kitchens and through the guards' mess hall to the training grounds. As he expected, Eowyn Hunter was sparring with another guard, honing his prowess with the sword and besting his opponent far too easily. The quality of the fighting skills among the royal guard left rather a lot to be desired. Not for the first time, Davynn thought that some time under Yna's tutelage would make a world of difference. But, after today, that would no longer be his problem.

He waited until Eowyn had disarmed his opponent and called the young man over.

"Sir Davynn, is there something I can do for you?" Eowyn, ever the loyal and dutiful lieutenant, asked.

Davynn took a deep breath. *Am I really doing this?* "I am promoting you to captain of the guard," he said.

Eowyn looked perplexed. "I don't understand, Sir Davynn. You are the captain of the guard."

"Not any more, son," Davynn said.

"But, sir..."

Davynn cut the new, and disbelieving, captain off. He stepped farther into the arena to address the guards that were present. "Eowyn Hunter is now your captain. I trust that you all will show him the same respect and loyalty that you have shown me these many years."

He didn't wait for a reaction. Instead, he turned on his heals and walked back into the castle. As he passed Eowyn, he chucked the young man under the chin. "Close your mouth, son. You can't give orders if your mouth is full of flies."

His next stop was Arthur's chambers. The guards at the door, unaware that he was no longer their captain, snapped to attention. Davynn chose not to apprise them of the change in the chain of command.

"Am I disturbing you?" Davynn said, entering Arthur's sitting room and closing the door.

"Not at all," Arthur said. "How can I help?"

Davynn settled himself on a sofa facing Arthur. He struggled to find the right words. Feeling like he had to justify his decision and obtain Arthur's approval, he tried to come up with some way of saying what he had to say without giving Arthur the opportunity to oppose it. But nothing sounded right in his head.

Arthur watched the knight struggle with his grief and guilt, and finally decided to give the poor man an out. "When are you planning on leaving us?"

Davynn looked at Arthur, surprise and relief and caution written all over his face. "How did you know? I only just decided this morning."

Arthur leaned forward in his chair and clasped his hand between his knees. "I know because that is what I wanted to do when Alex died."

"Why didn't you?" Davynn hated himself for asking that. He'd just given Arthur the opportunity he had been hoping to avoid.

"At first, the thought of staying here was unbearable. I couldn't imagine staying here and being constantly reminded of her. Then I realized that being someplace where there were no reminders of her would be far worse."

"So, you think I should stay." Davynn was almost convinced himself.

"I think you should do what feels right for you and the children," Arthur said.

"You're not going to try to talk me out of it?" Davynn didn't know whether to be hurt or grateful.

"No, I am not," Arthur said as gently as he could. "As happy as it would make me if you did stay here, I would never expect you to stay just to make my life easier. What are you planning to do?"

"I am taking the children to Branwyke and we will live in Highmere Manor. I think it's time that I oversaw the management of the demesne first hand. The children have never been there; they should get to know their birthright."

Arthur had never been there either. Once again, he was made painfully aware of how little he knew about the kingdom and the people he ruled. Sok had been the one to choose to grant the village and farmlands of Branwyke to Davynn when he was knighted. *The elf really is a better king than I am.*

"I agree," Arthur said. "And it will give me a good excuse to get out of this castle once in a while. I will have to come check up on you."

Davynn smiled. "Thank you, Arthur."

"I suppose we are going to have to find a replacement for you," Arthur switched to business mode, to keep himself from having to deal with losing another friend just then.

"I took the liberty of promoting Eowyn Hunter to captain," Davynn confessed. "I know that's not exactly protocol, but..."

Arthur nodded in approval. He didn't know Eowyn well, but he'd heard Davynn speak highly of the young man. And he trusted the knight's judgement. "I will order Sok to make it official."

"Do you expect Sok to resist the appointment?" Davynn asked.

Arthur thought about it for a moment. "No. Well, he'll yammer on about policy and procedure for a while. Then I'll tell him it was my idea, on your recommendation. I suspect he will be far more resistant to you leaving than to Eowyn becoming captain."

Davynn stood up, ready to leave. "Thank you, Arthur. I told Caleb that I would be back soon, so I better keep my promise."

Arthur stood as well. "How are the children taking it?"

"Caleb has developed a fear of me leaving. Thinks I won't come back, like..." He couldn't finish the thought.

"Is it alright if I come down later to visit them?"

"I'm going to take them to Braydon Wood this afternoon. I want to see if Elder Dhonna and King Röggenar made it back from the Fae Lands safely."

"What on Thraeh were those two doing in the Fae Lands?"

"Did I not tell you?" Davynn asked. His mind had been on other things, of course. "While you were on Mysturna, they thought they would help by rounding up Willow for Harpur."

"Were they successful?"

"Not exactly," Davynn said. "They got caught by the Fae and Glynnis had to intervene."

Arthur wasn't sure he wanted to know the details. "Well, please let me know that they are okay when you see them."

"I will."

Davynn shook Arthur's hand and left to return to his family.

"Father!" Brodie hollered when Davynn entered the suite. "You came back!"

Sok took the news about Eowyn's promotion rather well. He did cite the proper policies and procedures surrounding such an event, but when Arthur ordered him to make it official and provide Eowyn with the insignia of his new office, Sok complied without further complaint. He remained unaware of Davynn's future plans, however. Arthur felt that now was not the time to drop that bomb on the elf. He would wait until after Anayah's funeral. *Whenever that will be!* Davynn hadn't spoken of it, and no one wanted to push the issue.

The following day, Sok found a couple of guards milling about at the entrance to the castle and dispatched them to find Eowyn and have him come to the council chambers.

Alone in the familiar room, he deliberately sat in a chair he had never sat in before. The change in perspective was uncomfortable. He looked at the room with fresh eyes and found details he'd never noticed before. There was a chip in one of the pillars at the back of the room near the exit that led to the stairs. The door itself was slightly crooked. To his left, he could look down the short passageway that led to the kitchens. Even the round, oak table looked different from this side; the reflection from the light of the wall sconces revealed a ripple in the wood that he had never noticed. He realized how much he took for granted. Including Anayah. *Who am I going to squabble with now?* It was strange to recognize how important it had been to him to have someone who was willing to call him out when he overstepped or took a wrong turn. He had depended on her to challenge him, challenge his beliefs and convictions, and to keep his mind open to new points of view.

Suddenly, Sok no longer cared about punishing Berryl for his petty thievery. It was just stuff. Trinkets and baubles collected and, he suspected, all but forgotten by their previous owners. Their inconvenient disappearance had been remedied with replacements in some cases, or adjustment to life without them in others. Even the sentimental ones, like Meg's rag doll, didn't leave that much of an impact in the long run. Meg had survived quite well without it for eleven years. Those losses paled in comparison to knowing that Anayah would never again threaten to turn him into a toad.

The door to the council chambers opened and Eowyn Hunter walked in to find Sok staring at the chip in the pillar across the room. He cleared his throat to announce his own arrival and waited for the elf to acknowledge him.

"Sit," Sok said at last, still staring at the chipped pillar.

Eowyn pulled a chair out from the table and sat down. He followed Sok's gaze to the pillar and wondered what was so fascinating. "You wanted to speak to me?" he said at last.

Sok took a deep breath and pulled his eyes away from the pillar. "I do," he said. "Are you aware of the situation with Sir Berryl?"

"Davynn filled me in," Eowyn said. "I understand that he released Berryl."

"Not exactly," Sok said. He then went on to explain the plan for Berryl's rehabilitation.

"Wouldn't it be easier just to lock him up in the dungeons for a couple of years?" Eowyn said, unsure what to make of this bizarre strategy.

"One would think so," Sok said, "but Davynn has decided that his way is better, and Arthur supports his decision. I will need you to assign guards to watch over Berryl twenty-four-seven."

"Twenty-four-seven, sir?"

"It's an Earth code for all the time, day and night, every day." Sok didn't understand it any more than Eowyn did, but it sounded good. It was one of the few sayings Arthur used that amused more than it confused him.

Eowyn looked even more perplexed by the reference to Earth. He knew that Sok had been there before the Boundary in Braydon Wood was enclosed in an elven-built structure that prevented anyone from Epoh from Bounding to that world. But he was unaware of the adoption of its codes in Epoh. *Why not just say all the time?*

"I will get on it right away," Eowyn said, choosing not to probe into the code matter any further. "Where is Berryl now, sir?"

"Please call me Sok," Sok said.

"Yes, sir... uh, Sok." Eowyn squirmed in his chair. "I will do my best, sir... uh, Sok."

"Berryl is in his room, sorting through the items he stole. Over the next while, he will be returning them to their rightful owners. Making amends, Davynn calls it." Sok's gaze returned to the chipped pillar.

Eowyn kept his eyes on the elf. He wasn't sure if he was being dismissed or if he should wait until Sok clearly sent him on his way. He hadn't quite figured out how to wear his authority as Captain of the Guard, and, under the circumstances, he felt less than confident asserting himself. But sitting there soon grew awkward and he began to fidget in his seat. "Is there anything else, sssss... Sok?"

"Yeah," the elf replied. "Do your job."

"Sir?"

"Speak up when you have something to say. Act when you make a decision. Make decisions based on what you know to be right. Don't be afraid to make mistakes. Own them when you do. Be teachable, and teach by example. Nothing lasts forever, Eowyn, so enjoy every moment while you can. Appreciate what you have while you have it. That's your real job."

Sok stood up and drew a red and gold shoulder patch from his pocket. He held it for a moment, remembering when Arthur had presented an identical patch to Davynn when he became captain. It had been an elegant ceremony befitting the solemnity of the occasion. To simply hand it over to Eowyn like this seemed… unseemly somehow. So, he decided to improvise a ceremony on the spot.

He motioned to Eowyn to join him next to the table. "Eowyn Hunter, do you swear to uphold the peace, protect the citizens of Epoh, and lead the Royal Guard with courage and honour?

"I do," Eowyn said.

"And do you swear to serve not only with sword and shield, but with wisdom, fairness and an unwavering heart?"

"I do."

"Then by the will of the crown and the trust of the people, I name you Captain of the Guard. Stand tall, Eowyn of Colwygshire—may the light find you steadfast, and the dark find you fearless."

A little stunned, and not a little disappointed by the brevity of the isolated ceremony, Eowyn allowed Sok to pin the patch to his cloak. He wanted to say, "That's it?" but his expression said it for him.

"Don't worry, Eowyn," Sok said, clasping the new captain's hand, "I'll make sure you are recognized in a proper ceremony once things settle down around here. But with Davynn's unexpected resignation, we had to install a new captain and it's important that we make it official. If I have it my way, you will be knighted as well."

With that, Sok exited the council chambers, leaving young Eowyn to wonder what had just happened. He understood why Davynn had left his position, but Sok's odd behaviour was disconcerting. Not that he really knew the elf very well. The elf was considered a bit of a tyrant, and while Davynn had never demonstrated any disrespect for the elf, neither had he gone out of his way to dispel any preconceived notions on the part of the guards.

Eowyn took a moment to consider the implications. Davynn commanded respect from the men he led. He was firm, but fair with them all. He set clear boundaries and clear expectations. He listened before he judged. And he let his men draw their own conclusions about the king and his senior advisor. As long as no one openly expressed contempt toward the leaders of the kingdom without just cause, Davynn didn't interfere with their opinions and beliefs. From this new perspective of the hierarchy, Eowyn was beginning to see things differently. He had been trusted with an office of great influence, but he suddenly recognized that he couldn't fill Davynn's shoes, nor should he be expected to. If he was going to be successful, he would have to do it his way and fly or fall on his own merits.

He walked toward the back exit out of the council chambers. As he passed the pillar that Sok had been so engrossed by, he stopped to examine it. Other than a small chip in the plaster there didn't appear to be anything special about it. Eowyn shrugged and opened the door. He didn't notice the main door on the other side of the room open and close without anyone entering.

As he climbed the stairs to the king's chambers, Eowyn forced his shoulders back and lifted his chin slightly. He breathed deeply to calm and center himself, intending to walk into Arthur's rooms as confidently as possible. He wondered if he shouldn't have first sent a guard to announce him. The realization that he had no idea how to navigate his new position caused his shoulders to slump again. Then he saw the guards outside Arhtur's door and coerced them to stay put.

Rather than snap to attention as they would if Davynn had arrived, the guards were leaning against the wall next to the door, looking bored and, to Eowyn's eyes, rather less diligent than guards assigned to protect the king should look. Eowyn cleared his throat to get their attention.

"Oh, hey, Eowyn!" the first guard said. "What are you doing up here?"

Eowyn ignored the familiarity. "Is the king in?"

The guards were puzzled by Eowyn's demeanor.

"He is. What business do you have with the king?" the second guard asked.

"Captain of the Guard business," Eowyn said, pointing to the patch on his shoulder.

The guards' eyes widened.

"Is this a joke?" the first guard asked.

"If Sok sees that thing on your shoulder, you're gonna find yourself in the dungeons," the second guard scoffed.

"Sok is the one who put it there," Eowyn snapped. "Now stand up straight and keep your attention on what you're supposed to be doing."

The guards' eyes narrowed. "Davynn doesn't seem to mind if we lean against the wall," the second guard said.

This wasn't true, but he wanted to test the waters.

"Davynn is not in charge anymore," Eowyn said. "I am, though, and I expect that anyone under my command who is privileged enough to be assigned to guard the king do so in a manner that is befitting the task. Do I make myself clear?"

The guards' eyes shifted away from Eowyn as they struggled to reconcile the sudden change in command and the style in which it was being delivered.

"Yes, sir."

"Sorry, sir."

Eowyn waited until he was inside and the door was closed to release his held breath. He would have to keep his uncertainty under control if he was going to have any credibility.

Almost instinctively, Eowyn scanned the room to take stock of the situation. Arthur was sitting in the wing chair, holding a cup of ale in one hand and drumming the arm of the chair with the fingers of his other hand. His legs were crossed and he appeared relaxed.

"Ah, Eowyn," Arthur stood up when he saw the young captain. "Congratulations on your new appointment." He noticed the patch on Eowyn's shoulder and felt a pang of remorse for not having put it there himself. "I didn't think Sok would be so efficient in making it official."

He had, in fact, expected Sok to arrange an elaborate and formal ceremony with rituals and speeches and make Arthur wear his fancy crown and royal robes. He'd kind of hoped it would keep the elf occupied and prevent him from thinking too much about Harpur.

"He swore me in down in the council chambers a little while ago," Eowyn explained. "As long as it's official, I'm sure I don't need anything more, your majesty."

"Ah! A man after my own heart," Arthur said, appreciating the lad's humble attitude. "I think we are going to get along famously."

Arthur walked over to the table to refill his cup. He poured a cup for Eowyn and gestured for the young man to take a seat.

"I'm on duty, sire," Eowyn said, gently refusing the cup being offered to him.

"Yeah, well, so am I," Arthur replied. "But in our line of work, we're always on duty. That's no reason not to drink ale. If anything, it's a reason to drink it whenever we can." He paused, recalling Davynn's recent overindulgence. "Within reason, of course."

Eowyn accepted the cup and sat down. "Thank you, sire."

"Let's start with dropping the sire thing," Arthur suggested. "Just call me Arthur."

Eowyn took a sip of ale while he processed the king's... request? Order? This was all too new to him. "If you don't mind, sire, I would feel more comfortable properly and formally acknowledging your station."

Again, Arthur smiled. "Alright, we'll work up to that. Tell me why you are here."

The young man cleared his throat and looked thoughtful. "I just thought that I should come up and get my orders from you," he said, simply.

Arthur almost spit his ale back into his cup. He wasn't sure how to respond. Eowyn was brand new to this job and it hadn't occurred to him that the new captain would have no idea how things worked around the castle. He would have to speak to Davynn and get him to give Eowyn a mini-course in captaincy. "Well," he said, "I order you to do your job."

Eowyn frowned at the king. Then quickly unknotted his brows, lest the king think he was being insolent. "That's what Sok said," he said. "He told me to have fun with it, but..."

Arthur looked at Eowyn, bemused. "Sok told you to have fun being the captain of the guard?"

"Well, not exactly," Eowyn admitted. "He said to enjoy and appreciate things because nothing lasts forever. He said that was my real job."

Arthur smiled. "That elf never ceases to amaze me." He rubbed his chin and felt the stubble chafe against his fingers. "What else did he tell you?"

"He said that Berryl is to be kept under guard... twenty-four, seven?"

Again, Arthur looked bewildered. "He used that term?" Eowyn nodded. "Did he explain what it means?"

"All day and all night, every day and every night?" Eowyn hoped he understood Sok correctly.

Arthur's head bobbed in appreciation of Sok's grasp on the colloquialism. "That's right. The guards are meant to ensure that he doesn't continue to steal. Once he has finished making amends, he will be advanced to the position of citizen advocate."

"Citizen advocate, sire?" Eowyn frowned again.

"It will become his job to… filter through the complaints that would normally be presented at court and help people sort out their differences."

"Isn't that your job, sire?" Eowyn's frown deepened. He didn't understand how a king could delegate such an important duty to anyone, let alone a known thief.

"I will still hold court for the more serious disputes," Arthur explained. "But Davyn and I think that Berryl needs a purpose and some direction, and, from what I know about him, he is fair-minded. Becoming an advocate for the law is something that will help him overcome his unfortunate proclivity."

"But can you trust him?" Eowyn was astounded at Arthur's compassion for a man who had stolen so many things over the years.

"We'll see," Arthur said. "There are no guarantees that this will work. But I believe it is in all of our best interests to find out."

Eowyn lifted his cup and took a long, thoughtful draft. He was formulating a plan to oversee Berryl's unconventional punishment. But he had to first understand how he fit in. He knew that Davynn used to consult with Arthur regularly, but it seemed that it wasn't to get approval or follow orders. "When do I report to you, sire?"

"You don't report to me, as such," Arthur said. "You are in charge of the guards and it's up to you how you manage that. Join us for breakfast in the council chambers in the morning. That's when me, Sok, Bon, Hiro, Davynn and…" He almost said Anayah, but caught himself. "That's when we gather to check in and keep each other informed about anything important."

"Very well, sire, I will" Eowyn stood up and looked around for a place to leave his empty cup.

Arthur took the cup and placed it, along with his own, on the table by the window. "I'm looking forward to working with you," he said. "I don't suppose you know where Sok has gotten to?"

"No, sire," Eowyn admitted. "He left the council chambers before me. He didn't say where he was going."

Arthur sighed. *He'll turn up.*

Eowyn Hunter left the king's chambers feeling somewhat better about his unexpected promotion. But by the time he reached the main floor, his doubt had returned. *A king that doesn't give orders? What have I got myself into?*

After Eowyn left, Arthur made his way down to Hiro's laboratory. The whole world seemed to have been fractured by Anayah's death, but his talk with Eowyn had given him a small measure of hope. *Was Anayah the glue that had kept them all together?* He didn't think that was entirely true, but her sudden absence definitely impacted the once cohesive routine. They all needed closure. They needed to find a way back to normalcy—whatever that was going to look like. And they needed to sort things out for Harpur. He wondered how they were going to let Morgaine know if, and when, Bon made any progress with his plan. *We should all be figuring this stuff out together!*

He entered the laboratory to find it filled with dozens of dragon eggs. "Are these what I think they are?" he asked as he picked his way around the basketball-sized eggs.

Bon was holding one of the eggs, a shiny green one, examining it closely. "If you think they are dragon eggs, then, yes, they are what you think they are."

Hiro giggled. He was across the room shifting eggs into a neat pile. "They started appearing earlier this morning. We think they've finally stopped."

"Where did they come from?" Arthur was stunned.

"I cannot be certain at this point," Bon said, "but I suspect that Morgaine is responsible for their appearance."

"There's so many of them!" Arthur gushed. "And they're so small. I thought dragon eggs would be a lot bigger than this."

Bon set the shiny green egg down and picked up a sparkly purple one. "This is standard for dragon eggs. A dragon, upon hatching, weighs only about four and a half kilograms."

Arthur tried to imagine Harpur being that tiny. "They must grow fast."

"They do," Bon confirmed. "A dragon reaches its full size in only a few moon cycles. They don't actually mature, however, for eight to ten years. Once they are able to feed themselves, they are left to their own devices. Often young dragons will group together for protection until they are old enough to truly fend for themselves."

"So, their parents don't raise them?" Arthur picked up a blue egg with gold flecks and was surprised at how cold it felt. "Are you sure these eggs are any good?"

"Some of them are perfectly good, but I suspect that many of these eggs are quite old." Bon tapped his knuckles against the shell of an orange egg. He appeared satisfied by the sound and placed the egg in a pile with six other eggs on the work bench. "And no, they are not nurtured by their parents after they are able to feed themselves."

Arthur tapped the blue egg he was holding. He had no idea what he was listening for, but Bon soon assured him that it was a dud and directed him to add it to Hiro's growing pile.

"Interesting," Arthur said. "I always thought that Harpur and his mate had raised their sons. What were their names again?"

"Framanjesk and Phiercesten" Bon replied.

"Right. Weird names." Arthur picked up a white egg and tapped it.

"That's a good one!" Bon said and pointed to the pile on the work bench. While Arthur added the egg to the pile, Bon continued. "They are unconventional monikers for dragons, who typically take their names from a prominent quality such as their colour. Xzynthyrius, for example, is derived from xzynthyrite, a type of rare amethyst found only in the southernmost continent of Thraeh. Harpur took it as his name because it matched the colour of his scales. Karrys means graceful."

"Dragons name themselves?" Arthur was intrigued.

"They do," Bon said. "When they reach maturity, they announce the name they wish to be known as. Then the dragon community bestows them with a surname that reflects what the community sees in them. Usually, this is influenced by the reputation of the dragon."

264

"So, where does Dreamfinder come from?" Arthur asked, fully expecting Bon to have the answer.

"Xzynthyrius was known as a rather benevolent young dragon. He was fierce and strong, but was prone to show kindness and compassion. Rather than fight first and ask questions later, Xzynthyrius sought to understand. He had a gift for helping others and he was particularly known for the compassion he bestowed on what all dragons consider the lesser races, like humans and elves and dwarfs. Where most dragons could care less what happens to the lesser races, Xzynthyrius found ways of helping them thrive. He cared deeply for the well-being of all races and through his efforts, demonstrated how beneficial the lesser races really are. Look how he has utilized the humans, elves and dwarfs here in Epoh. The humans tend the land, the elves tend the forests, the dwarfs tend the mountains. Everyone prospers, everyone thrives. The kingdom isn't fraught with wars like some others are. There is peace here and it was like that for most of Harpur's reign. Dreamfinder reflects what the dragon community saw in Xzynthyrius."

"I never knew that," Arthur said, impressed. "Harpur never talked about his history much. But you make it sound like we are all just cattle."

"To dragons, that is, more or less, what you are." Bon said, excluding himself in particular and androids in general from ranking among the lesser races. He placed a ruby-red egg on the work bench.

Arthur considered this uncomfortable analogy. "That can't be true," he declared. "If we were just livestock, then why don't dragons eat virgin sacrifices? Why do they save them?"

Bon paused from his egg tapping to reassess his conclusion. "That is an excellent point, Arthur. Perhaps cattle is not the best comparation. Dragons do acknowledge the lesser races' intelligence and there is some measure of respect for it. They simply do not abide the willingness on the part of humans to sacrifice one of their own so arbitrarily."

Hiro giggled from across the room where his pile of eggs had grown to a precariously balanced mound. "I wonder if Harpur was ever offered a virgin as a sacrifice."

"According to Sok, he has. Edlyngton Bloomregaard attempted to bribe him with a virgin sacrifice once." Arthur said. "It was right before Harpur pretended to seek permission to act as Boundary guard on Earth when he went there to keep an eye on me. He was still keeping the full scope of his magic secret at the time, which makes no sense to me either. I mean why not just be yourself? Why pretend that you don't possess magic when you do?"

"Dragons, like all races, have their own idiosyncrasies. Somehow, somewhere, someone decided that keeping their magic a secret was an advantage and the rest of the dragons adopted the notion. I suspect that it makes them feel superior," Bon suggested.

Arthur snorted. While all this talk of dragons was fine and well, he was growing bored with tapping on eggs. "Davynn has resigned and Eowyn Hunter is the new captain of the guard," he announced as he bounced the toe of his boot off the shell of a brown egg.

"Ah," Bon said. "He is a fine young man. I believe he will do an excellent job."

"I agree," Arthur said, surprised at Bon's casual acceptance of this news. "He's a good lad."

"You don't sound like you're all that happy about it," Hiro observed.

Bon and Hiro both stopped what they were doing and stared at the contemplative king. When Arthur didn't elaborate, Bon prodded him. "What is bothering you, Arthur?"

"Everything is changing." Arthur picked up a blue egg focused on it. "Anayah is dead, Davynn is leaving… And Meg and Hart are… dragons. They won't be able to stay here either. What's going to happen if you are able to clone Harpur? I don't think I want him to become the dragon lord again."

The android and the Krist both nodded. Things had been irrevocably changed in the castle and the ripples were only just beginning to be felt. To Bon and Hiro, change was inevitable. Though Bon was not emotionally impacted, he did understand that people had to work through their emotions and that adapting didn't always come easy. Hiro, on the other hand, felt the emotions, but true to his kind, he processed them quickly and moved on. To him, Mezzi's disappearance was of more concern, simply because he didn't know what happened to her. He knew what had happened to Anayah and the twins, and he was involved in sorting out Harpur's problem. As far as Bon and Hiro were concerned, a little common sense was the best medicine in any situation.

Arthur sat down on a low stool and ran his fingers over the mottled shell. "You said that these were old eggs. Aren't they rotten?"

Bon returned to tapping and sorting, thankful for the change of subject. "Some are. But dragon eggs can remain viable for centuries. These were probably abandoned and left untended. Not every egg that gets laid hatches."

"There're so many of them," Arthur observed. "And you think Morgaine collected them and sent them here?"

"It makes sense," Bon said. "Who else would do this?"

Arthur tapped the blue egg and looked up at Bon, who shook his head. The dull thud indicated that the egg was no good. He placed it back on the floor and used his foot to roll it toward Hiro's pile against the wall. "When will you be ready to clone Harpur?"

"As soon as we finish sorting through these eggs. The processor is working and I will have more than enough DNA to proceed with the procedure. There are a few other small details to work out, but I am quite hopeful." Bon now had eleven eggs on the work bench.

"Well, I will leave you to it," Arthur walked toward the door. He nearly tripped over a deep-purple egg that had rolled across the floor and wedged against the end of the work bench. He picked it up and tapped it.

"Oh, how marvelous!" Bon said taking the egg from Arthur. "This one is perfect!"

"Do the colour of the eggs have anything to do with the colour of the dragon?" Arthur asked out of curiosity.

"Not necessarily," Bon said. "Often the dragon that hatches is similar in colour to its egg, but since we are genetically altering the embryo, it makes no real difference what colour the shell is."

Arthur nodded. "But the new Harpur will be purple, right?"

"He will be an almost exact replica of the old Harpur," Bon said.

Arthur started to exit the laboratory, then stopped again and turned back to the android. "And how long will it be before Harpur is really back to being himself?"

"I am working on a way to accelerate the growth process once the clone is hatched." Bon smiled reassuringly at Arthur. "It will require some magic enhancements, but I expect he will be his old self again withing a few weeks."

"How long does it take a dragon egg to hatch?"

"Once it has been exposed to fire, a couple of days."

"And how are you going to prevent Glynnis from sensing what you are doing?" Arthur was beginning to see the pitfalls in the plan.

"We will have to leave Epoh for that," Bon said. "Morgaine will assist us in finding a safe place to complete the process."

"It seems you have things well in hand," Arthur said. "Let me know if you need anything from me."

With that, he left the laboratory and made his way toward the council chambers. As he passed the kitchens, he heard a loud scream and the distinct clatter of pots being dropped. Abandoning his plan to look for Sok, he changed course and went to investigate.

Upon entering the kitchens, Arthur saw a new maid, Leia, pressed against the wall next to the big sink. A number of large pots lay at her feet. She looked terrified.

"What is going on?" Arthur asked. "Are you okay? Where is everyone?"

Leia stared across the room at Arthur. Then she pushed herself off the wall and threw herself against his chest. Instinctively, Arthur wrapped his arms around the distraught maid and tentatively patted her back in comfort. "What happened?" he asked.

Before Leia could answer, a voice filled the room with abject disapproval. "Here now! There'll be none of that in my kitchen!"

Arthur turned to see Finch marching toward them wielding a rather large wooden spoon. He moved to put himself between Leia and the hardwood threat. "Stand down!" he yelled over his shoulder. "I am your king!"

Oddly, Finch halted her advance and lowered the spoon. "King or not, you'll not be conducting yourself in such an unseemly manner here in my kitchen," Finch said, planting her chubby hands on her ample hips, the spoon still clutched in her fist.

Arthur released Leia and asked her if she was okay. The maid nodded and backed away from him, obviously still shaken. Then he turned back to face Finch. "And what unseemly manner do you think I am conducting myself in?"

"Snogging with a maid, of course!"

"I was not snogging with her!" Arthur was incensed. "She was frightened by something and I was comforting her."

Other members of the kitchen staff had filtered in behind Finch. They all looked uncertain about what they should do. Finch removed any doubt. "Get back to work! All of you!" Bodies hustled in different directions as the staff set about returning to their duties. At least half their attention remained on the king and the head housekeeper. "Frightened, was she?" Finch continued. "By what?"

Arthur looked at Leia. "What did happen?" he asked gently.

"I was washing the pots, like Mistress Finch told me to," Leia sobbed, "when something touched the back of my neck. I turned to see who was there and I swear that a woman walked right through the wall."

"Nonsense!" Finch snapped. "Women can't walk through walls."

Arthur agreed with Finch. Women can't walk through walls. "What did she look like?" he asked.

"I'm not sure," Leia said. "She was wearing a cloak. I only saw her back."

"Well, I'm sure seeing something like that would startle me too," Arthur said. "But she's gone now."

Finch harumphed. "Women walking through walls! I've never heard such a ridiculous excuse to get out of work in my life. Now pick up them pots and finish cleaning them. I'll be needing them for the pudding and vegetables. You've put me behind and I'll not tolerate you wasting another minute of my time."

Leia bent to retrieve the pots from the floor.

Arthur bent to assist her.

"That's no work for the king!" Finch barked. "The girl can do it herself."

Arthur ignored the head housekeeper and helped stack and carry the pots to the sink. Once they were safely placed in the basin, Arthur patted Leia's arm reassuringly and motioned for Finch to follow him into the little office. Muttering under her breath, the housekeeper complied.

"Go easy on her," Arthur said. "She's new to the job, but she's trying. Whatever she saw out there, it was real enough to her."

Finch snorted. "You have no idea what these maids are like, do you? They are always trying to get out of doing their work. I'll give her credit for creativity, though. Never heard that one before."

Arthur took a deep breath. Finch was not going to be moved from her belief that Leia was making up a wild story to get out of work. "If anything like this happens again, you are to report it to me immediately. Do you understand?"

Finch frowned at Arthur. "You want me to tell you every time a kitchen maid tries to get out doing her duty?"

"No, Finch," Arthur said with exaggerated patience. "I want you to report to me if anyone sees a woman walking through walls again."

"Why?" Finch was nonplussed. She couldn't believe that Arthur was taking this the least bit seriously.

"Because I am the king," Arthur said, "and I told you to."

Finch's frown deepened. She turned her back on Arthur and left the office. "Women walking through walls, indeed! What utter nonsense. Like I don't have better things to do than report to the king every time some lazy maid comes up with a wild story. It's not like she saw a ghost, for Harpur's sake!"

Arthur watched Finch waddle away. Then he, too, left the office to continue on his way to the council chambers. As he reached the kitchen door leading back into the hallway, Eowyn entered.

"Sire!" the young captain said. "What are you doing down here?"

"I was just checking on something," Arthur said. "What are you doing here?"

"I came to check on Berryl's progress," Eowyn said as if that should have been obvious.

"Right," Arthur said. "Well, I'd avoid the kitchens if I were you. Finch is in a mood."

"Isn't she always?" Eowyn replied.

Arthur had to chuckle. Eowyn had a point. "I'd like to talk to you about something else when you're done checking on Berryl. If I'm not in the council chambers, I'll be in my rooms."

"Very well, sire," Eowyn said. "Anything serious?"

"I'm not sure," Arthur said. "We'll talk about it later."

Arthur glanced back at Finch, who was still muttering about women and walls and lazy maids. Then he left Eowyn to his do his duty and headed down the hallway. He was just about to enter the council chambers when he felt a cold gust of air, almost as if someone with an icy hand had touched the back of his neck. He turned, but no one was there. He shivered involuntarily and continued into the council chambers.

The room was empty. Everyone, it seemed, was off doing their own things. Davynn was grieving for Anayah with his children. Bon and Hiro were occupied in the laboratory trying to clone Harpur. Harpur and Morgaine were Orhowyn only knew where, doing Orhowyn only knew what. Meg was probably practicing archery. Hart was probably studying how to be a dragon. And Sok was MIA. There were still a few hours before supper in the great hall. Hopefully, everyone would come together again there and things would feel more normal.

Arthur considered going to check in on Davynn, but remembered the knight was going to Braydon Wood and decided to return to his rooms instead. After Leia's strange encounter, he thought he should question the guards about the odd intruder they had seen earlier. While he had dismissed their concern, he was now beginning to wonder if there wasn't more to it.

Surrounded by eleven, small standing stones, the Well of the Ancients was a pool of crystal-clear water deep in Braydon Wood. Elves about to come of age came to this sacred place to receive their fates from their ancestors. It had been many years since Sok had first gone there and received a prophecy that changed his life forever. Expecting to be assigned to a guild and spend the rest of his life making jewelry or tooling leather, the young Sok had, instead, been instructed to give a gold coin to man carrying a silver fox. He had no idea that man would be Arthur and that he would find him on a different world, but, as fate would have it, Sok's curiosity had led him to Earth and there the prophecy had begun to unfold.

Since that fateful day, Sok had often wondered whether the prophecy had guided events, or if the events leading up to Arthur becoming king had been engineered by perception. Strictly speaking, Arthur had not been holding a silver fox; he had been holding a bag with the image of a silver fox emblazed upon it. At the time, and in the moment, Sok had been certain that he had found the right person and had not hesitated in pressing the gold coin into Arthur's hand. *But what might have happened if I had not done what I did? How would things have played out if I hadn't Bounded to Earth and hadn't run into Arthur?*

He approached the Well of the Ancients and looked past his own reflection into its depths. The last time he was there, Reine, the Singing Queen of Braydon Wood, had appeared after he had dropped dragonfoil leaves into the water. This time, he had no leaves; he had no offering to give at all. Instead, he simply leaned close to the water and called Reine's name. Elves seeking the guidance of the ancients were expected to leave an offering, which seemed to Sok to be an unnecessary step. *What good were bits of food or a libation to the Ancients? Either they will hear me and answer, or they won't.*

"Reine, if you can hear me, I need your help," Sok said to the water. "Anayah is dead and everything just seems... wrong now. I need to know what to do. I need you tell me if she's at peace."

The water remained stubbornly clear. Not a ripple marred its surface. All Sok saw was his reflection staring back at him.

He tried beseeching the Singing Queen with a plea for assistance again. "Please, Queen Reine! Please tell me what to do. I need to know if Davynn and Arthur and the twins are going to be okay. I need to know what's going to happen to Harpur."

His plea appeared to go unanswered. The water didn't change. Queen Reine failed to appear.

Sok scowled at the pool, then looked around for something he could use as an offering. As ludicrous as giving food or drink to a spirit seemed to him, Sok decided that it might be in his best interests to play along and follow the rules. But the immediate landscape offered nothing that he could improvise with. There were no berries yet. There weren't even any blossoms, the harbingers of future berries.

"Okay, so I don't have an offering to give you," Sok said to the water, "but that doesn't mean that I don't deserve your help. Can't you just talk to me because I'm asking?"

Apparently, not.

Apparently, the Ancients required some sort of offering before they would answer any questions. Reluctantly, Sok removed the gold ear cuff he always wore and balanced it on top of one of the standing stones. "Here!" he growled. "Take my favourite ear cuff, then."

Still nothing happened. The water didn't so much as undulate in response.

"Stupid well," Sok muttered as he backed away from the pool. "What a waste of time."

Sok, feeling defeated, started to walk away from the Well of the Ancients. Then he remembered his ear cuff and turned back to retrieve it. If the Ancients weren't going to give him any guidance, he wasn't going to let them keep his favourite ear cuff. But when he got back to the well, the ear cuff was gone.

"Seriously?" Sok said. Then, hoping that it had merely slipped off the standing stone he'd placed it on, he got down in his hands and knees and began to search the grass around its base. The ear cuff was not there. "Great! Just bloody great!"

He started to stand up again, intending to leave. As his eyes drew level with the top of the standing stones, Sok gasped in surprise. "What in Harpur's name are you?" he asked.

"I am known as a Sidhe. Although, strictly speaking, that is not correct."

"You look more like a he than a she," Sok said, taking in the tiny being that was standing on the standing stone where his ear cuff used to be.

The Sidhe was no more than six inches tall. It wore blue pants with a matching tail coat and had shiny flaxen hair that fell about its shoulders in miniature waves. A pair of iridescent wings sprouted from its back and its feet were clad in glossy black boots.

"Not she," the Sidhe said, "Sidhe. Sounds like she, but we threw in a couple of extra letters to differentiate us from the gender-specific pronoun. If it matters, though, I am a he Sidhe."

Sok had never heard of the Sidhe before. This minuscule creature standing before him was both fascinating and irritating. "Did you take my ear cuff?"

"I did!" the Sidhe said, patting his pants pocket. "Thank you! That was a generous offering. So shiny! I shall wear it with pride."

Sok opened and closed his mouth several times, wanting to say something, but feeling quite unsure how to respond. The ear cuff was half as long as the Sidhe was tall; perhaps he was planning on wearing it around his body, like a sash. The elf settled for sitting cross-legged so that he was, more or less, eye-level with the Sidhe.

"So," the Sidhe said, "you want to know what to do. I'm afraid that I can't tell you specifically what you are to do. I can tell you, however, that what you do decide to do will be the best course of action under the circumstances."

"That's not very helpful," Sok said. "Where is Queen Reine? I think I'd rather talk to her."

"Queen Reine is not available." The Sidhe mirrored Sok's sitting arrangement atop the standing stone. "I am your guide today."

"Then guide me!" Sok said.

"I just did," the Sidhe said.

Sok squinted his eyes and cocked his head. "I don't think you did."

"I think I did." The Sidhe scrunched up his face and tilted his head to one side.

Sok rested an elbow on his knee and stroked his chin with his fingers. "What's your name?"

"Sheldon," the Sidhe said.

"Sheldon?" Sok repeated.

"That's not my real name. My real name is terribly difficult to pronounce. I even have trouble with it sometimes, so I call myself Sheldon." Sheldon rested an elbow on one knee and stroked his chin.

"Are you going to mimic everything I do?" Sok asked.

"Imitation is the sincerest form of flattery," Sheldon replied. "I'm merely trying to let you know how much I like you."

"You don't even know me!" Sok countered.

"But I am a pretty good judge of character," Sheldon said, "and you seem like a nice elf."

"I am a nice elf," Sok said.

"Which is why you are so concerned about your friends," Sheldon said. "Only a nice elf would want to know if a dead friend is at peace."

"Is she?" Sok asked. "Is Anayah at peace?"

"Not particularly, no," Sheldon said. Then, when he saw the shock and sadness in Sok's eyes, he quickly continued, "The witch has some unfinished business to tend to before she can rest."

"What unfinished business?" Sok asked, not entirely sure that he wanted to know.

"I can't tell you that. Suffice it to say that Anayah needs to repair an artifact before she can... Do elves believe in an afterlife?"

"We live to be several hundred years old," Sok said. "Mostly we're good with that."

Sheldon nodded. "I see. Well, then Anayah needs to repair an artifact before she can move on to wherever it is that witches go when they die."

"Are you saying there *is* an afterlife?" Sok's curiosity got the better of him.

"I'm saying that witches believe there is," Sheldon said.

"Again, not very helpful." Sok scowled. "Okay. So, what artifact does she need to repair and… Wait! Is Anayah a ghost?"

"So, elves believe in ghosts, but they don't believe in an afterlife?" Sheldon surmised. "How does that work?"

"It's complicated," Sok said. "And it's irrelevant to our discussion. Tell me how I can help Anayah."

"I can't tell you that," Sheldon replied. "But Anayah can." The Sidhe looked skyward in thought. "I think."

"Ghosts can talk, can't they?"

"They can communicate."

Sok drew in a deep breath and let it out slowly. "Where is Anayah now?"

Sheldon shrugged. "I have no idea."

Sok stared at the Sidhe. "You're an odd little creature, aren't you?"

"I'm fairly standard for a Sidhe," Sheldon said, not seeming to take offence.

"What about Arthur and the twins? How are Meg and Hart going to fair now that they are dragons? Will Glynnis banish them from Epoh?" The twins were not the only ones to harbour this concern. Sok was quite afraid for them.

"The twins have some challenges ahead of them," Sheldon answered. "Arthur will follow in the footsteps of his ancestor. But you shouldn't worry about that too much."

How can I not worry about that? Sok wondered. "And Harpur? What becomes of him?"

Sheldon scrunched up his face as he searched for the right way to respond. "Harpur Diggins is long dead."

"No, he's not," Sok said. "His spirit is trapped in Karrys Evergreen's body. Bon and Hiro are trying to find a way to release him. Are you saying that they won't succeed?"

"I think you will find that Harpur Diggins' spirit is not *trapped* in the she-dragon's body at all." Sheldon suddenly stood up. "That's all the time I have for you, Sok. It's been a pleasure to be sure. I wish you well in all your future endeavors." Sheldon turned and moved to the edge of the standing stone. He took a position as if to dive into the water.

"Wait!" Sok shouted. "Don't go. I don't understand what you're telling me."

"You will," Sheldon said, "when you are meant to."

"That's it? That's all the help you're going to give me?"

Sheldon turned back to face Sok. "You ask too much of me. I am not here to tell you how things will be. If I did, you would make choices that could influence the fates of many others. I cannot give you such power. And you might end up thinking me a liar. Trust that life is unfolding exactly as it should. For everyone. Let yourself be surprised and delighted by events. Remember the advice you gave Eowyn Hunter this very day. Walk your own talk, Sok." The Sidhe chuckled.

"How do you know what I said to Eowyn?" Sok felt like he shouldn't have been surprised by that. But he was somewhat disturbed. "Why doesn't Davynn want to be captain of the guard anymore?"

Sheldon reached into his pocket and withdrew Sok's golden ear cuff. It appeared to have shrunken down to Sidhe size. He toyed with it for a minute. "The only constant in all the multiverse is change, Sok." He tossed the cuff to the elf who watched in amazement as it grew to its normal size and landed in his palm.

"Thank you!" Sok said, wrapping the treasured trinket around his ear.

Before Sok could ask any more questions, Sheldon dove into the Well of the Ancients and disappeared without making a splash or a ripple in the water. "You really aren't very good at this guidance thing," Sok called after the strange little being. He placed his hands on his hips and tried to ferret something useful out of his brief and enigmatic encounter with the Sidhe. *Anayah has to repair an artifact? Meg and Hart have challenges that they have to face due to being dragons. Harpur isn't trapped in Karrys' body. Arthur will follow in an ancestor's footsteps? Davynn wasn't captain of the guard anymore, but I still don't know what his plans are. I have to listen to my own advice. At least Sheldon didn't give me a prophecy to fulfill. Hmm... I think I need to find Anayah.*

Turning his back on the Well of the Ancients, Sok began to make his way through Braydon Wood to Colwygshire. By the time he arrived, evening had fallen and supper was being served in the great hall. Sok entered and made his way to the head table where he slipped into his seat on Arthur's right. The empty chair between them, reserved in Harpur's memory, felt like a mile-wide chasm and Sok decided it was time to close that gap. He shifted to his left and reached for a wine jug, from which he filled Harpur's unused cup. A gasp rose up from the crowd of people seated in the hall, causing Arthur to abandon his conversation with Bon and Hiro, who were seated in their appointed chairs at the end of the head table.

"What are you doing?" Arthur asked. "That's Harpur's chair."

"Harpur Diggins is dead, apparently," Sok said, "and change is the only constant in the multiverse. I would prefer not to have to lean across an empty seat just to talk to you."

Several questions popped into Arthur's mind, but he chose not to make a fuss in front of the supper guests. "We will talk about this later," he whispered to the elf.

"Indeed, we will," Sok replied, lifting his cup to his lips and taking a long drink of sweet wine. "I don't suppose you've seen Anayah lurking around anywhere, have you?"

Concern for Sok's sanity replaced Arthur's annoyance at the elf's audacity. "Are you okay?" he asked.

"I'm just dandy," Sok said. "Have you seen her?"

"No," Arthur said, cautiously. "Have you?"

"Not yet," Sok said. "I was hoping that you might have and could tell me where she's hanging out." Sok smiled at Arthur. "I think it's time you welcomed tonight's guests, don't you?" He raised his hand, signaling a footman to sound the trumpet announcing the king's nightly toast.

Arthur stood as another footman pulled his chair away to make room. He lifted his own cup and realized that it was still empty. A serving maid rushed forward to fill it, but Sok waved her away and poured the wine into the royal chalice. This obvious breach of protocol, elicited another gasp from the crowd and effectively rendered Arthur's prepared speech forgotten.

"Uh… Welcome!" Arthur said. "Uh… Enjoy your meal." He sat back down, dragging his chair closer to the table himself. The footman behind him was unprepared for the brevity of the king's speech and failed to do his duty. Unsure what to do, he stood blinking at the back of Arthur's head until Sok dismissed him with a wink and a nod. "What has gotten into you?" Arthur asked, forgetting that Sok was closer than he should be and leaning a smidgeon too close to the elf.

Sok pushed Arthur gently away. "I'm taking my own advice," he said. "I'm enjoying the moment."

Supper passed in relative silence. The crowd was watching for any other changes in the behaviour of the occupants of the head table, waiting for something more to gossip about during the entertainment that was scheduled to follow the meal. To their great disappointment, Arthur, Sok, Meg, Hart, Hiro and Bon, the only ones in attendance that night, carried on as if nothing was amiss. The meal ended and, as the servants cleared the tables, Arthur made his final announcements.

"Thank you all for sharing this meal with us tonight. As always, we are grateful for the efforts of Finch and the kitchen staff for preparing such a delicious supper." He raised his cup to the head housekeeper and the cooks. "I will be retiring early to my chambers tonight. In light of recent events, my family and advisors will not be staying for the entertainment, but I welcome you all to remain and enjoy the performances our esteemed Versifier to the King, Olly, has arranged for you. Good night."

To a smattering of polite applause, Arthur left the table and made his way to the exit leading to the stairs. The footman replaced the king's chair while the other members of the head table, scrambled to follow Arthur out of the hall.

"Orhowyn's wicked wings!" Hart complained. "I wanted to hear Olly's new song. He's written an ode to Anayah."

"I want to hear what's going on with Sok," Meg whispered to her brother. "What possessed him to sit in Harpur's chair tonight? Father did not look pleased."

Arthur stopped on the second floor and told the others to continue to his chambers. "I'll join you there shortly. I'm just going to check in on Davynn before we begin."

Sok veered off from the others and followed Arthur. "Should we send for Eowyn?"

Arthur paused. "I suppose we should. Also, make sure there's a place for him at the head table tomorrow night."

"Of course," Sok said, thinking that it was too soon to replace Davynn, but rather looking forward to the reaction of the supper guests. He wished he had thought of it earlier. "But what if Davynn decides to come back? The table isn't big enough to keep adding chairs."

"Then commission a bigger table." Arthur rounded the corner and headed toward Davynn's door.

Sok frowned. "Or, we could remove some chairs."

Arthur stopped. "The empty chairs stay."

"Arthur, they aren't coming back," Sok said quietly. "I think it's time that we let them go."

"The chairs stay!" Arthur continued toward to his destination.

"How about we keep them on the dais, but off to the side? That way your guests will still know you are remembering your lost loved ones, but there's room at the table for any changes." Sok did not continue walking.

As the elf suspected, Arthur stopped again. "The. Chairs. Stay."

Sok sighed. "We'll revisit this again later."

Arthur started walking again. Then stopped again. "Don't do this, Sok," he said. "I'm not ready for this."

Sok took a step back and looked Arthur squarely in the eye. "Keep Alex's chair. But move the others. Let those of us that are still here sit together like we should. Show the guests that we are united, rather than separated by our tragic losses."

This was a perspective that hadn't occurred to Arthur. *The only constant is change. We have to show the people that we can adapt; that we are not broken by loss.* "I'll think about it." Arthur turned, walked to Davynn's door, and knocked upon it.

Davynn answered the door and looked hard at Arthur and Sok as if he was deciding whether or not to invite them in. The king and the elf both affected aspects of innocence and waited respectfully for the knight to make up his own mind. Saying nothing, Davynn finally stepped back and held the door open for his friends to enter. *Might as well get this over with.*

Neither Arthur nor Sok had spent much time in Davynn and Anayah's suite of rooms. Though they had both been there before, they were both struck by Anayah's presence in the décor. The soft pillows on the sofa. The tapestries on the walls. The candles on the mantle. They wondered how Davynn was coping with the constant reminders.

"Are the children in bed already?" Arthur asked, perching on the edge of the sofa and clasping his hands between his knees.

Davynn nodded. "They are. Anayah liked them to be in bed fairly early."

Sok noticed one of the tapestries next to the fireplace ripple slightly like it had been disturbed by a breeze. He shifted his gaze back to Davynn, but kept the tapestry in his peripheral vision, ready to look should it move again. He was pretty sure he knew where Anayah's ghost was at the moment.

"How are you doing?" Arthur asked, unaware of rippling tapestries or Sok's interpretation of them.

"To be honest," Davynn said, "I'm angry."

Arthur remembered the anger he felt when Alex had died. He was never really sure what he was angry about, but there were moments when his wrath was solidly directed at Alex for leaving him. "I understand," he said. "Do you need anything? Is there anything we can do for you?"

Davynn shook his head. "I don't think so." The tapestry rippled again and one of the candles on the mantle guttered, then went out. "Orhowyn's rotting bones! This keeps happening." He stood up, retrieved a match from a box on the hearth and relit the candle. He was clearly aggravated.

Arthur and Sok exchanged a concerned look.

"Maybe it's Anayah letting you know that she's still with you," Sok suggested much to Arthur's complete horror.

"Sok!" Arthur yelled at the elf.

But before he could finish his admonition, a cold gust of air blew through the room, the fire in the hearth flared and all the candles in the room went out.

Arthur and Sok both jumped to their feet. Standing with legs apart and knees bent, the elf's hand went to the ever-present dagger at his hip. Arthur jumped back to avoid the razor-sharp point of the blade as Sok raised it defensively.

"Watch it!" Arthur shouted.

"Anayah?" Sok called out, sure now that the witch's ghost was nearby!

In the dim light, Davynn moved closer to Sok and took the dagger from him. "I'm going to relight the candles and then you're going to tell me what in Harpur's name that was all about."

Arthur glared at Sok and then went to assist Davynn with the candles. "Don't you have any lamps?"

"I think I do." Davynn handed Arthur a match. "But I don't know where Anayah put them. She always preferred candle light to lamp light." He struck the match in his own hand and lit the first candle. Then, taking it from its holder, he used the candle to light more.

"Can I have my dagger back?" Sok asked and was relieved when Davynn handed it to him pommel first.

"Keep it in its sheath," Davynn instructed.

The three friends settled onto the sofa and chairs. Davynn and Arthur trained their eyes on Sok.

"Well?" Davynn prompted.

Sok squinted his eyes and drew his lips into a tight line, concentrating on what he was going to say. "I think Anayah is a ghost."

Davynn leaned back in his chair, crossed one ankle over his knee and draped his hands over the chair's arms. "A ghost?"

Sok proceeded to describe his encounter with Sheldon at the Well of the Ancients. "Apparently, I am to help her repair an artifact."

Davynn looked at Arthur to see if he was buying any of Sok's story and was chagrined to see that the king was nodding his head in absolute acceptance.

"That tracks," Arthur said matter-of-factly.

Davynn's eyes shifted back to Sok. "You're both insane."

"How else do you explain what just happened?" Sok asked with a shrug. "We just have to figure out how to communicate with Anayah and find out what she needs."

"My wife is not a ghost." Davynn spoke softly, but Sok and Arthur heard the edge of irritated doubt behind his words.

Sok shrugged again. "Okay."

"Okay?" Arthur parroted.

"If Davynn doesn't want to accept that Anayah is a ghost, who am I to argue? Sooner or later, she will materialize and then we'll all see that I am right." Sok tapped his long fingers on the arm of the sofa.

"Actually," Arthur began, swiveling toward Davynn, "I think Sok might be right. There was an incident in my chambers earlier, and another one in the kitchens a while ago that kind of makes sense now." Davynn and Sok both waited for Arthur to enlighten them further. He told them about the guards' strange behaviour and their assertion that an intruder had entered his rooms. Then he told them about Leia's encounter with the woman who walked through the wall.

"That doesn't prove that Anayah is a ghost," Davynn said, denying the plausibility Arthur's account loaned to the situation.

Arthur could see the growing strain in Davynn's eyes. "Let's just put a pin in that for now, shall we?" Not sure exactly what Arthur meant by that, the knight and the elf remained silent. So, Arthur took advantage and changed the subject. "I came here to see if there is anything you need me to do for you. Can I help in any way with the arrangements for Anayah's funeral?"

Davynn took a deep breath. "Thank you, but no. I've decided to keep it simple, just those Anayah was closest to. The children want to take her ashes to Braydon Wood near the Boundary. Alexa thought that her mother would be happy close to a place that leads to another world. She loved hearing Anayah's stories about Bounding to different places and..." Davynn's voice trailed off.

"That sounds lovely," Arthur said. "When would you like us to gather?"

"I want to send word to Elder Dhonna first," Davynn said. "As soon as she is able to be here, we can..." Again, the knight's voice faltered.

"Of course," Arthur said. "What about Harpur?"

"What about him?" Davynn asked.

"You don't want to wait until he can be here?" Arthur suggested.

Davynn uncrossed his legs and folded his hands in his lap. He stared down at them for a long moment before he spoke. "Harpur hasn't been around for a long time. I'm not sure he deserves such a courtesy after everything he's done." Sok and Arthur exchanged worried looks, but before either of them could interject, Davynn continued, "I know how close Anayah and Harpur used to be. I've heard the stories. I also had to live with Anayah's grief after he was defeated, and her anger when he reappeared as Morgaine. When Anayah discovered what Harpur had done, how he tricked us all and then abandoned us, she was..." Davynn stood up and began pacing in front of the hearth. "Well, she was livid.

"Don't get me wrong, I liked Harpur well enough. But every bit of sorrow that Anayah endured was because of that dragon's recklessness. Being banished from Mysturna ate away at her. She might have hidden it well from all of you, but I saw the sadness and the grief. Not a day passed when she didn't talk about her aunt and Anabettah. I would sometimes find her sitting alone, rehashing everything that led up to Anabettah's death, trying to figure out what she could have done differently. She would obsess about it for hours sometimes. Not once did she ever blame Harpur, though. Not once did she ever hold him accountable for his part in it." Davynn paused. "But now I do."

Sok and Arthur did not reply. Davynn was grieving. He needed somewhere to direct his pain, someone to hold responsible for his loss. And Harpur, they both reasoned, was a reasonable target, in spite of Davynn's earlier claim that it was not Harpur's fault that Anayah was dead. It's not like Davynn was completely wrong about Harpur; the dragon had had his hand in all of it. But Anayah helped formulate the plan to lead Edlyngton Bloomregaard's evil wraiths into the Boundary. It was Anayah who had asked for Anabettah's help and had insisted that it would work. Which it did. The wraiths were destroyed. Unfortunately, so was Anabettah, and along with her, so was Analeetah's sanity. The thing was, Harpur's overarching goal was to save Epoh from a would-be tyrant and keep the peace. He had sacrificed a lot to do that: his own health and well-being, for example. Even knowing all of this, the elf and the king still struggled with where to place the blame.

Arthur knew that Davynn knew the whole story as well. He was, after all, the captain of the guard in Colwygshire, and had been a soldier when Bloomregaard had staged his coup. But grief changes one's perspective, and Davynn needed to justify Anayah's death somehow. Instinctively, Arthur could see where this was all going. Harpur's pending resurrection, so to speak, was a possibility that Davynn was struggling with. If Bon and Hiro were successful in cloning Harpur and returning his original spirit to the clone, Davynn would have to face his nemesis. At the same time, Harpur was loved and respected by his friends who had missed him and wanted him back; Davynn could hardly deny them the chance to reunite with the mighty dragon lord. As a friend to Davynn, Arthur had no choice but to give him the space and time to make his own decisions. Still, he couldn't quite bring himself to fully open that door for the knight. He wasn't ready to face more grief.

"I understand," Arthur said, looking pointedly at Sok who appeared to be coming to the same conclusions.

Sok narrowed his eyes and opened his mouth to speak. Then he thought better of it and stood up instead. "Are you joining us in the council chambers in the morning?" he asked.

Davynn shook his head. "I think I'd rather stay here with the children."

"Of course," Sok said. "Arthur? We should get going."

Reluctantly, they left Davynn to his thoughts and feelings and made their way silently back to Arthur's chambers.

Chapter Fourteen

Meg and Hart were listening closely to Bon's explanation of cloning. Well, Hart was listening closely; Meg was feigning interest by nodding whenever Bon's eyes shifted in her direction. She couldn't care less about how the android was going to make a new body and transfer Harpur's spirit into it from Karrys'. She just wanted to jump out the window, transform into a dragon, and fly over Braydon Wood for a couple of hours. She also had a strange hankering for venison—well done!

The discussion between Hart and Bon, with the occasional interjection from Hiro, was boring Meg to death. She considered excusing herself, but she wanted to see her father before she retired and she wanted to find out how Davynn was actually faring. Depending on Arthur's assessment of the knight's state of mind, Meg thought she might visit Davynn and the children in the morning, maybe offer to take the little ones to the market so Davynn could have some time to himself if he needed it.

While Bon droned on about the particular challenges in cloning a dragon, Meg's own feelings about it were wavering and she wondered why everyone was so keen to help Harpur at all. After all, Harpur got himself into this mess; it seemed only fitting that he should get himself out of it. Helping him had cost them all someone very dear to them. And it wasn't like Harpur could simply reprise his role as Dragon Lord of Epoh. It seemed to Meg that the sudden reappearance of a dragon who was supposed to be dead would dredge up all sorts of complications. She didn't totally understand dragon politics, but she'd heard enough to know that what Harpur had done was beyond the pale. At best, once Harpur's shenanigans were revealed, he would be banished by the dragons. More likely, though, he would be put to death anyway. This whole thing seemed to be nothing more than an exercise in futility. *Is Harpur doing this out of some sense of remorse for what he had done to Karrys? Is he merely trying to right a wrong? Or does he think that he will be welcomed back by his kind with open wings?* From the stories about the great purple dragon, hubris was one of Harpur's most palpable qualities.

Meg yawned.

She decided to give Sok and her father just a little while longer. Then she would excuse herself and hope that she didn't miss anything of any great importance. Catching up could be tricky with this bunch sometimes.

The princess was just about to bid the others good night when Arthur and Sok finally came through the door, effectively ending Bon's unbelievably dull monologue on cloning in a magical world versus cloning in a science-based world. The only truly interesting thing about it was that magic made it much easier, if not less unpredictable.

"How's Davynn?" Meg asked, perhaps a little too loudly.

"And how are you, Meg?" Sok said, plunking himself down beside her on the sofa. "It's so nice to see you too."

Meg rolled her eyes. "Hello, Uncle Sok. How are you tonight?"

"Pretty good," Sok said, "all things considered."

"What do you mean?" Hart asked. "Is Davynn okay?"

"He will be," Arthur said. "He just needs some time to himself right now."

Arthur helped himself to a cup of ale and sat down in the wing chair across from Meg, Hart and Sok, and next to the sofa currently occupied by Bon. Hiro was standing next to the balcony doors, looking up at the night sky.

Meg and Hart both turned toward Sok and waited for him to expand on all the things to be considered.

Sok and Arthur had discussed several things on the way from Davynn's rooms. They had agreed not to mention the possibility that Anayah was a ghost. There was no need to add that to the others' already full plates just yet. Finding Anayah and sorting that out was now Sok's project. In spite of the two incidents with the guards and the maid, Arthur was still struggling with the idea of Anayah's ghost now haunting the castle.

What they had not agreed on was what to do about the twins. Sok had made the pitch to send them away to keep them safe. Arthur believed they would be safer if they stayed in Colwygshire where he and the others could help them if need be. They just couldn't transform.

"A dragon is a dragon, whether it's a thirty-foot scaly beast, or it's in its tiny little human form," Sok had argued. "Glynnis is going to sense them."

"We've been back for several days," Arthur countered. "If Glynnis could sense them, he'd already have made it known to us."

"I think they would be better off in Andonsheer," Sok insisted. "They would blend in better there. And Morgaine is there; she could watch over them."

Arthur could see the logic. He just couldn't imagine having to send his children away.

"I'll think about it," Arthur had said.

"Why don't we ask Meg and Hart what they want to do?" Sok suggested. "They are adults now. It should be their choice."

"They aren't really adults yet," Arthur said. "They are only sixteen."

"And sixteen is an adult."

"Not where I come from."

"But it is where they come from!"

Arthur had no comeback for that. To him, adults did not become adults over night. It was a process. And it was a process that he wasn't quite ready to enter into. If they were on Earth, Meg and Hart would be in high school. They'd just be learning how to drive a car. They'd be applying for their first jobs. They'd be thinking about college. They'd just be starting to navigate their first romantic relationships.

Arthur's stomach did a repulsed dance in his abdomen. Like it or not, his babies were growing up. The process would have begun no matter where they lived. At least in Epoh, there were no cars!

Sok did not appear to be forthcoming, so the twins turned back to their father.

"All what things considered?" Meg asked.

"Nothing to worry about," Arthur said. "Sok is just being dramatic."

"We'll see how dramatic things get when…" the elf began.

"A bridge not yet built, let alone crossable," Arthur interrupted.

"You're wondering what to do about us, aren't you?" Hart said.

"What do you mean?" Meg stared at her brother.

"If I have to guess," Hart said, "Sok wants to send us somewhere safe and Father wants to keep us close."

"Well, I want to stay here!" Meg said. Her shoulder blades suddenly began to itch.

"Well, I think we'd be better off somewhere where being dragons isn't going to get us killed just because we're dragons." Hart directed his statement at Arthur, who looked at his son with a good measure of fear. "I finished reading that book that Morgaine told us to read," he turned to Meg, "and if Glynnis discovers what we've become, he has every right to try to kill us."

Meg was slightly horrified. "Or," she said, grasping at the only straw she could find, "we can kill him."

"It's not that simple," Hart said. "If Glynnis were to attack us, which is his right, and even if we were lucky enough to win the fight, we'd still be in the wrong according to dragon law. We are not welcome here anymore. We are a threat, even if we don't intend to be."

"I don't understand," Meg said, real terror beginning to grip like vise. The itch in her shoulder blades intensified.

"Epoh is Glynnis' territory. By dragon law, no other dragon is allowed to be here without his permission. The fact that we are in his territory without challenging him for rulership means that we are committing a crime. And that crime is punishable by death." Hart took a deep breath and waited for his words to sink in.

Sok gave Arthur an I-told-you-so look, but kept his mouth shut.

"Maybe it won't come to that," Arthur said, also grasping at ethereal straws. "Maybe Bon will finish cloning Harpur before Glynnis figures things out and Harpur will know how to handle things."

"Harpur is the reason we're in this predicament in the first place!" Hart said. "He's the one that put the sigils on our heads with his blood. He's the one who forced this on us. We were babies, for Orhowyn's sake! Honestly, I hope that Bon's plan doesn't work and that Harpur doesn't come back. He's never been anything but trouble. Look what he did to you, Father. I'd rather put my fate in Glynnis' claws than trust that interfering pillock to fix things."

Arthur felt his heart sink at his son's words. Hart was right, of course. But Harpur never intended this for the twins. He'd only wanted to ensure they were safe. Again, his allegiance altered. "Harpur did what he did because he loved you…"

"Arthur?" Hiro called from the balcony door. "You better come see this."

Arthur placed his cup on the low table between the sofas and rose from his chair. "What is it?" he asked as he approached the door.

Sok, Bon, Meg and Hart all rose and followed.

In the moonlight over Colwygshire, Glynnis was circling. Counter-clockwise.

"Shit!"

Swearing wasn't a thing that happened in Epoh and Arthur had fallen out of the habit of using profanity to punctuate his emotional responses to situations. But every now and then, an oath that started with Harpur or Orhowyn followed by a dragon body part just didn't cut it. Something stronger was required.

"Shit! Shit! Shit!"

Sok was the only one present who had any sense of the sentiment that Arthur was trying to convey. When Arthur had first arrived in Epoh, he'd used this— and other cuss words—frequently. While the elf had never quite grasped the correlation between excrement and disaster, he had come to accept that humans from Earth somehow did. He also accepted that Arthur's exclamatory announcement was likely to precede one of the king's infamous meltdowns. He had to take charge.

Motioning to the others to join him on the other side of the room, Sok left Arthur to work through the perceived crisis on his own. The priority was to get Meg and Hart anywhere outside the borders of Epoh. Now.

"You two," Sok said to the twins, "zap yourselves to Andonsheer. Look for Morgaine and stay with her until we can come and find you."

The problem with that plan was that Meg and Hart had never been to Andonsheer. Not knowing exactly where it was meant that they could end up... anywhere. Including inside a wall or a tree or a rock. Neither Meg, nor Hart were willing to risk the possibility of ending their lives in such a gruesome way.

"We don't even know what Glynnis wants," Meg protested.

"I think it's reasonable to assume he senses dragons in his kingdom," Sok said. "You need to get out of here. Now!"

"Sok is right," Hart said. "If Glynnis senses us, we do need to leave. If he's here for another reason, Father can send word to us. But I don't think we should attempt to zap ourselves to Andonsheer. It's too dangerous. Why doesn't Hiro take us there on the hover gilly. It can bend time, so we can get away before he realizes it."

Hiro giggled. He called the ever-present hover gilly to them.

"Your abrupt absence could confirm Glynnis' suspicions," Bon said. "I suggest that you prepare to leave, but wait until Arthur has spoken to him. There is a possibility that he has some other reason to speak to Arthur."

All eyes turned to Arthur, who was ranting next to the balcony door, arms flailing, feet pacing.

"Hopefully, that runs its course quickly. Glynnis isn't going to be happy if he's kept waiting too long," Sok said. Then he turned back to the group. "Bon has a point. But I'd feel better knowing you two are somewhere safe. I think you should leave immediately. It's up to you."

Meg and Hart looked at each other. It was clear that Meg didn't like the idea of leaving at all, but she didn't want to have to face Glynnis in a fight. As much as she wanted to protest, there wasn't time for further debate. "Let's go," she said.

Hart took her hand as they stepped onto the hover gilly with Hiro. Bon took advantage of Arthur having paced away from the balcony door to open it so Hiro could guide the hover gilly through. The moment the telekinetically controlled craft cleared the railing, Hiro forced it into a sort of psychic hyper-drive and they disappeared into the night. Sok held his breath as he watched Glynnis' big head snap toward the castle. Even from this distance, he could tell the big, bronze dragon had sensed the motion, if not the hover gilly's cargo. Glynnis continued to circle, though it seemed to Sok it was with less patience and more menace.

The cool air wafting in through the open doors was enough to kick Arthur out of his fit. He spun on his heels and looked at Sok and Bon. "Where is everyone?"

"Hiro took Meg and Hart to Andonsheer to look for Morgaine," Sok said. "You better get down to the field and talk to Glynnis fast. He's not going to like being kept waiting."

"Oh," Arthur said, disappointed that he didn't get the chance to take charge of the situation and be the one to save his own children. "Of course."

Accompanied by both Sok and Bon, Arthur made his way out of his chambers, down the stairs, across the expansive castle foyer and out into the Colwygshire night. They descended the wide steps and walked quickly down the paved road to the main city gate in the western wall. Already shut for the night, the iron portcullis barred their passage. They had to wake a guard to open the smaller door in the gate to let them out.

"I would dearly love to know how much we pay the guards to sleep," Arthur said to Sok as they waited for the sleepy guard to fumble through the keys on his belt to find the right one.

"They have very little to motivate them without any threat to keep them alert," Sok replied, not so much in the guard's defense as in Davynn's for never having forced the issue.

Arthur sighed. He caught Sok's veiled revelation and decided to accept it. Still, it rankled that the man was earning his keep with his eyes closed. "I will have to talk to Eowyn about this," he said, impressing his own veiled revelation of displeasure upon the guard.

"Good luck," Sok said.

They passed through the door and turned to their left to follow the city wall. There were torches lit on either side of the gate, but they only illuminated a small area in front of it. Beyond that, Arthur, Sok and Bon found themselves in the dark with nothing but the pale light of the crescent moon above to guide them. For Sok and Bon, this was no problem; both the elf and the android could see perfectly well in the dark. Arthur's human eyesight was no match for the enveloping darkness, so Sok and Bon each took an arm and led him into the field where they waited for Glynnis to land.

The dragon lord's huge body alighted ten yards away from the trio. He pumped his wings, sending a blast of wind in their direction, nearly knocking them off their feet.

"What took you so long?" Glynnis demanded.

"It's good to see you, too, Glynnis," Arthur said. "Why have you gotten me out of bed at this late hour?"

"Good one," Sok whispered, nudging Arthur's arm.

"There's a dragon in my kingdom again," Glynnis announced.

"Is there?" Arthur asked, feigning surprise. He was rather pleased with himself for keeping his anxiety in check; the meltdown had seemed to exorcise the worst of his fears. He'd always found being assertive the best way to deal with Glynnis. They dragon lord was more impressed with confidence than timidness and tended to be somewhat less threatening when Arthur presented an air of conviction. "And what would you like us to do about it?"

Glynnis snorted. "I would like you to tell me where it is so I can kill it."

"If I knew, I'd tell you," Arthur said, "but I am not aware of any dragon, other than you, of course, being in Epoh. Perhaps you're just sensing me. I have dragon blood in my veins and you are probably just picking up on that."

"It's not you," Glynnis snarled. "I know your scent. You smell like chicken. Probably taste like chicken too. No, the dragon I sensed was in the castle."

"You're mistaken," Arthur said, ignoring the barb. "You are welcome to transform into your human guise and come inside to check for yourself." Beside him, Sok stiffened.

Glynnis's eyes widened at Arthur's suggestion. He didn't know that Arthur knew the full scope of his magical abilities. "What are you talking about? I am a dragon. I do not have the ability to become human in form. Even if I did, why would I want to imitate one of you lowly creatures?"

"You're pissing him off!" Sok whispered.

"My mistake," Arthur said humbly. "I was thinking about the dragons on Alpha Centauri. I forget sometimes that the dragons on Thraeh are limited in that way."

"What are you doing?" Sok hissed.

"Dragons are dragons on any world," Glynnis growled. "And you are making up this Alpha Centauri."

"I assure you Alpha Centauri is a real place. But my point is that there are only a couple of rooms in the castle large enough to accommodate a dragon's body. If there was a dragon inside the castle, how would it get there? The doors are not big enough for a dragon to enter. And even if one did manage to get inside, there have been no reports of one. Surely, someone would have seen it. Unless, of course, dragons here can shapeshift and we just don't know about it. Surely, you can see how I got confused."

Sok relaxed a little. But only a little.

Glynnis' eyes narrowed and he released a puff of smoke in annoyance. He'd been backed into a corner and the only way out he could see was to acquiesce. "Indeed. It would be difficult for a dragon to enter the castle. That does not mean that there isn't a dragon somewhere in my kingdom."

"The only dragon I am aware of is you," Arthur said with an innocent shrug of his shoulders.

"Where is the little one?" Glynnis asked. "The one that giggles all the time."

"Oh, he's gone south somewhere," Arthur said dismissively. "I think he said he was heading toward the Crysteel Sea to look for some rare plant that grows on the shores of the Sands of Sancheera. He's kind of funny that way. Always looking for strange new plants to add to his collection."

"When did he leave?" Glynnis pried, thinking to trip Arthur up and turn the tables back in his favour.

Arthur looked at Bon. "He left just before we came out here to meet Glynnis, didn't he?"

Bon nodded. "I believe that is correct."

"If you were in bed, how would you know that?" Glynnis smiled smugly.

"Bon told me when he and Sok came to wake me to come talk to you." Arthur smiled an equally smug smile.

Glynnis growled. Foiled again. He knew that Arthur was lying; he just couldn't pin-point where the deception lay. With no other ploys to play, the dragon lord decided to give up. "Very well. But I will find the invader. And I will kill him."

"As you wish," Arthur said, stifling a sudden gulp of fear. "May I go back to bed now?"

Glynnis didn't answer. He turned away and prepared to launch himself skyward. Then he stopped and swung his head back around to face Arthur. "Little king," he began, "if I am challenged, I will request that in the event of my death, all humans are to be banished from Epoh."

Arthur wanted to ask Glynnis why he didn't exercise his prerogative to banish all humans from the kingdom himself, but his better judgement quelled his curiosity. *Why put the idea in his head?* "Isn't that up to the challenger if he wins?"

Glynnis didn't answer, but the look he gave Arthur suggested that Arthur had just been tested. And he had failed the test.

"I need a drink."

Bon and Sok both looked away from the retreating dragon lord and trained their gaze on Arthur.

"I need a real drink."

This, of course, confused Sok, but Bon understood the sentiment, if not the requirement. "I have some whiskey aging in barrels in the back of the laboratory," he said.

Arthur seemed rather pleased by this announcement. "That will do nicely," he said. Then he turned back toward Colwygshire. Now that his eyes had adjusted to the darkness somewhat, he was able to pick his way back to the gate on his own.

"Whiskey?" Sok asked.

"I think you'll like it, Sok," Arthur said. He turned to Bon on his left. "Thank you for your foresight, Bon. I don't know why I didn't think of asking you to brew some up for me sooner."

"Strictly speaking," Bon began, "whiskey isn't brewed."

"Whiskey?" Sok repeated.

"Brewed. Distilled. Whatever." Arthur was just looking forward to something stronger than ale. "How long has it been aging?"

"There is a small batch that is nearing fifteen years," Bon said.

"Excellent!" Arthur said. "We'll start with that."

"Whiskey?" Sok reiterated.

By the time they had walked back to the castle, after having to re-awaken the gate house guard to be let back into the city, Bon had explained in painful detail the process of distilling fermented grains to make hard liquor, or spirits, as he called them. The android was about to launch into the different types of whiskey and their histories, but Sok's eyes had glazed over and he was sorry he'd pressed for an explanation.

"Sounds awful," the elf said by way of cutting Bon's tedious narrative off, "but I'll give it a try."

The trio repaired to the laboratory where Bon fetched a small, spouted barrel from a back corner and placed it on the work bench.

"We need glasses," Arthur said, his mouth watering in anticipation.

"You're a wizard," Sok reminded the king, whose cheeks reddened with mild humiliation.

"Perhaps I should get some from the kitchens," Bon suggested and left the room without waiting for a reply. In spite of Arthur's recent successes with his magic, his friends were conditioned to his failures and were still of a mind that while he could indeed conjure two glasses, he could just as easily conjure something else. Such as a kitchen maid. Or worse, Finch herself.

Arthur shook his head at Sok. "It's a couple of glasses. I'm sure I could manage that."

"Bon wanted to get them," Sok said, to which the king responded with an eye roll.

When the android returned with the glasses, he filled each of them with a finger of the golden liquid from the barrel and handed them to his companions.

"Is that all we get?" Sok asked, holding the glass up and staring dubiously at the nearly empty vessel.

"Trust me," Arthur said, "this is enough." He held his glass up. "To better days ahead." Then he tossed the shot into his mouth.

Sok watched in appalled fascination as Arthur's face scrunched up and a violent shiver convulsed his body. "Ooh, lordy!" Arthur wheezed. "That's got some kick to it." He handed the empty glass back to Bon to refill.

"I think I'll pass," Sok said and placed his own glass down on the table.

"Aw, come on, Sok. Try it." Arthur repeated the ritual. This time he was prepared for the burn and the paroxysmal tremor that followed it was drastically less intense. "Another!" he said to Bon, passing his cup to the android.

"I have not tested the proof on this batch," Bon said. "You may want to take it easy. When was the last time you drank anything stronger than ale?" It seemed prudent to caution the king at this point, before the liquor took effect.

Arthur looked up at the ceiling, trying to recall that last time he'd had the pleasure of drinking such a fine, not to mention potent, single malt. "A long time, my friend. It's been a very long time."

"Then I advise you to sip it rather than shoot it," Bon said. "I suspect your tolerance is not what it used to be." He handed a third shot to Arthur, who was already feeling the warmth spreading through his body.

"You're a wise man, Bon," the king said, capitulating to the android's sensible advice. He turned back to Sok. "Go on, take a sip."

The elf looked at Bon, who assured him that it was perfectly safe. As long as he didn't overindulge.

"Very well," Sok said, lifting his glass to his lips and taking a tentative sip. "Oh! That is interesting!"

Arthur smiled. "Told you."

Sok took another, more substantive, sip. "I like it!" He downed what remained and shook off the burn much the same way Arthur had. "I see what you mean by it having a good kick."

"I take it my efforts have been successful?" Bon inquired.

"Indubitably," Arthur said with a decidedly Hiro-like giggle.

Sok accepted a second glass of whiskey from Bon, but chose to sip it slowly. "You better put that away, Bon," he said, pointing to the barrel. "I can see how this could get out of hand rather quickly."

Arthur agreed, albeit reluctantly. Part of him wanted to thoroughly drown his current sorrows, but he knew that would not help anything in the long run. Having had a taste, though, and knowing that there was more if he wanted it, he settled for the relaxing light buzz that was taking over his mind. "What are we going to do?" he asked as he watched Bon pick up the barrel with ease and tuck it back in the corner.

"About?" Sok replied.

"Everything!" Arthur said. "Harpur, the twins, Davynn, Anayah's ghost..."

"Anayah's ghost?" Bon interrupted. It was his turn at being taken aback.

As if on cue, a cold blast of air blew through the laboratory and a shimmering figure appeared near the doorway.

"Bloody hell!" Arthur shouted. He jumped up off his stool and staggered back away from the apparition.

"Ah, Anayah," Sok said like talking to ghosts was an everyday occurrence. "I'm so glad you could join us. We have much to discuss." He paused for a moment. "Are you able to communicate with us?"

The elf stood up, but did not approach the ethereal manifestation of his dead friend. Anayah's ghost did not reply; she simply stared at Bon with a pleading look in her pale eyes. Slowly, she raised her right hand and pointed at the android. Her mouth moved as if she was speaking, but no sound came out.

Sok could see from the growing desperation on her face that the effort to communicate was beyond her ability. The harder she tried, the more faintly she appeared. "Hey, Anayah!" he shouted, hoping to get her attention. "Slow down. Just take your time. We're here for you." That last statement gained a slight shift in Anayah's demeanor. She turned her gaze away from Bon toward Sok and she leveled a blazing glare in his direction. "Okay. It's okay. I know you're not happy with us right now. But we really do want to help you." That just seemed to make Anayah angrier. She balled her fists and disappeared.

"Way to go," Arthur said. But he was secretly relieved that Anayah was gone.

"At least I tried," Sok said over his shoulder. "I wish I knew what she was trying to say."

"I can help you with that," Bon said.

Sok and Arthur looked over at the android who was fiddling with something on his chest under his robes.

"Did you record that?" Arthur asked.

Sok was aware of Bon's ability to record things, but it creeped him out a little and he made a face at Arthur for bringing it up. "You're not going to do that thing with your eye where you make a little image appear in midair again, are you?"

"Actually, I am going to project a holographic reproduction of what we just witnessed over the table so we can study it," Bon said. "If I slow it down a bit, maybe we can read her lips and figure out what she was trying to tell us."

As a shocking green beam of light shot out of Bon's right eye, Sok picked up the remainder of his whiskey and tossed it back. Then he looked sadly at the spot on the work bench where the whiskey barrel had been only a few minutes earlier. Before he could look away, a spectral image of Anayah's ghost appeared on the table and he could hear his own disembodied voice saying, "Ah, Anayah! I'm so glad you could join us…"

"That's so cool," Arthur said. But he said that every time Bon projected a holographic image.

Sok grimaced and then grimaced again when he remembered that his glass was still empty. He turned his attention to the dragon eggs that were piled up against the wall and left Arthur and Bon to their *lip reading*.

"Can you filter out Sok's voice?" Arthur asked.

A moment later, the elf's words faded away, but they were replaced by a crackling noise that almost sounded like a voice. Arthur leaned closer to the image, though the sound was coming from a small speaker on Bon's chest.

"Can you enhance that?" Arthur asked.

Sok did his best to filter out Arthur's voice, but even he couldn't help being intrigued. He closed his eyes and trained his ears on the crackling.

Bon fiddled with the controls under his robe. It didn't help. "I am afraid that is as good as it is going to get."

"I think that's Anayah's voice," Arthur said. "I'm sure it's her voice."

"I believe you are correct," Bon said.

"How is it that we can hear her on the recording, but we couldn't hear her when she was speaking to us?" Arthur asked.

"My microphone is ultra-sensitive," Bon said. "It will pick up sounds that the human ear cannot detect." He restarted the projection and Anayah reappeared in miniature on the table. Because she was so small and so shadowy, Bon was unable to read her lips. Nor could he make sense of her crackly voice. When the recording ended, Arthur asked Bon to play it again.

"Damn," Arthur said again. "I still can't figure out what she's saying."

"She said, 'Harpur must not die. Find the walking stick.'," Sok said.

Bon stopped projecting the hologram of Anayah's ghost and turned to the elf, who was still looking at the pile of eggs. "Are you sure?" the android asked.

"How did you get that from the gibberish on the recording?" Arthur asked.

"I listened," Sok said. "And yes, Bon, I'm sure."

Bon seemed to be listening to the recording internally. "It is plausible," he conceded.

"So, what does that even mean?" Arthur asked, scratching his head.

"I think it means we have to find Harpur's walking stick," Sok said. He had picked up one of the dud eggs and was tossing it back and forth from one hand to the other.

"But that was lost... before I came to Epoh," Arthur said. "How are we supposed to find it?"

"I assume you are talking about a walking stick that belonged to Harpur?" Bon interjected.

"He carried it with him everywhere," Arthur said. "I never could figure out why he didn't try to find it himself. But after all this time, where would we even begin to look for it?"

Across the room, Sok sighed. "Why don't you just try conjuring it?"

Arthur stared at his senior advisor for a long moment. "I can try. I can barely even remember what Harpur's walking stick looked like. What if I conjure the wrong one?"

"At least you will have tried," Sok snapped. "Why do you resist your magic so much? Why can't you just be the wizard you were born to be?"

"Why can't you just leave it alone?" Arthur snapped back. "Why is it so important to you that I use my magic?"

"Because you don't seem to appreciate what a gift it is. Or how much easier you could make things for yourself, and everyone else, if you stopped being such a coward and…"

Arthur felt like he had been punched in the gut. He couldn't breathe. For several agonizing seconds he stood there, staring in disbelief at his best friend. "Did you just call me a coward?" he finally managed to croak.

Sok stopped tossing the egg and returned it to the pile. "If the shoe fits…" he snarled.

Arthur, close to tears, and overwhelmed with humiliation and anger, flipped Sok the bird. "Screw you!" he said. Then he stomped out of the laboratory.

"Wait! Arthur, I'm sorry. I didn't mean…" Sok called out as he started to follow the furious king.

But Bon stepped forward and caught the elf by the arm. "Let him go," the android said. "Now is not the time."

Sok yanked his arm free from Bon's grip, but did not continue to pursue Arthur. "He just doesn't get it."

"And maybe he never will," Bon said. "Not the way you do at any rate. Not everyone who possesses magic is meant to wield it, Sok. And Arthur is from a different world. He wasn't raised to be a wizard."

"I know." Sok hung his head in contrition. "It's just so frustrating to know that he could be a great wizard if he tried."

"Well, don't be surprised if his chambers are not filled with sticks—walking and otherwise—in the morning," Bon said with a knowing wink.

Sok snickered as he imagined Arthur attempting to prove him wrong. He rubbed his eyes and yawned. "It's late. I'll apologize tomorrow. I'm going to go to bed and try not to think about how awful I feel right now."

Bon watched the sulking elf leave the laboratory and recorded a hypothesis on the potential that anger had to motivate humans to acts of greatness.

Chapter Fifteen

Time-bending hover gillies are especially useful when avoiding dragons with invidious intentions. While Meg and Hart were grateful for the telepathically controlled contraption and its telepathic owner, they were heart-broken to be leaving Epoh with so much uncertainty and grief as their only luggage. Minutes after Hiro had whisked them out of Arthur's chambers, they found themselves floating over a lush jungle on their right and the edges of a desolate desert on their left. It was disconcerting to know they had travelled as far as they had from their home in Colwygshire in so short a time.

As the city of Andonsheer came into view, they realized that finding Morgaine might not be an easy task. It was much bigger than Colwygshire and, from their vantage point high above, they could see it was teeming with thousands of people all dressed in bright colours that swirled and mixed and separated again as the throngs shifted and moved through the streets.

"How are we going to find Morgaine in that?" Hart asked.

"How are we going to get through all those people with the hover gilly?" Meg asked.

"I'm going to drop you off outside the city gates," Hiro replied. "I'm sure you will be able to sniff Morgaine out eventually." He giggled at his pun, though he actually meant it quite literally.

As the Krist began their descent toward the city, Meg and Hart processed Hiro's words.

"You're just going to leave us here?" Hart asked.

"Alone?" Meg completed the thought.

"You'll be fine. Andonsheer is a relatively safe city. Most folks are friendly and welcoming. You shouldn't have any trouble." Hiro's attempt at reassuring the twins failed miserably.

"But we don't know our way around," Meg complained.

"And we don't have any money," Hart pointed out.

"Use your magic to conjure any money you need," Hiro said. "Make your way to the market square and ask for directions to a hostel. There are several scattered throughout the city."

"What about Morgaine?" Meg asked. "How are we supposed to find her?"

"Like I said," Hiro said and giggled again, "sniff her out."

Meg and Hart looked at the Krist in utter disbelief.

"You want us to go around Andonsheer smelling everyone?" Hart said.

"You are dragons," Hiro explained. "You have extraordinary senses now that you can use to your advantage. You will recognize Morgaine's scent when you smell it."

The twins both took deep breaths and were astounded at the information their olfactory senses picked up. They could smell the desert. And the jungle. And the city walls!

"Oh, my!" Meg exclaimed. "This is really weird."

"I can smell feet!" Hart said.

Hiro brought the hover gilly to the ground outside the main city gate that faced east toward the Sands of Sancheera and practically had to shoo the twins off of it.

"Can't you stay with us for a while?" Meg begged.

"You are adults now," Hiro reminded her and her brother. "Adults figure things out for themselves."

Neither of the twins expected such a terse dismissal from the Krist. But they suddenly realized how much they had relied on their father's protective nature. It was alarming to know that they were now completely on their own for the first time in their lives.

"What if Morgaine isn't here?" Hart asked.

"She's here... somewhere," Hiro said. "It's not like she can present herself as Karrys, is it?"

Hiro didn't wait for a response. He turned the hover gilly around and flew away, leaving the nervous twins to their own devices. It wasn't that he wanted to leave them there alone; the very idea was upsetting for him. But he had to trust that they would find Morgaine and all would be well. Had he known that Morgaine was not, in fact, in Andonsheer, he would have made a different choice. As it was, though, Morgaine was once again being held prisoner in a cell not far from where Meg and Hart now stood in practically paralyzed uncertainty.

After leaving Epoh, Morgaine Fayle had gone to hide in Andonsheer while Bon and Hiro worked on the processor. She had intended to lay low until they sent word on their progress. Harpur had never liked the city, mostly because it was too close to the enormous compound where his kind held their gatherings, a place he tended to avoid as much as possible. Karrys wasn't overly keen about being in Andonsheer either, but for a different reason. Namely, it was full of people.

Their decision to go there was practical. First, they could blend in and go more or less unnoticed by the general population. Second, dragons sometimes entered the city in their human guises and they were likely to come across one of their kind from whom they could get a feel for the political and social climate in the dragon community. It had been a long time since Karrys had defeated Harpur and subsequently abandoned Epoh, but dragons tended to have long memories and they didn't think it would be too difficult to gather some valuable intelligence on how their kin felt about the whole affair. Once Harpur and Karrys were free from each other, Karrys intended to return to the Sands of Sancheera and explain that she had been captured on another world, held prisoner, tortured and experimented on until she managed to escape. Not only was it true—she was missing enough scales to prove it—it would also enable her to return to a normal life as a dragon.

Harpur, on the other hand, would be much harder to explain. He was believed to be dead and gone, having been fairly and squarely defeated by Karrys. His resurrection after so many years would come as something of a shock. He would be scandalized for his crime of cheating death in such an unseemly and undignified manner. At worst, he would be sentenced to death anyway. At best, he would be mocked for having done it because he cared for and wanted to protect his human, elven and dwarven friends. He was already considered eccentric among his kind. Either way, he would be ostracized and the great purple dragon would become a pathetic laughing stock.

He'd had sixteen years to think about what he'd done. After the escape from the facility in which they had been imprisoned, Harpur's remorse was more than he could bear. His primary motivation for freeing himself from Karrys' body was simply to make amends, to give her life back to her. He didn't want to die, but he couldn't keep Karrys in what was essentially another kind of prison for the rest of her life.

Besides, it was weird being in a female body.

Karrys and Harpur had debated what he should do after they were separated. He considered taking over Glynnis' body, but his new ethics regarding possessing another being quickly put paid to that idea. They talked about going to the Dragon Council together and trying to pass off what he'd done as an act committed by his friends in Epoh. Again, the ethical considerations around throwing them under the wagon wheels, so to speak, were no better than taking over another dragon's body. Plus, there was no guarantee that the Dragon Council would not find Karrys complicit in the arrangement and punish her as well. His choices seemed to come down to two; confess his sins and take his lumps, or leave Thraeh forever. At all costs, though, Harpur was determined to ensure that everyone else involved came out of it relatively unscathed. That, however, was shaping up to be something he was unlikely to achieve. At least as far as Karrys was concerned.

They had been in Andonsheer for less than a day when they came across another dragon in human form. The woman, dressed in red and black, approached them in the market while they were purchasing meat pies for their lunch.

"I know you," the dragon-wizardess said.

"I'm sure you must be mistaken," Morgaine replied. She knew instantly that she was talking to another dragon, but she did not recognize the scent. Still, she instinctively felt uncomfortable and tried to dismiss the woman by walking away.

"I know I know you," the woman said, catching up to Morgaine and laying a firm hand on her shoulder.

"Take your hands off of me," Morgaine growled. "I don't know you and I don't want to." Again, she stalked away, hoping to lose herself in the crowd.

But the other dragon-wizardess would not be put off. She followed Morgaine through the market.

Karrys: What should we do?

Harpur: I'm going to duck into the next alley and become invisible.

Karrys: "How is that going to help? She will still be able to follow our scent.

Harpur: Not right away. The breeze is in our favour.

Harpur slipped into a narrow alley and vanished. Then he ran toward the opposite end.

Harpur: When I reappear, I'm going to change the way we usually look.

Karrys: And how is that going to help?

No matter how Harpur transformed their appearance, he couldn't do anything about their scent.

Harpur: It will throw her off. She's seen us as Morgaine Fayle and that's who she'll be looking for.

Harpur found a recessed doorway and stepped into it. Thankfully, there was no one around when he reappeared, still as a woman, but with short, blonde hair instead of Morgaine's trademark raven locks. To hide her missing right eye, he conjured a pair of round spectacles and shaded the lenses so no one could see the scarring. He completed the disguise with an outfit more akin to what an Andonsheer native might wear, a long, purple skirt, topped with an orange and yellow striped tunic, belted at the waste with a black sash. He traded the knee-high leather boots for a pair of sandals and instead of a hat, a pink scarf was tied around her head. Satisfied that there were no obvious similarities to Morgaine's typical style, Harpur headed back toward their original destination, the hostel.

Harpur: Upon further reflection, Andonsheer was not the best choice for a place to hole up.

Karrys: You think?

Karrys caught their reflection in a window and gasped involuntarily.

Karry: I thought you were known for your good taste!

Harpur: It's not that bad!

Though he, too, was eager to get back to their room where no one could see them.

When they finally arrived at the hostel—sans meat pies—Harpur sat down on the bed and tried to figure out where they could go and how he could get word back to Bon as to where they could be found. Thankful that Karrys wasn't nattering at him, Harpur considered and rejected a dozen different places for being either too far away from Epoh, or having too many dragons. There was only one place that came to mind where they would be safe: Whyte Avenue.

Harpur: It's perfect. We'll zap into the Boundary House and Bound to Earth. My old lair is still accessible and we won't have to worry about what we smell like. Well, not in the sense that a dragon will recognize us and turn us in to the Council."

Karrys: I don't like it there. There has to be somewhere on Thraeh we can hide.

Harpur: We're going to Whyte Avenue!

Just as he was about to zap them out of the hostel, the room was filled with red-black smoke and the dragon-wizardess they had met in the market appeared next to the bed. With her were two other dragons in human guise and before Harpur could react, one of the dragon-wizards clamped a collar around Morgaine's neck and the other snapped a pair of cuffs on her wrists. The collar and cuffs were magically enhanced to block the wearer's own magic. Harpur and Karrys weren't going anywhere.

"Karrys Evergreen," the dragon-wizardess said, "you are under arrest for abandoning your kingdom and failing to fulfil your sworn duties to its occupying lesser races. You will come with us to the compound to face the Dragon Council and answer for your crimes."

"Who are you?" Morgaine was incredulous.

"I am Astrideous Garaday," she said as if Morgaine should know that.

"Never heard of you," Morgaine said after a moment of reflection.

"I was there when you declared your intention to challenge Xzynthyrius Dreamfinder."

"Huh," Morgaine huffed. "I didn't notice you."

The insult was taken at face value. Astrideous clenched her fists and glared at Morgaine. "Well, you'll never forget me now." With that, she snapped her fingers and zapped herself, Morgaine and her two minions to the compound south of Andonsheer.

The moment they appeared in the compound, Astrideous and the other two dragon-wizards transformed. Morgaine, unable to transform due to the collar and cuffs she was wearing, remained in her human guise. She was surprised to see that Astrideous was a yellow dragon.

"Why do you wear red and black in human form when you're yellow?" Morgaine asked out of sheer curiosity. Typically, dragons wore clothing that was the same colour as their dragon scales.

"I am working undercover," Astrideous snapped. "Why are you dressed like a court jester when you are a blue-green?"

"I was trying to get away from you," Morgaine admitted. "But if you take these off, I'd be happy to change back into something more *appropriate*." She held her shackled wrists up.

"All in good time," Astrideous said. "First, we will see you safely locked up in the cells." She stepped away from Morgaine to speak to the two other dragons, who flew off as soon as she was finished talking.

"Off to call on the Council?" Morgaine asked.

"I'm sure they will be eager to convene when they hear you have been captured," Astrideous said. "I'm also sure you know the way to the cells. March!"

Morgaine started walking toward the north wall of the compound where a large opening led to a sloped tunnel leading to the cells. Harpur's plan was to cooperate until they got to the cell and then zap out the moment the collar and cuffs were removed. But when they arrived at the furthest cell on the right, Astrideous only removed the cuffs.

"What about the collar?" Morgaine asked.

"That stays on," Astrideous said. "But don't worry, Karrys, you can still transform into your natural state. The collar will adjust."

"Orhowyn's balls!" Morgaine muttered as Astrideous nudged her into the cell and then closed and locked the barred gate.

"What did you say?" Astrideous asked, unsure she had heard Morgaine correctly.

Realizing her mistake too late, Morgaine chose not to answer. Instead, she transformed into the impressive teal dragon that she was and leveled a sinister glare at her captor through the bars.

Something in Karrys' eye gave Astrideous pause and she backed away. "Never mind," she said. "I'll inform you when the Council is ready to hear your plea." With that she hurried from the cell block and left Karrys Evergreen alone with the possessing spirit of Harpur Diggins.

Karry: That was stupid.

Harpur: Slip of the tongue. Any thoughts on how we get out of this one?

Karrys: I was hoping you had a plan.

Harpur laughed out loud.

They fell silent, each of them lost in their own thoughts.

Karrys: This is the same cell where your friend... Elder Dhonna, I think her name was... was held when I sought a ruling on my defeat over you.

Harpur: I am aware.

It had taken some time for Harpur and Karrys to be able to communicate like this. Harpur didn't know what to expect when he took over her body, but he didn't anticipate that Karrys' thoughts and memories would remain, or that she could access his thoughts. When he first realized that Karrys was still very much alive and present, it took a great deal of effort to keep her thoughts from invading his. Of course, she was not happy with the situation and quickly understood how difficult it was for Harpur to concentrate. She chattered constantly, hoping that he would give up and leave. But he didn't. It was, in part, Karrys' endless invasion of thought that had caused Harpur to flea Epoh in the first place. After the confrontation with Anayah outside his lair, he was on the verge of going quite mad. He figured a trip to Earth would shock Karrys into silence.

That hadn't quite worked out as planned either. Karrys was even more upset at being taken away from her home world. On top of everything else, the culture shock and trying to adapt to life on Whyte Avenue made her worse. Then there was the problem of being in human form for an extended period of time. Harpur knew full well what that would lead to and so he decided to seek out and go to a world where dragons could be dragons. Unfortunately, that too had backfired and the result was less than auspicious. But it was during their imprisonment that they finally came to a truce and decided to work together to try to survive. In time they were able to control their thoughts and use them to converse. Now it appeared they had come full circle.

Karrys: I know. I was just making conversation.

Harpur: Then you also know that I don't want to talk about that.

Harpur snorted out of habit, and was surprised that a tendril of smoke emitted from his nostrils. He had assumed that the collar would suppress Karrys' dragon fire as well as her magic.

Karrys: That's interesting. Try breathing fire.

Harpur was ahead of Karrys on that one. He breathed deeply into his chest and released a rather satisfying plume of fire through the bars. The heat from the dragon fire was enough to cause the metal of the bars and the lock to start to melt.

Harpur: Did you know that the bars were ordinary iron?

Karrys: I did not, but what a peculiar oversight on the part of the builders.

Harpur: But is it?

Harpur lowered Karrys' head and peered at the opening between and around the sagging bars. He was not surprised to find that it had been warded.

Harpur: Do you think we are strong enough to break through once the bars are melted?

Karrys: I suspect that the warding is sufficient to keep us inside.

Harpur: Well, they are going to notice the damage to the bars. We might as well finish the job.

Karrys: For all the good it will do us.

Karrys didn't treasure the idea of an attempt to breach the warding.

Harpur, however, was nothing if not tenacious, so he blasted the bars with dragon fire until they were a molten puddle on the floor.

Karrys: You first.

Harpur: Cute.

There was a pile of junk against the eastern wall of the cell. Harpur maneuvered Karrys' body around, picked up a large chunk of metal, probably a strut from an old wagon, and threw it at the opening. Upon impact, the metal exploded, sending wickedly sharp shards back into the cell.

Karrys screamed as one of the shards pierced her left wing, which Harpur had failed to tuck in.

Harpur: It's just a flesh wound. It will heal in no time.

The explosion caught the attention of Astrideous, who was still outside in the compound. She rushed back to the cell, expecting the worst. From the look on her face, Harpur and Karrys could see that she was unaware of the fallibility of the iron bars as well.

"What have you done?" The yellow dragon snarled.

"I melted the bars," Harpur said nonchalantly through Karrys' mouth. "I was trying to escape."

If Karrys had control over her eyes, she would have rolled them.

Karrys: Be careful, you stupid oaf.

"This compound has stood for thousands of years," Astrideous began, "and hundreds of dragons have been in these cells. Then you come along and do this? You are a menace, Karrys Evergreen. A menace and a traitor. I hope the Council gets here soon and deals with you as harshly as you deserve."

Harpur: She really doesn't like you, does she?

Karrys: I think her opinion is actually aimed at you.

"You can't blame us… uh, me for trying." Once again, Harpur's tongue slipped dangerously.

"Us? Is someone in there with you?" Astrideous couldn't imagine how anyone else could be in the cell, but the plural could not be ignored.

"I was referring to the voices in my head." Harpur fashioned Karrys' face into a mocking grin.

Astrideous had no response to that. "I'll make arrangements to have you moved into another cell," she said and stormed away.

"I'll take the one closest to the exit!" Karrys called after her. "It will make it easier to escape once I figure out how to thwart the warding."

"Argh!" was all Harpur and Karrys heard in reply.

Karrys: Why must you provoke her?

Harpur: She kind of begs for it.

Karrys: She kind of does, doesn't she?"

Back at the castle in Colwygshire, Bon was busy preparing the viable eggs he had selected for the next step in the cloning process. Hiro had returned from Andonsheer and was doing his best to stay out of the android's way while still observing the complicated procedure, which involved much mixing and shaking and spinning of tiny vials filled with miniscule amounts of clear liquid. From time to time, Bon would extract an even more miniscule amount of the liquid and examine it under one of Hiro's favourite pieces of equipment, a microscope that Bon had built several years before.

"Is it ready?" Hiro would ask eagerly.

"Not quite," Bon would say, and Hiro would sigh. Or giggle. Or both.

While the intrepid scientists laboured in the laboratory, Arthur was in his rooms in the tower high above them. Sleeping.

Fueled by anger and a severely bruised ego, Arthur had returned to his chambers determined to show Sok that he was not a coward. The effects of the whiskey, however, were not conducive to accuracy in wielding his magic and the final result, before he crashed from exhaustion on one of the sofas, was a collection of thirteen walking sticks, none of which were Harpur's and all of which were cracked or broken, or otherwise scarred by Arthur's ineptitude at conjuring items he was unfamiliar with. If any good had come of his late-night conjuring debacle, it was that the effort had taken his mind off everything else that was going on and he was no longer worrying about Meg and Hart, or Anayah's ghost, or Davynn's grief, or Harpur's absence, or Berryl's kleptomania. All he could think about was Sok's insolent accusation and the fact that his best friend in the whole universe considered him a coward.

It was nearly dawn when he fell asleep and soon found himself dreaming about, of all things, baseball caps. Everyone in Colwygshire was wearing one, except Meg and Hart. In his dream, the twins refused to wear the caps, not even the ones that Arthur had so lovingly commissioned for them. Sad to learn that his gift was not appreciated, Arthur decreed that all baseball caps were illegal and anyone caught wearing one would be thrown in the dungeons. The first offender was none other than Sok himself, and Arthur took great pleasure at being the one to slam the cell door on the non-repentant elf.

He awoke with a start to find Sok standing next to the sofa with a tray full of pastries and two cups of jamba.

"Good morning! I see you have been busy," Sok said as he deposited the tray on the table next to the sofa and helped himself to one of the cups and a pastry. He sat in the wing chair and took a sip of jamba. "Any luck?"

"What are you doing here?" Arthur said. He sat up and rubbed his eyes.

"I came to apologize," Sok said around a mouthful of pastry. "I was out of line last night."

"So, apologize and then get out," Arthur said. After less than an hour of sleep, he was not in a forgiving mood. Especially now that Sok was aware of his failed attempts at conjuring Harpur's walking stick.

"Uh-uh," Sok said dismissively. "I'm here to help you find what you're looking for."

"All I'm looking for right now is some peace and quiet." Arthur flopped back down on the sofa and closed his eyes. "And some more sleep."

"You can sleep later," Sok said. "I know how to get the walking stick. And I know what we have to do with it."

Arthur couldn't help himself. He opened his eyes. "I'm listening."

"First, sit up and have some jamba," Sok said. "I need your full attention."

Arthur groaned. But he acquiesced and sat up again. He scratched the back of his head and reached for the jamba. Taking a sip, he leaned back to get comfortable, then, cued by a rumble in his stomach, reached forward and retrieved a pastry from the tray. "Go on."

Sok waited until Arthur was fully settled. "It occurred to me that there is a drawing of Harpur's walking stick in his life book. You can use that to focus on when you conjure it."

Arthur raised an eyebrow indicating his intrigue. *Why didn't I think of that?*

"Did you know that the walking stick was gifted to Harpur by the great Nyssira?" Sok asked.

"How would I know that?" Arthur asked. "And who is Nyssira?"

"You would know that if you had paid attention," Sok said. "It's in his life book."

"You mean the book that no one can read?" Arthur quipped.

Sok shrugged. "Well, that is one of its drawbacks, I'll give you that," Sok conceded. "But still, it's all in there."

"Anyway," Arthur deflected, "what about this Nyssira person. Why is he significant?"

"She," Sok stressed, "is significant because she made the walking stick." Sok paused to let that sink in. "Nyssira is a powerful sorceress from the Black North."

"And?" Arthur prompted.

"And she is the one who can use it to bring Harpur back."

"How?"

"Well, that I don't know," Sok admitted. "But when we find her, we can ask."

"Where do we find her?" The jamba was beginning to take effect and Arthur was getting into the spirit of things.

"I just told you, in the Black North." Sok sounded slightly exasperated.

"The Black North? Isn't that where Bloomregaard's wraiths were from?" Alarm bells were starting to go off in Arthur's head.

"I believe so," Sok said with another shrug, "but they are dead."

"They were dead when they were alive," Arthur pointed out. "What's to say there aren't more wraiths in the Black North?"

"I'm guessing there probably are," Sok said. "We'll just have to avoid them."

"So, you're suggesting that we... and I'm assuming you mean you and me... go to the Black North and look for the sorceress who made Harpur's walking stick and ask her to use it to bring Harpur back? What's wrong with Bon's plan to clone him? I think we are much better off letting Bon do his thing and not go to the Black North, and not have to avoid wraiths, and not look for a sorceress who we know nothing about!"

"Ah, but we do know a lot about the sorceress," Sok said. "I did some research on her last night after..." Sok thought better about mentioning the incident in the laboratory. "...I did some research last night and, according to the information that is available, she's... a decent sort."

Arthur was dubious. "Define decent sort."

"Nyssira is known for her benevolence," Sok paused, "more or less."

Arthur stared at his senior advisor. "You're kidding, right?"

Sok drained his cup and stood up. "Not in the least," he said. "Nor am I *suggesting* that we go to the Black North. We are leaving as soon as you conjure the walking stick." He headed to the door. "You'll need to pack some warm clothes, I hear it's cold over there."

"Sok?" Arthur said as the elf opened the door to leave.

The elf stopped, but didn't turn back.

"I'm still waiting for that apology."

Sok did turn around then. He looked at his best friend and said, "I am sorry, Arthur. You are not a coward and I was out of line saying that you are."

"Thank you, Sok. I'll be down shortly."

The elf nodded and left the king to the meltdown that was sure to follow.

Elder Dhonna and King Röggenar had arrived back at the elven city in Braydon Wood, bedraggled and hungry, two days after they were sent out of the Fae Lands by Glynnis Warwyrm. Hot baths, warm meals and a good, long sleep in Edler Dhonna's tree house were the only things on their minds. And once they had soaked the Fae Lands out of their systems, filled their bellies and rested properly, they were ready to make the short trip into Colwygshire to find out what had happened on Mysturna.

They had set out together the same day that Davynn had resigned and promoted Eowyn to take his place as captain of the guard and were about half way to the city when they met the knight and his children coming toward them in a light wagon. The elf and the dwarf moved to the side of the road and waited for Davynn to pull the wagon to a full stop.

"We were just on our way to the city," Elder Dhonna said, noting the strain on the knight's face.

"And we were just coming to make sure you made it home from the Fae Lands safely," Davynn said. "Climb in. We'll go back to Braydon Wood. The children are looking forward to spending some time there."

Elder Dhonna hopped lightly into the back of the wagon. It took some effort, but between her and Alexa, they managed to haul the short, squat dwarf in with them. As soon as they were settled, Davynn snapped the reins and the sorrel mare started forward at a jaunty trot.

In no time at all, they rolled through the gates to the elven city where two young elves met them and assured Davynn they would look after the horse while he was visiting. Alexa, Brodie and Caleb saw some friends playing in a clearing and ran off to join them. At first, Davynn was hesitant to let them go off by themselves, but Elder Dhonna assured him that they would be okay; Anayah brought them to Braydon Wood quite often and they were familiar with the elven children and knew how to find Elder Dhonna's tree house if they needed their father for anything.

"Where is Anayah?" Elder Dhonna asked when they reached the tree house. "We assumed they were back from Mysturna?"

Davynn had to fight to stay calm, but the look on his face belied his effort.

"Oh, no!" Elder Dhonna could barely breathe. "What happened?"

Davynn recounted the story as he had heard it from Morgaine. He ended the account with his retirement from the royal guard and his intention to move to Branwyke.

It was a lot for Elder Dhonna to absorb. The idea that her dear friend was dead was unthinkable. Anayah, so willfully strong, could not possibly be gone.

Röggenar took the shaken guild master's hand and held it gently. "Will there be a service for her?" he asked.

Davynn nodded. "The children want to take her ashes to Braydon Wood near the Boundary house. We would like you both to be there."

"What about Harpur?" Elder Dhonna asked.

Davynn frowned. "Morgaine has left Epoh," he said simply. "I don't intend to wait for him to be available."

Elder Dhonna could tell there was more behind that statement, and she sensed that Davynn was doing his best not to offend her by saying anything bad about Harpur. This was not the time or the place to poke that wound; she would save that for a more appropriate time.

"Is there anything we can do to help?" she asked instead.

"I don't know how to plan a witch's funeral," Davynn said. "I don't suppose you know anything about their rituals?"

Elder Dhonna looked at the grieving knight and smiled. "I'm afraid I don't. That's not a conversation Anayah and I ever had. But funerals are not for the dead, Davynn. They are for the living. You must say good bye to her the way that feels right to you. No matter what her kind's traditions are, she would be more pleased if it came from you, than if you simply performed a rite that has no meaning to you."

"Thank you, Elder Dhonna," Davynn said. "Will you help me plan it?"

"Of course, I will," she said. "I am honoured that you asked me."

The knight, the elf and the dwarf spent the rest of the afternoon reminiscing about Anayah, while they watched the children from the balcony of Elder Dhonna's tree house. The warm spring sun and the laughter of the children helped to sooth their pain. Davynn, especially, relished the smiles on Alexa, Brodie and Caleb's faces. He knew there would be more tears, but right then, their laughter was like a magical soundtrack for the stories he and Elder Dhonna were sharing about Anayah while Röggenar listened respectfully. All too soon, it

313

was time to leave and Davynn wished he didn't have to take the children back to the castle.

Dragons accused of crimes were not exactly deemed innocent until proven guilty. If a dragon was imprisoned, pending trial, for any reason, it was because there was incontrovertible proof that an offense had been committed. According to Astrideous Garaday, Karrys Evergreen's prolonged absence from Epoh was incontrovertible proof that she had abandoned the kingdom, and broken her oath to protect its citizens, both of which were serious breaches of the code of honour dragons liked to think they lived by. While it was indeed incontrovertible that Karrys had been away from Epoh for sixteen years, no dragon, other than Karrys herself, knew what had kept her away.

When word of her disappearance first reached the dragon community, the council had decided to hold a contest for the kingdom's rulership. Glynnis Warwyrm had won that contest by defeating eight other dragons. One of those dragons happened to be Astrideous' mate, a blue dragon named Raks Ojen. The fight between Raks and Glynnis was vicious and bloody. Glynnis gave no quarter to any of his opponents, and Raks, being the last of the eight to vie for rulership over Epoh, saw the worst of Glynnis' unrelenting brutality. Rather than blame the bronze dragon for her mate's death, Astrideous imputed her great loss onto Karrys and vowed to see her brought to justice. It didn't matter that the Dragon Council had decreed that should Karrys ever return, she be given the opportunity to explain herself before any judgement be made against her. Thus it was that when the Dragon Council convened, they were less than thrilled to find Karrys imprisoned by the vengeful Astrideous Garaday.

The compound was teeming with dragons of all colours when Karrys was led out of her cell and brought before the Dragon Council, a tribunal consisting of a red known as Themeela Sandward, a white known as Durnor Hornblower, and Khol the Black, Dragon Lord of the Kingdom of Rednow. As she took her place in front of the podium on which the council members stood, Karrys held her head high and showed no fear. Around her, hundreds of dragons whispered to each other, commenting on her missing eye and her audacious return after sixteen years. Some sympathized with her; others did not. But all were eager to find out what really happened.

Foregoing protocol and bypassing the conventional reading of the crimes of which Karrys was accused, Khol the Black stepped forward and peered at the collar around her neck. "Why is this thing around her neck?" he demanded of Astrideous.

Somewhat taken by surprise, Astrideous looked at the collar that prevented Karrys from using any of her natural dragon magic. "She is accused of the serious crime of abandoning her kingdom. The collar is there to ensure she does not escape before she is sentenced." Astrideous couldn't imagine why Khol had even asked. It wasn't the first time a dragon had been brought before the council with their magic subdued this way.

Khol looked at his fellow council members. "Do either of you recall Karrys Evergreen being accused of any such crime?" Themeela and Durnor both shook their enormous heads. "Neither do I. As I understand it, the Dragon Council at the time of Karrys' disappearance decided that if she ever returned, she would be given the benefit of any doubt and allowed to explain herself."

Astrideous felt her dragon fire begin to burn hot in her chest. This was not the way she had expected things to go. "Your Honours, Karrys Evergreen disappeared only weeks after defeating Xzynthyrius Dreamfinder and has been gone for sixteen years. The only conclusion is that she abandoned her kingdom and left its citizens unprotected."

Khol turned to Karrys. "Is that the only conclusion?"

"No, your honour, it is not," Karrys said with confidence.

"Can you explain why you left Epoh and where you have been all this time?" Khol asked.

"I left to go explore another world where I knew other dragons existed. I did not know that our kind was hated and hunted there, or that my magic would not work. I was captured and imprisoned. They would have killed me, but my teal scales were unknown there and so they imprisoned me. I was subjected to torturous experiments while I was there. If I could have returned to Epoh, I would have." Karrys kept her gaze on Khol as she spoke. Too late, she realized her mistake. Just as she finished delivering her brief account, she saw the recognition in his eyes.

"I see," Khol said, stifling a gasp. "I was unaware that you were of the sort who enjoyed exploring other worlds. That sounds more like something Harpur Diggins would have done."

Karrys gulped. *He knows. Orbowyn's ashes! He knows who I am.* "I am not the sort who enjoys exploring other worlds, especially after what happened to me." she said. "But everything in the kingdom was in good order and I thought I might try it. As you said, Harpur Diggins was an avid explorer. I thought I would see what compelled him to do such a thing."

Khol looked at Themeela and Durnor. Then he looked out across the compound at the crowd of dragons that were gathered to see what would happen to Karrys. He seemed to be deciding how to proceed.

"Bring me Harpur Diggins and Karrys Evergreen's life books," Khol suddenly boomed, causing a wave of murmurs to move through the throng.

Karrys was visibly shaken. Astrideous saw and smelled her fear and was certain that Khol had heard something in the teal dragon's testimony that rang false, and would ensure her criminal conviction. But what that could have been, the yellow dragon could not fathom. "I will get them!" she cried and immediately began pushing her way through the other dragons toward the library behind the cells in the compound where most dragons kept their life books. Harpur and Karrys' were not among them. Harpur's life book was safely stowed in the vault in Arthur's private chambers. Karrys' life book was hidden in Glynnis' lair.

Waiting for Astrideous to return gave Harpur and Karrys the chance to try to think of a way out of this newest mess. The collar prevented them from using Karrys' magic, but it did not prevent her from flying. The only problem with that was she wouldn't get far before they were brought down by a dozen or so other dragons. They were well and truly trapped, unless Harpur could convince Khol to remove the collar.

"She will not find the life books in the library," Karrys said to Khol.

"Of course, she won't!" Khol wasn't even trying to hide his anger. "Where are they?"

"They are safe," Karrys said. "I will not help you find them."

"What a surprise!" Khol sneered. "Care to tell me why?"

"I do not," Karrys said. "But I do wish to invoke my right to choose an advocate."

Humans in Colwygshire may not have understood what an advocate was, but dragons were very familiar with the concept. Rare though it was, any dragon accused of a crime had the right to choose a representative to protect them, even act as their champion if the need arose. The very fact that Karrys had asked for one now, threw Khol into doubt about his suspicions.

"And who do you call upon for this dubious honour?" Khol asked.

Any misgiving Khol was beginning to entertain about his suspicions was thoroughly crushed when Karrys looked him in the eye and said, "You. I choose you, Khol the Black, as my advocate."

The crowd around Karrys erupted into chaos as the news spread from dragon to dragon. Within seconds, dragons began launching into the air and flying in all directions, presumably to share the incredible development.

"You cannot do this," Khol said in a hoarse whisper.

"I can and I have," Karrys said. "Now you must step down from the council and take me to your lair where I will be safe and we can discuss my situation in private."

Plumes of black smoke rose from Khol's nostrils. There was nothing he could do. He leaned close to Karrys' ear. "You will pay for this, Harpur Diggins. I will kill you myself!"

"You can try," Karrys said, "but first remove this collar and let's get the hell out of here."

"The collar stays on," Khol said.

"I don't think so!" Karrys replied. "Now that I have an advocate, I am not to be unduly confined or restricted."

Reluctantly, Khol the Black removed the collar from Karrys' neck and tossed it onto the podium. "Karrys Evergreen has requested an advocate," he announced unnecessarily to the rapidly thinning crowd, "and she has appointed me to that position. We will return in two days' time to state her case before the council." He then turned to Themeela and Durnor. "Who is next in line to take a seat on the council?"

"Framanjesk, son of Xzynthyrius Dreamfinder," Themeela answered.

Another plume of black smoke rose from Khol's snout. Once again, he addressed Karrys. "Did you know this?"

"I did not!" Karrys said, trying to hide her own surprise at this unexpected development. "But good for him for stepping up and doing his civic duty."

"Fly, you bastard!" Khol then launched himself into the air and headed northwest toward Rednow. As soon as he cleared the wall, Karrys followed.

By the time Astrideous realized that the life books were not in the library and returned to the podium, most of the dragons were gone. The sky above the compound was filled with them, and the few that remained were waiting to take off. She stood, blinking at the nearly empty compound, wondering if her prisoner had somehow escaped. Nearby, a small, brown dragon was about to take off. Astrideous called to him. "What happened? Where are Karrys and the council members?"

"Karrys named Khol the Black as her advocate," the brown replied. "They've gone to his lair in Rednow to plan their strategy." He didn't wait to answer any more questions.

Astrideous roared in fury. The last thing she had been expecting was for Karrys to request an advocate, but to choose Khol the Black, a member of the current Dragon Council, was simply reprehensible. *Karrys is buying time. But for what?* the yellow dragon wondered. The only place she would get an answer was in Rednow, but going there was not an option. She couldn't just show up in another dragon's kingdom and expect to be welcomed. She would have to wait until the council reconvened. And that made her roar again.

Meg and Hart were sitting on a bench in the market square trying to figure out what to do next. They had searched the whole city for Morgaine and she was nowhere to be found. The only clue they had was her faint scent in an alley way the day they had arrived. Other than that, there was no sign of her and no one they asked recalled seeing a one-eyed, raven-haired woman in the city in recent days.

After two days of searching, the twins concluded that Morgaine must have gone somewhere else and, with nothing else to do but wait until someone, probably Hiro, contacted them, they decided to enjoy their freedom while they had it. They purchased clothing more in keeping with the local style, though Meg refrained from donning one of the brightly coloured skirts that the women of Andonsheer favoured. Instead, she kept her familiar leggings, but topped them off with a vivid red tunic tied at the waist with a dark green sash. Hart chose a pair of loose cobalt pants. Snug at the ankles, they billowed out from the waist in soft folds. Like most of the other men in the city, he picked out a short, sleeveless vest in a shade of burnt orange that only accentuated his pale, northern arms.

"You look ridiculous," Meg said, trying not to smile.

"But they are so comfortable." Hart was rather pleased with the way the pants fit and felt. "I'm going to take a few of these back home with me. They are fabulous."

"Rupert will have a fit when he sees those!" Meg observed.

Hart shrugged. "Rupert will love them."

They had noticed a lot of dragons flying over the city that morning, all heading southward and now flying in all directions. Picking up bits and snippets of conversation around them, they gleaned that there was a compound somewhere near the city and that the Dragon Council must be convoking. No one appeared to be alarmed about the proximity of hundreds of dragons gathering so close to Andonsheer; it was, apparently, not uncommon, nor did whatever brought them to the compound concern the citizenry. Meg and Hart were curious, though, and they trained their hearing on the voices around them, hoping to pick up more information.

"We could just ask someone," Meg suggested. "What if it has something to do with Morgaine?"

"I doubt it," Hart said. "Morgaine would never let herself get caught."

His words had barely left his mouth when Meg nudged him and pointed up at the sky. "Are you sure?"

Hart followed Meg's finger. A black dragon, closely followed by a teal dragon, flew over the city heading north. "Is that Karrys?"

"It looks like Karrys," Meg said.

"Where is she going?" Hart asked, standing up and craning his neck to keep the two dragons in view as long as possible.

"And who is the black dragon and what are they doing together?" Meg wondered aloud.

A passerby, overhearing Meg's question, stopped and looked skyward. "That is Khol the Black," the stranger explained. "He is the Dragon Lord of the Kingdom of Rednow. He's also a member of the Dragon Council."

Alarm bells went off in the twins' minds.

"Is he now?" Hart said to the stranger. "I don't suppose you know why the Dragon Council was here?"

"I heard a rumor that a dragon had been arrested," the stranger said, "but I can't tell you why. You'd be wise to keep your noses out of it, though. Dragons don't like us poking about in their business."

"Thank you," Hart said. "We were just curious."

"Well, best you keep your curiosity to yourselves," the stranger warned. "No one here will thank you if you bring the wrath of the dragons down on the city."

"Of course," Hart agreed. "We'd never think of it."

They watched the stranger walk away. As soon as he was out of earshot, Meg gripped her brother's arm and whispered, "We need to find out where the dragon compound is."

"You want to go to the dragon compound?" Hart was incredulous. "Why? You heard what that man said."

"We aren't going to get any information from the people here," Meg reasoned. "I think we need to talk to some dragons."

Hart looked at his sister. "So, you want us to... What? Walk into a dragon compound and just casually ask what's going on?"

"No," Meg said. "We can fly into the dragon compound and casually ask what's going on."

Hart stared down at Meg's eager face. "That sounds like a very bad idea."

"Oh, come on, little brother," Meg pleaded. "You're itching to transform as much as I am. This is our chance to fly again."

"But we don't even know where the compound is," Hart argued.

"How hard can it be to find out?" Meg said. "We know it's not far. If you don't want to ask someone, we can just leave the city, transform and fly around until we see it. If it's big enough to hold hundreds of dragons, it's big enough to see from the air."

"This is a very bad idea," Hart said again. "I think we should just wait until Hiro comes back."

"But we don't know how long that will be!" Meg was growing impatient with Hart's reticence. "Besides, didn't he say we are adults now, and that we should figure things out for ourselves? Karrys could be in trouble. I think we owe it to her—and to Harpur—to do what we can to help."

Hart *was* itching to transform and fly again. But Meg had a point; they were adults, and they were supposed to figure things out for themselves. He looked up as he scrambled to think of a good reason not to do what Meg was proposing, but nothing came to him. "Well, if we're going to do this, we better do it right away."

It was his turn to point upward. The sky was filled with dragons flying in all directions. "There might not be any dragons left in the compound soon."

Meg glanced up and then smiled. "Let's go!"

Arthur awoke to find Rupert rummaging through his wardrobe. The lanky valet was hunched over and Arthur could not see his head. It reminded the king yet again of the story of the headless horseman. For a moment, Arthur entertained the notion of pretending to still be asleep and wait for the skinny annoyance to remove himself from Arthur's personal space, but then Rupert stood up. He was wearing a baseball cap on his head. Arthur sat up in his bed and draped his arms around bent legs. He waited for Rupert to turn around, which he eventually did, holding a pair of hideous shoes in his hands.

Seeing Arthur awake and watching him caused the skittish man to yelp and drop the shoes. "I thought you were asleep," Rupert squeaked.

"I was," Arthur confirmed. "Now I'm awake. What are you wearing on your head?"

Rupert reached up and snatched the cap from his balding pate, then quickly raked his long fingers across his scalp to tame the ruffled wisps of remaining hair. "Nothing, sire!"

Arthur sighed. "Rupert, do you remember when I asked you to make hats like that for the twins?"

"Of course, sire," Rupert acknowledged.

"Do you also remember me telling you that they were very special and to keep them a secret?"

"Um…" Rupert tapped a bony finger against his lips. "Now that you mention it, I vaguely recall you saying something like that."

"Then why did Meg and Hart receive dozens of them as birthday gifts?" Arthur shouted.

Clearly rattled, Rupert fell to his knees. "Forgive me, sire! I needed the help of the tailor to get them just the way you wanted them. He must have told everyone else!"

"You assured me that you could do it yourself," Arthur said through gritted teeth. "You promised me that no one would know what you were making for me." Arthur tossed the covers back and swung his legs over the side of the bed. Tugging his nightshirt down, he walked to where Rupert was cringing on the floor. "Oh, for pity's sake, Rupert, stop groveling and stand up!"

Rupert scrambled to his feet bringing his constantly bobbing Adam's apple to Arthur's eye level. The king had to take a step back so he could look at something other than the yo-yoing larynx. "You know, Rupert, I trusted you to make the caps for Meg and Hart. They were supposed to be something special; mementos of my own youth on Earth. Now, because you failed to do as I asked, my special gifts to my children aren't special anymore!"

"I'm so sorry, sire!" Rupert's eyes started to well up. "I'll have them all removed. All but the ones you asked for..."

"That's not going to help!" Arthur was yelling again. "You can't just make all those gifts from all those people disappear. That would be rude!"

"You're right, sire." Rupert was shaking with panic. "I don't know why I even suggested such a thing. What would your majesty like me to do?"

Arthur looked ruefully at the quaking man. "I would like you to stop being my valet."

"What?" Rupert gasped. "Are you dismissing me, sire?"

"No!" Arthur waved his hand as if to shoo away the very thought. "Of course not. I just think that it is time for you to retire, that's all. I'll arrange for you to receive a pension, so you won't have to worry about money. I'm sure Sok can help you find some nice rooms somewhere in the city that won't cost much to rent..."

"You've given this some thought," Rupert said sadly. "I didn't realize you were so unhappy with my services."

Arthur rolled his eyes. He wasn't going to let Rupert guilt him into changing his mind. "Then you haven't been paying attention, Rupert," he said. "I have always been honest about my feelings about having a valet."

The sympathy card having failed, Rupert turned to begging. "I'll do better, sire. I'll commission clothes you like. I'll stay out of your way. Please don't do this to me. I didn't mean for anyone else to find out about the caps."

"I've made up my mind, Rupert." Arthur looked down at the shoes his valet had dropped. They were tan suede with pointy toes and three-inch heels. Giant gold buckles glinted on the uppers. They were at least four sized too big for Arthur. "You can keep the shoes, though."

Rupert quickly bent down and retrieved the footwear. "Before I go, would you like to see the mourning suit I had made for Lady Anayah's funeral?"

"You can keep that, too," Arthur said, believing that, even if it fit him, it was probably besieged by lacey embellishments and tacky buttons.

Rupert looked disappointed. As he shambled toward the door, he said over his shoulder, "Thank you, sire, but I will leave it in the wardrobe. You may change your mind."

Arthur didn't think that would happen.

Awash with relief, and putting the pending backlash from Sok out of his mind, Arthur dressed, brushed his hair and teeth, balanced his circlet on his head and made his way downstairs, intent on joining Sok and whoever else showed up in the council chamber. But instead of going directly to his destination, he decided to check on Berryl's progress. He took the hallway leading to the kitchens, but continued past them (in spite of the delicious aromas emitting from within) and followed the corridor to an intersection. To his right, there was a short passage that led to a door that he thought might open onto the kitchen gardens. To his left, another short passage ended with a locked and barred door that might have led down to the dungeons. Ahead was a longer hallway with doors on either side. It ended at a wall about forty feet away.

Arthur was sure they had come this way when Davynn first showed him the hoard of stolen stuff in Berryl's room, but he was also sure that they had turned a corner at some point and followed another longer passage to get there. He decided to go straight forward. Maybe this was the right hallway; maybe he had just imagined turning a corner.

As he made his way down the corridor, he tried opening several of the doors. Each one he tried was locked. When he reached the wall at the far end, he turned around and made his way back to the intersection. This time the locked and barred door was on his right. There was no point in going that way, so he turned to his left and went to the door he thought would open onto the kitchen gardens. This door was not locked, nor did it open onto the kitchen gardens. It did, however, open into another corridor that swept around the outside wall of the castle in a long, doorless curve to the left. It didn't look familiar, but now he was curious.

The windowless corridor was dark. There were unlit torches along the outside wall, but Arthur had nothing with him with which to light one. He'd never used his magic to start a fire before. He wasn't even sure how he would go about it. Still, he took one of the torches out of its sconce and pointed his finger at it. Nothing happened. *Magic is all about intention,* he reminded himself. *All I have to do is focus my intention on the torch…*

After a few tries with no result, Arthur was about to give up. Then he had an idea. *What if I just pretend I'm lighting it?* He closed his eyes and imagined that he was holding a lighter. Then he flicked the imaginary wheel and was immediately rewarded with a tiny, lighter-sized flame coming out of the top of his closed fist.

Impervious to fire, all he felt was the flame dancing warmly on his skin. It was an oddly comforting sensation and he watched it for moment, mesmerized by the flickering amber light, and proud of his ingenious method of visualizing the lighter to achieve fire. Finally, touching the flame to the torch, he was rewarded with enough light to make his way down the passage way. Instinctively, he blew the flame on his hand out and pushed the door closed. As soon as the door was properly shut, the other torches along the wall began to light up one by one.

"Huh!" he said aloud. "I guess I really am getting better at this."

He returned the torch he was holding to its sconce and started down the curved hallway, which seemed, the farther he went, to be spiraling both inward and downward. His steps slowed as he began to realize the impossibility of there being such a thing in the castle. In all the years that he had lived there, he had always stuck to the main rooms: private chambers, great hall, council chambers and kitchens. He had never really explored the bastion he called home. But this hallway made no sense. There were no curved walls in the main keep; only the turrets that stood at each corner of the castle were circular in construction. Suddenly flooded with trepidation, Arthur turned around and started walking back toward the door, thinking that he would ask Sok about this strange place. But after a short while, he noticed that he was not climbing up. The corridor was still spiraling downward. Arthur turned around again. The corridor appeared to be sloping upward, but as soon as he started walking back in the opposite direction, the slope changed and he found himself descending once again. If ever there was a time to panic, this was it. Arthur braced himself against the inner wall and let the meltdown begin.

While Arthur was freaking out in the mysterious corridor, Sok was leaving the kitchens. He had just ordered breakfast and was on his way to the council chamber when he thought he heard crying coming from outside the door that led to the kitchen gardens. It sounded like Arthur in one of his meltdown states. Unable to divine what could have possibly caused Arthur to have a fit in the kitchen gardens, he turned to his right to investigate.

The door opened, as it usually did, onto the gardens, and he stepped outside expecting to find Arthur ranting about some disaster. All he found were two servants with hoes, preparing the beds for planting in the coming weeks.

"Have you seen the king?" he asked the nearest servant.

"No, sir," the servant said, standing upright and stretching the kinks out of his back.

Sok could still hear the crying. "Are you sure he's not out here somewhere?" The elf looked around for any place Arthur could be hiding.

"I'm sure," the servant said. "We haven't seen him this morning."

"Who is crying then?" Sok asked, still sweeping his gaze back and forth across the gardens.

"Crying, sir?" the servant asked, somewhat perplexed.

"Yes, crying." Sok was annoyed. "Can't you hear it?"

The servant looked around as well. "No, sir. There's no one crying out here."

Sok wandered farther into the gardens, searching for the source of the wailing that the servants seemed oblivious to. Finding no one but the two gardeners, he stopped and cocked his head, trying to determine exactly where the sound was coming from. It was close; he was sure of that. Then another thought occurred to him.

"Have you seen a shimmery figure while you've been out here?" he asked.

"A shimmery figure, sire?" the servant who he'd been talking to asked.

"Why does everyone have to repeat everything I ask?" Sok glowered at the puzzled gardener. "Do you not hear me the first time?"

The gardener was growing nervous. "I heard you, sir," he said. "I just don't understand what you mean?"

"A ghost!" Sok said, throwing his hand up in the air. "Have you seen a ghost?"

The gardener dared not repeat the elf's words again. "I have not seen a ghost in the gardens, sir."

Sok looked at the other servant, who simply shook his head to indicate that he had not seen a ghost either.

"Well, that's good," Sok said. "If you do see a ghost, don't be alarmed. She's harmless." He paused. "Probably."

The two servants couldn't help but search the area for any signs of a ghost. "What should we do if we do see one?" one of the servants asked.

"Just ignore her," Sok said. Then he walked back into the castle.

The crying was louder near the door. He'd assumed it was Anayah, likely frustrated at being a ghost and unable to talk to anyone. He called out her name and waited, hoping she would appear. There was no response, no shimmery Anayah manifested. And the crying continued. Sok closed his eyes and listened carefully.

"I should never have come down here. What was I thinking? I'm going to kill Sok when I get out of here. He should have told me about this secret hallway." Then there was a pause. "Help! I'm trapped down here! Let me out. Someone let me out!"

That is definitely Arthur, Sok thought. He tried calling the king's name, but the ranting just continued. *Secret hallway? There is no secret hallway in the castle. Unless there is, and I just don't know about it.*

Sok, forgetting all about breakfast, began examining the walls on either side of the short passage way. He was looking for a hidden doorway or hatch of some kind, but the brick walls were solid and completely unforthcoming.

Confounded and deeply concerned, Sok started pounding on the wall on the left facing the doorway to the gardens. The ranting and crying had suddenly stopped. "Arthur! Arthur, can you hear me?"

All he got in return was Arthur, in composed mode, saying, "Okay! If the hallway wants me to go down, I'll go down. But when I get my hands on that elf..."

Alarmed and baffled, Sok stepped back from the wall and stared at it. He strained to hear more, but it seemed that Arthur had moved away. His voice had faded and not even Sok's sensitive elven hearing could pick up anything from... wherever Arthur was. He dashed around the corner and opened the first door on the right, which was a small storage room, and went inside. Several barrels stood against the wall to Sok's right. Opposite them were floor to ceiling shelves containing jars of food, prepared and canned by Finch and her staff. Arthur was not in the room. Sok retreated and closed the door.

"How is this my fault?" he asked aloud.

"Is everything alright, sir?"

Sok looked up to see one of Berryl's guards coming toward him. "I'm pretty sure everything is not alright," he said. "I think that our king has gotten himself into a spot of trouble." He walked back to the short passage and looked at the wall.

The guard, having spent a considerable amount of time with Sok and having learned that repeating back anything the elf said was not worth the effort, simply nodded and waited for more information. Or instructions.

"Well, don't just stand there," Sok barked. "Go find Eowyn. He's probably in the council chambers" *Eating my breakfast.*

"Yes, sir," the guard said, shrugging his shoulders. Before going to look for Eowyn, he opened the door to the storage room and looked inside. Finding nothing but a few barrels and shelves full of jars, he scratched his head in consternation. "That elf is crazy!"

There were only two dragons left in the compound by the time Meg and Hart found it and landed in its center. One was yellow, and looked to the twins to be not in good humour. The other one was blue and appeared to be looking for an excuse to leave. As intrigued as he was at seeing a pair of strange, metallic black dragons with opalescent streaks of purple and silver through their scales, the blue dragon backed away from the yellow dragon and launched into the air.

"Follow my lead," Meg whispered to her brother as the yellow dragon approached with a menacing glower on her face.

"And who might you two be?" Astrideous asked. She had never seen dragons with the twins' colouring before. She was certain that they were not from the Sands of Sancheera.

"Did we miss the Dragon Council?" Meg asked, ignoring Astrideous' demand for identification.

Astrideous looked at the twins with deeper suspicion. "I asked you who you are?" she repeated.

"The polite thing to do when welcoming newcomers is to introduce yourself first," Meg said haughtily.

Astrideous was aghast. "Who says you are welcome?"

"Are we not welcome, then?" Meg said. "I was under the impression that dragons from all over Thraeh were welcome in the Sands of Sancheera. We only wish to see the great desert. On our way, we learned that the Dragon Council was meeting and we thought we would stop to let the locals know that we come as friends. Are you a member of the council?"

Astrideous was unsure how to deal with this insolent young stranger, who seemed unphased by her assertiveness. Whoever these two were, they were not typical dragons. Not only were they oddly coloured, but the way the one that was doing all the talking expressed herself was… different. It wasn't uncommon for dragons from other parts of the world to visit the Sands of Sancheera. From time to time, dragons from other colonies did show up, but they showed deference to the local dragons. They did not refuse to identify themselves, nor did they make assumptions about their welcome reception.

"Who are you?" the yellow dragon demanded again.

Meg had been scrambling to think up names for herself and Hart. She had no idea that there were other dragon colonies and it never occurred to her that their appearance might be questioned. "I am Huckfinn Twain and this is Tomassawyer Twain." She stumbled over her words, as she made changes to the characters' names from the stories Arthur had told them when they were little. They were the first names to come to mind and she had to improvise to make them sound more dragonish.

Hart nearly choked and a blast of purple-black smoke escaped his mouth. "Apologies," he said, composing himself and taking over, rather than following Meg's lead. "My sister tends to be a bit more forward than etiquette demands in these situations. We are adventurers from… a distant land. We are indeed here to see the great desert and had heard that there was a trial being held here today. We thought we might learn how dragon law works in this part of the world, but it seems we have missed the proceedings."

If Astrideous was baffled by the way Meg had spoken, she was outright bemused by Hart. *A distant land? Adventurers? How stupid do they think I am?* Astrideous decided to play along to see where this bizarre encounter would lead. Perhaps these two would somehow make up for her earlier disappointment over losing her prisoner. She smiled at the twins, but the grin never reached her eyes; they remained full of skepticism and distrust.

"There was supposed to be a trial," she said, "but the accused chose an advocate and so the proceedings have been postponed until the day after tomorrow."

Hart had no idea what an advocate was, so he skipped over that and went on, "Oh, how disappointing. We will be long gone by then. Who was the accused, and what was she accused of?"

It was Meg's turn to choke. "Assuming the accused is a *she*," she said glowering a warning at her brother.

"He? She? What does it really matter?" Hart said, trying to sound casually dismissive of the gender specificity he'd inadvertently used. Then he turned his attention back to Astrideous. "You were about to say...?"

Astrideous couldn't figure out what it was, but something was terribly amiss with these two peculiar, albeit striking, dragons. She decided that playing along was not the best option after all and changed tack. "I was about to say nothing. I think it would be best if you continued on to the desert and stayed out of our business." She moved to her right to clear the way for the twins to take flight and pointed to the east. "The Sands of Sancheera is that way."

Meg and Hart exchanged frustrated looks. They could both see that the yellow dragon was not going to share any more information. Rather than push their luck with this one, they leapt into the air and flew toward the desert. Below them, Astrideous followed their path until they were out of sight. *Huckfinn and Tomassawyer Twain? I will have to look them up in the Dragon Registry.*

Hiro's arrival back in Andonsheer coincided with Meg and Hart's departure from the compound. Had he entered the city from the north instead of the east, he would have missed seeing two shiny black dragons approaching from the south. Fearing that they would veer to the east and go into the desert, Hiro kicked his hover gilly into time-bending mode and flew southward, hoping to catch their attention and signal for them to land and transform again. He dared not speculate on what had caused them to take their dragon forms and go anywhere near the compound. He was just thankful that he had spotted them at all.

Luckily, the twins both saw the hover gilly with their keen dragon sight and stayed their course, flying toward the city. They landed a short distance away from Hiro and then realized that they couldn't transform where they were. They didn't know if it was okay to talk to the Krist, so they just stood there gaping at the people near the gate who were gaping back at them. Dragons rarely landed this close to the city, unless they intended harm.

Hiro, too, was at a loss. But he decided to take the initiative and floated the hover gilly over to the big, shiny dragons. "What do you want?" he shouted at the twins as he pulled a slate and some chalk out of his satchel and wrote: SAY YOU MEAN THE PEOPLE OF ANDONSHEER NO HARM.

Meg and Hart read the brief instructions. "We mean the people of Andonsheer no harm," they said, more or less together.

Hiro looked over his shoulder at the people gathered. They appeared to be more curious than afraid, but he had to get Meg and Hart out of there. He wrote on the slate: FLY TO THE DESERT EAST OF ANDON. TRANSFORM AND WALK INTO THE VILLAGE. I WILL MEET YOU THERE.

The twins read the message and nodded at the Krist.

"Begone from here, dragons. You have no business with the people of Andonsheer, so leave us alone," he called out, shaking his fist at the twins.

Meg and Hart cast bemused looks down at the tiny Krist. Then they backed away, turned and flew off over the desert in what they hoped was the direction of Andon.

Hiro flew the hover gilly toward the gate and was greeted by a smattering of applause.

"What do you think they wanted?" one woman asked as Hiro guided the hover gilly through the gate.

"I think they were just curious," Hiro said. "But they won't bother us again, I'm sure." He continued into the city and floated around the market for a short time. He stopped at a few of the booths to examine the goods, but didn't buy anything. When he felt enough time had passed, he made his way to the north gate and crossed a wide swath of patchy grass to the road, which he followed until there was no one around. Then he pushed the hover gilly back into time-bending mode and flew to Andon to meet the twins.

It was hot and dusty in the little village at the edge of the desert. The few people who were out, were sitting on chairs in the shade, cooling themselves with hand-held fans and sipping on water from large, clay bottles. The arrival of the Krist on the hover gilly barely raised an eyebrow. He had been seen before; the only interesting thing about his arrival that day was that he was alone. They assumed he would help himself to water from the well in the centre of the village and then move on.

Hiro did not help himself to water from the well. He found a shady spot in a copse of scrubby trees on the south-west side of the village and sat on the edge of his floating chariot looking out at the desert. When he was settled, he pulled a sandwich and a flagon of ale out of his satchel and began eating the simple repast.

Seeing Hiro draw the food and drink from the satchel raised a few eyebrows, but no one approached him or asked how he did it. The people of Andon were a complacent bunch, preferring to leave strangers to themselves. If he didn't move by the time the sun began to set, someone would ask him about his intentions and probably offer him shelter for the night. Until then, or unless he did something to cause trouble, the heat would keep them where they were.

Hiro finished his sandwich and ale, then tucked the empty cup back inside his satchel. He was beginning to think that the twins had got lost. It shouldn't have taken them so long to get there. But just as he was starting to grow concerned, two young people walked out of the desert and, seeing him on his hover gilly, approached him with relieved smiles. Now, this did get the attention of the village folk. No human could survive the heat of the desert proper. Andon was about as close as anyone could get to the Sands of Sancheera without being burned alive in its high temperatures.

"Why didn't you come in on the road?" Hiro hissed. "How are we going to explain your being out in the desert?"

Meg and Hart both winced in contrition at their faux pas. It hadn't occurred to them that they should have been more discreet about their arrival.

"Let's not explain," Meg said. "Let's just leave."

Hiro cast a glance back at the villagers, some of whom were standing up and craning their necks to get a better look at the people who walked out of the desert. They might have been deciding which of them was going to venture over and inquire about what was going on. Or they might have been deciding what to do with two humans and a Krist who were behaving oddly. Either way, Hiro saw the wisdom in Meg's simple solution. "Get on," he said, standing up and moving to the helm.

Meg and Hart boarded the hover gilly and Hiro steered it out of the copse and up into the air high above the village. They soared northward away from the blazing heat and the puzzled citizens of Andon.

331

"That was not very clever of you," Hiro admonished. "They are going to wonder how two humans survived in the desert."

The twins mumbled their apologies. There was no point in trying to defend themselves. They both knew they had made a mistake.

"What were you doing in dragon form? Did you find Morgaine?" Hiro finally asked.

"Sort of," Meg said, answering his second question.

"We think that she got caught and was brought before the Dragon Council," Hart said. "We went to the compound to try to find out what was going on, but all we could learn was that the dragon that was on trial had chosen an… advocate?" He looked at Meg for confirmation.

"That's what the yellow dragon said," Meg verified. "Do you know what an advocate is?"

"It's sort of like a lawyer," Hiro said, only adding to the twins' confusion.

"What's a lawyer?" Hart asked.

"It's a person who helps others deal with legal problems," Hiro explained. "Dragons that are accused of a crime are allowed to choose an advocate to represent them before the Dragon Council. It hardly ever happens; taking an advocate is deemed to be a cowardly act. Dragons are expected to face the consequences of their actions with honour."

"But what if they are innocent?" Meg asked.

"If they are brought before the council, chances are they are not innocent," Hiro explained. "Dragons don't accuse each other of crimes without absolute proof. But what happened to make you think that Morgaine was the one on trial?"

"We couldn't find Morgaine anywhere in the city," Hart said. "Then this morning we saw dozens of dragons flying over Andonsheer. A short while later, we saw Karrys and a black dragon—who we found out is named Khol—fly back over the city to the north."

"Karrys was flying north with Khol the Black?" Hiro asked, astonished.

"That's what we were told by someone in the market right after we saw them fly over," Meg said.

Hiro thought about this new information for a while. "Assuming that the dragon on trial was Karrys," he began deducing out loud, "and she was flying north with

332

Khol the black, then Khol must be her advocate and they must be heading to Rednow to plan Karrys' case. Do you know when the trial is supposed to begin again?"

"In two days," Hart said.

Hiro banked the hover gilly to the left and started flying back toward Andonsheer.

"Where are we going?" Meg asked as she braced herself against the sudden turn.

"You two are going back to Andonsheer to wait for Karrys to return," Hiro said. "I have to go to the castle and let the others know what's happening here."

"But we don't know for sure what's happening here," Hart said.

"There is no reason for Karrys to be in dragon form and flying anywhere with Khol the Black other than she's been caught and he's her advocate," Hiro said.

Hiro deposited the twins near the main gate to Andonsheer. "Stay out of trouble!" he warned. "I'll be back the day after tomorrow with Sok and your father. We'll figure out a way to save Karrys."

Then the Krist was gone again.

Feeling a little helpless, the twins returned to the market square to while away the rest of the day. They bought some food and conjured some new outfits and watched the sky. Maybe Karrys would come back...

Chapter Sixteen

Khol the Black was furious. He ordered Karrys to a corner of his lair and told her to stay put and keep quiet. They hadn't spoken on their long flight back to Rednow, both being lost in their own thoughts, and now Karrys remained silent while her unwilling host paced back and forth outside the opening to the cave.

It was dark when they had arrived at the lair, a rather small space for a dragon to call home. It was half the size of the lair in Epoh, but what surprised Karrys was the size of Khol's hoard. Like most dragon's hoards, it consisted of shiny bits and gem-clad baubles, chests of gold coins and some fancy goblets, a few crowns and a number of swords. There was even part of a golden suit of armor. Karrys estimated that it was less than a quarter in volume compared to the mass of treasure Glynnis had inherited from Karrys when he won rulership over the kingdom.

Harpur: Maybe it's a space issue.

Karrys: Maybe he has another lair somewhere.

Harpur: Maybe he's just bad at amassing a hoard.

Just before dawn, Khol entered the lair and crawled on top of his stash. Karrys waited for him to say something, but the black dragon merely glared at her from his perch for a time. Karrys assumed that he was trying to intimidate her, but she just glared back and continued to wait.

Finally, Khol could take it no more. "Tell me everything," he said, resigning himself at last to being Karrys' advocate.

The teal dragon debated internally how much to tell and where to begin. It was obvious that Harpur's secret wasn't a secret anymore. How to couch what he had done without causing problems for anyone else was his biggest concern. In the end, he decided to tell the truth. It was Khol's job to find a loophole that would acquit him of any crime.

He started at the beginning, recounting his plan to survive any challenge for Epoh and how, as he slowly weakened due to all the time he had spent on Earth in human form, he had come to care so much for Arthur, Anayah, and Sok. He talked about Elder Dhonna and how they had become friends over the years, learning from each other and sharing their love for the land and the kingdom. He admitted that he knew that what he was doing was not exactly honourable and he made no excuses for his actions.

"What I told you at the compound was true," Harpur said through Karrys' mouth. "I was imprisoned on another world. I was starved and tortured. They took scales from my belly and my back.:" He paused to show Khol the damage to Karrys' plates. "If that earthquake hadn't happened, I might still be there. Or dead. I didn't abandon Epoh. I would never do that. You know that's true."

Khol had listened carefully to Harpur's tale. He'd been touched by the missing scales, knowing how horrific it must have been to end up disfigured in such a way. Being helpless to defend himself, Harpur must have suffered greatly. As must have Karrys, who had no choice in the matter. This was the sticking point for Khol; Harpur had taken away Karrys' right to choose for herself. He had condemned her to bear the consequences of his own decisions. Now she stood accused of abandoning her kingdom, not Harpur.

While it was obvious that Karrys was a victim and that he could easily argue for her acquittal based on having been imprisoned for the entire time she was missing, the fact remained that Harpur's spirit possessed her body and that was entirely beyond his ability to sort out.

"Why did you come back at all?" Khol finally asked. "Why not just go to another world after you escaped? Why put Karrys, and me for that matter, in such difficult positions?"

"I want to make amends," Harpur said. "I have a plan to free myself from Karrys so she can go on with her life as she chooses. I owe her that."

"Then what?" Khol asked. "What happens to you when all this is done? Do you just sail on to Arachovor?"

"Possibly," Harpur admitted. "Bon, the android who now lives in Epoh, has a plan to…" He didn't know how to explain cloning to Khol. "…make me a new body."

"You expect to come back from the dead and not have anyone question it?" Khol was incredulous.

"I don't really know what to expect," Harpur replied. "I suppose I will just have to take my chances before the Dragon Council."

"And isn't it convenient that your son, Framanjesk, is now a member of the council?" Khol snorted.

"I swear I didn't know that Framanjesk was in line for a seat on the council," Harpur said. "But I'm sure he will be impartial. It's not like we are close."

"Why would you think that?" Khol asked. "Framanjesk accepted your medallion from the Order of the Winter Dragons. Everything he does, he does in your name. I doubt very much he will be impartial."

Harpur was surprised by this news. He had no idea that Framanjesk felt any affinity toward him. There had been very little contact between him and his sons, particularly after his mate and their mother, Karryl, had challenged Khol the Black for rulership over Rednow, and lost. The last time he'd seen Framanjesk and his twin brother, Phiercesten, was just before he had lost Epoh to Karrys. They had come to petition for joint regency over Epoh, but Harpur had chosen to go through with Karrys' challenge and put his plan to take over her body in motion. They had accepted his decision and, according to Khol, had accepted his medallion from the Order of the Winter Dragons. At least Framanjesk had.

"Something else my absence denied me knowledge of," Harpur mused. "Perhaps he will recuse himself."

"Do you not see how far-reaching the effects of your actions are, Harpur Diggins?" Khol asked. Dragons were naturally vainglorious, but Harpur's hubris was highly abnormal.

"I am who I am," Harpur said. Then he looked away from Khol and out the entrance to the lair. "I am trying to set things right, Khol. No one needs to know about what I did to Karrys. Plead her case and get her acquitted. Once I am restored and she is free of me, I will turn myself in. I will accept whatever decision the council makes and I will not conspire to get out of it. You have my word. Help me give Karrys her life back."

Khol had every intention of getting Karrys acquitted. Astrideous would be furious, but whatever grievance she had with Karrys, it was theirs to sort out. He'd make sure that the yellow dragon came to understand that she could not use the Dragon Council to solve her personal problems. She was lucky that she wasn't brought before the council to explain why she had arrested Karrys when it had been decreed that Karrys was not to be charged before she had an opportunity to explain her prolonged absence.

He had always admired Harpur Diggins. The great purple dragon's audacity had often impressed him. Harpur was different. He did things his own way—never exactly mocking dragon tradition or convention—but always unapologetically. Part of him wanted to save Harpur, give him a second chance. Part of him wanted to throttle the idiot.

"How is this Bon creature going to make you a new body?" Khol asked. He did not know what an android was and he needed all the information before he could make a proper plan.

Harpur had hoped he wouldn't have to get into Bon's efforts to create a new body for him. He didn't understand the process himself, so he kept it simple and in terms he thought Khol would accept. "I don't know much about the actual method he intends to use. I believe it is an ancient procedure based on technology. Magic hasn't evolved yet on the world Bon comes from."

Technology was, indeed, ancient history. Khol had no interest in it, but he was intrigued that Harpur would put his trust in something so archaic. "And you trust this Bon to do this for you?"

"I do," Harpur said.

"And how will he get your spirit out of Karrys' body and into the new one?" Khol was grudgingly fascinated. "Is there ancient technology that will do that as well?"

The truth was Harpur had no idea how Bon planned to transfer his spirit when the time came. He suddenly recalled the procedure Bon had used to sort out Sok and Arthur's souls when they had become Entangled. Bon had to kill both the elf and the man to do it. *Funny, he didn't mention that when he pitched his plan to clone me.* "There is a way," Harpur began as he processed the possibility of having to die again in order to live. "It's a sort of blend between science and magic. Again, I don't know exactly how it works."

"Has any of this ever been done for a dragon?" Khol asked.

That hadn't occurred to Harpur either. "Not to my knowledge," he said, beginning to feel the first threads of trepidation, "but Bon wouldn't propose it if he didn't think it would work."

"You put a lot of faith in these *friends* of yours, don't you?" Khol asked.

"I do," Harpur said again. "They are good people. They have never let me down."

A contemplative silence fell upon the lair as the two dragons were once again absorbed by their own thoughts. While Khol mulled over the details of Harpur's story, Harpur tried to come to terms with what the future held. For himself, and for Karrys.

The sun had fully risen when Khol spoke again. "I will do my best for Karrys tomorrow. I'm confident that the council will agree that it was her imprisonment that kept her from looking after her kingdom. I see no issues coming from that." He stopped abruptly, unsure how to say what he had to say to Harpur.

Harpur didn't dare push Khol. He could see that the black dragon was struggling with what he'd just learned. It made Harpur wonder what he would do if he was in Khol's place.

At long last, Khol came to a decision. "I will keep your secret for the time being, Harpur Diggins. After the trial, pending Karrys is found innocent, you will be free to seek assistance from your friends to free Karrys. When your friend has completed this ancient procedure to make you a new body, you will report to me and we will go to the Dragon Council together with you under my arrest. But understand that I cannot help you once you stand before the council."

"I understand," Harpur said. "The procedure might not work. What then?"

"Have someone send me word," Khol said. "If it doesn't work, your secret will go to the grave with me."

Harpur nodded. It was more than he deserved. All he had to do was get through the trial for Karrys and then see how Bon was making out with the eggs.

"Thank you, Khol," Harpur said after a minute or so had passed.

"For what?" Khol asked. "I haven't done anything yet."

"For not saying how weird this is."

"Everything with you is weird, Harpur. I thought you knew that."

When Eowyn joined Sok by the door to the kitchen gardens, the elf told the new captain what he had heard. "And he said he was in a secret passage?"

"He said I should have told him about it! He's blaming me for getting trapped... wherever he is." Sok waved a hand at the unyielding wall.

"Why didn't you tell him about it?"

"I had no idea there was a secret passage in the castle," Sok said. "And if I did, I probably wouldn't have told him about it so that he wouldn't get trapped in it."

Eowyn tried to unravel the elf's logic and failed. "There must be plans for the castle somewhere," he suggested. "If there is a secret passage, it would be in the schematics."

"That's brilliant!" Sok said. "I should have thought of that myself!"

Without waiting for a reply, Sok dashed away, leaving the new captain to wonder if his promotion was a reward or a punishment.

"So, we're not meeting in the council chamber this morning, then?" Eowyn called out to Sok's retreating back. But he got no answer.

In very short order, Sok was in the archives, knee deep in scrolls he'd pulled off the shelves, opened and then discarded in his frantic search for the schematics for the castle. He'd seen them before. He just couldn't remember where they were.

The archives were housed in a low building adjacent to the castle. At one time, the building had been an office complex of sorts, where people went to buy permits and licenses, and pay their taxes. Since Arthur took the crown, many of these fees had been abolished. The administration costs far outweighed the revenue that was collected. People still paid taxes, but this had been simplified. Each household paid one gold coin for each person living in it, and each business paid five gold coins annually. Vendors paid one silver coin per day for the privilege of selling their wares in the market square and this was collected by the market manager on court days. The annual taxes were collected between the first and second full moon of the year. The year was divided into four seasons, each lasting roughly four moon cycles. The beginning of the wet season marked the beginning of the year. Arthur never did figure it all out, and his attempts at implementing a proper calendar never caught on. Mostly this was due to the fact that the moon cycles were shorter on Thraeh than they were on Earth and he didn't even know how many days there were in a year. He did not have the math or astronomical skills to sort it all out.

Now, only the archives remained, and it had fallen into something of a shambles. Sok `had planned to go in and sort it all out, but never seemed to get around to it. He was practically the only person who ever used the archives, though, so its disarray was at his own expense.

Half the morning passed before he finally found what he was looking for. The detailed schematics of the castle had been meticulously drawn on large sheets of parchment by some long-dead architect. There were front, back and side views of what the finished castle would look like. There were also several sheets with specific plans for each floor, including the dungeons, and four for the towers that graced the corners of the fortress. Everything outlined in the schematics was exactly as the castle was now, except for the tower on the south-west corner, which had been rebuilt after the original tower blew apart when Harpur had killed Edlyngton Bloomregaard's wraiths. Bloomregaard's body had never been recovered and it was presumed that he had exploded in a wave of black goo, just as the wraiths had. No one knew how he had controlled the wraiths; he must have been magically connected to them somehow, and their deaths meant his death as well.

Sok peered at the schematic for the first floor. Using his finger, he traced a path from the front entrance, through the council chambers, down the hallway to the kitchens and around the first corner to the door that led to the kitchen gardens. The room adjacent to the hallway and opposite to the kitchens was, as Sok had seen for himself earlier, a small storage room with a small window that looked out onto the gardens. As far as he could tell, there were no hidden rooms, or nooks or crannies in which Arthur could have become trapped.

The elf scratched his head. "What did he mean by, 'If the hallway wants me to go down, I'll go down.'?" he asked out loud. "Where in Orhowyn's rotting carcass is he?"

Taking *down* as a clue, Sok flipped the pages to the drawings of the dungeons. There were two levels, but neither of them showed anything but the mostly unused cells and the never-used torture chamber. Getting nowhere with the schematics, Sok rolled them back up and tucked them under his arm. He kicked a bunch of scrolls out of his way and left the archives in even greater shambles.

A few minutes later, the elf knocked on Davynn Willhart's door.

"I know you need your space and time," Sok said, pushing his way into Davynn's rooms as soon as the door opened, "but we have a problem and I need your help." He marched over to a table and started to spread out the schematics for the castle. "Oh, hi, Elder Dhonna! What are you doing here?"

The guild master and Davynn exchanged looks of disapproval at the interruption.

"Sok," Davynn said as patiently as he could, "Elder Dhonna and I are having a private discussion. You need to take whatever problem you have to Eowyn."

"I can't," Sok said. "This is not something that Eowyn can help with." Sok flipped through the sheets of parchment and pulled out the one that showed the layout for the main floor. "Arthur is trapped in a hidden room or something somewhere near the kitchen garden door."

This time the look Elder Dhonna and Davynn shared was of concerned confusion.

"What do you mean Arthur is trapped in a hidden room?" Elder Dhonna asked.

"I mean he is trapped in a hidden room! Why do people keep repeating what I say?"

The elf was obviously upset. Again, Davynn and Elder Dhonna looked at each other. They shrugged in resignation and joined Sok at the table where Sok told them what he had heard.

"And he blames me for this!" Sok summarized, causing the knight and the guild master to wonder if that was the true source of his distress. "I've gone over these drawings and I can't find any indication of a hidden room or passage. But there has to be something! We need to get Arthur out."

Davynn had lived most of his life in the castle. He knew every square inch of it and he had never even heard of a secret room or passage way. "Did you check this storage room? Maybe he just got locked in there." Davynn pointed at the drawing.

"Of course, I checked it," Sok said. "He's not in there."

Elder Dhonna bent over the table to take a closer look at the plans. "Are you sure he was on this floor?" she asked. "Maybe he is in a room on the second floor."

"I don't think so," Sok said. "His voice was coming from below, like he was underground."

"Did you check?" Davynn asked.

"Well, no," Sok admitted. "I'm telling you that he isn't up there."

"What is directly above the storage room?" Elder Dhonna asked.

Davynn didn't need to look at the plans. "Finch's room. I think you should go and take a look."

"What? Do you think that Finch got mad at Arthur and tied him up in her room?" Sok was being facetious.

Davynn played with that scenario for a moment. "It wouldn't entirely surprise me."

Sok scowled at Davynn. Then he thought about it too. "Me either," he admitted. "But I'm telling you his voice came from beneath the floor. And inside the wall."

Elder Dhonna picked up the parchment and turned to hold it up to the light of a lamp that was lit on the wall next to the table. "What's this?" she asked in surprise.

Sok and Davynn moved behind the guild master and stared at the parchment over her shoulders.

"What are you looking at?" Davynn asked.

Elder Dhonna indicated to the knight to hold his side of the parchment. "Here," she said pointing at two faint curved lines that started at the kitchen garden door and coiled around under the darker lines of the plans. She traced its path until it faded out about a halfway around the back of the castle.

"That's just a flaw in the parchment," Davynn said.

But Sok was already pulling out the schematics for the dungeon levels. Right where the curved lines faded on the first floor, a set of curved lines started on the dungeon floor and arched around in a smaller bend until it, too, faded out at the front of the castle. Sok then pulled out the parchment showing the lower level of the dungeons and held it up to the light. As with the previous schematic, faint curved lines started where the last one had ended. This one curled in tighter and faded out well inside the dungeons on the north side.

"It looks like a spiraling corridor," Sok said, stating the obvious.

"Through the castle?" Davynn asked. "That's impossible."

"Wasn't this castle built by a wizard after an attack on Epoh a few hundred years ago?" Elder Dhonna asked.

"Yes!" Sok exclaimed. "Ylemnir was his name. He travelled to Earth and had an affair with a human woman. He is Arthur's great, great, great... He was one of Arthur's ancestors. That's why Arthur possesses magic."

"So, a secret passage running through the castle isn't so impossible after all," Elder Dhonna said.

"Arthur must have stumbled into it somehow?" Davynn asked. Knowing that magic must be involved, he was no longer skeptical, but he was worried about Arthur now.

"Stumbling is about the only way Arthur could have gotten into it," Sok said sardonically. "How do we get him out?"

Elder Dhonna suggested that being a descendant of Ylemnir, Arthur was probably the only one who could access the passage. "There must be something in the archives about it," she said.

Sok dreaded the idea of having to search the archives for information on a secret passage in the castle after the state he'd left it in. "I've never seen anything. And I've read every book and scroll in the archives."

"Well, I think you better go and look again," Davynn said.

"It will take me all day!" Sok protested.

"Then you better get started," Elder Dhonna said. "Who knows where this leads? Do you really want to leave Arthur alone down there?"

Sok really didn't want to leave Arthur alone in a magical, secret passage that led to Orhowyn only knew where. The very idea was terrifying to the elf. He was certain, though, that there was nothing in the archives about it. *Unless…*

"There might be something in Harpur's life book!" Sok said.

Edler Dhonna, being the only one who could read Harpur's life book with ease, tried to remember if she'd ever seen anything about the castle itself in the book. "It's possible," she conceded, "but Harpur's life book is locked in the vault in Arthur's rooms. We can't get it without him."

Elder Dhonna was right. The book was locked away in the warded vault, secure and out of their reach. Still, he was determined not to have to spend the day sifting through the mess in the archives looking for something that he knew wasn't there. "We need Morgaine," he said.

"Morgaine can't come back here," Davynn reminded him.

Sok was at a loss. "What are we going to do?"

"You are going to look in the archives," Elder Dhonna said. "There has to be something there."

Sok decided not to argue. If there was anything in the archives about a secret passage, he'd have found it by now. "I'll go check the archives after lunch," he lied. He was hoping that some food and some time would inspire him and he would come up with a different plan. "Will you two be joining us in the council chamber this morning?"

Davynn and Elder Dhonna declined the invitation, assuring Sok that they had already made arrangements to eat in Davynn's room with the children.

Sok, feeling despondent, left Davynn and Elder Dhonna to continue with their private conversation and made his way down the stairs intent on going to the laboratory to see if Bon and Hiro might be able to assist him. He had just reached the bottom of the stairs leading to the back door of the council chambers when he was nearly run over by Hiro on his hover gilly.

"Sok! There you are!" The Krist giggled. "I've been looking for you and Arthur. You've got to come quick! Karrys has been captured and is going on trial before the Dragon Council the day after tomorrow. Where's Arthur? We need to pick him up and get back to Andonsheer right away!"

Sok blinked at Hiro as he tried to switch gears from Arthur's current dilemma to Karrys' current predicament. "What?" was all he could say.

Hiro repeated himself.

The elf suddenly understood Arthur's penchant for having meltdowns.

So, he had one.

Hiro stared wide-eyed at the elf as he blustered and fumed and seethed and raved with frustration. The Krist tried to make sense of the references to kings being trapped in secret passage ways, shambolic archives, useless knights and unhelpful guild masters, walking sticks and sorceresses from the Black North, uncommunicative ghosts, twins turning into dragons and dragons being nothing but pains in the ass, and, finally, something about Sok wondering if it was too late to join a guild and spend the rest of his life tooling leather.

When Sok eventually ran out of steam and collapsed against the wall, Hiro drew a large cup of jamba out of his satchel and handed it to him. "I take it things are not going so well here," Hiro said.

"I can't fix this," Sok said and took a sip of ale. "I can't fix any of this."

"Generally," Hiro said, "things tend to fix themselves. If you let them."

Sok thought back to a time when Harpur had told him much the same thing. *Trust the process.*

"Are the twins alright?" Sok asked, taking another drink.

"They could use some tutoring in dragon etiquette," he said, "but other than that, they are fine."

"Good," Sok said, draining his cup and handing it back to Hiro. "I'm not going to Andonsheer with you, Hiro. Neither is Arthur."

"But..." Hiro began. He wasn't used to Sok not diving in to save his friends.

"Arthur is trapped in a magical passage somewhere in the castle. I knew nothing about it, by the way," he added. "We don't know how he got in there, and we don't know how to get him out. So, I'm going to trust that he can figure it out himself. As for Karrys... Harpur... whoever they are, they got themselves into this mess, and they can get themselves out of it. I think it will be good for Meg and Hart to experience a bit of life on their own. They are smart, they'll manage. I am going to go to the council chamber and eat my breakfast. Then I'm going to go Braydon Wood and talk to the trees."

"But..." Hiro repeated.

Sok opened the door to the council chambers. "Care to join me?"

Sok didn't wait for Hiro to answer. He walked into the council chambers, pulled out a chair and started piling pancakes, eggs and bacon onto a plate. Across from him, Eowyn was already half finished his own meal.

"Did you find the schematics?" Eowyn asked.

"I did." Sok bit into a crispy slice of bacon.

"And?" Eowyn prompted. "Is there a secret passage?"

"There is."

"Do you know how to get his majesty out of it?"

"I do not."

Again, Eowyn found himself questioning his appointment. "What are you going to do?"

"I'm going to trust the process," Sok said.

Arthur, unaware that Sok had heard him in the throes of his meltdown, had steeled himself to follow the passage way to wherever it led. *It's just a hallway. Nothing bad is going to happen.* He repeated the mantra to himself as he descended down and around the spiraling passage that eventually ended at a wrought iron gate with a short length of chain that looped through the upright bars and was held in place by a shiny, silver lock.

Beyond the gate, he could see a dark room. The light from the torches on the walls of the passage only illuminated the first few feet of the room. Arthur pressed his face against the bars and let his eyes adjust to the dimness. There were tables and shelves strewn with bottles and jars and books. In the far corner to the right stood a fieldstone fireplace. Next to it, three brooms hung on the wall. A large circle was marked out on the floor in the centre of the room, and in the middle of the circle there stood a lectern that held a leather-bound book.

Arthur took hold of the lock and tried to wiggle it open. Nothing happened; he hadn't expected it to. He pulled on the gate to see if there was enough slack in the chain to let him slip through, but it was too short. He looked around for a key, feeling along the lintel stones above the gate, hoping to find one there. No such luck. Then he noticed a coat rack inside the room a couple feet to the left of the gate. On it hung a dark blue, velvety cloak. He reached through the bars with his right arm and just managed to grab hold of the soft material. He couldn't reach high enough to lift the cloak off the hook it was draped over, so he pulled it toward himself and let the rack fall with a clang as the metal hooks met the stone floor.

The cloak was thick and heavier than Arthur anticipated. He dragged it through the bars and laid it out on the floor to check for pockets. There were many pockets, and many of them were filled with packets and trinkets and vials and, to Arthur's surprise and delight, a long, slender stick that could only be a magic wand. He drew it out and pointed it at the lock on the gate, but the lock remained stubbornly fastened shut.

Not knowing what else to do, Arthur stuffed the cloak back through the gate and started back up the passage way, thinking that now that he had reached the bottom, he could return to the top. Within a few seconds, though, the passage switched from sloping up to sloping down and he soon found himself back in front of the locked gate. More frustrated than scared, he took a few deep breaths and tried to reason a way out. It seemed to him that he was meant to find this room. Why, he did not know, but he figured that the only way back up to the castle was through the room. He had to get inside so he could get out again. As much as this didn't make sense, it was the only thing that he could think of. He started searching for the key again.

He rechecked the lintel stones. He dragged the cloak out again and rechecked the pockets. He reached through the bars and felt along the inside wall on either side of the gate, feeling for a hook or a peg on which the key might be hanging. He even examined the walls on both sides of the gate in the passage for a loose brick, hoping that there might be a hidden compartment somewhere. None of his efforts produced a key. Then he noticed a small, leather satchel with a long strap laying on the floor next to the fallen coat rack. Thinking that it must have been hanging under the cloak, he squatted down and pulled the satchel free.

346

Much like the cloak pockets, the satchel was stuffed with paper packets and little, draw-string bags. Arthur dumped the contents out onto the cloak and started sifting through them looking for a key. To his great relief a tiny, silver key had tumbled out onto the fabric of the cloak with the other stuff. Arthur picked it up and inserted it into the lock. He heard a satisfying click when he turned the key and the lock popped open. He removed the chain and pulled the gates open. As he stepped inside, the room lit up, though he could not determine where the light was coming from.

Sok is going to love this! he thought as he made his way around the room from table to table and shelf to shelf. *If I can get out of here to tell him about it, that is.* He had quite forgotten that he had so recently believed that the elf knew about the passage way and hadn't informed him.

Putting any dire thoughts out of his mind, Arthur continued to explore what he had already began to think of as a wizard's laboratory. *I wonder who this belonged to,* he mused as he picked up a jar full of murky greenish-brown liquid and then quickly put it down when an eyeball bumped against the glass. He found a tray holding a skeleton of some long-dead creature resting on one of tables. This he passed by with a disgusted grimace.

Next, he wandered over to the lectern in the circle where the leather-bound book was and lifted the cover. He flipped through the pages and determined that the book was a grimoire, filled with spells and symbols and sigils with notes on their meanings and uses scribbled next to them. When he'd finished with the book, he made his way over to the wall where the three brooms hung. They were just brooms; they did not hold his interest. Below them was a large chest. He opened the lid and found several robes, two pairs of boots and a small box that was stuffed with jewels and an ornate dagger. He put it all back and made his way to the fireplace. A cast iron cauldron hung from a swinging arm above a metal grate. He pulled the cauldron toward him and peered inside. It was coated with a pinkish-orange residue that glowed eerily against the black interior of the pot. He pushed it back, then turned his attention to the mantle.

There were two empty, tarnished silver candle sticks on one end, four fancy tin boxes of varying sizes and shapes, and a silver frame—also tarnished—containing a sepia photograph of a woman sitting in a chair. She was dressed in a high-collared frock with a cameo pinned at the lace-trimmed neckline. Her hair was pulled up in a bun atop her head. Though she had a serious look on her face, she reminded Arthur of his mother. His heart clenched with a mild pang of regret.

347

He was about to try to leave again when the corner of an envelope sticking out from the mantle caught his eye. He reached up and slid it into his hand. Across the front, in slightly shaky calligraphy, he read his name.

The hair at the back of Arthur's neck stood up. He stared at his name on the envelope and tried to convince himself that it wasn't actually meant for him. *Arthur is a common name,* he told himself. *This has to be for someone else.* Yet he knew deep down that it was for him. In all the years he had lived in Epoh, never had he heard of anyone else named Arthur. He was the only one. None of this made any sense.

Finally, he flipped the envelope over. The wax seal on the back was dark blue with a stylized capital Y and three stars. He slid his finger under the flap above the seal and pulled it loose. Inside was a single sheet of high-quality, pale-blue stationery on which was written a short note:

My dearest Arthur;

You have found my laboratory at last! I have spent many happy hours here, honing our craft, and now it is yours to enjoy. Everything you need to become the great wizard that you are is here. I have waited a long time for you take the robes of power. Wear them proudly. Make me proud.

Yours

Ylemnir

Arthur looked over his shoulder at the cloak that was lying in a heap on the floor outside the gate and wondered if his leaving it there was disrespectful. He ran over and picked up all the bits he'd dumped out onto it and put them back into the satchel. He stood the coat rack back up and hung the robe and the satchel onto a hook. Then he carefully replaced the chain on the gate and locked it with the tiny, silver key. Putting the key in his own pocket, he started running up the spiral passage way. As he ascended, the torches behind him went out one by one, and he knew that this time he would make it back to the castle.

He reached the door at the top of the spiral and stepped into the short hallway between the kitchens and the storage rooms. The last of the torches went out as he closed the door and started toward the intersection. He was about to turn the corner when he stopped and returned to the door, opening it to be sure that the secret passage way was still there. It was. He breathed a sigh of relief and closed the door again.

He walked past the kitchens, through the empty council chambers and took the stairs to the top floor and his own private rooms. He needed to be alone for a while, though he didn't expect that he would have the luxury for long. The discovery of the secret passage and Ylemnir's laboratory had seemed to awaken something in him. He'd found a connection he didn't even realize he was missing. Everything that had happened since that fateful day when Harpur had witnessed him performing a simple feat of magic on Whyte Avenue suddenly made sense. He couldn't begin to fathom how Ylemnir had known he would find the hidden laboratory, but the fact that he did gave Arthur the sense of purpose he had been longing for all these years.

As the King of Epoh, Arthur was just a figurehead, a token, a symbol designed to give the human population a sense of protection and sovereignty. There were four races in Epoh, each with their own ruler—though Arthur used that term loosely—all under the over-arching aegis of a dragon. But there was no direct coordination or collaboration between the races themselves. Not that the Fae were likely to coordinate or collaborate... *but what if they did?*

Had Harpur been around, Arthur might have consulted him on developing a high council made of representatives from all the races. It had crossed his mind more than once. Now, though, he wanted only to return to the laboratory and learn more about his heritage. An odd craving after all the years he'd spent shunning his magic.

He was about to satisfy that craving when the door to his sitting room burst open and Sok came in with a tray laden with pastries.

"You missed breakfast!" Sok said.

Arthur plucked a pastry from the tray and took a bite. Trust the elf to anticipate and placate another hankering. "You're too good to me, Sok," he mumbled around a mouthful of flaky tartlet.

"I know," Sok said. "Could you return the favour and fill the jamba jug?"

Arthur waved his free hand and conjured up some of the warm, sweet wine, which the elf poured into two cups for them. After he had checked to make sure the jug was actually filled with jamba and not something else, like leftover kitchen grease.

While they sipped and chewed, neither of them mentioned the secret passage way, or anything else for that matter. But both were acutely aware that the other had something on his mind.

When his pastry was gone, and Sok still hadn't broached whatever was bothering him, Arthur decided to break the ice. "How is Berryl making out?"

"I believe that Eowyn was going to report on that in the council chamber this morning," Sok said, "but you failed to turn up."

Arthur leaned back into his chair and then leaned verbally into the game his senior advisor had just thrown down the gauntlet for. "I was... sidetracked."

Sok studied Arthur's face. Knowing that Arthur didn't know he knew about the secret passage gave him an advantage of sorts. But he was disappointed, and a little hurt, that Arthur wasn't eager to share the discovery with him. He sensed awe in his friend's expression. Maybe a little fear. Certainly, there was an air of excitement. Whatever Arthur had found, it had affected him personally, so Sok decided to give him time to absorb and process it.

"Eowyn needs some direction," Sok said.

Arthur was not expecting the game to end so soon. Or in such an anticlimactic way. "Oh?"

"I don't think he realizes he's part of your council of advisors now," Sok said.

"It's early days," Arthur replied. "Give him some time."

Trust the process. "I'm sure you're right," Sok said. "I'm expecting too much."

"We're all adjusting," Arthur said. "Eowyn has been thrown into the deep end, but he'll find his way."

"I do wish Davynn had consulted us before he promoted the boy."

"Would you have opposed Davynn's choice?"

Sok thought about it for a moment. "No, I don't think I would have. I like Eowyn. He's a good man, with a good, strong name."

"Uh... Eowyn's actually a girl's name," Arthur said. "I always wondered why his parents called him that."

"Eowyn is not a girl's name!" Sok argued. "Where did you get that idea?"

"From The Lord of the Rings! Eowyn was a shieldmaiden of Rohan."

"The Lord of the Rings? Rohan?" Sok felt himself falling down another Earth-based rabbit hole, but couldn't help himself.

Arthur began to describe the plot of the famous story, but Sok stopped him. "How do you know about that?"

"Everybody knows about it." Arthur was confused.

"But the bards stopped singing about it well before you came to Thraeh."

"I read the books! A few times!"

"There are no books about…" Sok stopped talking. He slumped against the back of the sofa with a strange look on his face. "Have you ever heard of Midd Thraehdamas?" Arthur shook his head. "Well, a long time ago, there was an incident there that was witnessed by a man from Earth who had come to Thraeh through a Veilrift."

"And?" Arthur asked. Then he, too, suddenly slumped against the back of his own chair. "You mean Tolkien was here? He wrote the books about something that really happened here on Thraeh?"

"According to Anayah, that's exactly what happened."

"Huh! That's incredible!" Arthur sipped his jamba. "Was there anyone involved named Eowyn?"

"The bards sang about an Eowyn," Sok confirmed, "but I don't recall what part he played in it."

"So, Tolkien must have used some of the real names of people involved. But why would he give a man's name to a woman?"

"Maybe he screwed up," Sok said, earning a glare from Arthur that said the elf had just committed literary blasphemy.

A knock on the door precluded Sok being turned into a toad, a threat Anayah had made many times, and now felt delightfully appealing to Arthur.

"Speak of the devil," Arthur said.

Eowyn didn't know what a devil was and, thinking it was an order from his king, had no clue as to how to speak of one. "Apologies, your majesty, I merely came to see if you had gotten out of the secret passage. I don't know if it is in regard to a… devil?"

Sok felt totally vindicated. "I'm not the only one who is vexed by your Earth-isms."

"Speak of the dragon?" Arthur suggested. Then he turned to Eowyn. "How do you know about the secret passage?"

"Sok told me about it. Said you were trapped in a secret passage."

Arthur turned to Sok. "So, you do know about it?"

"Well, I do now!" Sok said defensively. "I heard you having a meltdown through the wall."

"Why didn't you say anything?"

"Why didn't you?"

"Because I thought you knew about it and you just never told me."

"If I knew about it, why wouldn't I tell you about it?"

"I don't know. Did you know about it?"

"Not until I heard you through the wall."

"You really didn't know?"

"I really didn't know."

"Wanna see it?"

"I thought you'd never ask!"

Eowyn's hand strayed to the patch on his shoulder. He wondered if he took it off and gave it back if they would let him go back to being just a regular guard.

They reached the hallway leading to the kitchen gardens door and turned toward it. "Go ahead," Arthur said, "open it."

Sok, looking dubious, stepped in front of Arthur and opened the door. "Arthur, there's no secret passage here."

Arthur moved forward and looked through the door. All he saw was the garden on the other side. He stepped back and examined the doorway. "It was here a while ago," he said.

"This has always been the door to the gardens," Sok said. "Are you sure you didn't get into the passage some other way?"

"I'm sure." Arthur closed the door and put his hands on his hips. "I came down here looking for Berryl's room and I opened this door. And there was a winding hallway. I swear!"

Sok had a thought. "Have you ever opened this door before?" he asked.

Arthur combed through his memory. "I don't think so," he said. "Why would I?"

Because you're the king and maybe you should have come out to see how the gardens were doing once in a while. "Try it again," Sok said.

Arthur reached for the handle and pulled the door open. Both the king and the elf gaped at the result. There was the secret passage way. Arthur closed the door again. "You do it," he said.

Sok opened the door and looked out into the gardens. "That's interesting." He closed the door again and gestured for Arthur to try it one more time.

Arthur was happy to comply. He opened the door once again on the secret passage. "That's not even the best part. Come on." Arthur stepped into the passage and beckoned for Sok to follow.

"It's kind of dark," Sok complained, reaching for a torch. "I'm going to light this first."

"Just light the first one," Arthur instructed. "The rest of the torches will light automatically."

Sok lit the torch and pulled the door closed. As promised, the torches along the wall began to light up. "I like it," Sok said. "How far is it?"

"I'm only guessing," Arthur said, "but it's about the same distance to the bottom as it is to the market square from the castle."

"And what's down there?" Sok asked. He'd been looking around, but there was nothing to see but plain brick walls with identical wall sconces every few feet. He was already bored with the environment.

"You'll see!" Arthur said.

They walked in silence for a minute or so.

"You seem pretty excited about it," Sok observed.

"And you don't seem excited enough," Arthur said. "Something wrong?"

"Many things are wrong, Arthur," Sok said philosophically.

Again, they lapsed into silence.

Arthur started to wonder if he'd misjudged the distance. It seemed like it was taking far longer to reach the bottom this time. "We should be there by now," he said. "Something's not right."

Sok stopped walking. "Arthur, what did you find down here?"

Arthur stopped walking and turned around to face the elf. "I kind of want to surprise you."

"I can't count the number of times I've opened the door to the kitchen gardens," Sok began, "and every time I opened, it was just a door to the kitchen gardens. You open it for the first time and there's a secret passage. Does that make sense to you?"

"I am a wizard," Arthur said. "Let's keep going. I'm sure I just miscalculated the distance." He started walking down the spiral hallway again.

"Arthur, I need you to tell me what you found," Sok insisted.

Arthur stopped again. And turned around again. And walked back up to the elf. "Fine," he said. "I found a wizard's... laboratory?"

"I see," Sok said, intrigued. "Do you have any idea who it belonged to?"

Arthur reached into his pocket and pulled out the letter from Ylemnir. He handed it to Sok.

Sok read the brief missive and looked up at his friend. "Do you know who Ylemnir is?"

"He's the wizard that had an affair with my great, great, great... I don't actually remember how many greats she was... grandmother. According to the letter, he left the laboratory to me," Arthur answered.

"Does that not sound peculiar to you?" Sok asked.

"Well, I have been wondering how he knew I was going to show up here," Arthur said. "He died a long time ago. Didn't he?"

"He did," Sok agreed. "A very long time ago. So, how did he know you would find his laboratory?"

"Beats me," Arthur said with a shrug of his shoulders. "He must have had the ability to see into the future."

"It just occurred to me that maybe only you can get to the laboratory," Sok proffered. "Maybe the way is so much longer because I am with you and old Ylemnir warded it so that no one else could find it. Even if they are with you."

"Well, that's no fun!" Arthur said, wanting to reject the notion. "It's mine now. And I want you to see it. Doesn't that count?"

"I think we need to go back up to the top," Sok said. "Then you come back down and see if you can get to the laboratory. If you can, then we know that you can't take anyone there with you."

"Let's just try going on a little farther first," Arthur suggested. If we don't reach the room in the next fifty torches, we'll turn around and try your way."

Sok agreed, though he was almost positive that he was right. They continued down the passage, counting torches as they went. At fifty, they still had not reached the laboratory. With a sigh of disappointment, they turned around and started walking back to the top. In much less time than it had taken to get as far down as they had been, they were back at the door.

"Huh!" Arthur huffed. "That was weird."

Sok opened the door. They were back in the castle, in the hallway next to the kitchens. "Okay, you go back down without me and see if you make it all the way."

Suddenly, Arthur was tired and disappointed. It was getting late in the day and he didn't have the energy to go back down alone. "Let's try this again in the morning. We should be getting ready for supper."

Sok wanted to argue. He wanted to know for sure if his theory was correct. Instead, he smiled at his friend and said, "That's a good idea. We know the passage is there, and that you can access it through this door. We'll figure the rest out tomorrow."

There was a lot of action happening in the kitchens as they passed by on their way to their rooms. They peeked inside and saw several staff members laying food out on trays and stirring pots at the stove. They were singing and laughing and having a jolly time of it.

"Where's Finch?" Sok asked.

"Maybe the staff have mutinied and killed her and now they are celebrating their freedom," Arthur said. He waved Sok on and they left the cooks and maids to their revelry.

They stopped at the second floor where Sok's room was located. "Arthur, did you hear me when I said that Karrys had been captured and was going before the Dragon Council?"

Arthur looked down at Sok and saw the strain in the elf's eyes. "I heard you," he said. "I just don't know what we can do about it right now."

"I guess we just have to trust the process," Sok said.

Arthur was a little taken aback by Sok's acceptance of the situation. "Maybe we can figure that out tomorrow too."

"Maybe," Sok said noncommittally. "I'll see you in the great hall."

Chapter Seventeen

The day of Karrys' trial, the sun rose over the lands of Epoh, Rednow and Andonsheer as it usually did. With it, there also arose a sense of peace and acceptance among Arthur and his friends. No one had an elaborate plan to execute. They all had things to attend to, but not one among them felt like there was any need to force or control anything. They would each take the day as it came.

Khol the Black and Harpur—still in Karrys' body—left the lair in Rednow just before dawn. The proceedings of the Dragon Council would begin when all parties involved arrived. They wanted to get to the compound as early as possible, but not so early as to appear worried about the outcome. Khol would present the truth, or most of the truth, and then it would be up to the council members to decide whether Karrys had committed any crime.

As Karrys' advocate, Khol would speak on her behalf unless the council directed any questions specifically to the teal dragon before them. This was likely to happen; it was the job of the council to ferret out any discrepancies or anomalies in the accused's story. Khol assured Harpur that Themeela Sandward and Durnor Hornblower would probably accept the story as presented and move to absolve Karrys. Framanjesk was the wild card in the tribunal. Neither of them knew how he would react. There was a small chance that he might hold a grudge against Karrys for killing his father, but he couldn't use that overtly against her. He would have to convince Themeela and Durnor that she was lying about being imprisoned and tortured, and there was no evidence to refute that. At least none that Khol or Harpur could imagine.

As they flew over Andonsheer late in the morning, Bon, Hiro, Meg and Hart were in the market square, watching a puppet show. Well, Bon was watching the puppet show. The others were mostly watching the sky. Dragons had been flying back and forth over the city all morning and they were hoping to see Karrys arrive.

"There she is!" Hart said, being the first one to spot the teal dragon as she glided overhead with Khol the Black on her right.

Bon took his eyes off the puppet show and joined his companions in watching Karrys drift through the air toward the compound. Then he returned to watching the effigies on strings poke each other in the eyes and bop each other in the head with sticks, which made the audience laugh, though Bon could not fathom why this gratuitous violence was deemed in any way humorous.

"What should we do?" Meg asked.

"Nothing," Bon said. "I suspect that the trial will be over quickly and either Morgaine will appear here in the city. Or she will not."

"What if she doesn't?" Hart asked.

"Then Hiro and I return to Epoh and let Arthur and Sok know," Bon said.

Meg and Hart exchanged worried looks.

"What about me and Hart?" Meg asked. "What happens to us if Karrys is found guilty?"

"What happens to you if she is not found guilty?" Bon countered. "We have already established that you cannot return to Epoh at this point."

Hiro decided it was time to step in. "Don't worry, Meg," he said, "we'll figure something out. First, let's just wait and see what happens at the trial."

"I wish we could be there," Hart said.

"I do not think that is a good idea," Bon said.

The puppet show ended and all around them the audience started clapping and cheering. With Hiro and Bon both distracted by the activity of the people around them, Meg leaned close to Hart and whispered, "I think we should go."

"Do as you wish," Bon said, reminding Meg that his hearing was at least as good as her own dragon hearing.

"One minute you are all telling us that we're adults and we should make our own decisions, and the next minute you're ordering us around like children." Meg's sense of peace and acceptance was waning.

"Sometimes," Hiro began before the android could reply, "being an adult means making compromises. It isn't all about getting your own way all the time." This earned him a fierce glower from the princess. "Let me finish," he said and waited for Meg to settle down. "We all discussed this yesterday and we came to the consensus that it would be better if we all stuck together. You were the one who said that it would be best if you and Hart did not draw any undue attention to yourselves. That was an adult observation, Meg, and one that we all agreed was in all of our best interests. Tell us why you want to change the plan we agreed on and put yourself and us at risk now."

Meg lowered her gaze. She felt Hart squeeze her hand with his and tears began to well up in her eyes. "I'm sorry," she said. "I just feel so helpless now that I know Karrys is there and she's alone."

"I understand," Bon said. "We all feel helpless right now. But she's not alone. Harpur is there too."

Suddenly, Meg saw things quite differently. In reality, it wasn't Karrys on trial at all; it was Harpur. Harpur was the reason for everything that was happening; the trial, the stash of twelve dragon eggs that were hidden in the hostel they were staying at, the fact that she and Hart were part dragon… it was all because of Harpur Diggins and she began to wonder why this notorious purple dragon had so much power over them. Arthur and Sok, she was sure, would die for him. Anayah had died for him! At least she had died because of him. *Why are we helping him?* she wondered. *What are we really doing all this for?*

There were no simple answers.

Meg supposed that love had something to do with it, but just then it was all too big to sort through. "Shall we get some lunch, then?" she asked. "I'm hungry."

Next to her, Hart breathed a sigh of relief. He understood his sister's restlessness. He too would have preferred to be in the compound where he could provide moral support, if nothing else. And where he could see first-hand what was happening. At the same time, he was glad that he was with his friends and that he and Meg were not waiting alone to find out how Karrys' trial turned out.

"I'm kind of sick of market food," Hart said. "Why don't we find a nice shady spot somewhere out of the city and have a picnic? Hiro, can you conjure up some of that eggs and ham on the buns with the sauce? What is it called again?"

"Eggs Benedict," Hiro said with a giggle, his mouth watering at the prospect of eating one of his favourite meals.

"That's it!" Hart said. "Eggs Benedict."

One good thing about hover gillies was that they enabled their occupants to rise above the crowd. With everyone in agreement again, Meg, Hart and Bon boarded the little chariot and Hiro flew them over the walls and out of the city. He headed west, over the jungle that bordered Andonsheer in that direction and soon spotted a small lake a little to the south. From their vantage point high above the trees, they could see the dragon compound off in the distance behind them and to their left. It was writhing with gleaming dragon bodies that looked, from this distance, like living jewels glinting in the late morning sun. The trial had begun.

Khol the Black and Karrys Evergreen had landed in the cordoned off area before the podium where the Dragon Council was waiting. Themeela Sandward stood in the centre. To her left was Durnor Hornblower and to her right was Framanjesk, son of Xzynthyrius Dreamfinder. Though he had been granted the surname Greenheart when he came of age, he preferred to remind his kind of his lineage and rarely identified himself as anything other than the son of the great purple dragon. Harpur wondered if Framanjesk was making a statement by invoking his inherited name instead of the traditional one, and what this might mean for Karrys.

As soon as Khol and Karrys had landed, Themeela stepped forward and asked if they were ready to present their case. Khol replied that they were and the red dragon addressed the crowd. "We are here today to consider Karrys Evergreen's statement in regard to her absence from her kingdom for more than sixteen years. She has been charged with abandoning the Kingdom of Epoh and breaking her oath to protect the lesser races that live within its borders. By exercising her right to be represented by an advocate, Karrys Evergreen acknowledges the charges and does not deny either of these offenses. As her advocate, however, Khol the Black will attempt to convince the council members that extenuating circumstances prevailed and he will seek leniency for her transgressions. Once we are satisfied that all of the evidence is before us, we will deliberate privately and come to a consensus on how to proceed. Our decision will be final." Themeela turned her gaze on Astrideous Garaday, who was standing to left of the podium. "Do I make myself clear?" she asked as if to warn the yellow dragon that the council as a whole would not tolerate any interference.

Astrideous snorted a column of dark-amber smoke in the direction of the council members, but said nothing. She was not happy about being left out of the proceedings and wanted Themeela to know the level of contempt she felt about the way things were going.

The council had taken precautions, though. Knowing Astrideous was bent on revenge, for whatever reason, they had appointed six other dragons to keep an eye on her. They had been given the same collar and cuffs that she had put on Karrys when she had arrested the teal dragon and told to restrain her if she made any attempt to disrupt the trial.

"Khol, the Black," Themeela continued, "you may proceed."

"You have already heard Karrys Evergreen's account of what happened to her and why she was away for so long, but for the benefit of anyone who may not have been here two days ago and to ensure that the record is complete, I will repeat the account in greater detail." Kohl faced the council as he spoke.

"As you all know, Karrys Evergreen challenged and defeated Xzynthyrius Dreamfinder, also known as Harpur Diggins, for rulership over the Kingdom of Epoh. I was the witness at that challenge fight and confirmed that Xzynthyrius was killed at the hands of Karrys in a fair competition. Karrys, however, questioned the legitimacy of the kill; Xzynthyrius died as a result of falling onto the horn of a dragon who had once challenged him and lost, and whose skull Xzynthyrius had chosen to preserve in the meadow outside his lair. The horn penetrated his heart where he was missing a scale. A scale he lost during one of his adventures on another world and Karrys, not having inflicted the wound directly, decided to bring the matter before the Dragon Council to be sanctioned."

"Excuse me," Framanjesk interrupted. "How do you know how my father lost his scale?"

"Xzynthyrius told me when he petitioned me to be his witness at the challenge," Khol explained without skipping a beat. "He was deeply ashamed of his disfigurement, but he wanted me to know about it before he met Karrys in battle, so that she couldn't be blamed for any unfair tactics."

Framanjesk nodded. "May I ask why you are telling us this? What has the challenge between Karrys Evergreen and my father have to do with the charges before the council?"

"It speaks to her honour," Khol said. "She was prepared to forfeit her victory if the council deemed that she had not actually been responsible for Xzynthyrius' death."

Again, the young green dragon nodded. It seemed like overkill to him, but it did change how he saw Karrys, whose reputation as being rather ruthless had been his only point of view. "Go on," he said.

"Thank you," Khol said. "Karrys Evergreen assumed her role as Dragon Lord of Epoh. There was, as is typical when a new dragon takes over a kingdom, an adjustment period for the lesser races who lived there. Karrys had to assert herself with the people of Epoh, who had grown to love Xzynthyrius and were grieving his death. Being new to the role of overseer of so vast and important a kingdom as Epoh is, the time it took for those she swore to protect to accept her was stressful. When things settled down, Karrys decided to grant herself a brief respite and Bounded to another world where other dragons existed.

"Upon arrival in this new world, she discovered that her magic did not work and that dragons were feared and hated. Though she tried to defend herself, she was captured by a group of hunters and would have been killed except for the fact that her teal colouring was virtually unheard of. She was, therefore, imprisoned in a fortress and experimented on by humans. She was tortured. She was starved. They attempted to force her to eat virgins." He paused while a gasp of indignation rippled through the crowd. "Of course, she refused. They tore scales from her belly and her back.

"She was held in chains, never seeing the sun or feeling the wind beneath her wings, for sixteen years, until a massive earthquake struck the shoreline where the fortress was built and it crumbled into the sea below it. Karrys was hurled into the water and would have drowned, but a passing group of Drengrokil mercenaries happened to be sailing nearby and fished her out. They nursed her back to health and helped her find her way back to the Boundary so she could come home.

"She had no idea of how much time has passed on Thraeh while she was gone. She intended to present herself to the Dragon Council as soon as she could…"

"That's not true!" Astrideous shouted from beside Khol. "She was hiding in human form in Andonsheer when I arrested her."

The crowd erupted in angry protest at Astrideous' inadvertent confession. It took several minutes for Themeela to regain control and restore quiet to the compound. She nodded at the six dragons who were watching over Astrideous and one of them quickly clamped the magic-dampening collar around her neck.

The yellow dragon screamed and tried to fly away, but she was subdued and, with a nod from Themeela, dragged to the cells to be held until the council could deal with her.

Dragons were not expressly forbidden to enter Andonsheer in human form. They did it quite often, as a matter of fact. But they were forbidden to act as dragons or represent themselves as dragons when they did. Astrideous should have waited until Karrys had transformed from her guise as Morgaine Fayle, and confronted her as a dragon outside of the city. This breach of protocol was considered no less a crime than abandoning a kingdom.

"What is her problem with you?" Khol whispered to Karrys.

"I wish I knew," Karrys replied.

This was turning out to be the most exciting trial ever held in the compound. Usually, the charges were read, the evidence was presented, the council deliberated, and a sentence was handed down and carried out. It was all over and done quickly so the dragons could get on with less unsavory and more dragon-like things.

"As I was saying," Khol said once Astrideous was locked up and no longer an immediate threat, "Karrys had every intention of reporting to the Dragon Council. She was, as our friend told us, in Andonsheer in her human form, but only to try to gain some information on her status, if she could. Had Astrideous not arrested her, Karrys would have come before the council on her own."

Khol ended his statement and waited for Themeela to direct the next steps in the process, which the red dragon did after taking a moment to compose her thoughts. "Thank you, Khol," she said. "That was a very thorough and interesting testimony." She turned to her fellow council members. "Do either of you have any questions for Khol the Black or Karrys Evergreen?"

Durnor shook his head. He'd already made up his mind.

Framanjesk, however, did have a question. "Karrys Evergreen, why did you go to this other world? Do you often Bound to other places?"

Karrys and Khol were afraid someone would ask about her decision to Bound off-world. They had decided to stick, more or less, to the story that Karrys had originally told at her first appearance before the council. "I knew that Harpur Diggins often Bounded to explore other worlds. And I knew that some of the humans who lived in Colwygshire were his friends were from other worlds. I was curious, I suppose. I guess I just wanted to understand something beyond Thraeh and Epoh. I hoped it would help me relate to the people better."

"But why, then, didn't you go to one of the worlds that these people were from? Why go somewhere completely different? How would that help you with the people in Epoh?" Framanjesk probed.

"At the time, it just seemed like a good idea," Karrys said. "Like Khol explained, I knew there were dragons on that world and I was curious about them too. Had I known that my magic wouldn't work there, I might have gone to Earth or Mysturna instead. Or I might have picked a different world altogether."

Framanjesk frowned. That didn't make a whole lot of sense and it sounded more like something his father was reputed to do than something a dragon who was new to being a Dragon Lord would consider. He stepped forward and lowered his head closer to Karrys. "Karrys Evergreen, what aren't you telling us?"

It took all the willpower Harpur and Karrys combined had to keep from flinching. Rather than try to explain further, Karrys drew herself up to her full height and spread her wings out as far as she could in the confined space. She didn't have to point out the scars on her wings or the scales that were missing from her belly and her back. She stood there and let the young, green dragon rake his appalled gaze over the blemishes that covered her body.

Khol gently pushed Karrys' right wing back down. "What does it matter why she went to this other world? You can plainly see what was done to her while she was there. If this isn't proof enough that she did not abandon Epoh or break her oath, then find her guilty and choose her punishment. Do you want to be known as the council that demeaned and disgraced an innocent dragon so publicly?"

Framanjesk quickly backed away and averted his eyes from the wounded teal dragon he was expected to judge.

Themeela then moved forward. "I believe we have heard all we need to hear. We will retire to the Clearing to deliberate and make our final decision."

The red dragon didn't wait for Framanjesk or Durnor to say any more. She launched herself into the sky and flew westward over the compound. The other council members quickly followed.

Khol and Karrys were expected to stay in the compound until the Dragon Council returned. Depending on how each of them had interpreted the evidence, that could take the equivalent of hours. Or it could take days.

The black and teal dragons watched as most of their kind who had been present for the trial took wing and flew off. A few stayed, hoping that the Dragon Council would come to a quick decision, but they all retreated to the far corners of the compound away from Khol and Karrys.

"I'm sorry," Khol said.

"Thank you."

"I was talking to Karrys," Khol said.

"I know. She thanks you too."

That same morning, Sok and Arthur met in the council chambers for breakfast. A kitchen maid delivered trays of scrambled eggs, sausages, toast and seasoned hashbrowns. She also brought two large jugs of jamba, some fruit compote and a spread made from crushed nuts that was meant to mimic peanut butter. It fell somewhat short of the goal, but Sok loved it and dolloped gobs of it onto his eggs.

"You know that is supposed to go on your toast," Arthur said.

"Who says?" Sok said. Then he added more of the nutty spread to his toast as well.

"On Earth…" Arthur began.

"We are not on Earth," Sok interrupted. "On Thraeh, nutty butter goes on whatever the person eating wants it to go on."

Arthur filled two cups with jamba and passed one to Sok. "Fair enough," he said and raised his glass in a silent toast to the elf's stomach. "So, are you going to try to figure out the secret passage with me this morning?"

"I thought you already figured it out?"

Sok and Arthur looked up to see Eowyn entering the council chambers through the front door.

"It seems that the secret passage is warded against anyone but Arthur," Sok said. "We don't know why."

Eowyn sat down and started helping himself to breakfast. Like Sok, he spooned the nutty butter onto his eggs.

"That's supposed to go on your toast," Arthur said.

"I prefer the fruity stuff on my toast," the acting captain of the guard said. "This is better on eggs."

Arthur scowled. But in a good-natured sort of way.

"We are going to try to figure out how the passage way works after breakfast," Sok said. "Care to join us?"

Eowyn took a bite of his nutty-butter eggs. "Will it be dangerous?"

Sok and Arthur considered the potential for disaster and came to the same conclusion.

"Quite possibly," Sok said.

"Almost certainly," Arthur said.

"Ah, what the heck?" Eowyn said. "I've got nothing exciting going on today. Exploring a secret passage might be fun."

The back door to the council chambers opened and Davynn and Elder Dhonna came in.

"I see Arthur found his way out of the secret passage," Elder Dhonna observed.

"So, you did try to find me," Arthur confirmed.

"I told you that I did," Sok said defensively.

The knight and the guild master took seats at the table. They had eaten in Davynn's rooms with the children, but Davynn couldn't resist the steamy scrambled eggs. He helped himself to a plateful and then added a heaping spoonful of nutty butter on top of them.

"Orhowyn's horns! Does everybody ruin their eggs with that stuff?" Arthur asked.

"It's delicious!" Davynn said. "Have you tried it?"

"I'll pass," Arthur said.

"Tell us about this passage," Elder Dhonna said. "How did you find it, Arthur?"

"I just opened the door to the kitchen gardens and there it was," Arthur replied.

"And where does it go?" Davynn asked.

"To a wizard's laboratory somewhere beneath the castle," Arthur said.

"Ylemnir's laboratory?" Davynn deduced from the conversation they'd had in his rooms the day before.

"How did you know?" Arthur was intrigued.

"Ylemnir designed this castle," Davynn said. "And when we were looking at the schematics and saw the faint outline of a corridor on them, we figured he might have something to do with it."

"I'm surprised that no one knew about it," Arthur said.

"I'm surprised that you found it," Sok said, earning an exasperated eye-roll from Arthur.

"Can we all go and see this laboratory?" Elder Dhonna asked.

"Apparently, not!" Sok said. He went on to explain how he and Arthur tried to get to the bottom of the passage and were unable to get to the laboratory together. "We are going to try to figure out a way to dissolve the warding after breakfast. Would you like to come with us?"

"I would," Elder Dhonna said, giving Davynn a supportive look.

The knight and the elf had spent the afternoon the day before reminiscing about Anayah while they planned her memorial service. Elder Dhonna had gently tried to encourage Davynn not to spend all of his time in his rooms. This seemed like just the thing for him to do to keep him busy without having to take on a great deal of responsibility.

"I suppose I could tag along," Davynn agreed. "Will it be dangerous?"

"It will be fun!" Arthur declared.

When those who were eating had finished their breakfasts, the five explorers set out together to crack the warding on the secret passage. They arrived in the hallway and stood before the door to the kitchen gardens.

"Where's the entrance?" Davynn asked.

"Right there," Sok said, pointing at the door.

"That leads to the gardens," Davynn said.

"Yes, it does," Sok agreed and opened the door to reveal exactly what everyone expected to see—the enclosed gardens. He closed the door again. "But when Arthur opens it…"

Arthur stepped forward and opened the door. "Ta-da!"

"Wow!" Eowyn cried. "That's amazing!"

"Isn't it just?" Elder Dhonna stepped forward and poked her head into the passage that had replaced the gardens. "Is it safe for me to go in?"

"I think so," Arthur said. "Sok went in with me and nothing happened to him."

Sok reached out and pulled Elder Dhonna back. "I went in with Arthur. We don't know what will happen if one of us goes in without him."

"Good point!" Arthur said. "Best not to take any chances." He entered the passage and, as soon as he crossed the threshold, the torches began to light themselves.

"Wow!" Eowyn said again. "That's convenient." Boldly, he followed Sok through the door.

"It is, isn't it?" Arthur said, frowning at the torches. "Yesterday, I had to light the first one myself."

"Maybe you didn't," Sok said. "Maybe this is how it's supposed to work and yesterday you just assumed you had to light them yourself."

Arthur shrugged. Sok's supposition was entirely possible. The important thing now was that the torches were lit and they didn't have to traverse the passage way in the dark.

"Maybe one of us should stay here," Davynn said, looking at the walls that shouldn't have been there, "just in case." Never having learned to fully trust magic, even after being married to Anayah for so long, Davynn was hesitant to enter.

"It seems okay, so far," Eowyn remarked, moving farther into the passage to make room for Elder Dhonna.

"We'll be back shortly," Arthur said to Davynn. He understood the knight's discomfort and chose to respect it.

"Should we close the door?" Sok asked.

"Let's try it with the door open," Arthur suggested. "That way we can call up to Davynn and let him know how it goes."

"What if someone comes along and sees the passage?" Davynn was okay with staying behind to guard the door, but he wasn't all that keen to have the passage way discovered by some unwitting kitchen maid or one of the gardeners.

"Hmm…" Arthur cupped his chin in his hand and thought about the implications of the passage being noticed by someone before they had figured it all out and knew how it worked. "We need to find out if the door still functions as the door to the gardens even if someone is in the passage."

A bit of experimentation revealed that if Arthur was in the passage and someone else closed the door, it still opened onto the passage again, no matter who opened it, but if Arthur closed the door, the door opened onto the gardens normally. Having established Arthur's role in activating the passage, Arthur then tried going all the way to the laboratory alone with the door open. As it had when Sok was with him, the passage kept going and he could not get to the laboratory. He returned to the top and closed the door. This time he was able to get to the laboratory in a few short minutes. While he was there, he retrieved the satchel from the coat rack and brought it back up to the top to show the others and prove that there really was something down below.

Over the next few hours, they made several attempts to get someone other than Arthur to the laboratory. Nothing worked. Arthur could only get to the room at the bottom of the passage if he was alone and the door at the top was closed. They decided to stop after Sok was nearly crushed by the passage. Arthur had gone ahead of the elf, calling for Sok to follow when he reckoned that he was about half way down. As Sok began to descend, the walls of the passage started closing in on him from all sides. Soon he found himself crawling on his stomach.

"'Let's figure out the secret passage together,' he said," Sok mumbled. "'It will be fun,' he said." The elf stopped crawling when the side walls touched his shoulders. "Arthur, come back," he yelled down to the king. "I'm stuck!"

Arthur dashed back up the passage, fearing the worst. Thankfully, the walls opened up again as he drew near to the terrified elf. Helping Sok get back on his feet, he declared the experiment over. "I think we're done with this for now," Arthur said. "Let's get you out of here."

Sok did not argue. They returned to the top and Arthur closed the door on the secret passage way. "It's time for lunch," he said. "Let's eat in my chambers so we can brainstorm ideas on how to beat this thing."

Davynn declined, saying he wanted to eat with his children, but Elder Dhonna elected to go to Arthur's chambers. "Harpur must have known about this," she said as they made their way to the stairs leading to the tower. "I wonder why he never mentioned it."

That hadn't occurred to Arthur or Sok. But something else did.

"Harpur's life book!" the king and the elf said together. Then the four of them ran up the stairs, forgetting that they hadn't informed the kitchen staff that they would be having lunch in the tower.

The Clearing was, as its name suggested, a clearing in the jungle that happened to be next to a small lake, which happened to be the bucolic setting where Hiro and Bon, Meg and Hart were having their picnic. As the Dragon Council approached, the quartette of interlopers made the hasty decision to vacate the area and let the tribunal have its privacy.

Hiro guided the hover gilly over the lake to the north-west before veering around and bearing east again toward Andonsheer. The Krist and his passengers all assumed that the red, green and white dragons were the members of the Dragon

Council and they wished they could have hidden somewhere nearby to eavesdrop on deliberations. Bon reminded them all of how keen dragon's senses were and what folly trying to outwit them would be. So, back to the steamy, teeming streets of the city it was.

He didn't bother to mention that the dragons would be able to pick up their lingering scents in the clearing. But he did wonder what they would make of it. His own olfactory signature would be strange enough to the dragons, but what would they think of Meg and Hart's scent? How would they interpret the mixture of human and dragon odors?

Behind them, the Dragon Council landed in the Clearing one by one and did, indeed, register the odd scents left behind by Hiro, Bon, Hart and Meg, but they tucked the information away for another time. They were there to decide the fate of Karrys Evergreen, which is what they did. In very short order, the tribunal came to a consensus and returned to the compound to deliver their verdict.

Only a dozen or so dragons had remained in the compound in anticipation of a quick ruling by the council. A few others that were nearby, and saw Themeela, Durnor and Framanjesk's return, joined them. Most of the dragons who had been present during the brief trial believed they knew what the outcome would be and were more intrigued by Astrideous' dramatic outburst than the fate of a dragon who had suffered being tortured and disfigured. They would return for the yellow dragon's trial, but they were no longer concerned about the teal dragon's fate.

Khol and Karrys waited for the Dragon Council members to land and take their places on the podium before they approached it again. Khol was confident of an acquittal, but Harpur didn't dare allow himself to be so self-assured.

Themeela wasted no time in announcing the council's decision. "Karrys Evergreen, we find you innocent of all charges. You are free to go."

The anti-climactic end to the trial left Harpur feeling less relieved than he expected. It couldn't be this simple. Things were never this simple. But they had achieved, albeit sooner than they thought, absolution for Karrys, and with that so abruptly out of the way, it was now time to focus on freeing her of Harpur. And that, from the little Harpur understood about Bon's cloning procedure, was suddenly a prospect he was not looking forward to enduring. Through Karrys' mouth, he thanked the council and watched Themeela and Durnor fly away.

Framanjesk, however, remained on the podium and was looking intently at Karrys. "Was there something else?" Khol asked of the young, green dragon.

"Oh, I'm almost certain that there is," Framanjesk replied. "But unless *Karrys* wishes to confess…?"

The stress Framanjesk put on Karrys' name and the way he left his suspicions undefined gave both the black and the teal dragons a start.

"I have no idea what you mean," Karrys said with as much conviction as Harpur could muster. "I simply wish to get on with my life now, if you don't mind."

"Of course," Framanjesk agreed with a sardonic smile. "I don't mind at all." He launched himself into the air and flew into the desert beyond the wall.

Khol sensed the uncertainty in the teal dragon. "You're free," he said. "You know what you need to do."

"And it will be done," Karrys said. "You have my word."

Khol turned and prepared to leave the compound. "I will be waiting."

Karrys looked toward the cells where Astrideous was locked up. She and Harpur both knew that they should leave and send word to Bon right away. Instead, she entered the cell block and stood before the seething yellow dragon.

"I suppose you have come to gloat," Astrideous hissed.

"I have come to ask you why you did this to me," Karrys said. "Why do you hate me?"

"You are responsible for the death of Raks Ojen, my mate," Astrideous accused the astonished teal dragon.

"I've never even heard of this Raks Ojen," Karrys said. "How am I responsible for his death?"

"After you abandoned Epoh, Raks fought for rulership of the kingdom," Astrideous explained.

Karrys took a moment to process this information. "So, Glynnis Warwyrm killed him, not me."

"Raks would not have died if you hadn't abandoned Epoh," Astrideous insisted.

"I see," Karrys said. "But I have been acquitted of that charge, a charge I was falsely accused of in the first place."

"It doesn't matter!" Astrideous screeched. "You are the reason he is dead!"

Karrys turned away and left the cells without another word. This latest wrinkle (as Arthur used to say whenever a problem arose) was something that would have to be dealt with. But not today. Today, Harpur needed to find Bon and get on with keeping his word to Khol.

The immediate problem was finding out how Bon was coming along with his cloning process. The original plan had been for Morgaine to wait in Andonsheer until Bon was ready and came with Hiro on the hover gilly to let her know and to determine where the next phase of the plan would be carried out. It was Morgaine's job to figure out where that would be.

When she had first arrived in Andonsheer, she had been informed, quite inadvertently by another dragon in human guise that there were any number of eggs scattered throughout the desert that were not being tended to. Upon learning this, Morgaine went in search of these eggs and began zapping them to Hiro's laboratory in the castle. She had hoped that in doing so the process would be somewhat accelerated, and she had been right.

Then she had been arrested by Astrideous and now had no idea how that little diversion had affected the plan. *Have Bon and Hiro come to Andonsheer looking for me?* she wondered. *What if they did come and couldn't find me?* Getting things back on track was her the first priority.

The only thing she could think of to do was to return to Andonsheer and ask around to see if anyone had seen a tiny man and bearded man in grey robes going about in a floating chariot. If there was no indication they had been there, she would wait a few more days for them to arrive. If they had been seen, but were gone again, she would risk a trip to Epoh to check on what was holding them up.

As it turned out, there was no need to worry. On their return from the lake, Bon had suggested that they remain outside of Andonsheer and watch for the council to return. When they saw the tribunal, they would move to the east side of the city and watch for Khol the black and/or Karrys to leave, knowing that if Khol left alone, Karrys would not be leaving at all, in which case Bon and Hiro would return to Epoh to enlist Sok and Arthur's help in finding a way to save her. So it was that the android, the Krist and the twins saw Khol leave, and were so filled with fear about what this meant for Karrys, they weren't able to leap into action as they had planned.

Meg's reaction was to declare that she was going to transform into her dragon form and storm the compound to break Karrys out. It took a while to convince her that she should not do that, by which time Karrys flew over the compound walls and noticed the hover gilly and its four passengers on the road outside the main city gates. Relieved to see Bon and Hiro, and a bit confused by the presence of the twins, Karrys swerved closer and swooped low to get their attention.

It was Hiro who saw Karrys first. Not bothering to warn the others, he pushed the hover gilly forward and banked to the right to follow the teal dragon. It took a few moments, while they scrambled to keep from falling off the back of the hover gilly, for the others to realize what was happening, but once they caught sight of the teal dragon, they felt like maybe things were going to be okay.

Hiro had the good sense not to follow the dragon directly and had kept the hover gilly on a trajectory following the road out of Andonsheer to Andon while Karrys flew northward. When she felt they were far enough away from the city, she looped around and came up next to Harpur's friends. She told them to make for a small hillock farther to the north and to wait for Morgaine to find them there.

The Kirst immediately veered to the left and flew to a grassy mound that rose a little above the scrubby forest separating the Sands of Sancheera from the mountain range along the southern most border of Epoh. He landed and hopped down from the hover gilly along with Bon, Meg and Hart. Together, they speculated about where they might go to incubate the eggs and hatch Harpur's new body. Bon still hoped that Morgaine would be able to assist with the magic they required to accelerate that baby dragon's growth, but they would have to wait for the dragon-wizardess to confirm both of these things. Thankfully, Morgaine did not leave them to stew for long. As Karrys, she had flown farther north to land, transform into her human guise and zap herself to the hillock.

When she appeared, looking a little drained, she got right down to business. "Why are you two here?" she asked of the twins.

"Glyniss sensed us as dragons and was getting agitated," Hart said gruffly, somewhat affronted by the challenge in Morgaine's voice. "We went to Andonsheer, looking for you."

"Apparently, you were otherwise occupied," Meg added with the same measure of gruffness in her own voice.

Morgaine took a deep breath. "I am sorry," she said. "It has been a stressful few days. I did not mean to sound so…"

"Cranky?" Meg suggested.

"I see no need for all this posturing," Bon said. "Morgaine, the eggs are ready for the next phase. Where have you decided we should take them to hatch?"

"Them?" Morgaine asked. "How many bodies do I... does Harpur need?" Once again, Harpur had to remind himself to refer to himself in the third person.

"Twelve eggs have been prepared," Bon said. "I think that we need to have options in case anything goes wrong. Thank you for providing them, by the way."

"You're welcome," Morgaine said. "Where are they?"

"In our room in a hostel in Andonsheer," Bon said. Then, seeing Morgaine's worried expression, he added. "The room is locked and warded. The eggs are as safe as they can be, but we should retrieve them soon."

That meant returning to the city. Now that Karrys was free to come and go as she pleased, Harpur wasn't overly concerned about that. But he didn't want to be seen with his friends, lest another dragon recognize Morgaine and wonder why she was associating with them. Neither did he want to get separated again.

"Alright, let's all go back to Andonsheer. You four can settle your account with the hostel and gather your things. When you are done, I want you to follow the main road that passes the city to the south until you reach a fork in the road. I will meet you there and zap us all to where we need to go."

This all seemed straight forward to the foursome who promptly boarded the hover gilly again for their return to Andonsheer. On their way, Meg expressed her disappointment in not having taken the time to catch up with Morgaine on all that had happened over the past few days.

"There will be time for that later," Bon said. "I am certain that Harpur is eager to get on with things."

"I wonder where we are going." Hart said. "Do you think it's somewhere in the desert?"

"I highly doubt that," Bon said. "Harpur will choose a place where other dragons are not so likely to discover what we're up to."

Hiro giggled from the helm of the hover gilly. "I hope he doesn't plan on going into the desert. I wouldn't last very long."

Hart blushed at his oversight. While he, Meg and Bon would be able to withstand the heat in the Sands of Sancheera, Hiro would be crispy Krist in no time. "Sorry, Hiro, I forgot. But we can't go back to Epoh."

"Thraeh is a big world," Bon said. "I am sure Harpur knows of a few places where we can do our work without being discovered."

"Shouldn't we send word back to Father and Sok?" Meg asked. "They are probably worried about us."

Knowing Arthur, that was more likely a given than a probability, but there was no time for that now. They had to meet up with Morgaine in the market. And so, they flew toward their rendezvous with destiny.

Chapter Eighteen

Sok and Arthur, along with Elder Dhonna and Eowyn had raced up the stairs to Arthur's private chambers with the notion that there might be some information about the secret passage in Harpur's life book. Upon arrival, Arthur had retrieved the life book from the vault in his bedroom and had handed it to Elder Dhonna. She was the only one who could read the calligraphy with ease and so she was appointed the task of searching through the pages of the heavy tome to look for anything that might help them remove the warding that kept all but Arthur from reaching the laboratory at the bottom of the spiral passage.

After his close encounter with the walls of the passage, Sok was hungry. While Elder Dhonna settled on one of the sofas with the life book, Arthur, Sok and Eowyn launched into an argument about who should go all the way back down to the kitchens to have their lunch rerouted to the tower. Eventually, Arthur pulled rank and dispatched both the elf and the acting captain of the guard to go and get their midday repast.

"You could have just zapped yourself down there and been back in no time," Elder Dhonna said as she flipped to the next page and scanned the writing. "I see young Eowyn is starting to fit right in!"

Arthur laughed. "I fear we are ruining a good guard," he said. "But I needed to get them out of the way so can I ask you how Davynn is really doing?"

Elder Dhonna stopped scanning and looked up at the king, wondering how much of what Davynn had said to her the day before she could share without breaking his confidence. "He's anxious to get the memorial over with," she said at last. "Once that is done, I think he will be okay."

"What is he waiting for?" Arthur asked.

"He feels he must wait for Meg and Hart to return," Elder Dhonna said. "He doesn't want them to be left out."

"That's what I thought," Arthur said.

Elder Dhonna wanted to give Arthur some comfort, but had already reminded him of the twin's absence and she didn't want him to start fretting about them again. "I know that there is something in here about the castle," she said, changing the subject, "but I don't recall what it was."

"I wish I knew how things were going in Andonsheer," Arthur said, changing the subject back again. "I hate not knowing what the twins are up to. I wonder if they found Morgaine."

Elder Dhonna looked up from the pages of the life book and sighed. "Do you really want to know?" she asked. Arthur had been staring out the window, but he turned his gaze on the guild master, who tapped the life book with her finger. "If it's happening to Morgaine, it's happening to Harpur."

Arthur jumped up and relocated to the sofa next to Elder Dhonna. She flipped to the back of the book and started reading everything that had happened since Morgaine had left for Andonsheer. It ended with Karrys' acquittal.

"That's a relief," Arthur said when she finished.

"It is indeed!" Elder Dhonna said.

"But it doesn't say anything about Meg and Hart."

"No. It will only mention them if something they do has a direct effect on Harpur." The elf continued flipping through the book in search of a reference to the castle.

Arthur leaned back and rested his feet on the table. "I should probably get rid of all these walking sticks," he said.

Elder Dhonna paused her search again. "Why do you have so many of them?"

"I was trying to conjure Harpur's old walking stick, but I couldn't remember what it looked like, so…" He waved his arm at the result of his failed attempts.

"Why would you want to conjure that cursed thing?"

"Anayah's ghost told us to find it. We think it can help Harpur somehow."

Elder Dhonna could not decide where to start with that revelation, but Arthur didn't give her the chance to figure it out.

"Turn to the page with the walking stick so I can see what it looks like," he said. "I'll conjure it right now."

Elder Dhonna snapped the book shut. "I will do no such thing!"

"Why not?"

"Because it's cursed. Only Harpur and the sorceress who made it can wield it."

"I'm not planning on wielding it," Arthur said. "I'm just planning on finding it so that Harpur can wield it."

"I think you should leave it alone," Elder Dhonna cautioned. "It's far too dangerous."

Sok and Eowyn entered the room with trays laden with meat and cheese and bread and fruit. They placed them on the table by the windows and bade Elder Dhonna and Arthur to join them.

"Did you find anything about the secret passage?" Sok asked as they settled into chairs and began to select their lunches from the trays.

"Not yet," Arthur said, piling thinly sliced venison onto a piece of bread. "But Elder Dhonna says Harpur's walking stick is cursed and I shouldn't try to find it," Arthur said.

"Cursed?" Sok slathered butter onto a slice of bread.

"Yes," Elder Dhonna said, "the walking stick is cursed."

"Is that why Harpur was always so protective of it?" Sok wondered aloud.

"I guess," Arthur said. "But why would Anayah tell us to find it if it's cursed?"

"Speaking of which," Elder Dhonna interjected, "what is this nonsense about Anayah's ghost?"

Sok and Arthur stopped eating. Eowyn did not. But he listened intently.

Arthur left it to Sok to explain, and the elf went into great detail. When he was done, Elder Dhonna seemed to have drifted off and the others assumed she was processing the new information.

"Is that what you wanted to talk to me about earlier?" Eowyn asked Arthur.

"Yes!" Arthur had forgotten all about that. "I need you to watch out for any signs of a ghost in the castle and let me know if you see or hear anything."

"What kind of signs?" Eowyn asked. He had no experience with ghosts and wasn't sure he wanted any.

"A woman walking through walls," Arthur said. "Shimmery apparitions appearing and disappearing. That sort of thing."

"What did you bring back from Mysturna that belonged to Anayah?" Elder Dhonna suddenly came out of her reverie.

Arthur and Sok looked at each other and shrugged.

"Her ashes?" Sok suggested.

"No," Elder Dhonna dismissed the ashes. "It has to be something that belonged to her."

Again, Arthur and Sok both shrugged. Neither of them brought anything of Anayah's back, nor were they aware of anyone else having done so.

"We have to find out who brought what back," Elder Dhonna said. "Eowyn, is that something that falls under your purview?"

"You want me to question everyone who went to Mysturna and ask if they took something of Anayah's?"

"Yes," Elder Dhonna said. "We need to find whatever it is so we can help her cross over."

"No," Arthur said. "That would be a mistake."

His companions all looked at him blankly. Then Sok understood. "We need to try to talk to her and find out what she needs and what we have to do with the walking stick. If you ever manage to conjure it."

Arthur grimaced at the elf, then he got up from the table and went to Harpur's life book. He flipped through the pages until he found a picture of the walking stick. Focusing on the image, he raised his hand and a moment later, Harpur's walking stick appeared in his grasp. Mud and bits of sod clung to it, but it seemed to be intact.

"Ha!" he said to Sok.

"Don't touch it!" Elder Dhonna gasped. In exasperation, she joined Arthur and lifted up the life book to read what it said about the curse.

Reminded of the curse, Arthur quickly laid it down on the low table between the sofas. "How exactly does the curse work?" He wiped his hands on his pants as if that would remove any potential cursed-ness from his person.

"It seems that if anyone other than the sorceress Nyssira or Harpur try to wield it, it's power will be turned back on them," Elder Dhonna said.

"Then I will not wield it!" Arthur said picking up the walking stick again. He brushed off the worst of the dirt and grass and then took it into his bed chamber to stow it in the vault where it would be safe until they knew what to do with it.

"We really do need to find Anayah," Sok said when Arthur returned to the table.

"How do we find her?" Arthur said.

"There's a book on ghosts and how to summon them in the archives," Sok said. *Somewhere…*

"Good!" Arthur said. "You go find it. I'm going to go back to Ylemnir's laboratory to poke around some more."

Sok wanted to protest, but he couldn't tell exactly why Arthur wanting to go there bothered him. He'd have to monitor that situation closely. "I think we should finish out lunch first."

When they were done, Elder Dhonna looked again for any reference to the secret passage, but the only thing she found was reference to Harpur having warded it after Ylemnir had died. "I guess you will have to wait until Harpur returns and ask him to lift the warding." Then she announced she was going to go and check on Davynn and King Röggenar.

Eowyn was relatively sure that there was some captain-of-the-guard duty that he should attend to and invited Arthur to let him know if he could be of any further assistance.

When Elder Dhonna and Eowyn had gone off in their own directions, Sok turned to Arthur. "Don't stay down there too long," he said.

Puzzled by Sok's concern, Arthur agreed. But only to avoid an argument he didn't want to have.

The fork in the road was several miles past the dragon compound, which was a mile south of Andonsheer. When the hover gilly glided to a stop, its occupants were surprised, and relieved, to see Morgaine standing in the shade of an enormous plant with pink and green-striped, tentacle-like leaves that stretched up from the ground and curled outward at the top. The dragon-wizardess looked equally relieved to see them.

She stepped onto the back of the hover gilly and informed Hiro that he was to take them to the Boundary house in Braydon Wood.

"Why are we going there?" Hart asked.

"Because that's how we are going to get to Whyte Avenue," Morgaine announced.

After Arthur discovered the secret passage, he discovered something else. It was, in many ways a small discovery. In other ways, it was monumental.

Arthur discovered the joy of absolute, impenetrable, unadulterated privacy.

At first, when he descended to Ylemnir's laboratory, he was determined to find a way to get the passage to allow him to bring other people with him. He wanted to show his inheritance to Sok, Davynn, Eowyn and Elder Dhonna. But after an hour or so of pouring over his ancestor's note books and the great grimoire, he found himself tidying up the tables and shelves, making the space more to his own liking. He rearranged the furniture, such as it was. He figured out how to light the fireplace and he pulled the only comfortable chair over to it so he could sit and read without having to hunch over a table. He threw away the skeleton on the tray. He kept the tray, though, thinking that it might be useful someday. He moved the lectern out of the circle and placed it against the wall under the three brooms. He put the chest near the chair by the fireplace to rest his feet on.

Since no one else could join Arthur in the laboratory, Sok insisted that he check in regularly. In actuality, Sok just wanted to be sure that Arthur hadn't turned himself into a toad. When, on the second day, a large frog had made its way into the castle from the gardens, Sok spent an agonizing morning trying to figure out how to explain Arthur's new appearance to the twins when they returned.

Arthur, who was perfectly fine, walked into the council chambers to find the elf begging the frog to change back into the king and seal off Ylemnir's laboratory forever. "Please," Sok pled. "Meg and Hart could come back any time now. They can't find you like this."

Arthur tapped Sok on the shoulder and the elf nearly jumped out of his skin. "Who's your new friend?" he quipped.

"Oh, there you are!" Sok stammered. "I was just…"

"Put the frog outside and let's have lunch," Arthur suggested, stifling a laugh.

Sok released the frog in the garden and returned to the council chambers to eat lunch with his non-amphibian friend.

"Any luck?" Sok asked, mustering up his dignity again.

"Nope," Arthur replied. "Harpur seems determined to keep everyone out. Except me. I wonder why that is." He paused to take a bite of stew. "Any word from… anyone?"

"Nope," Sok said with a sigh. "I'm beginning to wonder if they have been imprisoned somewhere."

Arthur frowned at the elf. "It's only been a few days."

"You're taking this all rather well," Sok observed.

"I'm trying not to think about it too much," Arthur said. "When I do, I see images of them all with green skin and bulging eyes."

"Very funny," Sok said. "That could have been you."

"But it wasn't," Arthur said.

On the third day, Arthur began to appreciate the peace and quiet he experienced in the laboratory. No one could bother him there. No one could interrupt his thoughts or invade his space. It was... Nice! It was nice to be alone and have some time to himself. And he was learning new things about his magic and how to use it without straining himself. He mastered becoming invisible and with barely a thought, he could sit in his chair and have any book or instrument or ingredient come to him at will. If he was thirsty, he conjured ale. If he was cold, he lit the fire. In the laboratory, magic felt like second nature to him. He decided that, when he did eventually figure out how to lift the warding from the passage way, he would alter it so that no one could come down without him so that he could, if he wanted to, retreat to the laboratory and know he wouldn't be disturbed.

In the meantime, Sok was making progress on cleaning up the archives and putting the scrolls and books back in order. As he sorted and sifted and rearranged the collection, he kept an eye out for the book on summoning ghosts.

No one had seen Anayah's ghost since the night in Hiro's laboratory when she had instructed them to find the walking stick, which was now safely stowed in the vault in Arthur's room. Confounded by Anayah's persistent absence and lack of further elucidation on what they were supposed to do with it, Sok needed to lure the dead witch's spirit out in hopes of learning more. He reasoned that she had to still be in the castle somewhere. While sorting out the archives, he had finally come across the book on ghosts tucked in behind some loose scrolls that had been shoved haphazardly onto a shelf during some previous search for information. He had been tempted to abandon the archive at that point, but he was so close to finishing that he set the book down safely on a table near the door and completed the task before returning to his rooms to study the little tome.

With the archives back in order, Sok picked up the book and repaired to his room to read it, after stopping in the kitchens to grab a snack. Propped up against a stack of pillows, Sok settled himself comfortably and opened the book, which revealed that there was indeed a way to force a ghost to appear. Summoning a spirit was a relatively simple task and required no magical abilities to make it work. All Sok had to do was carve Anayah's name into a candle, light it, set it next to an item that belonged to her and wait for her to appear.

He couldn't very well ask Davynn for something of Anayah's. The knight was diametrically opposed to the idea of inviting the ghost of his dead wife to show up. So, Sok was obliged to pilfer a bracelet from the things that Berryl had stolen in order to do the deed.

The irony of this was not lost on the elf. But since the bracelet was already stolen and Berryl would not be able to return it to Anayah, he convinced himself that he was just borrowing it. Berryl had decided not to return Davynn and Anayah's things to the knight right away anyway, but would wait until after the funeral. Whenever that would be!

Reports from Eowyn indicated that Berryl's amend-making was not going well. The emotional toll it took on the man limited the number of items he could return to their rightful owners on any given day. Usually by lunch time, Berryl was a blubbering mess and no one was inclined to coach and console him through the process.

They had started with Arthur, who accepted Berryl's apology with grace and encouragement. After that, things took a downward turn. One of the maids slapped Berryl when he handed her a small basket that contained a collection of garters and stockings. A guard from whom he had stolen a sword, the cost of which had been taken out of his wages when he reported it missing, yelled at Berryl, calling him terrible names before insisting on being reimbursed. Some people simply took their items back without saying a much at all, and it was these ones that caused Berryl the most grief for some reason.

With the afternoons free, and Arthur being busy in his own laboratory deep beneath the castle, Sok was enjoying the opportunity to hunker down in his own room to perform the summoning ritual.

He carved Anayah's name into a candle, lit it and then set it down on his bedside table in the centre of the bracelet. While the candle burned, Sok decided to take a bath and began to fill the tub in the corner of his room. As was his wont, he added some fragrant oils to the steamy water and began to undress. He was down to his leggings when he remembered that he needed to set out a clean towel. When he turned to walk back to the wardrobe where the towels were stored, he nearly ran into a shadowy figure of a man he did not know.

Sok yelped and reached for the dagger that usually hung at his hip, but he had already taken it off and it was lying on the floor next to the tub behind him.

"Who are you?" Sok demanded. "What are you doing in my room?"

The shadowy man opened his mouth to say something, but vanished before he could speak.

Sok stared at the space where the man had stood. Unsure if what he'd seen was real, he took a step back closer to his dagger. As he bent down to retrieve the weapon, the shadowy man reappeared. The figure faded and darkened a few times before it stabilized and remained visible. Sok stood back up slowly, holding the dagger tight in his left hand.

"Why did you summon me?" the man asked.

"I didn't summon you," Sok said. "I don't even know you."

The man turned his head toward the candle.

Sok turned his head toward the candle. "Oh!" He said, realizing that the strange man was a ghost. "You're not Anayah. Where is Anayah?"

"I do not know any Anayah," the man said. "You summoned me with my bracelet. What do you want?"

"That's Anayah's bracelet," Sok said.

"That is my bracelet," the man said. "I ask again, why did you summon me?"

Sok scratched his head. "I was trying to summon Anayah. I don't know why you showed up." The elf walked over to the bedside table and frowned down at the candle and the bracelet. "Are you sure this is your bracelet?"

The ghost joined Sok by the bedside table. "I am sure," he said. "Are you sure you summoned Anayah?"

"I think so," Sok replied, bending over to check that he's spelled the witch's name correctly. "I carved her name into the candle."

"Is this Anayah a red-head with a bad attitude?" the ghost asked.

Sok stood back up. "That sounds like her."

"She must be the one who was trying to get through the veil when you summoned me." The ghost reached out and tried to pick up the bracelet, but his fingers went right through it.

"The veil?" Sok could not recall anything in the ghost book about veils.

"It separates this world from the spirit world," the ghost said.

"Huh!" Sok grunted. "So, Anayah isn't here in the castle?"

"Why would she be?"

"She was here a few days ago," Sok said. "I need to ask her something."

"She hasn't crossed over yet," the ghost said, "so you can try again. Next time use something that belongs to her."

"I thought I did," Sok said, looking back at the bracelet. "Did you lose this bracelet when you were…?"

"Alive?" the ghost finished for him. "I did."

"When was that?" Sok asked. He was beginning to put the pieces together.

"Shortly after the new king was crowned," the ghost said.

"Ah-ha! That makes sense." Sok tapped the side of his head. "Berryl must have forgotten who he stole it from and thought it was Anayah's."

"Berryl stole it from me?" The ghost sounded shocked.

"I'm afraid so," Sok admitted. "You knew Berryl?"

"Yes, I knew him. I can't believe he would steal from me. I was heartbroken when it went missing. It was a gift from my wife." Now the ghost sounded both sad and angry.

Sok attempted to put a hand on the ghost's shoulder and nearly fell over when it passed right through the apparition. "Sorry!" he said "Would you mind if I summoned you again sometime?"

The ghost seemed surprised. "I can't stop you," he said. "But why would you want to?"

"I've never summoned a ghost before, I would like to practice more," Sok said. His plan was a little on the wicked side, but figured he'd do it anyway. "What's your name, by the way?"

"Billy," the ghost said.

"Nice to meet you, Billy," Sok said. He raised his arm to shake the ghost's hand, but realized that it wouldn't work and dropped it again. "I'm Sok. It's been an absolute pleasure."

Sok retreated around the other side of his bed to put his shirt and dagger belt back on. He was smiling the smile of an elf with a full heart and a newfound appreciation for the afterlife.

"Ahem."

Sok looked up to see Billy still standing by his bed. "Is there something else?"

"If would be so kind as to blow out the candle, I'll be on my way." Billy pointed to said candle.

"Oh! Of course," Sok said hopping onto the bed and over to the other side. "I'm new to all this. I'll do better next time."

After Morgaine's unexpected announcement, she, Bon and Hiro, along with the twins, had arrived on Whyte Avenue on a summer morning before the street had come fully alive. They had zapped to the Boundary house in Braydon Wood where Morgaine had removed the lock and ushered the others inside. Only the elves and Harpur knew how to reverse the enchantment on the lock, so getting in was not an issue.

Upon landing on the roof of the building on which the Boundary was located, Meg and Hart dashed to the ledge and looked down on the street where Arthur had spent a good part of his life. The stories didn't do it justice. The cars, the people, the buildings were nothing like they had imagined.

Morgaine had indulged them for a few minutes while she prepared to zap all of them to the lair. Even this early in the morning, the hover gilly would be a cause for concern and she wasn't about to try to keep track of how many memories she would have to wipe. Hiro understood why he couldn't explore Whyte Avenue on it, but he was sad that he would have to keep it concealed in the lair. Meg and Hart were a little less understanding about not being able to start exploring right away.

"I will show you around once we get settled and can change into something less conspicuous," Morgaine assured them. "For now, we need to get these eggs to safety and let Bon get set up to do... whatever he has to do."

Harpur had chosen his old lair on Whyte Avenue for several reasons. First, there was more than enough room for Morgaine, Meg and Hart to transform into their dragon forms if needed. Second, though he hadn't planned on having to keep an eye on the twins, they were safer in the lair than left to their own devices on Thraeh. Third, there was plenty of room for twelve eggs and any subsequent baby dragons that may or may not hatch.

While Bon and Hiro dealt with the eggs, Morgaine reinstalled the kitchen and conversation pit. She hoped that a television would keep Meg and Hart occupied while they were there, and she had been right. The novelty of moving pictures with sound fascinated the twins and bought Morgaine some time to take care of a little errand.

"I'll be back as soon as I can," she had told them.

"But you said you'd show us around Whyte Avenue," Meg complained.

"And I will," Morgaine assured the princess. "I just have to fetch something we might need later. If Bon needs anything, conjure it for him. Hiro can make sure you don't go hungry. I won't be long."

With that, she left the lair, fully warded so Meg couldn't get out if she got a notion to explore without waiting for Morgaine's return. Then she bounded back to Epoh and zapped herself to the spot where Anayah had dropped the walking stick so long ago. Even in human form and invisible, she couldn't afford to take too long to look for it. Trying to keep watch on the skies for any sign of Glynnis and look for the walking stick proved stressful. She tried summoning it, but it did not respond.

She was about to give up when she noticed a strange patch of grass that had been recently disturbed. Upon further investigation, Morgaine was surprised to see a narrow channel in the dirt beneath the long grass that just happened to be about as long as the walking stick.

"Someone has already found it!" she said aloud. *But who? Glynnis? Arthur!*

Though she could not fathom why Arthur would conjure it out of its hiding place, her gut told her that he was the one who had. She had two options: go to the castle to get it from him and risk Glynnis sensing her unwanted presence; or returning after the eggs had hatched and she was certain it was worth the gamble. In the end, the one risk she wasn't going to take was that Arthur didn't know about the curse and would try to use it. She zapped herself to the castle.

Neither Sok, nor Arthur were anywhere to be found. Morgaine, checked the council chambers, Arthur's chambers and Hiro's laboratory, though she didn't really expect to find them there. She wandered through the market and stopped in at Skull's Keep, but they weren't there either. Her next stop was the north gate to look for Davynn.

"I haven't seen Sir Davynn since he retired, ma'am" the guard on duty said.

"Retired?" Morgaine repeated. This was unexpected.

"That's right," the guard said. "After his witch wife died, he left the royal guard."

"And who is in charge now?"

"That would be Captain Hunter, ma'am."

"Do you know where I can find Captain Hunter?"

"This time of day, he's either in the training arena, or the council chambers."

Morgaine sighed. She didn't have time to go looking for this Captain Hunter, or to find and talk to Davynn, or to keep looking for Sok and Arthur. Glynnis could have already sensed her presence and be on his way to Colwygshire. She had to find the walking stick and get back to Whyte Avenue.

"Thank you, anyway" she said to the guard.

"Do you want to leave a message for the captain, ma'am?"

"That won't be necessary."

Rather than waste time looking for a place to zap herself out of the guard house, Morgaine snapped her fingers and disappeared. Had she waited a few more moments, Eowyn would have walked through the door, and she might have saved both him and the guard from the confusing conversation that ensued. But she was in a hurry and went straight to Arthur's chambers.

It occurred to her that if Arthur had been the one to summon the walking stick, there was a very good chance that he had hidden it in the vault in his rooms along with the Amber chalice and the life book. Her instincts were proven right when she opened the vault and saw it lying on top of the life book.

"There you are, old friend," she said as she drew it out and held it up to examine it. She removed a blade of grass that was wrapped around the amethyst handle and brushed some dried dirt from the shaft. "Care to accompany me back to Earth?"

As she closed the vault and turned to zap herself to the Boundary House, she saw what she had been hoping to avoid; Glynnis was circling above the city.

"Orhowyn's empty eye sockets! That wyrm has got to go!"

But now was not the time to deal with Glynnis. In all fairness, Epoh was his kingdom and he had every right to protect it. By being there, Morgaine was in the wrong, and now that she was actually free to live her life as the dragon Karrys Evergreen, getting caught violating Glynnis' rights was not something either she or Harpur wanted to happen.

Morgaine zapped herself back to the Boundary House and quickly ducked inside. She had to hope that Glynnis was not aware that Harpur and the elves were the only ones with access to it. If he did, there could be questions. And Arthur would be the one Glynnis would turn to for answers. If only there had been a way to warn Arthur. It was bad enough that she had taken the walking stick without telling him. But there was nothing she could do about that now.

She entered the lair under Whyte Avenue and was relieved to see that Meg and Hart were still engrossed in the television. They were watching a show about two brothers who travelled around in a black Impala, hunting and killing monsters. The current episode was about a nest of vampires. The twins looked dumbfounded when the older brother cut off the head of one of the vampires, thus ending a gruesome battle in which he and his sibling had been ridiculously outnumbered. Morgaine anticipated a lot of questions.

"Ah! You're back," Hiro said as Morgaine approached. He looked at the walking stick. "Is that what I think it is?"

"It's my... Harpur's walking stick." Morgaine held it up. "I think we can use it to transfer my... uh, Harpur's spirit into the clone."

Bon stopped fussing with the eggs. "You really do not have to keep talking about yourself in the third person," he said. "We do know who you are."

"I don't do it for you guys," Morgaine said. "I do it so I don't give Harpur away."

Bon nodded and returned to arranging the eggs in a magically heated bed of sand that Hart had conjured. "With a bit of luck, you will not have to worry about that for long."

"You're not actually expecting all twelve eggs to hatch, are you?" Morgaine asked.

"The chances of that are slim. I cannot guarantee that any of them will hatch," Bon said, placing the last egg in the nest. "I have no way of being absolutely certain that any of them have even been fertilized. We will know in a few days if any of them are actually viable."

"What happens if none of them hatch?" Morgaine asked.

"Then we start again," Bon said. "If we can find more eggs."

"I sent you dozens of eggs," Morgaine said. "Surely, there must have been more than twelve that were useable."

"I am afraid that these were the only ones that were fresh enough to work with," Bon said. "Most of the ones you sent were too old."

Morgaine stared at the eggs wondering if any of them contained Harpur's new body. They had paid such a high price to get to this point. *Was it worth it? Am I worth the sacrifices everyone has made?*

Arthur was relaxing in his chair by the fireplace in his laboratory, reading one of Ylemnir's journals when he realized that he needed to check in with Sok. He had promised Sok that he would do so regularly, but this was defeating the purpose of having a private space and time to himself. He was near the end of the entry he was reading, so he decided to finish before making the trek up the passage way.

I have shattered the straight road of days. Time is no arrow; it is a great wheel, and blood is the spoke that lets a man ride its rim. Twice now, I have proved the law: the future will reveal itself only along my own line. A stranger's fate dissolves to smoke, but where my iron flows, the mists part and the future is mine to behold.

I have seen Arthur, in this very covert. He is reluctant of his magic, though his birthright will topple the crown from his head as he embraces the power I will give to him. And it is Harpur Diggins who will ensure his rise as king. This I cannot apprise the Dragon Lord of—lest he interfere and change the course of history yet to be. I shall think, however, on how to provoke him. The power of prophecy is now mine to wield; I shall use it to manipulate the beast to my bidding.

A bloodline drawn with wand of bone
Upon a polished onyx stone
Spin the wheel of time unseen
Reflect the future in the sheen

Arthur stared at the page in the journal. The implications were astounding, but he didn't have time to unravel them. Sok was waiting. He'd have to come back to this later. Tucking a feather he'd been using as a bookmark into the journal, he closed the book and left the covert. *At least this place has a cool name*, he thought as he pulled the gate closed and started up the passage way.

Sok was waiting for him at the top. "What took you so long?"

Arthur took note of the agitation on Sok's face and wondered what had set the elf off. "I was reading Ylemnir's journal." He hoped that by not asking, Sok would not tell him what was wrong.

"Well, you're going to have to limit your time down there," Sok said. "If I can't reach you when I need you, your being down there isn't going to work for me."

Arthur looked at his senior advisor and knew that he was going to have to come up with an efficient way of communicating. "What happened?" he asked, resigning himself to having to be a king again for a while.

"Glynnis wants to talk to you."

"What now?" Arthur groaned.

"There's only one way to find out." Sok turned and started down the corridor. "And where's your crown?"

Arthur had taken it off in the covert—no need for it there—and had forgotten to put it back on. He snapped his fingers and the circlet appeared on his head. "I don't know what you mean."

Sok looked back and scowled at Arthur. "If you can zap things in and out of your laboratory, why can't you zap me down there?"

Arthur had been considering this, but after the passage way's vehement refusal to allow anyone to accompany him all the way to the bottom, he wasn't comfortable risking a zap. "It's called a covert," he said. "And I'm not convinced the warding wouldn't stop me from zapping people down there."

Sok saw the logic in that, but he wondered if Arthur was worried about the warding, or if he didn't really want to zap anyone to the... *Covert?* Arthur adopting the wizardly argot was not a good sign.

They made their way out of the castle and to the main city gates. As usual, they turned left and followed the Colwygshire Road to the open field where their meetings with Glynnis always occurred. Neither of them could imagine what the Dragon Lord might want, but they knew it wouldn't be good.

"You don't think that Morgaine came back here, do you?" Arthur whispered.

"She knows better than that," Sok said.

Glynnis glided into the field and landed facing Arthur and Sok. "There's a dragon in my kingdom. Again!"

Arthur took a deep breath. "Thank you for telling us, Glynnis. What would you like us to do about it?"

"So, you deny any knowledge of it."

"Of course, I deny any knowledge of it! As far as I am aware, you are the only dragon in Epoh. I don't know why you keep bothering me with your paranoid delusions."

"Easy, Arthur," Sok murmured.

"I'm not paranoid! And I'm not delusional. There was a dragon in your castle, then it za... moved into Braydon Wood." Glynnis was clearly not pleased with Arthur's accusation.

"Then why are you talking to us and not going into Braydon Wood and dealing with it there?" Arthur was beginning to enjoy these verbal sparring matches with the bronze dragon.

"Because it isn't there anymore!" Glynnis roared.

"So, what's the problem? If it isn't there anymore, where did it go?" Arthur asked.

"That's what I want to know," Glynnis said. "It was in your castle before it disappeared."

"We've already been through this, Glynnis," Arthur said. "A dragon cannot fit in the castle. Unless maybe dragons can shapeshift...?"

Glynnis glared at the king and the elf, two tendrils of bronze-black smoke rising from his nostrils. "You know perfectly well that dragons cannot shapeshift. Stop trying to get me to say that they can."

"Then all that leaves us with is paran..."

"Oh, great and mighty Dragon Lord," Sok bellowed over Arthur, "we share your confusion, but alas, we truly do not know of any dragons being within the borders

392

of your great kingdom, and are as vexed as you are by their seeming to appear inside the castle. If we do come across any such an interloper within your domain, we will inform you forthwith, and without delay."

More than ever, Arthur wanted to retreat to his covert. He dropped his chin to his chest and pinched the bridge of his nose, shaking his head. In the moment it took Glynnis to preen his ego with Sok's bizarre speech, Arthur recovered. "What he said," he said.

Glynnis, suddenly feeling rather benevolent, stretched his wings in preparation for take-off. "That is more like it," he said, not wanting to appear too kindly.

Sok and Arthur watched the bronze dragon fly away. They could see his great head scanning Braydon Wood for any signs of another dragon, but he seemed intent on returning to his lair.

"What was that?" Arthur asked as they walked back toward the city gate.

"That was me saving your backside," Sok said. "One day, Arthur, you are going to push him too far, but unlike you, I am not impervious to fire and I really don't want to die that way."

Arthur started to laugh.

"What's so funny?"

"Can you imagine the look on Glynnis' face if he tried to roast me and I didn't burn?"

"No, but I can imagine the looks on everyone else's faces when the naked king returns."

Chapter Nineteen

Davynn was growing impatient. He wanted to have the funeral for Anayah and start making arrangements to move to Branwyke, but he also felt obligated to wait until Meg, Hart, Bon and Hiro could be there. And no one knew how long that would be.

"Can you give them a few more days?" Arthur asked.

They were gathered in the council chambers. Sok was pouring jamba into cups and passing them around the table. Trays laden with all things breakfast filled the centre of the oak slab.

"It's been weeks," Davynn said. "I can't wait any longer.

Arthur understood. Davynn needed closure. They all did.

The reality was that even if the cloning procedure worked and Bon was able to successfully transfer Harpur's spirit into it, Meg and Hart could still not return to Epoh. After the last encounter with Glynnis, having the twins in Epoh was just too big a risk to take.

"So, have the funeral now," Eowyn began, "and later, when Davynn gets settled and you've figured out what to do about the prince and princess, have another gathering in Branwyke. You could make a bit of holiday of it."

"That's a wonderful idea," Elder Dhonna added. "We can send word to Röggenar so he can join us there as well."

If it meant ending the delays, Davynn was inclined to agree to this option. He'd figure out what he would do with everyone coming to Highmere Manor later. The manor house could easily accommodate them all, but the thought of having eight guests descending on him all at once was already overwhelming.

"So be it!" the knight said. "We will take Anayah's ashes to Braydon Wood tomorrow morning at first light."

First light? Arthur thought. *My kingdom for an alarm clock!*

Instead of complaining, however, Arthur smiled at Davynn. "We'll be there!"

"Where is Röggenar anyway?" Sok asked. "I haven't seen him in a while."

"He has returned to the mountains," Elder Dhonna explained. "He was missing the mines."

Arthur looked around the table. The empty chairs tugged at his heart. *Will we ever all be together again?*

Sok slid a plate full of bacon, eggs, pan fries and toast in front of the king. "Eat up!"

Arthur thanked his senior advisor and then did as he was told.

In the lair beneath Whyte Avenue, Morgaine was pacing between the conversation pit and the egg nest. When she reached the nest, she stopped and looked at Bon, who would shake his head. Then she would turn and pace back to the conversation pit and stop again to check on the twins. Between the nest and the conversation pit, she glanced repeatedly at the walking stick, which was leaning against the cavern wall where Harpur's hoard used to be. She was certain it could help, but she didn't know how.

Karrys: You should go to the Black North and ask Nyssira how it works.

Harpur: That would require entering Everstar. And I'm not inclined to being trapped in that place.

Karry: You said once that she would do anything for you.

Harpur: Yes, but at a cost. I have enough to deal with without adding that crazy sorceress into the mix.

Karrys: There has to be a way to contact her.

Harpur: Nyssira is a bit of a hermit. She only talks to people when she feels like it.

Karrys: I think you should try.

Harpur: I don't want to owe her a favour.

Karry: Would that be so bad?

Harpur: The last time I did her a favour I ended up killing an innocent sorcerer.

Karry: I want this to work as badly as you do, but if you try to use the walking stick and something goes wrong…

Harpur: I know! But if we leave it to Bon to make the transfer, he has to kill you first. And by his own admission, he's never done it to a dragon before. I think we are better off trying the walking stick.

Morgaine turned around and nearly bumped into Meg.

"When are you going to take us up to see Whyte Avenue?" the princess asked.

"Later," Morgaine growled and tried to resume her pacing.

Meg stepped in front of the dragon-wizardess. "We want to go now," she said, crossing her harms and squinting her eyes. "You are driving everyone crazy with your pacing and muttering. I think you could use a little fresh air as well."

Bon looked up from the egg he was turning. "The princess is right," he said. "I think we should all go."

Hiro giggled and Hart leapt over the back of the sofa to join them. Out-numbered, Morgaine exhaled heavily and agreed to a tour of Whyte Avenue.

"But we can't go out dressed like this," she said.

Starting with Hart, she conjured up a pair of jeans and a t-shirt. Then she did the same for Hiro. Bon studied their attire, then used his own technology to mimic the current male fashions more suited to a middle-aged man on Whyte Avenue. He chose a pair of kakis and a polo shirt. Morgaine decided on a pair of leggings and a figure-hugging tank top with spaghetti straps.

"What about me?" Meg asked.

Morgaine smiled slyly and snapped her fingers.

"You're kidding, right?" Meg was mortified.

"You look cute, big sister," Hart said. "You'll turn the heads of every boy on Whyte Avenue."

"Not in this, I won't!" Meg said, pulling at the hem of the short, pink skirt Morgaine had conjured for her. "It barely covers my behind!"

Morgaine laughed. "Your father would be so proud of you right now."

"For going out half naked?"

"No! For not wanting to!"

Meg was confused. "Please, Morgaine. This is... uncomfortable."

"Oh, alright!" Morgaine changed the pink mini-skirt for a pair of denim capris and a coral, V-necked t-shirt. "Better?"

"I think so," Meg said. But she still looked uncomfortable.

When they reached the street, Meg pulled Morgaine back a few steps behind the guys. "What is this… undergarment I'm wearing?"

"It's called a bra," Morgaine said with a smirk. "It's Earth's answer to the corset."

Meg frowned. "I hate those too."

"I'm with you there," Morgaine said.

The first lesson Morgaine had to teach Meg, Hart and Hiro was how to cross the streets safely. They were fascinated by the traffic lights. Soon, Meg and Hart were racing each other to the corners to be the first to push the button for the crosswalk signals like five-year-olds. Morgaine considered quelling the immature antics, but decided that the novelty would wear off in good time. She smiled through the strange looks people gave her when Meg would squeal, "Ooh! We can go now!" when the light changed.

They stopped at a candy store with a picture of Marilyn Monroe made entirely out of jelly beans in the window. Meg and Hart loaded up on sweets while Morgaine and Hiro each settled for a chocolate bar. They wandered through the Army and Navy store, then crossed the street and spent a good hour in an enormous bookstore. From there, they made their way east to Arthur's old apartment building.

"Can we go in?" Hart asked.

"I'm afraid not," Morgaine said. "Someone else is living there now. I don't think they would appreciate us invading their space."

Morgaine led them back the other way and took them into Prophecy Comics. "This is where your father worked when I... Harpur met him. Back then it was called Fox Comics."

Together, the five Epohians meandered through the aisles, looking at comic books while Morgaine explained who the different, strangely-dressed characters were. Meg was particularly taken by a character in a black mask with pointy ears sticking out of it. He wore a cape with scalloped edges and a belt filled with gadgets. On his chest was a yellow oval with a silhouette of a bat in the centre. Morgaine permitted the princess to purchase a first issue copy. Hart was only mildly interested and declined the offer to choose a comic for himself.

What the prince was interested in surprised Morgaine. "People here are wearing the same kind of hats that we got for our birthday," he observed. "How would anyone back home know about them?"

"I think your father commissioned them for you, but someone let the secret out and the others came from people who were trying to impress the king." Morgaine watched the young man as this hypothesis sank in.

"So, people had them made for father, not us?"

"I'm sure not everyone did it for that reason," Morgaine explained. "Some may have thought that it was a new royal fad and wanted to show respect by emulating it. But there were very likely several who had more selfish reasons for gifting them to you."

Hart frowned. "Are grownups always so complicated?"

"No," Morgaine said. "When they're sleeping, they're okay."

Hart snickered.

They had reached O'Bryan's Pub and Morgaine stopped and handed Meg and Hart each a small, laminated card with their pictures on them. "If anyone asks to see your ID, hand them these."

Meg held up the card. "What are they?"

"They are what will allow you to eat in this restaurant," Morgaine said. "On Earth, you have to be nineteen to eat in an establishment like this."

"That's stupid," Meg said.

"Nevertheless, that's the law."

"What kind of establishment is it?" Hart asked, looking up at the sign above the door.

"It's sort of like Skull's Keep," Morgaine explained. "We'll eat supper here and then go back to the lair."

The evening repast consisted of pints of Guiness all around, butter chicken curry and fresh chocolate chip cookies, topped with ice cream and drizzled with Irish cream. Bon's polite refusal for either food or drink was received with something less than gracious acceptance. Morgaine tipped the server with a twenty-dollar bill that she conjured—probably from the till—to appease the minimum order rule and explained that her friend suffered from a potentially debilitating condition that required a strict diet. Feeling somewhat abashed, the young woman slipped the tip into her apron pocket nonetheless.

I don't suppose there is an archery range anywhere close by?" Meg suggested as they drew near to the alley where the entrance to the lair was.

"No," Morgaine said, "but if you're good, I'll take you to an escape room tomorrow."

"An escape room?" Hart was intrigued.

"You'll love it," Morgaine said.

"I'd rather shoot a bow and arrow," Meg complained.

"Depending on how long the eggs take to hatch, maybe we can go do some axe-throwing before we return to Thraeh."

They entered the lair through the magical door and Bon went straight to the eggs. "If you are planning on axe throwing and escape rooms, you have time."

Morgaine, magically sealing the entrance, had dared to hope for better news. "How much longer?" she asked as she approached the nest.

"We could have a couple of baby Harpurs as early as tomorrow," Bon said.

"And how does that give us time for escape rooms and axe-throwing?" Morgaine asked. She leaned over and rested her hands on her knees so she could get a closer look. Two of the eggs were rocking slightly in the sand.

"They have to grow," Bon explained. "And unless you have some way of making them mature faster, we are going to be here a while."

"I think I can enchant their food," Morgaine said. "Will accelerating their growth have any adverse effects?"

"I am as new to this as you are," Bon said noncommittally.

"You are aware that my... Harpur's life is hanging in the balance here?"

"You really do need to stop speaking in the third person," Bon said. "It is confusing."

"You should experience it from this side," Morgaine said. "But how do you think this is going to go?"

Bon turned two of the eggs. "So far, things are going according to plan. It is early days, though."

"I'm going to transform and get some sleep," Morgaine said. "Wake me if anything happens."

Arthur and Sok were the first to arrive in the council chambers on the morning of the funeral. While Sok went to the kitchen to order jamba and a light breakfast, Arthur placed the urn holding Anayah's ashes on the table and took a seat to wait for the others. It was early and he wasn't quite awake, but he was conscious enough to know that something wasn't right. When he had retrieved the urn from the vault, something was missing. Sok had been urging him to hurry from the other room and, in his sleep-deprived stupor, it didn't register that the walking stick was not where it was supposed to be.

He had laid awake well into the night, thinking about what he had read in Ylemnir's journal. ... *though his birthright will topple the crown from his head... What an odd thing to write.* There were other things in the entry that bothered him as well, but that part he found most disturbing.

Sok returned with jamba and cups on a tray. "I ordered pastries," he said as he poured himself and Arthur their morning beverage. "We can have a proper breakfast when we get back."

Arthur accepted the jamba with a nod and a grunt that might have been a semi-conscious thank you. He was leaning on the table with his head propped up on his hand, staring at the urn.

Sok sat down and sipped from his own cup. "I tried summoning Anayah."

"Uh-huh."

"A ghost named Billy showed up instead."

"Uh-huh."

"I'm going to try again later."

"Uh-huh."

Sok sighed. "Hopefully, she shows up and can tell me what we need the walking stick for."

Arthur sat up, suddenly wide-eyed and wide awake. "The walking stick!"

"Yes, Arthur," Sok said. "We need to try to find out what we need it for."

"It's gone."

"What are you talking about? It's in your vault."

"No, it's not. It's missing! When I got the urn, it wasn't there."

"That's impossible. Only you and Harpur know how to…" Sok paused. "Ah! That explains Glynnis' visit."

Arthur frowned at the elf. "What do you mean?"

"Glynnis sensed a dragon in the castle. Morgain must have come back and taken the walking stick." It made sense to Sok.

"But she doesn't even know that we have it," Arthur said.

"That's right," Sok said, seeing the hole in his logic. "Maybe she came back for Harpur's life book and saw the walking stick and took it."

"The life book is still there, though," Arthur said. "Why, if she came for the life book, would she leave it and take the walking stick? And why didn't she tell us?"

"Why didn't who tell you what?"

Arthur and Sok turned to see Eowyn enter the council chambers.

Sok informed the captain of the guard what had happened.

"We don't know that Morgaine came back here," Arthur said.

"Who else would take the walking stick?" Eowyn countered.

"Who else could have taken the walking stick?" Sok added.

Arthur had to admit that made sense. "Then why didn't she tell us?"

"She was probably in a rush," Eowyn said. "Didn't want Glynnis to find her here."

"Well, how did she know that the walking stick was in the vault?" Arthur was determined to find another answer.

"Does it matter?" Sok asked.

"It does if Morgaine wasn't the one to take it," Arthur said.

"If Morgaine wasn't the one to take what?"

Davynn, Elder Dhonna and the children filed into the council chambers, and Sok, again, explained what had happened.

Davynn helped Caleb get into a chair. The boy's nose barely cleared the table top. "How did Harpur's walking stick get into your vault?" he asked as he settled into a chair next to his youngest son.

401

"Arthur put it there," Sok said.

"Why?"

"Because Anay…" Sok began.

"Because we learned that it might be useful in helping Harpur somehow." Arthur glared at the elf.

Davynn looked from Arthur to Sok and decided not to pursue it. "Have you had breakfast?"

His question was answered by the arrival of a kitchen maid with a tray of fresh pastries. She set it down in front of Arthur, bobbed a quick curtsy, and retreated back to the kitchens.

Elder Dhonna reached for a pastry and cut it in half for Brodie and Caleb to share. "This will tide them over until Joy gets here with the basket she is preparing." Then she cut another pastry and gave half to Alexa. She took a bite of the half she'd kept for herself, ignoring Davynn's look of mild disapproval.

The knight shrugged and took a pastry and a cup of jamba for himself. They had to wait for the children's nanny to bring the food basket anyway; he might as well enjoy the food in front of him.

Arthur thought that this was a good opportunity to ask how Berryl was coming along with the task of returning the stolen items.

Eowyn had to finish chewing the bite of pastry in his mouth before he could answer. "He's almost done! He was asking how long it would be before he starts his new position."

Arthur turned to Sok. "Have you drafted the job description for Citizen Advocate yet?"

"No," Sok said, "I have not."

"Why is that?" Arthur asked, annoyed by the elf's procrastination.

"Because I don't know what a Citizen Advocate is!"

"I explained it to you," Arthur replied. "What is the problem?"

"The problem is that…" Sok paused and looked at the children. This was no time for an argument about castle administration. "…I need your help to clarify a few points. I was hoping we could meet privately later today."

Arthur groaned inwardly. He wished he hadn't brought it up. A meeting would mean he couldn't go down to his covert. And he really wanted to read more of Ylemnir's journal. "Of course. But I have to check on something in the covert first."

Sok was going to protest, but Brodie cut in, asking, "What's a covert, Papa?"

"I don't know, son," Davynn said, "but I'm sure it's not a place a young knight-to-be would want to go."

"Actually, it's a wizard's…," Arthur started to explain what a covert was to the lad.

"Actually," Elder Dhonna spoke over the king, "it's time we got going. It's a long walk to the Boundary House."

Joy had just come in with a basket that Sok thought was far too small to hold enough food for them all. It was barely large enough to accommodate a light lunch for one, but no one else seemed to think this could be a problem. He wished that Hiro was there with his satchel, but at least they had Arthur if they needed him. And a proper breakfast would be waiting for them when they returned.

The solemn procession left the castle with Alexa in the lead, carrying her mother's ashes in the urn. Behind her, Davynn carried Caleb, and Brodie walked beside them. Next in line were Arthur and Sok, followed by Eowyn with Elder Dhonna holding his arm. Joy brought up the rear, carrying the basket. Arthur offered to carry it for her, but the young nanny would not even think about letting the king take over such a menial task. He tried volunteering Sok or Eowyn for the job, a suggestion that was met with the assertion that it was beneath their stations as well. Like Sok, Arthur was curious about what the basket contained. Unlike Sok, he wasn't concerned about how far it would go.

The streets were already busy with vendors bringing in their goods to sell at the market. Upon seeing young Alexa holding the urn, many realized what was happening and stopped to pay their respects and give Davynn their condolences. It took nearly as long to get from the castle to the city gate as it did to get from the gate to the Boundary House. Once they got there, they were all ready for a rest. And a snack. But Joy declared that the basket was off limits for the time being. She even smacked Sok's hand when he attempted to lift the corner of the cloth that she had so neatly tucked in around the sides of the basket to cover the contents, much to everyone's delight.

Davynn told Alexa to set the urn down by the Boundary House wall and then set to cleaning out the firepit, a remnant of the days when patrols were stationed at the Boundary to keep people from making unauthorized Bounds. Eowyn took Brodie to look for firewood and the others busied themselves righting the stumps that the patrols had once used for seating and pushing them into a ring around the firepit. Soon, the area was fit for the gathering and a cheerful little fire was crackling away in its centre.

Alexa retrieved the urn again and brought it to the circle of stumps. She looked at her father, who gave her a nod. The bright-eyed ten-year-old cleared her throat and looked around at the good friends who had come to say good bye to her mother.

"Papa didn't know the traditional… burial rites? …for witches, but Mama told me about them once when I was little." She paused while she gathered her thoughts. "When witches die, their friends write nice things about them on a piece of special cloth. Then they tie a knot in the cloth to hold the nice things people write in place and then burn it in a fire."

Taking her cue, Joy lifted the cloth from the basket and pulled out a stack of cloth squares and a handful of biros, which she passed around to everyone. Sok eyed the basket suspiciously.

"You can write more than one nice thing about Mama if you want," Alexa said. "We brought extra pieces of cloth."

Arthur felt his eyes well up and he had to keep blinking so he could see what he was writing. He wasn't sure if he was supposed to tie the knot in the cloth right away, or if he was supposed to share what he'd written with the others first. He waited until a couple of others had finished to see what they did, but they weren't sure either.

Davynn and Elder Dhonna helped Brodie and Caleb write what they wanted to say to their mother, then they filled in their own cloths with their own words for Anayah. Everyone was then done, except for Sok. The elf, scribbling madly, was filling out his third piece of cloth and reaching for a fourth. Each piece was covered from corner to corner with his elegant, flourishing cursive script. He was oblivious to the fact that he was the only one still writing.

When he reached for a sixth piece of cloth, Arthur nudged him with his elbow. "Are you going to be much longer?"

Sok looked up and saw everyone looking back at him. "Almost done!" he said, and started writing again.

He filled half of the cloth, then signed it: Love and Light, Silkhar Ornathan Kluupentarajhar, and added the elven rune for peace under his signature.

"Finally," Arthur said under his breath.

"Alexa, my dear?" Elder Dhonna asked. "Do we read our cloths out loud now?"

Arthur winced, hoping she would say no.

"Only if you want to," Alexa said.

"I do!" Caleb shouted. "I wrote: You are the prettiest Mama in the world. I miss you."

Arthur, Eowyn, Davynn, Joy and Elder Dhonna all choked back sobs.

"Mine says: When I am a knight, I'm going to marry a witch who is a nice as you are, Mama. I love you," Brodie said proudly.

Arthur conjured nine handkerchiefs and handed them out.

"Mine is private," Alexa said solemnly.

"That's okay, sweetheart." Davynn sniffled. "Mama knows what it says."

Elder Dhonna and Arthur also elected to keep theirs private.

Eowyn decided to share. "Dear Anayah, I didn't know you well, but I know you touched a lot of hearts and you will be sadly missed."

Davynn had two cloths; he read one of them. "You will be forever in my heart, my Love. I miss you so much." He had already tied a knot in the other one.

Joy tried to read hers, but broke down right after saying Anayah's name. Elder Dhonna moved to a stump next to the nanny and wrapped her arms around the girl.

Everyone looked at Sok and waited. Finally, the elf shook his head.

Next to him, Arthur breathed a quiet sigh of relief.

"What do we do now?" Eowyn asked.

Alexa sniffled and wiped her eyes with her handkerchief. "Tie a knot in them like this." She demonstrated by folding her cloth in four and tying an overhand knot in the middle of it. "Then when you feel like it's time, you throw the cloth in the fire."

One-by-one, the mourners dropped their cloths into the flames, then sat back down, thinking about Anayah while they watched them burn. As the flames caught on the fabric, the fire glowed dark red and the rising smoke turned crimson. They all knew then that Anayah had received their messages.

"That was lovely," Sok said, wiping the tears from his cheeks.

"We aren't done yet," Alexa said.

Joy, still distraught, lifted the basket and withdrew a flask and ten small glass cups. Alexa took them from her and filled each cup from the flask with a pale-rose liquid.

"This is eluvium wine," Alexa explained. "On Mysturna, the witches used a different flower to make the wine, but it doesn't grow here. Papa and Elder Dhonna said that it is okay if we use eluvium wine because Mama like eluvium flowers and it's okay for children to drink it. Uncle Arthur, you are our king. Would you please make a… toast? …to Mama?"

Arthur had just regained his composure and had to fight hard not to break down again. Taking a deep breath, he stood and held his glass of eluvium wine level with his heart. "Anayah was the first witch I ever met. She was a good friend and a wonderful wife and mother. She lit up the castle with her beauty, her wit and her charm, and not infrequently with her temper." He paused while Davynn, Sok and Elder Dhonna all chuckled. "She was there for Meg and Hart and me when Alex left us. And now we have to be here for each other now that she is gone. Anayah, you will never be forgotten. May you rest in peace wherever witches go. To Anayah!"

"To Anayah!" the others echoed as they raised their glasses and then drank to their mother, wife, or friend.

After the toast was done, Alexa picked up the tenth glass and the urn. "Now we have to give Mama a drink too," she said.

For a moment, Arthur thought she was going to open the urn and pour the wine into it. Instead, she handed the urn to Davynn, who placed it inside a trunk hole in an old oak that grew next to the Boundary House. When he was done, Alexa poured the wine onto the ground at the base of the tree.

"Good bye, Mama," she whispered as she watched the liquid soak into the earth.

This seemed to mark the end of the rite. Joy and Elder Dhonna gathered up the cups and returned them to the basket, while Davynn and Eowynn smothered the fire with dirt.

"There's nothing to eat in that basket, is there?" Sok whispered to Arthur.

"I don't think so," Arthur said.

"I don't suppose you could..." Sok waved his hand, mimicking Arthur's conjuring gesture.

Unsure what etiquette demanded in this situation, Arthur declined. "Maybe we should wait until we get back to the castle."

"Okay," Sok said, "but if I faint from lack of nourishment on the way there, you get to carry me."

No one else mentioned food. Though Caleb did ask if he could pick some Faeroot leaves to munch on and was encouraged to do so by Elder Dhonna.

When they left the clearing and were out of site on the trail leading to the Colwygshire road, a tall, cloaked figure with a bronze sheen to his skin stepped out of the bushes and walked over to the oak where Davynn had placed the urn. He didn't touch it, but he read the inscription engraved into it: Anayah of Mysturna—a simple epitaph for a complicated witch.

"The lesser races are such an odd lot," Glynnis said. "I do not know what Harpur Diggins ever saw in them."

He had been keeping an eye on the Boundary House ever since he felt the presence of another dragon nearby. He was sure it had been Karrys Evergreen, but he could not figure out how or why she seemed to disappear there. As much as he hated the idea, he decided that he would have to spend more time in Colwygshire in his human form and start keeping closer tabs on what the lesser races were up to.

The first hatchling emerged from its shell while Morgaine and the twins were playing mini-golf at the mall two days after their first foray down Whyte Avenue. Morgaine had conjured a fully electric Jaguar and magically enhanced it to be an autonomous vehicle. Harpur had enjoyed driving when he lived on Whyte Avenue, but things had changed and Karrys was less than excited about moving about in a car at all. Harpur may have been in command of the body they shared, but Karrys was a terrible passenger.

The twins were loving every minute of their time on Whyte Avenue. The day before, they had been to an escape room, and had gone axe-throwing, followed by a 3D movie in D-Box seats where Morgaine was more entertained watching Meg and Hart's reactions than she was by the movie.

The morning of the day the baby dragon hatched, they had started out at the zoo, then rode the roller coaster at the mall and were now putting their way around an 18-hole, black-lit mini-golf course while they waited for the sealion show to start.

At first, Morgaine enjoyed seeing the twins experience life on Earth for the first time. They were like kids in a candy shop, all smiles and squeals of delight. If Karrys hadn't been so uncomfortable with it all, Harpur might have enjoyed it more, but her constant chatter about the inherent dangers she saw in everything they did was driving Harpur crazy. And Hart's abysmal putting skills were not helping.

Meg and Hart, but Meg especially, were giddy with the information overload from the past two days. They wanted to know what other things they could do and places they could go, and on the way back to the lair after the sealion show, pestered Morgaine for options.

"Tomorrow, I will take you to the art gallery and the museum," she said.

Something more passive was in order. Karrys seemed less anxious about this and refrained from making a fuss. She was aware that Harpur was growing agitated and knew better than to keep pushing. As much as she wanted to leave Earth and return to Thraeh, they had to see Bon's plan through. Nagging Harpur would only lead to him taking some desperate action to try to fix things. So, she watched and she waited quietly.

As Morgaine parked the Jaguar, Meg and Hart were arguing about what they were going to watch on TV that night. Meg had developed a fondness for reality shows while Hart was more partial to documentaries, particularly those pertaining to science and history. Much to Morgaine's relief, something else was waiting for them.

"It's so tiny," Hart said, leaning closer to look at the squawking, flailing infant.

"It's not purple," Meg said, concerned that something had gone wrong.

"All baby dragons are the colour of sand when they first hatch," Bon explained. "His scales will take on their proper colour as he grows."

"He's kind of cute," Meg said, eliciting a grunt from Morgaine, who remained on the other side of the room.

"He needs to feed," Bon said.

Hiro handed a small chunk of raw meat to the android, who turned and beckoned Morgaine to do the honours. "I think it would be best if he imprints on you," Bon said.

They had discussed this and agreed that Morgaine should be the first to feed the babies, but the dragon-wizardess needed some encouragement from Bon before she could cross the room and take the meat from him. Kneeling down next to the nest, she concealed the meat in her hand and reached out to let the baby dragon sniff her knuckles. He nudged her hand, trying to get to the food, but she made him wait until she was ready to give it to him. When she finally opened her hand, the baby tore it from her fingers and swallowed it whole. Immediately, he began nudging her hand again, looking for more.

"He's a feisty little thing, isn't he?" Hart said as Morgaine repeated the process.

"Look!" Meg squealed. She pointed to another egg that had started rocking. "Does that mean another one is going to hatch?"

Bon confirmed that it was a good sign. "We will soon find out."

Over the course of the evening, three more eggs hatched. Two of the babies died shortly after they emerged from their shells. The other one, a perfect replica of the first, was hale and hearty. By the next morning, Bon had deduced that the remaining eight eggs were not likely to hatch. At Meg's insistence, though, he agreed to give them one more day.

"We cannot keep them much longer," Bon explained to the princess. "The heat from the sand will soon degrade the shells and they will crack. You do not want to experience the smell of dragon eggs that have gone bad."

Meg was heartbroken over the deaths and the duds. "What will you do with them?" she asked the android.

"I will burn them," Morgaine said. "At nightfall tonight, I will take them somewhere remote and destroy them completely."

"How will you choose which clone to transfer your spirit into?" Hart asked. One of the baby dragons was perched on his shoulder and was nipping at his hair.

"I… Harpur will take whichever one is strongest when the time comes," Morgaine said.

"Then we'll take the other one to the Sands of Sancheera and set it free, right?" Meg asked.

"We'll see," Morgaine said, warning Bon and Hiro with a look to say nothing more.

Hiro produced a meal of fettuccini alfredo with grilled chicken, garlic toast and a Caesar salad for their dinner. They ate in a silence that was broken only by squawks from the baby dragons and pronunciations of approval by Meg and Hart. Otherwise, they remained preoccupied with their own thoughts. The moment the twins had finished eating, they raced to the conversation pit where their argument over what show to watch picked up where it had left off earlier.

Morgaine sighed and rose from the table. "I will choose what we watch tonight," she said, extricating the remote control from Meg's hands.

She pointed the device at the TV on the wall above the fireplace and deftly clicked the buttons until she found what she was looking for. She settled into Harpur's favourite spot on the sofa and adjusted her seat until she was comfortably reclined. Ignoring the twins' eye rolls and sighs of exasperation, she pressed play. Thus, the twins were introduced to the classic, late-twentieth-century action film genre. And Morgaine enjoyed a peaceful evening watching a bare-foot hero save the day from the evil machinations of a charismatic, but ultimately doomed bad guy. To keep the mood light and the twins from asking a million questions during the movie, Morgaine conjured large bags of popcorn and giant cups of cola.

Now that the incubation process was over, Bon and Hiro had little else to do but join in and watch the movie too. They left the baby dragons in the nest and made their way to the conversation pit.

"Ah," Bon said, recognizing the iconic film. "Did you know that 'Yippee-ki-yay...?'"

"No spoilers!" Morgaine said, cutting the android off.

Arthur tried to make a break for his covert as soon as they arrived back at the castle. Sok, however, reminded him of his kingly obligation to complete Berryl's appointment as the citizen advocate by showing him the 37 petitions that had accumulated since the last court day.

"The sooner you approve the duties of the position, the sooner Berryl can relieve you of..." He shuffled through the petitions. "...at least half of these cases."

"How close is he to finishing returning all the stuff to its owners?" Arthur directed this question to Eowyn.

"He's almost done," Eowyn said. "Some of the owners have moved; a few are deceased. There's a small pile of things that he cannot remember who he stole them from. But he's made great progress, and as soon as you decide what should be done with the leftovers, he can… advance to his new job."

"Sok, see to the items that Berryl can't return," Arthur ordered.

"Why me?"

"Why not you?"

"Eowyn, see to the items that Berryl can't return," Sok said to the captain of the guard.

"Why me?"

"Oh, for Orhowyn's sake!" Arthur exclaimed. "If Berryl is certain that he can't return them, donate them to a thrift store or something."

"What's a thrift store?" Sok and Eowyn asked in tandem.

"A second-hand store," Arthur explained. "You know, a place where people take things that they don't want anymore, but are still useable."

"Never heard of such a thing," Sok said.

"Well, what do people do with stuff like that?" Arthur asked. Again, he was reminded of how unaware he was of the culture in Colwygshire.

"They take it to the market. There's a stall where people leave things for others to take and use if they want them." Eowyn was surprised that the king did not know this.

"Then do that," Arthur said. "Problem solved."

"I will check with Berryl, then dispatch a couple of guards to see to it," Eowyn said.

"Good!" Arthur turned to leave the council chambers.

"Hold on!" Sok called the king back. "We're not done yet."

Arthur sighed. "Okay. Show me what you have so far."

He sat down at the big, oak table and took the partially finished job description from his senior advisor. Giving it a quick scan, he handed it back. "Looks good to me."

"What do you think about the part where Berryl collects a fee from the petitioners to review their cases?"

"He can't do that!" Arthur looked at the paper again, searching for any reference to a fee.

"How else is he going to get paid?" Sok replied.

"He'll get paid like any other castle employee," Arthur said.

"Clearly, you haven't thought this through," Sok said. "The castle accounts are very precise. There's no room in the budget for another paid position."

Arthur frowned. Sok had tried going over the accounts with him many times, but he'd never understood them and lost interest rather quickly. "Then close the charge account at Skull's Keep and pay Berryl out of those funds."

Sok gasped. "You can't be serious!"

Now, Arthur smiled. "I never approved that account, so now I'm disapproving it."

"It seems we have come to an impasse," Sok said, gathering up his papers and tapping them on the table to line them up. "We shall discuss this later."

Arthur watched his senior advisor walk out of the council chambers. That was his cue to retreat to his covert.

Chapter Twenty

The baby dragons were growing fast. But not fast enough for Harpur.

Bon estimated that, at the rate the enchanted food was accelerating their growth, it would take about three weeks on Earth for them to reach maturity. But there was another, more serious, problem to contend with; being confined and unable to fly, their wings were not developing properly.

"And you cannot continue stealing cows to feed them," Bon said to Morgaine. "There have been reports on the news about cows going missing. One network showed a video of a cow vanishing from a corral. People are going to start to panic."

Morgaine had seen it. "No one believes it," she said. "They think it's been tampered with. If the authorities prove it hasn't been tampered with, they will just say that it has and cover this all up. I'm not worried about that."

"Even so," Bon said, "the missing animals are not going unnoticed. Perhaps you can pluck a bear or a deer out of the wild next time."

Morgaine had chosen to conjure cows to feed the hatchlings from nearby farms because they were docile and easy prey for the young dragons. She didn't want to bring wild animals into the lair, due to their unpredictability, but Bon had a point. She'd had to bring in eleven cows to sate the hatchlings already. By the time they matured, they would require dozens more. And the gore in the lair was less than desirable.

"Then we will transfer Harpur's spirit into one of them tonight," Morgaine declared impulsively.

"You want me to put your spirit into a hatchling?" Bon asked.

Morgaine looked at the frustrated replicas and sighed. They were only three days old and while they had grown considerably, they were still technically babies. The idea of having to go through those early stages of development again did not appeal to Harpur, though Karrys found the prospect quite amusing.

"We can't stay here for three more weeks," Morgaine said. "If you transfer Harpur's spirit into one of them now, he can zap to a remote area at night and work his wings to make sure they aren't stunted."

Bon glanced over at the twins, who were watching a sequel to the action film they had seen the night before, then looked back at the dragon-wizardess. "I suggest you wait until after the scaleshift to do the transfer. It would be less uncomfortable for you and by then the magic will have stabilized enough that your experience should allow you to handle any problems that might occur."

Morgaine watched the hatchlings, both curled up and sleeping soundly. "How long until the scaleshift begins?"

"At the rate they are growing, scaleshift should be complete within a week." Bon's gaze drifted back to the twins.

Morgaine's eyes followed. They needed to talk privately about how to deal with the twins. Morgaine nodded toward the exit and motioned for Hiro to come with them.

"We'll be back shortly! If the hatchlings wake up, just leave them be; they can feed on the rest of the carcass from this afternoon," Morgaine called casually. They left before the twins had a chance to ask any questions.

From the alley, Morgaine zapped herself, Bon and Hiro to the rooftop where the Boundary was located. She conjured some folding chairs from a nearby dance studio that was currently closed and invited Hiro to produce some ale from his ever-present satchel, which he did.

"Whatever happens next," Morgaine began as she settled into her chair, "Meg and Hart have to be... managed."

Neither Harpur, nor Karrys had anticipated having the twins around for this part of the plan. But leaving them to their own devices in Andonsheer was not an option, and now that they were stuck with the prince and princess, they had to find a way to finish what they started without any teenage angst interfering. Meg had already expressed concern over destroying the unviable eggs. No one wanted to deal with her reaction to destroying the second, unnecessary clone, though they knew that it was inevitable.

Bon suggested that Harpur choose which clone he wanted to keep and take care of the other one and the eggs right away. That would leave them with one less mouth to feed and give Meg time to come to terms with what had to be done.

"Is there any difference between the two clones?" Morgaine asked.

"Physiologically, there are differences due to the mitochondrial DNA from the egg donors. One is physically more powerful, but has a calmer disposition. I suspect he will be the larger of the two when he matures. The other one is leaner, but fiercer. I have noticed his aggressive tendencies, particularly when they feed."

"I thought they would be exact replicas of Harpur," Morgaine said. She was obviously a little shaken by this news.

"Unfortunately, an exact replica is impossible to achieve under the circumstances," Bon said. "There could be other minor differences as well."

"Such as?"

"The eye colour might not be exactly the same as yours was, and there could be traces of the mother's colouring in the scales. We won't know for sure until after the scaleshift is complete."

Morgaine leaned back and looked up at the evening sky while inside her Harpur digested the information. Had he known all this before, he might not have been so quick to go along with Bon's plan. Realistically, some variation in eye or scale colour shouldn't be a big deal. And being young and strong and healthy again was more important than having a slightly larger or smaller body. The intention was to free Karrys Evergreen and give her life back to her. If the price he had to pay to make things right for Karrys was to look a little different than he used to, he should be grateful. Instead, he felt a measure of fear seize hold of him as another thought sprang up like a dragonfoil tree.

He had promised Khol the Black that he would turn himself in to the Dragon Council and confess what he had done. No one would believe him if he looked even marginally different than he had before he died. There would be no way to prove he was Harpur Diggins; the council would see a stranger. And they would think him insane.

Then a worse thought presented itself.

Morgaine sat up straight, a look of horror on her face. "Will I... will Harpur be sharing the body and spirit of the clone?"

Bon had anticipated this question, and he only had a theory to offer. "If the clones were left to grow and mature on their own, they would, of course, develop their own personalities. Their experiences would shape them the same way that your experiences shaped you. I believe, however, that your personality will dominate and that, in time, the clone's natural disposition will fade into insignificance. Whichever body you choose, it is too young to have established any preferences. It hasn't had any experiences on which to base opinions or beliefs. You will bring all that makes you Harpur Diggins when I transfer your spirit into it. It is possible, however, that there will be some inherent traits that you will have to adjust to."

"Like what?"

"The way you walk, for one," Bon said. "Your bite. Flying style. Almost assuredly, your voice will be different."

Morgaine relaxed a little, but only a little. "Will I look the same when I shapeshift into my human form?"

"No," Bon said. "Your human guise may be similar, but it will not be exactly as it was before."

"So, all I will retain is my consciousness," Morgaine said, forgetting to speak in the third person. "Essentially, we are just repeating what I did to Karrys, but in a body that won't care that it's been taken over. How is this any better?"

"Karry will be free," Bon said, "and you may be able to have a good life again too."

"How?" Morgaine nearly wailed. "I have no kingdom to rule. I can't go back to Colwygshire to be with my friends. Not that they'd want me there. I have nothing. And I will have stolen another dragon's life in the process."

Hiro, who had not contributed to the conversation, finished his ale and tucked the cup back into the satchel. He hopped down from his chair and looked at Morgaine. "The Harpur Diggins I knew would not wallow in self-pity. He would find the opportunity in the situation. He would make a plan. And one way or another, by the scales of Orhowyn, he'd find a way to put that plan into action."

Morgaine was taken aback by the Krist's assertive rebuke. Part of Harpur wanted to fry the diminutive being on the spot. Hiro had no idea how Harpur had been affected by the things that had happened to him. On the other hand, he'd have said the same thing if their roles were reversed.

"Everything happens for a reason, *Harpur*," Hiro continued.

"Oh, you're not going to lay any of that New Age crap on me now, are you?" Morgaine snapped so she wouldn't flinch at the use of Harpur's name.

"It's not New Age crap," Hiro said. "The reason everything happens is because everyone makes choices."

"I don't understand."

"Everything that happens is a consequence of a choice," Hiro explained. "The reason you are in this situation is because you chose it."

Morgaine had to take a moment to let that sink in. "I didn't choose this outcome!"

"Oh, but you did! You may have hoped for a different result, but this is the result you got. Now, you have to make another choice. If you pay attention to the results of your previous choices, you may just make a better one this time."

"You make it sound like everything is my fault! I didn't choose for Anayah to go off and try to defeat Analeetah on her own."

"How did we get to that?" It was Hiro's turn to be taken off-guard.

"I believe we are getting off track here," Bon interjected. "We came here to decide how to proceed with the cloning. And what to do about the twins."

Hiro hopped back up onto his chair and Morgaine shifted in hers. There was clearly more to be settled, but Bon was right; they were there to sort out the cloning conundrum and figure out how to keep the twins from making a bad choice.

"What do you propose?" Morgaine addressed the android.

"I propose that you choose a clone tonight. Then, when the twins are asleep, remove the remaining eggs and take care of the other clone. When the clone you choose has completed its scaleshift, we go ahead with the transfer and get back to Thraeh. We can decide where to send the twins later." Bon looked from Morgaine to Hiro, waiting for their response.

"What exactly is the scaleshift?" Hiro asked. He'd been curious since Bon first mentioned it in the lair.

"When a dragon hatches, its scales are soft. The scaleshift is a stage of development when the soft scales sluff off and are replaced by the hard armor scales of the adult," Bon explained. "It can take several weeks for the process to run its course, and during that time the dragon experiences a great deal of discomfort. They can become quite unruly!"

"I see," Hiro said. "And how long will it take the clone to go through this stage?"

"At the accelerated rate of growth," Bon said, "a day. Give or take a few hours."

"Will we be in any danger while this is going on?"

"The twins and I won't," Morgaine said, "but you and Bon will need protection. I will make a cage for him so he doesn't accidentally set you two on fire."

"Are we in agreement, then?" Bon asked as Hiro considered the implications.

Morgaine exhaled forcefully. "What do we do about Meg and Hart?"

"Hart won't be a problem," Bon said. "He is a sensible lad. Meg, however…"

"Yeah," Morgaine said as she stood up, "I'll probably have to make a cage for her too."

Sok and Arthur finally managed to hash out the job description for Berryl's new position as Citizen Advocate. They also found the money to pay him in a hidden account that King Gnik's financial officer had established, and, upon further examination, had been slowly siphoning off of for many years before the monarch's unfortunate demise at the hands of Edlyngton Bloomregaard. A considerable amount of money remained in this slush fund; enough to cover Berryl's wages for the rest of his life. And then some. How Sok had not noticed the odd discrepancy before this, Arthur did not know, but he was glad that its discovery had ended the elf's argument against paying Berryl anything at all. Sok was glad that he got to keep the castle account at Skull's Keep in the bargain.

Now that the accounts were all accounted for and the position of Citizen Advocate was sorted out, Sok needed Arthur to sign off on the financial report and officially authorize Berryl's appointment. As was becoming an all-too-frequent occurrence, though, Arthur was unreachable in his covert and it was well past the time he was due to have checked in.

Hoping that Arthur had gone to his chambers, Sok climbed the stairs and entered the king's private rooms. It was getting close to supper time, and it was entirely possible that Arthur had gone straight to his rooms to change. There was no sign of the king, and the guards assured Sok that they had neither seen, nor heard, the king inside all afternoon. There were signs that someone had been there. The towel cabinet was blocking the entrance to the bathing chamber.

"Do you know why this is here?" Sok asked the guards.

"The king asked us to help him move it into the bathing room, sir," one of the guards said.

"But why is it blocking the door?"

"It's too tall to fit through the bathing room's door, sir," said the other guard. "His majesty told us to leave it there and he would deal with it later."

"Why didn't he just zap it into the bathing room?" Sok asked, nonplussed by the whole affair.

"Couldn't rightly tell you, sir," said the first guard. "Perhaps it didn't occur to him."

Sok shook his head, muttering under his breath and ushered the guards back out into the hall. He was about to close the door when he noticed a piece of slate on the low table between the sofas. It appeared to have writing on it. Curious, Sok went over to the table and picked it up. The words were clearly written in Arthur's hand. They seemed to have been written in chalk. It read:

SOK, WHEN YOU FIND THIS, WIPE OFF WHAT I WROTE AND WRITE SOMETHING ELSE ON IT. A.

Sok frowned at the eight-inch by ten-inch slate. "What has he done now?"

He retrieved a small towel from the towel cabinet and wiped off the words. Then he looked around for something to write with. There were two biros on Arthur's desk next to the book shelves, but neither of them worked on the hard surface of the slate. He checked the table to see if Arthur had provided a piece of chalk and did not find one.

He examined the slate to see if there might be a compartment hidden on the underside, but the slate was solid. When he flipped it back over, he saw his own hand print on the top surface and realized that all he had to do was use his finger to write a message with.

SOMETHING ELSE.

A moment later, the words faded away and were replaced with a new message:

HA-HA!

Before Sok could reply, Arthur appeared in a puff of amber smoke.

"Pretty cool, hey?"

"You're late," Sok said, though he was impressed with Arthur's invention.

"I was waiting for you to find the whisperglyph."

"The what?"

"The whisperglyph! That's what I'm calling this." Arthur pointed at the slate.

"Whisperglyph?"

"I was going to call it an arkanote, but I like whisperglyph better. What do you think? Now, I don't have to keep zapping up here and you can send me messages when you need me." Arthur grinned proudly at his senior advisor.

"Or you could spend less time down there and I wouldn't have to pack around a heavy chunk of rock everywhere I go." He hefted the whisperglyph for effect.

"I know. I'm trying to find something lighter to make them from, but so far slate is the best material for transmitting messages."

"You do that," Sok said, not wanting to reveal how wonderful he thought the whisperglyph truly was. "In the meantime, I need you to sign these." Sok thrust the documents and a biro at Arthur.

While Arthur signed the financial report and Berryl's official appointment document, Sok wiped Arthur's message from the slate and wrote a new message. "How long does the message stay on the slate?"

"Until whoever receives it wipes it off of their slate." Arthur handed back the signed documents. "What did you write?"

"You'll see it when you read it on your slate," Sok said. "Where is your slate, by the way?"

"I left it in the covert," Arthur said.

"So, if I wipe this off now, you won't see what I wrote on your slate?"

"You can't wipe it off your slate," Arthur said. "It will stay there until I wipe it off my slate."

"That sounds like a design flaw," Sok observed.

"This is a prototype," Arthur said defensively. "But thanks for the feedback. I'll work on making it more efficient." He tried to peek over the top of Sok's slate to read the message, but the elf clutched it to his chest. "Fine. If you don't need me for anything else, I'll just zap back to the covert and keep working."

"It's time to dress for supper," Sok said. "You'll just have to wait until tomorrow to find out what I wrote."

Arthur rolled his eyes. "Do you know what Finch is serving tonight?"

"Mutton stew," Sok said.

"Oh, good!" Arthur said as he headed to his bed chamber to change. "I hope she makes that delicious corn bread to go with it."

"Say, Arthur?" Sok called out. "Why didn't you just zap your towel cabinet into the bathing room if you wanted it in there?"

Arthur popped his head around the door and looked at the offending piece of furniture. "Didn't think of that!" He waved his hand and the cabinet relocated.

"Some wizard you are," Sok said quietly. "You can make a whisperglyph, but you can't zap a towel cabinet from one room to another without being told."

"What did you say?" Arthur asked returning from his bed chamber dressed in a fetching poet's shirt tucked into a smart pair of pants. He was slipping his arms into a tailored jacket.

"Where's your crown?" Sok said, giving the king an approving look.

"Right! I'll be back in a sec." Another puff of amber smoke replaced Arthur in the room. A few moments later, he reappeared with his crown on his head and a sly smile on his face. "Ready?"

"Ready," Sok said as he followed Arthur out.

As he reached back to pull the door closed, Sok glanced down at the whisperglyph. The message he'd written—*THIS IS AWESOME!*—was gone and a new one was in its place.

I KNEW YOU'D LIKE IT.

Sok smiled and followed Arthur to the great hall.

Morgaine started with the eggs. She and Bon gathered them into the bags they had been transported to the lair in and the dragon-wizardess zapped them and herself to Elk Island where she transformed and burned them to ash. When she returned to the lair, the clone she rejected was sedated and sleeping soundly in the mound of sand that had so recently held the eggs.

Harpur had chosen the stronger, calmer one of the two clones, reasoning that it would at least be closer in stature to his original body when it matured. The smaller clone was less attractive, with beady eyes and a narrow snout. Harpur wanted a more majestic and less devious aspect when all was said and done. He tried not to think about the possibility that he might not get to enjoy it for very long.

The twins had fallen asleep on the sofas in the conversation pit and were peacefully oblivious to the activity around the nest, thanks to Hiro's sleeping draught, which he had slipped into their beverages a short time earlier. Morgaine confirmed that they hadn't so much as stirred while she was out destroying the eggs and then turned her attention to the clones.

"How much sleeping draught did you give him?" Morgaine asked.

"Enough to keep him quiet while you…" Bon whispered as he drew a finger across his neck.

"It's sad that he never got a chance to fly," Hiro said. "How will you do it?"

"Efficiently," Morgaine replied. "I'll be back before sunrise."

The clone that was to become Harpur's new body blinked in surprise when his nest-mate vanished. He leaned over and sniffed the spot where the other clone had been sleeping. Bon and Hiro stepped back, unsure how the young dragon was going to react.

"Get the meat ready," Bon said to Hiro, referring to a large chunk of deer meat they had laced with sleeping draught—just in case.

Hiro handed the android the meat and took another few steps back. "He doesn't look happy."

The clone turned to look at Bon and Hiro. He lowered his head and narrowed his eyes, shifting his gaze between the android and the Krist. Slowly, he spread his wings out in a menacing gesture of disapproval and confusion. A soft orange glow bloomed on his chest, the first signs of the dragon fire that would soon become a formidable weapon.

Bon stood his ground, keeping his own eyes locked on the hatchling's reptilian stare. He wasn't concerned about being burned; the clone's dragon fire would not present any significant threat until after his scaleshift. His claws and wings and teeth were another matter, though, and Bon could only hope that the lack of natural socialization and development would keep the young dragon from attacking.

The clone took a step toward Bon, flapping his wings and screeching loudly. A thin wisp of smoke escaped his maw with the deafening howl. Bon tossed the piece of meat, aiming for the clone's open mouth, but he missed his mark and the venison bounced off the hatchling's beaked snout. It was enough, however, to distract the clone, who snatched it up and swallowed it whole.

"Did the twins wake up?" Bon asked without taking his eyes off the clone.

"No," Hiro replied. "The sleeping draught is doing its job."

A few more tense seconds passed while they waited for the sedative to take effect. Finally, the clone lowered his wings and stopped shrieking. His eyes glazed over and his lids slowly closed. A moment later, he fell to the floor, blessedly quiet and quite unconscious.

Bon turned to Hiro. "A round of shookin, perhaps?"

"I think that is a grand idea!" Hiro giggled and went to the table to set up the game.

Morgaine zapped herself and the hatchling to a remote area on the north shore of Mud Lake in Elk Island National Park. A few bison lingering nearby showed no interest in the sudden appearance of a woman and a dragon in their midst. A passing glance was all they could afford the intrusion on their moonlight rest. Until, that is, Morgaine transformed and was substituted by an enormous teal dragon. A bellow from a startled bull jolted the small herd into action. They thundered away from the lake shore, crashing through the bush to get away from this new threat.

Karrys watched the bison stampeding westward and briefly entertained the idea of making one of them a late-night snack. The hatchling stirred at her feet, pulling her attention back to the gruesome task before her. Through her eyes, Harpur Diggins studied the small creature. The idea that this small dragon carried his DNA and was, more or less, a part of him was profoundly disturbing to the old dragon. It had been created for him and of him, and killing it was suddenly as repulsive a prospect as any Harpur had ever known.

Karrys: I'm not raising it for you.

Harpur: Of course not. I wouldn't ask you to.

Karrys: What will happen to it if you...?

Harpur: He might survive.

Karrys: It's the equivalent of a two-year-old dragon, but it's never flown, never hunted. You know it won't survive on its own.

Harpur: Shouldn't we give him a chance?

Karrys: The only reason the other one stands a chance is because it will have your experience to see it through. But don't think for a heartbeat that you aren't going to face some difficult times trying to catch its body up to your skill.

Harpur considered Karrys' words and realized that he wouldn't even be old enough to take a name when his spirit got transferred into the clone's body. He might not even have the capacity to speak yet, though that would happen soon. He would be in no position—the business with the Dragon Council notwithstanding—to care for another young dragon.

Karrys: You have grown too soft, Xzynthyrius. End it now. Let it know peace in Arachovor. We need to get out of here before we are discovered.

Harpur wanted to rage against this. He scrambled to think of a way to save the clone and at least give it a chance to survive. But he knew that Karrys was right; he was getting too soft.

With a growl that shook the trees, the teal dragon bent down and took hold of the drowsy hatchling by the neck. Lifting the mewling little thing off the ground, she bit down, snapping his neck. A couple of vicious shakes and he hung limp and dead in her mouth.

Dropping the body to the ground, the teal dragon set it alight with her dragon fire. The tiny body burned quickly and soon there was nothing left of the hatchling but a small pile of fine ash.

"I am sorry, Little One," Harpur said through Karrys' mouth. "You will be safe among the Nameless in Arachovor."

Becoming invisible, Harpur launched the stolen body he occupied into the sky and flew west over the Rocky Mountains until the sorrow and regret melted enough that he could face his future again.

Just before sunrise, Morgaine returned to the lair under Whyte Avenue. She joined Bon and Hiro at the table. Their game of shookin was just winding up.

"How did it go?" Bon asked gently. He could see the pain in the dragon-wizardess' eyes.

"How do you think it went?" Morgaine snapped.

Hiro reached into his satchel and produced a warm cup of coffee for her. "This will be over soon," he said.

"Not soon enough," Morgaine growled. She looked at the clone. He was sleeping off the sedative in the nest. "How long until the scaleshift again?"

"A few days," Bon replied. "No longer than a week."

Morgaine turned away again and sipped the coffee. *It's going to be a long week.*

Sok sat in the council chambers. Alone. He felt contemplative—in a jittery, anticipatory way. Part of him still wanted to go to Andonsheer to find out what was happening with Harpur. Part of him wanted to stay put and let things unfold as they may.

His life at the castle had fractured. Anayah was dead. Arthur was becoming obsessed with his magic. Davynn was leaving. Bon and Hiro were essentially still the same dogged scientists they had always been. *But for how long?* Elder Dhonna was growing distant; she hadn't been seen since the funeral. Eowyn had brought a refreshing new perspective to the table. The twins were dragons. It was unlikely that they would ever be able to return to Epoh. And then there was Harpur. After all they had gone through to help him, he was probably going to end up dead anyway.

The court petitions were piling up. There were more complaints and requests sitting on his desk than there had ever been and Arthur didn't seem at all interested in hearing them. He thought about handing them all over to Berryl, but he believed that the new Citizen Advocate needed to be eased into the position. Maybe he could go through the petitions and assign a few of the easier ones to Berryl first.

He had purchased a fine leather satchel to carry the slate in and he pulled it out, planning on demanding that Arthur come up and do his duty as the king. Then his stomach growled. It was not yet time for supper, but the afternoon was waning and there was little time left to accomplish anything anyway.

Hmm… Sok thought. *I wonder…*

DO YOU MIND IF I HOLD COURT IN YOUR PLACE TOMORROW? he wrote on the slate.

GO AHEAD Arthur wrote back almost immediately.

Sok stared at the words on the slate. This did not bode well, but it would provide a good distraction from… Well, everything else.

I WILL DRAW UP A PROCLOMATION GIVING ME AUTHORITY TO RESOLVE THE PETITIONS.

SOUNDS GOOD.

Sok scowled at the slate. YOU CAN SIGN IT WHEN YOU COME UP FOR SUPPER.

OKAY.

At least he's responding, Sok thought. Then he snickered. CAN I WEAR THE CROWN?

NO!

I THOUGHT NOT. WHAT ARE YOU WORKING ON?

STUFF.

Hopefully, he's finding something lighter to make the whisperglyph out of, thought Sok. He looked at his hands and decided that a manicure would be nice. He would suggest, stupid as it was, that Arthur create an instant manicure system.

He put the slate back in the bag and went to his office to write the proclamation. He kept it simple.

By order of King Arthur of Epoh, Sok, Senior Advisor, is hereby granted the authority to hear any and all petitions brought before the Colwygshire court, and to decide upon them as he sees fit, from this day forward.

"That should do it," Sok said aloud. "But I need someone to record the proceedings." He considered asking Davynn to do it, but didn't think that the knight would be terribly interested. The only reasonable candidate he could think of was Berryl. *It will be good training for him,* Sok thought. *But I'll have to keep an eye on the pen when we're done.*

With the proclamation written and ready for Arthur's signature, and a decision made in regard to someone to record his decisions, Sok felt better. He tucked the proclamation into his pocket and returned to the council chambers to find the bag with the slate buzzing and vibrating on the table. He stopped and cocked his head, furrowing his brows.

Tentatively, Sok reached out for the satchel and lifted the flap so he could see the slate inside. There were words written on it, but he had to pull it all the way out to read them. As soon as he touched the slate, it stopped buzzing and vibrating, so he pulled it free of the bag and turned it to read the message.

ANY WORD FROM ANDONSHEER?

YEAH! HARPUR IS DEAD. THE TWINS ARE IN DRAGON JAIL. AND MORGAINE KILLED THE DRAGON COUNCIL.

In a puff of amber smoke, Arthur appeared on the other side of the table. "Orhowyn's cold cadaver! What are we going to do? We have to get Davynn. And Elder Dhonna. We need a plan!"

Sok laughed. "Relax. It's not true. But I'm glad to know that all it takes is a disaster to get you out of that... What do you call it?"

"You can be a real jerk sometimes, Sok." Arthur slumped into the nearest chair. "It's called a covert."

"Since you're here..." Sok reached into his pocket and took out the proclamation. "Sign this."

Arthur unfolded the paper and read it. "From this day forward?" He arched an eyebrow.

"As required," Sok said.

Arthur scrunched up his face and shook his head. He was going to say no and have Sok re-write the proclamation. Then he changed his mind. "Okay." He picked up the pen Sok had slid across the table and signed it.

That was a little too easy, Sok thought as the retrieved the pen and the paper. "So, what stuff are you working on down there?"

"Want to come and see for yourself?" Arthur stroked his chin and grinned at the elf.

"I'd love to," Sok said, "but I don't fancy being crushed by walls today."

"I solved that problem," Arthur said. "We can just zap down to the covert."

"When did you figure that out?" Sok asked, surprised that this was the first he was hearing about it.

"Earlier today," Arthur said. "I was reading Ylemnir's journals and the warding spell Harpur must have used was written out in detail. You still can't use the passage, but I can zap us down there any time."

"Well, thank you for letting me know." Sok felt a surge of anger toward Arthur. *He's deliberately leaving me out.*

Arthur felt the anger wafting off the elf like the scent of bacon from the kitchens. "Sok, everyone needs something that is their own. On Earth, my thing was comic books. I loved them. I read them. I collected them. I studied them. I sold them. I read up on their creators. They gave me comfort. They let me see myself as someone special. Since I've been here, I have had nothing that was my own. This crown…" He touched his head, then remembered he had swapped it for a royal-blue, pointy wizard hat. "…*the* crown, isn't mine. It never was. Being a king wasn't mine. It's been fun and it's been interesting, but it doesn't give me a sense of identity; I don't feel like a king. Does this make any sense to you?"

"Why now?" Sok asked. "Why, after all these years of avoiding your magic are you suddenly… obsessed with it?"

Arthur saw confusion and fear in Sok's eyes, reflections of the elf's world falling apart around him. "We're all changing, Sok. All of us."

"I'm not!" Sok shouted. "I was super happy with things just the way they were. My thing was being here, being senior advisor to the king." He made a face at the pointy wizard hat. "I broke away from the traditions of my people for… this! And now it's all going away. I don't want it to change, Arthur.

"Nothing stays the same forever, Sok," Arthur said as gently as he could.

Sok looked at Arthur. "What will become of me?"

Arthur thought about what he had read in Ylemnir's journal about his crown toppling from his head. He had not found any other references to him losing the crown and he didn't want to alarm the worried elf any more than he was. "Maybe you will become the king."

Sok scoffed at him. "Have you not figured out how all this works yet? A human has to be king of the humans."

"Like you said, everything is changing." Arthur conjured an apple and bit into it. "The fact is you have been more of a king to the humans in Epoh than I ever was. I wouldn't be surprised if, one day, you do wear the crown."

The elf scowled. "Thanks for trying to cheer me up."

Arthur shrugged. "Any time! Why don't we have supper sent up to my rooms tonight?"

"That's a good idea," Sok said. "I will inform Finch."

"Let me," Arthur offered as he stood up. "That's not a job for the future king."

As Arthur walked away, Sok wondered if he wasn't losing his mind. *Me? King? When dragons dance and the Faefolk fly!*

Meg woke up and stretched. She felt groggy, as if she had overslept or had too much ale, a drink she was becoming accustomed to, if not learning to truly enjoy. But neither of these were the culprit; Hiro's sleeping draught, slipped into her and Hart's beverages the evening before was the reason for the brain fog. Morgaine, Bon and Hiro wanted to be sure that the twins would not wake up while they dealt with the non-viable eggs and the second clone. They had to get them out of the lair and ensure they were properly disposed of quickly and quietly.

She rose from the sofa, confused about not being in the bed Morgaine had conjured for her, and looked around. Hart was still sleeping on the sofa a couple feet away, his head lolling to one side and his mouth gaping open. Bon, Hiro and Morgaine were sitting at the table, talking softly over steaming cups of coffee. The enticing aroma of bacon stirred her senses.

She stood and turned to check on the hatchlings. Seeing only one, Meg scanned the rest of the lair searching for his nest-mate. There was nowhere the hatchling could hide, though her mind would not accept that he wasn't still there.

"Where is he? Where is the other hatchling?" she demanded, spinning frantically to face Morgaine, Bon and Hiro. Their somber expressions answered her question and tears welled up in her eyes. "Why?" she moaned.

Morgaine was too exhausted to deal with any histrionics. She looked at Bon and Hiro, hoping one of them would step in and console the princess, but neither the android nor the Krist took the hint. She drained her cup of coffee and went to the conversation pit to do damage control.

Meg's crying woke Hart. He sat up slowly and looked at his sister. "Meg? What's wrong? What happened?"

Meg pointed toward the nest. Seeing that it was far less occupied than it had been the night before, he turned and glared at Morgaine.

"Okay, both of you listen up," Morgaine said. "You both knew what was going to happen. So, if you think that I'm going apologize or mollycoddle you through it, you're going to be disappointed. It's done. Find a way to get over it, because I'm not going to spend the next week or so cooped up with you two sniffling and giving me dirty looks for doing what had to be done. Now, get cleaned up and eat your breakfast. Then we're going to the museum."

The dragon-wizardess returned to the table where she ignored Bon and Hiro's raised eyebrows.

"I hate you," Meg whined under her breath.

"Don't waste the sentiment," Morgaine said over her shoulder. "I hate myself enough for the both of us."

Court went better than Sok had expected. Berryl proved to be a fine recorder of the proceedings and seemed content to have a purpose once again. Before they opened the doors to the great hall to let the petitioners in, Sok had given Berryl specific instructions on how he wanted the petitions recorded. From the 37 petitions that were before the court that day, Sok had weeded out 23 that, from his vast experience, he deemed minor and told Berryl that these would be the first cases he would be handling on his own.

"You've read the list of your duties," the elf said to the eager citizen advocate. "You will listen to both sides of the petition and negotiate a settlement, which you will record and attach to the original petition for me to review. If you are unable to reach an agreement, you will record your efforts and advance the petition to me. You will brief Arthur and me on it and we will make a final decision. You will then convey that decision to the petitioners in writing. Do you understand?"

Berryl nodded. "I do."

"Good! After today, all petitions will go through you first. I've arranged an office for you next to the archives. When you receive a petition, you will rate it according to the system I have devised. Did you familiarize yourself with it yet?"

"Each petition is rated on a scale of one to five," Berryl recited. "A one is responded to in writing with my decision. No need for the petitioners to come to court. A two or a three, I receive in my office by appointment and decide on there. A four or a five is scheduled for court and will be heard and decided on by King Arthur."

"Or me," Sok added. "Go on."

Berryl wasn't entirely comfortable with Sok having been given the authority to make decisions on behalf of the king, but he dared not voice his opposition at this delicate stage. "Or you," he concurred. "All responses, decisions and referrals are to be attached to the original petitions and handed in to you for review and your signature."

"And what do you do if a petitioner doesn't accept your decision?"

Berryl blinked in confusion at the elf. "I... I don't know, sir," he stammered. "I don't believe that was covered in the documentation you gave me."

Sok sighed. Berryl had been doing so well. "Page ten, paragraph six."

Berryl flipped through the stack of papers Sok had given him. He was unaware that of the 19 pages, Arthur was aware of only the first two, which were the ones that contained the original job description that he and Sok had composed. There was a total of 64 rules, regulations and their accompanying penalties should any of them be breached. How could he possibly be expected to know them all on his first day?

"Ah, yes," Berryl said. "I respond in writing to remind them all decisions of the office of the Citizen Advocate are final and I am to levy a charge of five silver coins, due upon receipt of the letter, for inconvenience and failure to comply with the laws of the court in such matters."

"And?"

Berryl scanned the next paragraph. "And I am not to bother the king with it. Ever!"

"Right!" Sok said, satisfied that Berryl knew his place. "Call in the first petitioners."

Sok heard the remaining fourteen petitions and ruled on them swiftly and without hesitation. As each petitioner entered the great hall, the routine didn't change. It began with looks of confusion on the faces of the petitioners upon seeing Sok sitting on the throne. Berryl then read the proclamation, signed by Arthur, giving Sok the authority to hear and rule on the petitions. Thrown off as they all were, the petitioners stammered through their presentations. Sok then stroked his chin as if he was contemplating the case, a gesture that only served to increase the petitioners' discomfiture. Then he pronounced his ruling, all of which included small fines.

For the most part, the petitioners were too stunned to protest. Only three spoke up against the levy, and their efforts were met with a choice: pay the fine or spend a night in the cells at the north gate. Sok considered threatening them with a night in the dungeons, but he was pushing his luck with the fines in the first place. In all the years that Arthur had been king, not once had he fined a petitioner. And he only threatened time in the dungeons or cells when the petitioners became unruly or belligerent. Never had he been forced to follow through.

Berryl ended the cases by having the petitioners sign the ruling and delivering a firm reminder that, like the king's decisions, Sok's rulings were final. There was no avenue of appeal. A copy would be delivered to them before the next court day.

By lunch time, they were done and Sok thanked Berryl for his services. "I expect all of those with the copies on my desk by the end of the day."

"But, sir," Berryl said, "I won't have time to make copies of all these and hear the remaining cases and write up the decisions in such a short time. Perhaps I could have an assistant?"

"An assistant?" Sok could not believe his ears. "Berryl, you have been given an opportunity that you don't deserve. I would think you'd be a little more grateful."

Berryl hung his head. "Apologies, sir," he mumbled. "I will stay up all night if I must, but I will get this done for you."

Sok felt a small measure of remorse for his harshness. "Have them ready by lunch time tomorrow."

"Thank you, sir!" Berryl was relieved.

Sok picked up the satchel containing the whisperglyph and left the great hall. He was surprised to find Arthur waiting for him in the council chambers. Lunch was already laid out and a cup of ale was ready for him.

"How was your first day as Hand of the King?" Arthur asked as Sok entered the room.

Sok sat down and pulled his ale closer to him. "I'm guessing that is some sort of promotion."

"It is, indeed!" Arthur said. "I've decided to grant you the authority to act as my second in command. You have all the same authority as me. You just can't wear the crown."

Sok reached for a bowl of stew and a thick slice of bread. "I'm afraid I have to decline."

Arthur cocked his head to one side in surprise. "You can't decline. I am the king and I have decided to make you my Hand."

"I have no desire to be groomed for a position I can never hold," Sok said. "But thank you for trying."

Arthur removed his crown and placed it on the table. "Then I will ask you, not as the king, but as your friend to do this for me."

"So you can spend all your time in your covert and shirk your duties while you play great wizard of the land? I don't think so."

"Our world is changing, Sok." Arthur dipped his own bread into his stew. "I haven't seen my children for days. I don't even know where they are or if they are okay. Maybe I am spending too much time in the covert, but it's keeping me from going mad with worry. You have always been better at this than I am. Please, Sok, do this for me. At least until we hear from the twins, or Harpur. I know you want to. Otherwise, you wouldn't have used the phrase 'from this day forward,' in the proclamation."

Sok knew that would bite him in the ass. He leaned back in his chair. "Very well. But only until we hear from Harpur or the twins. What exactly does a Hand of the King do? And where did you come up with that title?"

"It's another Earth thing," Arthur admitted. "I borrowed it from a story I like. You pretty much get to run the show when I'm not around. You report to me and I correct you if I think you've overstepped."

"What constitutes over-stepping?" Sok asked innocently.

"Fining petitioners in court."

Arthur smiled smugly as the elf's mouth drop open. "How…?"

"Maybe I am the great wizard of the land." Arthur winked. "Make sure you return the fines to the petitioners. And I'm going to need to see those additional pages you added to Berryl's job description."

Sok frowned at Arthur. "You were there, weren't you?"

"I assure you I was in the covert all morning. I just came up to get lunch ready for us." Arthur took a bite of gravy-soaked bread and followed it with a spoonful of stew.

Sok's frown deepened. He didn't believe Arthur, but he decided to let it go. Sooner or later, he'd find out how Arthur knew about the fines and the additions to the job description. He dug into his stew and thought about how to word the proclamation declaring him Hand of the King.

Hand of the King! It did have a nice ring to it.

Eowyn entered the council chambers and took a seat. He ladled stew into a bowl and helped himself to a slice of bread. "Sorry I missed court this morning, I had to deal with an incident at the market. How'd it go? Anything I should be aware of?"

"Ask Arthur," Sok said, throwing Arthur a sardonic glare. "He *wasn't* there."

Eowyn paused his spoon on its way to his mouth. "What?"

"Ignore him," Arthur said. "What incident?"

"An argument between three of the vendors," Eowyn replied. "I've filed a petition with Berryl. They will appear next court day."

"Was it serious?" Sok asked.

"Berryl said it was... a four? I don't know what that means, but he said you would sort it out."

Sok looked at Arthur, not sure how the king would feel about the rating system.

"You can keep the rating system," Arthur said, adding a bit more mystery to how he came by his knowledge.

Eowyn's eyes shifted between the king and the elf. "Are either of you going to tell me what is going on?"

"I will brief you later," Sok said. "We're still working the flies out of Berryl's new position."

"Bugs," Arthur corrected. "You work the bugs out of something new."

"Flies are bugs," Sok countered.

"But not all bugs are flies!" Arthur said.

Eowyn poured a cup of ale and took a long drink. He'd been captain of the guard long enough now to realize that this could quickly get out of hand. A change of subject was in order. "Any word from Harpur?"

"None," Arthur said. "I'm getting worried."

"How long is this... what did Bon call it?" Eowyn still could not wrap his head around how the android could make a new body for Harpur.

"Cloning," Arthur said. "I don't know how it works exactly. But I sure wish someone would let us know what's happening."

"Why don't you go to Andonsheer and look for them?" Eowyn asked.

Arthur sighed and shook his head. "I don't know if they are even still there, much less where to start looking for them."

"You were in court today!" Sok exclaimed.

"I was not in court today, Sok," Arthur said.

"Well, then why don't you do whatever you did to find out what happened in court and find out what Harpur is doing?" Sok suggested.

"I tried," Arthur said despondently. "I can't find them anywhere."

Sok could only deduce from Arthur's response that he had discovered some magical means of spying on other people. "I'm not comfortable with being watched without my knowledge."

"Relax, Sok!" Arthur realized where the elf was going with that. "I'm not going to spy on anyone. I just wanted to check in and see how things were going this morning. I promise I will not watch you just for the sake of watching you."

"That doesn't make me feel better! Just knowing that you can listen in or see what I'm doing any time you want is a little disconcerting."

"Well, all I can give you is my word."

"Swear on Alex's grave," Sok said, folding his arms and narrowing his eyes.

"I swear on Alex's grave that I will not spy on you unless…"

"No, not unless anything," Sok said. "You will not spy on me period!"

"Fine." Arthur stood up. "I swear on Alex's grave that I will not spy on you."

Sok wasn't completely convinced, but what could he do about it? He decided to go to Braydon Wood and visit Elder Dhonna after lunch. Some time among the trees would calm his anxiety.

"Where are you going?" Sok asked as Arthur made his way to the door.

"For a walk," Arthur said. He opened the door and started to leave.

"You forgot your crown!"

Arthur returned to the table and reached across it to pick up the diadem. As he stretched forward, he placed a hand on Sok's arm as if to keep his balance. "I'd forget my head if it wasn't firmly attached somedays," he quipped.

He put the crown in place and turned back toward the door. He stopped next to Eowyn's chair and laid a hand on the young captain's shoulder. "You're doing a great job," he whispered. Then he left.

"That was weird," Eowyn said.

Sok nodded in agreement. "What were we talking about?"

Eowyn scratched his head thought about it. "I can't remember."

"Oh, well," Sok said, pushing his empty stew bowl away. "It must not have been important."

Outside the council chamber door, Arthur made a mental note not to tell Sok that he had learned how to wipe memories and to be careful about saying anything about being able to spy on people in the future.

I really am the great wizard of the land, the thought as he left the castle and headed toward the market.

Chapter Twenty-one

A grumpy, one-eyed dragon-wizardess and two surly teenagers entered the Royal Alberta Museum shortly after its doors opened to the public for the day. Morgaine was wearing a bizarre combination of a purple top hat with a black band and a knee-length teal trench coat, cinched at the waist by a matching belt. A black eye-patch hid the empty socket behind it. The twins were more casually, and far less conspicuously attired in jeans and t-shirts.

As they passed the reception desk, the attendant called out to them, politely asking if they would like to pay. Morgaine didn't break stride. She waved her hand over her shoulder, magically overriding the necessity of an admission fee.

"Why are we here?" Meg whined as she caught up to Morgaine.

"Because I said so," Morgaine snapped.

Hart lagged behind deliberately. He was wise enough to know that challenging Morgaine in her current mood was not a good idea. Besides, he didn't care why Morgaine had brought them there; he was already mesmerized by a cast of an Albertosaurus skeleton, a replica of a Columbian mammoth, and a 1918 Curtis JN-4C biplane, all on display in the lobby. The dinosaur skeleton was particularly fascinating. He had never seen a dragon without wings before.

"Hart!" Morgaine's unhappy voice drifted across the lobby.

Hart caught up to Morgaine. "Sorry," he said. "But I saw that dragon skeleton and then that girl…"

"That's not a dragon," Morgaine explained. "It's a dinosaur."

"But…"

"But nothing!" Morgaine hissed. "Just stick close to me."

"So, why did you bring us here?" Hart asked.

"Because I thought you would be interested in the dinosaurs," Morgaine said somewhat softly. "And I wanted to distract Meg from…"

"Was there no other way?" Hart asked.

Morgaine stopped walking and turned to face Hart. "When we leave here and return to Thraeh, I… Harpur is going to be a preadolescent. At least his body will be. He has to face the Dragon Council and then whatever decision they make afterward. If he is lucky enough to live through that, he will have to survive to adulthood. Again! He has the benefit of his experience to help him, but the other one would be on its own. He had no parents to watch over him. And his first days—essentially years—were not normal for a hatchling. He wouldn't have survived anyway."

"Meg and I could have taken care of him," Hart said.

"How?" Morgaine asked. "You don't even know half of what it's like to be a dragon."

"I read that book you told us to read. I know what it's like."

"Erudition cannot replace experience," Morgaine said. "I told you to read that book because I wanted you to understand the difference between being a dragon and being human. I wanted you to know that in spite of your abilities, you are not a dragon. And you never will be."

"That's not true!"

Morgaine growled. "You sound like your sister!"

"We didn't ask for this!" Hart said, his voice rising. "You did this to us. So, stop treating us like we're stupid and teach us how to be dragons!"

A passing couple stared at the prince like he had two heads.

"Keep your voice down!" Morgaine ordered. "We will talk about this later."

Still grumpy, still surly, the three Epohians wandered through the exhibits until the grumpiness and surliness softened and began to melt away. Hart was the first to lighten up. The exhibits instilled him with a sense of wonder. The morning passed and by mid-afternoon, they had seen everything there was to see. Morgaine, however, knew that there was much more to the Royal Alberta Museum and she decided to treat the twins to a behind-the-scenes look at what lay below the public galleries. She led them to a secluded corner on the second floor and zapped them into the basement.

Invisible, they made their way down a long corridor and through a set of doors into a vast storage room filled with artifacts of all kinds. A lone man was working at a bench to the right of the entrance, cataloguing items from a box on the floor beside him. He wore headphones and so did not hear them come in. To be safe, Morgaine steered the twins to the left.

"What is this place?" Meg whispered.

"This is where they store artifacts that they can't put on exhibit," Morgaine replied.

"Why don't they just get rid of it?" Hart asked.

"Some of it is extremely valuable," Morgaine said. "Some of it might be used again, or sold or given to other museums at some point."

They made their way to a climate-controlled vault in the back corner of the room. In it were stacks of books and historical documents. This was Harpur's favourite part of the museum; the hidden truths of a world that seemed to like to keep them that way. During his time living on Earth, he had spent many pleasurable hours down there, poking into the minds and lives of long-dead souls who wrote about the world as they saw it. It never ceased to amaze him how a simple letter to a friend or colleague could change history.

Meg had no interest in any of it, so she was posted by the door to watch for anyone coming into the vault. But Hart immediately began to rifle through the binders and folders filled with letters, contracts, treaties, proclamations, and genealogies, not understanding much of what he read, but fascinated all the same. He soon turned his attention to the volumes lining a shelf in the corner of the vault. With his head tilted to one side, he scanned the titles, but didn't find anything of any great interest. Until his eyes settled on a leather-bound tome without a title on the spine. He drew it out and flipped it open.

"Look at this!" he exclaimed.

Morgaine lifted her eyes from the scandalous diary of a politician's wife. "What is it?"

"I'm not sure," Hart said, "but it doesn't seem to belong here."

Morgaine put the diary down and accepted the book from Hart. "You're right! This doesn't belong here."

"Someone's coming," Meg whispered.

Morgaine thrust the book back into Hart's hands and zapped them all back to the lair.

The more anxious Arthur grew over the whereabouts of the twins, Morgaine, Bon and Hiro, the more time he wanted to spend in the covert. He felt like he had stepped into a different world at a different time when he was there. All his problems seemed to stay *above*, as he had come to think of everything outside of the covert. He was calm and focused, his magic flowed seamlessly and his confidence grew with every new spell he tried. The best part of it, though, was the solitude. He could think, and no one could interrupt him.

Ylemnir's journals were a constant source of inspiration. Filled with conceptual innovations, they reminded Arthur of Michaelangelo's musings. Ylemnir had spent months on a flying machine and, as Arthur read the entries, he realized how close the wizard had come to perfecting it. With a few modifications, Arthur was sure he had the solution to the hover gilly problem that Bon and Hiro had been working on for years. He had inadvertently proposed an anti-gravity propulsion system not long ago, but Ylemnir's ingenious combination of magic and technology knocked that idea right over of the castle walls.

Ylemnir had quaintly named it Dragon Wing Serum, though it wasn't a serum at all, nor a potion, nor a tincture, nor even a liquid of any kind. It was wax! A candle without a wick.

Arthur set to carving some complicated runes into a wax tube and, after assembling the components he found in a crate in a corner, inserted them into the housing between two fans carved out of rock. Immediately, he understood the first problem with the system: the fans had to be hand-cranked to get them moving. *It shouldn't be too difficult to put together a pull-rope*, Arthur thought. *Though I wonder why he didn't just use magic?*

There was nothing in the wizard's journals to explain this. The notes, triple-underlined and circled, clearly said: With the right hand, engage the left fan in a deosil direction. With the left hand, engage the right fan in a widdershins direction. Arthur had to look both deosil and widdershins up before he could attempt to *engage* the fans. Alas, time and neglect had taken their toll and the fans refused to spin.

Arthur was about to disassemble the contraption when his whisperglyph started vibrating on the table next to his chair. He glanced over and read the message:

GLYNNIS IS CIRCLING

Damn! What now?

Athur, heeding the warning in Ylemnir's journal, made sure that the wax tube with the runes was properly contained in a box so the magic it was imbued with didn't activate and perform some Fae-like mischief. Then he zapped himself above and joined Sok in the council chambers.

"Do you think this means that Harpur or the twins have returned?" Arthur asked, making Sok jump.

The elf had been staring at his whisperglyph, waiting for a reply. "Orhowyn's horned head, Arthur, you just took ten years off my life."

"You're an elf," Arthur said, taking a seat, "you can spare a few."

"Very funny. But I suppose a human would see things that way."

"Apparently, Ylemnir lived to be almost two hundred years old," Arthur said. "As his direct descendent, my lifespan could actually rival yours."

"Are you saying that I'm stuck with you?" Sok reached for a tart from a tray on the table.

"For the time being," Arthur said, helping himself to a tart as well. "But shouldn't we be going to see what Glynnis wants?"

Sok's face screwed up with guilt. "I lied. Glynnis isn't circling."

Arthur took a bite of his tart, buying time to quell his annoyance. Sok was struggling with something big, and he knew he had to be patient with him.

"What's bothering you?" Arthur finally asked.

Sok swallowed. "I don't want to be your Hand—whatever that means. I see no point in doing your job for you just because you no longer feel like doing it."

"You've been doing it all along anyway, Sok!"

"Be that as it may, I don't think this is the right way to do things."

Arthur picked up another tart. "So, what you're really saying is that you don't mind doing my job, you just don't want to do it in an official capacity."

"What I'm saying, Arthur, is that I don't want to do it alone."

"I see." Arthur nodded. He bit into the tart and chewed thoughtfully. "What do you suggest?"

"I suggest you stop spending all your time in the covert and help me get through…" Sok threw his hands open wide. "…this!"

"What is *this*, exactly?"

"Eowyn being the new captain. Davynn leaving. Anayah not responding to my summonses. Berryl's new role in things. Harpur, Bon, Hiro and the twins being off Orhowyn knows where, doing Orhowyn knows what! This! All this!" Sok plonked his own tart down on the table and crossed his arms in frustration.

441

"And what do you suppose I can do about it?" Arthur asked. "Eowyn is doing a great job. Davynn's leaving is his choice—I can't stop him. I don't know why you even want to summon Anayah's ghost. Just keep a couple of guards watching Berryl for a while, until we know he's over his kleptomania. As for Harpur, Bon, Hiro and the twins, I've been trying to find them. They are either heavily warded, or…"

Arthur stopped. All the colour drained from his face.

"Or what?" Sok demanded.

Arthur stood up. "That bastard!"

"What? What do you think Harpur has done?" Sok was alarmed.

"Want to take a little trip with me?"

"Where?"

"Whyte Avenue!"

Morgaine and the twins arrived in the lair to find it in a state of chaos. The dining table was overturned and partially burned. The sofas were ripped to shreds. The chandelier that had hung over the conversation pit had been torn down and smashed to pieces. The neat nest of sand was now strewn throughout the cave. And the hover gilly lay crushed at the base of the back wall. The hatchling was screeching and flailing about on top of the kitchen counter, spewing weak, but furious flames in the direction of the pantry door. Bon and Hiro were nowhere to be seen.

Quickly assessing the situation, Morgaine shushed the twins so they wouldn't draw the hatchling's attention. Then she conjured a large cage and zapped the intensely irritated young dragon into it. Momentarily dazed by his sudden relocation, the hatchling squawked pitifully at the dragon-wizardess, whom he had imprinted on when he first hatched. When she didn't end the extreme discomfort he was experiencing, he resumed screeching and threw himself at the cage bars.

In order to use her calming magic to sedate the hatchling, Morgaine had to touch him. She became invisible and zapped herself into the cage. Her disappearance was enough to distract the hatchling. He stopped thrashing his wings and tail long enough for Morgaine to move to his side and put her hands on his neck.

His eyes closed and his head drooped. Soon, he was sleeping, albeit fitfully, and the dragon-wizardess breathed a sigh of relief.

"What got into him?" Meg asked when Morgaine reappeared in the kitchen next to the pantry.

Morgaine didn't answer right away. She went to the pantry and pulled the door open to find Bon and Hiro huddling against the back wall. Their robes were singed and their faces were streaked with soot, but otherwise they seemed to be okay.

"I'm sure glad to see you!" Hiro giggled as he emerged from the pantry, but his smile vanished when he saw the ruins of his hover gilly on the other side of the lair. The Krist walked over to it and fell to his knees in despair.

"Can you fix it?" Bon asked as he, too, came out of his hiding place.

"The hover gilly is the least of my concerns at the moment," Morgaine said. "What happened here?"

Stepping over broken bits of furniture, they moved out of the kitchen and were joined by Meg and Hart in front of the cage.

"I believe the scaleshift started sooner than expected." Bon pointed to the hatchling's haunches. "You can see where some of the juvenile scales have started to sluff off."

"I barely remember going through it myself," Morgaine said, "but I don't recall it being so bad that I felt the need to destroy things."

"I can only assume," Bon said, "but the accelerated growth and development must also be intensifying the symptoms. I should have anticipated this and been better prepared. I am sorry."

"No need to apologize," Morgaine said. "This is new to all of us. How long do you expect this to last?"

"My calculations are, it seems, off by quite a bit. I had thought the scaleshift would begin in three or four days and last approximately twenty-four hours. Now, I cannot be sure how long it will last. It could be over quickly, or it could take longer. As you said, this is new to all of us; there is no basis for comparison."

"Why didn't you sedate him?" Hart asked.

"We tried," Bon said, "but he wouldn't eat the medicated meat. We slipped into the pantry while he was tearing down the chandelier. Thankfully, he didn't see us going in. He must have smelled us, though."

"You're lucky he doesn't know how to open doors!" Meg said.

"That we are!" Bon replied.

Indeed, several chunks of meat were littered throughout the lair among the wreckage. Morgaine announced that she was going to tidy up, and set to magically repairing the damage while Bon and the twins gathered up the hatchling's food. When order had been restored again, Morgaine approached Hiro and knelt down beside him.

"I am not familiar with the magic that powers your hover gilly," she said gently. "Do you want me to try to repair it anyway?"

Before Hiro could explain that the hover gilly was beyond repair, Arthur and Sok entered through the enchanted doorway to the lair.

"I told you we'd find them here," Arthur said.

"It's just not the same without Harpur's hoard taking up half the space," Sok observed.

The others all stared at the newcomers, some with open mouths. Then Meg ran to her father and threw her arms around him.

"How did you get here?" the princess cried.

"The same way you did, I suspect," Sok said, earning an eye roll from Arthur.

Extracting himself from his daughter's death grip, Arthur smiled down at Meg. "I'm so glad you're safe." He chucked her under the chin.

"What are you doing here?" Morgaine asked. She stood up and approached Sok and Arthur.

"Mostly, we came to ask you the same thing," Arthur said. "Whatever possessed you to bring the twins here without telling me?"

Morgaine crossed her arms defensively. "I couldn't very well leave them alone in Andonsheer," she said, "and this was the safest place I could think of to bring the eggs to hatch."

"Is that the clone?" Sok asked, spotting the caged hatchling. "Why is he in a cage?"

"Trust me," Hart said, "a cage is the best place for him."

"Did he do that?" Arthur asked, pointing to the crumpled hover gilly.

Everyone looked at the twisted heap.

"That and more," Meg said. "You should have seen this place a while ago. The poor thing was driven mad by scaleshift."

"Scale what?" Arthur asked.

"Nothing you need to concern yourself with," Morgaine said.

"So, are you still Harpur-Karrys-Morgaine, or…?" Sok asked.

"We have not attempted the transfer of Harpur's spirit into the clone as of yet," Bon said. "We are waiting for the scaleshift to be complete."

"Again, what is that?" Arthur asked.

Bon explained the process of scaleshift to Arthur and Sok. "We are hoping it passes quickly so we can get on with the transfer."

"Isn't he kind of young?" Sok asked.

"He'll grow into me… uh, Harpur," Morgaine said.

"Now, I'm even more glad we came," Sok said. "I can't wait to see this!"

Morgaine did not look pleased. Suddenly, the lair felt very crowded. But while the dragon-wizardess outwardly conveyed annoyance, inwardly, Harpur was happy to see them. "Well, if you're going to stay, you're going to have to conjure your own beds."

Through the exchanges of greetings, Hart studied his father. There was something different about Arthur, but he couldn't figure out exactly what it was. Still holding the book that Morgaine stole from the museum, the prince approached the king and extended his hand to him.

Arthur looked at Hart's outstretched hand and felt a little pang of sadness and a good measure of pride. Hart was growing into a fine young man. He shook his son's hand, and then pulled him in for a hug.

"What are you reading?" Arthur asked.

"I'm not sure," Hart admitted, flipping the book open and thumbing through the pages. "I found it at the museum."

Arthur could see that the book was old. Hart didn't buy it in the gift shop. "What do you mean you found it at the museum?"

"Morgaine, Meg and I were looking through an archive in the basement, and when I saw this book…" Hart looked up at his father and saw the question on his face. "I didn't steal it! Morgaine did!"

Arthur looked at the dragon-wizardess. "You stole a book from the Royal Alberta Museum?"

In the kerfuffle with the hatchling and the arrival of additional guests, Morgaine had forgotten all about the book. She joined Hart and Arthur and lifted the book out of the prince's hands.

"This book doesn't belong in the RAM," she said. "This book doesn't even belong on Earth."

Like Hart had just done, Morgaine carefully flipped through the pages, admiring the illuminated illustrations and the delicate calligraphy. As the others all gathered around to see the alien tome, she turned the pages slowly so they could all see the gilded sigils that dominated the top of each leaf.

"This is the codex of the Ice Dragons," Morgaine said.

"The Ice Dragons are a myth!" Sok exclaimed.

"You know them as The Order of the Winter Dragons," Morgaine replied, "but I assure you they are not a myth."

"You mean that little magic club that Harpur belonged to is a front for gods?" Sok was incredulous.

"It was hardly a little magic club," Morgaine admonished. "And, yes, the OWD is how the Ice Dragons survived."

Sok turned this over in his head. The Ice Dragons were a race of demi-gods that legend said roamed Thraeh long before the fire dragons evolved. When the humans, elves and dwarves evolved and human technology developed, the Ice Dragons died out. Or so the legend went.

"But…" Sok was about to argue the point when Morgaine gasped.

"What's the matter?" Meg asked, squeezing in closer to try to see what had alarmed the dragon-wizardess.

"It can't be!" Morgaine whispered.

"What can't be?" Arthur asked.

Morgaine lowered the book and looked at the twins. "I think I... I think Harpur turned you into Ice Dragons."

"What?"

"What?"

"What?"

"How?"

Morgaine carelessly flipped more pages, searching for confirmation of her unwanted theory. She finally stopped at a page with a sigil labelled: Protection. Then she flipped back to the page with the sigil that caused her alarm. It was labelled: Power of Averborn. The two looked almost identical.

Sok caught the book as it slipped from Morgaine's hands, deftly managing to keep the places of the two sigils. He read the description of the Protection sigil first.

"To protect an item of value, inscribe Protection upon the surface using chalk or charcoal for temporary effects. Blood delivers a permanent influence. Oil delays the reaction. Use sour whine to reverse the sigil. Incantations specify the scope of the effects."

Sok looked up from the book. Morgaine was staring into the distance, clearly distraught. He turned back to the Power of Averborn and continued to read.

"It is forbidden to inscribe the Power of Averborn upon any living thing." Sok turned the page to see if there was more information. "That's all it says."

Bon laid a hand on Morgaine's arm. "You drew the Power of Averborn sigil on the twins when they were infants."

Morgaine nodded. "We must return to Thraeh. We have to get Meg and Hart to Averborn. They have to walk the labyrinth."

"Why?"

"What will happen to us if we don't walk the labyrinth?"

"Where is Averborn?"

"Are the twins in danger?"

Morgaine turned to face Harpur's friends. "I made a grave mistake."

"How grave?" Arthur asked. "What is going to happen to Meg and Hart?"

Looking at Arthur, the dragon-wizardess swallowed. "Everything is going to be okay. If the twins go straight to Averborn and walk the labyrinth and make an offering at the pool in the centre, they will be just fine."

"Define just fine," Arthur demanded.

"If they complete the ritual, they will have both the power of the Ice Dragons and the magic of the fire dragons. They will be…"

"They will be what?" Arthur shouted. "What have you done to them?"

Morgaine couldn't seem to say the word.

Sok closed the book and took a deep breath. "I think what Harpur is trying to say is the twins will be gods."

Meg and Hart exchanged looks of awe.

"Good!" Hiro said with a giggle. "Only a god can repair the hover gilly!"

Elder Dhonna sat on her balcony, sipping tea. She had just returned from Colwygshire where she had gone to check in with Arthur and Sok to see if there had been any word yet from Harpur. The past days, since Morgaine's sudden appearance along with Harpur's unexpected return from the dead, had been tumultuous and emotionally draining. Laying Anayah to rest, on top of everything else that was going on, was more than the guild master could bear. Her grief was deep and consuming. The closure she hoped the funeral rite would bring didn't quite meet expectations. Losing Harpur had been hard; losing Anayah was somehow worse.

Her walk to the castle earlier in the day turned out to be an exercise in futility. No one knew where Sok or Arthur had gotten to. Eowyn suggested that they might be in Arthur's covert, but there was no way to reach them. She was welcome to hang out with him in the council chamber, and as much as she wanted to get to know the young man better, she opted, instead, to visit Davynn and the children while she waited. The knight, however, had taken Alexa, Brodie and Caleb to Braydon Wood for the afternoon. Edler Dhonna felt an ache of disappointment that he hadn't thought to include her.

Why would he, you old fool? He owes you nothing, she chided herself.

Below her, other elves came and went on their daily errands. Many waved a hand in greeting; a few stopped to offer compliments on the medicinal gardens and commend her on how well the guild was doing under her supervision. But she felt an emptiness beneath the accolades, like the words were a façade covering hollow sentiments. She smiled and thanked them anyway, disguising her own hollowness.

She finished her tea and forced herself to go to the guild house before ennui could swallow her whole. Intending to putter in the gardens, even if all she did was pull weeds, Elder Dhonna couldn't allow herself to sit and fret about things. Sinking her feet into the soil and feeling the warmth of the earth on her hands was about the best medicine she could think of for what was ailing her.

Taking the walkways through the canopy, Elder Dhonna strolled along at a contemplative gait until she reached the junction where the boardwalk branched off and led to the guild house. There was an open expanse of about 40 feet between her and her final destination from which she could look down on the gardens. Below her, guild members were busy tending to plants that would become powders and tinctures and unguents they would use to augment their own magical healing powers. A small group of elves were preparing the kilns to dry a crop of ironvale, a thick ground cover that grew best in rocky terrain and was used to bolster the immune system. Another group was stretching a length of netting between two poles to support the jamba berry vines. While most jamba berries were cultivated by the vintner guild, the healing guild grew them for medicinal purposes. Jamba berries were good for the skin and made a delightfully fragrant shampoo.

Satisfied that all seemed well, Elder Dhonna started to cross the suspension bridge from the main walkway to the guild house. She was half way across when she happened to look up. High above, she saw two dragons flying north. Seeing two dragons flying together like that was rare, though it was not unheard of. They were too high up to make out any details; she couldn't even tell what colour they were. She watched them until they disappeared in the distance, wondering where they were going and what they might be up to. Once they were out of sight, though, she shrugged her curiosity off and continued on to indulge in a couple of hours of gardening therapy.

Chapter Twenty-two

The atmosphere in the lair beneath Whyte Avenue was thick with fear and resentment, liberally mixed with an annoying sense of excitement. Meg and Hart had just learned that Harpur's inadvertent use of a forbidden sigil had not just turned them into dragons; they were, essentially, gods. With all the power and responsibility that came with it. At least they would be if they successfully completed the rite at Averborn. But while the twins were thrilled—more or less—Arthur was mortified.

After the initial shock of realization finally wore off, Morgaine tried to explain Harpur's mistake in such a way that it didn't sound in any way life-threatening to the twins. Which it was... possibly.

The problem was that the twins had inherited fire dragon blood from Arthur, who had received it from Harpur, who had used it to resurrect Arthur after he had died in a car accident on the corner of Whyte Avenue and 104 Street nearly 26 years earlier. The Power of Averborn sigil, when inscribed in blood, imbued the recipient with all the power of the original Ice Dragons, which is why it was forbidden. The blood of a fire dragon, invoking the power of the Ice Dragons resulted in a hybrid of opposing energies that would eventually vie for dominance. In the end, either the ice would quench the fire and the twins would freeze to death, or the fire would overpower the ice and Meg and Hart would literally melt.

"Unless they walk the labyrinth at Averborn?" Arthur asked for clarification.

"And make an offering at the pool," Sok added.

"What sort of offering do we have to make?" Meg asked.

"Well, that's the tricky part," Morgaine said. "The offering has to be the heart of a fire dragon that you sacrifice."

Meg winced in disgust.

"We have to kill a dragon and rip out its heart?" Hart was as horrified as his sister.

"You both have to kill a dragon and cut out their hearts." Morgaine had to force herself not to look away.

"Any volunteers?" Arthur sneered at the dragon-wizardess.

"I will gladly let you take my heart," Morgaine said.

"After my spirit has been transferred into the hatchling," Morgaine amended on Harpur's behalf.

"I'm not going to kill a baby dragon!" Hart declared.

"Why do you get to kill the hatchling? I think I should get to kill it!" Meg sounded hysterical.

"Neither of us are going to kill *Harpur!*" Hart said, stressing the dragon's name to remind Meg who she was actually talking about. "There has to be another way."

"There isn't," Morgaine said. "And killing the hatchling only solves half the problem. You will need to kill another dragon."

"I'm not killing Karrys, either," Hart said. Next to him, Meg was sizing up Morgaine, wondering if she could take her. Hart looked at his sister and was appalled. "And neither are you."

"Karrys is about to get her life back," Morgaine said. "She is not part of this."

"So, where do we get another dragon?" Arthur asked. If no one else was prepared to sacrifice Harpur to save his kids, he was.

"No one is going to kill Harpur or Karrys," Bon spoke up. "There is another way."

Throughout the debate, Bon had been studying the codex. Morgaine had not been wrong about the need for the twins to make an offering of a dragon heart, but according to the codex, there was an option.

"Esrioas Grithhall," the android said to six blank faces, "and the Blade of Isenwyld."

Morgaine was the first to recover. "Esrioas Grithhall can't still be alive! She was ancient when I was a hatchling."

"Who is Esrioas Grithhall?" Sok asked.

"False hope, I should imagine," Morgaine said, grimacing.

"According to the codex," Bon continued. "Esrioas Grithhall is the Guardian of Averborn. She is the one who is responsible for passing on the knowledge of the Ice Dragons to the dragons of Thraeh who belong to the Order of the Winter Dragons. It says here, 'Should Esrioas Grithhall's life end before the Ice Dragons return, her name shall fade from the page's memory and the sigils shall vanish with her.' I assume that means that as long as she is still alive, her name will remain visible in the codex."

"Where do we find her?" Hart leaned closer to Bon so he could read the codex.

"If she is still alive," Morgaine said, "she is in the Temple of Averborn. You can't miss it; it was built on the north pole of Thraeh."

"Have you ever met her?" Meg asked.

"Harpur met her once," Morgaine said, "when he was initiated into the Order of the Winter Dragons."

Sok listened to the exchange, but his attention was on the codex in Bon's hands. "How did the codex get here?" he mused aloud.

"That is an excellent question," Morgaine said. "It is supposed to be in the Temple of Averborn."

"Who cares how the stupid book got here," Arthur said. "How do we save my kids?"

Morgaine looked from the anxious father to the calm android. "Bon? What does the book say?"

Bon paraphrased the codex. "It merely says that Esrioas Grithhall is the appointed Guardian of Averborn until such time as the Ice Dragons return."

"How does that help Meg and Hart?" Arthur was still stuck on his children turning into blocks of ice or melting into puddles of goo.

"I cannot say for sure that it does," Bon admitted, "but rather than have them murder two of their kind, I should think that it would be worth a trip to the temple to talk to Esrioas. She might be in a better position to guide the twins."

That made sense. Though Harpur was convinced that Esrioas couldn't possibly still be a live, Bon had a point. Until his spirit was transferred into the hatchling, however, neither he, nor Karrys was in a position to get them to the temple to find out. Sending them there on their own seemed to be the only option, but... *What if Esrioas is dead? What will they do then?* All he could do was to have faith in the twins.

Morgaine proposed sending Meg and Hart back to Thraeh and having them make their way to the temple, a plan that Arthur was outwardly opposed to.

"We can't send them off to the north pole on their own! What if this Esrioas is dead? What if they are too late? What if they freeze? Or melt? What if they have to kill innocent dragons, and they're still too late?"

"You know, Arthur, this would all go a lot smoother if you would just go off into a corner and have a meltdown while the rest of us work out a plan," Morgaine said.

Hart then realized what it was about his father that was different; Arthur was calm. He exuded an air of confidence and even courageousness.

Sok agreed with the dragon-wizardess. "You know you're going to come to the same conclusion we already have anyway."

Arthur glowered at Sok and Morgaine. Then he turned to the twins. "What do you two want to do?"

Somewhat taken aback by their father's level-headedness in the situation, Meg and Hart were unsure how to reply. Of course, they both wanted to go to Averborn and look for the guardian. Whether or not saying that would tip the balance and send Arthur spiraling into a full-blown tizzy, was a toss-up. Either way, they knew they were going back to Thraeh. Stepping closer to each other in a gesture of solidarity, the twin exchanged glances and nodded in agreement.

"We want to go look for Esrioas," they said in unison.

"Very well," Arthur said, "that's settled. How do we get them there?"

He didn't see Sok and Morgaine's eye-rolls or head-shakes.

It was quickly decided that Morgaine would accompany Meg and Hart through the Boundary and unlock the Boundary house door for them. Once the twins were on their way north, she would return to the Whyte Avenue lair to wait for the hatchling's scaleshift to end, so they could move forward with the transfer of Harpur's spirit. Sok and Arthur, much to Morgaine's chagrin, elected to stay and see how things went with that. When asked who was in charge back in Colwygshire, Sok lied and assured Morgaine that Eowyn had everything under control.

"If he needs help," the elf concluded, "I'm sure Davynn will advise him."

Arthur's sudden interest in the ceiling told the dragon-wizardess otherwise, but she decided to let it go. Hopefully, their business in the lair would be done soon and they could all return to their own world before anything else went wrong.

Before Morgaine and the twins left, the dragon-wizardess gave the hatchling an extra dose of magical sedative. She noted that the scaleshift had progressed considerably in the short time since her return from the museum, a promising development that gave her hope.

When the trio arrived in the Boundary house in Epoh, Morgaine gave the twins their final instructions. "The moment you get out of here, transform and fly as high as you can as fast as you can. Head north over the mountains. You will see the labyrinth right away. Fly straight over it and keep going until you see the temple. It's made of ice; you can't miss it. If Esrioas is still alive, she will come out to greet you. Do not enter the temple unless she invites you inside. If she isn't there or if she can't help you, do not go back to Epoh!"

"Where should we go?" Meg asked.

"Stay there," Morgaine said. "When we're done here, I'll come find you."

"And if she can help us?" Hart asked.

Morgaine shrugged. "Then I'm sure you will be able to find us." Morgaine unlocked the Boundary house door and let the twins slip out. "Good luck!" she said, then locked the door and Bounded back to Whyte Avenue.

Karrys: Are you sure it was a good idea to send those two off on their own to Averborn?

Harpur: Not even a little bit!

"Look!" Meg said as she and Hart flew over Braydon Wood. "Elder Dhonna is on the walkway by the guild house.

Hart looked down. Even from such a great height, he could make out the guild master's shock of bright-red hair. "I think she sees us."

The twins waved at the elf, though she could not see them doing so, and flew on toward whatever fate had in store for them.

Eowyn knocked on Davynn's door. When the knight opened it, the young captain barged inside. "Sok and Arthur are still missing!"

"Come on in, Eowyn," Davynn said sarcastically.

"This is serious!" Eowyn said. "What if they have been kidnapped?"

Davynn stroked his chin. "I hardly think that is likely. They probably went down to Arthur's… whatever he calls it… and lost track of time."

"No, I don't think so," Eowyn insisted. "Sok wouldn't miss supper without a good reason."

It was uncharacteristic of the elf to vanish without a word. Sok was nothing if not a dutiful upholder of protocol. If he knew he and Arthur were going to miss supper in the great hall, he would have notified Finch.

"Has supper been served yet?" Davynn asked.

"Not yet," Eowyn said.

"And you're sure they aren't in Arthur's chambers?"

"I just came from there," Eowyn said. "The king's rooms are empty."

Davynn was only mildly worried. Everyone was out of sorts since their return from Mysturna. They would show up eventually. In the meantime…

"Joy! Get the children ready. We are going to dine in the great hall tonight!"

Eowyn was shocked. "Can you do that?"

"Why not?" Davynn said. "There's no point in letting Finch's feast go to waste."

Eowyn could hardly disagree. "May I join you?"

"The more, the merrier!"

Alexa, Brodie and Caleb had never had supper in the great hall. They endured Joy's fussing over their attire and their hair. Caleb even stood still while the nanny washed his face. When they were ready, she presented them to their father and told them to enjoy the evening.

"You're coming too," Davynn said.

"But I'm not dressed!" Joy protested.

"You look fine!" Davynn assured her. "But if you like, you can wear something from Anayah's closet. We have time."

"Oh, I'm sure I couldn't do that!" Joy was flabbergasted.

"And I'm sure that you can." Davynn smiled at the flustered nanny. "How about the blue dress you admire so much?"

"Are you sure, sir?" Joy's reluctance was turning into excitement.

"Go!" Davynn said. "We aren't going without you."

Joy ran into the bedroom and changed. A few minutes later she returned wearing a midnight-blue gown with a scoop neck and sheer sleeves. She had brushed and braided her silky blonde hair and borrowed a pair of satin slippers that matched the gown. Barely able to contain her glee, she spun around in a circle to show off how pretty she felt.

"What do you think?" she asked. "Am I fit for supper in the great hall?"

"You just need one more thing," Davynn said as he disappeared into the bedroom.

Joy watched him go, wondering what he could possibly be referring to. He returned with a single strand of pearls, which he fastened around her neck.

With tears of delight in her eyes, Joy thanked Davynn.

"You look beautiful," Eowyn said, opening the door and offering Joy his arm.

Together, they entered the great hall and, at Davynn's insistence, took seats at the head table. The guests all stopped and stared at the audacity of the knight to presume that he could bring his children, much less his nanny, to supper. And to sit at the head table?! It was scandalous!

But Davynn ignored the whispers and the pointed fingers and, other than having to remove Caleb from Arthur's chair when they first arrived, the evening went surprisingly well. Joy sat between the boys on the left, and Alexa sat between her father and Eowyn on the right. Periodically, the nanny and the captain of the guard leaned forward and tried to catch each other's eye, exchanging shy smiles when they did. Between the first and second courses, Davynn changed places with Joy so that neither of them would end up with sore necks from stretching them so far. Another ripple of disapproval wafted through the hall.

To the children's delight, Davynn allowed them to stay for some of the entertainment after the meal. To Olly's consternation, he had to make some last-minute changes to the program; several of the songs he'd chosen were not appropriate for young ears. But the Versifier to the King had a large enough repertoire to provide child-friendly entertainment that wouldn't also bore the other guests.

He began with a little ditty that he often sang for his own children. "Welcome, young ones, to the great hall. It is an honour to sing for you tonight." Olly strummed his lyre. "This first song is called, The Goat Who Would be King!"

Caleb squealed with delight. It was his favourite song of late. The little boy stood on his chair and joined Olly as he sang:

There once was a goat with a crown on his head,
He snuck in the hall and he leapt on a bed.
He pranced through the pantry and sampled the pies,
With a wink in his eye and a bleat of surprise!

(Clap, clap!)

"Make way!" cried the goat, "I'm the lord of this land!"
He waved his hoof high with a pie in his hand.
He butted the butler and danced in the rain,
And all of the children cried, "Do it again!"

He summoned the chickens, he knighted a sheep,
He gave out new titles before falling asleep.
The maids were in stitches, the knights were aghast
For no one had seen such a goat with such class.

(Clap, clap!)

"Make way!" cried the goat, "I'm the lord of this land!"
He waved his hoof high with a pie in his hand.
He butted the butler and danced in the rain,
And all of the children cried, "Do it again!"

So, if ever you dine and your pie goes a-miss...
Look out for the goat with ambitions of bliss!

The guests, having abandoned their earlier disfavour over the children's presence, laughed as Caleb all but stole the show. His antics on the chair, clapping and dancing, reminded everyone that they didn't have to take life so seriously; sometimes it was okay to set conventions aside and just let loose.

"Looks like you have a future bard on your hands," Eowyn said when the song ended.

"As long as he's happy and healthy, I don't care what he becomes," Davynn replied.

As the evening wore on, the children eventually grew tired. The excitement of eating at the head table in the great hall and all the singing and dancing that followed wore them out. Oddly, Brodie was the first to nod off. At some point, he had worked his way onto Arthur's ornate chair where he curled up and fell asleep. Davynn took that as his cue to gather Alexa and Caleb and take them back to their suite.

With the little ones finally tucked in, Joy announced that she was going to change back into her own dress.

"You are welcome to keep the dress," Davynn said. "And the pearls."

Joy released the clasp on the necklace. "This belongs to Alexa now. I think Anayah would want her to have it."

Davynn nodded and accepted the string of pearls. "Then we will let her decide. But, please keep the dress. You look stunning in it."

Joy blushed. "Thank you, Sir Davynn."

Eowyn cleared his throat. "May I escort you to your room?"

The pretty young nanny accepted the handsome captain's offer, and they left Davynn's rooms smiling coyly at each other.

Davynn sighed and closed the door behind them. "Orhowyn's stolen hoard! Looks like I'm going to have to find a new nanny to take to Branwyke!"

The lair was peacefully calm when Morgaine returned from sending Meg and Hart to the Temple of Averborn. The hatchling was still unconscious. Bon was setting up a table with vials and beakers and other paraphernalia. And Arthur was instructing Hiro and Sok on how to tell time on an analogue clock.

"The day is divided into twenty-four hours. Each hour has sixty minutes, and each minute has sixty seconds. Starting at midnight, the hours are numbered one to twelve, which brings us to noon when the hours are again numbered one to twelve. Between midnight and noon, the hours are referred at the a.m., or anti-meridian. Between noon and midnight, the hours are referred to as the p.m., or post-meridian. Before noon is the morning, and after noon is the afternoon and evening. Got all that?"

"Why is it called midnight if it is the beginning of the morning?" Sok asked.

"Because the twenty-four hours that make up a whole day are also divided into daytime and nighttime. The whole day begins approximately in the middle of the night, so... midnight."

"Then why isn't noon called midday?"

"It is," Arthur said. "Noon is just another name for midday."

Morgaine made her way over to where Bon was setting up his equipment. "I'm surprised Arthur hasn't tried to introduce a calendar and a time-keeping system in Epoh."

"He did," Bon said, "but he could not do the math."

"Could you do the math?"

"I could," Bon said, laying a nasty-looking scalpel on the table, "and I did."

"So, why isn't Epoh riddled with clocks and calendars?"

"Mostly because I believe Arthur would not adjust well to a six-day week and a fourteen-month year." Bon looked up and smiled conspiratorially at Morgaine.

Morgaine laughed. "And a nineteen-hour day would likely kill him!"

"So, you can do the math too! I am impressed."

"Nah," Morgaine said, "Ylemnir was a bit of an astronomer and he figured it out."

"Arthur's ancestor?" Bon asked. "Why then are there no calendars and clocks in Epoh now?"

"Harpur discouraged it," Morgaine said.

"May I ask why?"

"Because it would lead straight back to technology," Morgaine said, "and if that were to happen, magic would be lost again. Harpur sees no point in going backwards."

Bon nodded. He added a vial of glowing green liquid to the array of vials on the table. "The hatchling is almost through the scaleshift. We can begin the transfer in another few hours."

Morgaine looked at the clone. His scales had darkened to a deep purple and taken on the metallic sheen of an adult dragon's armor. His wings, however, had a reddish hue to them, and there were streaks of crimson visible in the scales on his haunches. The effect was not unattractive, but Harpur couldn't help feeling disappointed that his new body would not be solid amethyst in colour.

As if he'd read Harpur's mind, Bon interrupted the dragon-wizardess' thoughts. "I could provide you with a permanent dye to cover the red."

Morgaine laughed. "Thank you, Bon, but can you see Harpur dying his wings and scales?"

"I can," said the android. "From what I recall, you were rather fastidious about your appearance."

Morgaine grew pensive. "I wonder what my human guise will look like."

"I expect there will be subtle differences," Bon replied. "Hair colour, skin colour, eye colour will not be exactly as it was before. Your physique is likely to be different. You may be taller, or shorter, stalkier, or leaner... We won't know for sure until..."

"No, Sok! *Sunday* is the first day of the week!

"Then how is it the last day of the *week-end?* That makes no sense!"

"He has a point," Morgaine said. "Wait until Arthur tries to explain long weekends to him!"

"Indeed," Bon said. "And leap years!"

Morgaine laughed.

"Will you discourage Arthur from trying to implement timekeeping in Epoh as you did with Ylemnir?" Bon asked.

"It's not my call," Morgaine said with no trace of mirth. "I'll be lucky to live more than a few days once we return to Thraeh."

"You are worried about what the Dragon Council will decide?"

"I'm more worried about how to convince them that I actually am Harpur," Morgaine said. "No one is going to believe a juvenile who claims to be Xzynthyrius Dreamfinder. Especially when he's a different colour."

"So, do not even try," Bon said. "Take a different name and reestablish yourself as you see fit."

"I can't do that. I promised Khol that I would turn myself in."

"What would happen if the cloning procedure did not work and you were unable to turn yourself in?"

"I was to arrange for someone to inform Khol if that were to happen."

"Then inform him! Become a new dragon!"

"The whole point of this is to restore Harpur's honour," Morgaine said slipping back into the third person.

"I thought the whole point was to give Karrys her life back."

The timekeeping lessons fell apart when Sok decided that a thirteenth month made more sense than twelve. "There are thirteen moon cycles!" he insisted.

"But there are only four seasons," Arthur countered. "And you can't divide thirteen by four evenly."

"But the seasons start on random days in the middle of the months!"

"But you can't start the year on a solstice!"

"Why not?"

"I don't know!" Arthur flipped the calendar he was using to explain how time was measured on Earth closed and conjured himself a fresh bottle of beer. "I'm going to watch TV."

Hiro pulled the calendar toward himself and opened it up. He understood the system of days, months and years perfectly. "You do realize that this calendar is tailored for Earth?" he asked the exasperated elf.

"What do you mean?"

"It wouldn't work on Thraeh. As least not in its present form. It would have to be redesigned for the length and number of days in a year on our world."

"We've managed quite well without clocks and calendars for a long time," Sok observed.

"I'm not suggesting that we implement it," Hiro said with a giggle, "just that it would be an interesting challenge to work out a system of timekeeping for Thraeh."

"Well, you have fun with that," Sok said. He rose from the table, having had his fill of regimented scheduling systems, and joined Morgaine and Bon. "What's all this stuff for?" he asked as he reached for one of the vials of liquid on the table Bon had set up.

Bon gently pushed the elf's hand away. "It is for the transfer of Harpur's spirit from Karrys' body into the hatchling. Please, do not touch anything."

"Why don't you just use the walking stick?" Sok asked. "I assume that is why Anayah told us to find it. And why you stole it from Arthur's vault."

"It isn't stealing if it belongs to you," Morgaine said.

"It belongs to Harpur!"

"In case you forgot, at the moment we are still one and the same."

"We have been discussing the walking stick," Bon interjected. "Harpur does not know how to wield it for such an operation."

"Nyssira would know," Sok said.

"How do you know about her?" Morgaine asked.

"I looked it up after Anayah's ghost told us to find the walking stick."

"There's information about Nyssira in the archives?"

"Not a lot, but there is some in Harpur's life book."

"When this is done, I'm moving that life book somewhere safe." Morgaine was annoyed.

"If we hadn't looked into the life book, Arthur wouldn't have been able to conjure the walking stick."

"And I could have just gone to the old Boundary location and got it quickly instead of having to risk drawing Glynnis' attention by going to the castle to look for it."

"We were just trying to help," Sok said. He looked past Morgaine and Bon. "The hatchling is waking up."

The young dragon lifted his head and blinked at his audience. He was groggy from the magical and allopathically derived sedation he had been subjected to, but he managed to push himself up and stretch his wings. A smoky yawn escaped his maw.

"Wow!" Sok said. "He looks… different."

Indeed, the hatchling's scales were now entirely those of an adult dragon. The deep purple sheen, highlighted with crimson streaks across his back and hind legs, gave him a majestic appeal. Like Harpur's, his eyes were violet. He settled onto his haunches and folded his wings across his back.

"The scaleshift appears to be over," Bon said.

"I thought Harpur's new body was supposed to be an exact replica of his old body," Sok said. "Harpur didn't have red streaks like that."

"The mitochondrial DNA of the…"

Morgaine placed a hand on the android's arm to get his attention and then shook her head. "Don't go there with him."

"Of course," Bon agreed. Then he clasped his hands behind his back and turned to the elf. "I did the best I could."

"It looks great!" Sok said. "But no one is going to believe that's Harpur."

"We are well aware," Morgaine said. She shifted her gaze to the table with the paraphernalia for the spirit transfer. "I still think I'd rather try to figure out how to use the walking stick."

"How hard could it be?" Sok asked. "Just draw your spirit into the walking stick and then send it into the hatchling."

"Oh, come on! Open your eyes, you zebra!"

Morgaine, Sok and Bon all turned toward the conversation pit and Hiro looked up from his calculations. Arthur was shaking a fist at the TV.

"Hockey playoffs," Morgaine huffed dismissively. "Tends to bring out the worst in some people."

"What are hockey playoffs?" Sok asked.

"If you don't understand the Gregorian calendar, you are not going to understand hockey playoffs." Morgaine patted the elf on the shoulder.

He continued to watch the television screen. He recalled seeing a similar scene the first time he had come to Harpur's Whyte Avenue lair right after he'd given Arthur the coin that started their Entanglement. But the costumes were different colours, except for the men in the black and white striped shirts; those were the same. He wondered why they didn't have sticks like the others. Then Arthur yelled again.

"You've got to be kidding me! Are you blind?"

"Can the little people in the TV thing hear Arthur?" Sok asked.

"No."

"Then who is he yelling at?"

"It's complicated," Morgaine said. "Can we get back to the problem at hand?"

Sok decided that was a good idea. The sooner they got Harpur out of Karrys/Morgaine and into the hatchling the sooner they could get Arthur back to Epoh and away from hockey playoffs, which were clearly affecting his mind.

"It's Harpur's walking stick…" Sok got back to the problem at hand. "…so, he should know how to use it."

"I do! He does!" Morgaine snapped, more annoyed at having to remember to speak in the third person.

"Then what's the problem? Suck your… Harpur's spirit out of… yourself with it, and then send it into the hatchling. Seems simple to me."

"No! No, no!" Arthur bellowed from the conversation pit. "Get a real goalie!"

"And do it quickly!" Sok added. "I'm not sure how much longer Arthur is going to last."

"Arthur is fine!" Morgaine said. "And it's not that simple. What if the walking stick draws out both our spirits?"

"Then Bon can kill you both and put Karrys' spirit back into you… her, and your… Harpur's spirit back into the hatchling."

"I believe that would require a spell," Morgaine said.

"You are a wizard… ess?" Sok pointed out.

"Dragons don't do spell work."

"Well, you have a wizard sitting right over there." Sok pointed at Arthur. "Although, I'm not sure he's fit for any sort of magic at the moment."

"Arthur!" Morgaine called out.

"What?" Arthur answered without taking his eyes off the screen.

"We need your help."

"Fifteen seconds left in the period," Arthur called back.

"Now, Arthur!"

"Fine!"

Arthur put his beer bottle down and turned to climb over the back of the sofa out of the conversation pit. As he did, a loud buzzer sounded and the crowd went wild. Arthur spun back around to face the TV.

"What happened? Did they score? Who scored?"

"Edmonton," Morgaine said. "Now get over here."

"You made me miss it," Arthur grumbled. "What do you want?"

"I think Morgaine wants you to use Harpur's walking stick to draw his spirit out of Morgaine and put it into the hatchling." Sok peered at the TV screen. There was a lot of hugging and bottom patting going on.

"Very funny," Arthur said. "The walking stick is cursed. I'm not touching it."

"I will wield the walking stick," Morgaine assured the hockey-deprived king. "I just need you to come up with a spell that will ensure that I only draw Harpur's spirit out of me and leave Karrys' spirit where it belongs."

"Oh, sure, that's easy." Arthur snapped his fingers and handed Morgaine a piece of paper with an incantation scribbled on it. "Here you go."

"Hey!" Hiro shouted from the table where he'd been calculating the precise length of days for Thraeh. "That has my calculations on it!"

"Sorry, Hiro," Arthur said, snatching the paper from the dragon-wizardess and taking it back to the Krist. "Slight miscalculation. No pun intended."

He jotted down the spell on a fresh piece of paper and took it to Morgaine.

"And it's sep-ar-at-i-GO, not sep-ar-At-i-go. That's very important. You can say spirizontus any way you want to."

Arthur conjured another bottle of beer and returned to the conversation pit to watch the game, which had gone into overtime.

"Who is he and what did he do with the real Arthur?" Morgaine asked.

"Yeah," Sok said, shaking his head, "his skills have improved since he got back from Mysturna."

"Okay!" Morgaine said. "Let's do this!"

Chapter Twenty-three

The vast tundra that contained the labyrinth known as Averborn opened up before Meg and Hart as they passed the high mountains bordering Epoh to the north in all of its late-spring glory. The flat terrain was dotted with gold stones, between which a dusty-green groundcover blossomed with red, orange and yellow flowers. Here and there, tufts of buttery grass sprouted defiantly from the thin layer of soil. As they soared northward, the gold stones started to form a looping pathway.

The labyrinth of Averborn, was almost a mile in diameter. From the entrance to the centre pool, the path was just over 20 miles long. Meg gawked in awe at the intricate and perfectly symmetrical 11-circuit layout.

"It will take us days to walk the labyrinth," she said to Hart.

"We can easily walk that in one day," Hart said.

"Are you kidding? It's huge?"

"It's not as big as you think. The path doesn't even look wide enough for a dragon to walk without knocking the stones out of place."

"Well, let's hope that this Esrioas has a way to help us without us having to walk the labyrinth."

The vista changed little as the twins flew on. Grey rocks replaced the gold stones, and the dusty-green ground cover grew sparse. To the west, the tundra gave way to low, undulating hills covered in a mossy blanket of yellow-green fuzz. But soon, all they could see was mile after mile of dull greenish-grey rock. Nothing grew at all this far north; the landscape was bleak and unforgiving in all directions.

Meg and Hart were just beginning to think that they had missed the temple, when a ray of reflected evening sunlight flared like a beacon fire in the distance ahead of them.

"We're almost at the top of the world," Hart said.

"Race ya!" Meg surged forward, pumping her shiny black wings hard to gain the lead.

Behind her, Hart laughed. As he was in their human forms, he was the larger and stronger of the two dragons, and he had no difficulty in catching up and passing her well before they reached the temple. He was also the less impulsive of the two. His speed gave him the advantage of being able to survey what lay before them. The temple was much smaller than he had expected. Its walls were comprised of jagged spires of ice that scattered cerulean light in all directions, making the towering pillars appear unnaturally cheerful in their bleak surroundings. An arched entrance, guarded by an intricate filigreed portcullis, dominated the front of the temple, which sat on the edge of a wide moat, filled with black water. No bridge led to the entryway. Hart wondered if they would have to swim to the temple.

Slowing down to give himself more time to assess the situation, Hart banked to his left to circle around. The temple had an abandoned air to it. In spite of Bon's assertion that Esrioas must still be alive, nothing he could see, or sense, indicated that there was any life within miles of the palatial sanctuary of the Ice Dragons. Hope faded as he glided down in a lazy spiral and came to land at the edge of the moat.

"Looks like no one is home," Meg said as she landed next to him and strained to peer through the portcullis on the other side of the moat.

Morgaine had said that Esrioas would come to them if she was indeed alive. "Let's just wait here a while and see what happens."

"I don't suppose there's any game nearby that we can eat," Meg said, looking around the desolate landscape.

"I don't suppose there is." Hart's own stomach rumbled.

Neither he, nor Meg had ever fed in their dragon forms, and his human nature blanched at the thought of it. He tried to imagine burning a deer alive and then tearing it to pieces to devour. *I can wait*, he decided.

Inside the temple, an ancient, silver dragon stirred. She raised her weary head and smiled. "At last," she whispered.

With an effort, Esrioas Grithhall crawled out of her lair beneath the Temple of Averborn and climbed the winding passageway to the temple far above. There was a time when she could reach the top in a flash. But time and age, as it does with all living creatures, had slowed her down, and it was completely dark by the time she made it to the portcullis.

Across the moat, two young dragons sat side-by-side, waiting patiently in the cold of the night. She watched them through the ornamental gate, taking in their black scales, shimmering with purple and silver flashes in the pale moonlight. She had always known there would be two, but she always assumed they would be icy-blue, the colour of the Ice Dragons. As magnificent as these ones were, they did not fit the legend as she had learned it as a hatchling prior to becoming the Guardian of Averborn. Besides their colour, there was something else strange

468

about them. Their scent was off. It had been a long time since she had been around any people, but she was certain that she smelled the odor of humans clinging to them.

How odd.

Esrioas hesitated. The lore was clear that the Ice Dragons would return, that they would come as a pair, and that they would possess the qualities necessary to unite all the races of Thraeh. It never occurred to her that a human-dragon hybrid was even possible.

If they can't prove they are Ice Dragons, I can always kill them.

She glanced at the altar of ice on the other side of the temple. On it, rested Isenwylm—*cold steel*—the blade of the Ice Dragons. It gleamed brightly as if assuring her that it was ready to do her bidding. Then she touched the portcullis with her talons and stepped back as it dissolved out of sight.

"Hale and welcome, strangers," Esrioas called across the moat. "What business brings you to the Temple of Averborn?"

Meg and Hart stood up and bowed before the ageless, silver dragon.

"We come seeking Esrioas Grithhall," Hart called back. "We wish to walk the labyrinth so we can take our places as Ice Dragons on Thraeh."

"Have you an offering?" Esrioas asked.

"We do not," Meg said. "We are hoping that Esrioas will advise us. May we come in?"

Esrioas sniffed the air again. The pervading scent of humans both intrigued and disturbed her. Combined with the fact that these young dragons knew of the ritual, but had no offering, she decided that, if nothing else, she would hear a good story that night.

"You may."

Meg and Hart did not know how they were supposed to cross the moat. Neither of them treasured the idea of stepping into the black water. They didn't even know if dragons could swim. Before they could ask Esrioas what they should do, the surface of the water in the moat started to ripple and swell, and a wide, stone bridge rose up out of its depths.

When the bridge settled, Esrioas beckoned Meg and Hart to cross it and stepped away from the door so they could enter.

"Welcome," the silver dragon repeated as the twins passed through the arch.

The temple was a single room, large enough for a dozen full-grown dragons to fit in comfortably. There were no windows, and the only fixture was a narrow altar that curved along the far wall. On the left side of the alter sat three skulls; one human, one elven, and one dwarven. On the right side, Isenwylm rested on a white mantle of fur. The tunnel leading down to Esrioas' lair opened to the left of the temple's arched entrance.

"I am Esrioas Grithhall." The silver dragon introduced herself. "And you are…?"

"My name is Hart, and this is my sister, Meg." Again, he bowed respectfully.

"A brother and sister! How delightful," Esrioas crooned in her pebbly voice. "And you wish to walk the labyrinth, but you have no offering."

The old dragon was testing Meg and Hart. They should have known that it was her heart that they needed for the offering at the centre of the labyrinth.

"We are hoping there is another way," Meg said.

"There isn't." Esrioas laid down and crossed her front legs. "If you were indeed Ice Dragons, you would know that."

"Harpur Diggins told us…" Meg began.

Esrioas' eyes widened. "Harpur Diggins? He is dead. When did he tell you… whatever he told you?"

"Harpur isn't dead," Meg blurted. "Well, he did die, sort of. He had our father transfer his spirit into another dragon—Karrys Evergreen—and… Well, technically, that means he isn't really dead."

Esrioas stared at Meg for a moment. Then she shifted her gaze to Hart. "Perhaps you have something to say that makes sense."

Hart shifted nervously. What Meg had said made perfect sense—to him. But he could see how it could sound somewhat convoluted to another dragon.

"What my sister just told you is true," he confirmed. "Harpur Diggins lost the challenge for the Kingdom of Epoh to Karrys Evergreen, but before she burned his body, our father used the Amber Chalice to transfer Harpur's spirit into Karrys' body so he could continue to rule Epoh."

Esrioas had to concede that Harpur Diggins could conceivably come up with such an absurd scheme, but she could not fathom any other dragon being willing to participate in it. "And who is your father?"

"King Arthur of Epoh," Hart said.

There was no guile in the young dragon's tone, which only contributed to Esrioas' disbelief and confusion. "Your father is the human king of the Kingdom of Epoh. How exactly does that work?"

"Technically, we're not dragons," Meg said. "You see, when we were babies, Harpur drew a sigil on our foreheads. He thought he was drawing Protection, but he accidentally drew the Power of Averborn."

"A few weeks ago," Hart jumped in, "we were visiting Mysturna so we could get one of Harpur's scales back from the Forest of Dheersha so Bon could make a clone and get Harpur's spirit out of Karrys... Bon's an android, by the way... and while we were there, we ran into Frode of Ordyr and things got a little tense in the camp and, I think, the stress caused Meg and I to turn into dragons, but we didn't know it was because of the sigil that Harpur drew on us. We didn't find that out until yesterday when we found a book of Ice Dragon sigils in the museum and brought it back to Harpur's lair on Whyte Avenue, and that's when Harpur told us to come here and walk the labyrinth, but we didn't want to kill innocent dragons for their hearts, so here we are, asking for your help so we don't melt or turn into blocks of ice."

This was not how Esrioas envisioned this day unfolding. The return of the Ice Dragons was supposed to be a dignified event. A pair of crystalline ice-blue dragons would arrive at the temple on gossamer wings and take her heart, releasing her from her vow and vigil. Instead, she was entertaining two human-fire-dragon hybrids who were spinning as ridiculous a tale as she had ever heard. And she'd heard many.

Then again, if Harpur Diggins did, indeed, have a hand in things, the ludicrousness of it, if not the details, made perfect sense. She had always admired Harpur's audacious and unconventional tendencies. He was courageous and curious and completely unapologetic. Yet he never—at least not until now—strayed from being one of the most honourable dragons every to fly the skies of Thraeh. She could not reconcile how the great purple dragon, Xzynthyrius Dreamfinder, could possibly have stolen the body of another dragon, just to keep his kingdom. And a female dragon's body?

Poor Harpur. Poor Karrys Evergreen!

Esrioas could only hope that the teal dragon wasn't conscious through Harpur's spiritual occupation of her body. For now, though, all she could do was try to stitch the ragged pieces of Hart's brief synopsis into a cohesive and coherent history of events. If she was going to sacrifice herself, she had to know that it was for the legitimate return of the Ice Dragons to Thraeh. So far, she was nowhere near being convinced.

But by the time the sun rose again, Meg and Hart had answered all of Esrioas' questions, and she had a clearer picture of how and why they were standing in her temple, expecting to be welcomed as the demi-gods they claimed to be.

"It is a pity that you did not bring the book of sigils with you," Esrioas said. "I cannot imagine how it came to be on this other world you spoke of."

"Harpur doesn't know either," Hart said. "She... Morgaine... he was quite shocked when I showed it to him in the museum."

"It must be confusing to be speaking to Harpur and looking at Karrys, or Morgaine, when you do so."

"At Harpur's insistence, we referred to him as Morgaine or Karrys, depending on which form he took at the time," Hart explained. "But you're right, it was a bit strange."

"I have no doubt." Esrioas rose and turned toward the tunnel to her lair. "I need some time to consider all that you have told me. Feel free to remain in the temple if you wish. I will return by nightfall with my decision on what to do with you both."

"Is there somewhere we can get something to eat?" Meg asked, ignoring the implications of Esrioas' last words.

"There is a heard of elk roaming the plains to the west of the labyrinth," Esrioas said. "You can go there to hunt, or you can conjure one here. But please do not eat it inside the temple."

"How do we activate the portcullis?" Hart asked.

Esrioas looked at the gate. "I will leave it open for you."

The twins were tired, as well as hungry. The idea of flying all the way back to the labyrinth and then having to look for the herd did not appeal to either of them. And, while Meg was game to try dragon-fried elk, Hart wasn't ready to kill and devour one of the beasts.

"Let's go outside and transform," he suggested. "Then we can conjure something that isn't still alive to eat."

Meg snickered at her squeamish brother. "Okay! But we are going to have to learn how to do it sometime."

"Do demi-gods even have to eat?" Hart asked as they started across the bridge.

"I don't even really know what a demi-god is," Meg said.

"Well, let's hope that *we* live long enough to find out. Did you see the way Esrioas kept looking at that sword on the altar?"

"I did. When we go back inside later, make sure we are standing between it and her."

"Wouldn't it be better to stand by the door, so we can get away if we need to?"

"She could ward the door," Meg said. "I want to be able to get to the blade first if it comes to that."

They transformed and Hart conjured steaming bowls of stew with dumplings. Meg conjured two large cups of jamba to go with the aromatic meal.

"Do you think Esrioas would mind if I took a nap in the temple?" Hart said, stifling a yawn.

"I might not make it back to the temple before I pass out," Meg said, not stifling a yawn.

They clinked glasses and ate in silence.

The hatchling, awake, and fully sated after a meal of fresh and unmedicated venison, watched Morgaine through the bars of the cage. He was calm, but alert, following her every move. Perhaps he was hoping that she would bring his nest mate back. More likely, he wanted her to let him out of the cage.

Bon and Hiro were watching Morgaine as well. She was pacing, holding the walking stick and worrying at a finger nail with her teeth. It was the one that was slightly mottled, with a dark streak running down its length. She was trying to decide if she should use the walking stick, or let Bon kill her, transfer Harpur's spirit into the hatchling, and then bring her back. Every now and then, she would stop and pick up the paper with the spell Arthur had written out for her.

As for Arthur and Sok, after the hockey game ended—badly, if Arthur's sullen mood was any indication—they had settled in the conversation pit with a large platter of nachos to watch a movie. Westerns had made a comeback, but this one was a western-fantasy called *On the Wings of Grace*. It was about a bank robber who finds a dragon egg that hatches, and he ends up raising it. Arthur thought it was brilliant! But it confused Sok.

"If there are no dragons on Earth, where did they get the dragon for the movie?" the elf asked.

"They didn't," Arthur said. "The dragon isn't real. None of it is real."

"It's right there, Arthur!"

"It only looks like it's there. This movie was generated by AI—artificial intelligence."

"How can intelligence be artificial? And if it is artificial, how can it generate anything?"

"Just watch the movie."

Sok ate more nachos.

Morgaine continued to pace.

Arthur enjoyed the next two scenes without interruption.

"If there are no dragons here, how does this artificial intelligence know what they look like?" Sok asked.

That was a very good question. Arthur looked over at Sok with a blank expression.

"Before I went to live in Epoh, I always thought that the appearance of dragons was influenced by dinosaur fossils. Maybe dragons are universally consistent whether they are real or mythological."

Sok wanted to ask what dinosaurs were, but figured that would only confuse him more. He quelled his curiosity with more nachos. And Arthur got to enjoy another half a scene in peace.

"I wish Harpur would make up his mind and get this over with," Sok said.

"Maybe I should go over there and knock Morgaine out like Harpur did to us on Mysturna, so Bon can do his thing," Arthur suggested.

"He'd kill you when it was over," Sok said.

Arthur glanced over his shoulder at the hatchling. "I think I could take him!"

Sok laughed. "He isn't going to be that small forever, Arthur."

"True," Arthur said. "More beer?"

"Yes, please."

While Bon had the patience of… well, of an android, even he was beginning to show signs of losing it. "Harpur, do you not want to do this?"

Morgaine stopped pacing and looked at Bon. "I do."

"Then might we get on with it?"

"I suppose we should," Morgaine said. "But…"

"You won't feel a thing," Bon said. "It will all be over in ten minutes and you will be as good as new."

"Literally," Hiro said and giggled.

Morgaine sighed. "Which do you think is better? Your way, or the walking stick?"

"There are risks inherent with either method," Bon said.

Arthur couldn't take it anymore. He paused the movie, which baffled Sok even more, and climbed over the back of the sofa out of the conversation pit.

"Just use the spell I gave you and get it done!" he all but yelled. "We are tired of watching you wearing a trench in the floor. What is the big deal anyway?"

"The big deal, Arthur," Morgaine growled, "is that it could fail."

"You didn't seem to be too concerned about that when you made me and Sok go through the procedure on Mysturna. And you didn't seem too concerned about it when you had me use magic to put your spirit into Karrys."

"Do you want me to say that I am afraid?"

"You don't have to say it! We can all see that for ourselves. But dillydallying because of it isn't going to make it any easier. So, put on your big boy… or girl… pants and either cast the spell with the walking stick or let Bon do the transfer, so we can all go home!"

"Fine!" Morgaine snapped. "But if I die…"

"You're already dead! You died sixteen years ago!"

That was it! That was the moment of truth that Harpur had been avoiding. Sixteen years ago, he had convinced himself that he was taking over Karrys' body because he wanted to be able to continue to be there for his friends. He knew that his plan might not work, and he had accepted that risk. Had Arthur failed in casting the spell with the Amber Chalice, his spirit would have gone on to Arachovor and that would have been the end of it. He'd have no control over anything that happened in Epoh after that.

But that is exactly what had happened anyway. Arthur, Sok, Anayah, Davynn, Elder Dhonna, Bon and Hiro had all managed to get along without him. The only thing he had achieved was to force Karrys into a situation that had caused her pain and torment.

And yet, she had forgiven him. She was even rooting for him. There was no way to hide her thoughts or feelings from Harpur, so he knew that she was sincere in not wanting revenge. In spite of the damage to her scales and the loss of her eye, she genuinely cared about him. He wondered if he would ever be able to forgive himself.

The people in this lair, and the others back in Epoh, owed him nothing. Still, here they were, doing their best to help him.

"I want to try using the walking stick," Morgaine announced.

No one opposed this idea, so she picked up and re-read the spell Arthur had written for her until she was sure she had memorized the incantations and could recite them flawlessly. She was about to begin, when it finally occurred to her that this would not work.

"What's wrong?" Arthur asked. "The spell will work."

"No, it won't," Morgaine said. "Once my spirit is in the walking stick, there will be no way to get it from there into the hatchling." *Damn that Nyrissa!*

"What do you mean? All you have to do is say the next incantation… Oh! I see."

Arthur took the paper from Morgaine and studied the spell. He'd constructed it in two parts. First, Harpur, who was the only one in the room who could use the walking stick, would recite the opening incantation to draw his spirit out of the Morgaine's body. Next, he would recite the second incantation to send his spirit to the hatchling. But, of course, Harpur could not speak through the walking stick and the walking stick was incapable of wielding itself.

"I think I've got it!" Arthur said at last. "What we need to do here is to make the transfer through the walking stick instead of to it. The trick is that the walking stick has to be in Harpur's control the entire time."

"Which means that it can't be done." Feeling defeated, Morgaine put the walking stick down and turned to Bon. "I guess you're up."

"Now, don't be hasty," Arthur said. "Can the hatchling understand us? Can he follow instructions?"

Morgaine looked at Arthur. "He's just gone through scaleshift, so he has the mental and emotional capacity of a ten or twelve-year-old human."

"Great!" Arthur said. "So, he will be able to do what you tell him to!"

"Why can't he talk yet?"

Sok had just joined the others. He had tried to use the remote to un-pause the movie, but not knowing what all the buttons were for, he had only succeeded in muting the audio and changing the program to a documentary on the history of traffic cones. Sok could simply not understand why people were lining bright-orange witch's hats up along roadways, or how they didn't crumple when they got crushed by the terrifying vehicles people used on Earth.

"He will. When he's ready," Morgaine said.

Sok asked Arthur to conjure an apple and thanked him when the juicy, red fruit appeared in his hand. "I'm so glad you're finally getting the hang of your magic."

Arthur shook his head at the elf. "Anyway... If you ask the hatchling to hold onto the walking stick and not let go until you tell him to, will he do it?"

"I'm not going to risk having him wreck it," Morgaine said. "It's cursed. Who knows what will happen if he breaks it, or inadvertently uses his magic while he's holding it?"

"What's the worst thing that could happen?" Arthur asked.

"He could kill all of us!"

"Why don't you try mildly sedating him?" Hiro suggested.

Arthur looked at the hatchling, then at Bon. "If we did that, would the sedative affect Harpur when he transferred into the hatchling?"

"The hatchling's sedated neurological processes would dictate Harpur's experience, resulting in altered perception, cognition, and awareness."

"So, yes, then."

"That is what I said," Bon confirmed.

"What about hypnosis?"

"The result would be the same," Bon said, prudently leaving out the scientific details. No one but Hiro ever seemed to fully appreciate it.

Arthur grasped his chin and tried to come up with some other option. "It's too bad you couldn't just do a one-way, permanent Vulcan mind-meld."

Morgaine snorted derisively.

"That is not a bad idea," Bon said, snapping his fingers like he had just debugged the universe. "I should have thought of it myself."

All eyes, including the hatchling's, flicked toward the inspired android.

"Mind-melding isn't a real thing," Morgaine said.

"That is not, strictly speaking, true," Bon said. He scanned his internal files for a bit of data he had picked up in his early days as a time-traveling, virtual, anthropological archaeologist.

When he found what he was looking for, Bon refocused and smiled at his lair-mates.

"There was a study conducted on Ignis Mundi by a colleague of mine who determined that, in their formative years, dragons learn by absorbing the experiences of mature dragons. It is as if they take on the minds of other dragons and actually know how to perform tasks without the steep learning curve most creatures must go through to master... flying, for example."

"But they can't be taking that part of the other dragon's mind," Arthur reasoned. "They would only be copying it. Otherwise, dragons would have to keep absorbing experiences from each other all the time."

"You are right," Bon said. "They employ a kind of reverse telepathy to copy from the minds of other dragons. However, we are dealing with a clone who already has a basic imprint of Harpur's nature embedded in his biological composition."

"How does that help?" Arthur asked, growing both oddly and increasingly interested. "All this means is that the hatchling can learn everything that Harpur... and, presumably Karrys... has experienced, but it doesn't get Harpur out of Karrys and into the hatchling."

"I have not finished," Bon said. "My colleague observed two cases where pre-adolescent dragons whose parents were fatally injured suddenly developed skills that they should not have yet mastered. The injured adult appeared to focus intently on the infant as if it was willing its knowledge and experience into the its prodigy before it expired."

"I still don't see how that helps in this situation," Arthur said. "The injured adult, knowing it is going to die, makes a last-ditch effort to give its offspring every possible advantage for survival. All we'd end up with is a backup. Harpur would still be stuck in Karrys."

Morgaine was watching the exchange between Arthur and Bon with a sense of awe. Arthur's calm and practical approach in determining Harpur's immediate fate was unexpected to say the least.

"What happened to him?" Morgaine whispered to Sok.

The elf smiled. "Anayah died," Sok said. "And he's been spending a lot of time in Ylemnir's covert."

"He found the covert!?"

"He found himself."

Sok finished eating his apple while he pondered the implications of Morgaine's question about the covert. Clearly, Harpur knew it was there all along. If they managed to get Harpur sorted out, he would definitely be sitting the ex-Dragon Lord of Epoh down for a serious heart-to-heart. One step at a time.

Morgaine put the troubles with the transfer aside and tried to fit this newest wrinkle into the list of things that would need to be dealt with when all this was over. Harpur would have to face the Dragon Council, and if he survived that, the twins were now demi-gods. They were barely past childhood as humans. They had no clue yet what it meant to be dragons, let alone all-powerful immortal dragons! But Arthur's discovery of the covert was, by far, the most difficult thing for Harpur. It meant that he would not be the King of Epoh for much longer.

To pass the time after their naps, Meg and Hart flew back to the labyrinth and landed in its centre next to the pool. Seven standing stones surrounded the pool, with just enough room between them for a single dragon to stand and gaze into the clear water.

"I wonder what they do here," Meg said.

"Rituals and rites, I imagine," Hart said.

"Like throw dragon hearts into the pool," Meg suggested.

"Like that," Hart agreed.

"Seems barbaric," Meg said.

Hart didn't disagree. "I think that the offering of a fire dragon heart has something to do with the Ice Dragons. I'm pretty sure dragons don't ritually sacrifice their own kind on a regular basis."

"Did it say anything about that in that book you read?"

"There was nothing about rituals in it. Other than a couple of rites of passage that, as far as I can tell, are rather loosely adhered to."

"Like what?"

"Like the First Blood Flight." Hart looked up at his sister, who was waiting for him to continue. "Young dragons have to successfully capture prey while flying. They can't burn it first; they have to grab it off the ground and bring it back to the flight they belong to. Then they burn it and let the others eat it."

"Hmm…"

"I don't think we have to worry about doing stuff like that," Hart said.

"I wonder why humans don't seem to have things like that."

"Father used to tell us about holidays on Earth. I'd like to try Christmas."

Meg tried to recall the different holidays Arthur had told them about. "Is that the one where the guy in a red suit climbs down peoples' chimneys and put presents under a tree?"

"That's the one."

"I think Father made that up."

"He swears it really happens."

Meg rolled her eyes. "Why would anyone cut down a tree, bring it in their house, put a bunch of coloured balls on it just so some man in a fancy suit knew where to put the presents?"

Hart gave Meg a puzzled look. "It's the part about the tree that bothers you?"

"Well, yeah! Why cut down a perfectly good tree like that?"

"Right, silly me."

Hart walked away from the pool and followed the path of the labyrinth for a short distance. He adored his sister, but sometimes she had a very unusual way of looking at the world. From the time they were little, all she wanted to do was become a knight. It didn't matter to her that knighthood was reserved for men and that the world expected her to aspire to finding a husband and producing children. As the official heir to the throne, Meg's interest in archery and sword fighting didn't so much as raise an eyebrow in Colwygshire. People thought it was conscientious of her to understand how armies worked, but they did not expect her to actually fight, should fighting ever be called upon.

As second in line for the crown, Hart had never coveted his sister's position. Becoming the King of Epoh required that Meg turn down her place on the throne, and losing his father. A prospect he didn't want to think about, or be rewarded for—if being king could even be considered a reward.

Recent events, however, had set an even heavier burden on his shoulders. If what he understood about the old gods and demi-gods that legend told had once ruled the world of Thraeh, he and Meg were now possessed of immense power and longevity. Immortal wasn't precisely the right term; but, as demi-gods, they could conceivable live for thousands of years. *What*, he wondered, *would Thraeh be like a thousand years from now? And do I want to be around to find out?*

"We should probably head back to the temple," Meg called out, interrupting her brother's reverie.

Hart turned toward the pool and looked at Meg. She was as beautiful in dragon form as she was as the tiny, curly-haired, archery champion she was born to be. And she loved being a dragon. He knew that if there was a way out of what lay ahead for them and he took it, Meg would too. Perhaps he was better off not knowing. Either way, someone was going to end up being resentful.

"I'm right behind you," Hart said.

He waited until Meg had flown past him before he launched into the sky and followed her back to the north pole.

Esrioas was still in her lair beneath the temple when they arrived. There wasn't much to look at. The ice walls were bare and the skulls and sword on the altar were of little interest. So, they did what all dragons do when they are bored; they curled up on the floor and closed their eyes to sleep.

The silver dragon emerged from her lair, as promised, just before the sun set for the day. She had made her decision. Though she would never know if she was making a mistake, it was time for her watch to end.

Meg was first to wake. She nudged Hart as she rose to her feet and spread her wings out enough to form a wider barrier between Esrioas and the altar where the Isenwylm lay. Hart, of course, took a more subtle approach, keeping his wings folded, but stepping forward to place himself protectively in front of Meg.

Esrioas smiled. "You have nothing to fear from me," she said.

"So, you believe us?" Hart asked.

Esrioas cocked her head to one side in thought. "Belief is a tenuous thing. But sometimes that is all we have."

Meg's wings relaxed a little. "You will help us, then?"

"Pick up the blade," Esrioas ordered.

The twins turned and looked at Isenwylm. An icy blush of frost spread over the steel sword, glowing blue in the fading light. Meg reached out and lifted it from the fur mantle. It felt small in her hand as she wrapped her talons around it.

Across the room, Esrioas' smile broadened. She was pleased that the female had been the one to claim Isenwylm. The male would be the voice of reason. And, she suspected, he had his work cut out for him.

Meg held Isenwylm with a confidence that only an experienced sword-fighter would know—another good sign. But the next few moments were crucial. Isenwylm had to accept Meg. Only then could she take her place as an Ice Dragon and rule as a demi-god over all of Thraeh.

"What do I do with it?" Meg asked.

"I think the better question is: What is it doing to you?" Hart asked in alarm.

The blue-tinged frost that covered the blade was spreading across Meg's hand and up her arm. Wherever it touched her, her black scales faded to cobalt-blue. Gone were the silver and purple streaks; in their place touches of gold sparkled in the glow from the sword.

Meg seemed frozen, unable to release Isenwylm from her grasp. A cry of pain, so loud it cracked the ice walls of the temple, tore through the air, and Hart leapt toward his sister, intent on ripping the sword from her hands.

But Esrioas, old as she was, crossed the room and stopped him. "Do not interfere!"

Hart, horrified, stepped back. "What is happening to her?"

"Isenwylm has accepted her," Esrioas said. "She is becoming an Ice Dragon."

It had taken a while for Bon to convince both Arthur and Morgaine that the transfer of Harpur's spirit into the hatchling could—conceivably—work without them having to risk activating the walking stick's curse, or the need to kill anyone. His hypothesis was, if a dying dragon could will its life force into its offspring as his colleague had observed, then Harpur could do the same thing with the hatchling.

Neither Harpur, nor Karrys had ever heard of such a thing, but as the debate went on, heating and cooling as logic and imagination collided, a consensus was eventually reached. Arthur modified the spell for the umpteenth time and handed it to Morgaine.

"You've got to be kidding!" The dragon-wizardess looked at Arthur in disbelief. "I'm not saying this."

"Oh, come on!" Arthur grinned. "It will work. Just humour me."

It was late and Morgaine was tired. Too tired to argue anymore. She approached the cage and, speaking quietly to the hatchling, reached into the cage to scratch the side of his head just behind his jaw. The young dragon welcomed the attention and moved closer to the bars. He emitted a soft growling noise, not unlike the purring of a cat. Morgaine then reached out with her other hand and placed it on the opposite side of the hatchling's head.

"Spread your fingers out more," Arthur coached the dragon-wizardess from a few feet away.

Morgaine rolled her eyes, but complied. "I feel stupid doing this."

"It will be great," Arthur said. He waved his hand at her to hurry her along.

Morgaine took a deep breath, then rolled her shoulders and adjusted her stance. The hatchling continued to watch her intently through the bars.

"My mind to your mind. My thoughts to your thoughts," Morgaine said.

Behind her, Arthur, giddy with fatigue at such a late hour, had to stifle a giggle. "This is awesome," he whispered. "I wish I had a camera."

Morgaine's jaw clenched, but she managed to keep her focus on the hatchling. "My mind to your mind. My thoughts to your thoughts," she repeated.

Several minutes passed. Then suddenly the hatchling's eyes opened wide and Morgaine snapped her hands back out of the cage. They both stood there, staring at each other.

"Did it work?" Arthur asked.

Morgaine ran her hands over her body, then she held them to the sides of her head. "I'm… me! I'm… just… me!"

In the cage, the hatchling tried to speak. All that came out of his mouth was a gravelly, squeak.

"Harpur?" Arthur approached the cage. "Is that you?"

The hatchling nodded. He tried to say something again. The only sound he could produce was the same hoarse squawking noise. A large tear rolled down his cheek and fell to the cage floor.

Arthur pumped the air with his fists. "It worked! It worked! I can't believe it! Harpur is Harpur again!" He bounced over to Morgaine and threw his arms around her. "Praise Spock, it worked!"

Morgaine extricated herself from Arthur's embrace and turned to Harpur. "Can you get out of the cage?"

Harpur looked around at his prison. He tried to make the cage disappear. It flickered a few times, but remained solidly in place. He squawked in frustration.

"Take it easy there, little fella," Arthur said, quite unable to contain his delight.

Harpur glared and shot a plume of purple-red smoke at him.

"Whoa!" Arthur said, backing away. "I was just joking."

Sok and Hiro joined the others by the cage.

"What's wrong with him?" Sok asked.

"Nothing a bit more growing and maturing will not cure," Bon said. "He has to adjust to his new body. And it to him. I dare say that by morning, Harpur will be in full command of his faculties again."

"Is there no way we can get him out of the cage?" Sok asked.

"Harpur's magic conjured it," Morgaine said. "Only Harpur can make it disappear."

"I can't believe that worked," Arthur said again. "That was the coolest thing I've ever seen."

Morgaine seemed agitated.

"What's the matter?" Sok asked her.

The dragon-wizardess was choking up. She could barely talk through the sobs she was trying so hard to suppress. "I... I miss you!"

In a flash of teal smoke, Morgaine zapped herself into the cage. Harpur, tears flowing steadily from his own eyes, drew her to himself and folded a wing around her.

"Let's give them some privacy," Arthur said, turning away from the emotional scene in the cage. "O'Bryans is still open. Let's say we all go get a beer."

Isenwylm had accepted Meg and now she stood before Hart and Esrioas feeling powerful and utterly unsure of what had just happened to her. She focused on her hand, still gripping the sword, then scanned the rest of her body.

"I'm blue."

"Not precisely the right colour of blue," Esrioas said, suspecting that the blackness of Meg's scales had not completely succumbed to the transformation, and not wanting to think about what that meant, "but you are an Ice Dragon now."

"But I haven't walked the labyrinth yet. I thought I had to do that first."

"Isenwylm has accepted you. There is no need for you to walk the labyrinth." Esrioas shrugged.

"What about Hart?" Meg looked at her brother. For some reason, his black scales offended her.

Esrioas sighed. "If your brother wishes to take his place as your Icewright, he must complete the rites. If he survives, he to will have the power of the Ice Dragons."

"Icewright?" Hart asked.

"Of course he wants to be my Icewright!" Meg said. "He's my brother. He will serve me as my right wing."

"Excuse me?" Hart blurted. "Serve you?"

Meg was too busy trying to figure out how she knew what an Icewright was to respond. Then she realized what she had said and her thoughts turned to reconciling her assumption that Hart would willingly serve her in any capacity, even as her second-in-command. "Figure of speech," she mumbled.

"Hold on," Hart said. "Before I commit to being relegated to the status of servant, what exactly are these rites you mentioned? And what is an Icewright?"

Esrioas chose to downplay the connotations of being a servant to Meg. The siblings could sort that out for themselves. If Hart made it that far.

"You must harvest the heart of a dragon and then walk the labyrinth with it. If it is still beating when you reach the pool in the centre of the labyrinth, you may offer it to... Well, to your sister, since she is the only living god on Thraeh at the moment. If she accepts it, you will be transformed as she was and become an Ice Dragon too."

"Demi-god," Meg corrected. She clamped her mouth closed, again wondering how she understood any of what Esrioas had just said.

Hart shook his head. "No thanks. I think I'll just stay the way I am."

"You can't!" Meg admonished. "The Power of Averborn and your fire dragon blood will destroy you. You have to be purified by ritual or you will die."

"Or," Hart said, "You can fix me. You're a god now..."

"Demi-god!" Meg snapped.

"Semantics, Meg. You can still fix this."

"Can I?" Flustered now because she didn't know if that was true or not, Meg turned to Esrioas.

"He's right. The only real difference is a demi-god isn't immortal. But in the end, even gods don't last forever." The silver dragon's patience was waning quickly.

Meg looked at the sword in her hand, then back at the altar. "Is there a scabbard for this thing?"

"I can't believe that I waited around here for nearly five thousand years just to have you two Fae-brained fire-bloods show up!" Esrioas was ready to kill herself just to end this. "Fix him or don't. I don't care. But if he's not going to harvest my heart, I'm going back to my lair."

"Harvest your heart?" Hart felt sick.

"That's the deal, sonny," Esrioas said.

"Wait!" Meg had a great idea. "I'm like the Queen of the World now, right?"

"Sadly, yes."

"Then I can grant Hart the Power of Averborn just because I want to, right? He doesn't have to harvest your heart if I say he doesn't."

Esrioas thought about it. "What kind of god... demi-god doesn't want a little drama and pageantry to go with her divinity? You know, you two are ruining this day for me!"

Meg and Hart both gave the silver dragon confused looks.

"You mean you want me to rip your still-beating heart out of your chest?" Hart asked sarcastically.

"Well, no," Esrioas admitted. "I'd fight you tooth and talon all the way!"

"You're ancient!"

"And you're... What did you say? Sixteen? Still wet behind the horns!"

"I'm sure my brother could hold his own," Meg said, though not as confidently as she intended.

"I am not going to kill you!" Hart declared. He turned to face Meg. "I'm not!"

"Would it help if Hart walked the labyrinth anyway, and maybe took a vow or something?" Meg was desperately looking for a way out that didn't leave Esrioas disappointed. Although, she was having difficulty understanding how getting out alive could be disappointing.

"A little," Esrioas said grudgingly.

"Fine! I'll walk the labyrinth!" Hart turned to leave the temple. When he reached the gate, he stopped. "Wait! I don't want to be an Ice Dragon. I want to be a scientist. I want to find ways to bring science and magic together to make the world a better place."

Then he saw the sadness in Meg's eyes.

"If you really don't want to be an Ice Dragon, I won't make you," Meg said softly. "But I can't do this without you."

487

When it came right down to it, Hart didn't think he could go on living without Meg either. "Okay, big sister, we'll do this together. But I'm not going to be your servant."

"But the Queen of the World is supposed to have an Icewright at her beck and call," Meg said.

"What is an Icewright again?"

"It's just a fancy demi-god word for the guy who is at my beck and call."

"How do you know that?"

Meg looked at Isenwylm. "I think the sword told me. But I don't need an Icewright to boss around. How about you be in charge of science and magic?"

"And what will you be in charge of?"

Meg winked. "Everything else, little brother. Everything else."

Esrioas Grithhall watched the black and blue dragons walk out of the temple and cross the bridge. Meg stopped on the other side of the moat and conjured a scabbard for Isenwylm, which she then strapped to her back between her wings. After they flew away, she turned back to the altar and rearranged the skulls in the middle of the long slab of ice on top of the fur mantle.

Touching each of the skulls in turn, she said, "Good night, Korgren. Good night, Tiq. Good night, Ylemnir."

Chapter Twenty-four

Arthur, Sok, Bon and Hiro returned to the lair to find Morgaine and Harpur curled up together, sleeping in the cage. Except for Bon, they were all a little tipsy; it was something of a minor miracle that he managed to get them all to go to bed without waking the dragons. The volume of the shushing alone was enough to wake the dead, and the inapposite giggling didn't help. Bon rarely wished he possessed magical abilities, but a mute button would have been a blessing.

Eventually, the lair grew quiet though, and Bon was left to enjoy the remainder of the night in peace. He carefully repacked the accoutrements he'd prepared for the transfer of Harpur's spirit into the hatchling, both thankful and a bit disappointed that he had not had to use them. He had performed the procedure enough times to be confident in his proficiency, but he'd never done it for a dragon before. He'd have liked to have documented those results.

As it was, he did get to witness a phenomenon seemingly unprecedented among dragons from Thraeh. How these ancient and noble creatures were not aware that they could share their minds was a mystery, and one he would probably never solve. It was still good to know that there was an option to the surgical procedure should it ever come up again.

With nothing else to do until the others woke up, Bon settled himself in the conversation pit and wirelessly connected his auditory systems to the large-screen television above the fireplace. He found a documentary on the life of Genghis Khan and entertained himself by tallying the number of inaccuracies the program claimed as facts. He was tempted to dash off a few emails and set the *experts* right, but that would only unleash a maelstrom of outrage and debate. Humans on Earth tended not to appreciate being corrected, and the appearance of a time-travelling android would have a detrimental effect on Earth's timeline.

Harpur was the first to wake. It took a few minutes for him to get reoriented and remember how he got inside the cage—and the hatchling.

He saw Bon on the sofa, watching the muted television, and looked around for the others. Hiro was lying on the floor next to the crumpled hover gilly; whether he was actually asleep or not wasn't clear, but the Krist did not stir. Arthur and Sok were snoring on cots that Arthur must have conjured for them. And Morgaine, of course, was curled up next to him. There was no way he would be able to move without waking her.

But he wanted to test his magic. His attempt, the night before, to get rid of the cage had not gone well. His magic was there and working; it just wasn't stable enough to complete the task as he wanted it to. He needed to try something simpler.

A cup of coffee would be nice.

In order to drink it, though, he would have to transform into his human form. And the prospect of doing that filled him with dread. He had no idea what he would look like.

The first time he had transformed into a human, he had been a fully grown and mature adult dragon. The tall, broad-shouldered man with the violet eyes and skin the colour of poisonwood was the only human form he'd ever experienced. He had control over his hair—bald—and his beard—a neat and narrow line along his jaw. His choice of attires was up to him. But other than aesthetics, he had no control over the size and shape of his body. Generally speaking, a dragon's human guise was derived from its dragon physiology.

His best guess was that he would be a boy, about 12 or 14-years-old in appearance. A gawky teenager, probably not even old enough to shave. Harpur winced.

I don't need coffee that bad!

Then he spied his walking stick on the floor a few feet away from the cage where Morgaine had left it the night before. Telekinesis was a simple enough thing to start with. He focused on the walking stick, willing it to come to him.

At first, nothing happened. The walking stick remained where it was, completely still.

He tried again. This time, the walking stick twitched, but that is all it did.

"Need any help?"

Harpur looked up to see Arthur standing next to the cage. With a cup of coffee in his hand.

"No!" Surprised by the sound of his own voice, Harpur cleared his throat. "No, thank you."

Arthur had to take a sip of his coffee to keep himself from laughing. Harpur's voice was quite a bit higher in pitch than it used to be.

Harpur, more determined than ever, concentrated on the walking stick. This time, it rose from the floor and floated smoothly into the cage. A sigh of relief, accompanied by a thin wisp of purple-red smoke, escaped from his mouth.

"Well done!" Arthur said. "Are you going to stay in that cage forever?"

"I'm waiting for Morgaine to wake up," Harpur whispered. "I don't want to disturb her."

"Right," Arthur said. He pulled a chair from the dining area over to the cage and sat down, crossing one ankle over his knee. "How are you feeling?"

"What part of not disturbing Morgaine did you not get?"

"I'm awake," Morgaine groaned.

The dragon-wizardess opened her eyes and looked around. Like Harpur, she needed a few minutes to clear her head. One hand fluttered up to her throat; she wasn't used to speaking for herself.

Harpur lifted his wing so that Morgaine could sit up. They exchanged looks of sadness and confusion. Being separated was proving to be much more difficult than they had anticipated.

"Are you alright?" Harpur asked gently.

Morgaine stood up and tugged her vest into place. "I think so."

"If you will zap yourself out of the cage, I will attempt to get rid of it." Harpur smiled. But it was a rueful smile.

When he was alone in the cage, Harpur examined its structure. Zapping it back to wherever it came from should have been dragon's play to him. A quick gesture with his talons, or a wave of the walking stick, and it should vanish completely.

And it did.

The problem was that Harpur vanished with it.

Meg and Hart stood at the entrance to the labyrinth. They could see the pool in the centre a half mile away, though it would be a 20-mile trek to reach it.

"Why am I doing this again?" Hart asked.

"Esrioas didn't get the dignified ceremony she was expecting. The least you can do is walk the labyrinth for her."

"She's not even here to see me do it."

491

"I know," Meg said, "but if I want the dragons of Thraeh to respect me as a god…"

"Oh, you're a full-fledged god now!"

Meg flicked Hart on the leg with her tail. "If I want the respect of the dragons, I need to be true to my word."

"Again, no one is here to see me do it. No one will know."

"I'll know," Meg said. "And so will you."

Hart scowled at his sister. "You think I'm going to blackmail you over not making me walk twenty miles before you grant me the Power of Averborn."

Meg looked away from her brother. She had a decision to make.

"Meg?" Hart sensed her reluctance. "What is it?"

Meg sighed. "The truth is that I don't know how to grant you the Power of Averborn."

"That's not good, Meg."

"I know," Meg said. "I keep getting little flashes of information… from Isenwylm, I think. But it doesn't make a lot of sense. It's like things just pop into my head when I need them, but I don't really know what they mean." She looked at her brother. "I was hoping by the time you finished walking the labyrinth, Isenwylm would tell me what to do."

Hart did not envy his sister's position. "Maybe we should go back and ask Esrioas. She might know."

"No," Meg said. "I don't think that's a good idea."

Hart didn't either, really. The silver dragon was quite annoyed with them in the end. "Well, you became an Ice Dragon when you picked up the sword. Why don't I try holding it? Maybe it will accept me too."

"Never!" Meg shouted, taking them both by surprise. "I mean, that won't work. Isenwylm can only be wielded by one person… uh, god… uh, whatever, at a time. I am the one that it accepted; we're kind of bound to each other now."

"The sword told you that?"

"I just know that's how it works," Meg said. "I don't know how I know that."

Hart blew out a heavy breath. "Okay. Well, let's think about this. You said that things pop into your head when you need to know them, right? So, why don't you just start to grant me the Power of Averborn and maybe it will come to you?"

"That won't work." Meg began to fidget on her feet. "I think you have to walk the labyrinth."

"Okay, why?" Hart wanted—needed—to have faith in his sister. He could feel her panic starting to rise. If he kept her focused on finding a solution, they might get through this without him turning into a giant block of ice, or dissolving into a big, black puddle of goo.

"The labyrinth will protect you," Meg said.

"You're sure about that?"

"I think… Yes! You have to walk the labyrinth."

Hart raked his gaze across the enormous pathway before him. If Meg was right, walking the labyrinth would buy them five or six hours; more if he walked slowly. He stepped into it far enough so that his entire body was on the path.

"Meg?" he said to get her attention. "Go find Harpur."

"Harpur's on Earth. How am I supposed to get into the Boundary house?"

"You're a god. You'll figure it out."

Thankfully, she didn't argue. Hart watched his blue sister fly toward the mountains. When she was a mere speck in the sky, he started to walk the labyrinth.

Arthur, choking on his coffee, spat a mouthful of it across the floor. Eyes watering, he gasped for breath and pointed at the spot where the cage—and Harpur—had been only a moment before. Beside him, Morgaine yelped, drawing the attention of Bon, who had missed the whole, shocking event.

Sok sat up on his cot and tried to make sense of what was happening while Bon and Hiro, who had not, in fact, been asleep, rushed over to Arthur and Morgaine. It only took a second for the elf to put it all together.

"Well, that's not good." Sok swung his legs over the side of the cot and stood up.

"Ya think!?" Arthur croaked. "What in Orhowyn's name are we going to do now?"

Arthur had been holding himself together rather well in recent days. The thought of a magically-challenged adolescent dragon being on the loose somewhere in the city of Edmonton, however, was beyond his ability to process without a meltdown. He clasped his hands at the back of his neck and closed his eyes.

"No! No! No! No! No! This can't be happening!"

But it was. Harpur had zapped himself Orhowyn only knew where. And there wasn't a thing any of them could do about it.

Still, they tried.

"Harpur conjured the cage from somewhere," Bon said. "All we have to do is identify places where cages are kept. There cannot be that many."

"The cage could have come from anywhere in the world," Morgaine said. "He talked about the zoo, though. He felt bad that the animals were caged up all the time."

The dragon-wizardess was drawing from her memories of Harpur's experiences on Earth. Without being able to connect directly to his mind, her own memories of his memories were all she had. It wasn't the same.

"The cage was more suitable to a circus than a zoo," Bon observed.

"I thought it was a portable jail cell," Sok said. He didn't dare ask what a circus or a zoo was.

"I don't think it was any of those things," Hiro said. "It had no doors."

"That is correct," Bon said. "I should have noticed that myself. But that does help us."

"How?" asked Morgaine.

"It must be a prestidigitator's prop. An illusion." Bon was certain that was it.

Only Hiro was brave enough to ask for an explanation.

"Forgive me," Bon said. "I was attempting to spare you any confusion. Magicians on Earth are illusionists; prestidigitator is another word for magician. I suspect that Harpur conjured the cage from just such a person's inventory. If we can find out where any magic shows are scheduled locally, we can probably find Harpur."

"So where do we find these prestidi… whatever people?" Sok asked. "And could someone get me a cup of jamba?"

Morgaine conjured three mocha lattes that happened to have just been prepared for a now angry customer by a baffled barista in a café on Whyte Avenue. "There is no jamba here," she said, handing one each to Sok and Hiro, and keeping one for herself. "This will have to do."

Sok took a sip. "What is this fluffy white stuff on the top?"

"It is called whipped cream," Bon said. "Now, back to the problem at hand. We must find the library. We will be able to access the Internet there."

"A library is an archive, right?" Sok asked. "And the Internet is…?

"A library is indeed an archive, of sorts," Bon confirmed. "And the Internet is how we will be able to locate any nearby magic shows."

"You're in charge!" Sok said to the android. "I have no idea what anything you've said means. But if it will help us find Harpur, we're behind you all the way."

"We've got to go to the library!" Arthur's meltdown had come to its usual decisive conclusion. "We can access the Internet and research places where the cage might have come from."

Arthur headed toward the exit.

"Great idea!" Sok called after him. "Wish we had thought of that!"

They had all just left the lair when Harpur reappeared. He had only been gone for a few minutes and finding the lair empty was as alarming to him as his disappearance had been to the others.

"Where in Orhowyn's name did everyone go?"

"I don't know, but I need to find Harpur Diggins! Fast!"

Harpur spun around to see a cobalt-blue dragon standing next to the exit of the lair.

"Who are you?" he demanded.

"Who are you?" the cobalt dragon demanded back.

"I am Harpur Diggins. And this is my lair. How did you get in here?"

The cobalt dragon laughed. "You are not Harpur Diggins!"

There was something familiar about the blue dragon's laugh. Harpur blanched, suddenly, as recognition settled in. "Meg?"

"At your service," Meg said. "Are you really Harpur?"

"As a matter of fact, I am," he answered indignantly.

"Huh! I thought you'd be taller."

Harpur knew things weren't likely to go well for him in his human guise. Elated that his magic was working, the realization that he'd mistakenly zapped himself along with the cage had left him momentarily discombobulated. Unfortunately, the sudden appearance of the cage on the theatre stage he'd conjured it from in the first place, was almost witnessed by a couple of stage hands who were there early to set up for the afternoon matinee. His only saving grace was that the lights were still off; shock and darkness were on Harpur's side. He transformed seconds before one of the stage hands flipped on the overhead flood lights. He knew he'd been seen. It was too late to just zap himself away again.

"Hey, you!" the first stage hand shouted. "What are you doing in there?"

"I'm just testing the cage for this afternoon's show," Harpur said, with the cracking voice of the adolescent boy he now was.

"You're not Marvelous Mervin!" the other stage hand said.

"I'm his son." Harpur smiled as charmingly as he could. "Marvelous Mervin Junior."

The first stage hand pointed at a life-size cutout of Marvelous Mervin that was leaning against a trunk behind Harpur. Marvelous Mervin was a pudgy, blonde, white kid, not much older than Harpur's human form looked to be.

"Mac," the stage hand said to his colleague as he lunged at Harpur to restrain him, "call the cops!"

Harpur didn't hesitate. He didn't bother to wipe the stage hands' memories either. He simply zapped himself back to the lair.

"Give me a day or two," Harpur said sarcastically.

Meg started to laugh again. "You look like a little boy wearing his father's clothes."

Indeed, Harpur felt like a little boy wearing his father's clothes. He hadn't had a chance to see himself in a mirror yet, but he knew he was not the strapping, broad-shouldered man he once was. His face was devoid of whiskers, though a smattering of peach fuzz adorned his upper lip. He hadn't had time to think about his attire, so he had defaulted to the old Harpur's fashion choices, a black-leather duster over a black shirt, vest and pants. A creamy silk ascot was neatly knotted beneath his smooth, dark chin, and held in place with a ruby pin. A red-banded top hat sat on top of his thick, tightly curled hair. His eyes were pale mauve, flecked with red.

"And you look… blue! What happened to you?"

"Isenwylm," Meg said. "Hart and I went to the Temple of Averborn and Esrioas told me to pick up the sword. Apparently, I am now an Ice Dragon…"

"Ice Dragons are supposed to be pale blue," Harpur interrupted. "There is no variation in their colour."

"Well, we can sort out what colour I'm supposed to be later," Meg said. "Right now, I need your advice."

"Where's Hart?" Harpur asked, sensing that the prince was the reason for the needed advice.

"He's walking the labyrinth. I think."

"You think?" Harpur was growing alarmed.

"It just occurred to me that time is different here than it is on Thraeh. So, now I'm not exactly sure what he's doing."

"Does he have a dragon heart for an offering?"

"No." Meg faltered. "He can't bring himself to kill another dragon. Esrioas offered to let him kill her and take her heart but…"

Several colourful words filled the lair as Harpur nearly lapsed into an Arthurian meltdown of his own.

"Can you help us?" Meg was beginning to panic again too.

"Bloody teenagers!" Harpur snarled. "Get back to Averborn! Make sure Hart stays in the labyrinth."

"What if he's not there anymore?"

Harpur looked up at the frightened cobalt dragon. He couldn't tell her that if Hart wasn't in the labyrinth, he wasn't... anywhere. "He'll be there. And I'll be there as soon as I can. First, I have to find your father and the others and get them back to Epoh."

"But..."

"Go!" Harpur tried to yell, but his voice cracked again.

Meg vanished from the lair.

"What a mess!"

Harpur: I should have just let you kill me!

But Karrys didn't hear him; she wasn't there anymore. Harpur was on his own.

Eowyn knocked on Davynn's door. When the knight didn't answer, he had to will himself not to cry. Arthur, Sok, Bon and Hiro were all missing—had been for far too long—and now he feared that Davynn was missing too. Along with the children and...

"Joy!" Eowyn pounded on the door again. "Joy, are you in there?"

It was as if all the members of the royal court were being abducted.

Is the kingdom under siege? Are we being attacked by an invisible enemy?

The young captain of the guard was at a total loss. Nothing like this had ever happened under Davynn's watch. And there was no one left that he could turn to for guidance.

Except...

Eowyn made his way to the stables and ordered a groom to saddle his horse. Maybe Elder Dhonna could shed some light on what was going on. Davynn seemed to trust her, and it was a much better alternative to making the three-day trek through Braydon Wood to Glynnis' lair to see if the old wyrm knew where Arthur and the others had disappeared to. That would be his last resort.

The ride to the elven city helped to calm his nerves. The fresh air and sunshine buoyed his spirits and, by the time he arrived at Elder Dhonna's tree house, he'd almost convinced himself that he was worrying over nothing; that Arthur, Sok,

Bon and Hiro were just off tending to the business of freeing Harpur and they would all come back soon.

Elder Dhonna welcomed Eowyn to her home with a cup of tea and some freshly-made biscuits. "What is troubling you?" she asked as Eowyn settled himself on a comfortable chair on her balcony.

"Arthur and Sok have disappeared," he said matter-of-factly. "It's been a couple of days now."

"It is odd that they would leave the castle and not say something," Elder Dhonna agreed. But she wasn't ready to leap to conclusions. "They probably went to Andonsheer to check on how things are going there."

"That was my first thought," Eowyn admitted, "but they should have said something. To someone!"

"That is out of character. For Sok especially," Elder Dhonna said. "He tends to be rather obsessive about protocol. But, in my experience, both he and Arthur can also be full of surprises. I daresay that they will turn up and wonder why you were upset with them." She patted the young man's arm. "Give it another day. Sok won't let Arthur miss court."

Eowyn wondered if he should tell her about the changes to the court system that had recently been implemented. Then he wondered if he should prepare Berryl in case Sok and Arthur didn't return on time. That wasn't Elder Dhonna's problem, though.

"I can't find Sir Davynn either," he said instead.

"No..." Elder Dhonna replied hesitantly. "And you won't."

"What do you mean?"

"Davynn has taken the children to Branwyke," Elder Dhonna said sadly.

Now Eowyn was angry. "Without even saying good bye? What is wrong with everyone? Have they all lost their sense of responsibility?"

Elder Dhonna watched the weight of this news fall heavily on the young captain. She understood why he was upset; Davynn's departure had upset her too.

"We all knew he was planning on leaving," Elder Dhonna said. "He would have left sooner, I believe, but at first his sense of responsibility made him wait. To be honest, I encouraged him to go."

"Why?"

"So that he and the children could begin to heal."

Eowyn felt awful. He hadn't considered the knight's grief. "I suppose I should be happy for them."

"Yes," Elder Dhonna agreed. "They have a wonderful new life waiting for them at Highmere Manor."

Eowyn helped himself to another biscuit. They were delicious. Unlike any of the sweet treats that he'd eaten at the castle, the soft mounds of buttery goodness melted in his mouth.

As he swallowed the last bite of his biscuit, another thought occurred to Eowyn. "Did Joy go with Davynn?"

Elder Dhonna smiled. "I believe that she stayed in Colwygshire."

A tide of hope washed over him. "I should probably check on her when I get back to the city and see if she is okay."

"I think that she would like that."

Eowyn wanted another biscuit, but thought that he might be making a pig of himself. "I should go and let you get to the guild house," he said. "I've taken enough of your time."

"I will not be going to the guild house today," Elder Dhonna said. She lifted the plate of biscuits, offering Eowyn another.

He took a biscuit, gratefully. "Thank you. Off to forage in the woods, then?"

"Packing my belongings," Elder Dhonna said.

"Oh?"

"I will be joining Davynn and the children at Highmere just as soon as I know that Harpur is okay."

"I didn't know that elves were allowed to live outside of Braydon Wood." Eowyn was shocked. Then he realized how dumb that must have sounded. "Except for Sok, of course, but he's not a normal elf."

Elder Dhonna looked at the young captain. "Whatever makes you say that?"

"Have you met Sok?" Eowyn countered.

"Yes, well, you do have a point. But elves are free to chose lives outside of the forest; they just don't often do so."

"Why are you leaving?"

That was a good question. Elder Dhonna had been taken aback by Davynn's invitation to join him and the children at Highmere Manor. "There's plenty of room," he had said, "and we would love to have you with us."

"It seems that I have an impulsive side too," she answered with a wistful smile.

"I wish you well, Elder Dhonna," Eowyn said. He stood up and walked over to the rope ladder, ready to take his leave.

"It's just Dhonna, now."

Harpur was in a quandary. Meg and Hart needed his help in Averborn. But with Arthur, Sok, Morgaine, Bon and Hiro loose in Edmonton, doing Orhowyn only knew what, he was loath to leave.

It was a reasonable assumption that they had gone looking for him. His inadvertent disappearance must have come as something of a shock. The logical thing to do was sit tight and wait for them to return. But who knew how long they would be? And, in the meantime, Hart's life was in danger. If he tried using his Ice Dragon powers and his fire dragon powers at the same time, he'd be in for a very rough and agonizing time.

Why didn't Esrioas help them?

"Probably because they wouldn't let her!" Harpur said out loud in answer to his question.

There really was only one choice.

"I won't have Hart's death on my conscience too."

Harpur conjured a pen and some paper and scribbled a note directing Arthur and the others to return to Epoh and wait for him there. He looked at it in dismay; his once elegant handwriting was replaced with a jerky scrawl. But it was—more or less—legible.

"Penmanship will have to wait. I'm coming, Hart!"

He zapped himself to the Boundary on the roof top across Whyte Avenue and leapt into its centre. Using his magic, he unlocked the Boundary house door and stepped into the small clearing in Braydon Wood. Taking a moment to breathe in the familiar scent of the woods, he turned to relock the door. A glint of reflected sunlight coming from the large oak caught his eye, and he looked up to see Anayah's urn nestled in the hole in the trunk.

"Damn it, Davynn! Couldn't you have waited just a while longer?"

There was no time to linger, though. He would have to return later to pay his respects. If he could…

Harpur moved away from the Boundary house, transformed, and flexed his wings. *This ought to be interesting*, he thought as he bunched up his haunches and sprang into the air.

Penmanship was not the only thing his new body needed improvement on. While his mind knew exactly what to do, his wings did not have enough strength to keep him in the air. The hatchling's confinement in the lair had, as Bon had predicted, stunted his wings' development. There was no way he was going to be able to fly all the way to Averborn; he would have to zap himself there.

Finding Hart standing in the centre of the Labyrinth was a huge relief. Meg was there, looking harried while her brother—the one in danger—comforted her.

"How're you doing?" Harpur asked the stoic black dragon.

"Who are you?" Hart replied.

"That's Harpur," Meg said.

Hart frowned. "I pictured him bigger."

Harpur quelled his annoyance and ignored the thoughtless jibe at his appearance. "So, why didn't you do as you were told and get a heart for the offering?"

Hart frowned. "I was hoping that Esrioas would have an alternative. Barring that, I thought that my sister, the goddess, could fix me."

"Even goddesses have their limitations," Harpur said. "Did you even try, Meg?"

Meg looked uncomfortable. "I think something went wrong when Isenwylm accepted me. It's kind of like I am two dragons now, but the Ice Dragon part of me is… sort of stuck behind the fire dragon part of me. I can't seem to get all the Ice Dragon stuff to work properly all the time."

Interesting…

Harpur didn't know enough about Ice Dragons to be certain of what had happened to Meg. If Isenwylm had accepted her, which it clearly did, she should

502

have all the powers of an Ice Dragon. Hopefully, this was just a matter of her being inexperienced and she would eventually learn how to use her powers to their full extent. For now, though, it seemed that she had become a semi-demi-goddess. And Hart would just have to suck it up and kill another dragon to harvest its heart.

Seemed simple enough.

"You're just going to have to find a dragon heart, Hart," Harpur said.

"I am not going to kill a dragon!"

"Esrioas offered to let him kill her, but…," Meg said.

"She didn't offer to let me kill her," Hart said with strained patience. "She offered to let me fight her to the death."

"So, what's the problem?" Harpur asked. "That's her job."

Hart glared at the small, purple dragon. "Go away!"

Harpur rolled his eyes and turned to Meg. "Go get Esrioas and bring her back here."

"I can't just leave Hart," Meg said.

"I will stay with Hart. Go get Esrioas."

When Meg didn't move, Harpur lost his temper. "I may look like a juvenile dragon. But let me remind you that I know a thing or two more than you two do about being any kind of dragon. Now, get your ass in the air and go get Esrioas!"

"Watch your tone with me, buster," Meg growled across the pool, "or I'll…"

Harpur watched as Meg tried to reconcile the words that came out of her mouth. She was aghast at her own audacity, so he knew he just had to stand his ground.

And hope that the Ice Dragon in her didn't suddenly get unstuck.

"Or you'll what?" Harpur challenged.

Meg's bravado faltered as Hart nudged her with his wing. "Just be glad that my father likes you. If it wasn't for that, I'd…" Another, harder, nudge made her stop talking.

Harpur cocked his head and leaned toward her, silently calling her bluff.

"Fine!" Meg huffed. "I'll go get her!"

She didn't wait for a reply.

"You know, she's as scared as I am?" Hart said after Meg had flown far enough away that he felt comfortable confessing his fears.

"Of course, she is," Harpur said as gently as he could. "She doesn't want to lose her brother."

"I'm not a fighter, Harpur," Hart said. "And I'm not a killer."

"All dragons are fighters," Harpur said. "And they only kill if it's necessary."

"But I'm not a dragon. Not really." Hart trained his eyes on his sister's shrinking form in the sky. "I'm a sixteen-year-old kid who likes science. That's who I am."

"That's who you were," Harpur said. "But now you're more than that. And you can still do that too."

Hart didn't respond.

And Harpur didn't push. He had to find a way to convince Hart that his fate was sealed. He'd worry about dealing with the overwhelming remorse he felt later. Right now, though, he had to figure out how to stop Hart from making things worse. For everyone.

"Why did you do this to us?" Hart asked, breaking the silence. He looked directly at the small purple dragon.

Harpur sighed heavily. "I thought I was doing a good thing," he said. "I knew that I wasn't going to be around to see you and Meg grow up; I wanted to protect you."

"There's a very fine line between helping and interfering, isn't there?"

"Finer than I realized," Harpur admitted. "I am sorry for what I did to you."

Hart snorted. "If I do this... If I kill Esrioas and take her heart, will you swear to leave Epoh forever and never interfere with any of us again?"

Harpur's heart lurched in his chest. "If that is what you want, I swear it."

"Tell me how to kill her."

Arthur read the note that Harpur had left for them in the lair.

504

The library had been closed when they arrived. It was, after all, far too early in the day for it to be open. Arthur had zapped himself inside anyway, and with the help of his magic, had managed to boot up a public computer and access the Internet. Thankfully, Google was still a thing; he did a quick search and found three venues where magic shows were taking place in the city. By process of elimination, he chose the one that was most likely to include an illusion involving a large, doorless cage. It was scheduled to take place at a little theatre just off Whyte Avenue.

When he and the others arrived there, a police vehicle was parked by the front entrance and two officers were scolding two stage hands for wasting their time. It seemed that they were not happy about being called out to investigate a teenager who allegedly vanished into thin air after appearing out of thin air with a large cage.

"He must have gone back to the lair," Arthur deduced—correctly, as it turned out.

They found the note on the table, and eagerly agreed to follow the directions Harpur had left for them.

Until, that is, Hiro refused to leave without his hover gilly. "I can't just leave it here."

"You said it's not fixable," Sok argued. "Can't you just get a new one?"

"It's not that simple," Hiro said. "Hover gillies are divinely constructed. The only way I can get a new one is if Meg and Hart are really gods and will make one for me. Or fix this one."

"I'm sure they'll be happy to make you a new one," Arthur said. "And if they aren't, I'll tell them they have to."

Sok laughed. "You think you will be able to order demi-gods around. Just because they are your children, Arthur, doesn't mean they will obey you."

"It's not like we have to carry it," Morgaine said. "We can zap it back with us and Hiro can ask Meg and Hart to mend it or replace it."

"So, you got that from a god?" Arthur asked.

"I am acquainted with a variety of deities," Hiro said. "But none of them ever come to Thraeh."

Arthur and Sok eyed the mangled hover gilly, wondering who would get to toss it through the Boundary.

"If you two will be so kind as to carry my equipment," Bon said, "I will carry the hover gilly."

He didn't have to ask them twice! The king and the elf took the boxes and bags from the android and left the zapping to Morgaine, who got them all to, and through, the Boundary, and then on to the castle. When they reached the council chambers, the dragon-wizard announced that she would go on to Andonsheer, so as not to arouse Glynnis' suspicions, and that Harpur could meet her there when he was ready to face the Dragon Council.

She left in a puff of teal smoke and the others settled into chairs around the table while Hiro dispensed a hearty snack of meat and cheese and bread and ale from his satchel.

"It's good to be home," Arthur said, raising his cup to the others.

"I wonder where Harpur is," Sok said.

"I wonder where my kids are," Arthur said.

"They are at Averborn," Bon said, "becoming Ice Dragons."

"Of course, they are." Arthur sipped his ale. Then he turned to Bon. "I think I might need something a little stronger than this. Bon, would you mind getting the whiskey?"

As the android left to stow his equipment in the laboratory and fetch the whiskey barrel, the door to the council chambers opened. Eowyn stopped dead in his tracks and stared at Arthur, Sok and Hiro while he decided whether he wanted to hug them or hit them.

"Where have you been?"

"Oh, hey, Eowyn!" Arthur said. "I see you kept the castle standing. Thank you."

"It's been days!" Eowyn barked. "I've been going crazy wondering what happened to you."

"Sorry about that," Arthur said. "We didn't mean to be gone that long."

"It was only a day on Earth," Sok observed.

"You went to Earth?! Why?" Veins were popping out on the young man's forehead.

"We figured out that's where Harpur went and we just wanted to make sure everything was okay."

Something caught Eowyn's eye behind Sok and Arthur. He looked up. His eyes grew wide and his mouth dropped open. Slowly, he raised his hand and pointed toward the back of the room.

Sok, Arthur and Hiro followed Eowyn's gaze.

"Anayah!" Sok sang out. "I've been trying to reach you."

Anayah's ghost drifted farther into the room and stopped next to the table on Sok's right. She stared accusingly at the elf.

"Harpur must not die," the apparition said in an eerie voice.

"It's okay, Anayah," Sok said. "Harpur has his own body again. He's going to be fine."

"Harpur must not die," she repeated.

Bon returned with the whiskey barrel and put it down on the table. He immediately started recording the event.

"I thought you said you couldn't summon her," Arthur said. He drained his ale and stood up to fill his cup from the barrel.

"I didn't," Sok said. "And I couldn't. I don't know how she got here."

"Perhaps this has something to do with her appearance," Bon said, extracting Anayah's wedding band from his pocket and holding it up for all to see. "I meant to give it to Davynn, but we left in rather a hurry and I did not get the chance."

Seeing that everyone else was so at ease with a ghost in the room, Eowyn gathered his wits and composed himself. He took a shot of whiskey from Arthur and tossed it back without thinking. His face, pale from the shock of seeing a ghost, turned bright red from the shock of the burning alcohol.

"You okay, there, buddy?" Arthur asked, slapping the captain of the guard on the back to get him breathing again.

"Orhowyn's teeth and talons!" Eowyn wheezed. "What *is* that?"

"Whiskey," Arthur said, taking a prudent sip from his cup.

"Find the walking stick," Anayah moaned.

"We already did!" Sok said. "Harpur has it!"

Anayah's face contorted into a look of horror. "Harpur must not die."

Before anyone could say anything else, Anayah faded away and disappeared.

"Yeah," Arthur said, as he took his seat again, "it's good to be home."

Chapter Twenty-five

Esrioas Grithhall and Meg landed near the entrance to the labyrinth where Hart and Harpur were waiting. It had taken some effort for Meg to convince the silver guardian of the temple to come with her, but Esrioas had finally relented. Since her strange encounter with the strange candidates for Ice Dragons, she had felt somewhat displaced. She had been waiting for the return of the demi-gods for nearly 5,000 years and to have two bumbling human-fire dragon hybrids show up and claim to be Ice Dragons had been a disturbing outcome. That Isenwylm had accepted either of them was peculiar, but having the other one refuse the rite, was beyond the pale.

Now, apparently, he had changed his mind, and since she had taken a vow, she was determined to see this debacle through to its end.

Harpur watched the old, silver dragon land far more gracefully than one of her advanced age should have been capable of. As was customary, he bowed before her. "Esrioas, it is good to see you again."

"You've changed," she said as she folded her wings across her back.

"And you are as beautiful as ever," Harpur said, thankful that she had refrained from commenting on his stature. Esrioas snorted dismissively, but Harpur saw the gleam in her eye. She enjoyed the flattery.

"Shall we get on with it, then?" Esrioas asked, looking at Hart.

Harpur stepped in front of the nervous young dragon. "Hart has been under the protection of the labyrinth. Will he be safe if he comes out to face you in battle?"

"That is a ridiculous question, Harpur Diggins. No dragon is safe in battle until they have won."

"You know what I mean," Harpur said. "Will his condition remain stable until he has faced you?"

Esrioas turned to Harpur. "His *condition*, as you call it, is of your making. Don't you know?"

"If I did, I would not be asking." Harpur forced himself to stay calm. He needed to learn as much as he could before Hart and Esrioas fought.

"A thousand years ago, I warned you to stay out of the affairs of the lesser races. Now, look what your meddling has accomplished. Instead of true Ice Dragons returning to Thraeh, this... this Fae-headed pair of Heartforgers have laid claim to Isenwylm's wisdom and power. You should be locked up, Harpur Diggins! Locked up and forgotten!"

"You will most likely get your wish soon enough," Harpur said.

Esrioas did not comment. She turned her attention back to Hart, sizing him up, looking for weaknesses. She could smell his fear and see it in his eyes. But she would not underestimate him. Hart was young and strong; his fear could be his greatest strength.

She moved away from the labyrinth out into the rock-strewn plane, wondering if this was going to be her last day on Thraeh. Would Hart burn her body if he won? Would Harpur remember what to do with the skulls in the temple? Neither of those things would matter to her if she lost, which she was prepared to do, though not without a fight. If Isenwylm had not accepted the female, she would not be doing this.

No regrets, she thought as she turned to face her opponent.

For a moment, Esrioas was puzzled. She expected to see a full-grown, black dragon ready and waiting to attack her. Instead, a handsome young man with light-brown hair stood twenty-five yards away, aiming a loaded crossbow at her. His hands were shaking, but he had a determined look in his eyes. Then she realized what was happening, and she started to laugh.

"Do you really think that little toy of yours is going to bring me down?"

Esrioas rushed toward Hart, her chest aglow with the dragon fire she intended to burn him to death with. When she got within ten yards of the quaking youth, she drew back her head and opened her mouth to release the flames.

"Now!" Harpur shouted across the distance.

Hart pulled the trigger, loosing the bolt. He didn't wait to see what happened. Wheeling around, he ran as hard and as fast as he could back toward the labyrinth. A short blast of heat from the dragon fire washed over him, but the flames didn't reach him. A loud shriek told him that he'd hit something, but he didn't stop running until he heard the sickening thud of Esrioas' body hitting the ground. When he did look back, Esrioas lay dead with the crossbow bolt sticking out of one eye. Hart dropped to his knees and vomited.

"Well done, son," Harper said as he and Meg approached. "Now you have to harvest her heart."

There was no time for sympathy. Hart needed to cut Esrioas' heart out as quickly as possible. Harpur conjured a dagger and put it into the nauseated prince's hand.

"Do it quickly," Harpur urged.

Hart looked at the blade. He wanted to stick it into Harpur for putting him in this position in the first place, but he stood up and staggered to Esrioas' body.

With a cry of anguish, Hart plunged the blade into her chest. Hacking at the thick, silver scales, he finally managed to expose her heart. He could barely see what he was doing through the tears that cascaded from his eyes, but he pulled the organ out and cut it free without hurting himself. As he passed the others on the way back to the labyrinth, he shoved the bloody dagger back into Harpur's hands.

"Just remember your promise," he snarled.

"What promise?" Meg asked. She watched Hart as he walked purposely on. When Harpur didn't answer, she grabbed his front leg with her talons. "What promise?"

"It's nothing," Harpur said. "Go look after your brother."

Meg wasn't sure what she should do. She wanted to know what Harpur had promised, but Hart looked traumatized and she didn't want to leave him alone. "You will tell me when this is over," she hissed, then turned and followed Hart.

Harpur walked over to Esrioas. "I'm sorry, old friend," he said. "This wasn't how things were supposed to turn out. You did a good thing today, though, saving Hart. Those two are special. Annoying as hell sometimes, but they will do us all proud in the end. You didn't die for nothing."

It took a little more effort than it should have to burn Esrioas' body, but soon enough Harpur's dragon fire reduced it to ash. He watched as a brisk breeze picked up the remains and carried them across the planes. They sparkled silver-grey in the late afternoon sun.

"Safe travels to Arachovor," Harpur whispered.

Harpur was halfway back to the labyrinth when he stopped to watch the twins. It seemed that Hart must have ran the twenty-mile path to the centre, for he and Meg were both standing next to the pool and gazing into the water. Esrioas' heart was nowhere to be seen; Hart must have already made the offering. As he looked on, Meg drew Isenwylm from the scabbard on her back and touched Hart's shoulder with it.

Does she think she is knighting him?

A howl of pain reached Harpur's ears. Hart's black scales were changing colour, and clearly the transformation was not an easy one. Soon, the reluctant fire dragon stood in the centre of Averborn, now a cobalt-blue Ice Dragon.

When the transformation was complete, Meg and Hart both looked over at Harpur. Meg's expression was one of gratitude, a silent acknowledgement of his help in getting Hart to do the terrible thing he had to do to be with her. Hart's eyes, however, were narrowed with contempt. There was no mistaking the message behind the penetrating stare: *You did this to me.*

As much as he wanted to go to them, Harpur realized that Meg and Hart needed space and time to figure out who they were—what they were—now. Eventually, Hart would come around, maybe even forgive Harpur one day. In the meantime, they were both now in possession of powers he didn't understand completely. He could teach them how to be dragons, but he couldn't teach them how to be Ice Dragons. They had to figure that out for themselves. All he could do was hope that they didn't destroy the world in the process.

Harpur wanted to leap into the air and fly dramatically into the sunset, but his wings would not allow that. So, he bowed to the demi-gods, and then zapped himself away from Averborn.

Harpur's appearance in the council chambers was a conversation stopper, to say the least. Arthur and Sok, both well into their cups, and Eowyn, Hiro, and Bon had been debating the meaning behind Anayah's words and the look of horror she had given them upon hearing that Harpur was in possession of the walking stick. They all agreed that the walking stick was somehow intrinsic to Harpur's survival. But how was a mystery to them all. But when a teenage boy, wearing a top hat and an expertly knotted ascot, materialized in almost the exact spot Anayah had appeared, the debate came to an abrupt halt.

"Where's Morgaine?" Harpur demanded as he took a seat at the table. "You were all supposed to wait for me here."

Harpur had decided to take the direct approach and act as if his appearance was completely normal. As frustrating as it was to be trapped in a child's body, he reasoned that, with the aide of magic, his growth would continue to be accelerated, and he would not look like a "a boy wearing his father's clothes" much longer.

Arthur leaned toward Sok. "Is that Harpur?" he slurred.

"I think so," the elf replied.

"Ask him where the twins are," Arthur said.

"Where are the twins?" Sok obeyed.

"Are you two drunk?" Harpur looked at the whiskey barrel, then back at the inebriated pair.

Arthur thought about it for a few moments. "Yes!" he said. "We are drunk."

Harpur shook his head. He addressed his next question to the three sober members of the assembly. "Do you know where Morgaine is?"

"She has gone on to Andonsheer," Bon provided the answer. "She felt it was prudent not to stay in Epoh and risk drawing the attention of Glynnis. She asked that we tell you to meet her there."

That made perfect sense. Harpur, too, did not want to stay in Epoh any longer than he had to. But he did want to make sure that everyone had gotten safely back to the castle. He also wanted to talk to Bon about the twins.

Something wasn't right. Ice Dragons were supposed to be pale-blue, as if they were made of ice. The darker, albeit appealing, cobalt colouring that Meg and Hart had adopted was unexpected and troublesome, especially when paired with Meg's admission that her Ice Dragon powers felt like they were stuck behind her fire dragon powers. The fact that Isenwylm had accepted her was a good sign, but it was of small comfort if she couldn't properly access her powers, much less understand them.

"Bon, I need you to do something for me," Harpur continued.

"If I can," Bon said.

Harpur explained the anomaly to the android. "Try to find out what might be happening to the twins. I'd be very grateful."

Bon immediately started scanning his files.

"Eowyn," Harpur said to the new captain of the guard, "I may not be able to return to Epoh after I face the Dragon Council. But I suspect that things here will be quite different in the coming months. You need to be prepared."

Eowyn's brows furrowed. "What do you mean?"

"I wish I knew," Harpur replied. "It's just a feeling I have. Promise me that you will stay alert, though. Make sure that the royal guard is ready for… anything."

Taking orders from a kid rankled at first. Eowyn had to remind himself that the boy, so earnest and   intense, was actually a mature and long-lived dragon. "I need something more," he said. A feeling was not enough information to act on.

"I can't give you more," Harpur admitted. "But get Davynn to help you. He's good at anticipating the unexpected."

"Even if Sir Davynn was here," Eowyn began defensively, "he no longer leads the guards."

"Davynn is gone?" Harpur asked. "Where is he?"

"He's taken his family to live at his holdings in Branwyke," Eowyn said. "Elder Dhonna will be joining him there after she knows you are alright. I believe she is waiting for the results of your meeting with the Dragon Council."

Harpur was taken aback by this news. *Elder Dhonna leaving the Healing Guild? Davynn moved to Branwyke?* He wouldn't be more surprised if Arthur were to abdicate and Sok became the king.

"I see," he said. "That is interesting."

"Elder Dhonna would be grateful if you were to go and see her," Eowyn suggested.

"I will do my best," Harpur said.

There was no time for that now, though. Harpur needed to get to Andonsheer and keep his promise to Khol the Black. He stood up and pushed his chair in, preparing to leave. "Try to get these two up to their rooms." He pointed at Arthur and Sok, who were singing an off-key version of a song about lost salt shakers and misplaced blame. How Sok knew the lyrics to the classic rock song from Earth was anybody's guess.

"We'll take care of them," Eowyn assured the youthful dragon-wizard.

Bon snapped out of scanning mode. "There is very little information on the Ice Dragons. They are, as you know, demi-gods. I did find evidence of an incompatibility between fire dragon physiology and that of an Ice Dragon. According to the lore, if an Ice Dragon possess the body of a fire dragon, their magic will conflict, resulting in a gruesome death for the fire dragon. However, there is a ritual that allows the power of the Ice Dragon to exist alongside the magic of the fire dragon. Unfortunately, the two cannot combine. There will always be a division, between them, as if the Ice Dragon part is the alter ego of the original fire dragon."

Harpur exhaled sharply and ran his hand across the back of his neck.

"…But it's my own damn fault!" Arthur finished the song and held up his cup to clink it with Sok's.

That was Harpur's cue to get moving. *I wish I was in Margaritaville.* He thanked Bon and Eowyn, and asked Bon to impart that information to the twins, should they come back to Epoh. And then he zapped himself out of the council chambers.

The scrubby forest that stretched between the southern mountains of Epoh and the vast desert of the Sands of Sancheera provided Harpur with the privacy he needed to learn to fly. He would not zap himself into the compound to face the Dragon Council. His pride would not allow him to do that.

It took three days to get his wings to begin to cooperate. The first day was spent hopping from hill to hill, clearing to clearing, with more than a few crash landings when his wings gave out. The problem, he soon realized, was that he was growing too fast. His wings did not have the time to adapt to his constantly changing weight. Compressing a dozen years of growth into a few short days without the benefit of any flying practice to develop them, his wings could not keep up.

By the end of the third day, however, Harpur's cloned body seemed to have reached its full size. Still, he could only fly short distances and he didn't dare attempt altitudes of more than a couple hundred feet. It was an improvement, though, and he felt confident enough to move forward with calling the Dragon Council to hear his case.

First, though, he had to send word to Kohl the Black. He had promised to let him know when he was ready to face the Dragon Council. He composed a missive and zapped it to Rednow, hoping that the black dragon would respond right away.

He found Morgaine in the Andonsheer market, sitting on a bench, looking annoyed. He sat down beside her and rested both of his hands on the top of the walking stick.

"It's about time," the dragon-wizardess said.

"You recognized me?" Harpur wasn't sure if he was pleased or disappointed. He no longer looked like a boy, which did please him. His human guise was now that of a young man in his early twenties.

"The top hat and walking stick gave it away," Morgaine said. "How do you want to do this?"

Straight to the point. Harpur admired that about her. "I guess we wait for Kohl and then call the council and wait for them to convene."

"I've already alerted them," Morgaine said. "They can convene today."

"Efficient, aren't you?" Harpur said, wondering why she bothered to ask him how he wanted to proceed.

"I just don't see any point in delaying the..."

"Inevitable?" Harpur finished for her. "So, you believe they will rule against me?"

"How could they not?" Morgaine said. "You took over my body. You took over my life. That is a crime, Harpur."

Harpur sighed. "You are right. But there is something you aren't saying. What is it?"

Morgaine closed her eyes to keep her emotions from showing in them. "I know why you did it. I know that you were not trying to hurt me. If things had worked out the way you thought they would, I actually would have had a better life, even if I wasn't in control of it. You have a special way of looking at life. You taught me what it means to care about others. I would not have looked after the people of Epoh the way you did."

Harpur sighed. "I'm not sure I deserve your forgiveness after everything I put you through, but thank you, Karrys Evergreen. Your kindness means more than you will ever know."

Morgaine opened her eyes and stared at Harpur. "Why did you call me Karrys?"

"Because that's who you are." Harpur stood up and held out his arm for the dragon-wizardess. "Shall we?"

"I'm going to fight for you, Xzynthyrius Dreamfinder."

There were only a few dragons in the compound when Harpur and Karrys arrived. A couple dozen mingled in small groups within the enclosure, while Themeela Sandward, Durnor Hornblower, and Framanjesk stood on the dais against the eastern wall. No one recognized the great purple dragon with the red streaks through his scales who stepped up to the dais where dragons accused of crimes faced the council.

Harpur said nothing. Protocol demanded that the Chair of the Dragon Council convene the trial and address him first. Themeela, though, had no idea what the trial was about, or what crime the dragon before her might have committed. All Karrys had told them was that the matter concerned Harpur Diggins and that they needed to hear a confession. Curiosity, more than anything, caused the council members to agree to convene.

"I call this… meeting to order," Themeela called out. There was no formal accusation of a crime, so she could hardly declare it a trial. "We will now hear from the… this dragon who stands before us. What is your name, and what do you have to confess?"

"My name is Xzynthyrius Dreamfinder," Harpur said. "I am here to confess to a crime I committed sixteen years ago and throw myself upon the mercy of the Dragon Council. However, we are waiting for Kohl the Black to arrive before I begin."

A stunned silence filled the compound. The only sound was the shuffling of feet and wings as the dragons who had come to witness the mysterious trial moved in closer behind Harpur. While Themeela and Durnor's mouths gaped open in disbelief, Framanjesk's gaze shifted to Karrys, watching her reaction closely.

"You are not Xzynthyrius Dreamfinder! He is long dead, killed by Karrys Evergreen in a challenge for the Kingdom of Epoh. What game are you playing at? Who are you?" Themeela was incensed at the nerve of this stranger to the Sands of Sancheera.

"Hear me out," Harpur said. "I beg of you."

Framanjesk looked at the dragon who was claiming to be his father. The resemblance to Harpur was obvious. But for the colouring of his scales, the dragon could be who he said he was. "Let him speak," he said to Themeela. "I am curious about what he has to say."

"Very well." Themeela stepped back. "What is this crime you claim to have committed?"

Harpur scanned the skies, hoping to see Kohl the Black. The Dragon Lord of Rednow was gliding over Andonsheer, much to Harpur's relief. He hadn't expected Karrys to call the council; she knew that Kohl was to be notified first. But he understood her need to get this over with.

The previous Chair of the Dragon Council landed and moved up to stand behind Harpur and Karrys. His presence seemed to calm Themeela. Whatever this turned out to be about, with Kohl involved, she would defer to his recommendation if things proved to be more complicated than she expected.

Harpur, after receiving a nod of encouragement from Karrys, stood up tall and cleared his throat. He told his story from the beginning when he first met Arthur on Whyte Avenue and how he had then gone to live on Earth so he could keep an eye on the unwitting wizard. He included pretending to get Edlyngton Bloomregaard's permission to do so in order to keep his magic secret from the humans in Epoh. He recounted how Arthur had walked into a burning dragonfoil tree and came out unscathed due to having been resurrected with Harpur's blood, and how that had led to Arthur becoming king. He told them about Alex and the twins and how he had placed the wrong sigil on their foreheads. Then he described how Arthur had used the Amber Chalice to transfer his spirit into Karrys' body, and how he had then fled to the world where they had been held prisoner and tortured. He concluded his tale with an explanation of how Bon had used technology to create a clone, which was why his colouring was slightly different from his old body.

When, at last, he finished talking, another prolonged silence befell the compound. No one so much as twitched for so long that Harpur began to wonder if he had bored them all to death.

Then Durnor stepped forward. "So, you claim that you used necromancy to bring a human back from the dead, you then brought that human and his mate from his world to ours, along with a witch, a machine man, and a Krist—whatever that is—from a different world. You allowed the human to become the king in your Kingdom, and you brought technology from other worlds. You used a forbidden sigil on human infants, who you now say are Ice Dragons. You stole the body of another dragon so you could keep living and remain the Dragon Lord of Epoh. But you ended up a prisoner on another world until you miraculously escaped. And then you had this machine man you say you brought here make you a new body from a stolen dragon egg and transfer your spirit out of Karrys and into it? Is that all that you've done?"

"I think that about sums it up," Harpur said.

Durnor and Themeela looked at each other in disbelief. Then they burst into uncontrollable, almost maniacal laughter.

"That's the most absurd story I've ever heard!" Themeela cackled.

Behind Harpur, the other dragons that were present also started to laugh. Except for Kohl. The black dragon winced at the way his kind were behaving. On the dais, Framanjesk seemed to share Kohl's feelings on the matter and looked with disgust at his fellow council members.

Orhowyn, let this humiliation be my punishment, Harpur thought as he stood there waiting for everyone to settle down again.

Karrys moved closer and stood next to Harpur in a show of support.

Framanjesk studied Harpur, looking for any indication of insincerity. If only half of what the purple-red dragon had said was true, he deserved to be punished. But were any of his actions actually crimes? Taking over Karrys' body was deplorable. But what actual harm had he directly caused her? If everyone would just stop laughing, he would ask the teal dragon for her opinion.

Then there was the matter of the purple-red dragon's real identity. He was barely past drathescence, though he comported himself like a seasoned and experienced dragon—like Harpur Diggins. And it was clear that the mocking laughter was being stoically endured. This was a dragon with pride and dignity. Again, like Harpur Diggins.

Framanjesk was torn. If this was his father, he needed proof. The story was outlandish, but not outside the realm of possibility where Harpur Diggins was concerned. Everyone knew how unconventional the great purple dragon was. But, if he got sufficient proof, should he make an example of Harpur? Or should he defend him and let him live? There was much to consider, much to unravel. *And what role did Kohl the Black play in all of this?*

"Enough!" Framanjesk shouted over the din. "I want to hear from Karrys Evergreen."

"Don't be ridiculous, Framanjesk," Themeela scoffed. "This poor creature before us is clearly delusional. We should lock him in the cells for a moon cycle for wasting our time. Though we should also thank him for the entertaining afternoon he provided. I see no point in listening to anything Karrys has to share. In fact, she could benefit from a night or two in the cells as well."

Karrys scowled at the Dragon Council Chair. "I have done nothing wrong!"

"I thought you were going to fight for me," Harpur whispered.

"Sorry," Karrys said. "I didn't mean…"

"I know what you meant," Harpur assured her. "This isn't going the way I expected it to."

"Does that surprise you?"

Harpur didn't answer.

"Still, I would like to hear what Karrys has to say," Framanjesk insisted. "Why did you call us here, Karrys? What is this dragon to you?"

"He is my friend!" Karrys said without hesitation. "I want to see him vindicated. What he has told you is all true."

"I would think," Framanjesk said, "that you would be angry about having your life stolen from you in such an unsavory manner. Yet you call Harpur Diggins your friend. I'm confused, Karrys Evergreen. Why do you not seek revenge? Is it perhaps because this is not Harpur Diggins?"

"I assure you this is Harpur Diggins," Karrys said. "And I don't want revenge. The last sixteen years sharing his mind, I have learned the histories of places I would never have seen on my own. I have gained insight into the world and lives of humans, elves and dwarves... even the Fae. I've been privileged to see a different perspective. Harpur Diggins may have taken away my choice, but he gave me so much more in return."

Harpur was humbled by Karrys' speech. If she had these thoughts when his spirit was in her body, she had somehow kept them largely to herself. He shifted his wing to touch hers; he wasn't sure he could speak without losing his composure.

Framanjesk still detected no insincerity. But, as touching as all this was, it wasn't proof. "I think you are right, Themeela," he said. "A night or two in the cells will do them both good."

Harpur groaned, and Karrys gasped.

"Finally," Themeela said, "someone's making sense!"

"Have I been found guilty, then?" Harpur asked.

"Durnor looked at Harpur. "You come here claiming to be Xzynthyrius Dreamfinder—who we know has been dead for some time—and regale us with a fantastical tale of necromancy and body-snatching. The only thing you are guilty of is having a vivid imagination. Let him go."

"I believe what my esteemed fellow council member means is that your story is intriguing. I think we need to talk to a few of your friends, get their side of things." Framanjesk watched Harpur closely and was not disappointed to see a flash of fear in his eyes.

"There is no need for that," Kohl said, stepping forward. "Leave the citizens of Epoh out of this."

"Why is that?" Framanjesk said. "Will they not back him up? Or are you afraid that they will?"

"I couldn't care less about the citizens of Epoh," Kohl said. "They are Glynnis' to deal with. I know that this dragon is telling the truth. And I believe that you do as well, Framanjesk. Karrys has confirmed it, make your decision."

Themeela and Durnor looked at the son of Xzynthyrius Dreamfinder. Neither of them knew what to do. Both hoped that Kohl's interference would be enough for the younger member of the Dragon Council.

"They might enjoy a trip to the south!" Framanjesk said. "Don't worry, *Xzynthyrius*, we won't harm them."

Harpur and Karrys were marched to the cells and locked in. As a concession to their cooperation, they were not fitted with the magic-dampening collars.

"Framanjesk?" Harpur called as the green dragon retreated from the cells.

"What is it?"

"Your name means free to follow one's heart."

Framanjesk stopped. Only the real Xzynthyrius Dreamfinder would know that. Framanjesk was a name made up by his mother, Karryl. As was his brother's, Phiercesten (to rule with honour). They had taken them as their first names in honour of the stories Karryl had told them when they were still hatchlings.

Why you wily old wyrm!

Framanjesk continued on his way. He would bring his father's friends from Epoh regardless. It would buy him time to think of a way to make sure Harpur was— as Karrys wished—vindicated.

Arthur woke up unable to tell the pounding in his head from the pounding at his door. A piteous moan escaped his dry lips as he attempted to roll over and pull a pillow over his head.

That was a mistake.

The covers flew off and Arthur jumped out of bed. He flung open his bedroom door, nearly ran over Sok, who was the cause of the pounding on the door, and dashed across the sitting room to the bathroom where he threw up into the sink.

"Are you ill?" Sok said from the bathroom doorway.

"Aren't you?" Arthur groaned. And threw up again.

"I feel fine. Did you eat something that didn't agree with you? Perhaps I should engage a taste tester."

"I don't need a taste tester," Arthur growled. "It's called a hangover. You should be feeling at least as bad as I do."

"I can't imagine why," Sok said. "But you need to get well soon. Glynnis is circling."

"Tell him I'm sick," Arthur said, pressing his sweaty face against the cool stone wall.

"I would but…" Sok tried to think of a good way to tell Arthur what was going on. "Actually, you need to come see this for yourself."

"See what?" Arthur groaned again.

Sok entered the bathroom and pulled Arthur away from the wall. With his hands on the king's shoulders, the elf steered him through the sitting room and out onto the balcony. "That!" Sok lifted Arthur's chin and directed his face in the direction he needed him to look.

It took a while for Arthur's eyes to focus. And when they did, his hangover was instantly cured.

"Orhowyn's rotting innards! That's not good, Sok."

"It's definitely not normal," Sok said.

Glynnis was, indeed, circling above the city in lazy circles. There was no urgency in the slow pumping of his wings. He seemed to be enjoying a casual flight above his kingdom under the clear blue late-spring sky. He spotted Arthur on the balcony and a sinister smile spread across his face.

"We're waiting," he called out.

We being the operative word in that brief declaration. Glynnis was accompanied by five other dragons.

Arthur turned away from the unprecedented flight of dragons circling over his city and went to his bed chamber to change. He'd have liked to have had a bath before facing the Dragon Lord and his entourage, but a fresh shirt and clean pants was the best he could do. As he led Sok out of his private rooms, he conjured two cups of jamba.

"No bacon?" Sok asked as he took the warm beverage from Arthur.

"How can you eat after last night?" Arthur's stomach was still protesting the previous evening's over-indulgence in whiskey.

"It's morning. I'm hungry," Sok said.

"Well, I'm impressed. Elves must have a much higher tolerance for alcohol than humans." Arthur conjured a rasher of bacon for his second in command.

They made their way through the empty streets to the gate. The appearance of six dragons had sent the citizenry of Colwygshire running for cover. A few brave souls peeked out through their windows, and Sok and Arthur waved cheerfully, hoping to put their minds at ease. For the most part, they got nothing more than dirty looks in return.

The gate was locked and there was no guard in the guard house. While Sok looked for the key, Arthur looked for the guard. He found him cowering in a closet.

"What are you doing in there?" Arthur demanded. "And why did you close the gate?"

"There are six dragons out there!" the guard said with a shaky voice as if that explained everything.

"You do realize that if they were going to attack the city, they wouldn't be coming in through the gate, right?" The guard blinked at the king. "And with the gate locked, no one could get out."

"I didn't think of that," the guard said. He sidled out of the closet past Arthur and handed a set of keys to Sok.

"Do you guys not pay attention during training?" Sok mocked, taking the keys and exiting the guard house to open the gate.

As usual whenever Glynnis summoned them, Sok and Arthur turned to the left and followed the city wall to the open field. They walked through the tall grass, still kissed with morning dew, and stopped about ten yards away from the bronze dragon. Behind him, a green, a white, a red, a brown, and an orange dragon stood in a line. Each of them looked uncomfortable to be there.

"Good morning, oh, wise and powerful Dragon Lord," Arthur called out. "What brings you and your friends to our fair city?"

"Your presence is required in Andonsheer," Glynnis said. "My *friends* are here to take you and the elf, the android and the Krist, the knight and the witch, the prince and the princess, and the elf who goes by the name of Elder Dhonna to the dragon compound to answer to the Dragon Council. Where are the others?"

Arthur and Sok exchanged curious looks. This had to have something to do with Harpur.

"On behalf of myself and the others, I must respectfully decline your invitation," Arthur said. "If the Dragon Council wants to speak to us, they can come here and do it."

Sok held his breath and watched the five strange dragons. The green, white and red ones seemed to take exception to Arthur's flippant dismissal of Glynnis' command.

"I think they are here," Sok whispered to Arthur.

"I think so too," Arthur whispered back.

They both knew that the dragons could hear them. The whispering was for effect. And by the look on Glynnis' face, they could tell that he wanted to impress the Dragon Council. Sok and Arthur took a good measure of satisfaction from seeing him fail.

"It was not an invitation!" Glynnis roared. "Gather the others and prepare to go to Andonsheer."

Arthur took several steps to his right, looking past Glynnis at the green, white and red dragons. "You three are the Dragon Council, am I right?"

Framanjesk, Themeela and Durnor all looked at each other, stunned by the human king's insolence. And Glynnis' tolerance of it!

Themeela stepped forward. "You have been asked nicely to gather your people and prepare to come with us," she said. "We will not ask again."

"Or," Arthur said, picking a piece of imaginary lint from the sleeve of his shirt, "you can tell us what this is all about."

Themeela drew her head back. The orange glow of her dragon fire bloomed across her chest.

"Arthur," Sok hissed a warning through clenched teeth.

Framanjesk, ever the diplomat, stepped forward as well. "You must be Arthur. I believe that you were a friend of my father's. Harpur Diggins?"

"I was," Arthur admitted casually. "What of it?"

"A dragon has come to us, claiming to be Harpur Diggins. We simply wish for you and your people to come with us to either corroborate or refute his claim. We promise that no harm will come to any of you. Once you have told us your side of the story, we will return you safely to your home here in the beautiful Kingdom of Epoh." Framanjesk smiled in a friendly manner.

"Save your used-car-salesman schtick for someone else," Arthur said, eliciting six plumes of colourful smoke from the assembly of dragons. "I will go with you, but you are to leave the others alone."

"This is not a negotiation!" Glynnis snarled in a last-ditch attempt at impressing the Dragon Council.

"And we are not at your beck and call, Glynnis!" Arthur snapped. "As the Dragon Lord of Epoh, you are sworn to protect us. Yet here you are, allowing five strange dragons to enter Epoh and permitting them to spirit us away without even bothering to inform us what this is all about. I have offered to go with them. Take it or leave it!"

Sok wanted to disappear. He made a mental note to stop accompanying Arthur to these meetings with Glynnis. One of these days, Arthur was going to get him fried.

To his great relief, the green dragon with the diplomatic personality, agreed with Arthur. "The human makes a good point. We apologize for the intrusion. But it is a matter of some urgency. I'm sure you can appreciate that we cannot have one of our kind going around claiming to be someone he's not. We will take you with us for now. But if you cannot satisfy our need for answers, we will return for the others. Do we have an accord?"

Arthur pretended to consider the green dragon's proposal. "I need to confer with my Hand first."

"With his what?" Themeela asked in confusion as Arthur and Sok walked a short distance away and commenced arguing.

Framanjesk was more baffled about something else. "What is a used-car-salesman schtick?"

Glynnis sighed. "Who knows? He says weird things like that all time. I think he makes it up just to irritate me."

"Whatever he means," Durnor said, "you have to admire his courage."

"Indeed," Framanjesk agreed.

Arthur and Sok's conflict finally ended and Arthur returned to address the green dragon. "How long should I expect to be away?" he asked.

"If all goes well, we should be able to have you home in a day or two," Framanjesk answered.

"Jeez-Louise!" Arthur exclaimed, adding to the dragons' collective confusion. "How many questions do you have for me?"

"As many as we need to get to the bottom of things," Themeela replied.

"All right," Arthur said. "I just need another quick word with Sok. Be right back."

"This is why I never challenged anyone for a kingdom," Themeela said. "I'd kill all the lesser races within a moon cycle."

The brown and orange dragons were growing increasingly anxious. They didn't like being in another dragon's kingdom and the bizarre antics of the human and the elf were grating on their nerves. They asked to be dismissed and took off as soon as Themeela said they could go.

"I'll only be gone for one or two days," Arthur said to Sok.

"I don't like this, Arthur. What if you get into trouble down there?"

"At the first sign of a problem, I'll zap myself back here. Don't worry, Sok. What could possibly go wrong?"

So many things! Sok thought as Arthur turned away again.

"Okay, who gets to fly me back to Andonsheer?" Arthur said.

"It will be my pleasure," Framanjesk replied.

Prudently, Sok didn't wait for Arthur and the Dragon Council to leave. He had no intention of sticking around to deal with Glynnis on his own. Besides, he needed to try to find Meg and Hart and send them to Andonsheer to keep an eye on Arthur.

While all around him, people were panicking and running for cover, Jack y Lebard had stood outside of Skull's Keep watching the six dragons circling above the city. They hadn't seemed the least bit interested in attacking Colwygshire. Only Glynnis kept looking toward the castle, waiting, Jack assumed, for the king to make an appearance.

Of all the odd things that had been happening recently, this was the oddest. Five strange dragons within the borders of Epoh? He had to find out what this meant.

By the time he reached the market, it was all but deserted. A few vendors refused to leave their valuable wares unattended and had stayed, but otherwise not a soul was to be seen. He nodded at them as he rushed past, not stopping to ask if they knew what was going on. When he reached the main road from the castle to the gate, the dragons were all descending to land in the field on the south side of the city. From where he entered the broad roadway, he saw Arthur and Sok opening the gate and going through it to meet the dragons. Reasoning that they would not do this if they thought the city was in danger, Jack continued down the road arriving at the gate at about the same time Arthur and Sok stepped away from the dragons to argue about who should or should not go to Andonsheer.

"Halt!" the guard said as Jack was about to pass through the gate. "I can't let you go out there."

"Why not?" Jack asked.

"There are dragons out there!" the guard said as if he was talking to a child. "It's not safe. I will have to ask you to return to your home and stay there until the situation has been resolved."

Jack stroked his chin. "I wasn't aware that there was a situation," he said.

The guard eyed the publican suspiciously. "I just told you that there are dragons out there. That is the situation."

"Look, son," Jack said kindly, "I know you're just doing your job, but I think I can take care of myself."

He continued toward the gate.

"If you take one more step," the guard said, "I will arrest you."

Jack stopped and turned back to the guard. "For what?"

"For disobeying an order from a member of the royal guard," the guard said. He tried to sound authoritative, but the fact that six fire-breathing dragons stood only a few yards away made it difficult.

Jack didn't have a chance to respond. Sok ran back through the gate and kept running as he shouted to the guard, "They're leaving. You can go back to sleep now!"

The guard's cheeks burned red.

"Never mind," Jack said. "I don't want to go out anymore."

He ran after Sok, but the agile elf was faster than Jack and the publican couldn't keep up. He made it less than halfway to the castle before Sok vanished through the tall, arched doors.

Resting his hands on his knees while he caught his breath, Jack wondered what had happened to Arthur. *Why didn't the king come back with the elf?* Looking to the south, he could see three of the dragons flying away from the city. They were some distance away already, but he could see something in the green dragon's talons. *Is that the king?*

Jack decided that it was time to get some answers. He walked the rest of the way to the castle and went inside to look for Sok.

Chapter Twenty-six

Arthur was deposited inside the compound and told to wait in front of the platform. The oppressive heat of the desert and the jungle that the compound was sandwiched between bore down on him. He thought about conjuring a water skin and maybe a chair and an umbrella to shade him from the sun, but he didn't want to use his magic in front of the Dragon Council. At least not yet.

While Themeela and Durnor took their place on the dais, Framanjesk walked toward an enormous structure on the north side of the compound. Arthur deduced that must be where Harpur was being held. He was proven right when, a short time later, Framanjesk emerged from the structure, followed by a much larger Harpur. And Karrys. Arthur tried to keep his expression neutral as the three dragons made their way across the compound and took their places, Framanjesk on the platform, and Harpur and Karrys on either side of Arthur, solving the shade problem for him rather nicely.

"Are you alright?" Harpur asked.

"I could use some water," Arthur said.

"This man is not used to the heat. Could someone please bring him some water?" Harpur asked.

Themeela scowled. Humans were such a nuisance. She dispatched a nearby dragon to fetch Arthur some water.

"Where are the others?" Harpur asked Arthur.

"No one else was available," Arthur said. "You're stuck with me."

The dragon that Themeela had sent for the water returned and handed a flask to Harpur, who, in turn, handed it to Arthur. It was cold and wet, but it tasted awful. Arthur spit it out on the ground and earned himself a threatening glare from Durnor.

"Is something wrong?" the white dragon asked.

"Yeah," Arthur said, "it tastes like a swamp." He placed the flask down on the front edge of the dais. "I'll manage without."

Harpur pretended not to have noticed.

The compound was filling with dragons. Word had spread about Harpur's confessions and now that the Dragon Council had reconvened, more of the colourful beasts had come to see what the outcome would be.

Finally, Themeela called the meeting to order and introduced Arthur as the King of Humans in the Kingdom of Epoh and stated that he was there to assist the council in determining the veracity of the, as of yet, unknown dragon's claims.

"Do you know this dragon?" Themeela asked Arthur.

"I do," Arthur said.

"Well? Who is he?" Themeela was already exasperated.

Arthur looked up at Harpur, who nodded for him to answer. "His name is Harpur Diggins."

Murmurs rippled through the dragons behind him.

"Are you certain that this is Harpur Diggins?" Themeela asked.

"I am."

"Did Harpur Diggins not die in a challenge for rulership over Epoh some years ago?" Framanjesk asked.

"He did."

"So, this is not Harpur Diggins," Framanjesk said.

"No, this is Harpur Diggins," Arthur insisted.

"Is he the *same* Harpur Diggins?" Framanjesk asked.

Arthur caught the inflection in Framanjesk's voice. He wasn't entirely sure if the green dragon was leading him with it, but he decided to take a chance.

"Obviously not!" Arthur said confidently. "The Harpur Diggins who was the Dragon Lord of Epoh was a solid purple dragon. This Harpur Diggins has red streaks through his scales. Surely, you can see that."

"What are you doing?" Harpur hissed. "Tell them the truth."

Arthur ignored him. He watched Framanjesk and waited for the next question.

"So, you are saying that this Harpur Diggins is not the same Harpur Diggins who raised you from the dead and brought you to Epoh?"

"That is what I am saying."

"And this is not the same Harpur Diggins who placed the Power of Averborn sigil on your infant twins' foreheads.

"He is not."

"Arthur, stop it!" Harpur was growing angry.

"You have had your chance to speak," Framanjesk said. "Do not interrupt again."

Harpur stared at his son. He didn't speak, but he shook his head, pleading silently for Framanjesk to stop manipulating the truth.

"And this is not the same Harpur Diggins who got you to use your magic to transfer his spirit into the body of Karrys Evergreen."

"That particular Harpur Diggins is dead."

"How long have you known this Harpur Diggins?" Framanjesk asked.

Arthur paused. "Not long. A few days," he said.

"Have you ever known this Harpur Diggins to do anything that might be construed to be a crime?"

"I have not."

Harpur rolled his eyes. "I…"

"Shush!" Karrys, Arthur and Framanjesk all said.

"Why, then, would he come here and tell us that he did all those things?" Themeela asked.

This was a corner that Arthur had hoped not be get backed into. He wiped the sweat from his brown with his sleeve and exhaled sharply.

"The Harpur Diggins who raised me from the dead, and put me on the throne, and stole Karrys body, and used a forbidden sigil, and did all those other questionable things was a good dragon. He cared about this world and he cared deeply about the people, not just in Epoh, but in the rest of Thraeh—and other worlds—too. He never intended for things to happen the way they did. He tried to do things the right way, but his plans didn't always work out as he expected them to. Honestly, it was the people he tried to help that screwed things up for him. But he never gave up on us. And he never once stopped being the best example of a dragon there ever was. You ask me why I think this Harpur Diggins came here and said he did all those things? I think it is because he wants all dragon kind to know how noble and honourable the original Harpur Diggins was. And I think he wants to live up to the high standards that Harpur Diggins set for us all."

When Arthur finished talking, a smile spread across Framanjesk's face. "Thank you, King Arthur. Unless anyone else has something to add, I believe we are done here."

Themeela was not sure how she had managed to lose control over the proceedings. She was aware that Framanjesk had worked some ploy, but she couldn't figure out exactly how he had maneuvered the human king the way he had. Frankly, she didn't care. Harpur Diggins was long dead and no longer able to do "questionable things." And if this strange admirer of the great purple dragon wanted to call himself Harpur Diggins, well, so be it.

"You are free to go," she said to Harpur and Karrys. "Please don't come before us with any more nonsense again."

Harpur thanked the council members and then looked down at Arthur. "Let's get you back to Epoh," he growled.

The dragons who had gathered in the compound were abuzz with speculation about what had just happened. Like Themeela, many were sure that something had been left out, but they could not fathom what it was. None of them understood the part about the android making a new body for Harpur Diggins' spirit, and while they thought that might be at the crux of it all, they chose to gloss over it just as smoothly as Framanjesk and Arthur had. It was just simpler that way.

Harpur felt somewhat cheated by the whole affair. While Framanjesk seemed to be rather pleased with himself, Harpur wanted to throttle the cheeky sod.

Arthur just wanted to get out of the compound. "If you don't mind, I will zap myself back to the castle."

Harpur was about to protest, when a cold wind suddenly blew across the compound. Around him, conversation stopped as all eyes turned to the north.

"What now?" Themeela said.

"Who are they?" Arthur asked, craning to get a better view of two cobalt-blue dragons approaching from the same direction of the icy wind.

"*They*," Harpur said, "are your children."

"My children are black!" Arthur never thought he'd hear himself say those words. "That sounded different in my head."

"It's complicated," Harpur said. "Stay here. I better go see what they are doing here."

Harpur launched into the air, but immediately landed again.

"What's wrong?" Karrys said, seeing the look of consternation on Harpur's face.

"The twins have done something to the air. I can't fly."

Karrys didn't believe him. She leapt upward. And then came down. Hard. "It's like there is no air!"

"I told you."

Arthur took a deep breath in. "The air seems fine to me. It's a little cold, but we're still breathing."

Hart landed on the roof of the cells. He looked cranky.

Meg made her way to the platform. Framanjesk, Themeela and Durnor had to scramble out of the way so she could land. As soon as she had folded her wings, she drew Isenwylm from the scabbard on her back and held it up.

"I am Meg of Averborn," She cried. "Wielder of Isenwylm. You will release the prisoner immediately!"

"Oh, for the love of Orhowyn!" Harpur walked over to the platform. "Meg, what do you think you're doing?"

"I'm rescuing you," Meg said. "Everything's going to be all right."

"I don't need rescuing," Harpur said. "Thanks to your father, the Dragon Council is letting me go free."

"Oh." Meg looked disappointed. "Did you say my father? He's here?"

Meg looked around Harpur and saw Arthur standing next to Karrys. He waved. She waved back.

"But thank you," Harpur said. "Now, could you undo whatever you did to the air so the dragons can fly?"

The newly formed Ice Dragon looked out at the host of dragons, many of whom were hopping up and down like airborne nobility suddenly demoted to common reptiles. She couldn't help but feel proud of the feat she'd just accomplished. At the same time, she couldn't bear to watch the undignified antics of the increasingly terrified dragons.

"Sorry," she said, removing what amounted to a clever curse.

With no warning to let them know their launches would work again, several dragons collided in the air and crashed back down again. Much screeching and flapping ensued.

"Oh, Meg," Arthur sighed.

"My intentions were good!" Meg said defensively.

"We need to get out of here before someone realizes that we are connected and they throw me back in the cells forever," Harpur said. "Arthur, do you want a ride back to the castle, or not?"

"Why are they blue now?" Arthur asked.

"I'll explain everything when we get back to Epoh." Harpur wanted to crawl into a lair and never come out.

"We can't all go back to Epoh," Arthur said. "What about Glynnis?"

"Oh, we took care of Glynnis," Meg said. "It's safe for us to be in Epoh now."

Harpur's heart was filled with dread. "Meg, what did you do?"

"We didn't hurt him," she said. Then she giggled. "We just put the fear of the Ice Dragons into him. It was awesome!"

"Can we go now?" Harpur said. Then he caught Hart's eye and remembered his promise. "Actually, you three go on ahead. I need to speak to Hart privately."

Meg put Isenwylm back into its scabbard and offered her hand to Arthur for the flight back.

"Um, no offense, Sweetheart," Arthur said, "but I think I will fly back with Karrys."

"What makes you think that I want to carry you all the way back to Epoh?"

"Fine," Arthur said, climbing into Meg's hand, "but if she drops me...."

"I won't drop you, Father. How hard can it be to carry someone while I'm flying?"

Arthur looked pleadingly at Karrys. "You sure you don't want to carry me?"

"You'll be fine," Karrys said. "But if she does drop you, you can always zap yourself to the ground."

"Yeah, 'cause that went so well last time I fell from a great height."

Hart waited for Meg, Arthur and Karrys to fly away, then he flew down from the roof of the cells to meet Harpur on the compound grounds. Now that the other dragons were able to fly again, they were vacating rapidly. The icy wind Meg had used to herald her arrival, and the sight of Isenwylm had caused no small measure of concern. But it did give Hart and Harpur some privacy.

"How are you doing?" Harpur asked.

"I am adjusting," Hart said.

He was angry. And scared. Having super powers thrust upon him, whether he wanted them or not, was overwhelming. One day he was a young man, just coming of age, and the next he was a demi-god in a world where gods had been long-forgotten. Not only did he have to learn how to live with that, he had to keep his recklessly over-confident sister in check. If today's little demonstration was anything to go by, Hart would have his hands full. Harpur fully understood the lad's resentment toward him.

"I intend to keep my promise," he said. "I am going to say good bye to Elder Dhonna and pay my respects to Anayah first, though."

Hart looked away and Harpur sensed the conflict the young dragon was wrestling with. When, at last, Hart nodded his approval, Harpur felt a light wave of hope rise up inside him. In time, Hart would find a way to forgive him. In the meantime, he would give Hart some space.

"Thank you for coming here today," Harpur continued. "I appreciate that you wanted to help me."

"I didn't come here for you," Hart said, still not making eye contact. "I came to make sure Meg didn't do anything too stupid."

"Well, thank you for that as well," Harpur said. "She is going to need a lot of help in the coming days."

Hart snorted. A thick plume of purple-black smoke rose between him and Harpur. They both watched as it slowly dissipated.

"Hart, I…." Harpur grappled for something reassuring to say. But he knew so little about what the twins had become and could think of nothing that didn't sound trite and patronizing.

"I know," Hart said. Then he launched into the air and flew north to Epoh.

Harpur waited until Hart was far enough away that he could follow at a respectful distance. As he prepared to fly away himself, he noticed a yellow dragon standing next to the gates on the west side of the compound watching him.

Astrideous Garaday, the dragon who had blamed Karrys for the death of her mate. She had been charged with falsely accusing Karrys of abandoning Epoh when the Dragon Council had clearly intended to give the teal dragon the benefit of the doubt. Harpur had quite forgotten about her.

He considered talking to her to find out how the Dragon Council had ruled. Obviously, she had either been acquitted, or her punishment had been mild. But there remained a glint of bitterness in her eyes. *A warning?* Harpur wondered. He decided not to rekindle that wee fire of singe and sulk, and leapt skyward. Epoh was calling him home.

One last time.

Epilogue

Harpur took his time flying back to Epoh. Hart had granted him leave to pay his respects to Anayah and to say good bye to Elder Dhonna before leaving the kingdom permanently, neither of which he looked forward to. His banishment from Epoh weighed heavy on his heart, though he couldn't fault Hart for making the demand. The young prince could have done much worse and Harpur was grateful that Hart had no real idea of the extent of his powers yet.

Landing in Braydon Wood, Harpur transformed into this human form and made his way to the oak tree next to the Boundary house where Anayah's ashes were nestled into a hole in its trunk. The plain urn with the simple inscription seemed to mock him. Anayah deserved something... more than this. A monument, a mausoleum, a proper grave with a proper headstone at the very least... Something more than a hole in a tree. He felt a wave of anger toward Davynn for this unseemly disposal of Anayah's remains.

"It's okay."

Harpur spun around to see who had spoken. His eyes fell on a sight his mind struggled to reconcile. Next to the Boundary house stood Anayah, Analeetah, and Anabettah, each of them a shimmering apparition of immense beauty. They wore gowns of ivory. On their brows were delicate, inverted tiaras, each one adorned with a single large gemstone: Anayah's with a ruby; Analeetah's with a black sapphire; and Anabettah's with a diamond. Their faces were pale, but glowing with a serenity that enveloped Harpur with a sense of calm.

"It's okay," Anayah repeated. "Alexa chose this place for me. I am at peace, Harpur Diggins. Do not trouble yourself with remorse. I chose my own path."

All Harpur could do was shake his head in disbelief. He desperately wanted to believe in Anayah's forgiveness, but seeing her standing there and hearing her words nearly tore his heart in two.

"Fate and free will are the strangest of companions," Anabettah said softly. "Together they form a paradox from which there is no escape. You chose more wisely than you imagine, Harpur Diggins. Your destiny has not yet been fulfilled."

Harpur's mind raced to make sense of the silver-haired witch's words. Again, he heard forgiveness in them; a forgiveness he didn't deserve. But before he could find any words of his own, Analeetah stepped forward.

"Thank you for bringing Anayah back to me," she whispered. "Thank you for freeing me from my madness." She reached for Harpur's walking stick and he let her take it, quite unable to resist.

The raven-haired ghost returned to join the others and Harpur watched helplessly as Anayah and Anabettah both took hold of the staff along with Analeetah. A red, black and silver mist swirled around the walking stick, thickening until he could no longer see it, and the witches, with eyes closed, began to chant.

Their voices filled the clearing, rising and falling in rhythm with the cadence and harmony of their chant. With it, the mist rose as well, and Harpur watched, bewildered, as a dark green vapor was drawn out of the walking stick and devoured by the swirling haze of black, red and silver.

They are lifting the curse, he thought. *But how?*

When the green vapor had dissipated completely, the witches ended their chant and opened their eyes. Analeetah turned back to Harpur and held the walking stick out for him to take. He hesitated, but only for a moment as he took in the changes the witch's magic had made to it. The amethyst top was larger and richer in colour. Below it, a gold band, studded with rubies now encircled the polished ebony shaft. Gone were the teeth marks from a time when Harpur had had to carry the walking stick in his mouth while he was in dragon from. It appeared longer, stronger, and thicker than it used to be.

Harpur took it and continued to examine it closely. He knew he should say something. Thank you seemed appropriate. But he couldn't seem to form the words.

"The curse is lifted," Analeetah said. "Set right the wrong that remains."

The three spectral witches faded away, leaving Harpur alone and dazed. He stood staring at the spot they had occupied, willing them to return, tears pouring from his eyes. He had killed them. Yet they had forgiven him.

Will I ever be able to forgive myself?

The walk from the Boundary house to the elven city provided Harpur with the time he needed to compose himself. He had one more thing to do before he left Epoh for good. He had to say good bye to Elder Dhonna.

He tried to focus on what he would say to her, but his thoughts kept returning to Analeetah's parting words; *Right the wrong that remains.*

What did she mean?

There were so many wrongs he felt he had to atone for. His actions and decisions had affected so many people. Davynn had lost his wife. Arthur had lost his children—more or less. Meg and Hart had been forced into an existence they never asked for. Sok and Elder Dhonna had lost a friend. Bon and Hiro had been displaced. And Karrys... Karrys had her life stolen from her. And of all of them, Hart was the only one who seemed to hold any of it against him.

They had all been upset—even angry—with him. But they had all helped him anyway. And now, here he was with a healthy new body, fit and strong again. He'd gotten what he wanted. But his friends had paid the price.

Dhonna was sitting the balcony of her tree house when Harpur arrived. She watched him cross the grassy clearing, taking in his youthful appearance. If it hadn't been for the top hat and the walking stick, she would never have recognized her oldest and dearest friend. Even after all that had transpired, she felt a little thrill flutter in her heart as he climbed the rope ladder and stepped onto the balcony.

"Elder Dhonna," Harpur said, removing his hat and bowing slightly from the waist.

"It's just Dhonna, now," she replied and waved at a chair as an invitation for him to sit.

"You'll always be my Bella Dhonna," Harpur said.

"You look good," Dhonna said. "But you really do need to grow your beard back."

Harpur chuckled and rubbed his chin. "As soon as it decides to be a beard again, I will."

"I see you have a new walking stick."

Harpur held it up and looked at it like he didn't recognize it. "It isn't new. The curse has been lifted. Apparently."

Dhonna raised her eyebrows. "Nyssira better be careful then."

Right the wrong that remains. Harpur suddenly knew what Analeetah had meant. He has sworn to get his revenge on the sorceress of Everstar, but until now he'd been unable to touch her.

"And what is this 'just Dhonna' all about? An elf without a guild is... unheard of."

539

"I will be joining Davynn and the children in Branwyke," she said. "He's going to need help with the little ones. And I will be closer to Röggenar."

Harpur looked at the retired guild master with surprise. "Röggenar? I should think his wife would not approve."

Dhonna slapped Harpur's arm in playful admonition. "It's not like that! He has become a good friend. Davynn and I are going to take the children to the mines after I get settled in Highmere."

"Well, that ought to be interesting." Harpur smirked. The dwarven mines were dark and dirty. He couldn't imagine Dhonna crawling around in them.

"I think it will be fun," Dhonna said. "And where will you go now? Back to the Sands of Sancheera?"

Harpur stood up and hefted his walking stick. "I am planning on going to Earth for a short time. There is a particularly interesting woman there, whom I intend to engage as my biographer. After that, Bella Dhonna, I have a wrong to right in the Black North."

Dhonna stood as well. She hugged her new old friend. "Be well, Harpur Diggins. You are loved and cherished."

"As are you, Bella Dhonna," Harpur said, wrapping his arms around her. "Thank you."

Harpur would not be seen again in the Kingdom of Epoh for a very long time. But he did sneak back now and then to check on his friends and make sure they were doing okay. In the meantime, he had a biographer to hire. And a date with destiny in the Black North.

Acknowledgements

My undying gratitude goes out to my editor and sister, Peggy Thiessen. I cannot thank you enough for your help in bringing this story to life.

About the Author

Saoirse Temple is the author of the *Bounders of Epoh* trilogy—*The Fire of Orhowyn*, *The Amber Chalice*, and *The Power of Averborn*—as well as the *Dear Diary Style Files*, a humorous series on writing craft. An editor and book coach by trade, she delights in helping stories find their sharpest, brightest forms.

When she isn't writing or wrangling words, Saoirse can often be found sketching dragons, dreaming up new worlds, or coaxing inspiration out of a strong cup of tea.

Discover more at: **www.saoirsetemple.com**

The custom scene break symbol used in this book was created by Saoirse Temple. Visit https://www.saoirsetemple.com/category/all-products to purchase scene break symbols for use in your publications. To order your own custom scene break symbol, contact Saoirse directly at: saoirsealtemple@gmail.com

Follow Saoirse on

Facebook: www.facebook.com/saoirsetempe

Instagram: @saoirsealt